ROXIE'S PROTECTORS

MARISA CHENERY

CONTENTS

ROAN'S FALL

As a hairstylist, Ansley has seen and cut a lot of people's hair, but when Roxie shows up for her appointment with a very large, gorgeous man, Anlsey can't take her eyes off him. Nor can she stop her body's reaction to Roan when Roxie asks her to cut his hair as well. But things seem to go steadily downhill when Ansley's curse—her ability to say the first thing that comes to mind when around a man she is attracted to—rears its ugly head. When Roan growls at her to hurry up, Ansley knows her mouth has done it to her again.

Even through the harsh chemical smells in the hair salon, Ansley's scent is like a punch in the gut to Roan. Knowing she is his mate, and a mortal, it has him fighting the urge to claim her as his own. Hoping to ease into telling her he is a werewolf, Roan prays he has the control to take things slow. But when it comes to Ansley, he must fight the wolf inside him or risk scaring away the one woman who was meant for him.

CHAPTER ONE

Roan pulled open the glass, front-entrance door and stood on the threshold. He scanned the large open-concept space. He so did not want to be there. However long he had to stay would be pure torture. If given a choice, he would rather face down a hundred armed men in battle than go inside that place.

"Well? Are you going to stand there all day or what? You're going to make me late for my hair appointment." Roxie gave him a hard shove from behind.

Reluctantly, Roan stepped into the hair salon and then moved aside so Roxie could enter after him. He tried not to take many deep breaths. The smell of perm solution, hair dyes, and other such chemicals assaulted his sensitive werewolf nose. Considering Roxie was a werewolf too, he had no idea how she could stand the harsh smells. If they bothered her, she showed no signs of it. She walked to the front desk and gave her name to the receptionist.

Roxie rejoined him and led the way to one of the unoccupied pansy-assed-looking straight-backed chairs that lined the wall. Roan sat slowly, expecting the chair to break once he settled his full weight on it. The spindly wood legs didn't look as if they were made to support a man of his size. Being six foot nine and weighing over two hundred and sixty pounds, he was by no means a lightweight. As he planted his ass on the seat and leaned against the backrest, the chair groaned ominously, but it held together. Roan looked at Roxie, who had taken the empty seat next to his.

She shook her head and sighed. "If you're this uncomfortable, you should have let me come alone like I wanted to in the first place."

He scowled. "It's my duty to protect you."

Roan took his duty seriously. Roxie was special. She was the foretold one, the one who now ruled over all the werewolf packs. For hundreds of years, he, along with his brothers- and sister-in-arms, had trained to be the foretold one's protectors. Even though she thought she could take care of herself, he and the rest of her protectors weren't prepared to leave her unguarded. Even if it meant he had to sit inside a mortal hair salon while the fumes from perm solution slowly burned away the lining inside his nose.

Roxie scowled back at him. "Since I'm stuck with you, would you at least loosen up a bit? People are staring. You look as if you're ready to kill the next person who looks at you the wrong way."

Roan did a quick scan of the room. Roxie was right. Every gaze—all female—was turned their way. Some of the mortal females looked as if they were ready to run if he so much as said boo, while a few gave him looks that said they liked what they saw.

The chair creaked as he shifted his weight and turned back to Roxie. "What's the holdup?"

"Ansley is finishing with another client, then it'll be my turn."

"I thought you had an appointment."

"I do. Sometimes Ansley gets a little bit behind. I don't mind waiting."

"Well, I do. The faster I can get the hell out of here, the better."

Roxie eyed him. "I'm guessing you've never been to a hair salon before."

Roan snorted. "This will be my first and only time."

"Then where do you get your hair cut?" Roxie looked pointedly at his shoulder-length hair.

"Saskia cuts it for me." Saskia, his sister-in-arms and his leader, tended to take care of things like haircuts and such.

Before Roxie could say anything more, the girl from the front desk came around it and called her name. "Roxie? Ansley is ready for you now. If you want to follow me back, we'll get your hair washed."

Roan would have followed Roxie, but she shoved him back down on his chair and shook her head. "Park it, buddy. I'll be perfectly fine. You'll be able to keep an eye on me from here."

Roxie followed the girl to one of the sinks at the very back of the room where another woman waited for her. Roan figured the other woman had to be Ansley, Roxie's hairdresser. He ran his gaze over her. From what he could see of her from that distance, she was pretty enough. Her looks didn't compare to a female werewolf's, their race was known for their extreme goodlooks, but hers appealed to him nonetheless. She wore her straight, brown hair down past her shoulders. He couldn't see the color of her eyes, since she was in profile as she motioned Roxie to sit on the chair in front of the sink.

Roan spent the next half hour bored out of his mind while he watched Ansley cut Roxie's hair. The two women chatted away, sometimes laughing over something one of them had said. At one point, both turned their heads to look directly at him. He crossed his arms over his chest and stared back. He gave Ansley a cursory glance before he focused on Roxie. There was something about her smile that said she had to be up to something.

He soon found out he hadn't been too far off in his thinking. Once Ansley finished with Roxie's hair, Roxie beckoned to him. He'd made a mistake by volunteering to be the one to escort her today. Standing, he walked to the back of the salon. Prepared for just about anything when it came to her, he wasn't at all ready when he caught his first faint whiff of Ansley. He had the sensation of being punched in the gut while he filtered her scent out from the many others in the building.

He barely managed to hold back a growl of need as he drew even with the women. His gaze fixed on Ansley—his mate. Even though the harsh chemical smells that hung in the air burned the inside of his nose, Roan couldn't stop himself from dragging in great gulps of her scent. His cock went instantly rock hard inside his jeans. He looked her up and down. She really was a small thing. She couldn't be any taller than five-foot-three. Her hazel-eyed gaze locked with his light-blue one. Her lips parted slightly, and she craned her neck to look up at him. He fought the urge to yank her to him and see if her lips were as kissable as they looked.

"Well, well. Isn't this interesting," Roxie said with a chuckle.

Roan dragged his gaze off Ansley and turned to Roxie. "What?"

"I think you just got more than you bargained for by tagging along with me." Roxie wrapped her arm around Ansley's shoulders. "Ansley, this is my friend, Roan Haver. Roan, Ansley ended up having her next client cancel at the last minute. She's kindly agreed to let you take that opening."

He shook his head. Even though he spoke to Roxie, Roan kept his gaze on Ansley. "I don't need my hair cut."

"It's my treat," Roxie said. "You can trust Ansley. She won't shave you bald."

Ansley chuckled. "God, no. It would be a shame to cut off all that great-looking hair. I promise to be gentle."

With a curt nod, Roan followed Ansley to one of the sinks. He was in trouble, but he walked to his doom anyway. With the mating urge already riding him hard, once she laid hands on him, it would be three times worse. He would have a hard enough time trying to hide the hard-on he sported, but it would take all of his self-control to hide what he truly was from her. If he didn't watch it, he'd be growling while his eyes glowed with arousal.

Since Ansley was mortal, Roan didn't think she even knew werewolves existed. He found himself stuck in a Catch-22 situation. He wanted her to touch him, even though he could very well lose control if she did. Reluctantly, he sat on the chair and pushed back until his neck hit the sink. She leaned in to turn on the water, and he knew he was a goner.

*

Ansley ran the water and tried to look as if she knew what she was doing. Normally, she could wash a client's hair without much thought, but that wouldn't be the case this time. She was having a hard time focusing on anything but the very large, exceptionally gorgeous man who waited for her to wash his hair. Her heart thudded against her ribs. She pushed Roan's hair back so it fell into the sink. Much to her disgust, her hands shook. It wasn't as if she was afraid of him. Yes, he towered over her and probably could snap her in two without even trying, but those things didn't cause her to shake. No, she didn't fear him. Quite the opposite, in fact. Just the mere sight of him caused her body to go up in flames.

When Roxie first pointed Roan out, Ansley had taken one look at him and felt her mouth fall open. After she managed to stop staring at him as if he were a large piece of chocolate she wanted to savor, she'd tried to keep her attention focused on the task at hand, but more often than not, she found her gaze straying to where he sat. To say she was attracted to him would be an understatement. His male-model good looks and large, muscular body had her wanting to touch and lick every inch of him.

After Roxie found out Ansley's next client had cancelled, she asked if Roan could take that opening. Ansley had been quick to agree. Not that she thought she would have a shot at him. Guys who looked like him did not go for girls like her, but cutting his hair would at least give her a chance to have him up close and personal for a little while.

Now she stood shaking like a teenage girl with her first crush. The way Roan had intensely stared at her while he walked to join them had taken her breath away. She'd thought it could be lust in his light blue eyes, which sent her body into overdrive. Her breath had caught and her nipples had tightened beneath her t-shirt. Her pussy had throbbed as wetness pooled between her legs. The way he looked her up and down when he'd come to stand in front of her made Ansley think of hot, sweaty sex that lasted all night.

Ansley took a deep breath and tested the water to make sure it wouldn't be too hot, then proceeded to wet Roan's thick, light-brown hair. As she washed it, her thigh pressed against his shoulder. That small contact was enough to send a wave of awareness through her. She rinsed out the shampoo and her gaze fell on Roan's face. He had his eyes closed. She visually traced his firm lips, straight nose, chiseled cheekbones, and square jaw as she shampooed his hair for a second time. She had to resist the urge to climb onto his lap, sprawl on top of him, and kiss him until they were both breathless. With her luck, he would more than likely dump her on her ass if she ever tried such a stunt. She dragged her gaze away and leaned closer while she massaged his scalp.

A strangled noise that sounded close to an animalistic growl drew Ansley's gaze back to Roan's face. Her hands went still as she caught the intense look in his now-open eyes. Her mouth suddenly dry, she swallowed and licked her lips. He made the same strangled sound, and for a split second, she swore his light-blue eyes glowed.

Thinking her eyes had to be playing tricks on her, Ansley quickly finished washing Roan's hair. After she toweled it dry, she had him sit in her chair. His gaze followed her in the mirror in front of him as she draped a cape over him and did it up at the back of his neck.

She picked up her scissors and a comb from the small counter in front of Roan before she turned back to him. "How would you like me to cut your hair?"

Roan's gaze locked with hers. "Just a trim."

Ansley nodded and went to stand behind him. She combed out the snarls of his long hair. "So, you're a friend of Roxie?"

"You could say that."

When he didn't offer anything more, Ansley tried to think of something else to say to keep the conversation going, a feat, considering she was so turned-on she could barely think straight.

After she rejected more than one likely subject, she blurted out, "Are you single? Considering how good-looking you are, I can't picture you being single." She cringed inside. Real subtle. Not. Where the hell had that come from?

Roan stiffened his shoulders. The chair creaked. He seemed to be holding on to the armrests in a death grip. "Can you just hurry it up?"

Way to go, dumbass, she berated herself. *Now he thinks you're an idiot.* Her curse, at least she called it her curse, had just risen its ugly head. Whenever she became attracted to a man, especially a hunky one like Roan, her mouth spewed nothing but garbage. She'd driven away more than one man that way. Ansley focused on the back of Roan's head as she trimmed the ends of his hair. Now more embarrassed than aroused, she kept her mouth shut and made sure she didn't make eye contact with him in the mirror. Given the way he stiffened every time she touched him, she figured he couldn't wait to get away from her.

She didn't take any longer than she needed to finish his

haircut. When she went to pick up the hair dryer, Roan stopped her. "Let it dry on its own."

With a nod, Ansley stepped back behind him and undid the cape. She was just pulling it off when Roxie came over. She looked from Ansley to Roan, then scowled.

"What did you say to Ansley, Roan? The tension between you two is so thick you could cut it with a knife." Roxie gave Roan a meaningful look. "I thought you would have used your time more wisely, if you know what I mean."

Ansley had no idea what Roxie meant by that last part, but she quickly jumped in before Roan could answer. "It wasn't Roan's fault, Rox. I sometimes don't think before I speak." She turned to Roan. "I'm sorry. I should have kept my mouth shut. I'm sure you don't need someone like me asking about your personal life. You probably get enough women throwing themselves at you. Not that I was throwing myself at you. Okay, I'm going to shut up now."

Her face heated. Ansley figured she couldn't shove her foot any further into her mouth than she already had. She snuck a quick look at Roan and her heart tried to beat out of her chest as their gazes met. He stared at her as if she were the only woman in the room, which had her body going up in flames once again. A deep ache inside her pussy caused wetness to pool.

Unable to tear her gaze away, Ansley watched Roan's nostrils flare. He took a deep breath, then walked closer and crowded her with his big frame. She backed up until her butt hit the counter behind her. He didn't stop until their bodies were almost touching. She grabbed the edges of the counter to keep herself from pulling his lips down to hers so she could kiss him senseless.

Roan bent his head until their noses almost touched. "You can throw yourself at me any time you wish." He pushed his hips against her so she felt the large bulge in his pants. "I think it would be something we both would enjoy."

Ansley had to bite the inside of her cheek to stop the moan of need that threatened to push past her lips. The feel of Roan's hard cock pressed against her stomach made her pussy clench. She clutched the counter behind her as he lowered his head even more. Her breath caught, thinking he would kiss her, but instead of going for her lips, he pushed his face into the crook of her neck and took a deep breath. If she didn't know better, she would think he sniffed her. He pulled away to meet her gaze once more, and she felt as if her legs had turned to rubber.

As Roan's gaze locked on her lips, he asked, "When do you get off work?"

"Uh...uh, six."

Roan gave her one last look that made her blood heat even more before he turned and then walked out of the salon. Ansley stared at the door and tried to force her body to cool down. The sound of Roxie chuckling brought her out of the daze he'd put her in.

"I'd better catch up with Roan." Roxie gave Ansley a wink. "Don't do anything I wouldn't do." She went to the front desk to pay.

Ansley sat in her chair once Roxie left the salon. She looked at the large clock on the wall. There was another four hours to get through before she could leave. She had a feeling it would be the longest four hours of her life.

CHAPTER TWO

Roxie jumped out of the car and hurried to the front door of her house. Roan let her go inside before he slowly followed. He figured he would let her tell the others about what had taken place between him and Ansley at the hair salon. It wasn't as if he was embarrassed about it, quite the opposite. He'd always secretly longed to find his mate. He just hadn't expected the mating urge to hit him quite so hard when he did find her. With lust pounding through his body, walking away from Ansley had been the hardest thing he'd ever done. Even now, he had to fight the urge to get back in the car and go to her. The only thing that stopped him from returning to the salon and claiming her as his mate was the fact she was mortal. If she'd been a werewolf, he would already have had her under him, surging inside her.

With a sigh, Roan headed to the house. He wanted to take things slow with Ansley. He didn't want to scare her off. It would be a lot harder on him than her. Until he claimed her fully as his mate, the mating urge wouldn't loosen its grip on him. Even his dreams would be filled with erotic dreams of her, of touching and tasting her.

Once inside the house, he followed the sound of voices to the living room. He skipped his gaze over the occupants of the room. Roxie and her mate, Beowulf, sat on the loveseat while his two brothers by blood, Skylar and Jager, were sitting on the large, sectional couch with his brother-in-arms, Leif. From the looks of pity all his brothers gave him, Roan knew Roxie had told them about Ansley.

Roan headed to sit on the sectional next to Leif, but the other male held out his hands to ward him off. Leif shook his head. "No way are you sitting next to me. I don't need you rubbing off on me. I'm quite happy without a mate, thank you very much."

Roan rolled his eyes and shook his head before he sat on the large armchair across from his brothers. He expected as much from Leif. Leif loved women too much to want to find a mate, not that he would have much choice if the right woman came along. Roan only had to think of Eli, his sister's mate. Eli had felt the same way Leif did, but he'd fallen hard for Saskia and couldn't be happier.

"It isn't as if I'm contagious, Leif," Roan said. "And I didn't plan this. You wait until your turn comes."

Leif gave him a look of abject horror. "That will be the day hell freezes over. I like that I can have my fun, then walk away when I want."

Even with that type of attitude toward women, Leif still managed to get any woman he wanted—mortal and werewolf alike. "I'll have fun throwing that back in your face when you find your one and only." Roan turned to his other two brothers. "Well? I'm sure both of you have something to say."

Jager spoke first. "As long as you can keep your dick in your pants long enough to help protect Roxie, I couldn't care less."

That was Jager—always short and to the point. His brother wasn't one to mince words. "Thanks. I'll try not to turn into a sex fiend." He looked at his other brother. "What about you, Skylar?"

Skylar shrugged. "I'm happy for you. I'm just glad it's you and not me. I'm not ready to take on a mate."

Roxie drew Roan's attention her way when she quietly cleared her throat. "So, Roan, are you going back this evening to see Ansley?"

"Yes." Not that he had much choice in the matter. As it now stood, he would probably drive himself crazy thinking about her until he saw her again.

"I thought you would. I'm going to give you one piece of advice—tell Ansley what you are before you sleep with her. From personal experience," Roxie gave Beowulf a hard stare, "it isn't exactly easy to accept the whole mated thing if you aren't told what to expect."

Beowulf pulled Roxie under his arm. "I don't see you complaining."

"Not now, but I didn't take the news of you being a werewolf all that well in the beginning, if you remember."

Beowulf turned to look at Roan. "Roxie's right. It's best to be upfront right from the start."

"I'll take that into consideration. Now, if you don't mind, could we change the subject? Talking about Ansley is making me a little antsy, if you know what I mean."

As Beowulf and Roxie talked about Wulf's Den, the nightclub Beowulf owned, Roan let the conversation wash over him. With half an ear, he listened to his brothers and Beowulf discuss who would be going to the nightclub with him and Roxie that night. At least Roan wouldn't be expected to go along with them. With the mating urge riding him, he doubted he would be any good to them anyway. The demands of his body would be a lot harder to ignore until he made Ansley his. Until then, he wouldn't be good for much of anything.

* * * *

For the rest of the day, Ansley found herself distracted by thoughts of Roan. She couldn't help wondering if he would really show up when she got off work. He hadn't exactly asked her out, just what time she was finished. As the hours went by, she felt more than sure Roan wouldn't show up. Yes, he'd looked at her with arousal in his eyes, but that didn't mean he wouldn't change his mind after he had some time to think about it.

By the time six o'clock rolled around, Ansley had herself thoroughly convinced Roan would be a no-show. After cutting her last client's hair, she cleaned up her workstation, then headed out. Once she hit the sidewalk, she looked around. As she'd suspected, he didn't seem to be anywhere in sight. Trying not to let it bother her, she headed to the parking lot behind the salon. A large bowl of ice cream was in her future, along with a glass or two of wine.

She'd just reached the driver's side of her Pontiac Sunfire when a heavy hand landed on her shoulder. With a shriek, she swung around to see who had come up behind her.

Her eyes widened in surprise. "Roan? What are you doing here?"

"Why do you look so surprised? I told you I would be back."

Ansley shook her head. "No, you didn't. You just asked me what time I got off work."

Roan's brows drew together. "You didn't think I was coming back." He said it as a statement, not a question.

"Why would I? It isn't as if you asked me out on a date."

He crowded her back against her car. He put his hands on the roof on either side of her, effectively caging her in. In his deep voice now gone husky, Roan said, "Well, I'm asking now."

Ansley swallowed. "You're asking me out on a date?"

Roan smiled. "Isn't that what you wanted?"

With Roan this close, she had a hard time thinking straight. "Are you…are you sure you want to go out with me? You're so good-looking, and let's face it, I'm no beauty queen. You could find someone much prettier than me. Compared to you, I'm—"

He cut her off with his lips. At first, Ansley held herself perfectly still, but then Roan's mouth moved on hers. His tongue swept the seam of her lips. Her eyes drifted shut, and she opened for him. He threaded the fingers of one hand through her hair and held her in place, his tongue pushing inside.

She lifted her hands and fisted the front of his T-shirt as he explored the inside of her mouth. He tasted of sin and hot, wild sex.

Deepening the kiss, Roan ran his other hand down her side to her bottom and hauled her closer. Ansley moaned. The hard length of his cock nestled against her stomach. In response, her pussy grew wet. Her nipples went taut beneath her shirt. She wanted to strip off her clothes and rub her naked body against his. It'd been so long since a man had kissed her. Her sex-starved body ached to have his hard length deep inside it.

Roan placed one of his muscular thighs between her legs and pushed against her pussy. Ansley moaned into his mouth. The pressure sent shockwaves of pleasure through her sex. Using his T-shirt to pull him even closer, she hungrily kissed him back, rubbing herself against his thigh. She arched her back as he cupped her breast through her shirt.

The blast of a car horn out on the street jerked Ansley out of the sexual haze that had taken her over. She pulled back and looked at Roan. She sucked in a breath. His light-blue eyes glowed mutedly. She blinked in surprise.

At her sharp indrawn breath, Roan shut his eyes and rested his forehead against hers. "Just give me a second." His voice came out in a half growl.

Ansley held herself still as Roan took a couple of deep breaths. "Roan? Are you okay?" When he continued to hold himself stiffly, she asked quietly, "Did I do something wrong?"

He lifted his head to stare at her.

She noticed his eyes no longer appeared to glow, making her think once again she'd been seeing things that weren't there.

"Why would you think you did anything wrong?" he asked with a scowl. "You didn't. If anything, you did everything right." He palmed one of her cheeks. "The problem is, I promised myself I would take things slow with you. Take the time for us to get to know each other better. Right now, it's taking all my willpower not to throw you onto the hood of your car and take you until you scream my name."

Ansley's mouth formed a round "O" while images of what he wanted to do to her played through her mind. She could easily picture herself lying on the hood of her car with her legs wrapped around Roan's waist as he pounded into her. It made her pussy ache and wetness leak into her panties.

With a half growl, Roan took a step back. His chest rapidly rose and fell as he dragged in deep breaths. His hands fisted at his sides. "Whatever you're thinking about, stop it. I can smell your arousal, and it's playing havoc with what little self-control I have left. This may have been a mistake." He took another step back.

Afraid Roan would turn and walk away, Ansley quickly blurted, "Don't leave. Why don't you come back to my place?"

In a blink of an eye Roan had her once again trapped against her car while he loomed over her. "I think I need to learn why you keep thinking I'm going to walk away from you. If I had my way, I would take you to my bed and never let you out of it again."

Ansley gulped. "So, does that mean you want to come back to

my place?"

Roan chuckled. "You do realize that by asking me to your place, you'll be playing with fire. Are you willing to risk the chance of getting burned?"

"I'm willing to risk it."

God, she was more than willing to risk it. Just the idea that Roan wanted her made her knees go weak. Never in a million years would Ansley ever have thought she had a chance with a man like him. He was every woman's wet dream.

He dragged a finger down her cheek. "You may be willing to take that chance, but I'm not, just yet. How about we get something to eat first? Then we can see about going back to your place after that."

Even though she hadn't eaten since lunch, she probably wouldn't be able to eat much with Roan sitting so near. He made her hungry for other things besides food. She nodded. "All right. There's a great steakhouse on the way to my apartment."

"Sounds good to me. I'll follow you. My car is just over there."

Ansley looked in the direction Roan pointed. An unfeminine but longstanding love of sports cars allowed her to recognize his car. The Lexus IS F Performance in metallic gray had to have cost double what she made working at the hair salon in a year. It also made her Sunfire look like a dinky car when compared to his. Obviously, he had money as well as good looks.

After telling Roan the name and location of the restaurant, in case they became separated, Ansley got into her car. He crossed to his and then climbed in. As she led the way to the restaurant, she had to wonder when the ball would drop. It invariably did when she found herself attracted to a man. Roan seemed to be perfect in every way. It would only be a matter of time before she said or did something to drive him away. When it came to men, she tended to be her own greatest enemy.

* * * *

Roan gazed down along Ansley's slim, curvy body as she took the chair across from his at the restaurant. He wanted to strip her naked while he licked and kissed every inch of her. The kiss they'd shared in the parking lot had just fanned the flames of his arousal to even greater heights. It had been better than the headiest wine.

With the scent of her arousal swirling around them, Roan had had a hard time reining back the wolf inside him. It wanted to claim her as his mate as much as the man did. Somehow, he'd managed to hold himself back from acting on what his body screamed for him to do. He just hoped he would be able to do it again, because he had every intention of tasting every part of Ansley before he left her this night.

Ansley shifted on her chair. She stared at the menu that sat on the table in front of her, then bit her bottom lip. It made him want to replace her teeth with his own. As if she sensed him staring, she met his gaze, then quickly looked back down at the menu. He grinned. She was such a bundle of contradictions. At times she seemed outgoing, while at others she came across as being shy.

Once the waitress came, they gave her their orders. Roan ordered the largest steak on the menu and asked for it to be as rare as he could get it. Ansley ordered a salad. After the waitress left, he said, "You could have ordered more than a salad, Ansley."

"It will be enough." She gave him a nervous smile.

He hoped she wasn't one of those mortal women who only ate enough to keep a bird alive. He would have to break her of that if that turned out to be the case. Roan liked his women slim, but not to the point of skin and bones.

Having never really been on a date before, Roan had asked Roxie for some pointers. As a more than thousand-year-old warrior werewolf, dating hadn't exactly been high on his list of things to do. If he needed a woman, he usually sought out female werewolves who were willing to give him a night or two of pleasure in their beds and nothing more. And he never slept with mortal women. He'd wanted to avoid the hassle of having to hide what he truly was from them. The irony that his mate had turned out to be mortal, and he now had to somehow get her to accept him for what he was, hadn't been lost on him.

He cleared his throat. Roxie had told him that at this point on the date he should be asking Ansley questions about herself so he could get to know her better. "How long have you worked at the hair salon?"

Ansley fiddled with her fork. "Two years. I've been a hair

stylist for five. Where I work now pays more than the first place I worked. What about you? What do you do for a living?"

Roan had to think about that one. He didn't work, per se. He'd spent hundreds of years training to be one of the protectors of the foretold one. Most of his adult life had been spent training with a sword while he waited with his brothers and sister for the foretold one to be born. And it wasn't as if any of them needed to work. Being alive as long as he had, a person tended to accumulate more than enough money over the years. Plus, it helped that Dirk, one of his other brothers-in-arms, had a knack for investing.

In the end, he said, "You could say I'm in the protection business."

Ansley's gaze skipped across his chest and shoulders before she looked at his face. "Let me guess, you're a bodyguard. You're certainly strong enough to be one."

"You could say I'm one."

"Have you guarded anyone famous?"

"Ah…no. No one famous. Right now, I'm between jobs." Roan hated having to lie to Ansley, but until she knew what he truly was, that little untruth wouldn't do her any harm.

At that point, the waitress showed up with their food. Roan dug into his steak with gusto. It wasn't as rare as he liked his meat, but other than that, it tasted good. As all werewolves did, he liked it to barely touch a grill, and so rare it could practically get up and walk off his plate.

Roan lifted his eyes to see if Ansley enjoyed her salad. When their gazes collided, his cock instantly went rock hard. She hadn't touched her food. She stared at him as if she wanted to eat him instead. Just like that, he forgot about his meal, almost forgot where they were. With her heated gaze locked with his, he wanted nothing more than to throw her onto the table and sink his aching cock inside her.

Knowing that if Ansley continued to stare at him that way he would more than likely forget himself, Roan decided to hell with the whole date thing. If he didn't get a taste of her soon, he would go insane. His wolf didn't like being restrained. Having his mate nearby and unable to touch her made it throw back its head and howl.

Roan kept his gaze locked with Ansley's. "How about we take

our food back to your place? I'm suddenly in the mood for some privacy," he said in a gruff voice.

Ansley licked her lips and nodded. The smell of her arousal washed over him, making his cock grow even harder. Roan pulled his gaze away, then caught the eye of their waitress and signaled her over.

Ten minutes later, he ushered Ansley out of the restaurant while he carried their packaged food in a plastic bag. He only took long enough to give her a hard kiss before he left her and got into his car. As he followed her, he prayed she didn't live too far from the restaurant.

CHAPTER THREE

Ansley checked her rearview mirror to make sure Roan was still driving behind her. He was. She tried to take a deep, steadying breath, but that did nothing to stop her heart from pounding with excitement. When she and Roan had locked gazes across the table at the restaurant, she'd known exactly what they were going to do once they reached her apartment. Her body had reacted in the most elemental way when he said he wanted some privacy, in his gruff voice. Not usually one to hop into the sack with a guy she'd just met, she would make an exception for Roan. Whenever she was around him, she seemed to be in a perpetual state of arousal.

At her apartment building, she stuck her arm out of the car window and motioned for Roan to park his car in the visitors' parking area on the opposite end of the parking lot. She pulled into her space and then got out of her car. She'd just closed the car door when two large hands landed on her shoulders. With a yelp, she turned to find Roan standing behind her. For the second time that day, he'd been able to come up behind her without her hearing him.

She looked past him to see his Lexus parked at the far end of the parking lot. "How did you get over here so fast?"

"I ran."

He must have run fast. She let him take her hand and lead her to the front entrance of her apartment building. Now that she had him there, Ansley had second thoughts, but not about sleeping with him. She regretted inviting him to her place. Her small one-bedroom apartment probably didn't compare to where he lived. With her salary, she'd been lucky to afford this apartment, and it could in no way be called fancy. More on the cheap side, it had no secured entrance or underground parking garage. It didn't even have an elevator, since the apartment building only had three floors.

If Roan noticed the lack of an elevator as Ansley led him up the stairs to her third-floor apartment, he didn't say anything. Once she had her door unlocked, she pushed it open and went inside. He followed her. She flipped on a light before she turned to find him locking the door behind them. He did a quick scan of the apartment before his gaze returned to her.

She gave him a half smile. "I know it's small, and probably not what you're used to, but it's all I can afford right now. I'm trying to save money so I can open my own shop sometime in the future."

Roan put their food on her small kitchen table before he came to stand in front of her. "I didn't come here to check out your apartment, Ansley. I came here to be with you."

He pulled her into his arms. He took her lips in a heated kiss. She dropped her keys and purse to the floor before wrapping her arms around his neck. Her body liquefied as he licked and then gently bit her bottom lip before he pushed his tongue inside her mouth. She went to her tiptoes and pushed closer. He was so much taller he had to practically bend over to kiss her.

As Roan increased the pressure of his lips, Ansley sucked on his tongue and threaded her fingers through the long hair at the back of his neck. He picked her off her feet and continued to kiss her while he walked to her couch. He laid her on it, then followed her down. It barely accommodated both of them. He positioned them so they lay on their sides, with him on the very edge.

Ansley threw her leg over Roan's hip. He trailed his hand down her side to the bottom of her T-shirt. He shoved under it and cupped her breast through her bra. He rubbed his thumb back and forth across her already taut nipple. When she moaned and pressed her breast closer, he took hold of her shirt and removed it, then threw it over his shoulder onto the floor. Her bra quickly followed.

Roan rolled her nipple between his thumb and index finger while he nibbled his way along her jaw. Needing to feel his skin next to hers, Ansley grabbed the bottom of his T-shirt and raised it to his chin. He lifted his head only long enough pull it off before he made a trail of kisses down to her chest. Wetness leaked from her pussy into her panties, soaking them. He cupped her breast and circled her nipple with his tongue just before he sucked it deep inside his mouth. With each pull, there was a corresponding sensation in her sex. She clenched her inner muscles as her body readied itself to be filled.

Ansley gasped. Roan alternated between sucking and flicking her nipple with his tongue. The hard length of his cock pressed against the inside of her thigh. Wanting to feel just how big he was, she reached down and cupped him through his jeans. A low growl rumbled out of his throat from deep down in his chest as she stroked him. He lightly dragged his teeth over her nipple. She undid his jeans and then reached inside to wrap her hand around his thick shaft.

With another low growl, Roan quickly undid her pants before he pushed them down past her hips, taking her panties with them. Once he had them completely off, he released her breast and trailed his hand to the part of her that ached to be filled. He claimed her lips in a hard kiss as he stroked her wet pussy with a finger before he pushed it inside her core.

Ansley pumped her hand up and down his cock in the same rhythm as Roan slid his finger in and out of her pussy. Once his second finger joined the first, she moaned into his mouth. He thrust harder, faster. She squeezed her pussy around his fingers. She bucked her hips, and her body coiled tighter. As if he sensed it wouldn't take much to send her over the edge, he stroked her clit with his thumb while his fingers worked inside her. With a loud moan, she shattered. Her inner walls clutched his digits as she came.

She relaxed against him. The last wave of pleasure receded, but Ansley wanted all of Roan, not just his fingers. She trailed hers up his hard shaft to the head of his cock. She rubbed the bead of pre-cum she found there into his skin. He left her mouth and buried his face in the crook of her neck as she fisted his erection. He pumped his hips against her.

Feeling the pleasure once again build inside her, Ansley shifted until her sex came into alignment with his cock. With her hand still wrapped around the base of his shaft, she moved forward until the head butted against her wet opening. She flexed her hips and pressed down to take his tip inside her pussy.

Roan lifted his head and growled loudly. He placed a restraining hand on her hip to hold her still. "No," he said in a strained voice.

Ansley opened her eyes to find that Roan's eyes glowed as he stared at her. Even though what she saw couldn't possibly be real, his eyes continued to glow, even after she blinked. She found it oddly arousing. Despite his large hand on her hip, she flexed her hips and took a little more of his cock inside her.

"Stop, Ansley," Roan said between his gritted teeth. "You don't know what you're doing. I'm only hanging on to my self-control by a thread."

She tried to take more of him, but Roan's grip on her hip tightened. "I thought this was what you wanted." She moaned. "I know I want it."

With a growl that couldn't be mistaken for anything but animalistic, Roan pushed her away as he fell off the couch onto the floor.

Not sure exactly what she'd done to cause such a violent reaction from him, Ansley silently watched him pick himself up.

He stood in front of her and looked down at her. His chest rapidly rose and fell. His cock stood erect from the open front of his jeans.

She didn't understand. It was obvious he wanted her. She reached out, but he shook his head.

He shoved his shaft inside his jeans and then did them up. He snatched up his T-shirt from the floor and yanked it on.

"Roan?" Ansley asked bewilderedly.

"This was a mistake. I shouldn't have come here." Without another word, Roan turned and then let himself out of her apartment.

Feeling as if Roan had just slapped her, Ansley got off the couch and gathered up her clothes. Hurt, with no real understanding of why Roan had run from her, she headed for the bathroom to take a shower. She'd thought things had been going well. Obviously, she'd done something wrong. It wouldn't be the first time a man had changed his mind about her once things got intimate. Her last boyfriend, who had only lasted a couple months, hadn't liked that she tended to be a bit aggressive in bed. When she'd held herself back, he'd ended up dumping her because he found her too cold.

Ansley stepped into the shower. The warm water ran over her. As she washed Roan's scent off her skin, she wished she could just as easily wash away the memory of how good it had felt to be held in his arms.

* * * *

Roan couldn't get away from Ansley's apartment fast enough. As he sped down the highway toward the Golden Gate Bridge, he tried to leash his wolf. It wanted to go back to her and finish what they'd started. He couldn't believe how close he'd come to giving in to his urge to claim her as his mate right then and there. As she'd come apart in his arms, with her moans filling his ears, he'd told himself that would be enough until he felt ready to explain to her what she was to him. When she'd taken the head of his cock inside her body, he'd had to fight himself, and the wolf, to keep from sheathing himself to the hilt in her welcoming heat.

He drove across the bridge and then headed for Marin County where he and his brothers and sister lived. The mansion was large enough for the seven of them, actually, now eight, since Eli, Saskia's mate, had moved in with them. In his current mood, Roan wished he lived alone.

Once he arrived at the mansion, Roan drove up the long drive and then parked his Lexus in the spacious six-car garage before he headed inside the house. Feeling as if his nerves had been stretched to their limits, he went to see if anyone else was home. He found Saskia and Eli in the living room, watching a movie on the large LCD screen TV. They were cuddled together on the couch. The sight of them made him long for Ansley.

Saskia turned her head in his direction when Roan walked into the room. She looked him up and down. "You look as if you're about ready to snap. I take it your evening didn't turn out like you'd planned."

He ran a hand through his hair. "I damn near fucked it up."

"What happened?" Eli asked. "Did you tell her about you being a werewolf, and she didn't take it well?"

Roan shook his head. "I haven't told her about that yet."

"Then what's the problem?" Saskia asked.

"I came pretty damn close to claiming her."

"I thought you wanted to take things slow with Ansley."

"I do, but it's turning out to be a lot harder than I thought it would be. I think I may have screwed things up."

"Why?"

"Let's just say I pulled the same stunt you did with Eli when you found yourself mated to him — I ran."

Saskia and Eli hadn't known they were mates when they'd first met. Eli being a mortal at the time, naturally, hadn't shown the signs a male werewolf displayed when he'd found his mate. It'd been so unexpected, Saskia had run from Eli right after their mating bond had been formed.

Saskia cringed. "You didn't."

"Oh, but I did. It was either that or finish what we'd started."

"What are you going to do to fix it?"

"I haven't got a clue. Right now, I need to work off my frustration." He gave Saskia a pointed look. "Time to return the favor I gave you when you came running home from Eli's."

Saskia smiled and got off the couch. "I'll get my sword and meet you downstairs." She looked at Eli. "Are you going to join us?"

Eli gave her a heated look. "I'd better not. You know how seeing you swing that sword of yours turns me on. I don't think Roan would appreciate it if I stole you away too soon."

She bent and gave Eli a quick kiss. "Maybe later I'll have to do a little sword practice of my own in our room."

Turning, Roan said in a sharp voice, "I'll be downstairs." He walked away from the couple before he did something stupid, like put his fist through the wall.

* * * *

In the basement, which they'd converted into a training area, Roan watched Saskia cross the room with sword in hand to stand in front of him. She swung the weapon in an arc to loosen up. He did the same with his. She wouldn't take it easy on him. She never did, which he now counted on. He needed to do something that would distract him from thinking about Ansley. Something that would tire him out. And Saskia would be the woman to give him what he needed.

At first glance, Saskia didn't look as if she would be a match for him, but looks could be deceiving. With her long, light-blonde, almost-white hair, flashing violet eyes and slim build, someone would think he could disarm her and have her at his mercy in a matter of seconds. That was so far off the mark it wasn't even funny. She hadn't been chosen to be the leader of six, large, lone-male werewolves for nothing. She could hold her own against any of them.

At Saskia's nod, they circled each other with their swords raised. While most werewolves their age had given up the sword long ago and chose to fight in wolf form if the need ever arose, Roxie's seven protectors still used the sword—their weapon of choice. Roan made the first strike, which she easily blocked. Circling each other again, he waited for another opening, then struck out at her. This time, sparks flew when their blades met.

Saskia and Roan parried and thrust. The sound of their swords clashing filled the room. Neither of them tried to hurt the other. This was for practice only. By the time he held up his hand to indicate he'd had enough, he and Saskia were sweating and out of breath.

"Feel better now?" Saskia asked while she panted.

He wiped the sweat out of his eyes before he answered. "A bit. At least I now should be able to sleep."

"That bad, is it?"

"I'm sure it isn't as bad as when you and Eli are away from each other for any length of time." Once mated, werewolf couples couldn't stand to be apart for very long. The longer away, the more anxious they became until they were together again, which usually ended up with the mated pair having sex.

"Just tell Ansley what you are, Roan. You're not doing either of you any good by holding off, especially not you."

25

He snorted. "Yeah, I'll just blurt out I'm a werewolf and that she's my mate and we'll live happily ever after. Ansley will think I need to be locked up with the rest of the crazies."

"You could always go wolf in front of her. She wouldn't be able to deny the truth then."

"No, but she could very well run away screaming. Or drop dead in a faint. I don't think she's as strong as you are, Saskia. She's a bit on the timid, shy side."

"I think you're second-guessing yourself too much, Roan. How long do you intend to drag this out? How long do you think you'll be able to last before you break and claim her without telling her the truth?"

"To be honest, I haven't a clue. Right now, seeing how long I can keep myself in control is the least of my worries. After the way I left Ansley, I wouldn't be surprised if she's more than a little pissed off with me."

Saskia closed the distance between them and gave Roan a hug. "I'm sure she'll forgive you. After all, you two are meant to be together."

Roan hugged her back. "I can only hope so."

CHAPTER FOUR

After a fitful sleep with his dreams filled with erotic images of Ansley in his bed, of her moaning his name as he took her over and over again, Roan headed to Roxie and Beowulf's house. It was his turn, along with his two brothers-in-arms, Dirk and Kye, to watch over Roxie. Not that she allowed them to do much more than sit around, taking up space. Even though she didn't think she needed their protection, Beowulf was more than grateful. She might think they were overdoing it, but it would only be a matter of time before someone made a move on her.

The person who worried them most was Miles—Saskia's brother by blood. At one time, he'd been chosen to be one of the foretold one's protectors, but that soon changed when he decided he wanted to have control over the foretold one rather than be a protector.

Roan found his brothers with Roxie, inside her second-floor office. Even though she didn't need a job, since Beowulf had more than enough money and then some, she continued to work at the web design business she'd started before she met her mate. As a self-proclaimed Internet junkie, she had told him she loved her job too much to give it up.

Kye sat on one of the chairs near Roxie's desk, looking bored out of his mind. Dirk, on the other hand, stood behind her chair, completely absorbed in what she worked on as she pointed to something on the monitor of her desktop computer. Roan shook his head. Dirk and Roxie would be up there for hours. Dirk, the only one of them who had completely embraced the technological age, now did all his investments through the Internet. Once Roxie had found out he was computer savvy like she was, she'd taken it upon herself to teach him everything she knew about web design. Something he had been interested in learning.

Knowing the other two were too absorbed in what they were doing to have heard him come into the room, Roan caught Kye's eye. "If you need me, I'll be outside in the back. I have to make a phone call."

Kye covered a large yawn with his hand. "Sure, go ahead. Not much is happening here. I don't know how those two can stare at that computer monitor for hours on end and not get a headache. My eyes would be crossing by now, especially if I had to look at that gibberish Roxie calls HTML code."

Roan chuckled. "I guess it helps if you can understand what you're looking at."

"I guess." Kye settled lower on his chair. "I think I'll catch some Z's until they decide they've had enough."

Having been in Kye's place more than once, Roan couldn't blame him. He slipped out of the room and then headed to the kitchen. He stepped through the sliding glass door and pulled his cell phone out of his jeans' front pocket before closing the door behind himself. He searched through his contact list until he found Ansley's work number, which he'd programmed into his phone earlier.

Once someone picked up on the other end, Roan asked to speak to Ansley. Put on hold, he patiently waited for her to answer. When she did, he said, "Hey, Ansley. It's Roan."

"Oh. What do you want?" Ansley asked in a clipped tone.

She was not happy to hear from him. "I thought we could get together again tonight."

Ansley didn't reply right away. "Why? So you can run out on me again?"

"Ah, look, that had nothing to do with you. Okay?"

"Sure, it didn't. You couldn't get away from me fast enough."

"I had my reasons for doing what I did. Let me see you tonight and I'll explain everything."

"I don't think so. Being humiliated by you once was more than enough. I have to go. I'm in the middle of cutting a client's hair. Bye, Roan." Ansley hung up before Roan could say anything else.

He couldn't leave things the way they now stood. Roan hit redial and once again asked to speak to Ansley after the other end picked up. This time the girl who answered told him Ansley wouldn't take any phone calls right now. After he hit the end button to hang up, he let out a low frustrated growl.

"Your soon-to-be-mate giving you a hard time?"

Roan looked up and realized he hadn't been alone out there. Beowulf sat at the patio table with a newspaper in his hand. Roan joined him. "You could say that. I have no one to blame but myself, though."

Beowulf folded the newspaper in half and then placed it on the patio table. "Having a mortal mate who knows nothing of our kind tends to make things a little more stressful."

"You're not kidding. By taking it slow, I now have Ansley not wanting to talk to or see me. Roxie told me to explain everything to Ansley before I claimed her, but I don't know if I can keep this up."

Beowulf chuckled. "I know Roxie means well, but sometimes it's best to go with instinct. I might not have told her I was a werewolf at first, and what it meant to be mated to one, but in the end it all worked out."

"What about giving Ansley a choice?"

Beowulf gave him a hard stare. "If you explain everything to Ansley and she refuses you, will you just walk away?"

Roan ran a hand through his hair. The very idea that Ansley would refuse him made him want to throw back his head and howl. "No, I wouldn't walk away. She's mine."

"Then don't give her a chance to refuse you. Roxie would call me a Neanderthal if she heard me tell you this, but I'm going to say it anyway. Go to Ansley, throw her over your shoulder, and take her someplace where you two can be alone. Then show her exactly how good it can be being mated to one of our kind."

Beowulf got up and then walked into the house. Roan stayed outside as he thought over what the other male had said. He was torn between doing what every fiber in his body demanded he do, and what he thought would be fair to Ansley. Once he finally reached a decision, he stood and went back inside.

On his way to the front door, he walked past Beowulf, who wished him good luck. Confident Beowulf would tell his brothers where he'd gone, Roan walked out the door and then headed for his car. Ansley was about to find out he wouldn't be so easily put off.

* * * *

Arriving at the hair salon, Roan parked his Lexus in the parking lot at the back of the building and then headed around to the front. More prepared this time for the harsh chemical smells that seemed to permeate the whole place, he tried to breathe shallowly as he yanked open the glass door before he stepped inside. He ignored the stares of the staff and clients, keeping his gaze glued on Ansley while he walked to her chair. Now that he was attuned to her scent, he easily picked it out from the harsher smells around him. It caused the wolf inside him to come to life.

Ansley had her back toward him. She was putting the final touches on the hair of the client she had in her chair. With the element of surprise on his side, he grabbed her shoulder, spun her around, and brought his lips down onto hers. At first, she didn't respond to his kiss, but when he threaded his fingers through her hair and hungrily slanted his mouth across hers, she melted against him with a sigh. She might be angry with him, but that didn't stop her from wanting him. More than satisfied with her response, Roan ended their kiss. Then, doing what Beowulf had suggested, he bent down and picked her up over his shoulder.

As soon as he straightened to his full height, Ansley struggled. Roan slapped her shapely ass. "Stop that, or I'll do more than tap you on the butt." To show her he was serious, he turned his head and nipped her bottom.

With a shriek of outrage, Ansley reached down and slapped him on the ass. "Roan, put me down this second. You can't just barge in here and haul me over your shoulder like a sack of potatoes."

He snorted. "I just did, babe. Now I'm taking you out of here."

"Like hell you are. I have other clients waiting."

Roan turned and met the gaze of one of the other girls, a pretty brunette who worked in the salon. "Can you tell your boss that Ansley has to take the rest of the day off? For personal reasons." When the girl gave him a small smile and nodded, he said, "There, Ansley, you don't have any more clients to worry about today. Where is your purse?"

Ansley slapped him on the butt again—hard. "I'm not telling you."

The girl Roan had spoken to came around him and pulled open the bottom drawer on the counter in front of Ansley's chair. She reached inside and took out what he presumed was Ansley's purse.

"Here it is," she said.

Roan smiled and took it from her. "Thanks."

"Sherry, how could you?" Ansley wailed at his back.

Sherry gave Roan a wink. "Ansley, if a guy this good-looking came into the shop, kissed me the way he did you, and threw me over his shoulder—honey, I wouldn't fight him."

Spinning around, Roan headed out of the salon. He heard whispered comments as he walked by the other people. More than one woman said she wished a man would come and sweep her off her feet as he'd done to Ansley. Outside, he kept her captive over his shoulder and walked to the parking lot.

"Put me down, Roan."

"I don't think so."

"All the blood is rushing to my head. It isn't exactly comfortable."

"We're almost at my car. I'll put you down then."

Obviously not satisfied with his answer, Ansley pinched his butt. "Put. Me. Down. Now."

Roan grunted, the only outward sign to show her he'd felt her pinch. "No. You only brought this on yourself when you hung up and then refused to talk to me. You left me no other choice."

At his car, he opened the passenger door and put Ansley inside. He buckled the seatbelt around her before he shut her in and then hurried to the driver's side.

She turned to glare at him as he settled in the seat before he started the car. "What about my car?" she asked.

"We'll come back for it later." He pulled onto the street and headed in the direction of Ansley's apartment.

Ansley crossed her arms over her chest and stared out the windshield. "Why are you doing this?"

"I'm not letting you go that easily."

"Says the man who said last night was a mistake? How else would you expect me to react? I let you do things to me and then you left me naked on my couch, wondering what the hell I'd done wrong."

Roan cringed. "I know it looked bad from your perspective, but I really did have a very good reason for doing what I did. Once I explain everything, you'll understand." He shot a quick glance in Ansley's direction, only to see she stared daggers at him.

"I'm sure that bullshit line works on some women, but it won't work on me. I have no intention of listening to a word you have to say, and you can't make me."

That was like waving a red flag in front of the wolf's face. "We'll see about that."

They drove the rest of the way to Ansley's building in silence. After Roan parked the car, she got out before he had even shut off the engine. He caught up to her just before she reached the front entrance. He smiled to himself as she stomped up the stairs to her apartment. His mate might be on the shy side, but once riled, she had no qualms about standing up for herself. This was a trait that would hold her in good stead, in her role as a mate to a werewolf.

Ansley unlocked the door and then walked inside. Roan closed it behind them. She threw her purse on the kitchen table.

"How about we sit on the couch and I'll say what I came here to say," he said.

She made no move to go into the small living room. Ansley leaned back against the kitchen table and glared at him. "I don't think so. I'm not going anywhere near that couch while you're here."

He crossed the distance between them until he stood close, but not so close as to make her uncomfortable. "Fine. We'll talk here. About last night—"

She quickly cut him off. "I told you I don't want to hear it. Just leave, Roan."

"I'm not going anywhere."

"This is my place, not yours. I decide who I invite over, and I didn't invite you."

"I can understand you're a little pissed off with me right now."

"You think?" Ansley asked sarcastically. "Let me make this clearer for you. Get. Out."

Ansley had no idea; the harder she pushed him away, the more the wolf inside tried to take over. With the mating urge still riding him, Roan had a harder time holding back the wilder side of his nature. "No."

"Fine. You can stand there all day, for all I care. It doesn't mean I have to be in the same room with you." Ansley walked by him and headed for her bedroom.

Once she turned her back on him, what little control he still had over the wolf snapped. It no longer could wait to claim Ansley as his mate, to mark her with his scent, and make her his. Roan caught the bedroom door before she slammed it in his face. He crowded her, forcing her to back farther into her room. With a low growl of need, he cupped her face and brought his lips down to hers.

He pushed his tongue inside her mouth. The taste of her caused his erect cock to harden even more. Just like in the hair salon, Ansley didn't fight him. The heady scent of her arousal wafted around them as she moaned and pressed her body to his.

Roan angled his lips over hers. He dropped his hands to cup her bottom and haul her up against his erection. It was his turn to moan when Ansley shoved her hands under his T-shirt and dragged her nails down his back. He picked her up off her feet and crossed the room to the bed in two long strides.

He placed Ansley on the center, then followed her down to lie on his side next to her. Their tongues twined while he shoved his hand under her top and cupped her breast. He tugged at her already taut nipple. With his lips and tongue, he left a wet trail on her skin, making his way along her jaw to the side of her neck. He lifted his head only long enough to pull her top off, over her head. Reaching under her, he undid the clasp of her bra, and then pulled it off too.

Ansley arched her back as he trailed kisses along her collarbones and down to the top of her breasts. Roan shifted lower on her body, then circled her tight nipple with his tongue. As she threaded her fingers through his hair to hold him to her, he opened his mouth and sucked the taut peak deep inside. His cock jerked as she gasped and dug her fingernails into his scalp.

While he sucked on her nipple, Roan trailed his fingers across her stomach to the top of her jeans. He made short work of undoing them. He hooked the waistband with his fingers, pushing them down past her hips.

Ansley kicked off her shoes.

He yanked her pants the rest of the way off, then shifted lower on the bed. He released her nipple, then kissed his way down to the top of her panties, settling his upper body between her spread thighs and kissing his way even lower. The smell of Ansley's arousal filled his head. A growl pushed past his lips as he dragged his tongue along her pussy through her underwear.

She bucked beneath him.

Roan swirled his tongue inside her belly button as he tugged her panties down and off. Once again settling between her legs, he pushed on the inside of her thighs to spread her legs even farther apart and licked her from bottom to top. He moaned and growled at his first real taste of her sex. "You taste even better than you smell," he said in a husky voice.

Dipping his head once again, Roan laved her pussy with the flat of his tongue. He lapped at her until Ansley's hips rose off the bed. He circled her clit once before he sucked it into his mouth. She moaned and gripped the sheets beneath her. He licked and sucked, pushing one, and then another finger inside her wet core. He pumped them in and out as her inner walls clamped down around them.

He continued to pleasure her with his fingers and tongue, taking her to the brink of her orgasm before he pulled back. He slipped from the bed, then kicked off his shoes before taking off his socks and removed his T-shirt. Ansley's hot gaze caressed him while he undid his jeans and pushed them down past his hips. Her stare locked on to his cock, which stood erect from his body. Now naked, Roan got back on the bed and settled his hips between her legs.

He took her hand and led it to his erection. He closed his eyes and moaned at the feel of her fingers wrapped around his shaft, and allowed her to pump her hand up and down his thick length a few times before he pulled it away. Roan opened his eyes to find

Ansley staring at him. He knew what she saw — his eyes would be glowing mutedly. It wasn't something he could control when aroused.

Roan rested his weight on his bent arms and pressed the tip of his cock against her slick opening. Ansley gripped the tops of his shoulders and wrapped her legs around his waist. With one thrust, he sheathed his cock to the hilt inside her pussy. The feel of her wet heat wrapped around his shaft made him growl deep inside his chest. They were a perfect fit.

With their gazes locked, Roan pulled back, then surged inside her body once again. He kept the pace slow and steady until Ansley lifted her head and dragged her tongue across his skin where his neck and shoulder met. Then he rode her harder. He cupped the back of her head to hold her in place.

"Use your teeth instead of your tongue," he urged.

Ansley did as he asked. He stiffened in anticipation. She dragged her teeth over the spot once before she latched on to him with her teeth. No longer able to hold himself back, Roan pounded into her. She lifted her hips to match his strokes as he sank his cock inside her over and over again.

As his release edged nearer, a part of his soul reached out to Ansley. When a part of hers reached out for his and wrapped around it, making them one, he braced his upper body onto his hands. His shaft rubbed her clit with each stroke. She gripped his biceps as her release overtook her. Her strong inner walls clutched his cock while she came. It was enough to send him over the edge into his own release. He moaned and growled. His shaft pulsed, emptying deep inside her, filling her with his cum.

Still hard, Roan rolled them to their sides with Ansley's leg over his hip. He tucked her head under his chin as he fought to catch his breath. She was now his. He held her close. Ansley relaxed against him. He'd taken her choice away. Hopefully, she would understand why he'd done it, because there would be no going back. For better or worse, they were now mated.

CHAPTER FIVE

Ansley lay curled around Roan, listening to the sound of his heart beating. Ending up in bed together had been the last thing she expected when he'd carried her out of the hair salon. She'd been more than a little angry with him, but then he'd kissed her, and she'd forgotten all about her anger. One possessive kiss and the man sent her body into intense arousal. And he had known it, had used it to his advantage. The snake.

She shifted slightly and bit back a moan at the feel of his cock still buried inside her, thick and hard. Ansley had no idea how Roan had managed it. Even though he had come, he hadn't lost his erection. She didn't think most men could achieve that feat, not that she'd had a whole lot of experience. Making love to him, by no means, could be compared to the two other men's performance who she'd slept with in the past. He blew them right out of the water.

It wasn't just that the sex had been mind-blowing, which it'd been. There were a couple of other things that set him apart from the rest. For starters, what was up with the glowing eyes and animal-sounding growls he'd made? If she let herself think about those things too closely right now, she could very well freak out. She pushed those aside. It was what had happened while they'd made love that concerned her more. And *something* had happened. Ansley had felt it. It was as if a part of her had reached for Roan, then joined with a part of him. *How could that be?* She had to have imagined it, but it'd felt so real.

Ansley pulled back in Roan's embrace so she could look up at him. His light-blue eyes still had a slight glow to them. She didn't think any contacts existed that made them do that.

Feeling a little freaked, she took a deep breath, and said, "Roan, your eyes. They glow. Why? And I don't know if it was just my imagination, but something happened while we made love." Roan leaned forward to claim her lips, but she placed her fingers on his mouth to keep him away. "You said you would explain everything."

Roan pulled away and kissed the tip of each of her fingers. "Later. Right now, I want you again."

Ansley bit her bottom lip.

Roan sucked the tip of her index finger into his mouth. He swirled his tongue around it.

"You're trying to distract me."

He flexed his hips to sink his hard cock a little deeper inside her. "The explanations can wait. I want to make you to come while you scream my name."

Roan held on to her thigh as he pumped his hips between her legs. The feel of him moving deep inside her caused her arousal to build once again. This time when he went to claim her lips, she didn't push him away. She sucked on his tongue. He growled into her mouth. The sound pushed her arousal even higher.

Ansley threaded the fingers of one hand through his hair and kissed him with nothing held back. Once Roan growled again and held her closer, she grew bolder. She pushed at his shoulder, getting him to roll onto his back. With his cock still buried deep, she straddled his hips. She sat up, then slowly rode him. As she moved up and down on his shaft, his eyes once again glowed, this time brighter.

Roan thrust his hips to match her strokes. Reaching up, he cupped her breasts. She tightened her inner walls around his thickness as he lifted his head and sucked one of her nipples into his mouth. Ansley moaned. With each pull, she felt it deep inside her pussy. She rode him faster, all the while her orgasm inched closer. He trailed one hand down her body to where they were joined. He stroked her clit. With a keening moan, her head fell back. Her body climaxed around his cock.

After the last wave of pleasure receded, Roan lifted her off him and placed her onto her stomach. He moved behind her as he took hold of her hips and urged her to her knees. He dragged the flat of his tongue up the curve of her spine before he kneeled between her spread thighs. Ansley rested her upper body on her bent arms. The tip of his cock probed her wet entrance before he surged inside her.

Roan held her in place with his hands on her hips and pistoned into her. He took her hard and fast. Another climax built as he pumped his cock in and out of her. She clutched the sheets and pushed back to meet each of his strokes. He grew even harder. She fell over the edge, moaning his name. He growled and moaned and pushed into her one final time. She gasped with pleasure as his shaft pulsed deep inside her.

Sated, Ansley collapsed onto the bed. Roan pulled his still-hard cock out of her and moved to lie next to her. He lifted her off the mattress and placed her on top of him so she lay sprawled along him. Panting to catch her breath, she kissed his chest. He wrapped his arms around her. Totally relaxed, she snuggled closer and her eyes drifted shut.

* * * *

Unaware she'd fallen asleep until Roan gently shook her, Ansley blinked her eyes open and lifted her head off his chest to give him a half smile. "Sorry. I didn't sleep very well last night. I hope I didn't drool."

Roan stroked his hand down her back to her bottom. "You can sleep later. Why don't you get dressed and then throw some clothes into a suitcase? I want us to be on the road in about fifteen minutes."

Her brows drew together. "Where exactly are you taking me? And why do I have to pack some clothes?"

Roan slid out from under her and got out of bed. "We're going to my place. And you need clothes because you'll be staying the night."

Ansley had a hard time trying to keep her thoughts straight with Roan completely naked. The man had the bod of a body builder. He was all muscle, without an inch of fat on him anywhere. She sat up and ran her gaze across his thickly muscled chest, then down to his washboard abs. She dropped it even lower until she came level with his large cock, which was semi-erect. It lengthened and hardened.

A large T-shirt smelling like Roan smacked her in the face. Pulling it off, Ansley complained, "Hey! What did you do that for?"

Roan picked his jeans off the floor and then put them on. Much to Ansley's dismay, he tucked his now-erect cock inside and then did up the button. "If you kept looking at me like that, we'd never get out of here."

"And that would be bad because…?"

He leaned toward her and braced his hands on the mattress. His lips hovered over hers. He said, "I would much rather get you into my bed, which is a lot bigger than yours. It'll give me more room to lick every inch of your body before I take you, over and over again."

His deep husky voice went straight to Ansley's pussy, causing it to ache with arousal. "As long as I get to lick every inch of your body, I'm game." She gave the large bulge in his jeans a pointed look.

Roan's eyes glowed for a split second before he jerked away. "Ah, shit. Now I'm not going to be able to think of anything else but having your tongue on me." He gathered her clothes off the floor before he threw them on the bed next to her. "Get dressed and pack a suitcase. And don't take any longer than you have to. Just remember, the more time you spend in here, the longer it'll be before you can do all those delicious things with your tongue." He snatched his T-shirt off the bed, then picked up his socks and shoes before he left her alone in the bedroom.

Ansley jumped off the bed and got dressed in record time. It only took her a few minutes to dig her overnight bag out of the closet. She shoved some clothes and a hairbrush into it before she left the bedroom and went to the bathroom to get her toothbrush. After she came out, she found Roan standing impatiently by the apartment door.

She picked up her purse from the kitchen table before, then went to join him. "What about my car? It's still parked at the salon."

"Do you have to work tomorrow?"

"No."

"Then it can stay there for now. We'll get it for you sometime tomorrow." With that said, Roan opened the apartment door and then ushered her into the hallway.

Ansley closed the door and locked it. He took her overnight bag from her and laced the fingers of his other hand with hers. She let him lead her down the stairs and outside to the parking lot. In no time flat, he had them inside his Lexus and they drove down the street.

Ansley watched the scenery go by. She had no idea where Roan lived, but when they crossed the Golden Gate Bridge and headed for the North Bay area, she realized he must live in Marin County. It was a very affluent area with its share of ridiculously expensive mansions. If he lived there, he had more money than she'd first thought.

Once Roan pulled his Lexus onto a long private drive, and Ansley got her first look at the mansion up ahead, she swallowed. Now she knew why he hadn't wanted to stay overnight at her hole-in-the-wall apartment. Compared to his house, her place looked like a slum.

As Roan parked in front of a large six-car garage, Ansley asked, "Do you live here by yourself?"

Roan pulled the keys out of the ignition and smiled. "No. I share the house with my five brothers, sister, and her ma...her husband."

Ansley's eyes widened. "Five brothers and a sister? And you can live together without killing each other?"

"Mostly," Roan said with a chuckle. "Actually, two of my brothers are by blood. The other three and my sister, we sort of adopted each other."

"What about your parents? Do they live here too?"

"No. My parents died a long time ago."

"Oh. Sorry."

"It's okay. Let's go inside."

Ansley got out of the car while Roan collected her overnight bag from the backseat. She looked at the large house. If he lived with his brothers and sister, there was a good chance at least one of them would be inside. Somehow, her relationship with him had gone from basically being non-existent to meeting-the-family stage in a matter of hours. She didn't know how she felt about that. Just because Roan and she'd had sex didn't mean they now had a commitment and would get married. Not that she wouldn't mind being able to keep him as her own, but realistically, the chances that they'd work out for the long haul were not very good. Not with her track record when it came to relationships.

Roan came around to her side of the car and took her hand. Once they walked through the front door, Ansley heard more than one male voice coming from somewhere inside the house.

"I take it some of your brothers are home?"

With a quick sniff, Roan nodded. "All of them are."

Considering Ansley had only heard two different male voices, it made her wonder how Roan knew all five of his brothers where home. She walked beside him as he headed farther into the house. The sound of male laughter fell away once she and Roan stepped through the entrance to the large living room. Her mouth fell open when she got her first look at the five, very large, very muscular men who sat there. It looked as if an underwear model convention took place in Roan's home. With their gorgeous faces and well-muscled bodies, they could have made a fortune off their looks alone. She couldn't stop staring at them. She'd never seen so many good-looking men all in one place before.

Roan snarled beside her. "Maybe introducing you to them isn't such a great idea, after all."

One of Roan's brothers, one of the two who had their long hair pulled back in a ponytail, got up from the couch and walked to where they stood. His features were very similar to Roan's, right down to the same light-brown hair and light-blue eyes. Ansley guessed this had to be one of Roan's true brothers.

"Don't be a prick, Roan," his brother said. He looked at Ansley. "Introduce us." The other men got up and came to stand before them as well.

Roan stepped closer and pulled her under his arm. "The a-hole demanding I introduce you is my true brother, Jager. Our brother, Skylar, is the other one with his hair in a ponytail."

Ansley gave Jager and then Skylar a tentative smile. Skylar shared his brothers' good looks.

Roan continued. "Dirk is standing on Jager's left. Next to him is Kye. And beside Skylar is Leif."

Her gaze settled on each of the men. Dirk had blond highlights in his dark-brown that fell past his shoulders. His eyes were dark green. Kye had dark-blond hair that just touched the top of his shoulders. His brown eyes looked into hers, and he nodded in her direction. Leif's short, auburn hair was the most conservative of the bunch. When she met his blue-eyed gaze, he winked at her, then proceeded to look her up and down. Standing in the midst of these six men who all stood well over six foot six, Ansley felt awfully short.

Roan pulled her even closer to his side. "This is Ansley."

"She's just a little thing," Jager said. "I bet she weighs next to nothing, too."

"You won't be finding out," Roan said through gritted teeth.

Leif pushed Jager out of the way so he stood in front of her and reached for her hand. He quickly pulled back when Roan snapped his teeth at him.

Roan gave Leif a pointed look. "You'll keep your hands, and paws, to yourself."

Leif chuckled. "Just wanted to be friendly. With your scent all over her, and seeing that mark on your neck, I don't need to be told who she belongs to."

Ansley felt her face flush when she looked at Roan's neck and saw the bite mark she'd left on his skin, peeking out from under the collar of his T-shirt.

Leif chuckled again. "I think I just embarrassed her. Sorry, Ansley. There's no reason to be ashamed about leaving your mark on Roan. It'll just let any female wer—"

Roan cut Leif off before he could finish his sentence. He loudly cleared his throat. "Enough, Leif."

Leif looked from her, then to Roan, who he gave a look of pity. "I get it. Your best intentions went out the window, didn't they? That's why you brought her here. Well, good luck with that."

Ansley only listened to what Leif said to Roan with half an ear. With all these hunky men around her, she had a hard time not staring at each of them. They all looked as if they'd walked off a cover of a romance novel. Each one of them exuded confidence and sex appeal. She doubted any of them had trouble getting a woman. Not that she was interested in Roan's brothers in that way. Roan's good looks attracted her more than his brothers' did.

Noticing the room had gone completely silent, Ansley looked at the men who stood around her. From the scowl on Roan's face, she realized she'd been caught staring. She gave him a sheepish smile.

"Hey, as long as they're here, I'm going look. I'm not dead, you know." Ansley cringed when the last word left her mouth. That hadn't exactly been smart to tell the man she'd just slept with that she'd been ogling his brothers. Her cursed mouth had done it again.

Instead of getting mad or berating her, Roan picked her up and walked out of the living room. Once they were out of sight, Ansley heard his brothers making bets about when she and Roan would leave his bed.

Roan reached the bottom of the stairs that led to the upper level and hurried up them.

Ansley felt her face flame red. As first impressions went, she had to say the one she'd made sucked. Not sure if she could face his brothers again, she put her head on his shoulder and let him carry her away.

CHAPTER SIX

Roan didn't let her down until he had them behind the closed door of what Ansley presumed had to be his bedroom. She only managed to get a quick look at the very solid, masculine furnishings and large bed before he pulled her to him. He took her lips in a demanding kiss as he lifted her so he could grind his erection against her pussy. Just like that, her embarrassment slipped away, replaced by an intense wave of arousal. She even forgot about his brothers downstairs. All that mattered was getting closer to the hard bulge in his pants.

Once she squirmed against him, Roan let her slide down his body until her feet touched the floor. He took a step back and slowly took off his clothes. Ansley watched his every movement while she stripped out of hers. After they were naked, she closed the space between them and ran her hands up his chest to the tops of his shoulders. She went on tiptoe, cupped the back of his head, and tugged until his lips touched hers. She nipped and licked at his mouth until he opened for her.

She swept the inside with her tongue and brushed the tips of her breasts against his chest. Roan growled softly. She left his mouth and pressed her lips along his firm jaw to his ear. She swirled her tongue inside it before she took his earlobe between her teeth and gave it a small tug. He moaned, and she left his ear and kissed a path down the side of his throat to where his neck and shoulder met. He stiffened and went to wrap his arms around her as she licked the bitemark.

Ansley pulled back and shook her head. "Let me have my way with you this time. Remember, I said I wanted to lick and kiss every inch of you."

Roan dropped his hands and groaned. "You make me want to howl, in a good way."

Stepping close again, Ansley licked and kissed her way along the thick muscles of his chest and down to his flat nipples. She held on to Roan's sides and licked one small nub with the tip of her tongue before she sucked it between her teeth. He ground his hard cock against her as she moved to his other nipple and did the same to it.

She continued her downward trail to his washboard abs. His stomach muscles quivered as she licked her way down even farther. Ansley went on her knees before Roan and looked up at him. His light-blue eyes glowed mutedly. She turned her attention to his erect cock and rubbed the drop of pre-cum on the tip into his skin before she wrapped her hand around his shaft. She flicked out her tongue and ran it around the head.

He groaned and pressed his hips closer.

With a firm grip on his erection, Ansley stroked her tongue along Roan's full length. An ache built inside her pussy. She grew wet with desire. She licked the tip of him, then opened her mouth to take as much of his length as she could handle inside. His hands threaded through her hair and he moaned and growled deep inside his chest. He pumped his hips while she sucked. Pleasuring him in this way aroused her even more. She drew on him harder and brought up her other hand to cup the heavy flesh between his legs.

Roan's movements grew jerky. His cock hardened even more. "Enough, Ansley. I need to be inside you. Now."

He pulled her to her feet. Roan lifted her into his arms as he took her mouth in a heated kiss. Ansley wrapped her legs around his waist and ground her wet pussy against his hard shaft. He switched his grip to her bottom, then positioned the tip of his cock at the entrance to her body. He flexed his hips, and sheathed himself to the hilt with one stroke. She held on to him tightly, and he carried her to the bed, keeping their bodies joined. Each of his steps drove his shaft deeper inside her.

Roan placed her on the center of his large bed so she lay on her back. Supporting his weight on his bent arms, he slowly thrust into her.

Ansley moaned into his mouth at the feel of his thick, hard cock working in and out of her. Stretched and filled, she matched his strokes. She clutched his erection with her inner muscles, increasing her pleasure.

He angled his strokes higher on her body so his shaft rubbed her clit, and pumped his hips faster.

Ansley's release built deep inside her pussy. It wouldn't take much to push her over the edge. She lifted her head and nipped the bite mark on Roan's neck. He moaned loudly before he turned slightly to the side to give her better access. Knowing how much he'd found it a turn-on when she'd bitten him before, she bit down on the same spot and held on with her teeth. She didn't break the skin, but she did it hard enough to leave another mark on him.

Roan cupped her bottom and lifted her hips as he pounded into her.

Ansley continued to hold him with her teeth until the first flutter of her orgasm started. Once it hit, her head fell back and she moaned. With her pussy clutching his shaft, gripping his cock in a tight fist, his moans joined hers as he too came deep inside her.

Ansley held Roan tightly after he collapsed on top of her. His cock was still a thick, hard length buried inside her pussy. It made her wonder if he would always be able to sustain an erection even after he'd come. If he could, he would spoil her for other men. She would expect the next guy to be able to keep it up for just as long as Roan could.

Roan propped himself up on his arms and kissed the tip of her nose. "What are you thinking about?"

She smiled. "You."

He smiled back. "I hope they're all good thoughts and not bad."

"Oh, they're definitely good. I can't help but notice your little talent here." Ansley gave his still-hard cock a squeeze with her inner muscles. "I have a feeling the more I sleep with you, the more the chances are I'll expect every man I take to my bed to be able to do the same."

Ansley had kept her words teasing and light, so she didn't expect the kind of reaction she got out of Roan. His upper lip curled up on a loud growl. She found her hands held over her head and pressed to the mattress by one of his before she had time to protest.

He took her lips in a hard kiss that left her breathless once he lifted his head. "The only man in your bed will be *me*," he said in a husky voice. "There will *be* no others."

She stared at him, not sure Roan meant what she thought he meant. "What do you mean? Are you saying you already know I'm the one for you? That soon I can expect you to get down on bended knee and ask me to marry you?"

"I don't need to do that," Roan replied. He pulled back until his cock was almost free of her body, then pushed back into her. "You're already mine."

Roan claimed her mouth in a hard kiss. This time he took her hard and fast. He hooked one of her legs over his arm and pounded into her.

Swept away by the sensations that surged through her, Ansley could only hold on to him. His thick cock plunged into her over and over again until she reached her release. Coming at the same time, his head fell back with a howl that she would have thought sounded too animalistic to be human if she hadn't been limp and sated with pleasure.

He pulled his still-hard cock from her body, then lay on his back and gathered her close so she lay on her side with her head pillowed on his chest.

Beyond relaxed, Ansley's eyes drifted shut, and she snuggled closer to Roan.

* * * *

She and Roan ended up making love for most of the night. Inconceivably, he'd been able to keep his erection for hours at a time. He'd also taken her in every position imaginable. Near dawn, he'd finally allowed her to sleep more than an hour. Not that Ansley had complained about the way he'd kept her up most of the night.

Ansley stretched and slowly came awake. She cringed a bit at all the aches she had in the intimate places of her body. She smiled to herself. After the marathon of sex she and Roan had participated in, she guessed it was to be expected. She hadn't ever had that much sex at one time.

She turned her head toward the other side of the bed and found the spot where Roan had slept beside her empty. Ansley rolled to her side and pressed her face into his pillow. His scent still lingered on the pillowcase.

She rolled onto her back and pulled the covers up to her shoulders. Not knowing exactly where Roan had gone, and not wanting to run into one of his brothers or sister if she went in search of him, Ansley decided she would just stay in bed until he came back. After the minutes ticked by and he still hadn't returned, she wondered if she shouldn't get dressed and look for him, after all.

Just as she was about to get out of bed, the bedroom door slammed open. Ansley let out a small shriek and pulled the covers up to her chin when Leif entered the room. He gave her a smile and lifted his arm to show he carried her overnight bag, which she'd left downstairs the day before.

"I thought I'd bring this up to you," Leif said while he placed it on the floor next to the bed. He gave her a smile that Ansley felt sure more than one woman had found hard to resist.

Keeping a stranglehold on the sheets, Ansley gave Leif a tentative smile. "Ah, thanks."

Leif made no move to leave. "Did you and Roan have a chance to talk during the night or did he keep you too...busy...for conversation?"

Ansley felt her cheeks heat as she blushed. How was she supposed to answer that question? No way in hell she was going to tell Roan's brother that Roan had been too busy screwing her brains out to have had any kind of conversation during the night. "Um...well..."

Leif chuckled. "I'm going to take that for a no."

A loud growl suddenly filled the room. She looked in the direction it had come from to find Roan framed in the doorway, much to her relief. His brows grew thunderous when his gaze landed on Leif. With two long strides, he crossed the room to his brother and grabbed Leif by the back of his T-shirt. Roan also took hold of the back of Leif's jeans and literally threw him out of the room.

Ansley cringed when she heard Leif hit the opposite wall in the hallway. Leif's loud cursing told her Roan had been far from gentle. Of course, the sound of the ruckus drew the rest of the occupants of the house to Roan's bedroom door, which still stood wide open. Naked under the sheets, she wondered if the situation could get any worse. It did.

After Roan's brothers found out what the commotion had been about, they all told Leif off. Somehow, while they talked loudly over each other, Jager, Skylar, and Dirk ended up inside the bedroom with Roan, while Leif and Kye stayed in the hallway. Luckily for Ansley, the first three had their backs to her and hadn't noticed her in the bed.

A long, shrill whistle soon cut through the men's voices. They fell silent and covered their ears with their hands until the whistling stopped. From her position on the bed, Ansley watched a woman, accompanied by another man, walk into the middle of the gathered men. This had to be Roan's sister. She gave each of her brothers a look that said she'd heard more than enough. She took charge of the situation.

Roan's sister pointed at Leif. "You should have known better. Going into Roan's bedroom while Roan wasn't there, you were only asking for trouble. And well you know it." She turned to Kye. "Make sure Leif goes downstairs and stays there until we come down for breakfast." Kye nodded, then waited for Leif to walk past him before he too, left.

She turned to the rest of her brothers. "Jager, Skylar and Dirk, get the hell out of Roan's bedroom unless you want to be thrown out the same way he threw Leif out."

Each man looked around as if they'd noticed where they were for the first time. None of them turned to look at her. They filed out one by one until only Roan's sister, the man who'd arrived with her, and Roan remained. Ansley found herself in awe of his sister. She'd managed to rein in all her brothers with very little effort, which Ansley thought had to be no small feat. Even though Roan's sister was tall for a woman, her brothers still towered over her, and had three times the muscle mass.

His sister cinched the belt of her housecoat tighter around her waist. She walked into the bedroom and went to Ansley. Her long, light-blonde hair looked a little mussed, as if she'd just gotten out of her bed.

She smiled. "We haven't been properly introduced yet. I'm Saskia York." She nodded in the direction of the hallway. "Over there is my husband, Eli."

Ansley nodded at Eli, then returned Saskia's smile. "I'm Ansley Conry. Nice to meet you."

"Likewise. Sorry about that. Leif tends to be a bit of a knucklehead at times. He's harmless. He just wanted to yank Roan's chain."

"Which he succeeded in doing," Roan said drolly. He came to the bed and sat next to Ansley. He turned to her. "I hope he didn't bother you too much before I threw him out."

Ansley shook her head. "No, he didn't. He just brought up my overnight bag and asked if you and I had a chance to talk yet." Roan and Saskia exchanged a meaningful look. Ansley could only guess what it meant.

"I'll have a chat with Leif," Saskia said to Roan. "He had no right to ask that. I'll make sure he keeps his nose out of where it doesn't belong."

Roan got up and kissed Saskia on the cheek. "Thanks. Now if you don't mind, I'm sure Ansley would like to get up."

Saskia nodded. "I'll see the two of you downstairs shortly." She went back into the hallway to her husband. Eli wrapped an arm around Saskia's shoulders. "Just don't take too long or you'll end up with nothing to eat for breakfast. The food supply is starting to get a little low. For punishment, I think I'll send Leif out to do the grocery shopping."

As the other couple walked away, Roan shut the bedroom door. He came back to the bed and lay on top of the sheets next to Ansley. "If I'd known Leif would pull a stunt like that, I wouldn't have left you alone."

Ansley turned to her side and brushed her lips against his. "No harm done, but I can think of a way for you to make it up to me," she said in a husky voice.

Roan chuckled. "After last night, I thought you would have

had enough of me by now."

She lifted herself on her elbow and ran her gaze down Roan's body. He wore a pair of jeans and nothing else. "I don't think I'll ever get enough of you."

He reached over and slapped her on the butt. "Insatiable, aren't you?"

"Only when it comes to you."

"I'm glad you feel that way, but I think you'd better get up before I never let you out of here. For one thing, you must be starved. I know I am. And Saskia wasn't kidding when she said we'd better not take too long. There's a good chance my brothers will eat all the food before we get down there, if we aren't lucky. You can have the bathroom first." Roan pointed to the en suite. "There's a shower in there, too. Help yourself."

At first, Ansley thought maybe she could persuade Roan to change his mind, but her stomach growled. Considering the two of them had not once left his bedroom last night, not even to eat supper, she ran on fumes. With a sigh of regret, she slipped out of bed and then grabbed her overnight bag on her way to the bathroom. She felt Roan's gaze follow her as she stepped inside, until she shut the door. She decided she would satisfy her hunger for food, then her other one.

CHAPTER SEVEN

After she and Roan had showered, they went downstairs. Ansley still couldn't get over the size of the house, or the luxuriousness of it. She would never have guessed in a million years that he and his brothers lived in a mansion so tastefully decorated. From what she'd seen so far, it looked as if a professional had decorated it. Given the amount of money he and his family had to have to afford a place such as this, she figured they probably had used an interior designer.

Once they reached the large front foyer with its black-and-white-checked marble floor, Roan led Ansley toward the back of the house. Even before they arrived at the kitchen, she smelled the scent of food cooking. Her stomach rumbled.

Roan pushed Ansley toward the large table that sat in the middle of the big room. "Sit next to Saskia and Eli, and I'll get us some food."

Much to her surprise, all of Roan's brothers sat at the table calmly eating. She'd thought they'd be rowdy, same as they'd been upstairs earlier. She took the empty chair next to Saskia, then looked down the table. The men nodded in her direction when she met each of their gazes, except for Dirk, who hadn't looked up from the financial section of the newspaper he was reading.

Roan returned with two plates that each held a very large omelet. He set one in front of her before he left to get the two cups of coffee sitting on the counter. Ansley looked at her plate. She was hungry, but she wasn't that hungry.

Saskia leaned over and whispered into Ansley's ear, "Don't worry about it if you can't eat all that. The guys tend to forget that not everybody can eat like they do."

"If I ate this much all the time, I would be as big as a house," Ansley said, laughing.

"Same here."

Roan came back to the table and handed Ansley a cup of coffee. "I hope the two of you weren't talking about me when I wasn't here."

Saskia rolled her eyes. "No. I just told Ansley that she didn't have to feel obligated to eat all that food you gave her. You must think she eats like a horse like you do."

"Sorry about that, Ansley." Roan pushed his plate closer to hers. "You can put what you don't want on my plate. I'll eat it for you."

After cutting the omelet in half, she pushed one part onto his plate. "That should be enough." Once Roan moved his food back in front of him and dug in, Ansley turned back to Saskia. "So, how long have you and Eli been married?"

"Just a little over a month."

"You're still newlyweds, then?"

"You could say that," Eli said from Saskia's other side. He gave his wife a heated look.

A muffin flew by and hit Eli dead center on his forehead. "Knock off the goo-goo eyes, Eli," Leif said. He sat across and a little down the table from Eli. "Take it to the bedroom so the rest of us don't have to be subjected to it. We *are* trying to eat, you know."

Eli chucked the muffin back at Leif. "You're just jealous that you don't have what Saskia and I have."

"Hell, no. I like being a free agent."

"Your time will come. Take it from someone who once thought the same way you do."

Ansley ate her omelet while Leif and Eli bantered back and forth. It was obvious Eli had been accepted as another brother. Roan moved his chair closer to hers so their thighs were pressed against each other. He placed a hand on top of her leg and squeezed. Such a simple gesture, but it made her body respond to his touch. She reached under the table and put her hand on his hard thigh while she continued to eat. She'd just taken a sip of coffee when he moved to the inside of her thigh and gently brushed between her legs with his knuckles. She had to quickly swallow the liquid before she choked on it.

Taking a quick peek at Saskia to make sure she couldn't see what took place under the table, Ansley stroked her hand up Roan's thigh and skimmed her fingers over the bulge in his jeans. He stiffened for a fraction of a second before he rubbed her pussy with the side of his hand. It took all her concentration to act as if nothing was going on.

With more boldness than she thought she possessed, Ansley cupped Roan's cock through his jeans and gave him a squeeze. His sharp, indrawn breath told her she had to be getting to him same as he was getting to her. Another muffin hit him square in the chest. Ansley quickly pulled her hand off him.

She looked up to find Leif staring at her and Roan. "Would the pair of you cut it out? It's bad enough we have to put up with Saskia and Eli. If you want to make a move on each other, please take it somewhere I'm not. I can smell the pair of you all the way over here."

Ansley shifted uncomfortably. She had no idea what had come over her. She usually didn't do things like fondle a man while in the company of his family, and where anyone could see what they were up to. Embarrassed at being caught, she jerked her gaze down to her plate and kept it there. Leif's words acted like a bucket of ice water on her arousal.

"You're walking a fine line, Leif." Roan snarled. "If you don't like the smell, you can always leave."

Ansley resisted the urge to turn her head, lift her arm, and give her armpit a sniff. Since she'd just had a shower, she didn't think she smelled bad. She kept her head down and concentrated on finishing her food. Everyone around the table suddenly went silent. She didn't have to look up to know they all had turned their gazes her way.

"Ah, shit," Leif said, breaking the silence. "I'm sorry, Ansley. I didn't mean to embarrass you. I only thought to give Roan a hard time. I know you and he don't have any control over it."

She had no idea what *it* was, but she decided it would be best to let it go. She looked up to meet Leif's gaze. He wore an apologetic expression. "No need to apologize, Leif. To be honest, it doesn't take much to make me feel embarrassed. I think I spend half my life feeling like that, mostly from my own doing. My curse makes sure of that."

"Your curse?" Roan asked with a chuckle.

Ansley turned her gaze to him. "Well, that's what I call it. You've already been subjected to it. There are times when I say pretty much whatever happens to be on my mind at the time. I also tend to say things that, if I'd really thought about them, should have been kept to myself."

Roan put his arm along the back of her chair and leaned in to kiss her cheek. "Then you and Jager should get along famously. He says whatever he has on his mind, too, but unlike you, he doesn't give a shit how people react to it."

She turned her head to look in Jager's direction at the end of the table. He shrugged. "What can I say? I like to be direct, and to the point. It's what makes me so lovable."

Everyone but Ansley broke out in laughter. Skylar, who sat closest to Jager, punched him in the arm. "Yeah, you're about as lovable as a rattlesnake when you're in one of your moods. You get pissed off, and you make damn sure everyone around you knows about it and why."

Jager crossed his arms over his wide chest. "Nothing wrong with being out in the open about how you feel."

Roan pushed back his chair and stood. He held his hand out to her. Ansley took it and allowed him to pull her up. He spoke to the room at large. "Now that Ansley has finished eating, she and I are going out for a bit. I promised I would take her to get her car. We'll be back later." He turned to Saskia. "If you don't have other plans for me, that is."

Saskia waved them away. "Go. Roxie will understand, not that she feels she needs us there, anyway. Eli and I will go with Jager and Dirk."

"Then, Ansley and I are out of here."

Ansley let Roan walk her out of the kitchen. Leif's words about her and Roan not having any control over *it* played through her mind. She couldn't help but think this *it* was somehow connected to the talk Roan had originally wanted to have with her before they'd ended up in bed together at her apartment. Maybe if they kept their hands off each other long enough, they could have that talk sometime soon, but she wasn't going to bet on it.

* * * *

After they collected her car from the salon's parking lot, Roan and Ansley went to her apartment. Determined to prove she could be around him and not think about hot, sweaty sex, she threw her overnight bag onto her bed and then returned to the living room to sit on the couch next to him. She sat sideways so she faced him and crossed her legs in front of her. He put his arm on the back of the couch and turned his body toward her.

"You know you don't have to sit so far away," he said in a husky voice. "There's plenty of room over here."

"I'm staying right where I am. I thought maybe we would talk for a bit, get to know each other better. If I get any closer, the last thing we'll do is talk."

Roan gave her a crooked grin. "I can guarantee it'll be more fun than talking."

Ansley rolled her eyes. She shook her head. "Talk first, then maybe I'll let you do what you want with me."

"Fine. Have it your way. What do you want to talk about?"

Even though Ansley promised herself she wouldn't touch Roan until after they had their chat, she couldn't stop her gaze from running over his body. Telling herself to stop it, she jerked her attention back up to his face.

"I don't know. There was something you wanted to say to me yesterday before..." She let her words trail away. Ansley didn't think it'd be a good idea to bring the subject of sex into the conversation. "Why don't we start there?"

Roan stiffened for a second before he inched a little closer. "How about we talk about you instead? You know more about me than I do about you."

"Okay. What do you want to know?"

He reached across the couch and played with the ends of her hair that fell over her shoulder. "Let's see. Something easy to start with. How old are you?"

Having Roan play with her hair like that, Ansley found it harder to concentrate. "I'm twenty-six. What about you? How old are you?"

"I'm a lot older than I look." Ansley wondered if Roan had been deliberately vague on purpose when he quickly added, "We're supposed be talking about you, not me. What about family?"

Ansley didn't usually like to talk about her parents, mostly because she never knew them. Since Roan had introduced her to his family, she figured she might as well tell him why he would never be in a position to meet hers. "I don't have any."

"How old were you when you lost your parents?"

She took a deep breath. "As far as I know, my parents are alive and well."

Roan gave her a confused look. "I don't understand."

"My parents were teenagers when I was born. They chose to give me up for adoption shortly after my birth. They also signed papers stating they didn't want me to have any contact with them once I reached my maturity."

"What about adoptive parents?"

She shook her head. "I grew up in an orphanage."

Roan shifted his hand from her hair to the upper part of her arm. He rubbed it with comforting strokes. "So, you basically have been alone all your life?"

"You could say that."

He gathered her close and put her on his lap. "Well, you don't have to be anymore." Roan nuzzled the side of her neck.

Ansley shivered when he pressed feather-light kisses against her skin. She wrapped her arms around his neck. "We talked about me, now it's your turn. Are you finally going to tell me what you wanted to say, or do I have to force it out of you?" Roan pushed her off him so fast she ended up on the couch in an undignified heap. "What did you do that for?"

He ignored her question as he stood and turned to face her. "Why don't you pack some more clothes, then I'll take you out for some coffee or something before we head back to my place."

Given Roan's reaction, Ansley got the distinct impression he now wanted to avoid this talk he'd wanted to have with her. She had no idea why, but she decided not to press the issue.

She sat straighter and looked at Roan. "You want me to stay over at your place again?"

He gave her a sexy smile. "Of course I do. Actually, why don't you pack enough clothes for the week?"

"Are you sure, Roan? Not that I'm complaining, but don't you think you're taking things a little fast? The last boyfriend I had, we didn't reach the stage of staying overnight at each other's place until we'd dated for a month."

Roan picked her up from the couch and kissed her until her toes curled. He pulled back and crushed her to him. "Let's get one thing straight, here. I'm not like your other boyfriend. I'm much more than just that. Never forget it." He kissed her breathless again. "Go pack your clothes. I'll wait out here for you."

He slowly let her slide down his body until she stood on her feet. Ansley tried to slow her rapidly beating heart as she went to her bedroom to pack. If Roan wanted her to stay at his place for the week, she would stay for the week. She just prayed to God that during that time she didn't do or say something to screw it up.

CHAPTER EIGHT

The next morning, Ansley woke up at seven o'clock on the dot, a talent of hers. She never needed an alarm clock. Somehow, no matter the time, she managed to wake up when she needed to be awake. Quietly, not wanting to awaken Roan, who snored softly next to her, she slipped out of bed. She grabbed her suitcase and brought it with her as she carefully closed the en suite bathroom door behind her.

In a matter of minutes, she'd washed her face, brushed her teeth and hair, and gotten dressed. Normally, she would have taken a shower before heading to work, but she really didn't have time for it. She had a longer drive than she normally would.

She slipped back out into the bedroom and then collected her purse before tiptoeing to the closed door. Roan slept on. Ansley smiled and blew him a silent kiss. She would let him sleep. He'd earned it. They hadn't really slept much during the night. At least one of them should be able to sleep in.

Ansley slowly closed the bedroom door behind her, then tiptoed down the stairs, not wanting to wake up the other occupants of the house. At the front door, she unlocked the deadbolt and the lock in the doorknob. After she opened it, she turned the lock on the knob so it would engage behind her.

Thankful her car hadn't been parked in the large garage, she started it, and then headed to the street. Ansley had only been on the road for ten minutes when she realized she missed Roan. She ignored the feeling and turned on the stereo. The music helped distract her, but the need to be with him seemed to persist. She told herself she was being ridiculous. She'd just left him. How could she be missing him already? And it wasn't as if she wouldn't see him again. She planned to do her shift at work and then return to his place afterward.

By the time Ansley reached the salon, she felt as if a whole year had passed since she'd last been with Roan. It just didn't make any sense. The real need to be with him, to touch him, to kiss him, threatened to override everything else. Her body ached for his.

After turning off the car, Ansley gave herself a shake. "Get over it."

Had she become so obsessed with Roan, he had become the center of her universe? She hoped the hell not. If she didn't stop it, she would end up more than devastated if he were to change his mind about how he felt about her and left. She would probably end up turning into his stalker, begging him to take her back. Not something she ever wanted to see herself doing. She walked into the salon and hoped her inner turmoil didn't show on the outside.

Sherry was the first person to see Ansley. She followed her to her chair. "So? How was Mr. Tall and Muscular?"

Ansley put her purse away, then turned to Sherry. "Who?"

"Oh, come on, Ansley. You know exactly who I mean. So, how was he in bed?"

"Who says we slept together?"

Sherry gave her a stare that silently asked, *What do you take me for?* "Sure, you didn't sleep together," she said sarcastically. "Give me a break. That hunk of a man did not come in here, kiss you senseless, then carry you away over his shoulder just to say hello. I bet he screwed your brains out."

Ansley's lips twitched. "You do have a way with words, Sherry."

"That's why we get along so well."

"So true," she said with a laugh.

"Well? I'm waiting."

"You're not going to let this go, are you?"

"Nope. I want all the juicy details."

"I don't know about juicy details, but I will say Roan has the stamina of three men, and knows how to use it."

Boy, did he know how to use it. Ansley hadn't thought she could orgasm so many times until she'd slept with Roan. Thinking of how he'd used his hard cock along with his mouth to make her come over and over again, intensified the need to be with him. She roughly pushed those thoughts aside before she completely lost it.

Sherry groaned. "It figures he would be a god in bed. I have only one piece of advice for you—don't let him go. Men like that, they're damn hard to come by."

Ansley smiled. "Oh, believe me, I have no plans to let Roan go any time soon."

"Good." Sherry looked at the front desk where a client stood, waiting. "I'd better get back to the front. We'll have to continue our talk about your new boyfriend later. I'll have to see if I can get more details out of you." She gave Ansley a wink before she left.

The client turned out to be Ansley's first one of the day. As she washed the woman's hair, her thoughts wandered to Roan once again. Her need for him seemed to get stronger as time went by. She didn't know how much more of this she could take. Determined not to let it get the better of her, she clamped down on it and tried to ignore it the best she could.

* * * *

Roan came awake with a start. Something wasn't right. All his senses went on alert. He quickly scanned the room. Nothing seemed amiss that he could see. What had caused him to be dragged out of sleep? He reached for Ansley and found the spot next to him empty. He sat up. The sheets were cool to the touch.

He threw back the covers and his gaze fell on Ansley's suitcase that sat on the floor close to the bathroom door. He relaxed slightly when he saw it, but the feeling of wrongness didn't go away. He stood with his hands on his hips and tried to sort out what exactly he felt. It hit him like a ton of bricks.

He quickly pulled on a pair of jeans while he swore up a storm. He hoped Ansley hadn't done what he thought she had, but what he felt inside said she'd done exactly that. Roan pounded down the stairs and then headed for the kitchen, just on the off chance she would be there. Instead, he found Eli and Saskia sitting at the table, sipping coffee. It was still early enough, the others hadn't gotten their asses out of bed yet.

"Did you see her?"

Saskia answered without having to be told who he referred to. "No, we haven't seen anyone this morning but you."

"Damn it."

Roan agitatedly ran his hand through his hair. Now that he'd claimed Ansley as his mate, being separated from her was going to play hell with him. He'd known it would be bad, but he hadn't known it would cause this driving need to be with his mate.

He turned and hurried to the front door. Not surprisingly, he found the deadbolt unlocked. He stepped out only far enough to see Ansley's car no longer sat parked in front of the garage. Roan stormed back inside and almost collided with Saskia and Eli.

Saskia crossed her arms over her chest and stood to block his path. "You didn't tell her she was your mate, did you?"

"No, I didn't." Saskia arched a brow. "I chickened out, okay? I was waiting for the right time to tell Ansley everything." He barely managed to bite back a growl. "Fuck. How did you and Eli survive this? And why the hell did you run from him in the first place if this was what you would have to go through? I either want to climb the walls or punch something."

"Don't bring me into this. This is all your doing. You could have avoided this if you'd told Ansley right from the start. I'm sure she's suffering too, but unlike you, she has no idea why. Do you know where she would have gone?"

This time Roan didn't hold back the growl that built inside his chest. It wasn't directed at his sister, though. He totally directed it at himself. Saskia was right. Ansley had to be suffering, and probably wondered what was wrong with her.

"She mentioned yesterday that she had to work today. We got involved doing other things and it slipped my mind."

Eli laughed. "I'm sure it did. I know how self-involved Saskia and I were in the beginning." He grunted when Saskia's elbow connected with his ribs. "Hey, it's true."

"Don't encourage him." She chastised her mate. "Well, Roan. You'd better go and fix this before it gets much worse. And for God's sake, tell Ansley the truth. She deserves that much from you."

Moving faster than any mortal could, Roan ran up to his bedroom and then finished getting dressed. A few minutes later, he was out the door and had raced to his car. The drive to San Francisco seemed to stretch his nerves to almost the breaking point. Once he crossed the Golden Gate Bridge, he realized he was in trouble. The closer he was to Ansley, the harder his cock became. He knew what would happen when he saw her again. He would be inside her in a matter of seconds, and she would be just as needy as he. He just hoped he could get them somewhere private before he tried to rip her clothes off.

At first glance, the parking lot behind the hair salon seemed full, but Roan managed to slip into the last empty space when he found it. This did not bode well for privacy. He gripped the steering wheel until his knuckles turned white, and took some deep breaths. It helped a little, but not by much. He finally slid out of the car and then walked to the salon.

Roan yanked open the door before he headed straight for Ansley. She appeared to be in just as bad shape. Her hair was mussed as if she'd repeatedly run her hands through it. He spared only a glance at her chair to see no one sat there. He didn't stop until he stood in front of her. He smelled her arousal with each breath, which caused his to ratchet even higher.

Through gritted teeth, he said, "Washroom. Now."

Ansley quickly spun around and headed to the very back of the salon. Roan followed her into the small washroom, shut the door, and locked it behind them. She threw herself into his arms a second later, her lips seeking his. She pulled up his shirt and undid his jeans. He groaned when she wrapped her hand around his aching cock.

Knowing he would have to make this quick, and quiet, if possible, he undid her pants and shoved them roughly down her hips, taking her panties with them. Roan lifted her off her feet once her jeans cleared them. Ansley wrapped her legs around his waist as he pressed her back against one of the walls. He pushed his jeans down only far enough to free his cock, then positioned himself between her thighs and sank into her wet pussy with one thrust. She moaned into his mouth.

The feel of her warm wetness closing around his shaft made Roan want to growl, but he kept his mouth sealed to hers. He reared back, then pumped into her. Ansley tried to pull her lips away. He didn't let her, knowing full well any sounds they made would alert everyone in the salon to what happened inside the washroom.

He cupped her bottom, then raised and lowered her on his cock. He plunged in and out of her body at a fast pace. Ansley dug her fingernails into the tops of his shoulders and squeezed his shaft with her inner muscles. Roan pumped his hips once, twice, and then they came at the same time. They moaned into each other's mouth, her pussy milking his cock in a tight fist as he came deep inside her.

Once they could breathe normally again, Roan pulled his still-hard cock out of Ansley and then let her stand on her feet. She leaned against him for a few seconds before she bent down to retrieve her panties and jeans.

"Roan, what was wrong with me? Whatever it was, it's gone now. You had to have felt it too, because you were as desperate for me as I was for you."

He shoved his cock back inside his jeans before he zipped them up while Ansley dressed. "Not here. Do you think they'll let you leave?"

"I don't know. Gail, the owner, is already in. She's probably not impressed that I'm in here with you. She's kind of a hard woman to get along with."

"Tell her you have to leave, that an emergency came up. All I know is I can't stay here all day with you."

"Then go back home and I'll meet you there when my shift is over."

Roan ran his hand through his hair. "And go through what we just went through again? No fucking way."

Ansley's brows drew together. "Being apart is what caused this? Whatever it is?"

He placed his hand over her left breast. "We're a part of each other now, babe. Neither one of us will be able to stand being separated for long periods of time. The longer we're apart, the worse it'll get. Now, talk to your boss so we can get the hell out of here."

*

More confused than anything, Ansley left the washroom with Roan at her heels. All heads in the salon seemed to turn their way. She ignored the stares. She went to the front counter where Gail stood. The older lady scowled. Ansley could tell Gail was already pissed off with her, and figured her boss wouldn't be inclined to let her go early.

Ansley took a deep breath. Roan came to stand at her back. "Gail, I need to leave. A bit of an emergency came up."

Her boss looked from Ansley, then to Roan and back to Ansley again. "An emergency, huh? I think the emergency is standing behind you. You left early the other day because of him."

"I really do need to take the rest of the day off."

Gail sneered. "I don't pay my employees to take time off whenever they want. You leave now, don't bother coming back. There are plenty of other hairstylists who would be more than happy to take your chair."

Before Ansley could say anything else, Roan said from behind her, "Then Ansley quits. She doesn't need this job anymore. We'll be by tomorrow to pick up her final paycheck."

Roan would have led her away then, but Ansley refused to budge. "I can't quit, Roan. I need this job to pay my rent and bills."

He brushed a quick kiss against her lips. "No, you don't. I have more than enough money to look after us."

Shocked speechless, Ansley let him walk her away a few steps before she found her voice again. "Wait, Roan. My stuff. I'm not leaving it behind, or my purse."

Roan changed direction and headed for her chair. Ansley collected her purse, then looked around for something to put her hairdryer, curling iron, and the rest of her tools of the trade in.

She turned to find Sherry standing beside her with an empty box. "Thanks."

Sherry smiled. "No problem. Just make sure you call me."

Ansley didn't have many friends, but she considered Sherry one of her closest. "I'll do that."

Roan took the box and then shoved her things into it. In a matter of seconds, they had put all her belongings in it and walked out the door. Ansley looked back one final time and met

Sherry's gaze. Her friend waved, then silently mouthed to call her. Ansley only had enough time to wave back before Roan pulled her out the door.

CHAPTER NINE

Inside Roan's Lexus, Ansley watched large privacy gates swing open. He had only let her take her car back to her apartment before he ushered her into his. When she asked where they were going, he'd only told her he was taking her to see Roxie. She had no idea what her connection with Roan had to do with Roxie, but she decided to wait and see what he had planned.

Once the gates opened all the way, Roan drove past them and then up the long drive to the large mansion. She hadn't known where Roxie lived. Even though Roxie had been coming to her for the last couple years, Ansley really didn't know much about the other woman. So it came as a bit of a surprise to learn she lived in a large house, the same as Roan and his family did. It made Ansley feel like the odd man out.

Roan parked at the top of the drive before he got out. Ansley slid out on her side and then came around the front of the car to meet him. He took her hand and gave it a reassuring squeeze. He led her to the front door. He rang the doorbell, then stepped back to wait for someone to answer it.

Roxie opened the door a few seconds later. She smiled and waved them inside. "Come on in. It's nice to see you again, Ansley." She closed the door and directed her attention to Roan. "I didn't expect you today. Jager and Dirk are already here. I thought you and Ansley would be a little busy."

Roan cleared his throat as if he'd suddenly become nervous about something when Roxie led them into her large living room. "I brought Ansley here because I thought you would be able to help her understand when I tell her about me."

Roxie spun around and crossly stared at Roan with her hands on her hips. "Are you telling me you claimed her without explaining everything to her, even after I told you not to do it that way?"

"Well, you see, things got a little out of hand." Roan let out a squawk when Roxie reached up and grabbed him by his ear. "Rox, that really hurts. Let go."

"No. And it's supposed to hurt, you idiot. Now get over here and let's see if I can make this right for you."

Roxie didn't let go of his ear. She kept hold of it as she led him to the large sectional couch before she forced him to sit. Ansley had to cover her mouth with her hand to hide the smile that spread across her lips. It was quite comical to see Roan, who stood much taller than Roxie, being led about by a woman half his size. Ansley went and sat next to Roan, who rubbed his abused ear.

Roxie sat on the couch so she faced them, then looked at Ansley, and asked, "Okay, what exactly has Roan told you about your relationship with him?"

"Not too much, really," Ansley said cautiously. The serious expressions on Roan's and Roxie's faces made her worry a little bit. It didn't take a genius to guess he had kept something about himself from her. "He only said that we're now a part of each other, and we won't like to be apart for long periods of time."

Roxie leveled a hard stare at Roan. "You told her that much, but not the reason behind it?"

Roan sighed. "I had to tell her something. She went to work this morning while I slept. When I woke up, she'd already been gone for over an hour."

Roxie dropped her head to her hand and shook it. "Yup, you couldn't have messed things up any worse then you already have." She looked up. "Roan, tell Ansley the truth."

"Now? You don't want to gently ease her into it?"

"No. Sometimes it's best just to get it all out in the open at once. And it's not as if she has much choice in the matter, now does she?"

Now worried, Ansley kept her gaze locked on Roan. He turned to her and grabbed her hand. She didn't know if she wanted to hear what he had to say.

Roan took a deep breath. "Please try not to freak out when I say this, okay? I never meant to take your choice from you. I tried to tell you the other day at your apartment, but you acted as if you didn't want anything to do with me, and my control snapped."

"Just spit it out, Roan."

"All right. Ansley, we're mated. That's why we can't be separated for long without needing to be with one another. The mating bond, the joining of our souls, happened the first time we slept together. I knew you were my mate when I met you at the salon. I knew if we made love that would be the result."

"Mated? I don't understand. Only animals take mates. The last time I looked, I wasn't one."

Roan's eyes glowed mutedly. He made a very animal-like growl. "I'm not completely human, Ansley. There's a part of me that *is* an animal."

Ansley shot off the couch to stand in front of Roan. No longer could she try to talk herself into believing his eyes didn't really glow, or that he didn't growl like a wild animal would. "That's not possible."

"It is possible." Roan reached for Ansley, but she crossed her arms over chest.

She narrowed her eyes. "If it's possible, then what exactly are you?"

Roan stood, but kept his distance. "I'm a werewolf, Ansley."

"A werewolf? There are no such things as werewolves. Next you'll tell me vampires, fairies, and evil trolls exist, too." Roan gave Roxie a pleading look. Ansley chuckled. "Oh, come on, Roxie. Don't tell me you believe this werewolf nonsense." She gasped. Roxie's eyes glowed just as Roan's did.

"Sorry, Ansley," Roxie said. "I'm a werewolf, too. Same with Beowulf."

Ansley's gaze shot back to Roan. "Your family? Are they werewolves too?"

"Yes."

"Your eyes, it has to be a trick you're both playing on me. They aren't glowing by themselves."

"It's no trick. I didn't want to do it this way, but I can't think of anything else to prove to you that Rox and I are telling you the truth."

She backed up a step. His body shimmered and blurred. It all happened so quickly. One minute Roan stood in front of her, and the next, a wolf had taken his place. One that had light-brown fur and light-blue eyes, the same as Roan's. Ansley shook her head and backed up even more until the back of her legs hit the coffee table. She flailed her arms to keep her balance. One of them hit the crystal vase that sat on the table. It smashed onto the hardwood floor with a loud crash.

The wolf stepped closer, but Ansley held up her hands to ward him off. "Keep the hell away from me," she yelled. The wolf stopped dead in his tracks.

Jager suddenly ran into the room, holding a huge sword. "What's the matter? Are you okay, Roxie? I heard a crash and someone yelling."

Ansley didn't know who to keep her gaze on. The wolf, and Jager, with his sword, seemed equally dangerous to her.

Roxie groaned. "Put the sword away, Jager, before you upset Ansley more than she already is. And, of course, everything is fine. I thought I told you not to come running with your sword drawn at the slightest noise. We discussed that the last time you did it."

Jager lowered his sword slightly. "I apologized then. How was I to know you and Beowulf were fooling around? The noises you made, I thought someone was trying to kill you."

"For the love of God, Jager, would you just shut up already?" Roxie asked. "Now, give me the sword. I don't want you scaring anyone else with it."

Jager lowered his weapon even more and shook his head. "I am not giving it to you. I told you, I feel naked without it when I'm not at home."

Ansley's heart jumped into her throat. Roxie's body shimmered and blurred, but unlike Roan, she didn't shift into a wolf. She changed into what could only be described as half-wolf and half-human. Her body was covered from head to toe in light-golden-brown fur. She now stood taller than Jager, and looked much stronger. With a swish of her tail, she stalked to Jager and then easily took the sword from him.

In a gruff voice, Rox said, "You'll get it back before you leave. Now, out. We have a situation going on here. Ansley isn't taking the news of Roan being her mate, or us being werewolves, very well. With your mouth, I think you'll just make things worse."

Jager leaned around Roxie and gave Ansley a weak smile. "Sorry, I didn't mean to make things worse." He left the room.

Roxie shifted back to her fully human form and came to stand next to Roan, still in his wolf shape. She stroked the top of his head. "Roan, why don't you leave Ansley and me alone for a bit?"

The wolf nodded before he turned and padded out of the living room. Roxie put the sword on the floor at her feet and then sat on the couch once again. She patted the spot next to her.

"Ansley, why don't you sit and we'll talk about this? I know it's all very confusing and a bit scary."

Finally finding her voice, Ansley shot back, "How would you know? You're a werewolf."

"I wasn't always one. I've only been a werewolf for the past year. I used to be a mortal just like you."

Feeling more than a little overwhelmed, Ansley slowly went to the couch and sat on the far end of it, as far away from Roxie as she could get. "What happened? Did you get bitten by a werewolf?"

Roxie chuckled. "No. Usually, a mortal can't be turned into a werewolf by being bitten by one. You have to be born one."

"You just said you weren't always a werewolf."

"My case is a little different. A spell turned me, one that was written specifically to turn me. You see, I'm *special*." Roxie did air quotes when she said the word special. "A few thousand years ago, it was foretold a werewolf with a special mark on his or her wrist would one day rule over all the werewolf packs—the foretold one. Well, it turns out I'm the foretold one." She held out her left arm.

Ansley looked at the black Celtic-style markings that banded Roxie's left wrist, then gazed back up at her face. "Why are you telling me this?"

"I'm trying to give you a little more insight into Roan. He, along with his brothers and sister, have trained for hundreds of years to be my protector. Even though they all went lone wolves long ago, I have never met a more loyal bunch of people. Roan would never hurt you, Ansley. Nor would his family. They protect their own. They welcomed Eli into the family with open arms when he and Saskia mated, even before he chose to become a werewolf. They'll do the same with you."

More intrigued now than she would admit, Ansley's brows drew together. "I thought the spell was only for you."

"Originally, yes, but as I said before, I'm special. Besides being able to shift into my half-wolf and half-human form, which no other werewolf can do, I have a little bit more magic inside me than they. If I perform the spell, a mortal can be turned into a werewolf."

"You keep calling everyone who isn't a werewolf a mortal. Are you telling me werewolves are immortal?"

"Not exactly. Our lifespans are much, much longer than a mortal's. We can live three thousand years. We also can heal much faster and survive wounds that would kill a mortal."

Ansley swallowed. "How old is Roan?"

"He's slightly over a thousand years old. I think one thousand and eight, to be exact."

She felt all the blood drain out of her face. Spots appeared before her eyes. "A thousand years old. That means he'll live for another two thousand."

Roxie shifted closer and rubbed Ansley's back. "Just breathe, Ansley. Don't faint on me. Roan will get upset with me if you do. I don't want him to accuse me of mistreating his mate."

Ansley took a couple of deep, cleansing breaths. Once her vision cleared, she gave Roxie a weak smile. "I'm okay now. Can you please tell me what it means to be his mate?"

"For starters, it's more permanent than marriage. As Roan said, your souls have joined. There's no undoing it. And, as you found out from firsthand experience, it isn't pleasant being separated from your mate."

Ansley fisted her hands on her lap. "So, let me get this straight. The first time we made love, we mated; and technically, we're as good as married. Roan knew he would tie me to him forever in this way when we first met, and still he went ahead and did it anyway. Without giving us the chance to get to know each other." Her voice rose with each word she spoke. "Nor did he even try to tell me anything about his being a werewolf before he went ahead and made love to me."

Roxie snorted. "That basically says it all. Beowulf did the same thing to me. I reacted about the same way you are now."

"You two must have worked it out. You seem crazy about each other."

"Yes, we did, in a roundabout way. I'm going to say this, even though it sounds kind of cornball, but deep down inside, you must have fallen in love with Roan the first time you laid eyes on him. If you hadn't, your souls never would have joined. I want you to think about that, because I'm going to offer you something that will bring you closer to him."

"The spell?"

"Yes. I don't want you to give me your answer now. Hell, you can take as long as you want. Years, even. My offer is open-ended. Now I'm going to get Roan back in here. I can hear him pacing in the kitchen."

Ansley couldn't hear any noise. If anything, the house seemed as silent as a tomb.

Roxie smiled. "Werewolf hearing. We can hear, smell, and see, three times better than a mortal."

After Roxie left her alone, Ansley prepared herself to face Roan again. Talking to Roxie had helped, but she still felt a bit overwhelmed by everything she'd learned. It wasn't every day a girl found herself married, no, mated, to an over-thousand-year-old werewolf.

As for Roxie's offer to turn her into one, Ansley didn't know when, or if, she would be able to take that step. It all depended on how Roan really felt about her, and she about him. She would like to believe their souls joined because they fell in love with each other at first sight, but she was too practical to believe that could be possible. Neither one of them had declared love for the other. To be quite frank, she had no idea if she loved him. Her feelings for him were still too new. She hadn't had the time to really examine them closely. He'd barged into her life, and she hadn't been able to think straight since.

CHAPTER TEN

Roan stepped into the living room and found Ansley on the couch. She stared off into space, appearing lost in thought. He had no idea if that boded well for him or not. Cautiously, not wanting to startle her, he crossed to her and took the seat next to her.

"I'm so sorry, Ansley. I never planned to spring it on you like this. I wanted to take things slow."

Ansley kept her gaze fixed straight ahead of her. "I don't know what to think, Roan. What Roxie told me...it's an awful lot to digest all at once."

"I know. Roxie had told me to be up-front with you right from the start. You have to understand, when a male werewolf finds his mate, the mating urge sinks its claws into him and doesn't let go until he has claimed his mate. It's hard to ignore when the wolf inside is howling for you to take what belongs to you." When Ansley didn't say anything or look at him, Roan sighed. "I know it doesn't excuse what I did, but can you at least try to forgive me?"

"Do you love me, Roan?" Ansley's voice sounded flat, emotionless.

Roan blinked at the sudden change in topic. "What?"

"I asked if you love me."

No longer able to stand the distance Ansley had put between them physically and mentally, he pulled her onto his lap. He put a hand under her chin and forced her to look at him. "Of course I love you, Ansley. You're my mate."

"Are you sure it's love and not lust? Are you sure it isn't this mating urge forcing you to feel what you think is love?"

Roan scowled. "It isn't just the mating urge. I love you. The mating urge never would have kicked in if you weren't the one meant for me. Do you have any idea how long I've waited to find my mate?"

"Roxie told me you are over a thousand years old. She also told me about the spell."

"And?" Roan held his breath, waiting to hear what Ansley's answer would be.

"I'm not ready for that. I don't know if I'll ever be."

He released the breath he'd been holding. "What are you saying?"

"You say you love me, but I don't know if what I feel for you is love or not. I've never been in love before. I have no idea what it is. I didn't exactly grow up knowing the love of a mother or father. I don't know if I'm even capable of it. I'm just so confused right now."

Roan pulled Ansley's head down to his shoulder and rubbed her back. "I won't ask anything from you that you aren't ready to give. Just know that I'm not going anywhere—ever. You're mine. For now, that's enough for me. We'll work out the rest as we go along."

Some of the tension left him when Ansley snuggled closer into his embrace. At least she hadn't rejected him outright. The way she'd reacted when he'd gone wolf, Roan had been worried she would want nothing to do with him.

At that moment, Jager popped his head into the living room. "Sorry, never mind me." He walked to the couch and then picked up his sword where Roxie had left it on the floor.

Much to Roan's surprise, Ansley lifted her head and shook her head in Jager's direction. "You better not let Roxie catch you with that. She may kick your butt instead of just taking it from you the next time. And given how big she looked in her half-wolf and half-human form, I would say she would have no problem doing it if she wanted to."

Jager shrugged. "She can always try," he said with a smile.

He'd just stepped into the hallway when Roan heard him say, "Oh, shit."

The next voice he heard was Roxie's. "I thought I took that from you already."

Jager replied, "Well, I took it back."

"You know how I feel about it," Roxie said. "Now hand it over." Jager obviously didn't do as she'd asked, because she said, "Give me that damn sword, Jager."

The next thing Roan heard were the sounds of heavy footfalls taking off at a run and another much lighter set following them.

Roxie's voice drifted to him as she chased after Jager. "You can run, but I'm still going to take that sword away from you."

Roan and Ansley looked at each other, then burst out laughing. Ansley was the first to recover. "Are they always like this?"

"Not all the time. The sword just happens to be a bone of contention between them. Roxie's just afraid Jager will hurt somebody with it."

"Would he?"

Roan shook his head. "No. Jager can handle a sword better than most of us. He doesn't make mistakes like that. As you may have guessed, he's so attached to the thing you would swear he had been born with it in his hand."

Ansley's face grew serious. "You have a sword too, don't you?"

"Yes. All my brothers have one. Same with Saskia. That's our weapon of choice."

"I think I would like to see your sword, Roan," Ansley said softly. "I have to admit Jager looked pretty hot with his raised like that. It made me think about other raised swords."

Roan growled low in his throat. "You'd better be thinking about my sword and not Jager's. I would hate to beat the crap out of my own brother."

Ansley smiled. "It most definitely was yours I thought about, since you know how to use it so well."

With another growl, Roan kissed Ansley until she grew pliant against him. He urged her head onto his shoulder and wrapped his arms around her, holding her tight. She would still need some time to come to terms with everything she'd learned today, but he felt more than pleased that the distance she'd tried to put between no longer existed. Later he would show her how much he loved her. And, if she made the decision to stay a mortal, he would show her he would stand by it and wouldn't force her into becoming a werewolf. He'd already taken one choice away from her. He wouldn't take this one from her too.

* * * *

Roan crossed swords with Jager in the training area in the basement. After Ansley and Roan had left Roxie and Beowulf's place, they'd gone to Roan's house, actually, her house too, now. She and Roan had had a long talk. He'd told her everything about himself, even what it was like to be a werewolf. It had helped her to be more accepting of what he'd done. And it helped her to understand the whole mated business. She had strong feelings for him — the strongest she'd ever felt for a man — but she still didn't know if she would call it love. She wished she could tell him she loved him in return when he told her, but Ansley wouldn't just say the words because he wanted to hear them.

During their talk, Roan had explained why he and his family had trained so hard to protect Roxie, the foretold one. According to Roan, Roxie was more than just special. She could do things no other werewolf could, much more than just being able to shift into a half-wolf and half-human form and having the ability to use a spell to turn mortals into werewolves. Since she ruled over all the packs, it made her vulnerable. If another werewolf somehow managed to get control of her, they could use her as a figurehead. Roan told her about Miles, Saskia's true brother, who at one time had been trained alongside his sister to protect the foretold one. That was before he'd decided to switch sides and covet the foretold one for his own.

The sound of swords clashing brought Ansley out of her musings. She followed Roan's movements with her gaze. Since he was shirtless, she could easily see the muscles in his arms and shoulders bunch when he swung at Jager. Each man's hits were controlled. Not once did they draw blood.

Soon, Roan stepped back and held up his hand. "That's enough for one day, I think."

"Are you sure?" Jager swung his sword in an arc in front of

him. "I could do this all day."

Roan nodded toward where Ansley stood off to the side. "Unlike you, I have something more important in my life than my sword."

"Since I'm no longer wanted, I guess I'll leave you two lovebirds alone. I'll tell the others that you and Ansley will be fooling around down here and not to disturb you."

Roan shook his head. "Jager."

"What? Isn't that what you want to do?"

"Would you get the hell out of here?"

With an unrepentant smile, Jager headed up the basement stairs, leaving Roan and Ansley alone.

Ansley crossed to Roan. "You definitely were right about Jager. He says whatever he wants, and doesn't give a crap what other people think."

"We've tried breaking him of that habit over the years, but I don't think he'll ever change."

"Will he tell the others we're fooling around down here?"

"Of course, but Saskia will soon set him straight. She usually does."

"I still can't get over the fact Saskia is the leader of you all."

"It wasn't on a whim that she was picked for that position. She knows how to put each and every one of us in our place. She's also lethal with a sword. She's the only one who can best Jager in practice."

Ansley stared at the sword Roan held. "Can I?"

Roan stepped to her side and then put the pommel in her hand. "You got it? It's pretty heavy."

The way she'd watched Roan swing it, Ansley didn't think it could be all that heavy. She nodded. "Okay, I got it." Once he let go, she soon found out how wrong she'd been in that thinking. The tip of the sword thumped onto the floor. It took using both her hands to lift it back up to her waist. Her arms soon shook with the strain of holding the heavy weapon. "I think you'd better take it, Roan."

He easily took it from her and held it as if it weighed nothing. "I told you it was heavy."

"The way you and Jager handled them, you wouldn't think it was."

Roan put his arm around her shoulders and steered her toward the stairs. "I've had years of practice. How about I take a shower, then we can watch TV or something?"

"I guess."

Instead of staying downstairs on the main floor, Ansley followed Roan up to their room. They planned to move the things out of her apartment to the house the following day. She decided she would see where she could fit her dresser into the room while he was in the shower. Most of her furniture, she would have to either sell or give away to charity. Not that she cared. None of it held any sentimental value.

Ansley sat on the bed after Roan went into the bathroom. Since he'd left the door open, she easily heard him undress before the water turned on in the shower. It didn't take much for her to picture how he would look, the water running down his naked body. His arms would flex while he ran the bar of soap all over himself. Her pussy ached and wetness pooled between her legs as she pictured him running his big, soapy hand up and down his cock as he washed it.

She stood, walked to the bedroom door, and locked it. She stripped off her clothes and then dropped them to the floor. She crossed to the bathroom. After revealing what he was, Roan hadn't once tried to initiate sex. If Ansley didn't know better, she would think he held off, afraid she would reject him. Not that she would have. They were mates, and nothing would change that. She may not be able to tell him she loved him, but she could show him with her body that he meant much more than what she could say in words.

Ansley slipped into the bathroom, then walked to the glass-enclosed shower. Roan had his back toward her, with his head under the running water. She pulled open the door, and then stepped inside behind him.

Roan spun around. "Ansley?"

She gave him a smile. "I hope you didn't expect another woman to get in the shower with you."

"I thought you were going to wait out in the bedroom for me."

"I decided I would much rather join you." She stepped closer and pressed her lips to his chest.

Roan moaned. "Are you sure?"

She dragged her tongue across his nipple. "Why wouldn't I want to?"

His hands fisted at his sides. "I thought maybe you would need more time to get your head around what I am."

Ansley slid her hands down Roan's back to his ass. She rubbed herself against his cock, which had grown thick and hard between them. "I'm over my initial shock. And right now, all I can think about is making love to you."

As if that had been all he'd waited to hear, Roan threaded his fingers through her hair and took her mouth in a hard kiss.

Ansley pressed closer and rubbed her taut nipples against his chest. She sucked his tongue into her mouth. She reached between them and took his hard cock in her fist, then pumped up and down his length.

Roan growled softly. He cupped one of her breasts and thumbed her nipple. The fingers of his other hand trailed down her body to her pussy. He found her clit and rubbed it before he pushed a finger inside her.

"You're already wet for me."

"What are you going to do about it?" Ansley asked coyly. She squeezed his cock even harder.

"First, I'm going to taste you."

Roan pulled out of her grasp and then went down on his knees. He nudged her legs apart and used his fingers to spread the lips of her sex. Ansley gasped at the first stroke of his tongue. He flicked her clit with it before he sucked it into his mouth. She held on to his shoulders and rocked her hips. Waves of pleasure shot through her when he pushed two fingers inside her. He pumped them in and out while he continued to suck and lick her.

Ansley's moans filled the shower as he continued to work her, pushing her ever closer to an orgasm. It was all she could do to keep upright. Her legs shook. If she hadn't been holding on to Roan, she would have fallen.

Roan spread his fingers as he moved them inside her, stretching her. "Come for me, Ansley," he half-growled. "I want to taste you when you come."

He sucked on her clit harder. Ansley called Roan's name as her climax tore through her. He replaced his fingers with his tongue. He lapped and sucked until the last wave of pleasure receded.

Weak, Ansley sank to her knees in front of Roan. "My turn."

She bent and circled her tongue around the head of his cock. Roan threaded his hands into her hair and groaned. She opened her mouth and took just the tip of him inside. Sucking, she wrapped her hand around his shaft and pumped it up and down. His hips bucked. He growled deep inside his chest. The sound of his growls made her body liquefy.

Ansley took hold of his shaft at the base and took more of his length inside her mouth.

Roan's cock grew even harder. He pumped his hips when she alternated between sucking and swirling her tongue around the head.

She would have continued to pleasure him this way until he came, but he had other ideas.

He pulled away before he turned her so she faced the glass shower door. Still on their knees, Roan came up behind her. He took hold of her hips. His cock slipped between her spread thighs and probed the entrance to her body.

Ansley rocked back against him, rubbing her wetness along his thick shaft.

With a growl, he sheathed himself to the hilt inside her with one stroke.

Ansley placed her hands on the glass door. Roan pulled back until he was almost free of her body, then surged back inside. She clamped her inner walls around his shaft as he pounded into her. Moaning, she pushed back, matching his strokes. Her body coiled tighter once again. The feel of his thick cock stretching her, moving in and out, pushed her ever closer to orgasm.

Roan surged into her harder, faster. With one hand still on her hip, he reached around her and found her clit. He rubbed it as he bent forward, bit the top of her shoulder near her neck, and held on with his teeth.

Ansley cried out when she came.

He stiffened behind her as he too found his release. His cock pulsed deep inside her, filling her with his cum.

Ansley leaned her forehead against the cool glass. Roan was still buried thick and hard deep inside her pussy. "You're still hard."

He pumped his hips once. "Of course I am. All male

werewolves can keep an erection for hours, even after coming."

She pushed back until she leaned against Roan's chest. "It's a good thing that isn't common knowledge among mortal women or poor mortal men would never get laid."

Roan swirled his tongue inside her ear. "The only mortal woman I'll be sharing that information with is you."

"I'm not complaining. How about we go to bed and you can show me just how many times you can come. Maybe you can set a new personal best."

Roan pulled out of her, turned off the water, and then picked her up in his arms. He carried her to the bedroom and put her on the bed. "Now that is one challenge I'm more than up for."

CHAPTER ELEVEN

The next day, Roan and Ansley arrived at her apartment a little later than they'd first planned. It was already going on late afternoon. Considering they hadn't gotten much sleep during the night, they'd both slept in.

Instead of taking his Lexus, Roan had taken the black Cadillac Escalade SUV that belonged to his family. He'd figured they would be able to pack most of her things into it and then rent a truck later to get the furniture.

The first thing Ansley did once she arrived, was to go to the building's superintendent and give her notice. Even though she would have thirty days to clear out her apartment, she would be gone long before that deadline.

Glad she hadn't accumulated too much stuff over the years, Ansley packed her belongings into the boxes she and Roan had brought. With his help, the packing didn't seem to take as long as it would have if she'd been by herself. She hadn't forgotten how hard it'd been for her to move most of her things into the apartment alone. She'd only asked Sherry and her boyfriend to help with the heavy lifting.

By the time they'd packed everything into boxes, night had descended. Ansley stood and stretched her aching back. She took in all the boxes stacked on top of each other in her living room. What had originally looked like not much at first glance had turned out to be more than just a little. She hated moving, and hoped this would be the last move she would ever have to do.

Roan came into the room from the bedroom where he'd been dismantling her bed. "All done?"

"I think I got everything. It looks as if we're going to have to make more than one trip."

He glanced at the boxes. "I think you're right. At least we have lots of time. Why don't we just load up the SUV with the things you'll miss if you don't have tonight and we'll leave the rest for tomorrow. I'll ask Leif or one of the others to come with us. I'm going to have to get help moving the furniture, anyway. Plus, we'll have the rental truck by then."

"All right. You can bring the SUV to the back of the building. The super doesn't like tenants to use the front entrance when moving."

Roan gave her a kiss. "I'll be back in a few minutes."

After Roan left, Ansley pulled out the boxes she wanted to take with her. She decided they could just remove the drawers from of her dresser and take them too. It would make it much lighter for the guys to move.

Once Roan returned, he and Ansley started loading up the SUV. He seemed able to get up and down the stairs much faster than she did. Obviously, this was one case where being a werewolf had the advantage over being a mortal. He could carry a lot more than she could.

Her sixth trip up the stairs, Ansley had to sit for a few minutes on the couch to rest. Her legs felt like lead weights. Roan didn't seem tired at all. While she sat, he continued to take boxes downstairs.

One run while she rested, it took Ansley a few minutes to realize Roan hadn't come back up. Usually, he did it in a minute or less. Wondering what could be keeping him, she got up and then headed downstairs to the back entrance. She hoped the super hadn't decided to give him a hard time about them moving her things so late.

She didn't find Roan cornered by the super. What she did find had her frozen in place with fear. He stood by the back of the SUV while another man confronted him with a sword. Roan had no expression as he stared down his attacker. Ansley had to cover her mouth with her hand to stop herself from calling out to him. She didn't want to distract him. Neither man had noticed her standing on the other side of the glass door.

From one second to the next, the standoff ended. The man swung his sword at Roan. Even though he had no sword of his own, Roan avoided getting hit by jumping out of range. The man continued to swing at him, forcing him back until the men had disappeared around the side of the SUV.

No longer able to see them, Ansley quickly bolted outside. She didn't go too close to where the two men fought. Once she heard Roan and his attacker growl at each other, she realized Roan's attacker was another werewolf.

Feeling powerless, not sure of what she could do to help Roan, Ansley searched for something she could use for a weapon. Her best bet would be to look in the SUV, but if she distracted him now, he could end up hurt. Just as she was about ready to go back up to her apartment to get one of her kitchen knives, the attacker's sword skidded across the pavement not too far from where Ansley stood. Somehow Roan must have disarmed his attacker.

Her heart raced. Ansley went to the sword and picked it up. She tiptoed to the SUV, afraid of what she would find. She stuck her head around the rear of it and took a quick peek before she pulled back. Two large wolves snarled and clawed at each other where Roan and his attacker had been. With the sword gone, they'd switched to teeth and claws.

After taking a couple deep breaths for courage, Ansley hefted the heavy sword in both hands and stepped around the back of the SUV to the side where the wolves fought. She easily could tell which wolf was which. She recognized Roan as the one with the light-brown fur that matched his hair. The other had dark-gray fur. She focused on the dark-gray wolf as she slowly walked closer.

She tried not to think about what she was about to do. She focused on the fear she felt for Roan. He was her mate, her other half. No one would take him away from her. She loved him too much to allow anyone to hurt him. Ansley blinked. She *loved* Roan. Now that there was a chance she could lose him, she knew without a shadow of a doubt that she loved him, and had from the start. More determined to make sure she got a chance to tell him how she truly felt, she gripped the sword tighter.

Once she dared to get close enough to the wolves, Ansley used all her strength to lift the weapon as high as she could. She brought the flat of it down onto the dark gray wolf's back, putting all the force she had behind it. He yelped and went down hard to the ground. Roan took advantage of the situation and jumped onto the back of the dark gray wolf and took the back of his neck in his strong jaws. The other wolf yelped again and then went still when Roan growled and dug his sharp claws into the gray wolf's side. Defeated, the dark-gray wolf whimpered and put his tail between his legs.

Roan released the other wolf's neck, but didn't move away. The wolves shifted to human form at the same time. Roan rolled his attacker onto his back, then coldcocked him. Unconscious, his attacker went limp. Roan picked him up and carried him over one shoulder. He put the other man into the back of the SUV. He pulled out some rope and hog-tied him. Ansley stood quietly by, shaking as she waited for him to finish.

His attacker taken care of, Roan spun around and hauled Ansley to him in a tight hug. "What were you thinking, Ansley? You could have been seriously hurt. If anything happened to you…" He couldn't seem to finish his sentence.

"Nothing did." Roan squeezed her so hard Ansley could barely draw in a deep breath, but she didn't care. "If you think I would just stand by and let you get hurt, you have another think coming. You're my mate. I won't let anyone take the man I love away from me."

Roan went still. He released her enough so he could pull back and look at her. "What was that last part?"

Ansley smiled. "I said I won't let anyone take the man I love away from me."

She'd hardly said the last word before Roan kissed her so thoroughly Ansley's legs almost gave out and she barely remembered her own name. Once he lifted his head, he said, "If I didn't have to get rid of this trash," he nodded to the back of the SUV, "I would haul you up to your apartment and show you how happy you've just made me."

Ansley shivered with pleasure. "What are you going to do with him?"

"He's one of Miles' men. I'm going to take him to Roxie. As the ruler of the packs, she gets to decide his fate."

"What will she do to him?"

Roan chuckled. "To start with, he's going to learn his place. I hope he likes being stuck in his wolf form while chained up in Roxie's backyard like the dog he is. If that doesn't make him inclined to talk, I don't know what will."

Ansley bit her bottom lip and looked at Roan. "Since we're going to Roxie's, while we're there, I think I'll ask her if she has time to use that spell of hers."

Roan cupped her face in his hands. "Are you sure that's what you want, Ansley? I don't want you to do it if you're only doing it for me. I want you to do it because it's what you want."

She stood on tiptoe and brushed her lips across his. "I'm sure. I want us to have the thousands of years together the spell will give us. You're my mate. I want to be mated to you in every sense of the word."

As Roan kissed her tenderly, Ansley knew she'd made the right decision. No longer would she ever have to worry about being alone. Her wolf would always be by her side.

The End

JAGER'S MATE

Daylen is a cop, and a good one. When she discovers two men sword fighting in an alley during one of her nightly patrols, she confronts them, ordering them to put down their weapons. One of the men takes off running, surprising her with his speed. Only one man left, she knows she'll have to take him down when he ignores her demands. With her suspect in her grasp, her world turns upside down when he pins her to the ground and kisses her senseless.

Jager knows no wilting flower—werewolf or mortal—would ever survive as his mate, but this cop has all the right moves. Her scent leaves no doubt this mortal woman is his, and after tasting her lips, he knows claiming her will be a challenge. The bigger problem, however, might be her obsession to arrest him whenever they meet. As their passion flares, he'll do anything it takes to make her his mate.

CHAPTER ONE

Jager silently followed the lone wolf at a discreet distance. He kept his gaze locked on the other werewolf's back while he wove through the people who shared the sidewalk in this busy section of downtown San Francisco. More than a few of the buildings that lined the street were restaurants, bars, or nightclubs. He had spotted the lone wolf at one of the nightclubs.

He'd gone to the Hot Spot—which had been anything but—after Leif, his brother-in-arms, had heard a rumor going around about a lone wolf trying to recruit other lone wolves for a new cause at this nightclub. Leif had come by that information from a bar he liked to frequent to pick up female werewolves who were unmated and wanted to share their beds for a bit of fun. Leif's womanizing sometimes paid off when he came across a bit of information such as that.

The lone wolf ducked into an alley between two buildings at the end of the street where most of the crowd had thinned. Increasing his speed, Jager kept him in sight. Once inside the alley, Jager opened the front of his long, black duster and brushed it to one side as he reached for the hilt of his sword. It made a slight hissing sound when he pulled it free of its scabbard.

After taking a quick look behind him to make sure no mortals were able to see him from the opening into the alley, Jager stealthily walked halfway down the passage. It was quite dark, but with his keen werewolf sight, he could see just as well as if it were daytime instead of night. Only one weak, exposed light bulb shone above a door that opened onto the alley. His steps slowed when he caught the glint of light that suddenly flashed in his eyes. At the same time, he heard a sword being drawn.

A smile spread across Jager's face. It looked as if this lone wolf wanted to play. And that he carried a concealed weapon on him — more than likely having been strapped to his back under his leather jacket — marked him as one of Miles' recruits. The average werewolf didn't carry swords nowadays.

The sound of a low growl drifted to Jager after he came to a stop a short distance from the lone wolf. He looked the other werewolf over. Like all of his kind, the lone wolf was taller than the average mortal, but he was about an inch shorter than Jager, which put him at about six foot eight. He was muscular as well, but Jager figured he had a few extra pounds of muscle on him that the lone wolf didn't have. Strength-wise they would be close, but it all came down to how well the lone wolf could handle his sword. Jager planned to beat his ass, but he hoped the altercation would last longer than a few seconds. There was nothing more that Jager enjoyed than a good sword fight. Just the thought of it made his blood pump a little bit faster.

"So, lone wolf, you think you're man...or should I say werewolf...enough to take on the likes of me," Jager said as he stepped closer. "I'll give you fair warning. You point a sword in my direction, you'd better know how to use the damn thing."

The lone wolf snarled and growled menacingly at the same time. "Let me guess. You must be one of the Protectors who watch over the foretold one. Miles warned us about you."

Jager chuckled. "I'm sure he did. Yes, I'm one of the Protectors. And did dear old Miles tell you that he used to be one of us before he decided to go bad?"

"Miles told us how unfairly he was treated while he was one of the Protectors, and how he was given no choice but to leave and try to find the foretold one for himself."

Jager snorted. The only way Miles had been treated "unfairly" was when it had been decided by his grandmother, who had brought all the Protectors together, that his sister, Saskia, would lead instead of him. Miles had been so enraged he hadn't been chosen to be their leader he'd forsaken his sister and grandmother, swearing he would be the one to find the foretold one and use him or her for his own benefits. Now that Roxie had come forward and declared herself as the foretold one, Jager and the rest of her Protectors knew it would only be a matter of time before Miles made his move.

Raising his sword, Jager ran his gaze over the gleaming blade before he pinned a hard stare on the lone wolf. "Enough of the idle chitchat. How about we get down to business? The night isn't getting any younger, and I'm itching for a fight."

Instead of answering him, the lone wolf growled once more and took the first strike as he closed the distance between them. Jager easily blocked the blade and took a strike of his own. He felt a surge of hope that he might have a worthy opponent when the lone wolf circled out of range at the last minute. Grinning widely, he swung his sword up to meet the lone wolf's next blow. Fun and games were on.

* * * *

Daylen Reardon drove her police cruiser down the busy downtown street. She looked from right to left as she patrolled her regular beat. She didn't expect any trouble, but given the bars and nightclubs on this road, there was always a chance she would come across a few patrons who had indulged just a little too much. If she spotted an individual weaving down the sidewalk, she usually pulled over to make sure they had an alternative means of getting home besides getting into a car to drive.

She'd been a cop for the last five years, and loved the job. When she put on her uniform and strapped on her gun, she knew she was doing a service for her city to help make it a better place. Not that she thought she did it all by herself, but she liked that she was doing her part.

Nearing the end of the street, she slowed the cruiser, preparing to take the next left in her circuit. Daylen happened to glance out the passenger window at an alley sandwiched between two buildings. What she saw had her hitting the brakes and pulling over to the curb.

After she turned off the cruiser's engine, Daylen got out and locked the door behind her. As she slowly walked to the entrance of the alley, she pocketed the car keys and then pulled out her flashlight. She turned it on before she aimed the beam of light at what she thought she saw. The space was semi-dark, but she'd always had pretty good night vision. When the light hit the middle of the alley, she knew she hadn't been imagining what she'd seen from the cruiser.

With the flashlight still held in her left hand, Daylen unclipped her holster in case she needed to draw her gun while she quietly approached the two men who were going at each other with a pair of swords. Now *that* wasn't something she saw every day on her patrols.

Daylen didn't call out to the men, deciding to wait until she was a bit closer. She slowly walked nearer, and heard growling sounds that sounded all too animal-like. They were mixed in with the noise of the men's swords clashing. They were big brutes. One had short, black hair, was well over six-and-a-half feet tall, and wore jeans along with a black leather jacket. He appeared to be the one making the growling sounds as he swung his sword at his opponent. The other had long light-brown hair pulled back in a ponytail, was just a bit taller than the other man, and wore a long, black duster over his dark jeans. She also noticed he wore an expression of glee, and a smile that seemed to get wider with each blow that came at him.

Daylen shook her head. They had to be a couple of kooks. At first, she thought the swords couldn't be real, but when the black-haired man ended up catching the blade of the other's across his cheek and blood welled, she had her proof that they were. Just what she needed, a pair of crazies whacking at each other with real swords.

Having come close enough to the two men that she would be able to catch them if they decided to take off running, Daylen aimed the beam of her flashlight at their faces. "All right, boys, time to put the swords down," she said in her best loud-and-authoritative police officer voice.

Both men lowered their swords and turned to face her. Daylen opened her mouth to ask what the hell they thought they were doing when the black-haired man spun around, ran down toward the opposite end of the alley and disappeared into the darkness.

She blinked. The man had run so quickly she'd had a hard time tracking him. She'd never seen anyone move at that speed before. She hadn't even had a chance to yell at him to stop.

The other man hadn't moved from where he stood. Daylen focused her attention on him. With her flashlight once again aimed at his face, she had to admit he was one good-looking kook. A male model came to mind when she took in his chiseled cheekbones, straight nose, and firm, full lips. Against her will, her gaze settled on his mouth for a few seconds longer than necessary. If he hadn't been a crazy person, and she wasn't on duty, she would have liked to get to know him better. She might be a cop, but she was also a woman, and right now, she found herself more than a little attracted to the man before her.

Daylen pulled her mind back to the task at hand, and said, "Put the sword on the ground and take a step away from it."

The man's nostrils flared slightly when he took a deep breath. His gaze latched on to her, staring at her so intently Daylen found herself reacting in a way she shouldn't. His light blue-eyed gaze looked her up and down, leaving a trail of goosebumps under her uniform wherever it touched. Her breasts seemed to grow heavy, and her nipples tightened when his gaze settled on them. Her breath hitched at seeing the arousal that lurked in the man's eyes. He made no move to put down the sword he held.

She cleared her throat and tried again. "Put the sword down," she said, louder.

This time he slowly brushed the left side of his duster aside to reveal a scabbard that hung there. He sheathed the sword while he kept his gaze locked to hers. For a brief second, Daylen swore she saw his light-blue eyes glow mutedly as he closed the distance between them. With the beam of her flashlight still shining on his face, she had to think it was a trick of the light.

She put her right hand on top her gun. "Stay where you are, and put your hands behind your head. If you don't, I will draw my gun."

"What are you going to do? Handcuff me?" he asked in a deep, sexy drawl. "I may like that." He continued to slowly come toward her.

Daylen had yet to fire her gun in the line of duty. She didn't want tonight to be the night she had to, but if the man in front of her decided to pull out his sword again and think to use it on her, she would do whatever was necessary to take him down.

"Carrying a concealed weapon is a major offense. Resisting arrest will make it that much worse for you. Why don't you just cooperate and make it easier for the both of us?"

A grin spread across his lips, and Daylen had to admit that made the man look even sexier. "Sorry, but I'm not going to let you arrest me," he said.

Figures. The kooks never wanted to be taken away without kicking up a fuss. Not wanting this to draw out any longer than it had to, Daylen waited until he came within range. She dropped her flashlight and grabbed him by one arm as she used a karate move to kick his legs out from under him. Having caught him off guard, she managed to get him down face-first onto the ground with his hands behind him. She sat on his back, pinning his arms between her legs as she reached for her handcuffs that were in a leather case attached to her belt. With her other hand, she kept the side of his face pressed to the pavement.

The handcuffs now out of their case, Daylen started to read the man his rights. "You have the right to remain silent. Everything—"

She never got to finish. One second she had him pinned, ready to cuff his hands behind him, and then the next, he'd bucked her off. With a move faster than she could react to, he had her on her back with his large body on top of hers. He manacled her wrists in one strong hand as he grabbed the handcuffs and tossed them away.

Shit. Now she was in trouble. Even though his grip didn't hurt, Daylen couldn't break free of his hold. She tried to buck him off as he'd done to her, but he was solid muscle and didn't budge an inch.

Daylen gazed at him, not sure what he would do next. Instead of seeing malice in his eyes, he stared at her with intense longing. Against her will, her heart beat a little faster. The longer he held her gaze, the more her body reacted. Instead of being afraid of what he would do to her, she found herself becoming aroused. An ache pounded between her legs, and she breathed faster. And, if she was not mistaken, he was aroused as well. The hard length of his cock pressed against her thigh where he had her legs pinned between his.

He felt way too good pressed against her. That had Daylen trying once more to buck him off. She shouldn't be getting turned on by a guy who obviously had a few screws loose. She had to stay professional. He was the bad guy, and she was the cop.

When she arched her back again to try to throw him off, he made a low sound deep inside his chest that came damn close to something a wild animal would make. She instantly stilled.

He shook his head. "Keep doing that and I won't be responsible for what I do to you. I'm barely holding back as it is."

He shoved the collar of her shirt aside before he buried his nose in the crook of her neck and took a deep breath.

He dragged his tongue across the skin where her shoulder and neck met. "God, you smell good." He lifted his head and looked at the name tag pinned to the front of her shirt. "Officer Daylen Reardon, I would like to continue what's started here, but I don't think you'll be as cooperative as I want you to be. We'll have to finish this another time, but I'm not going to leave before I've gotten a taste of you."

Before Daylen knew what he was about to do, he brought his mouth down to hers and kissed her. His lips gently moved over hers before his tongue came out and pushed its way between her lips. He tasted her thoroughly, twining his tongue with hers.

The man might be a kook, but he sure knew how to kiss a woman senseless. Unable to stop herself from kissing him back, Daylen's body went up in flames with each stroke of his tongue. He licked and sucked at her lips as she found herself sinking deeper and deeper into a fog of arousal. Her brain seemed to only be functioning at half power. A part of her knew this was so very wrong, but another baser part of her had taken over and wanted more. The feel of his well-muscled body pressed against hers just sent her arousal to greater heights. She moaned softly into his mouth.

Then his lips were gone, along with the weight of his body that had been pressing on top of her. Now free, Daylen sat up and caught sight of the back of the man's duster as he ran down the alley in the same direction the other man had taken. He was gone.

What the hell is wrong with me? Daylen stood and grabbed her flashlight that lay on the ground not far away. Using its light, she found her handcuffs. If another cop had been present to see what had taken place, there would be questions as to whether or not she could do her job. And she wouldn't have been able to defend her actions. She'd just let a criminal kiss her stupid while she basically did nothing to stop him. And, if that wasn't bad enough, he'd gotten away, on top of it all.

She called herself the lamest woman to walk the face of the earth and headed to her police cruiser. Just as she got in on the driver's side, she remembered what he'd said before he'd kissed her — they would finish this another time. Whatever the hell he meant by *that*.

Daylen started the cruiser and then pulled away from the curb to continue with her patrol. She knew one thing. If she ever did see him again, she'd be more prepared. She wouldn't let his lips anywhere near her. Instead, she'd make him kiss the dirt as she cuffed his ass before hauling him off to jail. There was no way in hell she would let the man make a fool of her twice. No matter how attractive he was, and how he made her want things she shouldn't. She wouldn't think twice about arresting him. The man had better hope they didn't cross paths again, for his sake.

CHAPTER TWO

Jager ran to where he'd parked his black Chevy Camaro. He'd tried to pick up the trail of the lone wolf after he left the woman cop in the alley, but he lost it once he reached the street. The bastard must have had a vehicle parked there, and had made good his escape.

After getting into his Camaro and then pulling away to make the drive to Marin County where he lived with the rest of Roxie's Protectors, Jager thought about the woman cop, Daylen. She'd been totally unexpected, and not because she was a cop who happened to come across him and the lone wolf sword fighting. No, it'd been his reaction to her. One whiff of her scent and he'd become cemented in place. All his senses had been riveted to her, as if he'd suddenly developed tunnel vision and only she existed. The wolf inside him had thrown back its head and howled. And, inside his mind, the word "mine" had repeated itself over and over again. He'd at last found his mate.

Jager smiled as he remembered how she'd brought him down and then tried to handcuff him. She'd totally taken him by surprise. He hadn't expected her to use a karate move on him. Obviously, his mate was even tougher than she looked. Just listening to her ordering him to put down his sword in an authoritative voice, and while dressed in her cop uniform with her long, reddish-brown hair pulled back in a bun had been a turn-on.

Her brown eyes had been all business, even when she'd been checking him out, which was good. He needed his mate to be tough, not some flower who would dissolve in a fit of tears if he looked at her wrong. He was never one for watching what he said. He liked to say whatever was on his mind, no pussyfooting around.

Unlike his brother-in-arms, Leif, who never wanted to be tied down, Jager looked forward to claiming the one woman who was meant to be his. Though doing it would be a tad difficult. Other than the fact she was mortal, and more than likely had no idea werewolves existed, there was also the small point that she would try to arrest his ass if she saw him again. He would have to work around that. At least she hadn't been totally unaffected by him. When he'd kissed her, unable to keep from having one small taste of her before he'd left, and she'd kissed him back, it'd taken everything in him not to claim her as his mate right then and there on the ground in that dirty alley. The mating urge had ridden him hard, and that wouldn't have done anything to endear him to her.

After arriving at the mansion where he lived with his sister and brothers, Jager parked his Camaro in the large garage and then went inside. Once he stepped into the spacious foyer, he heard voices coming from the kitchen. He walked to that room and found Skylar, Roan, and Roan's mate, Ansley, there. Skylar and Roan were his true brothers. They all shared similar features, along with having the same light-brown hair and light-blue eyes. Ansley had Skylar sitting in one of the kitchen chairs with a hairdresser's cape around him while she trimmed the ends of his long hair. Ansley was a hair stylist and had taken over the job of doing haircuts from their sister, Saskia. Roan sat on the edge of the kitchen table and watched his mate work.

Jager crossed the room and grabbed a bottle of beer out of the fridge before he went back to the others. He pulled out one of the empty chairs and sat before he twisted off the beer cap and then took a big sip.

He put the beer bottle on the table, and said, "Aren't you looking pretty, Skylar, with your hair all nicely trimmed?" Jager chuckled when his brother flipped him off.

"Be nice, Jager," Ansley said. "And talking about trims, when are you going to let me cut your hair?"

Jager grabbed his ponytail and pulled it over his shoulder. It was getting long. It hung to the middle of his back when tied like that, but he liked it that way. He looked at the ends. "I'm good. I'll let you know when I want a haircut." Since Roan had claimed Ansley as his mate three months before, she'd cut everyone's hair who lived in the mansion, except for his.

Roan snorted. "If your hair gets any longer, people will think you're a woman from behind."

"Bite me."

"No thanks. I'd much rather bite my mate." Roan went to stand behind Ansley and nuzzled the side of her neck.

"Hey," Skylar said. "Enough of that. Please don't distract her when she's holding a pair of very sharp scissors near me. I only want a trim. I don't want my hair all cut off because Ansley chopped a big hunk out of it." Skylar usually wore his hair the same way Jager liked his, except it wasn't quite as long.

Ansley shoved Roan away. "Don't worry, Skylar, I would never do that. Roan will stay out the way. I doubt he'd want me to slip and get his hair instead." She opened and closed the scissors in her mate's direction.

Roan backed away. "I don't want to be shaved bald either." He pulled out a chair next to Jager and then took a seat. "So, how did tonight go? Did Leif's tip pay off?"

Jager nodded. "Yeah. I found the lone wolf at the nightclub where Leif said he would be. If not for one small interruption, I would have beaten him during our sword fight and forced some answers out of him.

At that moment, Leif walked into the kitchen. "What kind of interruption?" With his werewolf hearing, he had no problem hearing what Jager said, even before arriving in the kitchen.

A smile spread across Jager's lips. "A lady cop spotted me and the lone wolf crossing swords in an alley. The lone wolf took off when she showed up."

"Why didn't you go after him?" Leif asked.

"I couldn't. I was a little busy trying to get a grip on the mating urged that slammed into me while my mate ordered me to put down my sword so she could arrest me."

Leif cursed as he got up and went to the fridge. He took out a beer and gulped down two big swigs before he returned to the table with it. "Dear God, you're dropping like flies. First Saskia, then Roan, and now you find your mate. If I'm not careful, I'll be next."

Roan wrapped his arm around Ansley, now that she'd finished with Skylar's hair. "I wouldn't say that too many times out loud, Leif, or it might actually come true." He chuckled when Leif picked up his beer and chugged half of it almost in one gulp. He turned to Jager. "So, when do we get to meet this mate of yours?"

Jager scratched his chin. "Well, there's a bit of a problem, besides her being a mortal."

Ansley spoke up. "Does her being a mortal bother you?"

Jager knew why Ansley had asked that question. Before she'd mated with Roan, she had been a mortal, the same as Eli, Saskia's mate. They both had become werewolves with the help of Roxie, the foretold one. Not only was Roxie the leader of the packs because of the mark she had around her left wrist, she also had some extra magic inside her that the average werewolf didn't. One of her powers was her ability to turn a mortal into a werewolf with a magic spell and some of her blood. Because she was *so* special, they had become her Protectors. If it ever came out that she could do the things she could, they would have to worry about more than Miles trying to steal her away.

With a shake of his head, Jager said, "No, her being a mortal doesn't bother me. The problem is the fact I resisted arrest, and she'll probably try to cuff me when I get close to her again."

Skylar laughed. "She tried to cuff you? I wish I'd been there to see that."

Jager ignored him. "Anyway, once I got away from my mate, the lone wolf's trail had gone dead, but he was definitely one of Miles' men. He admitted to that."

"We'll have to tell Saskia. She'll want to know," Roan said. "So, what are you going to do about your lady cop?"

Jager shrugged. "Not sure, yet. At least I managed to get her name from the tag she wore. Are Dirk and Kye still with Roxie?"

They usually split their numbers and took turns watching Roxie, especially when she went to Wulf's Den with her mate, Beowulf. Beowulf owned the local nightclub where werewolves and mortals mixed, not that the mortals knew that.

Roan nodded. "Yeah, they are. They should be home in a

couple hours."

Jager grabbed his beer off the table and stood. "Good. I'm going to get Dirk to do his magic on the Internet and see what he can come up with on my mate." Dirk, though well over a thousand years old just like the rest of the Protectors, kept up his skills with all the new technology. He was an Internet junkie just as Roxie was.

Without another word, Jager walked out of the kitchen. He needed to be by himself for a bit. Now that he'd found his mate, the mating urge would ride him hard until he claimed her as his own. Even now, just talking about Daylen had caused him to become slightly aroused. He would be lucky if he didn't constantly walk around with a hard-on until she was his. And tonight, having listened to what Roan had gone through before he claimed Ansley as his mate, Jager expected to have one erotic dream after another about Daylen. The longer he waited to make her his, the worse the mating urge would ride him. Not a patient man by any stretch, he would have to act quickly.

Once he reached his bedroom, he shut the door behind him. He had plans to make. First and foremost, he had to find a way to get Daylen to overlook what she thought was her duty, and not want to arrest him. Once they got over that, Jager had a feeling he could get her to accept what was meant to be. If she didn't, he had no qualms about throwing her over his shoulder and locking her in a room somewhere until he'd persuaded her to see things his way. He threw himself onto his bed, then turned on the television on the far wall with the remote and grinned. He knew just what he would do to convince her to see things his way. Something they both would enjoy.

* * * *

When dawn started to lighten the sky, Daylen drove her cruiser to the police station. After a long night of patrolling, she was ready to go home and fall into bed. Once in her own car, a dark blue Ford Focus, she debated on whether or not to pick up some breakfast through one of the fast food drive-thrus, but in the end she decided against it. Her body needed sleep more than it needed food, especially since she had one more night shift to get through before she had a couple of days off.

Daylen arrived at the street where she lived, a neighborhood that was mostly made up of families with young children, then parked her car in the driveway of her three-room bungalow. Inside the house, she locked the door behind her before she headed to her bedroom to change out of her uniform.

As she locked up her gun in the metal fire-safe lockbox she stored in her closet, she once again found her thoughts drawn to the man she'd encountered in the alley. She seemed to be thinking about him way more than she should. For some reason, she couldn't stop herself from doing it. And it wasn't because he'd gotten away. No, she found herself mooning over what it had felt like to be kissed by him with his body pressed to hers. It pissed her off every time she did it. Daylen had never been, and never would be, the kind of woman to go all gaga over a man. And especially not one who went around sword fighting in dark alleys.

Daylen was too practical to lose her head over a man. Every relationship she had, she'd looked at as a partnership rather than a romantic love affair. If she found the man attractive, and he was willing to overlook the fact she was a cop, she let things take their natural course. The sex would be all right, but it was never blow-your-mind good. The relationship would usually peter out a few months down the road with no one getting hurt.

Now she'd found a man who could not only kiss like there was no tomorrow, he'd also just about blown her socks off while doing it. And the kicker was she wanted to see him again. She hadn't reported the incident in the alley. For some inexplicable reason, she didn't like the thought of another cop finding and arresting him. Daylen wanted to be the one to bring him in.

Disgusted with how much time she'd spent thinking about him, she went to the bathroom to wash her face and brush her teeth after she changed into a pair of pajama bottoms and an over-sized T-shirt. That done, she returned to the bedroom and got into bed. The dark shade pulled over the window blocked most of the light from outside. After closing her eyes, Daylen drifted off to sleep with the image of the man swirling inside her mind.

* * * *

Miles sat in an overstuffed leather armchair in front of the wall of windows in his penthouse apartment, watching the sunrise. He swirled the scotch in his glass before he brought it to his lips and took a drink. The news he'd received had been good and bad. He took another swallow.

The bad was that the Protectors had once again found one of the men he used to find new recruits. At least this one had been smart enough to get away before he led the enemy to their door. The last time the Protectors had found the place where he trained his recruits, Miles had to destroy it, taking some of his men with it. It'd taken him months to set up a new location, and to recruit the number of lone wolves willing to follow him. He couldn't afford a loss of that magnitude again, now that the foretold one had been found.

The good news had in a small way made up for the Protectors being on his trail once again. A wicked smile spread across Miles' lips. His man had made an interesting find before he'd managed to get away from the alley where he'd encountered Jager. And Miles knew it was Jager from the lone wolf's description. His recruit also mentioned Jager's reaction to the female police officer who'd interrupted their fight.

The sword-happy idiot had found his mate. Needless to say, Miles found that information quite useful. It wouldn't be that hard to find out who the woman was. All he had to do was have one of his men follow Jager to her. The dumbass wouldn't be able to stay away from her. Since she had to be mortal, it would hinder Jager's ability to claim her as his. If the Protectors happened to come too close to his new headquarters, Miles figured Jager's soon-to-be mate would make an excellent bargaining chip. And if Jager managed to claim her before Miles needed to use her, all the better. Mated werewolves couldn't stand to be away from their mates. They became extremely agitated, to say the least. It would be fun to watch Jager suffer while separated from his mate. It would just be one more incentive to get the Protectors to leave him alone. Given how honorable his sister and her brothers-in-arms were, they would do everything in their power to keep Jager's mate from harm. Their weakness would be his gain.

CHAPTER THREE

At the start of her next shift, Daylen walked into the large room her sergeant usually used for the short meetings before she and the rest of the officers went out on patrol. She crossed the space and sat in an empty chair next to one of the other officers.

He turned in his seat and smiled. "One more night and then the next two days are ours. Got any plans this weekend?"

Daylen shook her head and smiled back at the man beside her. She and Nick Winston had gone through the police academy together and then had come to work in the same precinct. At first glance, he looked liked one tough customer with his brown hair buzzed close to his scalp and his large, muscular body. Being six four also helped with the illusion. On the inside, he was a sweet guy who would go out of his way to help people.

"No," Daylen said. "No plans. I'll probably just veg in front of the TV. How's Allison? Any signs of that baby making an appearance any time soon?" Nick's wife, Allison, was pregnant with their first child and due any day.

Nick shook his head. "Not yet, but Allison is more than ready."

Daylen chuckled. "I bet she is. I think she was ready a month ago."

"At least she hasn't gone over her due date."

"Well, you know what to do if she does go past it. From what

I've read, sex apparently will jumpstart a woman's labor."

Nick grinned. "I told Allison about that when you told me the first time. Let's just say we've been putting that bit of advice to good use."

"I figured it would be no hardship for you."

At that moment, their sergeant walked into the room. The other officers settled down when he went to stand at the front. "All right, people. You all know what you'll be doing tonight, so I won't keep you long. While you're out, keep your eyes peeled for anything out of the ordinary."

"What would that be, sarge?" Nick asked.

"We've had a couple of reports that a wolf, or a very large dog, has been seen in the back alleys of the nightclub district. Normally, I wouldn't take this seriously, but we've had more than one person call over the last couple weeks, and the sightings have been in the same general area. This could just be someone's pet who has gotten loose, but if you do spot it, don't take any chances. Try to keep it cornered and then call for animal control to take care of it. That's it for tonight. Be careful out there."

Daylen filed out of the room with the rest of the officers. Nick walked at her side. "The nightclub district is your patrol," he said. "Have you spotted a wolf lurking about?"

"None so far." A wolf couldn't be any stranger than that sword fight.

Damn. Just like that, she found herself remembering the man in the alley. Even in sleep, she hadn't been able to get away from him. She'd had one particularly erotic dream starring him. It'd started off with him kissing her in the alley, but then the scene had shifted and they had somehow ended up in bed together — naked. In her dream, they'd made love, and it'd been the best sex Daylen had ever had. He'd rocked her world. At the end of it, she'd woken up wet and aching for a man she'd have to arrest if she ever saw him again.

Lost in her thoughts, she didn't realize Nick had been speaking to her until he grabbed her by the arm and pulled her to a stop. They'd reached his cruiser outside.

Daylen quickly pulled her thoughts together. "Sorry, what did you say?"

Nick gave her a look that said he'd probably already repeated himself more than once. "I said if you do happen to see the wolf, don't do anything stupid. You never know. The damn thing could have rabies."

"I doubt I'll see it. And I doubt it's a wolf. It's more likely some mongrel stray that happens to be on the large size."

"Even then, be careful."

Daylen walked backward toward her cruiser. "Stop worrying, mother hen. You know I don't do anything rash. If I don't catch you at the end of your shift, tell Allison I said hi."

"I will. Hopefully, I'll be calling you from the hospital over the weekend."

"I'll keep my fingers crossed for you."

* * * *

The night turned out to be uneventful for Daylen. Being a Friday, she kept a closer watch on the patrons who filed in and out of the bars and nightclubs. This day of the week tended to be a lot busier, and people seemed to drink a bit more than they did during the nights. Not too often, but at times, fights would break out as well.

Near the end of her shift, Daylen made one final sweep of her patrol route. With dawn fast approaching, things had settled down. As she neared the alley where the sword fight had taken place the night before, she slowed the cruiser, something she'd done each time she'd driven by it. Not that she thought the man would be stupid enough to show up at the place where he'd resisted arrest. She just couldn't stop herself from looking at the last spot she'd seen him.

Daylen's foot slammed on the brake when she saw the figure of a man standing just at the opening of the alley. His long hair was pulled back in a ponytail, the ends of it fluttering in the breeze. He wore the same black duster he'd worn when she'd first seen him. He waited until he made eye contact with her before he turned and ducked into the alley.

Not wanting him to get away from her this time, Daylen hit the gas and sped up to the alley. She rammed the cruiser into park and then jumped out, slamming the door behind her.

Inside the alley, she stopped short when she swept the length of it with her gaze and found it empty. *Where has he gone?* It'd taken her all of ten seconds to get there. He couldn't have run the length of it and disappeared in that short amount of time. Then again, he'd moved incredibly fast the first time she'd encountered him. Just to make sure he was indeed gone, Daylen walked down to the very end that opened onto another street, but there was no sign of him. She had to wonder if her mind had made him up since she seemed to be spending so much time thinking about him.

Just as she turned to head back to her cruiser, Daylen heard someone call her name. She looked at the opposite end of the alley and found Nick walking toward her. She met him at the halfway point.

"Nick, what are you doing here?" she asked.

"I saw your cruiser at the curb. Considering you weren't in it, I thought I'd see if you needed any help."

She shook her head. "I just thought I saw something and decided to take a closer look is all. If I had seen the wolf, dog, or whatever, I would have radioed in. There's nothing here. I thought you would have already gone to the station. This part of the city isn't that close to your patrol route."

Nick gave her a sheepish grin. "Okay, I came looking for you. I just wanted to make sure you were all right. I had a bad experience with a big dog when I was a kid, and I never really got over it."

"That's sweet, but totally unnecessary. I'm perfectly capable of looking out for myself, as you know. Having a black belt in karate, I can pretty much kick butt when I need to, be it man or dog. Now go to the station so you can get home and enjoy your weekend. I'll be right behind you." Before Nick walked away, Daylen gave him a kiss on the cheek. "That's for thinking of me."

A loud animal-like growl echoed through the alley. Nick and Daylen put their hands on the butts of their guns at the same time.

Nick swept the alley with his gaze. "Can you see anything? It sounded like it came from somewhere close by."

They did a thorough search of the alley, but she didn't see the animal that had made the growl. "Nope. Nothing. Whatever it was, I don't think it hung around. Let's go."

"You don't have to ask me twice."

As she and Nick walked out of the alley to their cruisers, Daylen couldn't shake the feeling that they were being watched. Before she got into the car, she looked one last time down the alley. It remained just as empty as it had been when they'd left it.

* * * *

Jager straightened from where he'd crouched on the upper level of the fire escape attached to one of the buildings that made up the alley walls. He'd had a good vantage point from up there to see what went on below. The shadows had also helped to hide his presence. After he'd let Daylen spot him, he'd climbed up the fire escape before she'd followed him. Being able to move faster than a mortal did have its advantages.

He'd been quite happy to watch Daylen when she'd done her search of the alley. Her scent had drifted up to him on the slight breeze, making him ache for her. His cock had hardened the instant she stepped into view. He had run his gaze over her face and body. She wasn't supermodel pretty like female werewolves were, but she was far from ugly with her full, kissable lips, high cheekbones, and sharp brown eyes that didn't seem to miss anything. Through her uniform, Jager had been able to see the faint outlines of a small, curved waist and more-than-a-handful breasts. Her attire did more to hide her body than not. He wanted to strip it off her and see what she would look like out of it. He also wanted to free her hair from its tight bun to see how long it was while he ran his fingers through it.

Then the male cop had arrived. Seeing how friendly they had been with each other, Jager had had to put a tight rein on his wolf. It didn't like any other males around his potential mate. Neither had the man. Until he claimed Daylen as his own, her being around other men would make the mating urge ride him all the harder.

He'd been able to keep himself in control up to the point where Daylen had kissed the male cop on the cheek. His wolf had wanted him to rush down to the alley and warn the other man away from his mate. Jager hadn't been able to stop the growl that had rumbled out of him.

Once he figured Daylen would have driven away, Jager

headed down the fire escape. Thanks to Dirk, he'd found out in which precinct Daylen worked. Dirk hadn't been able to find a telephone number or a home address. Obviously, being a cop, Daylen didn't want that kind of information to be common knowledge.

After reaching the alley, Jager took off at a fast run to where he'd parked his Camaro. From the conversation he'd heard between Daylen and the male cop, he figured she would be on her way to the police station since it was the end of her shift. He drove to the street where it was located and then parked at the curb across from it where he had a good view of the cars leaving the parking lot. He fully intended to follow her home. Fifteen minutes later, a dark blue Ford Focus pulled out of the lot with her behind the wheel. He quickly started his vehicle before he merged into the traffic and followed her at a discreet distance.

The sky had completely lightened by the time Daylen pulled into the driveway of a bungalow in a quiet neighborhood. He drove past the house and parked a couple of blocks away. He'd had all day to come up with a plan to be around her without her trying to throw him into jail. There was a good chance it would backfire on him, but Jager was willing to take that chance.

After getting out of his car, he quickly headed to Daylen's house. Once he reached it, he went to the side where the sun's rays had yet to touch. With a quick look around to make sure none of her neighbors would see him, Jager reached for the magic inside him that would allow him to shift to his wolf form.

With his hand held out in front of him, Jager watched it shimmer and then blur as he shifted. In a matter of seconds, a wolf with light brown fur took his place. On silent paws, he walked to the front door of the bungalow. He scratched at it. When it didn't cause any reaction from inside the house, he rammed it. Still not hearing any movement from the other side, he threw back his head and let out a loud howl. If that didn't get Daylen's attention, nothing would.

CHAPTER FOUR

The sound of a loud howl coming from the front of the house had Daylen rushing in that direction. She'd just finished changing into her pajamas. Knowing she wouldn't get any sleep until she found out what had made the noise, she yanked open the door to peer outside.

No sooner had she gotten it open, then a large, furry body darted past her and into the house. "What the hell?"

Daylen turned to find what looked suspiciously like a wolf sitting in the middle of her front entranceway hall, staring at her. On closer inspection, she noticed it was a male. Not sure what to do next, she stared back at him. The wolf soon broke off the staring contest, got up, and then headed down the hallway that led to her bedroom.

"Oh no, you don't," she called as she followed him after she'd shut the front door in case there were more strays out there.

This was one headache she didn't need. All she wanted to do was get a few hours of sleep. Since she didn't have to work for the next couple days, Daylen usually shifted back to sleeping at night instead of all day, which required her to only nap for a few hours before she got up again. That being the case, she didn't want to waste what little time she had chasing after what she thought was a wolf to get it out of her house.

Sure enough, the wolf had made a beeline straight to her

bedroom. When she entered the room, he opened his mouth in a way that almost made it look as if he were smiling. Almost as if he knew exactly what room that was.

Daylen tried not to make any sudden movements as she edged nearer. "All right, you, it's time for you to leave."

While she spoke, the wolf cocked his head to the side and wagged his tail. At least he didn't seem to be vicious. Actually, she had the feeling he was used to being around humans. It made her wonder if he was someone's pet and had somehow gotten loose. It would explain why he'd been so quick to run into the house after she opened the front door.

As she stepped even closer, the wolf remained where he was, still watching her every move. Just before she reached him, he closed the distance between them. He gently took her wrist in his mouth and pulled her toward the king-sized bed. Daylen knew better than to try to yank her arm free. The sharp points of the wolf's teeth were against her skin, but he wasn't biting hard enough to break it. If she tried to free herself, there was a good chance they could do some damage.

Once he had her at the end of the bed with her back toward it, the wolf released her. Daylen straightened to her full height and looked down at him. "And what exactly do you think you're doing? I'm not a new toy to play with, you know. You obviously have to belong to someone. You're tame. I really should call animal control right now, but I have no idea how long it'll take them to get here, and I really do need to sleep."

As if he'd understood what she'd said, the wolf jumped up and put his paws on her chest. Not expecting it, Daylen lost her balance and fell back onto the bed. The wolf hopped onto the mattress beside her and lay down next to her with his head on her upper chest.

Daylen tried to push him off, but that only caused him to put a paw on her stomach to keep her in place. She lifted her head to look at him. "Look, buddy, this isn't exactly what I had in mind when I said I needed to sleep." He licked her chin. She chuckled. "Kisses aren't going to butter me up, either. Since you seem friendly, I'm going to lock you in the bathroom, and once I wake up, I'll call for animal control to get you. Maybe they'll be able to find out who owns you."

She grabbed the wolf by the scruff of his neck and lifted him off her. She kept her hold on him as she sat up and then urged him to jump down. The wolf didn't try to resist when she pushed him inside the bathroom and shut the door behind him. Reassured he wouldn't be able to get out, Daylen locked the front door and then headed back to her bedroom. Being trapped in the bathroom for a few hours shouldn't bother the wolf too much. At least he would be safer there than wandering loose outside.

Covering a yawn with her hand, Daylen crawled into bed. She'd sleep, then she would take care of her new furry friend.

* * * *

Jager waited a half hour before he shifted to his human form, willing his clothes back on at the same time. He let himself out of the bathroom. That had gone better than he'd expected.

Silently, he stepped into Daylen's bedroom. He remained in the open doorway and gazed at her sleeping form beneath the covers. Her long, reddish-brown hair was spread over her pillow. When she changed out of her uniform, she had taken her hair out of its bun she'd worn. It hung just past her shoulders and had a slight curl.

Jager tiptoed closer to the bed, then looked down at his sleeping mate. The urge to touch her, to feel her under him, became a living, breathing thing inside him. Just being around her made him so hard he ached. All he wanted to do was join her on the bed and sink his cock deep inside her body. He took a deep breath and drew her scent inside his lungs. It was a heady mix of woman and Daylen. Forever etched in his brain, he would have no trouble picking it out in a crowd.

He stiffened when Daylen shifted in her sleep and then opened her eyes. As she opened her mouth, Jager jumped on top of her, pinning her beneath him, and put his hand over her mouth. Her brown eyes glared at him. He needed to keep her calm. From the number of minivans he'd seen parked in the driveways around her house, this had to be a neighborhood with a lot of young kids. Which meant her neighbors probably looked out for one another. That being the case, if she kicked up enough fuss to be heard outside, one of those neighbors would undoubtedly come running.

He locked gazes with her. "I'm not here to hurt you." From the expression in her eyes, Jager saw she didn't believe him. "I just want to talk. I'm going to take my hand off your mouth. Please don't scream. And if I'd wanted to hurt you, I would have done it before you awakened." When she just continued to glare at him, he slowly removed his hand from her mouth.

"You have some balls, breaking into my house. I may be off-duty, but I can still arrest you."

He grinned. "When you talk to me all cop-like, it turns me on." He shifted so the hard length of his cock pressed against her thigh.

Daylen stiffened. "So, you aren't going to hurt me, but you're going to rape me instead?"

Jager scowled. "No. I don't need to force my attentions on a woman. When we make love, you'll come to me willingly. I can't help the way my body responds to being near you."

"I don't think that will be happening any time soon," she said as she struggled to get free.

He pressed more of his weight on top of her to keep her in place. "Stop squirming."

The more she moved, the more turned on he became. With his duster open and only a thin sheet separating them, her breasts under the large T-shirt she wore were flattened against his chest. He wanted to reach between them and mold them in his hands, to pluck her taut nipples.

At her sharp intake of breath, and by the way Daylen's gaze had become riveted to his eyes, Jager realized they must be glowing. He closed them for a few seconds while he got himself back under control. Whenever he became aroused, or angry, his eyes would glow.

He opened his eyes, and said, "I think it would be better if we continued this conversation without you under me. It's playing havoc with my self-control."

"Look, whatever your name is —"

"Jager." When Daylen gave him a questioning look, he said, "My name is Jager."

"Well, Jager, you can't really expect me to calmly lie here and have a conversation with you. You're a criminal who has broken into my house."

"I'm not a criminal."

"Yeah, right," she scoffed. "In my books, resisting arrest, and now being here, would make you a criminal."

Jager sighed, feeling a bit exasperated. "Can you give the cop thing a rest? I'm trying to do this right. As for the sword fight in the alley, it's no concern of yours."

She shifted, which had Jager biting back a growl of need that threatened to push past his lips. "I hate to tell you, but it *is* my concern. You broke the law."

"Stop thinking like a cop." He was getting nowhere with Daylen.

"It's kind of hard, when that's what I am."

Feeling as if he'd run up against a brick wall, Jager did what he'd been dying to do since he'd walked into her house in wolf form. He bent his head and took her mouth in a heated kiss. At first, Daylen resisted him, but after he swept his tongue along the seam and nibbled her lips, they softened beneath his and she kissed him back.

Encouraged by her response, Jager kissed her deeper. He pushed his tongue inside and stroked it against hers. The taste of her made him groan. This was what he craved—holding Daylen in his arms with her scent surrounding him and the flavor of her on his tongue.

As he sucked her tongue into his mouth, Jager shifted and put a leg between hers and pushed up so it connected with her pussy. Daylen sighed softly and rubbed herself against his thigh. He should stop what he was doing. It would only make the mating urge ride him even harder, but he wanted this too much.

When Daylen tried to pull her arms free from where he'd trapped them at her sides, he freed her. She yanked the hair elastic out of his hair and tossed it aside. His long locks spilled forward, forming a curtain around their heads. Jager moaned against her mouth at the feel of her hands tunneling through his hair, holding him in place as she angled her lips across his.

His cock throbbed in time with his racing heart. God, he wanted her, wanted to strip their clothes off and take her until neither one of them could move, but he couldn't. He had to wait. If he were to make love to her now, their souls would join, which would complete their mating. Once that happened, there would be no going back. He wanted Daylen to know exactly what she would be getting herself into before he made her his.

No longer able to stand the sheet that was between them, Jager lifted himself from Daylen only far enough to grab it and yank it aside. He settled back down with his hips between her legs. His fully erect cock came up against her pajama-covered pussy. He growled softly as she rubbed against it.

He cupped her breast through her T-shirt and brushed her taut nipple with the pad of his thumb. Daylen moaned in the back of her throat and pushed herself closer. Jager closed his eyes to hide them from her, knowing they had to be glowing again.

Jager moved from her mouth, then licked and sucked a path down the side of her neck. "I have to touch you," he said against her skin.

He bunched the bottom of her shirt in his fingers before he shoved his hand under it. He molded her bare breast before he plucked her nipple. Daylen's fingers tightened in his hair as she pushed his head lower. Jager knew exactly what she wanted. He lifted her shirt to her chin and bent his head to her breast. He laved the tight peak with the flat of his tongue and then sucked it inside his mouth. She bucked her hips as she let out a breathy moan.

The smell of her arousal, and the sounds she made, pushed at the limits of his control, but Jager continued to suck at her breast. "I need to see how wet you are," he said once he released her nipple. "You smell so damn good. I bet you'll taste just as good as well, but that would be too risky." He trailed his hand down her side to the top of her pajama bottoms. He licked the underside of her breast, and asked, "Do you want me to touch you, Daylen?" He chanced a look at her and found she had her eyes closed. The sight of her face flushed with desire made his cock jerk.

"God, yes." Daylen panted.

Jager moved off Daylen so he lay beside her on his side. He rested his weight on a bent arm and watched her face as he shoved his hand down the front of her pajamas. She spread her legs wider when he dragged a finger along the seam of her pussy. He bit back a growl of need. She was more than wet for him.

Jager used a finger to spread her folds, then circled her clit with the tip before he pushed it inside her core. The feel of her warm wetness closing around it caused his cock to strain against the zipper of his jeans. He was so hard he was surprised he hadn't burst it.

Daylen's inner muscles gripped his finger while he slid it in and out of her pussy. He pushed another inside her. She moaned and lifted her hips, matching his strokes. Jager thrust faster and used the heel of his palm to rub her clit. Her wetness flowed around his digits, making him wish it was his cock moving deep inside her.

Daylen moaned. "Ahh...I'm going to..."

Jager continued to push her closer to climax. "Come for me, Daylen. Let me watch you fly."

Her breaths came in pants. She clutched the sheet beneath her as the first flutter of her orgasm caused her inner muscles to grip his fingers. Once she fell over the edge, Daylen let out a loud, long moan. Her pussy clenched around him.

Aching to claim her, fighting to maintain his control, Jager pulled his fingers out of Daylen and dropped his head to her chest. Once he was sure his eyes no longer glowed, he lifted his head. She was still breathing heavily with hers closed. She opened them after he brushed a gentle kiss across her lips.

"I'll be back this evening," he said as he got off the bed and stood. "If I stay here any longer, I'm going to do something I know you're not ready for."

Jager walked out of the bedroom. He unlocked the front door and then stepped outside. With the scent of Daylen's arousal on his skin, and the image of how she'd looked when she'd come, leaving her was the last thing he wanted to do. He gritted his teeth against the unfulfilled desire that made his cock throb painfully and took off at a run down the street. At least he now knew where Daylen lived, and that she wanted him as much as he wanted her.

CHAPTER FIVE

He was gone. Daylen heard her front door close behind him. He'd given her one hell of an orgasm and then just got up and left. Realizing her shirt was still pushed to her chin, she roughly yanked it down to cover her breasts.

What the hell was the matter with her? She'd never been the type of woman to get swept away by passion to the extent she lost the use of her higher brain functions. And she sure as shit had no business letting a man like Jager touch her so intimately. He was a bad guy. Good cops did not go around letting the bad guys make them come, no matter how good it'd been.

Disgusted with herself, Daylen sat up. Her body still thrummed with little aftershocks of pleasure. It also craved more of Jager's touch. A shiver went through her when her thoughts strayed to how good it'd felt to have his large body pressing down on hers, and how big his cock had felt against her pussy.

Daylen gave herself a hard shake. She had to snap out of it. Her reaction to Jager was totally uncalled for. When he came back that evening—and she had a good feeling that he would—she would steel herself against him. If he touched her again, she knew without a doubt she would let all her guards down as she'd done this time. One touch and the man turned her into a quivering pile of jelly. She could blame it on sleep deprivation, but she would only be fooling herself. Both times when he'd kissed her, there and in the alley, she'd hadn't been able to concentrate on anything but getting more of him.

She pushed thoughts of how good a kisser Jager was out of her mind, then remembered the wolf. She quickly stood before she went to the bathroom. She hadn't heard a sound out of him since she'd awakened to find Jager standing over her. Daylen soon found out the reason he'd been so quiet. The bathroom door stood wide open with no sign of the wolf anywhere.

"Terrific." At this rate, she wasn't going to get any sleep at all.

Daylen did a quick search of the rest of the house, but the wolf wasn't anywhere to be seen. The only thing she could think of was that somehow he'd managed to get out of the bathroom when Jager had broken into the house. He must have left the front door standing open. She figured he had to have picked her lock, since there were no signs of forced entry, and none of the windows were open. The wolf must have just walked out while she'd been busy with Jager.

She went to the front door one last time and opened it. No wolf sat on her front porch or ran around in her yard. He was more than likely long gone. Daylen just hoped he stayed out of trouble.

Daylen closed and locked the front door, then went back to bed. So far, this had been one hell of a strange morning. She crawled under the covers as sleep tugged at her. How much she was going to get remained to be seen, especially since what had taken place earlier in her bed played through her mind when she closed her eyes. She rolled to her side and punched the pillow, determined to forget about Jager and how he'd made her body go up in flames.

* * * *

The feel of someone shaking him had Jager reaching under the sheets for the sword that lay next to him. Not completely awake, he still managed to get it out from under the covers in case he needed to use it.

"Jesus, Jager. How many times do I have to tell you to knock it off with the sword already?" asked a very exasperated-sounding female voice. "And please don't tell me you sleep with that thing in your bed every night."

Shaking off the last vestiges of sleep, he looked up to find Roxie standing beside his bed with her hands on her hips. She stared down at him with an expression that matched the tone of her voice. Jager searched the room with his gaze and saw she'd come up to his bedroom alone.

"Yes, I sleep with my sword. What time is it?" he asked in a sleep-roughened voice. "And what the hell are you doing in my bedroom, let alone here at the mansion?"

Roxie shook her head. "Blunt as usual, I see. It's twelve thirty. As for what I'm doing here, well, when you didn't show up for your scheduled *babysitting* of me, and Leif arrived to take your place, I, of course, had to rush over here to find out why you were still sleeping."

Jager groaned and rubbed his forehead with his free hand. "Damn it. Leif told you."

"Of course he told me," Roxie said with a laugh. "The man is scared shitless he'll be next to find his mate." She reached up and brushed a length of her long, golden-brown hair over her shoulder. Her hazel eyes flashed with amusement. "Get out of bed. We're going to have a little talk."

He laid his sword back on the mattress. "Can't it wait? I think I got all of two hours of sleep."

Roxie crossed her arms over her chest. "No, it can't wait. Now get up."

When it didn't look as if Roxie had any intention of leaving, Jager figured she'd asked for it. After flipping back the sheets, he got out of bed to stand in front of her.

She let out a little squawk and turned her back to him. "You're naked! And...and..."

Jager chuckled. "Well, you did tell me to get out of bed. And I do sleep naked. As for being aroused, with the mating urge riding me, I don't have much control over that now, as you very well know."

"Just put something on."

Jager picked up the jeans he'd worn earlier but thrown on the floor, then slipped them on. "I'm decent. You can turn around now." Roxie turned and then went to sit on his bed. She reached for his sword, but he picked it up before she could grab it. He shook his head. "No, you don't. This isn't your house. It's mine.

I'm not going to let you take it."

Roxie wasn't always thrilled with the idea that he carried his sword wherever he went. She especially didn't like it when he came running with it drawn when he heard something out of the ordinary while he protected her. One simple mistake and she was forever trying to take his sword from him. If he'd known she and Beowulf were only having sex, Jager wouldn't have busted in on them with his sword drawn. He'd apologized more than once, but so far, she had yet to forget about that incident.

"Fine. Keep the damn thing," she said. "We're still going to have our talk."

"About what?"

"About you having found your mate."

"Why exactly does that warrant you coming into my bedroom and waking me up to talk to me?"

"Since your brother almost blew it with Ansley, I thought I would lay down some ground rules for you."

He gaped at Roxie. "Some ground rules?" he asked warily. "There are no *ground rules* when it comes to a male werewolf claiming his mate."

"With your mate being a mortal, there are now." When Jager opened his mouth to protest, Roxie stopped him. "I'm the one who holds the power to turn a mortal mate into a werewolf, remember? If you want her to have the lifespan of a werewolf instead of a mortal's, you play by my rules. I know what it's like to be blindsided with this whole werewolf mating business without having a clue as to what's going on. Lately, it seems to be a trend. Now sit your butt down."

"Ah, fuck me," Jager said as he glared at Roxie.

She smiled. "No thanks. I'll leave that job to your mate."

He ran his hand through his long hair and pushed it behind his ears. He'd kept it down ever since Daylen had pulled out his hair elastic. It still had to be on her bedroom floor somewhere. Jager could still feel her hands buried in his hair. His cock jerked before he pushed thoughts of Daylen away. They would just work him up even more than he already was.

"Roxie, is this necessary? I really don't need you to add any more stress on top of what I'm already feeling," he said.

She patted the spot next to her. "Stop your griping and sit

down. You're giving me a sore neck having to look up at you like this."

Reluctantly, Jager sat next to Roxie, knowing full well if he didn't let her say what she wanted to, he would never get her out of his bedroom. "Okay, I'm sitting. Hurry it up already."

Roxie shook her head. "I hope you aren't this rude when you're with your mate."

"I haven't had a chance to be rude. Most of our conversations have consisted of her ordering me to put down my sword so she can arrest me, or her telling me I'm a criminal who has broken the law."

"I heard your mate was a cop." Roxie laughed. "I also heard she got the take on you and almost managed to cuff you."

"Yeah, yeah. I'm glad everyone thinks it's so funny. Can we please get on with this?"

"All right. No more laughing at your expense. I promise." Roxie's face grew sober. "Now, the rules. First, you're not to take any advice from Beowulf on how to claim a mortal mate. He's the one who gave Roan the oh-so-excellent advice of not giving Ansley the chance to refuse him as her mate. And that worked out so well too. She freaked when she found out Roan was a werewolf. Just as I freaked on Beowulf when I found out about him."

Jager clearly remembered the day Roan had told Ansley. He'd been at Roxie and Beowulf's place when Roan had brought Ansley there to tell her. He'd thought Roxie would be able to help Ansley better accept what he was. Ansley hadn't exactly reacted well.

"All right. I won't go to Beowulf for advice, not that I intended to, anyway."

"Good. Rule number two. You will not claim your mate until you have told her what you are and what being mated to a werewolf entails. Which means no getting carried away in the moment."

"So far, I've managed to stay in control," he said.

"Rule number three. No using head games or coercion to get your mate to allow me to use the spell to turn her into a werewolf. It'll be her choice when, and if, she wants to take that final step."

"Not a problem." Roxie meant well, but her rules grated on his nerves. All this talk about claiming mates was only causing his mating urge to dig its claws deeper into him.

Roxie nodded. "Rule number—"

He cut her off. "I think that's more than enough rules. Give me some credit for not being a complete idiot. I know claiming a mortal as my mate is not the same as claiming a female werewolf. I saw how Ansley reacted. I was there, remember?"

Roxie's eyes narrowed as her gaze landed on the sword he still held. "I remember. I also remember you came in running with that weapon in your hand, ready to do battle when you heard raised voices."

"Don't even think about it," Jager said as he moved his sword well out of Roxie's reach.

She sighed, then stood. "Just promise me you won't sleep with that thing in your bed once you're mated. I'm sure your mate doesn't want to find you cuddling your sword instead of her some night."

"I don't cuddle my sword. I sleep with it, so it's always on hand in case I need it."

Roxie smiled. "Sure. I believe you."

After Roxie left the room, closing the door behind her, Jager grabbed two fistfuls of his hair and gave it a good yank. He'd have to get things settled with Daylen very soon. If he didn't, he could easily see Roxie driving him completely insane.

* * * *

Early that evening Jager went to talk to Saskia before he left to see Daylen. He found her in the basement with her mate, Eli. She was giving him another sword lesson. Since Eli had been a mortal up until recently, the same as Ansley had been, he'd never had an occasion to learn how to handle a sword. Given that Saskia was the leader of Roxie's Protectors, Eli had decided he should learn.

Saskia crossed swords with Eli. She was taking it easy on him, though Jager could see Eli's potential to become quite skilled. At least he already had the muscle mass that was required to swing the weapon for any length of time. As a personal trainer at his family's gym, Eli had been lifting weights for years.

When Saskia noticed Jager, she signaled Eli to lower his sword.

She pushed her sweat-dampened almost-white-blonde hair out of her eyes and walked to where Jager stood. "Are you going to see your mate?"

"Yeah. If I don't work on claiming her as mine soon, Roxie will continue to hound the shit out of me to make sure I don't screw it up."

Saskia chuckled. "Roxie told me about the rules she said you had to follow."

Eli went to stand beside Saskia and put his arm around her shoulders. His black hair was just as sweaty-looking as his mate's. "It makes me glad I was just a regular mortal before Saskia and I became mates. I would have hated to go through the mating urge and then have a bunch of rules to follow on top of it."

"Yeah, you lucked out with that one," Jager said. He turned to Saskia. "Is there any way we can put a muzzle on Roxie? I seriously don't think I can handle any more of her *talks*."

Saskia grinned and shook her head. "Sorry, I can't help you out with that one. She rules over all the packs, which includes us. Roxie can pretty much do what she wants."

"Well, you're no help," he grumbled.

"Go to your mate, Jager, and forget about Roxie. Also, don't worry about having to take your turn protecting her until you've claimed your mate. Roan was pretty much useless before he claimed Ansley. And you look to be just as stressed as he was."

Oh, he was stressed all right. The need to make Daylen his was a living, breathing thing inside him that would not go away until he'd made love to her. Plus, the lack of sleep wasn't helping any. After Roxie had left him, he'd tried to fall asleep, but he couldn't stop thinking about Daylen.

"You can say I'm stressed," he said. "I guess I'll leave you two to get back to your sword practice. I should be home later tonight."

As he walked away, Eli said, "Try not to get arrested."

Jager turned back around and flipped him off. He doubted he would ever be able to live it down that Daylen had almost gotten the better of him.

* * * *

Parked across the street from the entrance to the long driveway of the Protectors' mansion, a lone wolf sat in his car, watching who came and went. When a black Camaro pulled out onto the street, he quickly started his vehicle and then followed it. He smiled. The werewolf who drove the Camaro was the one his leader wanted information about.

Keeping a discreet distance, he followed the Camaro out of Marin County and into San Francisco. Once the werewolf pulled his car into the driveway of a bungalow in a residential area of the city, the lone wolf slowly drove by, making note of the house number and street name.

Sure Miles would be more than pleased to learn the address of Jager's mate, the lone wolf turned his car in the direction that would take him to their new headquarters. They now had something that would put one of the Protectors at a distinct disadvantage. And maybe this information would make up for the fact that Jager had cornered him in that alley.

CHAPTER SIX

The sound of someone knocking on her front door made Daylen jump where she sat on the couch, watching television. Ever since that morning, she'd been reacting to the slightest noise, thinking Jager might have returned as he'd said he would. She hadn't been able to stop replaying how it had felt to have him kiss her. Her body craved more of his touch, much to her disgust. And when she'd found the hair elastic she'd pulled out of his hair on her bedroom floor, she hadn't been able to throw it into the garbage. It now sat on her dresser. Just another sign of her weakening toward him.

Daylen stood and then walked to the front door. She figured it couldn't be Jager. He would more than likely break in again instead of knocking. She opened it and came face-to-face with the last person she'd thought she would see on her porch. So surprised to see it was Jager, Daylen only stared.

After a few seconds, he smiled, and said, "Does the sight of me leave you speechless? I must have left you with a better impression than I thought."

It was partly surprise—and something else Daylen didn't want to admit to—that made her remain in the doorway, unable to get her brain to function properly. As soon as her gaze landed on Jager, something inside her had stood up and shouted with joy. He hadn't even touched her and her nipples had already tightened beneath her long-sleeved T-shirt.

Almost against her will, her gaze lowered to his firm lips. Hers tingled as she remembered how it'd felt to have them moving across hers. Daylen had to snap out of it. She'd promised herself she wouldn't let him do that to her again, but all she could do was stand there like a twit and stare.

Jager chuckled at her continued silence. "I'm going to take your reaction as a good sign you no longer want to haul me away to jail." He brushed past her and walked into the house.

Daylen sucked in a breath as Jager's body came into contact with hers when he passed her. A shiver of arousal shot through her. A small ache pounded between her legs. She wanted to reach out, grab him by his long ponytail, and take his mouth with hers until neither one of them could think straight.

Then his words sank in. *Why* the hell wasn't she trying to haul him away to jail? Moving quickly, Daylen shut the front door and then came up behind Jager as he headed toward the living room. She ignored the thrum of arousal that surged through her and kicked out so her foot connected with the back of his knee. When he stumbled, she quickly kicked his other out from under him. As he fell forward, she jumped onto his back and used her weight to push him completely over. She straddled him and yanked his arms behind him. She held on to his wrists and pushed his hands to the center of his back.

Jager chuckled. "Damn, you got me again. I'm going to blame this on the fact that whenever I'm near you, I'm not my usual, observant self." He lifted his head and turned it to give her a sideways look. "Now that you've got me, let's see if you can keep me down."

With a show of strength, Jager surged beneath her and threw her off his back. Thrown onto her side, Daylen tried to get enough space between them so she could try another karate move on him, but he proved to be faster. His large hand wrapped around her ankle and pulled her toward him. He shoved her flat onto her back and then threw himself on top of her.

Her hands pinned between their chests, Daylen futilely tried to push him away. "Get off me," she said through gritted teeth.

Having him stretched out along her body with her legs trapped between his heavily muscled thighs made her blood heat, which caused the throb in her pussy to pick up tempo.

Not moving, Jager said, "We're going to have to work on this, Daylen. I wouldn't mind you jumping me every time you saw me if it led to you and I in bed, but I know that isn't what you had in mind when you kicked my legs out from under me just now."

Daylen arched her back to try to throw Jager off. She had to bite her tongue to stop the moan that threatened to break free when his hard cock ended up pressed against her lower abdomen.

"The only thing I have to work on is keeping you down long enough to cuff you," she said.

Jager shook his head. "Are we ever going to get past this point? I'd like to get over it so we can move on to more pleasurable things, like getting to know each other better in the most intimate of ways."

"I don't think so." That was the furthest thing from the truth. Daylen was weakening, wanting Jager to touch more of her as each second ticked by.

He gave her a knowing smile. "Now I know that's a lie." His gaze dropped to her chest, which caused her already taut nipples to tighten even more. "Your nipples are just begging for me to suck on them, and the scent of your arousal is like a drug in the air." Jager lowered his head until his lips hovered above hers. "I'm so hard for you right now I feel as if I'm about ready to come in my pants. Since I first saw you, I've done nothing but dream about having you under me as I sink my cock between your legs over and over again."

Daylen took a shuddering breath. What Jager had said, along with the intense look of longing on his face, had her pussy readying itself for him. Wetness leaked between her legs into her panties. She'd never been so turned on in her life. The thought of ripping off their clothes so she could rub against him made her pussy grow even wetter.

Jager closed his eyes and drew in a deep breath. He opened them again, and Daylen swore they glowed for a split second. "I need to touch you, Daylen. That delicious scent of yours just got stronger. It's got me in its claws, and I feel as if I'm going to die if I don't get a taste of you. Stop fighting this thing between us. Stop thinking like a cop. I know you want me."

With Jager's lips so close to hers, and the length of his hard body branding her everywhere they touched, Daylen's will to resist him shattered. She lifted her head to close the distance between their lips and covered his with hers. A loud groan that verged on a growl rose out of him as he took her mouth in a fiery kiss.

Able to turn her hands enough to put them against Jager's muscular chest, Daylen fisted the front of his black T-shirt. Having jumped in feetfirst, she stopped holding herself back. She no longer let herself question how ethical it was to want this man. For the first time since becoming a cop, she let herself be just a woman.

Their kiss became more passionate as Jager sucked her tongue between his lips. Daylen twined hers with his before she swept the inside of his mouth. He shifted so he no longer pinned her to the floor. He rested his upper body on his bent arms and rocked his erection against her stomach.

Free to move her arms, Daylen skimmed her hands up his chest to his broad shoulders. When she encountered the material of the duster he wore, she grabbed fistfuls of it and yanked. "Off. Take this off," she said against Jager's lips.

He pulled away from her mouth and moved to sit up, straddling her hips. "I'll gladly take off whatever you want me to." He kept their gazes locked, shrugged out the duster, and threw it to the side. He gave her a wicked smile. "I'll even take this off for you."

Daylen lowered her gaze. Jager undid the buckle of the leather belt around his waist that had his sheathed sword attached to it. He put that on the floor beside them. At this point, she pretty much didn't care that he'd been carrying a concealed weapon once again. She was more interested in the noticeably large bulge in the front of his snug-fitting jeans.

She licked her suddenly dry lips and pulled the bottom of Jager's T-shirt out of his waistband and then slowly pushed it up his body. Little by little, well-defined washboard abs appeared. Daylen swallowed. Unable to resist, she ran a hand over his stomach. His loud, indrawn breath caused her to still as her gaze shot back up to his face. He had his eyes closed while his large chest rapidly rose and fell.

"Don't stop," Jager said in a strained voice. "I love the feel of you touching me."

More than willing to comply, Daylen stroked along his skin. Jager's stomach muscles quivered beneath her fingers. She pushed his shirt as high as she could reach before he took hold of the bottom of it and roughly pulled it over his head and off. It was her turn to suck in a breath. His upper body was a sight to behold — all smooth skin. His chest was thickly padded with muscle, as were his shoulders and arms. She wanted to explore every inch of him with her hands and tongue.

Since she couldn't reach his upper body, Daylen settled for putting her hands on his hard, jean-clad thighs. As she kneaded them, and his erection jerked, it proved to be a temptation she couldn't resist. She ran her palms up Jager's thighs and settled them on his narrow hips. He made another half-growl and half-groan sound as she trailed one hand from his hipbone across the front of his jeans to his hard cock. She lightly stroked across it. His hips jerked in response.

"Touch me there, Daylen," Jager said huskily. "Feel how hard you make me?"

Her pussy clenched at his words. Panting with need, she reached for the button and zipper of his jeans. Once she parted the material, his engorged cock sprang free. The sight of him, thick and long, caused more wetness to leak out of her core. Daylen wanted to feel it buried deep inside her, moving in and out until she screamed her pleasure.

With her fingers, she traced the length of Jager's shaft, then circled the head. He moaned as a bead of pre-cum appeared on the very tip of his cock. Daylen circled his thickness with her hand, then pumped it up and down. He rocked his hips in time with her strokes, pushing himself tighter into her grip.

"Christ, that feels good," Jager said with a moan. "I'm about ready to explode, but not yet."

Jager pulled her hand off him and moved to lie at her side. He placed kisses along her jaw as he molded her breast in his large hand. While he dragged his lips to the side of her neck, he shoved a hand under her shirt. He pushed up the front of the sports bra she wore and took her nipple between his thumb and index finger, rolling it between them.

Daylen arched her back as Jager gathered the front of her shirt in his hand and pulled it, along with her bra, off. He flung them away and bent his head to take a taut nipple between his teeth. He gently bit down before he sucked it inside his mouth. She reached up and pulled his hair loose, then she buried her hands in the silky strands and moaned, holding him to her breast.

He soon shifted his attention to her other breast. She moaned again at the feel of him drawing on her nipple. Her pussy ached to be filled. Daylen reached for Jager's cock, but he pushed her hand away before she could touch him.

He lifted his head. "Not yet. You touch me now and I'll lose control."

Daylen groaned. "Losing control is good."

"Yes, but not this time."

Jager laved her nipple with the flat of his tongue, then blew across it.

Goosebumps rose along Daylen's skin, and she shivered. He kissed the underside of her breast as he hooked the top of her yoga pants with his fingers and pulled them past her hips. Once he had them down her legs, she kicked them free.

He shoved his hand down the front of her panties and palmed her pussy. A finger delved between her folds and pushed inside her core. "You're so wet," he said as he pumped in and out of her sex. "I have to taste."

Jager quickly pulled her panties off before he shifted to lie between her spread thighs. He kissed his way down her stomach and cupped her bottom. He lifted her to him and dragged his tongue along her pussy. Daylen cried out as waves of pleasure shot through her. They only intensified when he spread her open even more and lapped at her sex. He licked and sucked, circling her clit before he sucked on it as well.

Lost in wave after wave of pleasure, Daylen's orgasm built. She was so close to falling over the edge. With Jager, her body sang. He knew just where to touch her to give her the most pleasure.

Unable to hold still any longer, Daylen rocked her hips as Jager licked her sex. She moaned when one finger, and then a second, pushed inside her core. He sucked on her clit while he moved the digits inside her. With a strangled cry, she came. He continued to work her until the last wave of her orgasm subsided.

Instead of yanking down his jeans so he could sheath himself inside her, he rose between her legs and up her body. Jager moved to his side, then pulled Daylen onto hers next to him and brought her hand down to his engorged cock.

He held her to his chest, and said, "Make me come this way."

Daylen dragged her tongue across one of his flat nipples. "Come inside me instead."

Jager wrapped her fingers around his hard length. "I can't. Not this time."

Thinking maybe he couldn't because he didn't have a condom, Daylen relented. She squeezed his cock before she slid her hand up and down his shaft. As she stroked him, his cock hardened even more.

"That's it," Jager panted as he rocked his hips in time with her strokes. "I'm going to come. Just a little bit more."

Daylen pumped her hand faster, tightening it around his thickness. Jager held her closer and buried his face in the crook of her neck. The sound of his harsh breathing filled her ears as his erection pulsed in her fist. With a loud moan, he thrust into her grip one final time as hot jets of semen shot into her hand and onto her stomach.

Breathing hard, aroused again from bringing Jager to completion, Daylen allowed him to tuck her head under his chin and hold her close. Even though he'd come, his cock was still hard, but he made no move to do anything more than hold her.

With reason slowly returning, she lifted her head to look Jager in the face. The sight of his eyes glowing mutedly while he stared back at her made her stiffen. "What's with your eyes?"

Jager tried to push her head back under his chin, but she stopped him. He sighed. "Forget about my eyes right now. I just want to hold you for a little while longer before we get to the complicated stuff."

Daylen realized she lay naked in the middle of the hallway near the entrance to her living room. The TV played in the background. She gave Jager a hard shove on the chest until he released her, then scrambled to her feet. Needing time to let what had just happened between her and Jager sink in, she gathered her scattered clothes, went to the bathroom, and shut the door behind her.

CHAPTER SEVEN

Daylen disappeared down the hall, and Jager heard the bathroom door shut a few seconds later. He tucked his loose hair behind his ears before he stood. His jeans gaped open with his still-hard cock hanging out the front. The hand job she had given him had only whetted his appetite for her. Even if he had come deep inside her pussy, he still would have kept his erection. That was one advantage the males of his kind had over mortal ones — they could keep an erection for hours, even after coming several times.

After he stuffed his dick back inside his jeans and then zipped them up, Jager picked up his shirt from the floor before he put it on. He gathered up his duster and sword, but kept them in his hand. He found his hair elastic and put it into his pocket. Not sure how long Daylen would be in the bathroom he went into the living room and then sat on the couch to wait.

A few minutes passed before Daylen walked into the room, once again dressed. She stood in front of him with her arms crossed over her chest. Her cheeks still held a slight flush, and the scent of their lovemaking lingered on her skin. Jager forced himself not to reach for her, to let her make the first move.

Her gaze skidded over his sheathed sword beside him before she brought it back to his face. "I've decided I won't haul you off to jail. It seems every time you touch me, I lose my ability to think like a normal, rational person, but that doesn't mean I don't want some explanations."

Jager patted the empty spot next to him. "Sit down, Daylen."

She shook her head. "I don't think so. I need to keep my head, which is so out of character for me. I don't know if I like this weakness you bring out of me either."

"It's not a weakness. It's part of the process," he said in a matter-of-fact tone.

Daylen's brows drew together. "Part of what process?"

"It causes us both to lose our heads when we're near each other."

"What's this *it* you keep referring to?"

"The mating urge. Now sit down so I can give you the explanations you want."

She snorted. "The mating urge, huh? I would say that would be an apt description of what just took place on my hallway floor. It had a whole lot to do with pure, simple lust."

Jager sighed when Daylen made no move to sit next to him. "That's just the start of it. Are you going to sit down or not?"

Daylen gave him a hard look. "How can I trust you not to touch me again?"

He picked up his sword. "I swear on my sword, which is very near and dear to me, that I won't touch you while we talk. Unless you want me to, that is."

It took a few seconds, but in the end, Daylen gave a nod and took a seat beside him. She made sure there was good deal of space between them.

"See, that wasn't so hard," he said.

"All right, talk. You can start off by telling me what you were doing sword fighting with that other guy in the alley. And why the hell do you carry a sword around in the first place?"

If Jager wanted Daylen to understand about those things, he would have to tell her about his being a werewolf first. Now that he had her willing to sit and listen to him, he was a little reluctant to tell her the truth. He didn't think he would have to worry about her running from him in fright. She was too tough for that, but there was a good chance she wouldn't want to accept what he truly was.

He turned to face Daylen. "I promised Roxie I would follow

her rules, but right about now I want to say bugger them. There's something to be said about not giving you a choice."

Daylen shook her head. "You're losing me. Who is Roxie, and what choice am I supposed to make?"

"Roxie is a female who my sister, brothers, and I protect."

A funny look passed across Daylen's face. "A female? That sounds so —"

Flustered, Jager waved her question away. "Forget that. You don't need to know about her right now. Look, I don't know how to do this any other way but lay it all out on the table. I'm not known for being subtle."

"Then spit it out already."

Cursing Roxie and her damn rules, Jager said, "I'm a werewolf, and you're my mate. I knew the first time back in that alley when I smelled your scent. The mating urge has been riding me ever since. I want you as mine."

Daylen blinked a few times, then burst out laughing. "As a cop, I've seen a lot of weird shit, but seeing a real werewolf isn't one of them. Though I met a whacked-out druggie once who liked to howl at the full moon and pretend he was about to change into a creature who hungered to kill."

Jager scowled. "I'm not some whacked-out druggie. I'm truly a werewolf, and you are my mate. That's why you can't resist my touch."

Daylen slowly brought herself back under control, though a smile hovered on her lips. "Come on, Jager, a werewolf? You can do better than that."

"I'm not making it up."

Daylen snickered. "Maybe I should look out the window and see if there's a full moon tonight. I always say it brings out the crazies."

A little annoyed that Daylen would laugh when he'd told her the truth, Jager stood. It was obvious she would never believe him unless he gave her proof. Then that was what she would get.

Not giving Daylen any kind of warning, he reached for the magic inside him to make the shift from his human form to his wolf one. All humor drained from her face as he jumped up onto the couch and put his nose an inch away from hers.

"Holy shit!" She quickly moved away from him. "You're a

wolf," Daylen said in a quiet voice. "And you're the wolf I locked in the bathroom this morning."

Jager nodded. At least Daylen had recognized him in his wolf form. The way she stared at him, with fear and shock flitting across her face, he wasn't sure if this had been a smart move on his part.

Daylen pushed herself back into the corner of the couch. When he followed, she practically leaned backward over the arm to get away from him. "You can understand what I'm saying?"

Once again, Jager moved his head up and down. He let out a whine and tried to put his head under Daylen's hand so she would pet him. All that got him was a palm in the face as she roughly pushed him away.

She jumped off the couch. "No, no, no. I don't think I can handle this."

Jager realized he was doing more damage than good the longer he stayed in wolf form. He shifted to his human one. He stood and went to stand in front of Daylen. She held out her hands to keep him away.

"You don't have to be afraid. I would never hurt you. You're my mate," he said.

"Back up there. I'm not your mate. And, since you're laying it out all on the table, I'm going to be truthful here. I seriously can't see myself being mated to a freakin' werewolf." Daylen's voice rose a couple of octaves when she said those last two words.

"It isn't as if we'll have much choice in the matter. We were meant to be together. I know you're my mate, and I'll never be able to just walk away from you."

"Well, you're going to have to because I'm not tying myself, mated or whatever you want to call it, to you. Yes, I lust after you, but it doesn't go beyond that. And now that I know what you are, the lust part just isn't there anymore."

Already having his nerves stretched thin from the mating urge riding him, Jager had reached the end of his tether. He lunged for Daylen, took her by the arms, and yanked her to him. He brought his mouth down to hers and kissed her until the lust she said was gone flared between them. The scent of her arousal swirled in the air, giving testament to the fact she wasn't as unaffected by him as she wanted him to believe.

Jager continued to kiss her as he brought his hands down her arms and pulled them behind her back. He kept them shackled in one hand and lifted his head. He gave a grunt of satisfaction when he saw the glazed look in Daylen's eyes.

He spun her around, kept his grip on her hands, and walked her to her bedroom. Once inside the room, he looked around until his gaze landed on her uniform belt hanging from the closet-door handle. He stepped to it, taking Daylen with him, and opened the pouch that held her handcuffs. He pulled them out and then put the key to unlock them in his jeans pocket.

"What are you going to do with those?" Daylen asked as she warily eyed the handcuffs.

"Since you're not going to make this easy on me, I'm going to play by *my* rules now."

Jager slapped the handcuffs onto Daylen's wrists and pulled her back out into the hallway. It was time for Plan B.

*

"Where the hell are you taking me?" Daylen asked as Jager pulled her down the hall in the direction of the front door. She tried to yank her arm out of his grasp, but cuffed, she couldn't get the leverage she needed.

"I'm going to take you to my place and keep you there until you see reason."

Daylen dug in her heels, which had no effect on Jager whatsoever. "That's kidnapping, another criminal offense."

Jager pulled her to a stop and turned her so she faced him. "Do I look as if I care? We're mates. The sooner you admit that, the better off both of us will be. I want you, you want me, so no more trying to get rid of me. It won't work. Once you accept what we mean to each other, you'll wish you'd never fought it."

She couldn't believe the audacity of the man. "For your information, I don't want you."

Jager shook his head. "Do I have to kiss you again to show you how wrong that statement is?"

No, she didn't want him to kiss her again. She lost all will to resist when he did that. When his mouth claimed hers, Daylen no longer cared that Jager was a werewolf, or that he could shift into a wolf. Even now, her body wanted to feel his lips and tongue again.

When she didn't say anything, Jager gave a quick nod. "I didn't think you'd want me to, but I'm not promising I'll keep my lips to myself later."

Daylen's heart beat faster at the thought of Jager's lips kissing every inch of her. God, she was losing it. There she was handcuffed, about to be taken against her will to some place she didn't know, with a man who happened to be a werewolf, and all she could think about was how well he knew how to use his tongue.

Jager kept his grip on her arm and led her to the living room where he turned off the TV and all the lights. Before leaving the room, he scooped up his duster and sword. He steered her toward the front entrance hallway. He snagged her house keys off the key rack that hung on the wall next to the door. Before he opened the door, he got her to shove her feet into her running shoes that sat in front of the closet. For someone who was kidnapping her, he took his time to do everything someone would do if they were leaving the house for the rest of the night.

After he pulled the front door open, Jager walked her through it, then closed and locked it behind them. Daylen looked at the neighboring houses as he led her toward the driveway where a new-model black Camaro was parked. If one of her neighbors happened to be outside, all it would take would be one call for help and they would come running.

As if he knew what she'd been thinking, Jager said, "Don't even think about it. You can either walk nicely to my car, without kicking up a stink, or I can sling you over my shoulder and carry you there. I'm sure your neighbors would get an eyeful if I fondle that shapely ass of yours. I wonder what their reaction would be, you being a cop and all."

"Did anyone ever tell you you're a fucking asshole?"

Jager chuckled. "Actually, I get that quite a lot. I have a reputation for saying whatever is on my mind, no punches pulled. It tends to piss some people off."

"You think?" Daylen asked sarcastically.

He chuckled again. "You'll get used to it."

Jager pulled open the Camaro's passenger door and then

helped her inside. Once he had her settled on the seat, he strapped the seatbelt around her. Experiencing what it must be like for the people she'd arrested and stuck cuffed into the back of her police cruiser, Daylen watched Jager walk around the front of the car and then get into the driver's side. After he threw his duster and sword onto the backseat, he started the car before backing out of her driveway.

Her house grew smaller in the side-view mirror, and Daylen decided she would bide her time. Once Jager took the handcuffs off, he was going to find out what someone with a black belt in karate could do to a werewolf.

* * * *

Daylen's jaw dropped when Jager pulled onto a long drive of a house that could only be called a mansion. When he'd driven across the Golden Gate Bridge and into Marin County, she'd thought about the fact there were some swanky homes there, but she hadn't expected a werewolf to live in a place so rich. She really hadn't thought of where he would call home, but the mansion that loomed in front of the car was not what she'd expected.

Before she could stop herself, she turned her head to look at Jager and said with wonder, "You live here?"

He smiled as he parked in front of a large garage. "Yeah, I live here along with the rest of my family."

"How big is your family? This place is huge."

"There are nine of us altogether. You'll get to eventually meet them all. Not everyone will be home right now."

Hearing that somebody besides her and Jager would be inside the mansion, Daylen started to get her hopes up that she would be able to get free. She had to think that once one of his family members saw her with her hands cuffed behind her back, they would demand he release her.

Daylen kept her thoughts to herself as Jager got out of the car and then walked around to her side.

He undid the seatbelt and helped her out. Holding her upper arm firmly, he guided her to the front door of the mansion.

She and Jager had just stepped inside the large foyer when a man started down the stairs that led to the upper level. Daylen found herself unable to take her gaze off him as he took the steps and then walked toward them. He was just as tall as Jager, and just as exceptionally good-looking. And like Jager, from what she could see of it in his snug-fitting jeans and long-sleeved T-shirt, his body seemed to be all muscle. He wore his dark-blond hair on the long side with the ends touching the tops of his shoulders. His brown eyes skimmed over her with interest.

When he reached them, he smiled in her direction. "Who do we have here?"

Jager pulled her closer to his side. "This is Daylen. Daylen, this is my brother-in-arms, Kye."

"Under other circumstances, I would be happy to meet you," Daylen said to Kye. She twisted around so he could see her handcuffed hands.

Instead of being shocked and demanding that Jager let her go, Kye burst out into loud peals of laughter. In between, he said to Jager, "You're so screwed. Once Roxie finds out about this, she's going throw a shit fit."

"She can rag me out as much as she wants," Jager replied. "I did it her way, and it blew up in my face."

Kye seemed to sober a bit at that, but laughter still lurked in his eyes. "You told her what we are?"

Kye is a werewolf too? Daylen hadn't thought about Jager's family being werewolves as well.

"I told her," Jager said. "She reacted just about as well as Ansley did; not as bad, but close enough."

At that point, Daylen became fed up with Jager and Kye talking about her as if she wasn't standing right in front of them. "Can the two of you stop talking about me? I am right here. And I'm sorry, but when someone suddenly changes into a wolf, how else am I supposed to act?" She turned to look at Kye. "And are you going to do nothing about this?" She twisted around again and shook her hands at him. "According to California Penal Code Section 207, the punishment for kidnapping is serving up to eight years in a state prison."

Kye laughed again. "Yup, you can tell she's a cop."

"Well?" Daylen asked exasperatedly.

He shook his head and backed up a bit with his hands held

palm out toward her. "Sorry, but I'm not getting involved with this. I can see where Jager is coming from, though. If I were in his shoes and my potential mate outright rejected me, I probably would do the same thing."

"Plus, Kye is smart enough to know I won't tolerate another male interfering," Jager said.

Daylen looked from Jager to Kye and back to Jager again. A look of understanding passed between the two men. She couldn't believe Kye would do nothing to help her, but she really wasn't afraid of what Jager would do to her. If he had wanted to hurt her, he would have done it long before now. She was more annoyed with the fact she'd been so easily overpowered by him. It was a blow to her ego. She broke out of her musings when Kye spoke to Jager.

"You're going to break the last part of Roxie's rule number two, aren't you? You're going to get carried away in the moment without giving a full explanation."

Jager shrugged. "I'm already going to be in shit. I might as well completely bury myself."

There the two of them went again, talking over her as if she wasn't in the room. "Would the two of you knock it off with acting like I'm not here? And, Kye, what do you mean about getting carried away in the moment?"

Kye gave her a knowing smile. "You'll find out soon enough." He gave her a wink, then went to step past her and Jager. "And, Jager," he said as he turned to walk backward. "I wouldn't hold off doing it for too long. You've got her here, and everyone else has gone out, so you'll have the house to yourselves. I would use my time wisely before Saskia gets home. I doubt she'll be too upset, but you know how close she and Roxie have become."

Jager gave a nod. "Don't worry. It'll be a done deal by the time everyone comes home tonight."

"Then I'll leave you two to it." He smiled. "And Daylen, welcome to the family." Kye turned back around and walked out the front door.

CHAPTER EIGHT

With a yank on Daylen's arm, Jager got her moving again. The house sounded eerily quiet as he led her up the stairs. Usually, the mansion was filled with some kind of sound, considering how many people lived in it. For once, Jager was glad to have the house to himself. He was back on his own territory and knew, even if somebody did show up before he claimed Daylen as his mate, they wouldn't bother them.

Once he had Daylen inside his bedroom, Jager closed and locked the door behind them. He threw his duster and sword on top of the large wooden chest that sat at the end of his bed before he turned her to face him.

He reached up and gently brushed a lock of her reddish-brown hair off her forehead. "I realize you're probably pissed at me, but I knew you weren't going to be reasonable about me being a werewolf or the fact we're mates. You really didn't leave me much choice."

Daylen glared at him. "So, you thought putting me in handcuffs and then kidnapping me would make me more reasonable? What planet are you from?"

Jager smiled. "Well, at least you aren't cowering from me. I'd say we're off to a pretty good start. I wouldn't want my mate to be afraid of me. Pissed, I can handle."

"Good, because if you don't take these damn cuffs off me soon,

I'm just going to get more pissed off."

He wrapped his arms around Daylen and pulled her against his body. "How about we turn that anger of yours into something else?" He pressed his rock-hard erection along her hip.

Daylen bit her bottom lip, as if she were fighting to hold back a moan, but the telltale scent of her arousal perfumed the air. Jager smiled to himself. She might fight what he stirred inside her, but she obviously couldn't stop her body's reaction to his nearness. She only needed a bit more convincing that he was the male for her, then she would no longer fight what was between them.

Daylen tilted her head back so she could meet his gaze. "You don't like to lose, do you?"

"No. Not really."

"Neither do I. That's why I'm just as pissed off at myself as I am at you. Every time you touch me, you turn me into a weak-willed woman. I really, really don't like it. I should be able to resist you."

Jager chuckled. "Even though you aren't a female werewolf, you *are* feeling some effect of the mating urge. You're not meant to be able to resist me. It just means I'm yours."

She audibly ground her teeth together. "You aren't mine. And I'm not yours." When he nodded that he was, Daylen shook her head. "For Christ's sake, we just met. There's no possible way you can have *those* kind of strong feelings for me. You know nothing about who I am as a person. What you're feeling is just a good case of lust, nothing more."

Jager tapped his nose. "This told me you were the one I've been waiting for."

Daylen gave him a look that said she thought he'd lost it. "Your nose? Your nose told you I was *the* one?"

"One whiff of your scent and I knew. Plus, having my mating urge kick in helped as well." Jager bent his head closer while he spoke. He hadn't missed the way her breath had caught the closer he came.

With her gaze locked on his mouth, Daylen said, "What...what exactly is your mating urge?"

He dropped one of his hands to her bottom and squeezed, while he held her more firmly against him. "Every male werewolf goes through the mating urge when he finally finds his mate. It'll ride me hard until I've taken you."

"Taken me?" Daylen's words came out in a husky whisper.

"Yes, taken you. Made love to you until you know there will be no other man in your life but me. It's also the reason I've been walking around with an almost constant hard-on since I met you. I ache for you. And I won't find any relief from the mating urge until I've claimed you."

At his words, a rosy flush filled Daylen's cheeks and she slightly parted her lips. When the tip of her tongue came out and licked her bottom lip, he'd reached the end of his control. With a groan of need, he closed the distance between their mouths and took her lips in a gentle, languid kiss.

Daylen moaned, then mumbled, "More. Kiss me harder."

She sighed once he increased the pressure of his lips and pushed his tongue inside her mouth. Passion flared between them as he stroked hers with his. He dropped his other hand to her bottom and kneaded both cheeks while he ground his cock against her. The need to take her, to lower her to the floor and sink his erection deep inside her pussy beat at him, but Jager held it in check. He would take his time with Daylen, make it so she wanted him as badly as he wanted her.

Keeping his grip on her ass, he picked her up off her feet and lifted her onto the bed. He slowly lowered her onto her back on the mattress. He followed her down and stretched out on top of her.

Daylen squirmed beneath him and jerked her head to the side. "Take the damn handcuffs off, Jager. I want to touch you."

"Not yet," he said as he lifted off her and shifted to her side. He took hold of the waistband of her yoga pants and pushed them down past her hips. "I have to taste you again. Then I'll free you."

Once he had her pants down her legs, he slipped off her running shoes and socks before he removed the garment the rest of the way. He kneeled at her side and ran a caressing hand down the flat plane of her stomach. Daylen lifted her hips off the mattress in silent invitation to touch more of her.

Not sure how much longer he could hold himself back, Jager eased her panties down her legs and off. He quickly lay between her legs, his shoulders spreading them even farther apart. A low growl pushed past his lips as the scent of her arousal filled his lungs with each breath he took. His cock jerked as he bent his head and dragged his tongue along her sex.

Daylen panted. "Jager. Please."

He gently blew against her clit, which caused Daylen to moan. "I know, baby. I know exactly what you want."

Jager bent his head and licked her pussy, lapping up her juices as her body wept for him. He stiffened his tongue and pushed it inside her slick opening as Daylen's hips rose off the bed. The little sounds she made as he pleasured her had him about ready to explode in his pants. He circled her clit with his tongue before he sucked on it. Her cries increased in volume.

Jager sensed it wouldn't take much to push Daylen into a climax, and moved from between her legs to stand at the side of the bed. She whimpered in response. Looking at her, knowing his eyes had to be mutedly glowing, he held her gaze as he lifted his shirt and yanked it over his head. He reached inside the front pocket of his jeans and pulled out the key to the handcuffs. She quickly rolled onto her stomach.

With quick motions, Jager undid each cuff and then put them and the key on the bedside table. Now free, Daylen knelt on the bed and yanked off her top and bra. She moved closer and reached for his jeans and undid them.

"My turn to taste you," she said, as she pushed his pants over his hips and down his legs.

Jager kicked off his shoes before he stepped out his jeans and kicked them aside. He growled deep inside his chest as Daylen ran her hands down his sides to his hipbones. His cock bobbed at the intense way she gazed at it. The feel of her fingertips gently caressing his length brought another growl out of him.

Daylen inched even closer, and wrapped her hand around his shaft. Jager panted as if he'd just run a marathon, and silently watched her stick her tongue out and circle the head of his cock. He fisted his hands at his sides to stop himself from pushing her flat onto her back.

His eyes just about rolled back in his head as Daylen opened her mouth and took his erection inside it. The feel of her lips closing around him while she sucked had Jager moaning. Lost in a haze of arousal, he watched her pleasure him. His cock hardened even more. He wouldn't be able to last if he let her continue for much longer, but it felt incredibly good.

Unable to stand any more, Jager pulled free of her grip. He pushed her back and climbed onto the mattress. He followed Daylen as she shifted to the middle of the bed and then pulled him to her. He settled between her spread thighs. Her wetness coated his cock as he slid the tip of it inside her pussy.

"Look at me, Daylen," he said as he held himself above her.

Daylen opened her eyes and lifted her gaze to his. "Your eyes are glowing again," she said softly.

"I know. You make them glow."

Jager held her gaze, then surged forward and sheathed his cock deep inside her with one thrust. He growled low in his throat as he moved inside Daylen. With his weight resting on his bent arms, he surged in and out of her. At first, he kept the pace slow and steady, but when she held on to his biceps, wrapping her legs around his waist to take him deeper, he rode her faster.

As his orgasm inched closer, Jager felt the mating bond form between him and Daylen. A part of his soul reached out for hers. He knew the instant she felt it and when her soul reached for his. Her eyes widened. They moaned as their souls joined and became one. An intense wave of pleasure washed through him with the knowledge that she was now forever his.

Taking her harder, faster, Jager pumped his hips between her legs. The first flutter of Daylen's orgasm rippled along the length of his cock. He fought to hold his orgasm back, wanting to watch her as she found her pleasure. Her hands tightened on his biceps, and she arched into him as her pussy rhythmically clutched his shaft.

Before it ended, he put his hand around the back of her neck and lifted her head so her mouth came to rest low on his neck where it met his shoulder. The point of no return rushed up to meet him. "Bite me, Daylen," he said through gritted teeth.

She shook her head. "No."

"Do it," he panted. "Mark me as yours." When she nuzzled his neck, Jager groaned. "Hurry. I want to feel your teeth on me as I come inside you."

Daylen nipped his skin. Still working his cock in and out, he pushed her mouth closer. She bit harder, enough to break the skin. With a loud howl, Jager surged into her one final time. His shaft pulsed deep inside her pussy, filling her with his cum.

Once the last wave hit him, he released her and let her lie back down on the bed. Jager collapsed on top of Daylen with his head in the crook of her neck. The hard length of his cock remained buried inside her pussy.

Daylen ran her hands up and down his back. "You came, and you're still hard."

He rocked his hips into her. "I know. I can keep it that way for hours, no matter how many times I come. It's a male werewolf trait."

"I'm not complaining," Daylen said. She let out a small moan when he almost pulled free of her body only to sheath himself to the hilt once more. "Again?"

"Again," he said. Jager rubbed his cheek against one of Daylen's taut nipples, then sucked it into his mouth. Once he had her squirming beneath him, he lifted his head. "This time I want to take you as a wolf would take his mate."

He pulled out of her, then urged Daylen onto her hands and knees. He grasped her hips to hold her in position. Before he sank his hard cock inside her warm wetness, he rubbed the tip of it against her clit. She rocked back, trying to take him as he pushed into her.

She took him deeper in this position. Her inner muscles gripped his shaft in a tight fist as he moved in and out. Daylen pushed back in time with his strokes. He thrust into her while his cock hardened even more. Their mating bond grew more solid, drawing them emotionally closer together. The knowledge that she was his had another climax building inside him. He pumped his hips faster as she let out a whimpered moan. Her pussy fisted around his length, milking him, as she came once more. Jager pumped into her once, twice, then he, too, found his release.

Satiated, feeling more content than he'd ever felt before, he pulled his still-erect cock out of Daylen and then took her into his arms. He moved to his back and got her to lie on her side with her head pillowed on his chest. With the mating urge no longer digging its claws into him, Jager's eyes drifted shut. He'd let them sleep for a while, but there was still a lot of the night left to love her, and he was going to put it to good use.

* * * *

Daylen must have dozed off because when she opened her eyes again, the room was in shadowed darkness. Moonlight spilled in through the open curtains of the room's only window. She turned her head so she could look at Jager from where she lay snuggled against his side. His eyes were closed, and his chest moved with his even breathing. Even though there wasn't much light to see by, her eyes had adjusted enough to the dark she could make out most of his features. He was so good-looking he almost took her breath away.

To look at him, she would never guess Jager was a werewolf. He looked like a normal man, albeit an exceptionally good-looking one with a killer body. Now that she'd made love to him, the fact he was a werewolf didn't bother her as much as it had in the beginning. Even when she'd seen his eyes mutedly glowing while he took her, she found they only increased his sexiness.

And making love to him hadn't been like any of the encounters she'd had with other men. Yes, Jager was great in bed — he'd made her just about mindless with his kisses and touch — but something else had passed between them. And it was something she'd never experienced in another man's bed before. It almost seemed as if a part of him had reached for a part of her. When they'd touched and joined, Daylen had been filled with a sense of rightness, as if she really hadn't been complete until that moment.

Daylen found herself drawn to Jager more than she was before. She was more than content just to lie snuggled beside him while he slept. All the reasons she should push him away seemed to fly out the window. One bout of mind-blowing sex and she felt closer to him than she'd ever allowed herself to be with a man. And she'd only known him for a couple days. During that time, he'd turned her life upside down and had her acting out of character.

She suddenly stiffened as another thought came to her. "Oh, shit!" she said out loud before she could stop herself.

Jager jerked awake and looked around the room. "What? What's the matter?"

Daylen moved out of his embrace and sat up. "We didn't use any protection. What kind of cop am I? I'm on the pill, but we still should have used a condom."

"Is that all?" Jager asked as he once more relaxed. "Don't worry about it. We didn't need one."

"I beg to differ."

Jager sighed. "There's no reason to get upset. Werewolves can't get HIV or STDs, and I can't smell any of those sicknesses on you either. And, even if you did have any of them, you wouldn't be able to pass it on to me."

"You can actually smell when someone is ill?"

"Yes." He pulled her back into his arms.

She allowed him to tuck her head under his chin. "And you can't ever get HIV or an STD?"

"No. Werewolves never get sick, literally. Only mortals have that weakness."

Daylen tried to pull away so she could look at him, but Jager easily held her in place. "Mortals? What do you mean by that? The way you talk you would think werewolves are immortal."

Jager yawned largely. "Almost, but not quite." He hooked the blankets with his feet and pulled them over them. "Go back to sleep. I want to rest a little while longer, then I'm going to make love to you again and again and again."

A small thrill went through Daylen at his words. She closed her eyes, but sleep eluded her. *Werewolves are almost immortal?* What exactly had she gotten herself into?

CHAPTER NINE

The sound of someone pounding on the bedroom door brought Jager and Daylen awake at the same time. Daylen blinked at the bright light and lifted her head so she could see the clock on the bedside table next to his side of the bed. It was just after eleven thirty. Considering they had made love most of the night, she wasn't surprised to find they'd slept almost through the entire morning.

The loud banging resumed until Jager shouted, "Whoever is out there had better have a good reason for waking us up."

A woman's voice sounded from the other side of the door. "Oh, I have a very good reason. Kye told me what you did last night. Now open this door and let me see what damage you've done."

"Aw, Christ," Jager said under his breath. He said louder, "Roxie, go downstairs. Just give us a few minutes to get dressed and then you can commence with your reaming out."

There was a few seconds of silence, then Roxie said, "Fine, I'll be downstairs, but don't keep me waiting too long."

So the infamous Roxie, who wanted Jager to follow her rules, had shown up. Daylen was more than a little curious to meet her. Since Jager and Kye thought Roxie would give Jager crap for pulling the stunt of bringing Daylen there, Roxie obviously had some control over the men.

Jager threw back the covers and got out of bed. He stretched, giving Daylen a nice few of his tight ass. He turned and gave her a smile that said he knew she'd been staring. "You might as well use the bathroom first while I get dressed. If we don't get downstairs in what Roxie thinks is a fair amount of time, she'll only come pounding on the door again."

"What is Roxie to you? Is she a relation of yours?"

Jager snorted. "No. She's more like my boss. She rules over all the werewolf packs."

"So, she's like your queen or something?"

"Not a queen. There are no royal families in werewolf society. Roxie's just special. She's the foretold one. She can do things a normal werewolf can't. Being the foretold one also puts her at risk of being used as a figurehead if an unscrupulous werewolf ever got his or her hands on her. That's where my sister, brothers, and I come in. We're Roxie's Protectors."

Daylen ran an appreciative gaze over the front of Jager. The sight of his naked body made her wish they could stay in bed. The man hadn't lied when he'd said he could keep an erection after coming over and over again.

She jerked her gaze back up to Jager's face, and said, "So, you and your family are her bodyguards? And why do you sometimes call them your brothers- or sister-in-arms at times and just brothers and sister at others?"

"I guess we're closer to being bodyguards than anything else. We've trained for centuries, waiting for Roxie to be found. As for your other question, we aren't really all related. I have two true brothers—Roan and Skylar. As for the others, they were lone wolves, same as my brothers and I were. It was Saskia's grandmother who brought us all together to train and basically form our own pack, with Saskia, my sister, as the pack leader."

Daylen listened to the rest of Jager's explanation, but her mind had sort of frozen on the part where he'd said he and his family had trained for centuries while they waited for Roxie. *Centuries?* She remembered his comment from the night before about werewolves being almost immortal. Could Jager really be that old? She felt the blood drain away from her face when she thought about his penchant for carrying a sword. If he'd lived through a time when carrying one was part of everyday life, it would explain why he was so comfortable having it strapped to his waist.

Jager gave her a concerned look. "Daylen? Are you all right? You've gotten awfully pale all of a sudden."

"You said last night that werewolves were almost immortal. How old are you, Jager?"

In a matter-of-fact tone, he said, "I'm one thousand and ten. Since you asked me my age, what's yours?"

"I'm just a measly thirty years old," she said with more calm than she actually felt.

Yup, at over a thousand years old, Jager was an official card-carrying medieval warrior. The sword now made perfect sense. His great age had her verging on wanting to laugh hysterically out loud. And not in a good way. She'd just spent the night screwing the brains out of a man who'd seen history in the making.

Jager came and sat on the bed next to her, then lifted her to an upright position and took her into his arms. He rubbed a large hand up and down her back. "Just breathe, Daylen. I guess I shouldn't have just dropped the age thing on you like that."

"It's okay. I had to find out sometime." Daylen pushed away and then slid out of the bed on the opposite side. "I'll hurry in the bathroom so you can have it after me."

Before Jager could say anything to her, she raced into the en suite and then closed the door behind her, turning the lock once it clicked into place. She leaned her forehead against the back of the door and took a couple of deep breaths. She was in over her head.

* * * *

Once she'd splashed some cold water on her face, Daylen had pulled herself together enough so she could face Jager again. After she'd stepped back into the bedroom, he hadn't said anything as he'd walked past her and into the bathroom. By the time he finished, she was dressed.

They were now on their way downstairs, and they still hadn't said a word to each other. Before they reached the last step, Jager pulled her to a halt. Daylen gave him a questioning look.

"Just so you aren't caught off guard," he said, "you're about to meet my entire family as well as Roxie and her mate. I can smell all their scents. I've dumped a lot on you already. If you'd rather not be around a bunch of werewolves right now, I'll tell them to get lost."

Daylen slipped her hand in his. She was not the type of woman to back down from anything. She was getting herself back on an even keel. If she could accept that Jager was a werewolf, she'd have to come to grips with how old he was. They had yet to discuss how things were going to go now that they'd slept together, but she had a feeling she was about to find out exactly what it meant to be considered his mate.

Jager guided Daylen into a spacious living room with a large LED television and a couple of long, black leather couches. Along with those pieces of furniture, there were two matching black leather armchairs. Most of the seating was already taken up by his family. There was only an empty spot on one of the couches.

All heads turned Daylen and Jager's way after they stepped into the room. She recognized Kye, who sat in one of the armchairs. He smiled at her. Two of the men sitting on one of the couches looked so similar to Jager that Daylen guessed them to be his true brothers, Roan and Skylar. One of them wore his hair almost as long as Jager did, while the other's brushed the tops of his shoulders. All three men shared the same hair color and light-blue eyes. One had his arm around the shoulders of a woman.

The one thing Daylen immediately noticed was how extremely good-looking most of the occupants of the room were. The only ones who didn't have the supermodel look going on, though they were no means bad looking, were the woman who sat next to one of Jager's brothers, the man sitting beside a woman with white-blonde hair and the woman with golden-brown hair who happened to be glaring daggers at Jager. If Daylen had to guess, she would say that was Roxie.

Jager led Daylen to stand in front of the television and turned them so they faced the others in the room. He introduced her to everyone, leaving the man and woman who sat together in one of the armchairs for last.

"That's Roxie over there, and the man whose lap she's sitting on is Beowulf, her mate," Jager said.

Daylen smiled. "It's nice to meet you all."

Roxie slid off her mate's lap and came to stand in front of Daylen and Jager. She glared at Jager, then turned a smile on Daylen. "It's nice to meet you as well, Daylen, though I heard you were brought here under duress."

"Jager and I sorted it out in the end."

"You two may have sorted it out," Roxie said, "but I would like to know if Jager left out some major details."

"Did you run out and tell Roxie as soon as you left here last night?" Jager asked Kye as he turned his gaze on him. "I figured she would find out eventually. I just wasn't expecting someone to tell her so soon."

Kye shrugged. "What can I say? I went to Wulf's Den last night, and Roxie asked if I'd seen you before I'd arrived. I'm sorry, bro, but when she threatened to do all kinds of nasty things to me if I didn't talk, I caved."

Roxie loudly cleared her throat. "Well, I'm waiting, Jager. Did you tell Daylen everything?"

Not sure what *everything* was, Daylen decided to take some of the heat off Jager. "He did tell me about his knowing I was his mate as soon as he smelled my scent, and about the mating urge. He also told me how werewolves are almost immortal, and that he's over a thousand years old."

"And that was it?" Roxie asked with exasperation tingeing her words. "Incredible. Just incredible. So he never mentioned what it meant when you made love for the first time and your souls joined. You have to tell me you felt it. It isn't exactly something that just slides by without you noticing."

Daylen looked from Roxie to Jager, who happened to look a smidgen guilty about something, and then back to Roxie again. "So that's what that was. Jager never said anything about it. I thought maybe I'd imagined it."

Roxie rounded on Jager and poked a finger into the center of his chest. "I told you to give her a choice, you big lug." Poke. "Why didn't you listen to me?" Poke.

Jager grabbed Roxie's finger and pushed it away. "Stop poking me. Hey, having no choice has worked out for all the mated couples here in this room. Granted, Eli wasn't a werewolf when he claimed Saskia, and didn't have the mating urge to tell him she was his, but they still didn't have a choice. Roan and Ansley are happy. And Beowulf didn't ask first before he claimed you."

"Leave me out of this," Beowulf said with a chuckle from where he sat.

Roxie crossed her arms over her chest. "All right, knucklehead. Daylen has accepted you being a werewolf well. Shall we see how well she accepts what it really means to be a mate to one?"

Daylen met Roxie's gaze when the other woman stepped away from Jager to stand in front of her. Given how upset Roxie seemed to be about him not telling her all there was to know about being a werewolf's mate, Daylen braced herself for what was coming next. She had a feeling it would be another blow to her system.

"Now, Daylen," Roxie said, "I want you to stay calm, and remember, I'm just the messenger. If you want to punish someone after I've told you everything, I suggest you do it to the idiot standing beside you." Jager let out a low growl at that, but Roxie ignored him. "First of all, I suggest you get Jager to buy you a big-ass diamond ring, because you and he are basically now married." She flashed the large diamond ring and gold band she wore on the ring finger of her left hand.

Daylen swallowed. "Married? As in we're married, married?"

"Yup. As soon as your souls joined, that was a werewolf equivalent of a mortal marriage ceremony, only it doesn't have any witnesses and it's much, much more intimate. There's also no breaking that bond once it has been forged."

She looked frantically around the room, hoping Roxie was pulling her leg, but everyone had serious expressions. "You're kidding, right? I can't possibly be married to Jager. We barely know each other. Up until last night, I wanted to throw him into jail every time I saw him."

One of the men laughed, but it was quickly covered with a loud cough. Seeing as how Leif had his hand over his mouth and laughter lurked in his eyes, Daylen figured it had been him.

"That's why I told Jager to explain and give you a choice. As for getting to know each other, you'll learn quickly. The joining of your souls will take care of that. Now that you're mated, neither you nor Jager will be able to stand being away from each other for any length of time, especially in the beginning. A few hours away from him and you'll feel as if you're in a living hell. All you'll be able to think about is getting back to him."

Daylen turned to Jager. "You knew that would happen?"

He unwaveringly met her gaze. "Yes."

She didn't think. She just reacted. Taking Jager by the arm, she kicked out at the back of his leg. As he went down to the floor, she kept her hold on his arm, keeping it high and outstretched as she used her thumb to apply pressure to the underside of his wrist. She had him on his knees, leaning forward, with his arm held higher than his shoulder in a matter of seconds. He couldn't get out of that hold so long as she kept her thumb on the pressure point. Daylen had used that hold on more than one suspect.

"Now I can see why Roxie is a little pissed with you," she said. "There's one thing you have to learn about me. I don't like surprises like that." The room had gone completely silent. Daylen looked around to see everyone staring at her with surprise on their faces. "I have a black belt in karate, and I know a bit of jujitsu."

Leif, suddenly, burst out laughing. He laughed so hard tears ran out of his eyes and he had to hold his ribs. The others in the room broke out in varying degrees of laughter as well. Even Roxie had cracked a smile.

"I'm sorry," Leif said as he tried to bring himself back under control. "You have to admit it looks pretty good to see Mr. He-man-warrior-who-can't-be-separated-from-my-sword taken down so easily by a woman, and a mortal, no less. How many times is this? Twice now?"

"This would be the third time," Daylen answered.

That only sent Leif into another round of laughter.

Dirk, who sat next to Leif, elbowed him. "I'd cut that out if I were you. Jager will take it out on your hide."

While still laughing, Leif said, "It will be so worth it."

Daylen ignored Leif and turned her gaze on Jager. "If we're stuck with each other, you're going to have to stop keeping things from me. I don't do well with people who don't tell the truth or who purposely neglect to tell me things." She released him.

He stood and quickly put his arms around her waist when she would have put more distance between them. "Okay, I didn't exactly go about this in the right way. If you'd been a female werewolf, you would have already known these things. You being mortal just made it a little more complicated."

155

"Speaking of me being a mortal," Daylen said. "You said something about Eli not always being a werewolf. Does that mean now that we're mates I'll become one? Or do you have to bite me to turn me?"

"A mortal can't be turned from being bitten by a werewolf. Werewolves are born werewolves. Actually, to the general werewolf population, a mortal can never be turned."

Daylen frowned in confusion. "Then how did Eli get turned?"

Roxie broke into their conversation. "I think I should be the one to explain this one. I was once mortal as well, same with Ansley. There's a very old spell that will turn a mortal into a werewolf. I was the first mortal it worked on. It seems I have a little more magic inside me than the average werewolf. The spark of it deep inside us is how we make the change. Anyway, it has turned out that I'm the only one now who can use the spell. With a small of amount of my blood and it, I can make you and Jager truly mates in all ways. At least I think it'll still work in my condition."

"Your condition?" Jager asked before Daylen could.

"You might as well tell them, Roxie," Beowulf said when Roxie hesitated.

"There was another reason Beowulf and I came here this morning, other than me giving Jager shit." She paused, then smiled. "I'm pregnant."

CHAPTER TEN

The room went from being so quiet you could hear a pin drop to six people talking all at once in rather loud male voices. Daylen couldn't help chuckling when she saw the frantic faces of Roxie's Protectors. Even Jager looked as if someone had told him the world was about to be destroyed and he was the only one who could stop it.

"This means we're going to have watch Roxie even closer," Skylar said.

"We'll now have to do night shifts at Beowulf and Roxie's house," Roan said in a pained voice.

"Roxie won't be able to go to Wulf's Den anymore. It won't be safe for her and the baby," Kye added.

"I don't mind taking the first night shift," Dirk said.

"If Miles finds out about this, we're fucked," Leif said.

All Jager said was, "Fuck me."

Saskia hadn't said anything, but from the thoughtful look she wore, Daylen figured she was thinking about what Roxie had just told them.

As the men continued to talk over each other, Roxie put her fingers into her mouth and let out a shrill whistle. All the werewolves in the room stopped talking and covered their ears.

Now that Roxie had everyone's attention, she said, "Me being pregnant does not mean things have to change. So I'm going to have a baby. Countless women have done it."

Saskia finally spoke up. "That may be true, Roxie, but you aren't exactly just any other pregnant woman. You're the foretold one. We already know Miles will do anything to get his hands on you. We also know he's recovered from the loss of his last headquarters. His new one we have yet to find, but he's still recruiting lone wolves. Remember Jager managed to corner one of his men before the lone wolf got away. You being pregnant means we'll have to be extra vigilant."

Daylen cringed inside at Saskia's mention of Jager confronting the lone wolf. It was because of her that Miles' man had gotten away. Now able to see the sword fight from his standpoint, she realized she'd caused the Protectors to lose out on some valuable information. Since she was now technically one of them because she and Jager were mated, she figured her skills as a police officer could be used to help them find Miles' new headquarters.

Before Roxie could reply to Saskia, Daylen asked, "Who is Miles?"

Saskia answered. "Miles is my true brother. At one time, he was one of us, one of the foretold one's Protectors. He left, vowing to find the foretold one for himself when I was chosen to be the Protectors' leader. Miles figured it should have been him."

"What's his last name?"

"It's Jensen."

"Can you give me a description of him?"

"Miles is just about as tall as Jager, has the same hair and eye color as me, and has similar features."

"Where was the location of his last headquarters?"

Saskia rattled off an address in San Francisco's older warehouse district. She added, "I'm not sure why you need all that information about Miles. And the warehouse is no longer there. He blew it up because we got too close to him."

"It was my fault the lone wolf got away from Jager. If not for me, you probably would already have discovered the location of Miles' new headquarters. I'm going to fix that." Daylen asked the room at large, "Do one of you have a cell phone I can use?"

"You can use mine." Dirk pulled one out of the front pocket of his jeans and tossed it to her.

Daylen caught it. She punched in the number to her police

station. Once the other end picked up, she said, "Hey, Carey, it's Daylen. Can you put me through to Ted's line?" She waited for Ted to pick up. Once he did, she said, "Hi, Ted. I was wondering if you could use your amazing police detective skills and dig up some information for me."

Ted chuckled. "Anything for you, Daylen. What do you need?"

"I need whatever info you can get on a man named Miles Jensen." She gave Ted a description of Miles. "I also need you to look up who was listed as owning a warehouse that blew up some months back in the old warehouse district." Daylen quickly gave him the address Saskia had given her.

"No problem. I'll see what I can find and call you back at home."

"I'm not at home right now. I'm over at a friend's place. You can call me at this number." Daylen looked at Dirk, who told her the number to his cell. She repeated it for Ted.

"This may take me a while, especially finding the information you want about the warehouse."

"That's okay. I'm pretty sure I'm going to be here for most of the day."

After Daylen hung up, she tossed the phone back to Dirk. "Ted is one of the detectives at my station. He has a knack for finding information about people and places others can't. If he can find out who owned the warehouse, he may be able to trace it to another property that Miles may have recently purchased."

"Damn," Kye said. "Having a cop in the family is going to have some fringe benefits."

Daylen smiled. "I figure since I'm now a Protector too, I might as well start pulling my weight."

Jager shook his head. "Whoa, slow down there. You're my mate. I never said anything about you becoming one of Roxie's Protectors. You haven't even said whether or not you want Roxie to turn you yet. A mortal doesn't stand a chance against a werewolf. We're a lot faster and stronger than your kind."

Daylen narrowed her eyes. "My kind? Well, this *mortal* has gotten the jump on you more than once."

"That's only because you caught me off guard each time."

"Oh, really? Shall we test out your theory and see if I can still take you down head-on?"

"We don't just fight with our fists, Daylen. We fight with our swords, and if need be, in our wolf forms. As a mortal, you wouldn't be able to defend yourself against one of Miles' men."

"What's the matter, Jager?" she taunted. "Are you afraid I'll prove you wrong?"

Leif jumped up. "You've got him now, Daylen. That's one thing Jager can never pass on—a direct challenge."

Jager crossed his arms over his wide chest. "All right, Daylen. You want to do this, then let's see who has the right of it. I'd rather you found out here how much of a disadvantage you are at than while facing down one of Miles' men out on the street. I'll get my sword, and I'll meet you in the basement."

After Jager left the living room, Daylen and the others headed to the basement. She took in the weights and large open space. It had been set up as a training room. She stood in the middle of the open area while everyone else went to stand off to the side.

It didn't take Jager long to join them. He carried his unsheathed sword. Once he stood in front of her, he said, "Remember, I don't like to lose. I won't take it easy on you."

She smiled. "I wouldn't expect you to."

Without giving her any warning, Jager swung at her with his sword. She jumped out of the way. Daylen may not have the speed of a werewolf, but she was still quick on her feet. She spent the next few minutes dodging his blows while striking out at him with her hands and feet. Since he was doing most of the work, it would only be a matter of time before he tired enough for her to make her move.

Once the opportunity came, she quickly moved in and kicked out in a karate move that sent Jager's sword flying out of his hand. The triumphant smile that spread across Daylen's lips faded when he launched himself at her, shifting in mid-air to his wolf form. She jumped out of the way and just managed to avoid his sharp teeth.

Jager stalked her as he growled and snapped at her. Daylen took up a karate stance and waited for him to go on the attack. This time she'd be ready for him. As he leapt at her, she kicked out with a roundhouse that caught him right across the muzzle. He landed hard on the floor. Before he could get back up onto his paws, she jumped onto his back and used her weight to pin him to the floor while she wrapped her hands around his muzzle to stop him from trying to use his teeth to free himself.

"Well," Daylen said while she panted. "Do you admit defeat?" Jager let out a whine. Taking that as a yes, she let go of his muzzle and stood. His wolf form blurred and shimmered as he shifted.

Daylen touched her gaze on each of the other people in the room. They all were beaming at her. Roxie stood under the shelter of Beowulf's arm and clapped. "Way to go, Daylen," she said.

Saskia left her mate's side and came to stand in front of Daylen. "Now that I've seen your fighting skills, I think you're more than qualified to be considered a Protector. Being a cop, you definitely have the background for it."

Daylen smiled. "Thanks."

She turned to look at Jager. Seeing his stern features, the smile Daylen wore slipped. Without a word, he manacled her wrist with his hand and hurriedly walked her to the basement stairs. He didn't stop until they were upstairs and inside his bedroom with the door firmly shut behind them.

As Jager put his sword on the dresser and then turned to face her, she tried to ask, "Are you pis—"

Before Daylen could finish the sentence, he had her in his arms and his mouth moving greedily over hers. The hard length of his cock pressed against her belly. She wrapped her arms around his neck and rubbed herself along him.

Jager finally lifted his head once they were breathing heavily. "You were magnificent. You've made me so hard all I can think about is being inside you."

Daylen's heart beat faster as she gazed into Jager's mutedly glowing eyes. "I'll have to remember me beating your ass turns you on."

Jager kissed a trail from the corner of her mouth to the side of her neck and yanked at her clothes. "Only with you. I need you naked."

A deep ache throbbed inside her pussy. They'd made love so many times the night before, Daylen had lost count, but her body was in flames once again for Jager. They yanked at each other's clothes until they stood naked. He pulled her back against him. She moaned as her taut nipples brushed against his chest. The feel of his hard cock pressed against her bare skin had wetness leaking between her legs.

Jager took her mouth in a demanding kiss as he wrapped his arm around her waist. With his other hand, he cupped her breast. Leaving her mouth, he bent his head to swirl his tongue around her nipple. Daylen clutched his shoulders as intense waves of pleasure shot through her body when he opened his mouth and sucked her nipple inside.

The pulling sensation caused her pussy to ache to be filled. Daylen needed to touch more of Jager. She ran a hand down his chest to his hardness nestled against her stomach. She trailed her fingers along the length of his cock, then took him in her hand. He jerked his hips, pushing his erection tighter inside her grasp as she pumped up and down.

Jager released her nipple, then straightened, and said huskily, "That feels good, but being inside you will feel even better." He reached between her legs and worked a finger in and out of her core. "You're already wet. I don't think I can wait any longer."

Daylen moaned. "I'm not stopping you."

Jager moved his hands to her bottom and lifted her off her feet. Daylen held on to his shoulders. "Put your legs around my waist," he said in a voice that came out half a growl.

As soon as she had done as he'd said, Jager lifted her into position and impaled her on his erect cock in one stroke. He slowly sank to his knees to the floor. Once he moved to a sitting position, with her bent legs on either side of his hips, he took hold of her hips and lifted her up and down.

"Ride me, Daylen."

With his hard shaft filling her, deliciously stretching her, Daylen moved. Jager reached up to cup the back of her head as he brought her lips down to his. His tongue moved in and out of her mouth in time with the motion of their bodies. Able to control their lovemaking, she alternated between slow and fast strokes. She arched her back as his cock slid in and out of her pussy, which caused his hardness to rub in just the right spot to have her moaning.

Jager lifted his hips to meet each of her strokes. His erection grew even harder as she clamped her inner muscles around him. Faster she rode him, her body coiling tighter. Her orgasm edged ever closer. On the verge of coming, Daylen bent her head and dragged her tongue across the bite mark she'd made on his neck the night before. He stiffened, then bucked hard beneath her, lifting her knees off the floor.

"You like when I bite you there?" she asked softly.

"Call it a male werewolf's G-spot," Jager said in a half-growl. "You bite me there, and I'll come."

Already feeling the first flutter of her climax, Daylen bit down on Jager's neck where it met his shoulder as her inner muscles rhythmically clamped down around his cock. He wrapped his arms around her waist and held her tightly to him as he came. His loud groans mingled with her whimpered moans.

Daylen turned her head to the side, then rested her cheek on Jager's shoulder and collapsed against his chest. She panted for breath. All she could do was put her arms around his waist and hold on. His still erect cock kept their bodies joined.

Once she could breathe evenly again, she lifted her head to gaze into Jager's light blue eyes. "If this will always be the result, I'll most definitely have to get the drop on you more often."

Jager got her to sit up. He cupped the side of her face and brushed his thumb across her cheek. "Are you really okay with this, Daylen? With us?"

Each time they made love, their mating bond grew stronger. With him buried deep inside her while she looked at his gorgeous face, she couldn't picture herself being with another man. She and Jager just seemed to click. Daylen didn't doubt they would butt heads over things now and then, but it was inevitable, considering they had strong personalities. Could she see herself uttering the words to him that she'd never said to any man before? Eventually, but it was just too soon.

"Yes. I've come to care a great deal about you. I'm not ready to say anything more than that, but that doesn't mean I'm not committed to making this work. We have a few issues that need to be discussed, though."

A sexy grin spread across Jager's face. "I have deeper feelings than caring a great deal for you, but I can wait until you're ready. You're mine now. That's all that matters. Now, what are these issues you want to discuss with me?"

Daylen ran a caressing hand along the thick slab of muscles on his chest. "We have to talk about how our mating is going to affect me doing my job, and then there's the whole topic of Roxie turning me into a werewolf."

"Before we touch on either of those subjects, I think we'll be more comfortable if we move to the bed."

In a show of just how strong he was, Jager managed to get off the floor with her still held in his arms and their bodies joined. He carried her to the unmade bed and placed her on the center of it on her back as he followed her down. His movements had his erection moving inside her pussy, which caused Daylen to gasp with pleasure.

He rested his weight above her, and said, "There. Much better. Let's start with the easy one—your job as a police officer. You'll quit. You don't need to work. I have plenty of money for the both of us. As you said yourself, you're now a Protector. It's basically the same kind of job, except on a smaller scale. Besides, the long hours we would have to be separated while you did your shift wouldn't work out. We'd never make it." Jager slowly slid his cock in and out of her in a lazy glide.

Daylen took her bottom lip between her teeth and moaned. "All right. I can do that." Another moan pushed out of her as he continued to slowly thrust between her legs. "That feels good. How am I supposed to be able to concentrate while you do that?"

He chuckled. "I think you'll manage. Now what about you being turned?"

She found she had to think a lot longer about that one. With Jager moving inside her, Daylen was having a hard time focusing on anything but the pleasure that built inside her once again.

"Ah...ah, I think I need to know exactly what it means to be a werewolf before I can make that decision. You're over a thousand years old and practically immortal. Does that mean werewolves can't die?"

Jager reached down and hooked one of her legs over his arm as he pumped his hips a little faster. "We can die. We're just a lot harder to kill, and we're very long-lived. The oldest our kind lives around three thousand years. So if you let Roxie turn you, we'll have more than a few centuries to be together instead of a single mortal lifetime." His eyes glowed as he gazed into hers. "And, Daylen, I want to have every day of those centuries. I know the choice is yours, and you would have to eventually give up your family and friends, but I don't want to lose you before I have to."

She looked at Jager and saw what she could only describe as love shining in his eyes. She would take that final step to make them mates in every way. No man had ever looked at her the way he was now. "I really don't have any family. My mom died when I was ten, and my dad passed away three years ago. The only family I have is my dad's brother, his wife, and my cousins. We've never been close, even when my dad was still alive. So they won't miss me. The only close friend I have is Nick. He's a cop at my precinct. It'll be hard leaving him, but I'll have a few years before I have to worry about him noticing I'm not aging."

"Is Nick the cop you were talking to in the alley the other day?"

Daylen smiled. "You *were* watching us?"

"Of course. He's also lucky he never touched you or I would have had to take it out on his hide."

She reached up and tucked Jager's long hair behind his ears. "Nick is very happily married, and his wife is very pregnant with their first child. So he's no threat."

Jager bent his head and kissed her long and hard. After he pulled away, he asked, "So we've worked out the first topic of discussion, what about the second? From what you said about your family and friends, do I take it you're willing to let Roxie turn you?"

"More than willing," she said with meaning in her voice. "We're mates. We should be mates in every sense of the word."

With a low growl, Jager kissed her once again as he moved more forcefully inside her pussy. Daylen moaned into his mouth and held on to his biceps as he brought her arousal to a fevered pitch. As she came, he came with her. She put her arms around her mate and held him tight once he collapsed on top of her.

CHAPTER ELEVEN

Jager and Daylen had just gotten out of the shower in the en suite when someone knocked on his bedroom door. He quickly wrapped a towel around his waist and went to answer it while she stayed in the bathroom.

He cracked open the door to find Dirk on the other side with his cell phone held against his chest. "Daylen's detective friend is on my cell. I figured she'd want to talk to him."

At the sound of footsteps coming up behind him, Jager looked over his shoulder and saw Daylen with a towel wrapped around her, walking toward him. Once she reached his side, she said to Dirk, "I'll talk to Ted."

Dirk passed Daylen his cell phone. Jager and Dirk quietly waited as she talked to the man on the other end. After a few minutes, she ended the call and then handed it back to Dirk.

"Ted came through again," she told them with a smile.

Jager nodded and then turned to Dirk. "Tell the others that Daylen and I will be down in a few minutes."

Dirk nodded, then left to head downstairs.

Jager closed the bedroom door and turned to watch Daylen getting dressed. He lovingly ran his gaze over her body. She had curves in all the right places and had enough muscle on her that he didn't have to worry she would break in his arms. Even though she wasn't ready to tell him she loved her, he already loved her.

If he hadn't have been able to fall in love with her practically at first sight, his mating urge never would have kicked in to tell him she was his.

Realizing Daylen had finished dressing and he still only wore a damp towel around his hips, Jager dropped it to the floor and then scooped up his jeans. He felt her gaze following his movements as he pulled them up his legs before he fastened them at his waist. He went to his dresser and took out a clean dark-blue T-shirt. He yanked it on over his head, then turned to face her. Her eyes most definitely had a heated look to them that made him wish they didn't have to go downstairs.

As if Daylen had read his mind, she said, "Don't even suggest it. I have to tell the others what Ted told me. And besides, you just had me a minute ago in the shower."

He grinned. "You enjoyed it, though."

She shook her head and smiled. "Yes, but you're going to have to feed me first before we have another marathon of sex. If I don't get some food into me soon, I'll start wasting away."

Jager crossed to her and then put his hands on the sides of her waist. He brushed a gentle kiss across her lips. "We can't have that. After we've had our meeting with the others, we can go to the kitchen and get something to eat."

They left his bedroom hand in hand and headed downstairs. They found the others once again congregated in the living room. Much to Jager's surprise, he saw Beowulf and Roxie were still there.

After guiding Daylen to the couch to where Beowulf and Roxie sat, he had Daylen sit next to the other woman while he lowered himself onto the arm. He said to the other couple, "I thought the two of you would have left by now."

"We thought it best to stay to hear what that police detective Daylen knows could come up with," Beowulf replied. "Plus, if we'd left, Saskia would have sent a few of your brothers along to watch over Roxie. We didn't think it would be fair."

"Enough chitchat over there," Leif said from one of the armchairs. "What did your buddy have to say, Daylen?"

"Well, first off," she said, "Ted couldn't find anything on a Miles Jensen with the description I'd given him. No driver's license, no social security number and no properties under that name either."

Saskia nodded, and said, "Miles must be using an alias. He isn't stupid. He would know if he used his real name we'd have found him by now."

"Ted did manage to find out who the owner is listed for the warehouse. It's owned by a company named Denco Ltd. Ted also figures it has to be a dummy corporation, because he couldn't find anything else out about it. After he did a little more digging, he found an old factory that's no longer in use was recently purchased by a company named Wolfen Inc., which also happens to be a subsidiary of Denco Ltd."

Kye snorted. "Miles couldn't come up with better names than that? We'd never be able to guess a werewolf owned those properties with names like those," he said sarcastically.

Saskia spoke up before anyone else could add anything more. "What's the address of the factory, Daylen? Some of us will check it out while the others stay behind and watch over Roxie. Jager, since you and Daylen are newly mated and shouldn't be separated just yet, I suggest the two of you stay behind." As Daylen opened her mouth, Saskia said, "I know you're one of us now, Daylen, but you still have much to learn about werewolf kind." She smiled. "Plus, newly mated couples tend to be a little distracted. You and Jager will have more pleasurable pursuits on your minds."

Jager couldn't argue with that, and he guessed neither could Daylen since she closed her mouth and blushed slightly. He put an arm around her shoulders and pulled her over so she leaned against his side while Saskia split up the other Protectors.

In the end, she decided Roan and Ansley would stay behind with Jager and Daylen. Saskia, Eli, Skylar, Kye, Leif, and Dirk would be the ones to scout out the factory. Jager was a little disappointed that he would miss out on the action, but Daylen wasn't ready to face a pack of lone wolves if the factory ended up panning out. And he wanted her turned before she had to confront any of Miles' men. As a mortal, she was just too vulnerable.

* * * *

After the others had left to check out the factory, Jager and Daylen raided the fridge. Since it was already well past noon, he made her a thick sandwich layered with cold cuts, cheese and lettuce. Having eaten nothing since dinner the night before, she ate with gusto. He must have been just as hungry because his practically disappeared in two large bites.

Their empty bellies now taken care of, she and Jager joined the other two couples. The men eventually got on the topic of weightlifting and ended up heading to the basement to check out the weights while the women stayed in the living room.

Roxie smiled at Daylen, and said, "It would seem you've managed to tame the brash warrior. Both times I've seen Jager today he didn't have his sword strapped to his waist as if it were one of his vital organs."

"Does he really carry it around that much?" Daylen asked.

Ansley answered her. "Afraid so. And Roxie is forever trying to take Jager's sword from him."

Roxie snorted. "Not that I get it away from him for very long. He always manages to swipe it back when I'm not looking." She grew serious. "So have you really adjusted to the fact you're mated to a werewolf, Daylen?"

She nodded. "Yes. I'm a bit surprised by how easily I have. If you would have asked me last week if I believed werewolves existed, and that I would be a mate to one, I probably would have suggested I take you to nearest shrink. It has all happened so fast."

"That's the mating urge for you," Roxie said. "It makes you feel as if you're on a runaway train. It's even worse for the males. They can't focus on anything else but the woman who is meant for them."

Daylen had noticed how more controlled Jager seemed now that their mating bond was in place. "About this not wanting to be separated, is it really that bad?"

"Yes, it is," Roxie said. "And I'm speaking from experience. Ansley has gone through it as well."

The other woman shuddered. "You feel as if you've lost your mind. All I could think about was that something had happened to Roan, and that I had to get back to him, no matter the cost." Ansley smiled. "The only good side about the separation is the explosive sex that happens after you get back together. I only suggest that if you ever are separated from Jager for a long time, make sure you get away from other people as fast as you can or you'll give them an eyeful."

"I'll keep that in mind," Daylen said. "Maybe it won't affect me that badly. I've always been a bit of a loner. I'm sure I'll be able to handle it."

Roxie gave her a look that said she didn't think so. "If you're that sure of yourself, why don't you test your theory? Jager obviously didn't let you bring a change of clothes when he brought you here handcuffed last night. Why don't you go to your place and grab some and then come back? I bet even that short amount of time will get to you."

"All right, but I don't have my car here. How am I supposed to get to my place?"

"Take Jager's. I noticed it wasn't parked in the garage when Beowulf and I arrived. And if you're going to do this, you should probably slip away before he realizes what you're up to. He'll try to stop you if he finds out."

Daylen stood. "You're on."

She quickly left the living room and headed up to Jager's bedroom. The keys to the Camaro and her house sat on top his dresser. After snagging both sets, she hurried back downstairs and then slipped out of the mansion. As she drove the Camaro down the long drive and no hue and cry was raised, she figured she'd made a clean getaway.

* * * *

By the time Daylen arrived at her house, she already felt a little out of sorts, as if everything wasn't quite right. It was less than an hour since she'd left the mansion in Marin County and already she missed not being with Jager. If this was only the start of how it felt when she was away from him, no wonder Roxie hadn't believed her when she'd said she may not be as affected. Daylen could only think about getting back to him.

Once she was inside the house, she almost ran into her bedroom. Daylen quickly stripped off the clothes she wore and then put on fresh ones. She made short work of stuffing another change of clothing into an athletic bag.

Daylen was so distracted with thoughts of returning to Jager she almost missed the fact a man stood blocking her way to the front door. Moving faster than a mortal could, he had her by the throat and gasping for air in a matter of seconds. As she frantically tried to pry his hand off her, she realized this was the same lone wolf Jager had been fighting in the alley the first night she'd seen him.

The lone wolf eased his hold only enough so she could drag air into her lungs. "You recognize me, don't you, little cop? I can also smell Jager's scent all over you. He's claimed you as his mate. I'm surprised he let you out by yourself, but it does make this a whole lot nicer. You're his Achilles heel now." He dragged her toward the front door. "It's time for you to meet my boss."

Daylen dropped the athletic bag she'd been carrying and tried to punch him, but all that did was to have him throw her against the wall hard enough so her head cracked against it. With black spots flickering before her eyes, the lone wolf easily flipped her onto her stomach and then tied her hands behind her back with a length of rope he'd pulled out of his jacket pocket. He threw her over his shoulder and walked out of the house.

CHAPTER TWELVE

Jager put down the dumbbell he'd been using to show Beowulf one of the exercises he did. Something had suddenly felt not right. He frowned as he tried to figure out what the hell bothered him.

"What's the matter?" Roan asked. "You look strange."

"I don't know. If I didn't already know Daylen was upstairs with Roxie and Ansley, I would think she wasn't in the mansion. I feel as if I really need to be with her to make sure she's okay. I've never heard of the separation bothering mates when they're in the same place but not in the same room. We haven't been down here that long."

"It shouldn't be affecting you like that," Beowulf said. He looked at the basement's ceiling. "Maybe you should check on Daylen."

As Jager rushed up the basement stairs, Roan and Beowulf followed him. Once he reached the living room and only saw Roxie and Ansley there, he asked, "Where's Daylen?"

Roxie answered. "She went to her place."

Jager took a deep breath to stop himself from bellowing at Roxie. "And why did she go there alone?"

"She didn't want to believe how badly she would feel if the two of you were separated, so I bet her she couldn't go to her place for a change of clothes and come back here without feeling as if she'd gone crazy. And she took your car, by the way."

Jager wanted nothing more than to take Roxie by the shoulders and give her a good shake, but with Beowulf standing beside him, Jager didn't think the other male would let him manhandle his pregnant mate like that.

Instead, he took another deep breath and squeezed his hands into fists at his side. "I'm going to need someone to drive me to Daylen's house. Now."

"Since Roxie in a way caused this," Beowulf gave his mate a stern look, "we'll drive you."

Roan quickly said, "And Ansley and I will follow you guys in my car. Saskia will have my head if I don't go with you."

To Jager, it seemed to take a lot more time than was necessary for them to get on the road. Soon Beowulf's Mercedes Benz was on the highway with Roan's Lexus following closely behind.

Once they crossed the Golden Gate Bridge, Jager gave Beowulf Daylen's address. After they pulled onto her street and neared her bungalow, he saw his Camaro parked in the driveway. It made some of the anxiety he felt go away, knowing she was still there. As soon as Beowulf stopped the car, Jager jumped out of the back and then ran to the front door. He paused when he saw it stood slightly ajar.

He pushed the door wider, and called, "Daylen?" His gaze landed on the athletic bag that sat in the middle of the entrance hallway. "Daylen? Where are you?"

When she didn't answer, Jager quickly did a tour of the house. Daylen wasn't anywhere to be found. His gut told him something was very wrong. He returned to the front hall and saw Beowulf, Roxie, Roan, and Ansley had come into the house.

"She's not here," he said as he met their gazes. He took a deep breath. A low growl left his throat. "I smell the scent of another werewolf."

Roan nodded. "I smell it too. I don't recognize it."

"I do," Jager said through gritted teeth. "It's the scent of a lone wolf. The one I fought in the alley. Miles' man."

Jager would have barged out of the house and gone looking for Daylen if Roan hadn't grabbed his arm to stop him. "Hold up. You won't be able to find him on your own, Jager. He more than likely has a car, which means there won't be a scent trail to follow.

If he is Miles' man, he'll probably take Daylen to him. There's a good chance the factory Saskia and the others went to check out is his headquarters. They have to be there already. I'll call her and let her know what's going on. They'll be able to get Daylen back."

Feeling completely helpless, Jager nodded. As Roan took out his cell phone and called their sister, Jager felt as if he wanted to kill someone. Without thinking about it, he reached for his sword. His hand only encountered the material of his jeans, and he realized, for the first time in his adult life, he'd left his home without taking his sword with him.

* * * *

Unable to really move since her captor had used another length of rope he'd had in his car to tie her ankles together, Daylen could only sit in the front seat and watch the streets go by. Once busy downtown gave way to industrial buildings, she knew Ted had been right about the factory. It had to be Miles' new headquarters. That realization also gave her some hope. Saskia and the others who had gone along with her to investigate the factory should be there. Somehow Daylen had to make sure they saw her so they could get her away from the lone wolf.

Worried what Miles would do to her if his man managed to deliver her to him, Daylen also had to deal with the wild emotions going through her the longer she was away from Jager. He'd been right. There was no way in hell she would be able to keep working as a police officer. A ten-hour shift away from him would kill her. She'd been a fool to think she could handle this better than Roxie and Ansley had.

Once the lone wolf drove onto the street where the factory was located, and where Saskia and the others investigated, he slowed as he drove by a black Cadillac Escalade parked at the side of the road about a half block away from the building. He continued on and drove around to the back of the factory. After parking, he walked around to the passenger side and then hefted Daylen over his shoulder like a sack of potatoes.

He entered the building and took her to the main area of the factory. Outlines of the machinery that had been used at one time still marked the grimy cement floor. Unable to see what was in front of him, Daylen heard the lone wolf talk to someone who was out of her range of sight.

"Miles, I brought you a present. I figured you'd want her sooner rather than later." He put Daylen onto her feet and jerked her around to face Miles.

She found the man standing in front of her to be exactly as Saskia had described her brother. He had almost white-blond hair that brushed the tops of his shoulders. His eyes, the same distinctive violet color as his sister's, stared at the lone wolf with fury. Miles would be considered extremely good-looking, but the cruelty that lurked in his eyes took away from some of his handsomeness.

Miles backhanded the lone wolf. "You idiot. I never gave you permission to abduct Jager's mate. I wasn't ready to play that card yet. Now you've lost us the upper hand. With my bitch of a sister and her dumbass Protectors lurking around here, you've put me in a situation I had no wish to be in." As the lone wolf opened his mouth to speak, Miles backhanded him again. The lone wolf wiped a trickle of blood from the corner of his mouth. "Get out of here before I do more than bloody your mouth."

Once the lone wolf walked away, Miles centered his attention on Daylen. She lifted her chin and stared back. "Just let me go. No one has gotten hurt, and no damage has been done yet."

Miles chuckled. "You are a tough one." He pulled a knife out of the top of one of his boots and then cut the rope around Daylen's ankles. After he put it away and straightened, he roughly grabbed her by the arm and pulled her closer as he said, "Your presence does throw a wrench in the works, but I can use you to keep the Protectors at bay."

He jerked her arm to get her moving and took her outside to the front of the building. Miles called out, "You all might as well come out of hiding. I know you're there. Plus, I have something that belongs to you."

One by one, Saskia and the men with her appeared from different spots on the factory's property. They all came to stand at a cautious distance from Miles and Daylen.

Saskia took a step closer before she spoke. "Let her go, Miles. Your beef isn't with Daylen. Just let her go and you can walk away."

Miles shook his head. "As if there was ever a chance of you capturing me. You see, sister, you aren't the only one who inherited some of our grandmother's gift of sight. Mine may not be as strong as yours, but twice it has allowed me to see when you would be coming. The factory is useless to me now, and you'll find nothing inside it. I'll move on, and our little cat-and-mouse game will continue."

With a hard shove that sent Daylen sprawling painfully on the ground, Miles turned and took off at a run. Saskia rushed over to her and helped her stand. Kye would have gone after Miles, but Saskia said, "Let him go, Kye. We have Daylen back." She turned to Skylar. "Call Jager and tell him Daylen is safe, and that we'll get her to him as soon as we possibly can." She used a knife she carried to cut the ropes around Daylen's wrists. "Sorry you had to be introduced to Miles that way. He didn't hurt you, did he?"

Daylen shook her head. "No. The lone wolf had only just brought me here. Miles was more than a little pissed to see me. I guess I didn't work into his plans for the day."

"Be grateful for that. Come on. Let's get you to Jager. Both of you must be feeling the separation."

Now that she was no longer a captive the need to be with Jager pressed down on Daylen harder. It almost felt as if her very soul cried out for him. As she followed Saskia and the men to the Escalade that she'd seen parked on the street, her feelings for her mate were stronger than she'd wanted to admit before. The time away from him showed her that even though their relationship had taken off at lightning speed, she really did love Jager. Why else would her soul yearn to be with him so strongly?

Once they'd all crammed into the Escalade, Skylar, who drove, wasted no time getting Daylen to her bungalow. As they raced down the streets, she was surprised no other police officers pulled them over for speeding. If she had been on patrol, Skylar would have gotten a ticket by now, but in her present condition, she couldn't have cared less. She just needed to get to Jager.

After the Escalade pulled over in front of her house, Daylen jumped out and ran up to the front door. She burst into the bungalow and threw herself into Jager's open arms as he met her in the front hall.

Heedless of the others who'd been with Jager, and who quickly headed out the front door, Daylen met Jager's lips halfway when he claimed her mouth in a heated kiss. She moaned as she clutched the front of his shirt and pushed him up against the wall. The anxiety and sense that something had happened to him melted away now that she could touch him. They were replaced with the need to have his cock buried deep inside her, joining them in the most intimate of ways.

Daylen broke contact with Jager's lips and tugged at his jeans. Her breath came in labored pants as she opened his fly and took his hard cock in her hand. "I need to have you inside me. Right now."

Jager groaned and thumbed her nipple through her shirt. "I need you just as badly. It's the mating bond. The separation."

Daylen pumped her hand a few times on his shaft, then released it so she could tug Jager's jeans down past his hips. "I promise never to leave like that again. I was an idiot to think I would be strong enough to take it. Now make love to me."

Jager switched their positions and quickly undid her jeans and shucked them down her legs. Once Daylen kicked them the rest of the way off, he lifted her, pressed her back against the wall, and sheathed his cock inside her pussy with one stroke. She put her legs around his waist and wrapped her arms around his neck. He thrust his hips into her, causing her body to coil ever tighter. The head of his shaft butted against her cervix with each stroke in. She let out a whimpered moan as her climax thundered to the surface. With one final stroke, he buried his face into the crook of her neck and groaned loudly as he came with her.

Still feeling little aftershocks deep inside her pussy, Daylen pulled the hair elastic from Jager's hair and tossed it away. She ran her hands through the long, silky length of it.

Jager lifted his head and chuckled. "If you keep doing that, I'm going to run out of hair elastics."

Daylen cupped his chiseled face. "I like your hair better when it isn't pulled back. That way I can run my hands through it."

"If you like it that much, I can keep it down."

She grew serious. Locking her gaze to his, she said, "I love you, Jager. I don't want to ever lose you. I'll get Roxie to turn me as soon as she can."

Jager tenderly kissed. "I love you as well, Daylen. I think I fell for you the first time you brought me down in that alley. Knowing my mate can stand up to me turns me on like nothing else." He gave her a sexy grin. "I think we'll hold off on getting Roxie to turn you, at least for today. You're going to be a little too busy to have her use the spell on you. We have some lost time to make up, and I intend to spend it in bed with my mate."

Daylen smiled and gave his still-hard cock a squeeze with her inner muscles. "That can easily be arranged. I don't think I could come up with a better way to spend a Sunday than making love to the man I love."

With his strong arms supporting her, Jager pulled away from the wall and walked toward the bedroom. Daylen kissed the side of his neck. Once she reached where his shoulder and neck met, she bit him. The hall floor suddenly rose to meet her, and soon she didn't care that they never made it to the bed.

The End

LEIF'S SURRENDER

Jaden notices the sexy hunk in her cashier's line. But she knows with her plain looks and glasses he'd never notice her. So when he returns to the grocery store the next day and kisses her senseless in front of everyone, she can only hope she'll see him again.

Leif swears he'll never be permanently mated, but when he feels his mate at a grocery store while buying pregnant Roxie ice cream, his world turns upside down. Drawn to his would-be mate, he finds fighting his mating urge is harder than he expects. If he can only hold out long enough to let nature run its course, he can get on with his life. But resisting her is impossible, and he needs to claim her as his.

CHAPTER ONE

"You want me to do what?" Leif asked Roxie with a scowl.

"You heard me. I want you to run to the store and get me some ice cream."

"Why?"

Roxie rolled her eyes. "Well, I'd get it myself, but since you guys won't let me go anywhere alone now that I'm showing, you're going to have to get it for me. I ate the last of what I had last night, and now I'm craving ice cream—bad."

"Can't you get Jager or Daylen to get it instead?"

Leif hated going to the grocery store. He avoided it like the plague. The few times he'd gone shopping, he'd had the back of his heels run over by unobservant mortals with their carts, which was beyond annoying. Even worse were those who came to a sudden stop in the middle of an aisle, oblivious to those behind them.

"No, they can't," Roxie said. "They've gone a few times for me already. It's time you took your turn."

Leif made one last attempt to get out of it. "What about Beowulf? He's your mate. He should be the one getting it for you."

"He's not here, as you well know. It could be hours before he gets back from Wade and Taryn's."

Wade was Beowulf's younger brother. He and his mate, Taryn,

owned a winery in Napa Valley. Taryn had inherited it from her uncle, so once she and Wade became mates, Wade had moved in with her.

Damn. It looked as if he wasn't going to be able to escape making the dreaded trip to the grocery store. Knowing Jager, he'd probably put Roxie up to it. As one of Roxie's Protectors, they'd lived together for centuries. Jager had to have known Leif would balk at the idea. The big idiot was probably having a good chuckle over it too, knowing full well Roxie wouldn't back down. Jager might now be mated to Daylen, who used to be a police officer, but that didn't mean he still didn't do or say whatever the hell he wanted.

Leif breathed a heavy sigh. "All right. I'll get your ice cream this time, but don't expect me to do this too often."

Roxie smiled and put her hand on her distended belly. "Just think, in three more months, the baby will be here and I won't have any more cravings. Then you won't have to worry about it."

Leif turned on his heel, then left Roxie's mansion before he headed for his black Cadillac CTS. He climbed into the driver's side and then headed down the winding drive to the street. He was a warrior, having trained for centuries with the rest of the Protectors for the day when the foretold one would come. Roxie was the foretold one. It was his duty to protect her against being abducted by other werewolves to use as a figurehead to rule the packs. Running to the grocery store to buy ice cream wasn't part of the job description.

Leif pulled into the parking lot of the store closest to Roxie's place and found an empty space, then parked. He got out, slammed the car door a little harder than necessary, and then headed inside. Forgoing a shopping cart, he walked through the large store, searching for the frozen foods aisle. After he finally found it, he stood in front of the glass freezer doors staring at all the different types of ice cream. *Well, hell.* He'd forgotten to ask Roxie what kind she wanted.

He reached inside the front pocket of his jeans for his cell phone, then remembered he'd left it at home. He'd forgotten to charge it during the night, and it now sat on his dresser in his room doing just that. Wasn't this just his day? Making an executive decision, he opened the freezer and grabbed cartons of vanilla, chocolate, and butterscotch ripple. Roxie should like at least one of them. He juggled the ice-cold containers in his arms and walked to the checkout area.

Leif went to stand at the end of the express line and looked up to the front and groaned. An older lady was paying for her purchase, counting out change, one coin at a time. Hopefully, the other customers ahead of him wouldn't take so long. The ice cream was damn cold. Already his fingers were feeling numb. He was rethinking his decision to not take a cart, but he wasn't going to leave the lineup just to get one now.

The line inched forward until he reached the conveyor belt. More than happy to put the ice cream down—which was more than likely already starting to melt—Leif shook out his frozen hands.

He bit back a curse when the cart behind him pushed into the back of his thighs. Leif turned to find a woman who looked to be in her forties staring at him. She quickly apologized. He smiled and had the satisfaction of watching her jaw drop. After telling her it was okay, he turned back around and smiled even more. He was used to the effect he had over mortal women. Standing at six foot five, his body well-padded with muscle, and with his werewolf good-looks, he drew a lot of feminine stares. Not that he complained about it. He loved women. All women. Young, old, he flirted with them all. Most male werewolves longed to find their mates, the one woman their soul would join with, but not Leif. He never wanted to be that tied down.

Finally, at long last, it was his turn. He muttered to himself about pregnant women and their cravings, then took a deep breath once he came to stand across from the cashier. As if he'd been sucker punched in the gut, Leif froze in place and struggled to draw another big breath of air into his lungs. His cock went instantly rock-hard, and the unthinkable happened—his mating urge kicked into high gear.

Leif settled his gaze on the cashier, the woman who was to be his mate, and took in her mousy brown hair that she wore pulled back in a high ponytail. He couldn't see what color her eyes were behind her stylish glasses, because she was busy looking down as she rang up his purchases. Her face, he found cute in a plain sort of way. She wasn't ugly, but she was by no means a raving beauty. And she was not at all what he expected his mate to look like.

She might not be heart-stoppingly beautiful, but she appealed to all Leif's senses, in a big way. Her scent stirred his body like no other. He wanted to jump across the counter, rip the glasses off her face, pull her hair loose, and devour her lips with his. He wanted to hear her make little moaning noises as he ground his aching cock against her pussy. And his wolf wanted to claim her as his.

The sound of her voice brought him out of the haze of lust that had descended over him. He looked at her and asked, sounding like a complete idiot, "Wha...what?"

She lifted her gaze to his. Her eyes were brown. "I asked if you wanted paper or plastic," she said in a quiet voice that seemed to take hold of his cock and make it throb even more.

"Plastic is fine," he said.

His voice sounded gruff with need, even to his own ears. A spark of interest flashed in her eyes before she bagged the ice cream. Their fingers brushed when he handed her the money to pay. That simple touch caused his cock to jerk hard. Leif had to bite back a growl of need. If he wasn't careful, he'd be howling like the wolf he was, and his eyes would be glowing mutedly for all the mortals to see.

Once she handed him his change, he made sure their fingers didn't come in contact, and he found his gaze settling back on her face. The mating urge had well and truly dug its claws into him. Leif panicked. He grabbed the bag of ice cream and did the one thing his mating urge was *not* screaming at him to do—he hightailed it out of there.

* * * *

Jaden turned her head to watch the guy she'd just run up beat a hasty retreat to the store's exit. She let out a breathy sigh and turned back to cash out the next customer in her cash register's line. She went through the motions of scanning each item, but her mind wasn't totally there. It was still focused on the exceptionally good-looking guy who'd bought the three containers of ice cream.

She'd noticed him as soon as he got in her line. She would have had to be blind not to. He stood about a foot taller than she, had a body that made her want to drool, and a face that reminded her of a male model's. His not-too-short auburn hair had just brushed the collar of his black, formfitting T-shirt. The blue jeans he wore were faded and snug in all the right places. She'd had to fight not to let her gaze zero in on the front of them to check him out.

As he moved up in line, Jaden couldn't stop herself from stealing glances, knowing that looking at him was about all she'd be able to do. Men as good-looking as him rarely acknowledged she existed. With her plain looks and glasses, she was pretty much overlooked half the time. She was used to it, therefore, she never had any high expectations when it came to good-looking men.

When she'd asked him if he wanted paper or plastic and his gaze had latched on to hers, she'd had to blink a few times to make sure her eyes hadn't played tricks on her. He'd stared at her as if he were ready to jump over to her side and devour her in one bite. Jaden shivered just thinking about it. Having his blue-eyed gaze greedily lock with hers, had her wishing for things she knew would never happen. Her body, though, thought otherwise. Her nipples had hardened beneath her shirt, and her pussy had clenched with the need to be filled.

Of course nothing went beyond that. Once he'd paid, even making sure she didn't touch him inadvertently when she handed him his change, he'd practically run out of the store. He may have looked at her as if he wanted to devour her, but obviously that really hadn't meant anything. *C'est la vie.* That was the story of *her* life.

After she charged out the last customer in line, she put a sign on the end of the conveyor belt, directing customers to the next cash register. It was her break time, and she was ready for it. Working as a cashier for a large grocery store chain wasn't exactly her dream job, but it was better than not working at all. Her life was in a bit of a funk, and no matter what she tried, she couldn't change things. One day seemed to bleed into another.

As she headed for the small coffee shop inside the store, Jaden had to admit getting stared at by an exceptionally hot guy was a step away from the same old, same old. Who knew, if she was lucky, he'd come to the store again. It was kind of pathetic to think catching a glimpse of a good-looking guy, who she didn't have a chance in hell of ever really knowing, was the highlight of her day.

* * * *

By the time Leif arrived at Roxie's place, he still hadn't gotten himself totally under control. The shock of finding his mate hadn't worn off yet. It was like a bad dream come true. There was a battle going on inside him. His wolf side, and the mating urge that rode him, had him yearning to go back to the store and claim his mate. The part of him that liked being unmated and wanted to stay that way, fought it tooth and nail.

Leif turned off the car and grasped the steering wheel with both hands as he smacked his forehead on it a few times. He had to get it together. He could resist. All he had to do was stop thinking about her and how much he wanted to strip her naked and taste every inch of her body before he sank his aching cock inside her pussy. He'd be so deep inside her she'd never want to let him go. He could almost feel her inner walls clutching his shaft as he rode her.

He groaned and smacked his forehead on the steering wheel again. *Grrr*, he had to stop thinking that way. There was no way in hell he was going to sleep with her. If he did, their souls would join, and he'd be tied to her forever. Once werewolves were mated, they couldn't stand to be away from their mates for long periods of time. In the beginning, a few hours apart felt like days. Their minds would play tricks on them, making them think something had happened to the other. Leif didn't want that kind of commitment with a woman. Just thinking he was close to that very thing scared the bejesus out of him.

After giving himself a good shake, Leif grabbed the bag of ice cream off the passenger seat and then climbed out of the car. Before he went inside, he had to make sure he didn't show any outward sign of what had happened in the grocery store. If he did, Roxie would pick up on it and make his life a living hell. Like a dog, or a wolf, with a bone, she'd ride his ass until he eventually caved and went after his mate. He didn't need that kind of interference in his life, thank you very much.

He walked through the door and then headed to the kitchen to put the ice cream in the freezer. Leif had just placed the grocery bag on the counter next to the fridge when Roxie came into the room.

Leif kept his back to her and opened the freezer door. "You didn't tell me what flavor to get, so I picked what I thought you'd like."

As Roxie came to stand beside him and her shoulder brushed his arm, he couldn't stop himself from jerking away from the contact. He was still wound up as tight as a top.

"What's the matter with you?" Roxie asked. She ran her gaze over him. "You look a bit...tense. Did something happen while you were out?"

"No. Having to go to a grocery store tends to do that to me. So, are the flavors I picked all right?"

Roxie gave him another onceover, then looked at the ice cream containers he'd put into the freezer. "They're good. Chocolate, I'm kind of meh on, but I like the other two. And if shopping gets you this strung out, I won't send you again."

"I'll take my turn just so long as you don't expect me to pick up more than a couple of items."

He slammed the freezer door hard enough to shake the fridge. Why had he said that? Did he now have runaway-mouth syndrome? He couldn't go back to that grocery store. Ever. If he did, he'd be only setting himself up for his own doom. *Remember, dummy, you don't want a mate.*

He turned to face Roxie and found her staring at him with a strange look.

"What did my fridge ever do to you?" she asked.

"It slipped. All right?"

"Whatever you say."

Before Roxie could say anything more, he said, "I'm going to look for Jager."

"Why don't you do that? He's out in the backyard with Daylen, giving her another sword fighting lesson. She may not be able to disarm him with a sword yet, but she used her karate skills and knocked him on his butt. I never get sick of seeing that."

"Neither do I," he said as he left the kitchen.

Leif made a short detour to his car to get his sword out of the trunk before he headed to the backyard. Instead of sword practice,

Jager and Daylen were locked in a passionate embrace, kissing as if there were no tomorrow. Usually the sight of them—or one of the other two mated couples who lived in the Protectors' mansion—putting on such a display would leave him shaking his head. Now it just made him feel downright uncomfortable. It made him wish for things he didn't want *nor* need.

He walked closer to the couple and said what he'd normally say in such a situation. "Would the two of you go get a room? Is it necessary for me to see you sucking each other's lips off? You do anything more, and I'm liable to go blind."

Jager broke the kiss and moved to Daylen's side, then tucked her under his arm. "What's the matter, Leif? Jealous?"

"Hardly," he scoffed. He lifted his sword. "I came out here to see if you wanted some real competition."

"Hey," Daylen said. "I could take offense at that. I may not be as quick with a sword, but I can still kick both of your butts."

Jager kissed her temple. "Leif and I both know that, love. I, in particular, have learned that from firsthand experience, more than once."

When Jager and Daylen first met, she'd caught him sword fighting with another werewolf in an alley while she was on patrol. She'd even managed to get the drop on him, using a karate move her mate hadn't expected, and had almost ended up arresting him.

Daylen kissed Jager's cheek. "Don't you forget it. I guess I'll go inside and keep Roxie company while you two whack at each other." She headed across the lawn to the mansion.

Leif had just enough time to lift his sword to block Jager's when he swung it in his direction. Leif pulled his sword back to make a strike of his own. Jager's next blow had Leif spinning away. He used the momentum, making a slashing cut that would have sliced across Jager's ribs if the other male hadn't blocked it.

Letting the familiar rhythm of thrust and parry take over, Leif gave as good as he got. The stretch of his muscles, and the need to concentrate on Jager's next move, helped relieve some of the agitation the mating urge had caused. Leif had deliberately challenged Jager for that very reason. Jager was one of the best swordsmen of the Protectors. The man didn't go anywhere without his sword, and until recently, even slept with it in his bed.

The only one of the Protectors who could get the better of him was Saskia, their leader.

After fifteen minutes of intense swordplay, Jager backed up and lowered his sword. The tip of Leif's sword rested on the grass as he bent over, trying to catch his breath. "Give me a couple minutes." He panted. "Then we can go again."

Jager breathed just as hard. He used his hand to wipe sweat from his brow. "Is there something you want to tell me?"

"No. Why?"

"Well, for starters, you don't usually practice this hard. And for another, you're pounding on me as if you're trying to distract yourself from something."

Leif straightened. "You're the last person I thought would complain about a tough sword workout."

"Hey, I'm not complaining. The way you're acting just reminds me of how I was before Daylen and I became mates, and I had to convince Daylen not to arrest my ass every time she saw me." Jager gave Leif a hard stare, then scratched his chin. "If I didn't know better, I would say your mating urge has you in its claws and you're trying to ignore it. You weren't like this when we first arrived here, so I'm guessing it happened when you went to the store for Roxie."

Hearing Jager accurately guess what bothered him, Leif dropped his sword and jumped on the other warrior. Having caught Jager off guard, Leif knocked the larger man flat on his back and straddled his chest.

"What the fuck?" Jager said with a snarl.

Leif kept him pinned and lowered his head until he was in Jager's face. "Not a word. Do you understand me? Don't tell anyone, especially Roxie."

The scowl on Jager's face disappeared as he roared with laughter. "You found your mate," he said through peals of laughter. "You should see your face. You look as if the hounds of hell are after you."

Putting his hand over Jager's mouth, Leif quietly snapped back, "Would you keep it down?"

With a hard shove, Jager pushed Leif off him and then stood. His laughter had settled down to a chuckle. "So, it's true?"

"Yes," Leif said with disgust.

"You're a stupid fuck if you think you can run away from the mating urge. Accept it. Being mated is not as bad as you think. It's the best thing that ever happened to me. I never knew what I'd been missing in my life until I found Daylen."

Leif shook his head. "I will not accept it."

"So what do you plan to do? Just ignore it and hope it goes away?"

"That's exactly what I'm going to do."

Jager picked up his dropped sword and shook his head. "You're delusional if you think that. There is no *ignoring* the mating urge. What's the problem with her, besides you not wanting a mate? Is she a mortal?"

"Yes. There's *nothing* wrong with her. She's just not what I expected."

"She's ugly? If that is the case, you could always put a bag over her head while you screw her."

Leif let out a wolfish growl and launched himself at Jager, not liking the insult to his mate. Jager easily sidestepped him, then slowly backed toward the mansion.

"See, you've got it bad, Leif. You say you don't want her, but you're quick to defend her. You're buggered, man."

After watching Jager go inside, Leif picked up his sword. Shit, Jager was right. Of course the asshole had had to prove it to him in the most direct of ways. Jager may have been right, but that didn't mean Leif was going to meekly accept his fate. He was going to stay strong. He wasn't going to let the mating urge get the best of him.

CHAPTER TWO

Leif was in a foul mood. It was the next day, and he was once
again at Roxie's place. This time he was with Kye and Dirk.
He'd also volunteered to take another shift. Being there
would give him a good enough excuse not to talk himself into
going to the grocery store to see if his mate worked today.

He went into the kitchen, wondering if there was any coffee.
Sleep had not come easily last night. And what he did get was
filled with erotic dreams of claiming his mate. He'd woken up
with an aching hard-on. All he could think about was getting his
mate under him and taking her in every position imaginable.
Taking a cold shower this morning hadn't cooled his libido any.
Jerking off hadn't done much to take the edge off, either. Even
now, his cock was semi-hard.

Spotting the full pot of coffee, Leif crossed to it and then took a
clean mug out of the cupboard. It was almost noon, but it already
felt as if he'd been up for days. He needed caffeine, and lots of it.

Kye came into the kitchen and helped himself to a cup of coffee
as well. He glanced at Leif, went over to the fridge, took out the
milk, and dumped some into his mug. "You look like you didn't
get any sleep."

Leif shrugged. "It was just one of those nights when I couldn't
shut my brain off."

Kye put the milk back and then came to stand in front of him.

"I guess we'll be making another pot of coffee soon, then. Dirk and Roxie are upstairs again, doing whatever they do on her computer. Listening to them talk about it puts me to sleep."

Roxie was a web designer, and had been teaching HTML to Dirk for months now. He'd even coded a few web pages of his own. Not that Leif understood their technical speak anymore than Kye did.

"That should keep the two of them busy for hours," he said.

"Yeah, the two computer geeks are happily in their element."

"I wouldn't let Roxie hear you call her a computer geek," Beowulf said as he walked into the kitchen. He smiled at Kye. "I wish she'd stick to the computers, though. Lately, she's been experimenting with her magic to see what other neat tricks she has that the rest of us don't. And you know nothing good can come out of that."

Every werewolf had a spark of magic inside them. It was how he and the rest of his kind were able to shift into their wolf forms. Roxie had a little bit more than the average werewolf. She not only could shift into a wolf, she could also shift into a half-human/half-werewolf form. No other werewolf could do that.

She also could keep a werewolf in wolf form for twenty-four hours and freeze a person in place for as long as she wanted. Her great-great-great, etc. grandmother had been a mortal with magic of her own, or so Leif had been told. This magic had finally been passed down to Roxie, who supposedly was very similar in looks to her grandmother. Her grandfather, Royce, was still around to attest to that. Werewolves weren't immortal, but they were very long-lived, living up to three thousand years old. Royce was well over a thousand, and had found another mate who at one time had been a mortal, like his first.

Kye cringed. "I definitely don't want Roxie practicing anything new on me. She'd probably turn me into a toad or something just as awful."

Beowulf chuckled. "I don't think you have to worry about that. Do you think one of you could give me a hand? The new crib and change table need to be brought up to the baby's room and assembled."

Before Leif could say anything, Kye said, "I can help."

"Great," Beowulf said. "Since Roxie is busy with Dirk, I

thought we could get it set up for her."

Beowulf and Kye walked out of the kitchen. So much for the added distraction he was looking for. Leif was now left alone with his thoughts, which seemed to center around sex with a certain cashier at a certain grocery store. He took a sip of his hot coffee. This had to get better, but if he was going to be truthful with himself, the longer he held off claiming his mate, the worse the mating urge would get. And it wasn't as if he could search out another woman for some relief. Until it let him go, his cock wouldn't get hard for anyone else. God, he hated this.

He finished his coffee, put the mug on the counter and went to the fridge. He was in the mood for something to eat. He opened the door, but didn't see anything that appealed to him. He opened the freezer and spotted the ice cream he'd bought the day before. He reached in and took out the carton of vanilla.

He brought it to the kitchen table and opened it. Evidently, Roxie had already been into it, since a quarter of it was gone. Having a hankering for some, Leif grabbed a big spoon out of the drawer. Usually not much of an ice cream eater, he thought this one went down pretty good. It was a creamy vanilla with just enough sweetness. Before he knew it, he'd eaten well over half the container. There was nothing left but a few scrapings on the sides and the bottom.

"Oh, shit," he said in a murmur.

Roxie was going to kill him. Wanting to hide what he'd done, Leif dropped the spoon inside the carton, closed it, and hurriedly put it back into the freezer. What to do, what to do? He'd have to go to the grocery store and buy another one before she found out. Yeah, that's what he'd do.

Leif left the kitchen and planned to go upstairs and tell Kye where he was going when he saw Roxie coming down the stairs. She, of course, headed straight for the kitchen. He closed his eyes and waited.

Sure enough, he heard Roxie yell, "Hey! Who the hell ate all the vanilla ice cream? And who left a spoon in it?"

Leif decided it was better to make a getaway now and ran out of the mansion without telling Kye anything before Roxie came out of the kitchen. He was in his car and on the road to the store in less than a minute.

After arriving at the grocery store, all his senses came alive. Like a piece of metal drawn to a magnet, he headed inside. He sniffed the air, trying to single out one scent mixed in with the many. His mate's scent was there, but weak. Realizing what he was doing, Leif gritted his teeth and forced himself to walk to the freezer section. He was not there to search out his would-be mate. He would not try to find her. He would make his purchase and then get the hell out of there without seeing her.

Thinking that, he ended up doing the opposite. After he grabbed a carton of vanilla ice cream, he went unerringly to the end of the line where his mate's scent was the strongest. She was once again working the cash register for the express checkout.

The closer he came to her, the more her scent washed over him. His cock throbbed painfully, straining against the zipper of his jeans. The need to touch and taste every inch of the woman who had no idea what she meant to him just about overpowered Leif. The wolf inside him threw back its head with a howl of longing.

His body shook once it was finally his turn to pay. He tried to not look at her, but after he handed her his money, his gaze lifted to her face. She gave him a tentative smile, as if unsure of herself or what his reaction might be.

That small, sweet smile was just too much. With a groan, Leif leaned over the counter that separated them, wrapped his hand around the back of her neck, and pulled her lips to his. He hungrily kissed her, pushing his tongue inside her mouth to get his first taste of her. At first, her lips remained stiff and unyielding, but after he stroked her tongue, twining it with his, she kissed him back.

At the sound of loud whistles and catcalls, Leif jerked back to reality and to what he was doing. He abruptly released her and jumped away. His chest heaving as if he'd run a great distance, he looked at her. She stared at him, her glasses slightly askew, looking dazed. The scent of her arousal filled his nose. He had to fight the growl that threatened to push past his lips.

He snatched up the ice cream and dropped his gaze to her chest to look at the name tag pinned to her shirt. He only took the time to read it before he hurriedly walked away. With the taste of Jaden still on his tongue, Leif forced himself not to turn back and drag his mate away with him. He'd had one taste of her. It had to be enough.

* * * *

Jaden's brain had seemed to stop functioning. It took her more than a few seconds to gather her wits about her and remember where she was. She straightened her glasses as she tried to get her rapidly beating heart to slow. The left lens was smudged where his nose had brushed against it while he'd kissed her stupid.

Holy crap. The gorgeous guy had come back and kissed her as if there were no tomorrow. Kissed *her*, Jaden Pryce, the plain Jane who normally only attracted men who wouldn't know a dumbbell from a barbell. And what a kiss it'd been. The feel of his tongue stroking hers had set her body on fire. Wetness had pooled in her pussy while her nipples had tightened beneath her shirt, begging for some attention.

Ignoring the large smudge hindering her line of sight, Jaden rang up the remaining customers in her line before she closed her cash register for a quick washroom break. Out of the corner of her eye, she saw her friend, Vicky, shut down her register and follow.

Once inside the employee washroom, Vicky said, "You have to tell me who that hot hunk was who laid that kiss on you."

Jaden took off her glasses and ran them under the water in the sink before she grabbed some toilet paper from one of the stalls to dry them. "I have no idea."

"What do you mean you have no idea? From that kiss, I'd say you know each other pretty well."

Jaden put her glasses back on and shook her head. "It's true. I don't even know his name. I saw him here yesterday for the first time."

"Well, you must have made one hell of an impression if he came back today and kissed you as if he couldn't get enough of you. Why can't something like that happen to me?"

Jaden shook her head and smiled. "If I did, I have no idea how I did it. I doubt it'll happen again, and I doubt I'll see him again."

Vicky rolled her eyes. "If you believe that, you need your head seriously examined. A guy does not kiss a woman like that and then walk away forever. He'll be back. And I bet he'll hang around longer as well."

Jaden wanted to hope that would be the case, but she didn't have much confidence when it came to men. Yes, Mr. Gorgeous had kissed her senseless today, but he hadn't exactly stuck around afterward. At the end there, it almost seemed as if he realized he'd been doing something he shouldn't have. And he couldn't have been all that affected if he could just walk away without a word. She'd been lucky to even remain upright, let alone regain all her brain power. For a split second, when he'd stared at her after the kiss, her muddled mind had thought his eyes had glowed.

"Come on, Vic. Do you really think a guy like that would have any real interest in a woman who looks like me?"

"Stop selling yourself short. You're not that bad."

"I'm not that good either. Compared to you, I look like chopped liver."

Vicky was in her mid-twenties, blonde and blue-eyed with a face that had turned more than one male head when she walked by. She had no trouble getting boyfriends, and seemed to go through them faster than Jaden could keep track.

"I've offered to give you a makeover, and you always refuse. If you'd stop wearing your hair up in that tight pony tail and wore contacts, you'd get your fair share of guys."

"I told you I can't wear contacts. I tried them once, and I couldn't tolerate them. And I doubt changing my hairstyle would help that much."

"Fine, have it your way, but I still think you'll be seeing your hunk again soon." Vicky headed for the washroom door. "I'm going back to my register before both of us are missed. Don't take too long."

After Vicky left, Jaden stared at her reflection in the large mirror over the sink. Her lips were still a little puffy from being kissed. She touched them with her fingertips, remembering how it had felt to have his mouth moving over hers. It hadn't been the longest kiss in the world, but it was one she'd probably always remember. With a sigh, she tugged her ponytail tighter and left the washroom. She still had another four hours of her shift to get through. At least she had something to daydream about to help make the time pass more quickly.

* * * *

Leif managed to return to the mansion and sneak the new container of ice cream into the freezer with Roxie being none the wiser. He spent the remainder of the time there thinking about Jaden. The taste of her mouth, the feel of her lips against his, the texture of the soft skin at the back of her neck all seemed to have burned into his brain. Her scent was already permanently etched there. He would be able to latch on to it anytime, anywhere.

He stood at the living room window and watched Skylar's black Kawasaki Ninja ZX-14 motorcycle drive up to the front of the mansion. Skylar was attached to that bike as much as his true brother, Jager, was attached to his sword. Personally, Leif didn't know how Skylar could ride the thing, considering how low the handlebars were. Being a Supersport motorcycle, more suited for racing, the rider had to practically lean over the gas tank to reach them. Leif's back ached from him just thinking about how uncomfortable that position had to be for any length of time.

Skylar sat up, shut off the bike, and put down the kickstand. Skylar was to replace him and Kye. Dirk was going to stay overnight. Ever since they'd found out Roxie was pregnant, the Protectors had stepped up their protection duties. At least one of them now spent the night at Beowulf and Roxie's place. With Miles, Saskia's true brother—and at one time a Protector himself until he'd decided he'd rather switch sides—on the loose, they couldn't be too careful. If Miles got his hands on Roxie, especially in her condition, he'd use her to rule all the werewolf packs.

As far as they knew, Miles didn't know what Roxie looked like. They wanted to keep it that way, so they kept her well under wraps. And it wasn't as if the packs had a society paper that told everybody who was who. The leaders of every pack had come and sworn their allegiance to her, but the general population didn't know too much about her yet.

Leif met Skylar at the door once he walked into the mansion. "You can tell Kye I already left. He's upstairs with Beowulf. They've been working in the baby's room most of the day. Of course Roxie and Dirk are in her office doing their computer stuff."

Skylar nodded. "All right. Off on a hot date, are you?" he asked with a smile.

Leif stiffened. "No. Why would you say that?"

"You seem to be in an awful hurry to get out of here. I thought maybe you were going to Wulf's Den tonight to look for your next conquest."

Wulf's Den was the nightclub Beowulf owned. Werewolves and mortals went there. None of the mortals realized they were rubbing elbows with werewolves. Leif had picked up his fair share of women at the place.

"No," he said. "I'm not going to Wulf's Den tonight. Maybe I'm just in a hurry to get home, sit in front of the TV, and call it an early night."

Skylar burst out laughing. "Sure you are. What's the matter? Are you in a slump when it comes to finding women to sleep with? I haven't heard you bragging about taking a hot woman to bed for the last couple days."

Leif clenched his jaw and took a few deep breaths to keep from snapping his teeth at Skylar. As if he would sleep around on Jaden, now that he'd found her. She was the only one he wanted naked and moaning with pleasure in his bed. He wanted only her to stroke his cock, making him hard before she took him into her mouth. *Fuck.* There he went again, thinking about her as a mate. It wasn't going to happen. He wasn't about to give up his freedom. He liked it too much.

Not bothering to explain himself, Leif brushed past the other warrior and then headed outside. Before heading to the Protectors' mansion in Marion County, he'd go for a drive. He needed to get himself back under control before he went home. So far, Jager had kept his mouth shut about Leif finding his mate. He didn't need the others to figure it out as well.

After getting into his car, he drove onto the street and decided to drive wherever the mood struck.

CHAPTER THREE

What a long day. Jaden walked out of the grocery store, ready to go home, put her feet up, and relax in front of the TV. Her shift had ended up being longer than she'd been scheduled for. When one of the other girls had called in sick, the manager had asked her to stay for a few hours longer to help cover the shift. Not one to turn down the extra money, Jaden said she would do it. Now her feet and lower back ached from standing at her cash register for so long.

It was times like this that she wished she still had a car. When her old late-model vehicle had finally given up the ghost, she hadn't been able to afford to replace it. Not even another clunker. Jaden was now relegated to riding the bus to and from work, or anywhere else she couldn't walk to.

She crossed the parking lot, heading for the bus stop near the grocery store, and noticed the sporty black Cadillac parked close to the lot's entrance. If she were rich, that was the type of car she would buy for herself—one that cost an arm and a leg and had enough power under the hood to make an adrenaline junky envious.

Wanting to get a closer look, Jaden altered her course a little so she would have to walk right by it. She'd just peek inside to see if it was an automatic or manual drive. She always thought it was a shame that people who could afford sporty cars like that one ended up with an automatic transmission. Sports cars were meant to be manual drives.

At the driver's side, she stopped and looked inside. What she saw had her breath catching. The hot guy who'd kissed her earlier that day sat behind the steering wheel, smacking his forehead against it. Before she could think about what she was doing, she knocked on the closed window.

His straightened and turned his head to look through the window. Once his gaze latched on to her, he jumped. Jaden took a step back as he opened the car door and then slid out. His gaze never left her. He stared at her intently.

Jaden swallowed. He really was a big guy. Next to all those muscles and his much greater height, she felt small. She had to crane her neck to look him in the face. "Uh, sorry. I didn't mean to disturb you. I was just admiring your car, and then when I saw you smacking your forehead on the steering wheel, I..."

She let her words fall away. He didn't say anything, but continued to stare at her as he had both times she'd seen him in the store—with hunger blazing in his blue eyes. Her body, of course, reacted as it had before. An ache beat inside her pussy and wetness pooled. Every time she saw him, her libido kicked into high gear. She had to stop it or she'd end up not only being horny, but frustrated as well. He may have kissed her, but that didn't mean he would do anything more.

He had yet to say anything, and Jaden became uncomfortable. She cleared her throat and shifted her gaze to her feet. "As I said, I'm sorry. I'll leave you alone now." She'd begun to turn to continue on her way when his hand shot out and he wrapped his fingers around her wrist.

"Wait," he said. The husky tone of his voice sent a thrill through Jaden's body, straight to her pussy. "Don't go. Are you just getting off work?"

She turned back to face him. "Yes." A shiver of awareness zipped through her as he stroked his thumb along the inside of her wrist.

"I guess you wouldn't have eaten dinner yet. Would you like to go somewhere with me to eat?"

She blinked. "You want to take me out for a meal?" Jaden had to ask just to make sure she'd heard him right. He couldn't possibly want to take her out on a date. Could he?

"Yes. We could go to your place first so you can change." He stiffened, and said, "Shit. What the fuck am I doing?" He was so quiet she almost missed it.

Jaden yanked free of his grasp and slowly backed away. "Look, it's okay. I'll just be on my way. I don't want to miss my bus." She'd only taken a few steps when he captured her wrist again.

"Jaden, don't go. I...I'm having a hard time...just forget what I said."

"How do you know my name?" He glanced at her chest, and Jaden followed his gaze to her name tag pinned there. "Oh," she said, feeling her face take on a blush. "Right."

She looked up when he caressed a finger across her cheek. "Your cheeks turn a nice shade of pink when you blush," he said with a smile.

Of course that made her blush even more. "Uh, thanks."

"Since I don't have a tag, I'll tell you my name. I'm Leif."

Even his name was sexy. Jaden didn't think there wasn't anything about Leif that didn't scream sex. She pulled on her wrist, but he kept his fingers wrapped around it. "I really should go before I miss my bus. The next one won't come for another half hour."

"Forget the bus," he said as he pulled her toward the passenger side of his car. "I'll drive you, then we can go out for dinner."

Jaden yanked her wrist a few more times, but it didn't do any good. She found herself standing near the passenger door while Leif opened it. "It's really not necessary. I'm sure you'd rather be doing something else besides driving me home." *Like going out on a date with a gorgeous model who matches you in looks.*

Leif's answer was to pull her against his wide chest and lower his lips to hers. He kissed her hungrily, his tongue spearing into her mouth, before he lifted his head. His voice was even huskier than it had been as he said, "It really is necessary, and there is nothing I'd rather do than be with you right here, right now."

Jaden forgot to breathe. By the time she remembered to, Leif had gotten her into the passenger seat. He put the seatbelt around her, and the back of his hand brushed one of her breasts as he clicked it into place. She sucked in a breath at the contact. Her nipples tightened even more, the taut peaks brushing against her shirt.

Unable to find her voice, she silently watched Leif shut her door and then walk around the front of the car. He folded his large frame into the driver's side before he started the car. She closed her eyes. This had to be a dream. This couldn't really be happening. She wasn't sitting in a fancy sports car owned by a guy who was hotter than sin and about to let him drive her home. She counted to five and then opened her eyes again. She found Leif watching her with a bemused look on his face. Oh, my God. It *really* was happening.

He gave her a lopsided grin. "So, where to?"

*

Jaden squirmed on her seat. Her reactions to him made him even more attracted to her. She was a mixture of uncertainty and shyness. So different from the usual women he dated, she was like a breath of fresh air.

When his aimless drive had ended with him parked in the grocery store parking lot, Leif had sat there in disbelief for a few minutes. No matter how hard he tried to stay away from Jaden, he subconsciously always ended up doing the opposite. She drew him like a lodestone, and he couldn't fight the pull.

Frustrated, he thought to knock some sense into himself by bashing his forehead on the steering wheel. At the rate he was going, he'd end up cracking the damn thing. When someone had knocked on his window and he'd seen it was Jaden, everything he'd told himself about staying away from her flew out the window. He'd been out of the car in no time at all and stared at her with all the pent-up longing he'd tried so hard to bury.

Asking her out for dinner had slipped off his tongue before his brain could catch up with it. He wasn't going to be able to just walk away without spending some time with Jaden, so he'd decided to roll with it. Maybe if he got to know her better, he'd be able to appease his mating urge enough to let him leave her unclaimed after the meal.

Leif smiled, and Jaden's breath caught. "We can sit here all night if you want, but I'd much rather take you some place nicer than the inside of my car."

Jaden blushed again. "Oh. Sorry." She rattled off an address.

He pulled out of the parking lot. "Do you like Italian? I know a place that has the best Italian food."

"Anything is fine. I'm easy."

"You're easy, huh?" he said with a grin. "I'll have to remember that." He was rewarded with the pinkening of Jaden's cheeks once more, when he glanced in her direction.

"I-I didn't mean I'm easy, easy," she stammered. "I meant when it comes to food, I'm easy. I'm not picky."

He chuckled. "Relax, Jaden. I'm just having a bit of fun with you. I knew what you meant."

"Oh."

Once the silence grew between them, Leif asked, "Have you been working at the grocery store for long?"

"For about a year now."

"Do you like it?" Out of the corner of his eye, he saw her shrug.

"It's a job."

"So in other words, not really."

"It's better than some jobs I've had. That's about all I can say about it." She pointed toward the windshield. "There's my place. The second driveway on the left."

Leif pulled into the drive of small bungalow. It wasn't much to look at, and the neighborhood was an older one. To be polite, he said, "Nice house."

"It's all right, I guess. It isn't mine. I rent the basement from the older couple who own it and live upstairs."

Jaden got out of the car before Leif could get to her side. She led him to a side door, unlocked it, and stepped inside. He followed her in and then down a flight of stairs and through another door to a small basement that had been converted into a bachelor-type apartment. The tiny kitchen, living room, and bedroom were all visible, with no walls separating them. A below-ground basement, the apartment was gloomy. Leif had a feeling even if it had been the middle of the afternoon instead of evening, there wouldn't have been much light streaming in from the small windows set high in the walls. Personally, if he had to live there, he would have been claustrophobic within a week. The drop ceiling was low enough he almost had to hunch his shoulders so the top of his head wouldn't brush it.

Jaden went to the area that was her bedroom and pulled some clothes out of her dresser, then said, "Take a seat. I'll just be a few minutes." She walked to what had to be the bathroom and then shut the door behind her.

Leif sat on the couch that had seen better days. A small nineteen-inch TV sat across from it on an equally small stand. The place was no prize, but Jaden kept it neat as a pin. There was no clutter, and there didn't seem to be a speck of dust on any of the furniture. She obviously didn't have enough money to live better than this, but she appeared to be making the most of what she could afford. Seeing how his mate lived, he had to fight the instinct to take her away from all this and give her something better. Since he wasn't going to claim her as his, he couldn't do that.

Jaden came out of the bathroom wearing a pair of black jeans and a pink long-sleeved T-shirt. She carried her store uniform to her bedroom and put it on the bed before she walked to where he sat.

"Is what I'm wearing going to be okay?" She gestured to his jeans and shirt. "Going by what you have on, I figured we wouldn't be going anywhere fancy."

"No, it's casual."

"Good. I guess we should head out then."

Jaden headed for the door after Leif stood. He followed her as she walked up the stairs, his gaze falling to her ass. The jeans she wore hugged her hips and backside, showing off her curved-in waist a lot better than the dress pants she'd worn for work. Even the long-sleeved T-shirt molded her upper body in a flattering fit. Before she turned away, Leif had seen her generous breasts, something the grocery store's uniform did not reveal. He looked his fill at the back of her, and his cock hardened painfully. He quickly adjusted his erection before she could see it.

Back in his car, he drove them to the Italian restaurant he'd told her about. The interior had dark, wood paneling on the walls; red, thick carpet underfoot; and red-and-white checked tablecloths. Tt was family run and only had limited seating. Luckily for them, there was a table free, and they were quickly seated.

Once they were settled, with menus open in front of them, Leif said, "So, what do you do for fun when you're not working?"

Jaden lifted her gaze from her menu and looked at him. "Not much. I mostly sit at home and watch TV or read."

"You don't go out with your friends?"

Her gaze fell to the menu again. "No. I don't have what you would call close friends. I don't mind, really. I've always been a bit of a loner, anyway."

When the waitress came to take their orders, Jaden ordered the manicotti, and Leif asked for the spaghetti and meatballs. Once alone again, he said, "Nothing wrong with that, I guess."

Jaden snorted. "As if you would know anything about being a loner."

"Why would you say that?"

"Have you looked in the mirror lately? A guy like you is never alone. I'm sure you just have to snap your fingers and a woman falls into your arms. Which leads me to ask, why me?"

Leif latched on to the last part of what she'd said. There was no way he was going to tell Jaden she wasn't too far off the mark with her statement about women throwing themselves at him. And if he survived this evening, there would more than likely be many more years of it.

"What do you mean by why you?" he asked.

"I'll say it again, have you looked in a mirror lately? Why would a guy as good-looking as you—who could get any woman he wanted—want anything to do with someone as plain as me?"

The wolf inside him didn't like the way Jaden talked down about herself. Nor did the man. She may not have spectacular looks, but she wasn't ugly. If she only knew how she affected him, she wouldn't have asked that question. He still had a hard-on, and he ached to bury it deep inside her. He also wanted nothing more than to pull her to him and show her how wrong the perception she had of herself was. Someone had to have put that notion in her head. Whoever it was should count him- or herself lucky he didn't know the culprit or Leif would have gladly made someone pay.

He reached across the table and took hold of Jaden's hand, lacing their fingers together. Touching her made the mating urge dig its claws deeper, but Leif wanted, needed, to have some tactile contact with her.

After she lifted her gaze to his, he said, "When I kissed you, did it feel as if I didn't want you? Even now, I want to come around to your side of the table, take you into my arms and kiss you until neither one of us knows our names."

Jaden swallowed. "No, it didn't feel as if you didn't want me. I just don't understand why."

He lowered his voice so only she heard. "If we were alone right now, I'd show you how badly I want you. Let's just say the front of my jeans is about two sizes too small."

With his acute werewolf hearing, Leif heard her heart beat faster. The scent of her arousal perfumed the air around her. The smell of it made his cock jerk. Jaden may have a hard time understanding his interest in her, but that didn't mean she didn't want him.

As the air became charged with longing, the waitress appeared with their food. Leif reluctantly let go of Jaden's hand. She quickly put it on her lap under the table as her food was placed in front of her. Alone once again, she focused her gaze on her meal. He decided to let her have that space. He needed it to get himself back under control. He ate some of his spaghetti and forced his body to cool off. He couldn't let things blaze out of control between them. They would have their meal, he'd drop her back home, and then he would leave. He could do it. *No,* he had to do it. He didn't want the alternative if he couldn't walk away.

CHAPTER FOUR

J aden stole a quick glance at Leif as he drove them back to her place. She still felt a bit nervous around him, even though their meal had gone well. She hadn't choked on her food or dumped it on herself, which was a good thing. Most of her nervousness came from how good-looking Leif was. During the meal, she'd pinched herself under the table a few times just to make sure she wasn't dreaming. And hearing him say he wanted her had left her shaking. Stuff like that didn't normally happen to her.

Once Leif pulled his car into the driveway of her place and then shut off the engine, Jaden took off her seatbelt before she turned to face him. She really didn't want this evening to end. She thought of asking him if he wanted to come inside and watch some TV with her, but she didn't want to appear too pushy, or desperate.

Deciding to wait and see how Leif wanted to end the night, she said, "Thanks for dinner. The food was really good."

He took off his belt and turned slightly in his seat. "I told you they had the best Italian food."

"I'll have to remember it the next time I get a craving for Italian cuisine." When Leif didn't say anything more, but seemed to stare at her in that hungry way of his, she stammered, "Well...ah...I guess—"

Leif cut her off by cupping the back of her neck and leaning across his seat to kiss her. His lips moved sensuously over hers, angling for a better fit before he ran his tongue along the seam of her mouth. Once she opened for him, he deepened the kiss, stroking and sucking.

At her moan, he pulled back. The heat she saw in his eyes had her whispering, "Do you want to come inside?"

In answer, Leif got out of the car, walked around to her side, and opened her door. He held out his hand for her to take. Holding hands with their fingers laced together, Jaden let them into the house. He let go as they walked down the stairs, but as soon as they were inside her apartment, he pushed the door shut, and then took her into his arms. His lips hungrily claimed hers once again.

Jaden wrapped her arms around Leif's neck as he backed her into the middle of the living room. His hands skimmed down her back to her bottom. She shifted closer, and the hard length of his cock pressed against her belly. Her pussy clenched, liking how good he felt. She rocked into him, which elicited what sounded like a soft growl out of him. The ache of arousal between her legs increased, causing her juices to leak into her panties.

He backed her toward her bed and said against her mouth, "I promised myself I wouldn't do this, but the scent of your arousal is driving me crazy. I need to taste more of you."

Having slept with only two other men, and she'd hadn't gone to bed with them until they'd been dating for a while, Jaden felt no such reservations with Leif. His kisses made her desperate for him. Right now, her body didn't care they hardly knew each other. All it cared about was getting naked with the man in her arms.

After they reached the foot of her bed, Leif pulled off her glasses and put them on the corner of the mattress. He took hold of the bottom of her shirt and pulled it over her head. He let it fall to the floor. He stared down at her chest and thumbed her taut nipples through her bra.

"So beautiful," he said in a husky whisper. "They're just begging for me to suck on them."

He bent his head and kissed a path across her upper chest as he undid her bra at her back. Jaden lowered her arms to her sides so the straps slid down them, and the undergarment landed at their feet. She kicked it aside as Leif covered one of her breasts with his hand. He rolled her nipple between his thumb and index finger while his lips made a lazy path across her skin toward it.

By the time he reached it, she was practically panting. The feel of his tongue circling the taut peak made her moan. Leif put his other arm around her waist and slightly bent her back as he opened his mouth and sucked her nipple between his lips. His suckling caused more wetness to leak out of her pussy. With each pull, she felt it deep inside her core.

Leif moved to her other breast, lavishing the same attention on it as he'd done to the first. Jaden dug her nails into the tops of his shoulders, her arousal building by steady degrees. She rubbed against him; the feel of his hard cock made her ache to have it buried deep inside her.

He lifted his head and ground his erection into her. His blue eyes seemed to glow mutedly for a split second before the faint glimmer was gone, making Jaden question if she'd seen it or not.

"I want to see more of you. Will you let me?" he asked.

"God, yes," she said, going on tiptoe and taking possession of his lips.

Leif dropped his hands to the waist of her jeans. He made short work of undoing the button and zipper. Jaden sucked his tongue into her mouth as he pushed his hand inside the front of her panties. A finger brushed against her clit before delving inside her pussy.

"So wet," Leif said, as he brushed his lips along the side of her jaw. "I need to taste you there."

Leif pushed her jeans down past her hips so they pooled at her feet. With a gentle push, he had her sit on the bed. He nuzzled the side of her neck, then leaned into her until she fell back onto the mattress. Leif shifted so he stood with his legs on either side of hers. He rested his weight on his hands, above her head, and trailed kisses from the side of her neck to the top of her shoulder. He moved down her body and licked and kissed across both collarbones and to her breasts. He sucked each one into his mouth, swirling his tongue around her taut nipples until she panted, arching her back to push herself closer.

Leif continued his downward journey. By the time he'd kissed along her stomach, pausing to swirl the tip of his tongue inside her belly button, he was on his knees. He ran his hands along her sides, hooked the top of her panties with his fingers, and pulled them down to join her jeans at her ankles. He picked up one foot and took off her shoe and sock before he removed the other pair.

With a sweep of his hands, he pushed her jeans and panties all the way off, then moved to kneel between her legs. Using his upper body to spread her thighs farther apart, he lifted her legs and placed each of her feet on his hard-muscled thighs. Leif dragged his lips up the inside of her thigh. As he inched closer to her pussy, Jaden lifted her head to watch. The sight of his dark-auburn head between her thighs had her gripping the quilt under her in anticipation. He licked her wet core. She let out a keening moan, and her head dropped back down onto the mattress.

Leif lapped at her pussy. "You taste as good as you smell," he said.

His warm breath fanned over her clit when he spoke. Jaden lifted her hips, wanting more. With another strange growl, Leif licked her slick opening before stiffening his tongue to spear it inside her. She pushed down on his thighs with her feet and rocked her pussy against his mouth. Her core coiled tighter, her climax not too far off.

Oral sex had never been this good. From experience, Jaden had thought something was wrong with her since the other men she'd slept with hadn't ever been able to make her come that way. Obviously, it'd been their lack of skill, and not something physically wrong with her.

As Leif sucked on her clit and pushed a finger inside her, she panted, "Yes. Don't stop."

Leif inserted a second finger into her pussy to join the first. "Come for me, baby."

He continued to take her with his fingers as he alternated between licking and sucking on her clit. Jaden tightened her inner walls around the digits that moved in and out of her. She was so close. She clutched the quilt in tight fists and called out Leif's name, falling over the edge into ecstasy. Her pussy rhythmically clutched his fingers while she came, as wave after wave of pleasure washed through her. He kept pumping in and out until the last crest hit her. After it was over, she relaxed, unable to move.

Once she regained her breath and realized Leif hadn't moved from his kneeling position on the floor, she weakly lifted her head. He had his head down, with his forehead between her legs. His hands were curled into tight fists next to her hips. He clenched them so tightly the veins and muscles popped out along his arms. His thighs shook under her feet.

"Leif? Are you all right?"

At the sound of her voice, he stiffened even more. "I can't. I won't." His voice sounded muffled from being pressed into the mattress.

"What do you mean?" After that orgasm, her brain wasn't exactly firing on all pistons now. "You won't what?"

With one fluid move, Leif pushed to his feet. He stared down at her as she ran her gaze over him. His large erection strained against the front of his jeans. She sat up and reached out to stroke his cock, but he blocked her with a sweep of his hand.

"Don't," he said through clenched teeth. "Don't touch me, or I'm lost."

"Lost? You're not making any sense."

Leif didn't answer. Instead, he spun away from her, walked out her apartment door, and shut it behind him. The sound of his heavy footfalls going up the stairs, and then a few seconds later, the sound of his car starting, left Jaden wondering what the hell had happened. He'd given her the best orgasm of her life, then up and ran off. With the hard-to-miss hard-on he'd sported, she'd have thought for sure he would have wanted to finish what they'd started. It wasn't as if he hadn't wanted her. The way he'd kissed and touched her weren't the actions of a man who hadn't been as turned-on as she.

Jaden sat on the bed as her apartment grew darker. She couldn't figure Leif out. And right now, she had no clue if she would ever see him again. He'd left in one hell of a hurry. That didn't exactly make a girl think he wanted to be around her.

She picked up her discarded clothes, threw them into the hamper, and then walked to the bathroom naked. She needed to have a good long drenching in a hot shower. She wrapped the long strands of her ponytail around the scrunchie she wore to pull it back, forming it into a bun, twisting it tight enough so it would stay in place.

She turned on the water in the shower stall and then waited until steam filled the room. Leif was an enigma. He ran hot one moment, and cold the next. She'd just have to wait and see if he would drop back into her life again, or stay away for good this time.

* * * *

Leif sped toward Marin County and home as if the hounds of hell chased him. That had been too fucking close. He should never have gone inside her apartment after they finished their meal. He should have dropped her off, and then left, just as he'd planned, but he'd been too weak to resist the pull Jaden had over him. She'd stammered at him, unsure of herself, and he hadn't been able to stop himself from kissing her. And then his determination not to touch her had shattered.

He smacked the steering wheel with his palm. Once he'd kissed Jaden, he hadn't been able to stop. Her complete acceptance of him had been his downfall. One kiss had led to another, which led to him stripping her naked and feasting on her pussy until he made her climax.

The sound of her cries of pleasure still rang in his ears. Leif gritted his teeth as his cock jerked. He was still painfully aroused, and would probably stay that way until he washed Jaden's scent from his body. It was like his own personal aphrodisiac, keeping his shaft fully engorged.

And, of course, doing what he'd done with Jaden had not done him any favors. Oral sex with a would-be mate only increased the mating urge. He now had to look forward to a night of sex-filled dreams. The only way to stop them was to sleep with her, and he didn't want to do that. He'd really buggered himself.

After arriving at the Protectors' mansion, Leif parked his car in the large garage and then went inside. He headed for the kitchen to grab a cold beer out of the fridge. Just as he reached the doorway that led to the basement, Jager walked through it. He must have been working out, because he was bare-chested and had a small towel hung around his neck. There was a sheen of perspiration on his face as well. Just the person Leif didn't need to run into right now.

Jager stepped in front of Leif and looked him up and down. "You aren't looking so great." He sniffed the air. A large smile appeared on his face. "Well, well. Let me guess. Since you have the scent of a mortal female on you, obviously your mate, along with the scent of her passion on you, I'd say you got your taste of her but didn't fuck her."

Given every werewolf's acute sense of smell, it was no surprise to Leif that Jager had been able to pick up on all that with one sniff. It also meant Leif would have to get into a shower darn quick before he ran into any of the others.

"Piss off, Jager," he said as he brushed past him and continued into the kitchen. Jager followed him.

"You won't be able to fight it forever, Leif."

He pulled out a beer, twisted off the cap, and took a big swallow before he answered. "I was able to this time."

"Yeah, but for how long? Why torture yourself? She's your mate. You have to be at least halfway in love with her now, or she wouldn't be yours."

Leif scowled. Well, shit. Jager was right, but he wasn't going to tell the other warrior that. Just spending some quality time with Jaden had him wanting her more than he had before. He wanted to know everything about her. And by getting her glasses off, along with her clothes, he found she was even more attractive. If he wanted to be truthful with himself, a tiny, miniscule part of him wanted to wrap her in his arms and never let her go. The thought of spending the rest of his years waking up with her in his bed didn't seem as repugnant as it first had.

How long would that last? He honestly didn't know if he could stay true to one woman for that long. He was only a couple years over a thousand. Could he spend the remaining two thousand years of his life with the same woman even if she was his destined mate? Given his history of becoming quickly bored with his latest flame, the chances weren't very good. He didn't want to join his soul with a mate and find out years later it wasn't something he wanted. It wouldn't be fair to him or to her.

He shook his head. "I can't, Jager. It's not in me to be a mate."

"If you think that way, then you're an idiot. You're wired just like any other male werewolf. We all long to find our mates, to love and protect them."

"Well, I'm a living, breathing example of that not being true."

"Leif, you're fucked in the head. You're going to fall just like the rest of us who have become mated. In a way, I pity you, though. Your mating urge is going to have you so strung out you won't know whether you're coming or going. And when you break, and I can guarantee you will, your choice will be taken from you." With that cryptic remark, Jager turned and walked out of the kitchen.

Leif finished his beer in two large swallows and then thumped the empty bottle onto the counter. He got himself a second beer before he headed upstairs to his room. Much to his dismay, he found Saskia leaning against his door as if she'd been waiting for him. This night just seemed to get better and better.

She crossed her arms over her chest and gave him a knowing stare once he came even with her. "Claim your mate and be done with it, Leif."

He scrubbed his face with his hand. "You heard what Jager and I were talking about in the kitchen."

"Yes, but I already knew about you finding your mate before that. I saw it yesterday when you met her. I've just been keeping quiet about it to see what you would do."

Saskia had the sight. Just like her grandmother, she saw snatches of the future. It'd been her grandmother who had the vision about the foretold one.

"Well, if you saw it, then you already know I'm fighting it."

The corner of Saskia's mouth lifted in a half-smile. "I didn't need to see it to know that."

"I'm not going to claim Jaden," he said.

"Yes, you will. Your will is weakening already. As Jager said, you smell like you were doing some fooling around with your soon-to-be mate. And if you wanted to keep your distance from her, you wouldn't be referring to her by name."

Was everyone in his family not listening to what he wanted? He sighed. "It doesn't matter. I won't do it."

Saskia pushed away from his door. Her face took on a serious mien. "If I could, I would order you to take her as your mate, but this has to be your choice. That doesn't mean I can't pull you off protection duties until you decide to do what your mating urge must be screaming at you to do." As he opened his mouth to protest, she held up her hand. "Not a word. You have no say in the matter. I'm the leader of the Protectors, and I have to do what is best for the rest of us, and Roxie. If you're going to continue with this stupidity, then I have no choice but to pull you. Soon you'll be no good to anyone. So, as of now, you're off rotation."

Saskia walked away while he resisted the urge to beat his head against the wall. Now, a member of his own family had conspired against him. *Shit, shit, shit.* Could his life get any worse? He didn't want to be pulled off protection duty. He *needed* to be in the rotation. Without it, he would do nothing but think about Jaden with all the free time he'd have on his hands. He was so screwed.

CHAPTER FIVE

The next day at work, Jaden caught herself looking down her line of customers once again. She'd done it at least a million times already, hoping to catch a glimpse of Leif. Just like the other times, she didn't see him.

He'd been all she'd been able to think about until she'd gone to bed, and she'd started thinking about him again as soon as she'd woken up. She'd even been awakened a couple times during the night to the most erotic dreams she'd ever had—both featuring Leif. Maybe because of the great orgasm he'd given her, she now found herself obsessing about him. And she never obsessed over men.

Even though she'd told herself that what they'd done hadn't really meant anything to Leif, she couldn't stop thinking about him, wanting to be held in his arms again. It was stupid, really. After his departure last night, the chances weren't high he would want to see her again. Hadn't he said so himself that he couldn't and wouldn't. Jaden took that to mean he couldn't be with her. Not that she understood why. From her perspective, things had been going damn good.

After she finished ringing up the last customer in line, for now, Jaden lifted her head to find Vicky staring at her from the cash register across from hers.

"There's something different about you today," Vicky said as she studied Jaden closely. "I can't put my finger on it."

Jaden pushed her glasses higher up on her nose. "No, there isn't. Maybe it's just tiredness. I did work a longer shift yesterday."

Vicky shook her head. "No, that's not it. It's hard to explain, but there is *something* different. If I didn't know any better, I would say you got laid last night."

Jaden felt herself blush. "Don't talk that way. If Grant hears you, he'll give you hell for it."

Grant was their manager, and believed all his employees should be above reproach. He'd laid off another girl just because she'd tried to stand up to a customer who was verbally abusing her. He had told everyone he'd laid her off because she hadn't been working out as well as he'd thought she would. They all knew that wasn't true.

Vicky huffed. "Forget about Grant. Knowing him, he's probably in his office right now, seeing how far he can shove a stick up his butt just to keep himself all stiff and snooty. The pretentious ass."

Jaden covered her mouth with her hand, hoping to smother her laugh, but it bubbled out of her anyway. She could just picture Grant doing it, too. "You're bad," she said with another laugh.

Vicky waved her comment away with a flick of her hand. "So, are you going to tell me what you did last night that brought on this change to your appearance?"

Jaden instantly sobered and felt another blush color her cheeks. What could she say to Vicky? That the hottest guy she'd ever seen gave her an intense orgasm and then bailed on her right afterward?

When she didn't say anything, Vicky said, "Ah-ha. I think I know what did it. It was that kiss that hot guy gave you yesterday."

She rolled her eyes. "It was only one kiss. I doubt it was enough to change me that much. Remember, I don't even know his name." That little white lie wasn't going to hurt anyone.

"Maybe it's the prospect of seeing him again. I've been watching you. I've seen you trying to be oh-so-casual as you look at each customer who comes to your cash register. You're looking for him, aren't you?"

Jaden adjusted her glasses again. "So what if I am?"

Vicky smiled. "There's nothing wrong with it. It just goes to show, you have needs just like every other woman. And a man like that, I'd be watching for him at every turn as well."

"Well, I doubt I'll see him today."

"You never know."

A customer walked up to Jaden's cash register. She looked away from Vicky, essentially ending their conversation, and rang up each item. As for Vicky's last remark, Jaden did know. It was just wishful thinking on her part to assume Leif would just saunter into the grocery store, walk to her cash register and say he wanted to continue where they'd left off last night. She had to be realistic and face facts. For a girl like her to end up with a man like Leif, Earth would have to tilt off its axis and spin in the opposite direction.

* * * *

It'd been three god-awful, painful days since Leif had last seen Jaden. Tenaciously, he hung on to his resolve not to see her again, but he was losing the battle. His mating urge had not only sunk its claws into him, it was ripping and pulling with its sharp teeth as well. No longer able to watch over Roxie, he thought of nothing but Jaden almost the entire twenty-fours in a day. It was unending, and it was driving him insane with need. And nothing he did seemed to stop it. He'd even driven to Muir Woods, hoping shifting to his wolf form and going for a long run in the forest would help, but that was one mistake he wouldn't make again anytime soon. In his other form, his mating urge went off the charts, the wolf inside him more than willing to search Jaden out and force him to claim her.

And to make matters even worse, he basically walked around all day with a hard-on. He'd tried to find some relief by knocking off in the shower, but at this stage, it no longer worked. He could stroke his cock until his hand hurt, but he never reached climax. He had a feeling only sleeping with Jaden would end that pain. Leif had no idea if that was normal for a male in the throes of the mating urge, mostly because he'd never heard of another male werewolf ever refusing to claim his mate.

Now on the third day of unending torture, Leif paced the length of his room like the wild wolf he was. He'd been at it for hours. Every time he passed the mirror attached to his dresser he caught a glimpse of his glowing eyes. Along with his dick staying perpetually hard, his eyes glowed with the state of arousal he was in constantly.

By now, everyone in the mansion knew he'd found his mate, and that he wasn't thrilled about it. It was kind of hard to miss when he walked around with a huge bulge in the front of his pants and glowing eyes. He'd had every member of his family cajole, then yell at him, trying to persuade him to just go to Jaden. He refused all of them. Today, if they tried it again, he didn't know if he could still do it.

Leif suddenly stopped pacing as his bedroom door slammed open and three of his brothers-in-arms barged in. He growled and snapped his teeth at Roan, Jager, and Skylar. Since they were the only true brothers, they were all similar in looks as well as size. As they advanced on him, he realized he was sunk. There was no way he could get away from the three of them working together.

Roan rushed in to take hold of one of his arms while Skylar grabbed the other. Jager picked up his legs, holding on tight to his ankles. Leif arched his back, pulling on his arms and legs to get free, but he couldn't shake them off.

"Get the fuck off me," he said with a growl.

Jager shook his head. "Not going to happen. Enough is enough."

"Yeah," said Roan. "We've heard you pacing up here all day. Everyone has. This torturing yourself is going to stop — today."

They carried him through his bedroom door. "Where are you taking me?" he snapped.

"Out to your car so you can go to your mate," Roan stated.

Leif really fought them then. "No. I can't leave the mansion, let alone get into my car. I'll just head straight for Jaden."

"That's what we're counting on," Skylar said with a chuckle. "And just so you know, Saskia knows exactly what we're doing. She's also not here, so don't even think about calling for help. No one is going to save you."

Even though he struggled, muscles straining, trying to throw them off-balance with his weight, the brothers managed to get him out to his car. One of them must have moved it out of the garage to the front of the mansion. They wrestled him into the driver's side and then strapped him in. Leif noticed the engine was running.

Jager leaned into the car and slapped a pair of dark sunglasses over Leif's eyes. "We can't have mortals, including your mate, seeing those glowing peepers of yours. At least, not yet. Explanations of what you are can wait until after you've claimed her." He slammed the car door shut.

Free of the confines of his room, Leif couldn't ignore his mating urge anymore. He put the car into gear and peeled away down the large drive. It vaguely registered on him that the sky was just starting to darken. He drove straight to Jaden's basement apartment, unable to stop what was about to happen. The only thing that would save them would be if she wasn't home.

Leif pulled over to the curb in front of the house and parked. He got out of the car and then crossed the distance between it and the side door of the house in a few long strides, using his ability to move faster than any mortal could. If anyone saw him, he pretty much didn't care. All of him was focused on getting to his mate, of making her his.

He banged on the door, praying Jaden wouldn't be home, and then just as quickly praying she was. Once he heard movement on the other side of the door, he groaned to himself. His senses went on high alert in anticipation of her opening it.

As she swung it open, she asked, "Leif?" The tone of her voice said she was surprised to find him standing on her doorstep.

With her scent filling his head, he was beyond being able to form words. Longing and desire pounded through him, leaving no room for anything else. Only left with the need to act, he pulled her to his chest and took her mouth in a searing kiss, unleashing all his pent-up arousal.

He circled his arms around her waist and picked her up off her feet so he could kiss her without having to bend his head. He carried her over the threshold and then kicked the door shut before he walked down the stairs, all the while hungrily moving his mouth over hers. She put her legs around his waist, her pussy coming to rest against his cock, where he ached the most.

As he stepped into her apartment and shut that door as well,

Jaden buried her fingers in the hair at the back of his head and kissed him just as greedily. Her responsiveness caused a loud growl of need to rumble out of his chest. He carried her to the bed and put her on the center of it, following her down. With her legs still around his waist, his cock remained against her pussy. He rocked his hips, groaning into her mouth at the pleasure of it.

Leif lifted his head. Covering one of Jaden's breasts, tugging on her taut nipple that he badly wanted to suck, he said, "Tell me you want this."

Jaden arched her back into his touch. "Yes. God, how I want this. I've done nothing but dream and think about you touching me again."

A shudder racked him. She may not be a female werewolf, but Jaden was obviously feeling the effects of the mating urge as well. His bringing her to orgasm that night must have started the process that would make her his.

He took off her glasses, and put them on the small nightstand next to the bed. Leif then grabbed her hand and led it to the front of his jeans. "Touch me. I ache for you."

Jaden cupped him through the material of his pants before trailing her fingers upward over his full length. Once she reached his button and fly, she undid them both. He sucked in a breath as his cock sprang free, and she took him in her hand. She stroked it up and down, and he couldn't hold back the growls of pleasure that rumbled out of him.

As she circled the head of his dick, rubbing a bead of his pre-cum into his skin, Leif had to fight not to come there and then. Even though all male werewolves could keep an erection for hours at a time, even after coming several times, he wanted his first time to last a little bit longer.

In one pull, he yanked Jaden's T-shirt off over her head. He removed her bra just as quickly. Once he had her bared breasts in front of him, he bent his head and sucked a nipple into his mouth. He rocked his hips and pushed his erection tighter into her hand as she stroked his shaft. Leif sucked until she panted.

He groaned at the loss when she let go of his cock and yanked at the bottom of his shirt, lifting it up to his chest. To help, he grabbed the back of it and dragged it over his head, taking the sunglasses he wore with it. Not caring if Jaden saw his mutedly glowing eyes, he bent his head and sucked on her other nipple.

Jaden tugged at the top of his jeans, trying to push them over his hips. "Take these off."

He quickly obliged. Jaden's hand once again wrapped around his cock, squeezing him tight as she stroked it. He was about ready to explode. The scent of her arousal beat at him, making his shaft harden even more.

With no finesse at all, Leif tore off the sweatpants she wore, taking her panties with them. Feeling more animal than man, having pushed the mating urge to its limits, he used his thigh to spread her legs wider before he settled his hips between them. He tested her readiness to take him by stroking a finger against her pussy. It came away soaked.

With an animalistic growl, he positioned his cock at her entrance and seated himself to the hilt with one stroke. The feel of her wet inner walls closing around his shaft had Leif's eyes almost rolling back inside his head. Pleasure built in his gut and spread throughout his body. It increased a thousandfold as he moved inside her.

He rested his weight on his bent arms and worked his erection in and out of her pussy. "So tight," he groaned. "Feel so good."

Jaden's inner walls squeezed his shaft, making it an even tighter fit. She whimpered beneath him as she lifted her hips to match his strokes. He'd been with a lot of women over his long life, but none had given him this much pleasure. Leif usually liked to take his time when he had sex. Not with her. This joining, he wanted her hard and fast, wanted to hear her desperate cries of passion ringing in his ears as she strived for her orgasm.

He pounded into her faster. Just before his climax hit the point of no return, he felt it—the formation of the mating bond. He looked into Jaden's face and watched her eyes snap open, as she obviously felt it too. A part of his soul reached out for hers at the same time hers reached for his. They both sucked in a breath when they joined and became one. She stared at him in wonder, then cried out as she came. With her pussy milking his shaft in a tight fist, Leif drove into her one final time, threw back his head, and howled as his cock pulsed deep inside her, filling her with all he had to give. After the last tremor shook him, he collapsed on top of her and buried his face in the crook of her neck.

*

Jaden wrapped her arms around Leif's back as his much heavier body pushed her deeper into the mattress. He was a solid weight atop her, making it hard to take a breath, but she liked him there. Little aftershocks rocked her, twitching around his cock that was still deep inside her, and still very hard. She had no idea how he'd managed to keep his erection. She'd felt it when he'd come. She'd also felt something else pass between them just before they'd found their release. To describe what it felt like, she'd have to say it was as if they had joined not only their bodies but another part of them as well.

She shivered as Leif nuzzled her neck and gently scraped his teeth along her skin. He nipped her gently, then licked the same spot. He pulled back his hips until his cock was almost free of her body, only to push back inside.

With a gasp, she asked, "Again?"

"Again," he growled into her ear.

In a show of strength, Leif wrapped his arms around her, and holding her close, he sat up, taking her with him. He settled her bent legs on either side of his hips and then urged her to ride him. Being on top had his cock sinking even deeper inside her pussy while she impaled herself on him over and over again.

While she rode him, Leif cupped the back of her head and pushed her mouth to the side of his neck where it met his shoulder. She licked his skin, and he shivered beneath her.

"Bite me, Jaden. Mark me," he said in a voice husky with arousal.

"No." She shook her head. "I can't bite you."

"I want you to. Mark me as yours."

Leif pushed up into her hard enough to lift her knees off the mattress as she grazed her teeth along the spot he wanted her to bite him. She was never one for the kinky stuff in bed, but something seemed to take her over. Somehow knowing this would tease him, she dragged her teeth over his skin a few more times before she gently bit down.

He stiffened, his hands on her hips, urging her to ride him faster. "Harder. Bite me harder."

His cock seemed to harden even more, hitting a spot inside her pussy that had another climax building. Jaden gripped Leif's shoulders tight and bit him as hard as he demanded. He surged up into her and made one of those strange animalistic growls he'd made before. And just like that, she fell over the edge, whimpering against his skin as she climaxed. He came at the same time, holding her hips to his as his cock emptied into her pussy.

Tasting blood on her tongue, Jaden pulled her mouth away from Leif's neck to see she'd broken the skin where she'd bitten him. Horrified at what she'd done, she quickly said, "I hurt you. I didn't mean to."

Leif put a hand under her chin and forced her to look at him. "You didn't hurt me. I asked you to mark me, and you did."

Now just embarrassed that she'd let herself get carried away with the moment, she relaxed against his chest and rested her head on his shoulder. Adjusting her legs, incredibly she found Leif's cock still thick and hard inside her. She squeezed her inner walls around him, and he moaned. He'd come twice. It shouldn't be possible.

"Don't get too comfortable there," he said. "I'm not finished yet."

She sat back up. "I don't know if I can a third time."

"Yes, you can."

He bent his head to one of her breasts and circled her nipple with his tongue before taking it inside his mouth. He sucked on it while he held on to her hips and slowly raised and lowered her on his shaft. He continued to do it until she moaned.

Leif released her nipple with a pop, then lifted her off him, turning her so she was on the bed on all fours before he moved to kneel behind her. "I'm going to take you this way to truly make you mine."

He bent over her and nipped the back of her neck as the head of his cock nudged at her pussy. Straightening, he pushed forward, sinking his shaft inside her. Jaden gasped. He was in so deep she swore she felt him at the back of her throat. Then he moved. He held on to her hips, keeping her right where he wanted her, and surged into her with powerful strokes. Leif seemed to growl with each exhale he made. Jaden's pussy coiled tighter as her desire grew stronger.

She fisted the sheets under her hands, pushing backward to meet him. The orgasm she thought she wouldn't be able to have tore through her once Leif reached around her and stroked her clit with his finger. Whimpering his name, Jaden vaguely heard him howl like a wolf as he came.

Satiated and worn out from the intense sex she'd just had, Jaden let Leif lower her to her side so her back was pressed to his chest. Her last thought before sleep claimed her was that his cock was still hard, keeping their bodies joined.

CHAPTER SIX

L eif awoke to the sensation of a warm, female body wrapped around him. The feel of Jaden's breasts plastered to his side and her leg thrown over his thigh had his cock hardening. He ignored it as memories of the night rose to the surface of his mind.

He lay perfectly still and shifted his gaze to look at Jaden. Each breath she took was deep and even. He silently cursed himself with every swear word he knew. He'd taken her in every position imaginable, more than once, during the night, making them well and truly mated. And judging by the throbbing in his now fully erect cock, he was ready to go again.

He really had mixed emotions about being mated to Jaden. On one hand, the old part of him wanted to run away in horror. And on the other, the new part found what had passed between them to be something he never wanted to give up. Making love to her had been mind-blowing. Just one night of passion and he was addicted to her touch. And after the closeness they'd shared, he wanted to know everything there was to know about her, to know her better than anyone else ever had.

And it was probably a good thing he felt that way, because he'd claimed her as his mate, they wouldn't be able to stand being apart for any real length of time. Now he had the excruciating task of trying to figure out how the hell to explain that to Jaden as well as the fact that he was a werewolf.

Jaden stretched against him, her knee nudging his erection. She pressed her lips to his chest and kissed him. "Hmm, I see someone is awake before me, and raring to go."

She trailed her fingers down his body to his cock and took him in her hand. She pumped his shaft. Leif knew what would happen if he let this go much further, but with Jaden stroking him, he had a hard time getting his brain to function. With all the blood in his body rushing to his cock, that was no surprise.

"Ah...god, you're making me horny. Ah, Jaden, we should have a talk."

She let go and rolled on top of him, straddling his thighs. Jaden playfully shook her head. "Somehow, I really don't think you're in the mood for talking right now. I know I would much rather be doing something else."

Leif sucked in a breath as she bent to his chest and flicked one of his flat nipples with the tip of her tongue. His erection jerked against her stomach when she did it to the other as well. "We really need to talk, Jaden."

"It can wait. I have more important things to do."

Obviously, sometime during the night, Jaden had lost her shyness around him. She shifted lower on his legs as she licked, kissed, and nipped a trail to his abs, moving ever closer to his cock.

His breath punched out of his chest once her lips settled on his lower belly. "Jaden, seriously, we have...oh, Christ."

She'd taken a firm grip on the base of his shaft and circled the tip with her tongue. She proceeded to lick him like an ice cream cone. He lifted his head to watch. The sight of her laving the length of his cock while she used her other hand to fondle his balls had him lifting his hips off the bed. Leif just about lost it when she gave the head one last lick before opening her mouth and sucking him deep.

The suction had his balls drawing up close to his body. Her head bobbed up and down as she worked him in and out. Having his mate suck him off was the most erotic thing he'd ever seen. If he let Jaden keep this up, he wasn't going to be able to stop himself from blowing his load.

"Jaden." He panted with a groan. "Even though this feels so

damn good, you have to stop or I'll come."

She kept a tight grip on him, then released his cock and shifted her gaze to his face. "I want you to. I know you'll still be hard even after you do." She sucked him back inside the moist confines of her mouth.

She sucked on him hard, her cheeks hollowing as she worked her hand up and down the part of his shaft she couldn't take. His cock hardened to bursting point. The pleasure she gave him had him growling, thrusting his hips, pushing more of his length into her mouth. Then, for one suspended moment, he hung on the edge of coming before he crossed over it with a loud moan. Jet after jet of cum pumped out of him. Jaden didn't stop sucking until she'd wrung every drop out of him.

With a satisfied smile, she climbed up his body and positioned her wet pussy over his still hard cock. "My turn," she said.

She reached between them and took hold of his shaft before she slowly lowered herself onto it. They moaned in pleasure. Jaden put her hands on his chest as she rode him. Leif reached up to cover her breasts, squeezing and tugging on her nipples. He looked down at where their bodies were joined, watching her pussy taking his cock over and over again.

She sat up and rocked against him faster. Jaden angled her hips so her clit rubbed against his pubic bone, wringing a breathy moan out of her. Another climax built. Just when he thought he wouldn't be able to hold back long enough until she'd found her release, her head fell back and she released a keening moan. Her pussy rhythmically gripped his cock, sending him into an intense orgasm.

Once it was over, he put his arms around Jaden and pulled her down to his chest. His still-hard cock kept them joined. He kissed her sweaty forehead, realizing he was well and truly lost.

*

Jaden was just getting nice and comfortable sprawled out on top of Leif when he lightly slapped her butt, and said, "No more sleeping. We aren't staying in bed all day."

She pillowed her chin on top of her hands on his chest and met Leif's gaze. His eyes seemed to be normal again, not that she really believed they'd been glowing in the first place. Considering she'd thought she noticed the change only while they were having sex, Jaden had to chalk it up to her mind being fried with pleasure, distorting her sight. Being nearsighted, her eyesight wasn't exactly great to begin with. It was plausible she was seeing things. And as for the animalistic growls and wolfish-sounding howls, her ears must not have been working properly either.

She cocked her hips so his still-hard cock moved deeper inside her, and said, "Are you sure about that?"

Leif slapped her butt again and gave her a grin. "I'm positive, greedy woman. At this rate, you'll make me weak and feeble."

She raised a brow. "Yeah, right. I'm sorry, but I can't see you ever getting in that condition." Jaden nipped his chin, then sucked on the stubble-roughened skin.

Leif shivered. Instead of going for round two, he rolled her to her back, pulled out of her, and pinned her to the mattress. "I can see you aren't going to take pity on me. To make you behave, I'm going to get up and use your shower."

She sighed dramatically. "Oh, very well. Since my shower is nothing more than a small corner unit with no tub, we won't be able to share. You can shower first, then I'll take one."

"Do you have to work today?"

"No, not until tomorrow. Why?"

He kissed the tip of her nose. "Because once you're showered and dressed, we're getting out of here."

"And where exactly are we going?"

"My place, so you can meet my family," Leif said as he got up and stood beside the bed. "Where is the shower?"

Jaden gave his naked body an appreciative glance as she slipped out of bed to stand next to him. She'd explored every inch of him during the night. Leif's body was a work of art. She could probably spend an eternity running her hands and lips over all his muscles. And then there was his cock, which was long and thick and still hard, jutting out from his body.

Leif snapped his fingers in front of her face. "Jaden? The shower?"

She met his gaze and could tell from the look in his eyes that she'd been caught staring. Not embarrassed in the least—how could she be with all the things they'd done to each other during the long hours of the night—she said, "I'll show you."

Jaden walked past him and led Leif to her almost closet-sized bathroom. She pushed open the door and then went to pull out a clean towel from under the sink. After she put it on top the counter, she turned to find him stepping into the shower stall. He took up all the space. There was no way the two of them could fit in there at the same time.

"I'll leave you to it," she said as he shut the shower door and then turned on the water. "Just don't use all the hot water on me. The water heater isn't the best here."

"Gottcha," he said as he tipped his head back under the spray, having to bend his knees to do it.

Jaden went back to the bed and stretched out on it. A goofy smile spread across her face. Never in a million years would she have thought she'd spend the night getting screwed silly by a man like Leif. The other guys she'd slept with hadn't had anything near his stamina. It'd taken hours, and numerous orgasms, before he'd lost his erection. And boy, did he know how to use his cock. He'd made her come over and over again. If things didn't work out between them, she didn't know if she could go back to a regular guy.

That thought gave Jaden pause. Before Leif had shown up at her door yesterday evening, she'd thought for sure she would never see him again. She'd been shocked to see him standing there. When he'd pulled her into her arms and devoured her mouth, she hadn't wanted to question what had caused him to change his mind.

She listened to the sound of the shower running and shook her head. She wasn't going to exactly question him now, either. Whatever had caused it, she was quite happy with the way things had turned out. Having Leif say he wanted to take her to meet his family had to mean he wasn't going to skip out on her again. Didn't it? She shook her head. She had to stop second-guessing everything, something she regularly did more often than not. It was kind of a byproduct of her not being exactly confident about herself. If she really wanted to have things work out with him, it didn't take much thinking on her part to realize she couldn't let herself get that way around him. As good-looking as he was, she doubted he had self-confidence issues like she did.

Five minutes later, the shower shut off. Jaden lifted her head from the pillow as Leif stepped out of the bathroom with a towel around his hips. He ran a hand through his damp auburn hair and walked to the bed.

"The shower is all yours," he said. Before she could get up, he added, "How about I take us out for breakfast? I'm starved."

Jaden scooted off the end of the bed. "I'm hungry too." She smiled. "I guess we worked up an appetite."

Leif grabbed her arm and pulled her to him. He kissed her slowly and thoroughly until she breathed quicker. After he released her, he said, "Hurry up in the shower."

She didn't waste any time getting into the bathroom or starting the water in the shower. No way was she going to delay Leif's plans any longer than she had to. For the first time in a very long time, Jaden looked forward to what the day would bring.

* * * *

During breakfast at a diner-type restaurant not too far from Jaden's place, Leif became a little anxious. Having decided not to claim her as his mortal mate, he hadn't prepared himself for what he would do if he did. He had to tell her the truth about himself. There really was no choice in the matter. If he didn't, she would think it awfully strange that he wanted her with him all the time. Mortals who first entered into relationships didn't do that. They eased into making that kind of commitment. The mating bond he'd forged with her last night negated that.

He wasn't exactly scared to tell her he was a werewolf. It was just the thought of Jaden becoming afraid of *him* didn't sit well in his gut. He sure as shit didn't want to scare her away. Leif might not have wanted a mate, but he had one now, and he planned to do right by her. Letting her leave him so she would go through the inevitable separation anxiety was not something he wanted her to experience this early when it really wasn't necessary. She was his to protect and care for. And the first thing he would do would be to get her out of the tiny basement apartment. Christ, his room at the Protectors' mansion was the same size, if not bigger, than her whole apartment.

"What has you all silent and brooding?" Jaden asked as she put her fork onto her empty plate.

She tucked her hair behind her ear. It'd been a bit of a battle, but he'd managed to get Jaden to keep it down after her shower. He liked it better that way, than pulled back in a ponytail. "I'm not brooding. I just got lost in my thoughts."

"Well, they must have been pretty intense since you scowled while you stared off into space."

"Maybe it was thoughts of you that had me so distracted."

"Gee, thanks. Am I supposed to be flattered to know thinking about me makes you scowl like that?"

"Actually, yes," he said with a chuckle. "I was just thinking about how you'll react when you meet my family. We aren't exactly like your normal, run-of-the-mill family."

Jaden waved his concern away. "At least you have a family to introduce me to. I wish I could say I had one to bring you to meet."

"You have no family at all?"

"No. It has only been me for a while now. I pretty much grew up with just my mom. I haven't a clue who my father is. She never talked about him, and I never really got a chance to push the issue with her, either. When I was sixteen, a car jumped the sidewalk when she walked home from work and hit her. She was killed instantly. The driver was a twenty-year-old guy who'd had one too many drinks to have any business getting behind the wheel of a car."

Leif reached across the table and took Jaden's hand in his. "So what happened to you? Did you have grandparents to stay with?"

"Nope. My mom's parents had been up there in age when they had her, so by the time of her death, they'd already passed away. I was put into foster care for a couple years. Once I was eighteen, I moved out of my foster parents' place. I found a job, a place of my own, and I never looked back."

"Do you still have some contact with them?"

"Not really. In the beginning, they called on my birthday and at Christmas, but we've basically lost touch. I've moved to so many different places over the years, it got a little tedious to let them know every time I changed my address and phone number. Enough about me. What's your family like?"

Leif smiled and shook his head. "I'm not going to say too

much, or you'll back out of meeting them, especially if I tell you about Jager."

"He's your brother?"

"Yeah. You may find he'll take some getting used to. He likes to say whatever he's thinking. Let's put it to you this way, subtle, Jager is not."

Jaden laughed. "Is he really that bad?"

"At one time, yes, but now that he's ma…married, Daylen tries to keep him reined in as much as she can. She used to be a cop, so she knows how to handle Jager."

"I can't wait to meet them. Do you have any other siblings?"

"In total, I have five brothers and one sister. Besides Jager, one of my brothers and my sister are married."

"Wow, you have a large family. What about your parents?"

"No parents, just us."

"Well, at least you guys have each other."

Leif let the conversation end there as their waitress came to gather their empty plates and give them their bill. He put enough money on the table to cover it and the tip, and then waited for Jaden to stand before he took her hand.

Once he had them in his Cadillac and on the road to Marin County, they talked about trivial things. Much to Leif's surprise, he found it nice. Now with the mating urge no longer riding him, he found he could relax around Jaden and be himself.

He would be the first to admit that sometimes his sense of humor could be a little out there, but she seemed to get it. Even though they were mated—and for that to be even possible, his feelings for Jaden had to be running along the lines of love—he wasn't ready to admit he loved her. He liked her, a lot, but he still had doubts as to whether he was capable of that kind of strong emotion. Yes, he loved his brothers- and sister-in-arms. Those feelings weren't the same as giving his heart away to a woman, forever.

It would be darn close to that. He had to somehow convince Jaden to allow Roxie to perform the spell that would turn her into a werewolf. Allowing Jaden to have a regular, mortal lifespan was out of the question. They were mated, and there was no going back, so he wanted them to be true mates in every sense of the word.

Once they crossed the Golden Gate Bridge, heading toward Marin County, Leif decided he'd have to take his time and slowly ease Jaden into his life without dropping it on her all at once. The first step would be to introduce her to his family and take it from there.

CHAPTER SEVEN

Leif pulled his car onto a long drive that led to a large mansion. Jaden wasn't particularly surprised to find he lived in one. Considering the car he drove, there was no question in her mind that he wasn't hurting when it came to money. It only made sense.

Jaden stared out the window at the manicured lawns and perfectly landscaped flowerbeds. The mansion loomed in front of them. There were a lot of windows lining both stories, which meant there were a lot of rooms to be found inside. She could only ever dream of living in a place as rich as that.

As Leif parked his car at the front of a large detached garage, she said, "Your house is huge. You can't tell me you live here all by yourself. It looks as if you could house a small army inside it."

Leif chuckled. "You could say that. And no, I don't live alone. I share it with my family."

She blinked. "You all live together?"

Growing up, she'd wished for a bigger family, but now as an adult who'd spent most of that time living alone, she didn't think she could handle living with a family as large as Leif's. How did they get any alone time or privacy?

Once they were out of the car and walking toward the mansion, Leif said, "It's not that bad, living with them. We've lived under the same roof for years. I'm not saying we don't get on each other's nerves from time to time, but for the most part, we get along. Mostly because we work together as well."

"You do? And what exactly is it you do? You haven't told me."

"We're in the protection business."

Jaden believed that. Leif was muscular enough to kick ass as a hired bodyguard for somebody rich or famous. "You and your family must be doing well at it, to live in a place like this."

"Well enough."

Leif pushed open the front door and moved aside for her to step into the large foyer that had a black-and-white-checked marble floor. A large crystal chandelier hung from the middle of the cathedral ceiling. She'd never been inside a house this ritzy. A blond oak railing ran up the outside of the curving staircase that led to the second floor. It was the kind of place she only dreamed of owning if she ever won the lotto.

With a small tug on the hand he held, Leif pulled her to a stop and took a deep breath. "Damn. Roxie is here," he said quietly, almost to himself.

"Who?" she asked cautiously.

"Roxie. She's the woman my family and I protect. I was going to introduce her to you at some point, but I wasn't planning on doing it today. Maybe we can slip back outside before we're noticed, and we'll come back after she's gone."

Before they could move, a woman's voice called from somewhere at the rear of the mansion. "Leif! Don't you dare go anywhere. I can smell the two of you."

Smell the two of you? What did she mean by that? It wasn't as if she and Leif hadn't showered before they came there. How in the heck could anybody *smell* them from that great a distance away.

Leif groaned. "Too late. That was Roxie. We might as well brave the lion's den."

He led her in the direction Roxie's voice had come from. It turned out to be the kitchen. Two women were there. One, who could have passed for a supermodel with long, almost white-blonde hair, stood near one of the counters with another woman who looked to be about six months pregnant. She was eating a big bowl of ice cream. Her looks weren't nearly as spectacular as the first woman's, but she was better looking than Jaden considered herself to be. She also had long, golden-brown hair that she flipped over one shoulder as Jaden and Leif came closer.

Leif let go of her hand and put his on the small of her back. "Jaden, this is my sister, Saskia." The woman with the white-blonde hair smiled. "And the one stuffing her face with ice cream is Roxie."

"Hi," Jaden said.

"It's nice to meet you, Jaden," Saskia said in return.

"Yes, it is," Roxie added. "I never thought I'd see the day Leif would actually find his mat—"

Leif jumped closer to Roxie and put his hand over her mouth before she finished speaking. "I don't think Jaden is ready to hear that, if you catch my meaning."

Roxie glared over his hand at him. She yanked it away, narrowing her eyes. "Not another one. What is wrong with you guys?"

"Take some pity on Leif," Saskia said before Leif could reply. "He wasn't exactly capable of following your list of rules because of you-know-what. He fought you-know-what until we were left with no alternative but to send him out to do what had to be done."

Now completely lost, Jaden had no idea what the "you-know-what" Saskia kept referring to was. It was obvious Roxie and Leif did, from their expressions.

Roxie shook her head and gave Leif an exasperated look. "Stupid man. Why did you even bother? You know there's no beating the you-know-what. I told you one day this would happen."

Saskia chuckled. "We all did, Rox. I guess I'll let the others know Jaden is here." She left Jaden and Leif alone with Roxie.

"So why are you here, Rox? I thought you would be at your place, stuffing your face with your own ice cream and not ours. Did you run out, and none of the others would go to the grocery store to get you any?"

Jaden bit back a smile. That explained why Leif had come to the store and bought nothing but ice cream. Knowing where he lived, she now knew the grocery store where she worked wasn't all that close.

"Har, har," Roxie said. "Aren't you a funny one? Not. Skylar was telling Beowulf about the new motorcycle he'd bought. Since he hadn't ridden it to our place, he was boring the crap out of me by describing every minute detail about it to Beowulf. So I suggested we come here so Skylar could show it to him. Kye decided we'd all go in the SUV, because, God forbid, something might happen to me while on his watch. He's going to drive us back this evening and then stay overnight."

"Kye is just being cautious."

"Whatever," Roxie said, as she put her now-empty bowl onto the counter. "I'm going to see where my husband is. You can introduce Jaden to the rest of your family whenever you're ready."

After she left, Leif blew out a breath. "That went better than expected."

"She seems nice enough," Jaden said.

"She is, but I can tell she's getting fed up with us watching her closer than we used to. Because of her pregnancy, that's the way it has to be for now. Roxie is special, and tends to forget sometimes just how special she is. That's why we're here to protect her. Shall we see where the others are?"

"Sure."

With his arm around her waist, Leif guided her out of the kitchen. He seemed to always want to touch her in some way. Jaden didn't mind, though. It made her feel wanted. It also made her want him again. Just one little touch and he stirred her body to life. It was almost as if it tried to make up for the years of celibacy that'd been forced on it.

As if Leif had picked up on her thoughts, his nostrils flared as he stopped her and crowded her until her back hit the wall. Jaden put her arms around his neck when he settled his hands on her hips and lowered his lips to hers. She moaned into his mouth, sucking on his tongue once it pushed past her parted lips. He pulled her closer, and the hard ridge of his erection nestled against her stomach.

A loud cough had Leif pulling away from her mouth, but he kept her pressed against the wall with his body. He turned his head to look at the large man who stood a short distance away. Jaden quickly adjusted her glasses that'd been knocked askew while Leif had kissed her.

"Can I do something for you, Jager?" Leif asked.

"What is it you always tell Daylen and me when you catch us making out? Oh, yes, I remember now. Why don't you get a room?"

So this was the brother Leif had warned her about. Jager was just as tall and muscular. He wore his long hair pulled back in a ponytail. And just like Leif and Saskia, he had model good-looks. It made Jaden wonder if the rest of the family had been so lucky in the looks department.

Leif stepped away and pulled her against his side so they stood facing Jager. "I can see you're going to use this as an excuse to get back at me."

Jager chuckled. "I wouldn't pass this up for the world. Payback is a bitch, or so they say." He focused his attention on her. "You must be Jaden. I have to tell you I'm happy to see you didn't hoof Leif's ass out your door. We'll now be able to live with him once again."

"You're welcome, I guess," she said softly.

"Come on, then," Jager said as he nodded toward another part of the house. "Everyone is waiting to meet her."

She and Leif fell into step behind Jager as he walked away. Jaden stepped into a large living room that had a big widescreen television against one wall and found the room full of people. All conversation stopped when they entered.

She had to do a double-take a few times as Leif introduced her. The rest of his brothers turned out to be super good-looking and large. Roan, Jager, and Skylar looked so similar, there was no mistaking them as siblings. And Roxie's husband, Beowulf, fit right in with the rest of the hot-looking men. The only people in the room who didn't have the supermodel attractiveness going on were Roxie, Ansley, who was Roan's wife, Daylen, Eli, who was Saskia's husband, and, of course, herself.

Jaden still found it mindboggling that Leif lived with all these people—minus Beowulf and Roxie—and didn't find it overcrowded. Yes, the mansion was huge compared to her standards, but with this many people in the house at any given time, they'd be running into someone at almost every turn.

She and Leif sat on one of the couches, which were the only seats not taken. Once they were settled, Roxie asked, "So, where did you two meet?"

When Leif didn't offer up anything right away, Jaden answered. "At the grocery store where I work. I believe he was buying ice cream for you."

Roxie shot Leif a knowing smile. "Ah-ha. I knew something was up after you came back from shopping that time I sent you."

"Well, I wasn't going to be telling you, now was I?" Leif asked. "If I had told you I'd met Jaden there, you would have just used it to ride the hell out of me. I really didn't need that in addition to the urge driving me crazy."

Jaden looked at Leif. "The urge?" As he stiffened, she quickly added with a small laugh, "What's that? I hope it isn't something contagious."

"Yes, Leif," Roxie said. "Why don't you explain to Jaden what the urge is?"

Leif stood, yanking her up with him. "I'll show Jaden the rest of the house, now." He practically dragged her out of the room by her hand.

She was almost running to keep up with his longer stride. He didn't seem to notice that her shorter legs couldn't cover as much space as his long ones. He led her to the kitchen and then out the door to the back of the mansion. Leif didn't stop until they stood on the grass in the center of a large backyard. It'd been as beautifully landscaped as the front.

Jaden panted from her run out of the house, and said, "Can you at least give me some warning before you drag me around like a dog on a leash? Not everyone is a giant like you."

He gave her a sheepish look. "Sorry. I wanted to finish the tour."

She raised a brow. "Sure, you did. I think it's more along the lines of you wanting to get me away from Roxie."

Leif captured her in his arms and kissed her forehead. "Okay, you found me out. It's just..."

"It's just what?"

"There are some things I have to tell you about me, and I'm not ready to do that yet."

Jaden went very still. "I have to say that doesn't exactly make me think it's anything good. Please don't tell me you're married."

"No, I am not."

"Or that you're really gay."

"No! No, I'm not gay or bisexual. Believe me, I've never swung that way." He nibbled at the corner of her mouth. "I would think after last night, my sexual orientation would be quite clear."

She shivered as Leif moved to her ear and swirled his tongue inside it. "Those were the only things I could think of that you might be reluctant to tell me about."

"Since the thought even crossed your mind, I guess that means I should show you my room and remind you why thoughts of me being gay are completely unfounded."

"Hmm, I could go for seeing your bedroom."

Jaden lifted her face to Leif as he shifted his lips back to her mouth. He took it in a heated kiss. He ground his hips into her, showing her just how hard he'd gotten. Her pussy grew wet, knowing how good it was to have his thick cock inside her, stroking in and out. Even though she hadn't ever had this much sex in her life, she desperately wanted him again. If he pulled her down to the grass and stripped her naked to have his way with her right out there, she probably wouldn't stop him. He touched her, and she lost all her common sense.

"Arg, I'm going blind," Jager yelled out one of the open windows. "Would you two get a room already?"

Leif lifted his head, looked toward the mansion, and flipped his brother off. "I'm going to kill him."

"I guess we asked for it, standing out here in the open for anyone to see."

"Then it's time for us to go some place where we won't be disturbed."

Instead of heading back to the mansion as Jaden had thought he would, Leif took her hand and guided her to what looked to be a storage shed at the back of the property. He opened the door and then urged her to step inside. Once he stepped in behind her, he shut them in.

Since there weren't any windows, Jaden couldn't see anything. "I'm blind here."

"It's okay. I got you," Leif said as he pressed his body against the back of her.

"I thought you were going to show me your room." She sucked in a breath as his large hands covered her breasts, and he kneaded them through her shirt.

"I will, but I don't think I can wait long enough to have you. We'd have to get you back inside and all the way up the stairs."

Jaden relaxed into him. Her pussy throbbed as Leif slightly bent his knees and rocked his erection against her bottom. Wetness leaked into her panties. "I don't think I can wait, either."

"Good, because I'm going to have my cock inside you very soon."

That just made her even more breathless. Her head fell to his chest and she rubbed her butt against him. "And I want you there."

He brushed her hair aside and kissed the side of her neck. "Hold on to the shelf."

"What shelf? I can't see anything."

"It's right in front of you."

She blindly reached out until her fingers brushed against wood that was at about waist height. Jaden figured Leif couldn't see any better than she could and was about to tell him she'd found the shelf when he dropped his hands to her waist. He tugged her sweats down her legs to her ankles. Cupping her pussy through her panties, he stroked her. Not able to see, she had to rely on her other senses. The feel of him touching her in complete darkness only enhanced her pleasure.

Leif hooked the top of her panties with his fingers and stripped them down her legs to lay in a puddle on top her pants. He skimmed his hands back up to her hips and pulled her farther away from the shelf. She ended up slightly bent over. Then, with a knee between her legs, he pushed her to open them as far as she could with her pants around her ankles.

"Perfect," he said, running his hands under her shirt and pushing her bra up and over her breasts. "Stay just like that."

After giving each nipple a tweak, Leif kissed a path down her back to her bare waist, lowering behind her as he went. He skimmed his hand along the back of her calves and thighs. He followed the same trail with his mouth, one leg at a time. Once he reached the curve of her backside, he gently nipped the flesh there. Jaden gripped the shelf in front of her tighter. A pounding ache throbbed deep inside her pussy.

"Leif," she whimpered. "Now."

"I will. I just need a quick taste first."

Jaden practically went on her toes as he swiped her pussy with his tongue from behind. She moaned as a wave of pleasure swept through her. As he continued to lick, delving into her wet opening, she rocked against his mouth. God, did Leif know how to use his tongue. If he kept it up, she would come before he even entered her.

He gave her one last lick and then Jaden heard the zipper on his jeans being tugged down, along with the rustle of material. After Leif rose behind her, his cock brushed against her entrance with nothing between them. He rocked into her, stroking his shaft along her pussy, the blunt head gliding against her clit.

Wanting him inside her now, she shifted her hips as he pushed in from behind. The head of his cock slipped inside her pussy. With a strangled moan, Leif grasped her hips and sank the rest of his length inside her. He used her hips for leverage, and pumped in and out. Jaden gripped the shelf so hard the wood creaked beneath her fingers. Lost in the sensation of his shaft impaling her over and over again, she rocked back to meet his strokes.

Their harsh breathing filled the small shed. As her orgasm built, Jaden couldn't have cared less that they were in a garden shed with no lock on the door, where anyone who walked past could hear what she and Leif were doing. All that mattered was having his thick shaft pumping inside her.

Her pussy clutched Leif's cock as her climax took her over, and he half-growled and half-groaned. He surged into her one final time and stiffened while he, too, came.

Once she slowly came down from the sexual high, Jaden realized her legs and arms shook. If not for Leif holding her around the waist, she wouldn't have been able to keep herself standing. Each time she made love to him, it just seemed to get more intense. If not for exactly remembering where they were, she would have gone for a second round since his cock was still thick and hard inside her.

He pulled out and straightened her against him. He cupped the side of her face, turned her head toward him, and gave her a tender kiss. "I think we're going to have use the shed like this more often."

She chuckled. "If we do, I think we should figure a way to lock it from the inside. I don't know about you, but I wouldn't want one of your family walking in on us."

"You have a point there. I doubt they would, but with Jager, you never know. We'll figure something out for next time."

Jaden blindly fumbled to pull her panties and sweats back up while she heard Leif doing up his jeans. "This was nice, but I was really looking forward to seeing your room," she said.

Leif opened the shed door and guided her outside. Jaden had to shade her eyes with her hand until they adjusted to the bright sunshine. "I was thinking my bedroom would be the logical place for my tour to end. I can also show you my shower, which has enough room for two adults. Maybe you would like a tour of it as well?"

"I'd love to see it, along with a few other things," she said in a husky voice.

She ran her gaze suggestively over Leif's body and landed on the still prominent bulge in the front of his pants. Before she could protest, he scooped her up into his arms and ran with her toward the mansion.

CHAPTER EIGHT

L eif used the tips of his fingers and traced circles against Jaden's shoulder as she lay snuggled into his side. They'd made love in the shower and then in his bed — twice. They'd also fallen asleep for a few hours, which was not surprising, since they were expending a lot of energy making love. Soon he would have to get up and find them some food. They'd probably burned a ton of calories.

He wasn't ready to leave the bed yet. Leif was quite content to just quietly hold Jaden in his arms — something else that was entirely new for him. He wasn't what you would call a cuddler. Usually, after he slept with a woman, he made sure he satiated her to the point where she would fall asleep. That way, he could easily slip out of her bed without any fuss or muss.

With Jaden, he'd satiated her enough that she fell asleep, but he wanted to keep her close. This feeling had to be part of the reason she'd been destined to be his mate. After only a few short days of knowing her, he felt strongly for her. His hunger for her seemed to be unending. It was still in the early days, but he had a feeling he wouldn't get bored with her. The more he made love to her, the more he craved her touch.

Jaden stirred and lifted her head so she could look at his clock on the bedside table. She squinted. "What time is it? Without my glasses on, I can't see that well."

He turned his head and took a quick look. "It's a little after six."

She dropped her head back down onto his chest. "You do realize we've spent almost the entire day in bed."

"There's nothing wrong with that."

"Won't your family say anything? They have to know what we're doing up here."

"They do. That's why no one has come pounding on the door. With three other couples in the house, everyone knows when a bedroom door is shut, not to disturb the people inside."

Jaden stretched. "I think I could lie here with you for the rest of the night, but I should get up. For one thing, I'm hungry, and for another, I should be heading home soon."

Leif clutched her tighter. "Why? I can feed you, and you can even stay here in bed. I'll make us something and bring it up. Plus, I want you to stay the night."

She propped herself up on her bent arm and stared at him with an expression that said she was surprised by his offer. "Really? You want me to stay the night?"

"Yes, really. Why do you find it surprising?"

"Well, you spent the night with me last night, and we've been together ever since. I thought men liked to have their space."

He smiled. "At one time, that might have been true for me, but not anymore."

Jaden seemed to mull it over for a few seconds. "I don't know, Leif. It's very tempting, but I have to go to work tomorrow morning." She leaned down and kissed his lips. "If I stayed here tonight, I'd end up not getting much sleep, and I wouldn't be able to wake up to go into work."

"I promise I won't keep you awake all night. We'll get up early enough for me to drive you to your place so you can change into your uniform, then I'll take you to work."

She took her bottom lip between her teeth. It made Leif want to suck on it. "I'm really not sure. It would be an awful lot to ask of you."

"I don't mind. Soon, you'll be living here anyway."

"What did you just say?"

Leif gave himself a mental kick. He hadn't exactly expected to broach the subject of Jaden moving in with him in quite this way.

Since he had it out in the open, he decided to run with it anyway.

"I want you to move in with me, Jaden."

"You mean move into the mansion and share your bedroom with you?" At his nod, she sat up. "Don't you think you're rushing things a tiny bit? I didn't want to bring this up, but now I have to. The first time you came to my place you ended up running out of there, saying you couldn't do it. Now you want me to move in with you. I might not have that much experience when it comes to relationships, but I know just great sex won't make it last. And if we jump into it too quickly, it might not work out." As he opened his mouth to interrupt, she said, "Wait, let me finish. If we did break up, you'd be okay. I, on the other hand, would have to search for another place to live. On my wages, I'm pretty limited as to where I can go."

He sat up and cupped Jaden's face in his hands. "It'll work out."

"How can you be so sure?"

"I just know," he reassured her.

This would have been a great time for him to tell her what he was, and about her being his mate, but his tongue seemed to stick to the roof of his mouth, refusing to form the words. They were getting along so well right now, and he didn't want anything to mar it.

"Can I at least think about it?"

"Yes, and while you're doing that, I want you to think about quitting your job."

Jaden's eyes widened. "My job? You want me to quit my job?"

"Once you move in with me, you won't need to work. I have enough money to look after us both financially."

"Then what will I do? I'm used to taking care of myself."

He cupped the back of her head and brushed his lips across hers before he put their foreheads together. "It's time you let someone else take care of you. I want to be that person. Say you'll stay with me tonight." Leif kissed the side of her neck, nibbling his way down to the top of her shoulder. "Just say yes."

Jaden put her arms around his waist and leaned into him. "All right, I'll stay, but I'm going to work tomorrow. I'll use that time to think about everything else." She shivered. "With you kissing me like this, I don't think I can tell you no, anyway."

He covered her breast with his hand and squeezed. "I do have my ways."

"Yes, you do, but if you don't feed me soon, you won't be getting much further than this."

Leif let her go, jumped out of bed and quickly reached for his discarded jeans. "Then I'd better do something about that right now."

He gave her one more quick kiss, then left to find some food his mate would like.

* * * *

As promised, Leif did nothing but sleep next to Jaden during the night. Falling asleep with her in his arms, and waking up with her still there, was more than nice. He looked forward to many more of those.

He'd set his alarm so he could get Jaden to her place in time to change before she had to start work. Leif now sat on her bed, watching her pull on the slacks and blouse that were the grocery store's employee uniform. It really did nothing for her. It did a great job of hiding the curves he knew where just under her clothes. And as she pulled back her hair into a tight ponytail, he easily saw how other men could overlook her. As far as he was concerned, it was their loss and his gain.

Jaden put her glasses on once she finished with her hair. "I'm ready."

He stood. "What time do you get off work?"

"At four."

"All right. I'll be outside in the parking lot, waiting for you then."

She chuckled and shook her head. "And let me guess, you're going to take me to your place afterward."

"Of course." He gave her bed a quick glance. "No offense, but I don't really fit all that well in your double bed. My feet hang *way* over the edge."

"Yeah, I guess it wasn't made for a man of your size. I'll take pity on you and won't force you to endure that again."

"Which I'm grateful for. Let's go."

Once they arrived at the grocery store, Leif pulled into an

empty spot close to the front entrance. Before Jaden could get out, he leaned across his seat and gave her a kiss goodbye. "I'll be right around here, waiting for you when you get off."

"And I'll look for you." She gave him another quick kiss, then said, "I'm going to miss you."

"I'll miss you too."

Jaden opened the car door and then got out. She walked inside the store. Once she was out of sight, he started the car before he drove around to the side of the building. After he parked, he headed for the side entrance. Since he wasn't ready to tell her what being mated to him entailed, and he didn't want either of them to have to go through the anxiety of being separated, there wasn't much else he could do but hang out at the store. As long as he was inside, they would be fine. He just had to make sure she didn't see him, which meant he'd be playing hide-and-seek with her for her entire shift.

He caught sight of Jaden heading toward her cash register and ducked down an aisle. This wouldn't be much fun, but it was better than the alternative. It was going to be a long damn day.

* * * *

Jaden spent the hours until her break dealing with customers and thinking about Leif. She also couldn't stop thinking about his offer for her to quit her job and move in with him. It wasn't as if she loved her job, but to accept what he offered would be a huge leap of faith. As she'd told him the day before, if things didn't work out between them, she'd stand to lose a lot more than he would. She just had to decide whether she was willing to make that leap or not.

She also had to decide whether she'd be able to handle everything that came with Leif. She wouldn't be just moving in with him, she would be moving in with his entire family as well. Her feelings about it all were torn. She enjoyed living alone; she liked her privacy. On the other hand, being part of a big family was something she'd always wanted. There were times when being by one's self was overrated. Not having anyone around to help celebrate her birthday, Christmas, or the other holidays really sucked. If she moved in with him, she wouldn't have to face another one by herself.

And there was the fact she was falling for Leif in a big way. She could easily see it not taking much for her to fall completely in love with him. He must obviously feel something for her, or he wouldn't have asked her to move into the mansion with him. When he touched her, he made her feel as if she were precious to him, and that he never wanted to let her go.

Jaden could easily see this driving her crazy. What she needed was some advice from someone neutral. Knowing exactly who she could talk to about all this, she caught Vicky's eye and pointed to her wrist to indicate it was time for their break. There weren't too many customers around, and luckily, none of the other girls had called in sick, so they didn't have to cut their break short.

Vicky met up with her as Jaden walked toward the staff break room. "How did your weekend off, go?"

"Good." Jaden pushed opened the break room's door. They had it to themselves for now. She turned to face her friend. "I really need some advice."

"Okay. Lay it on me."

"I need some man advice."

Vicky grabbed her hand and led her to one of the chairs. "Sit. I'm all ears."

"All right. I'll get straight to the point. I met a man, and we ended up spending over twenty-four hours together this weekend. He slept over at my place the first night, and I stayed over at his last night. Now, here is where I need your advice. He wants me to move in with him."

"First of all, do I know this man?"

Jaden figured she might as well tell Vicky who Leif was. Her friend would eventually see them together, anyway. "It's the guy who kissed me at my cash register the other day. His name is Leif."

"I told you. Didn't I tell you? I knew you would see him again."

She rolled her eyes. "Yes, you told me."

"As for you moving in with him, how do you really feel about him?"

Jaden blew out a breath. "I like him—a lot. He makes me feel comfortable, and I enjoy being with him. There aren't any of those awkward silences. We just seemed to click from the very start."

"Since you've spent so much time together, you have to have slept with him. How is he in the sack?"

She felt a blush spread over her face. "Let's just say I would never have any complaints in that department."

"So, the man is a god in bed as well as looks like one. I'd say go for it."

"Well, there is one other thing I haven't told you about. He also wants me to quit my job. Leif is what you would call well-to-do. He says he has more than enough money to look after the both of us."

"The guy is rich too? Man, do you know how many times I've wished for a rich guy to come into the store, sweep me off my feet, and carry me away from all this? You'd be an idiot to tell him no."

"I wouldn't just be moving in with him. He lives in a mansion in Marin County with his big family. He has five brothers and a sister. The spouses of his sister and two of his brothers also live there."

"If it were me, he could live with fifty people and I'd still move in with him. If you like Leif that much, don't let him slip through your fingers. You'll find a way to make things work."

"I don't want to lose him, but don't you think this is all a bit rushed?"

"Look, if you feel that way, why don't you give it a trial run? Tell Leif you want to try it for a week before you give up your place and quit here. If it doesn't work out, you won't be left in the lurch. And if it does work, what's a week?"

She nodded. "I think you just gave me the answer to my problem. A trial run is a perfect idea."

Vicky patted her hand. "See, I'm good for something sometimes."

Jaden laughed. "It would seem so. I guess we should head back." After they stood, she said, "Thanks, Vicky. I really needed someone to talk to about this."

"I'm always here for you."

Now Jaden couldn't wait until the end of her shift so she could tell Leif about her decision. It wasn't exactly what he wanted, but she didn't think he would object to a trial run.

Jaden stepped back into the store and thought she caught a

glimpse of Leif just out of the corner of her eye. When she turned to look at that spot, no one was there. Obviously, she was thinking about him so much she was now seeing him when he really wasn't there.

CHAPTER NINE

That had been a close one. Leif had watched Jaden go to the break room with another cashier and decided to hang close by until she left. He'd already walked around the store so much, he now knew where to find everything in it. So far, he'd been able to keep under the other employees' radars. He didn't need one of them noticing he'd been there for hours and have him kicked out for loitering.

To be honest, he didn't know how many more times he could do this. If he had to do this all week, he could see himself losing his mind from boredom. He could only look at food for so long before his eyes crossed. Plus, it made him hungry. At least the store had a coffee shop. He'd managed to grab a cup of coffee and a muffin close to lunchtime, before Jaden had gone there to buy her lunch.

It wasn't all completely bad, though. Spying on Jaden all day allowed him to see what she was like when not around him. Able to see for greater distances than a mortal, he hadn't had to get very close to watch her. There were times when he swore she turned to look his way, but he wasn't worried she would catch him. Her glasses only improved her eyesight so much.

Her nearsightedness was something Leif hoped would go away once Jaden was turned into a werewolf. Not that he minded that she wore glasses. She looked cute when he accidently knocked them askew while kissing her. He just wanted her to have all the abilities a normal werewolf would have. Since neither Roxie nor the other mortals she'd turned into werewolves had worn glasses before the spell had been used, he wasn't sure what would happen to Jaden's eyesight.

He was getting ahead of himself. Jaden first had to accept him for what he was, as well as their being mates, before he made any mention of the spell. He hoped she would allow Roxie to turn her, but there was always the chance she would refuse. It might be selfish of him, but he didn't want to settle for one human lifetime with her. He wanted to live out the rest of *his* days with her at his side.

Leif walked down the aisle and headed for the opposite end of the store from where Jaden worked. He ignored the mortals around him, feeling as if he'd just been pole-axed. He loved Jaden. For a man who'd never thought he was capable of having that kind of emotion for a woman, it was a huge revelation. But it was true. His feelings for her had solidified into love.

A smile spread across his face. Now he understood what his mated siblings had meant about him not being able to escape it when it became his turn to find his mate. He'd been a fool to try. Even now, he couldn't picture his life without Jaden in it. Christ, he was even having a hard time remembering what it'd been like before her. She completed him. He'd thought he was good the way he'd been, but now that he could admit his true feelings for her, he knew how wrong that had been.

He'd have to tell Jaden what he was that night. And then he'd convince her to move in with him and quit her job. There was no point in putting it off. He'd also bare his soul to her. He chuckled to himself and shook his head. For a man who once thought doing that would doom him to hell, he couldn't wait for the opportunity to do it.

* * * *

At five minutes after four, Jaden walked out to the parking lot. She gave it a quick scan and found Leif's Cadillac parked almost in the same spot he'd used when he'd dropped her off. Smiling, she headed to it, and then got inside.

"You're right on time," she said.

"Of course I am. I wouldn't leave you hanging like that."

Leif gave her a thorough kiss that made her wish they weren't in such a public place, then he drove out of the parking lot. Once she noticed he took the route to her apartment, she said, "I thought we were going to your place."

"We are. I figured you would like to change and pack some clothes for tomorrow."

"How about I pack enough clothes for a week?" Jaden turned her head to look at Leif, to see his reaction to her words.

He gave her a quick glance before he turned his attention back on the road. "Does that mean you'll move in with me?"

"Well, not exactly. What it does mean is I'm willing to give you a week as a trial run."

"A trial run?"

"Yes. If, after a week, we haven't started to hate each other, I'll quit my job and move in with you permanently."

"How about the trial run only lasting three days?"

"A week."

"Four days."

"Are you trying to bargain me down?" she asked with a laugh.

He gave her a sexy grin. "Is it working? If not, I think I can come up with some ideas that will help sway you."

She laughed again, but inside, Jaden melted. She had a pretty good idea what Leif would do to win her over to his way of thinking. He'd use his body to persuade her, and it would work, too. One good bout of lovemaking and she'd be putty in his hands.

"All right, you win. Four days, but I'm standing firm on that. Not a day less."

Leif reached over and ran his hand up and down the top of her thigh. "You drive a hard bargain, but I'll still use my powers of persuasion to see if I can wheedle you down some more."

After they arrived at her apartment, Jaden didn't take very long to change out of her uniform and then pack it, along with enough clothes for four days. She also taped a note to her landlords' door to let them know she would be staying over at a friend's for a few days, just in case something came up.

In no time at all, she and Leif were back on the road, heading for Marin County. She watched the landscape go by, still finding it hard to believe there was a chance she would be living in such a rich neighborhood.

At the mansion, Leif took the small suitcase she'd packed and carried it inside while he held her hand. Instead of taking her upstairs to his bedroom, he put her suitcase down near the stairs and then headed them in the direction of the kitchen.

"I don't know about you," he said, "but I'm starved. I bet you are too, having to look at food all day."

"You build up a tolerance after a while."

"I doubt I ever would. I'd want to come home and eat everything in the house."

"I'm not saying there aren't some things I see and decide I should pick up after my shift is done. It's kind of the downside of the job. I've spent more money at the store than I should, at times."

"I'll have to take you shopping sometime and let you fill the cart up with whatever you want. My treat."

They found only Dirk inside the kitchen. He was at the stove, plating a steak he'd fried. He also had a large mound of mashed potatoes smothered in gravy on his plate.

"You're finally back," Dirk said as he turned and went to sit at the table.

"Where is everyone else?" Leif asked.

"Saskia, Eli, Roan, Ansley, Jager, and Daylen went out for dinner, separately. Kye and Skylar are with Roxie. I'll be heading over there as soon as I'm done eating."

Leif pulled out a chair for Jaden to sit. "Oh yeah, it's date night. And isn't this your day off?"

Dirk nodded and swallowed his mouthful of food. "Yes, but Roxie is helping with a project of mine. Before I forget, Saskia left a couple thawed steaks in the fridge for you and Jaden."

Leif went the fridge, and said, "I don't know, Dirk. Since you practically live over at Roxie's, you might as well move in with her and Beowulf."

"I don't think so."

Leif turned to Jaden with two packages of steak in his hands. "I think I'll throw these on the barbeque. How would you like yours done, Jaden?"

She looked at the T-bone steaks he held. "I like mine medium, but not too pink."

"Then yours will have to go on before mine." Leif turned to the stove and lifted the lids off the two pots that sat on it. "And it looks as if there are enough potatoes and gravy for us, so I don't have to make anything else. I'll just run out and get the barbeque fired up."

Leif walked out the back door to the patio. Now alone with Dirk, she turned to him and smiled. After meeting all of Leif's siblings, she'd noticed Dirk was the quietest of the bunch. He even used quiet, even tones when he spoke. With his friendly dark-green eyes and dark-brown hair with blond highlights, that just fell past his shoulders, she was sure he drew a lot of female attention, but he didn't come across as a man who would take much notice of it.

He smiled back. "While Leif is busy, I just want to tell you that I'm happy you're with him. He's a better man for it."

Jaden felt herself blush. "Thanks, but I'm sure I haven't had that much of an effect on him. We haven't even known each other for a week."

"Yes, you've definitely had an impact. Before meeting you, he had a bit of a roving eye when it came to women, but he's settled right down with you. We all told him one day he'd find the woman meant for him. He never wanted to believe us. And now, here you are."

"Thanks, I guess," she said, not sure what to say in response.

"Anyway, I'm happy to see you with Leif."

Dirk turned his attention to his food, leaving Jaden to think over what he'd said. She'd assumed Leif wouldn't have had any problem picking up women before meeting her, but she hadn't thought he was one of those guys who went from one woman to the next. It didn't seem like the Leif she knew. Whenever he was with her, he seemed only to have eyes for her. Not once had she caught him staring at another woman. Assuming what Dirk had said was true, Leif's asking her to move in with him would have been a monumental step for him to take. Maybe his feelings for her were a lot stronger than she'd thought.

Leif returned to the kitchen and washed his hands in the sink. "I have your steak on, Jaden. I figured we can just heat the potatoes in the microwave."

After he turned to face her, she stood and walked to him. "How about I do that since you're looking after the steaks?"

He wrapped his arms around her waist and pulled her close. "All right. That would be a big help."

Dirk pushed back from the table. "I'm done, so I'll leave you two alone to enjoy your meal." He put his plate into the dishwasher, and then walked out of the kitchen.

"I hope Dirk doesn't feel as if he had to leave because of us," she said.

"He knows he doesn't. Knowing him, he's probably in a hurry to get to Roxie's to play on the computer. They're both Internet junkies."

"Oh."

Leif brought his mouth down to hers. He swept the seam of her lips with his tongue before slipping it inside. Their tongues brushed against each other, tasting. Jaden leaned into him, getting swept away on the tide of passion he stirred inside her. At her moan, his kiss deepened. He angled his lips over hers for a tighter fit and ground his erection against her.

Before she completely lost the ability to think, Jaden said against his mouth, "Leif, the steaks."

He quickly let her go. "Crap, I almost forgot about them. We'll have to continue this later."

After he went outside, Jaden looked inside the cupboards until she found the plates. There was no question of what she and Leif would be doing after they ate. It looked as if she would be getting dessert once she finished her meal, after all.

* * * *

The sound of his cell phone ringing had Leif reluctantly leaving the warmth of Jaden's arms. They'd eaten and then hurried up to his room to make love. It'd been close as to whether or not they'd make it there. While they'd eaten, he'd used every opportunity to heat things up between them. He would never be able to look at another steak or mashed potatoes without getting aroused.

He grabbed his cell phone off his nightstand and answered the call. "Hello?"

"If you want that information you were looking for, you need to meet with me in an hour. Alone."

Leif recognized the gruff, male voice as a lone wolf he'd been working on to get information about what Miles was up to. "I'm not in the city right now. How about we set up another meeting?"

"No, it has to be tonight, or the deal is off. I found out what you wanted. Meet me in the parking lot behind the bar. You know which one. You have less than an hour, now."

Once the other end disconnected, Leif swore under his breath. He had no choice but to meet with the lone wolf. The information might be the lead they needed to flush Miles out of hiding again. The bastard had a knack for pulling a disappearing act.

Leif put his cell phone back and then turned to look at Jaden. The lone wolf had just complicated things between them. He couldn't bring her with him. It was too dangerous. She was a mortal, and could easily get hurt or worse. He didn't exactly trust this lone wolf. Leaving her behind was going to cause them to go through separation anxiety. It would be bad, since they were newly mated. Once they'd been mated for a while, like Roxie and Beowulf, they could stand to be away from each other for a few hours or so. Shit, he was going to have to quickly explain everything to her before he left, and he wouldn't have any time to reassure her or answer the inevitable questions she would have.

"Is everything okay, Leif?"

He sighed. "No. I have to go out, and I can't take you with me. Get dressed."

Jaden frowned, but she did as he asked. Leif quickly dressed as well, then headed for his walk-in closet. He came out with his sword and a leather jacket in his hands. He looked at Jaden. She was dressed, and her gaze was locked on his sword.

She swallowed. "Is that a sword you're holding?"

"Yes. Come downstairs with me. I don't have much time, but I have to tell you something."

Once they reached the foyer, he belted his sword onto his back and pulled his jacket on over it. He turned to Jaden and took her by the arms. She curiously gazed at him. He saw the confusion in her eyes. There was nothing for it but to tell her everything at once. He hoped he didn't scare the hell out of her.

"I have to meet someone, a lone wolf. He says he has some

information we need to help keep Roxie safe. There's a man named Miles, and if he ever got his hands on Roxie, he would use her so he could rule over all the werewolf packs in her stead. As her Protectors, we can't allow that to happen."

"Wait a second. Werewolf packs?"

"I'm a werewolf, Jaden. So are Roxie and the rest of my family."

"How can you be a werewolf? It's not possible."

"Yes, it is."

Hating that he could no longer ease Jaden into this, Leif let go of her and took a step back. He reached inside himself for the spark of magic that would allow him to make the change and shifted into his wolf form. She let out a small shriek and took a step back as she stared at him. He knew what she saw. Even in his wolf form, he was big. His fur was the same auburn color as his hair. He gave her a chance to take him all in, then he shifted back to human form.

Before she could take another step away, he took Jaden by the arms again. "I know you're probably having a hard time accepting what I am, but you have to listen to me. It's important. I've claimed you as my mate. The first time we made love, our souls joined. Being mated to a werewolf is very different from taking a mortal as a husband. With our souls joined, we won't be able to stand to be apart from each other for very long, which means after I leave, you're going to feel as if you haven't seen me in months, even though it has only been an hour. It could get so bad you'll feel like climbing the walls. You'll also think something bad has happened to me. Just try to remember I'm going to come back. I'll feel it as well, but I don't have much choice. Until Roxie turns you into a werewolf, you're too vulnerable as a mortal. I won't take the risk that something will happen to you."

Jaden's eyes had gone round behind her glasses. "Claimed me as your mate...turn me into a werewolf...Leif, I can't—"

He cut her off with a kiss. "The others will be home soon. Tell them I went to meet the lone wolf about Miles. They'll understand." Leif dropped his hands and walked backward toward the front door. "And tell them I didn't get to explain much about us. Saskia and the others will help you understand. I promise I won't be away any longer than I have to."

Knowing he was about to put them through hell, Leif turned and walked out the door without a backward glance.

CHAPTER TEN

She was going crazy. Jaden had never experienced anything like this before, and quite frankly, she never wanted to again. Her nerves were stretched thin. All she could do was pace back and forth across the large foyer. Leif had been gone for an hour, and it felt as if she hadn't seen him in almost a year. Every fiber in her being wanted, no, needed to be with him.

Along with feeling as if she were slowly losing her mind, what he'd told her about him being a werewolf and being her mate kept swirling around inside her mind. After watching him shift into a wolf, there was no doubt that what he'd said was true. At first, she'd been scared, but as the minutes ticked by after he'd left, she hadn't been able to hold on to her fear. Her anxiousness to be with him again kind of overrode any other emotion she felt. God, she missed him. She didn't care what he was. She just needed to have him hold her again.

Finally, some of the other couples of the house returned. Saskia, Eli, Roan, and Ansley arrived at the mansion at the same time. Saskia took one look at Jaden and rushed to her, worry clearly showing on her face.

"Jaden? Where's Leif?"

She stopped pacing, but she couldn't seem to cease wringing her hands. "He got a call on his cell. A lone wolf called who supposedly had information about Miles. He went to see him. Leif said you would know what that meant."

Saskia's look of worry increased. "I do. Did he get a chance to explain—?"

"About you all being werewolves and that I'm his mate? Yes, but I don't think as well as he wanted to. He was in a bit of a rush, but he did take the time to shift into his wolf form to make me believe what he'd told me."

"How long has he been gone?"

"About an hour. He told me it would get bad, but I wasn't expecting this. I don't know if I can take much more of it." Jaden crossed her arms over her stomach.

"We'll help you get through it," Saskia reassured her as she rubbed her back. "We've all experienced this since we became mated. Once Leif comes home, it'll end."

A cell phone ringing had Saskia reaching into her jeans' pocket. She pulled it out and looked at who was calling. She smiled at Jaden. "It's Leif. I'll put it on hands-free. Hearing his voice should help a little."

Saskia flipped the phone open. "Leif, you'd better be on your way back."

A male voice that wasn't Leif's said, "I'm sorry, sister dear, but Leif is a little...indisposed now."

"Miles, what have you done to Leif?" Saskia asked with a snarl.

"The nosy bastard got what he deserved."

"You better not have harmed him. Or I'll—"

"You'll do nothing. I didn't harm your precious brother-in-arms. He's taking a forced nap right now. No harm will come to him so long as you agree to a trade."

"A trade?"

"Yes, sister dear, a trade. The foretold one for Leif."

"We're her Protectors. We aren't going to just hand her over to you."

"You will, or Leif won't live to see another thousand years. I'll give you until dawn to think about it, then I'll call you again to tell you where to make the trade. For Leif's sake, you'd better make the right decision, because if you don't bring me the foretold one, I'll take my disappointment out on him before I put him out of his misery."

Miles disconnected, and silence reigned for a few seconds

before the others argued about what to do.

"We can't hand Roxie over to Miles," Saskia said.

"No," Roan agreed, "but we can't leave Leif with Miles, either."

"What if we made the trade with a decoy?" Eli asked. "You know, find another female who Miles wouldn't know, one who would be able to hold her own against him and be able to get away."

"Hmm, that could be an idea," Saskia said, but then she shook her head. "The only female I know who would be strong enough to take Miles down, besides myself, is Billie, and she and Royce are away on holiday."

Eli chuckled. "My sister will be upset that she missed the opportunity to kick some butt."

"We'll just have to come up with something else," Roan said.

Feeling even more desperate than she had before, Jaden said not very loudly, "What about me?" When she got no response, she said louder, "Use me instead of Roxie. I'll go."

The others stopped talking. Saskia gave her a sad look. "Jaden, you can't. For one thing, you smell like a mortal. Miles would get one whiff of you from a distance and he'd know. And being that you are mortal, it would be twice as risky as sending in an untrained female werewolf. At least she would have the ability to shift."

"Then do it," Jaden blurted.

"Do what?"

"Leif said something about Roxie being able to turn me into a werewolf. Then get her to turn me. That way I won't smell like a mortal."

"I don't know, Jaden. Once you're turned, it can't be undone. You have to know that we live a very long time. You would be living as a werewolf for at least a couple thousand years."

"I would be living those years with Leif as my mate, right? And I would be a lot stronger than I am now."

"Yes."

"Then I want it. Call Roxie and do whatever you have to do to get her to turn me."

When Saskia hesitated, Roan said, "I think we should let her. She and Leif are mated. If he sees his mate put in danger, he'll be that more protective of her. He'll claw through Miles and any of his men to get to her. Nothing will hold him back, especially after being separated from Jaden for so long."

Saskia sighed. "All right, you have a point there, but what if there is a slim chance Miles has seen Roxie from a distance? Jaden and Roxie have similar builds, even though they aren't the same height, but Jaden's hair isn't the same. She wouldn't be able to fool him even from a distance."

Ansley cleared her throat. "That's where I come in. Remember, I'm Roxie's hair stylist. I can color Jaden's hair to match hers and cut it the same way. It may be a tad shorter, but it won't make that much of a difference. As for the glasses, Jaden just won't wear them."

"I really can't see all that well without them," Jaden said.

"After you're turned, you'll have perfect vision, I'm sure," Roan assured her. "Since she was turned, Ansley's eyesight and hearing are now as acute as any born werewolf. The same will happen with you." He looked at Saskia. "Well, sis, what do you say?"

Jaden looked expectantly at Saskia, as did Ansley. Finally, Saskia nodded. "All right, we'll do it. Let's just hope Leif doesn't kill me afterward for putting his mate in danger."

* * * *

After one quick phone call, Roxie was on her way to the mansion, accompanied by the Protectors who'd been with her. Roan had taken Ansley to an open-late drugstore to buy the hair coloring kit needed to dye Jaden's brown hair to Roxie's golden-brown. They arrived a short time after Jager and Daylen had returned home.

While waiting for Ansley to return, Saskia had done her best to answer any questions Jaden had. Jaden now had a better understanding of werewolves, and what being mated to one entailed. She still couldn't get over the fact Leif had known she was his mate from her scent on that very first day she'd seen him. After what Dirk had said about Leif being a lady's man, it also didn't surprise her to learn he'd fought the mating urge to claim her as his. It also explained why he'd been so desperate to have her, that night he'd come to her place.

Jaden wasn't bothered that she hadn't been given any choice when it came to their mating. Leif was the man for her. Her feelings for him had grown deeper faster than she'd ever experienced before. And now that she was separated from him, she realized she never wanted to live without him.

Ansley had dyed her hair, and Jaden had just come down from showering out the color when Roxie, Beowulf, Dirk, Skylar, and Kye arrived. Everyone congregated in the kitchen while Ansley set to work cutting Jaden's hair. The men and Saskia had moved to one part of the kitchen while the other women gathered where Ansley worked.

Roxie pulled up a chair across from Jaden and met her gaze. "Are you still sure you want to go through with this, Jaden?"

"Yes, I'm sure." To distract herself from the rollercoaster of emotions she was almost constantly feeling because of not being with Leif, she asked, "How is the spell done?"

"It's pretty simple. I inject you with some of my blood, say the words of the spell and then you'll turn. That's why I brought these with me." Roxie opened a paper bag and pulled out two small packages holding rubbing alcohol wipes and a new syringe, one that looked like the kind diabetics used.

"I can handle that."

"Now I'm not going to lie to you, Jaden. Once I've said the words, it's going to hurt like a bugger, but it doesn't last for very long. Right, Ansley?"

"Roxie's right," Ansley said in return. "It only lasts a matter of seconds."

"Just remember what the outcome will be," Daylen said. "Once the pain is over, you'll be Leif's mate in every way."

"I should be able to handle it, then." Jaden listened to the sound of Ansley's scissors clipping away for a few seconds before she said, "While on the phone with Saskia, Miles called her sister, but called Leif her brother-in-arms. Wouldn't Leif be his brother too?"

Roxie shook her head. "The Protectors may call themselves brothers and sister, but they all aren't natural siblings. Roan, Jager, and Skylar are the only true siblings. They've been living together for centuries, so they've come to think of themselves as one big family. Saskia's grandmother was the one who brought them all together, basically forming their own small pack, with Saskia as pack leader. Miles is Saskia's real brother and, at one time, was a Protector until he went bad."

"I get it now. Miles needs you so he can rule the packs?"

"Basically. I rule them now since I'm the foretold one. Saskia's grandmother had the sight and was the one who saw my coming, hence the title of the foretold one. Saskia also has the sight, and recently, we learned Miles unfortunately has a bit of it as well. That's why he's been able to keep one step ahead of the Protectors."

"If he has the sight, why hasn't he been able to see you in one of his visions?"

Saskia, who had come to join them, said, "That's a good question. I haven't been able to figure that one out. I had the vision that led me to Wulf's Den where I knew the foretold would be found, but Miles obviously hasn't been able to pick up on you."

"Well," Roxie said, "I may have an explanation for that. You know I've been playing around with my magic to see exactly what I can and can't do. One of the things I've been doing ever since that night at the club, when you said how you found me, is to use my magic to shield myself. When you told me about Miles, I've been kind of specifically directing it to deflect him."

"You've been doing it all this time, and you never told me?" Saskia asked.

"I didn't know if it was actually working or not, but I have a feeling it must be."

"All right. Let's do a test. I know I can pick up your location if I concentrate hard enough, and a vision will come to me. Include me in this direct shielding you're doing for Miles."

Roxie closed her eyes for a few seconds, then opened them. "Okay, done."

Saskia got a faraway look on her face. A full minute passed before she shook her head and smiled. "Well, I'll be damned. I'm getting nothing but a blank."

"Then I guess it's working," Roxie said with a large smile.

"At least we don't have to worry about Miles learning your identity through a vision."

Ansley put down her scissors and picked up the hairdryer.

"I'm all done. Once I style it, it should look exactly like Roxie's."

Jaden closed her eyes as Ansley dried her hair. She'd let the others' conversations wash over her. It took almost everything she had not to go out and look for Leif, even though doing so would be a complete waste of time. Miles had him hidden somewhere in the city. It would take an army and more hours than they had, to be able to find him.

Ansley shut off the hairdryer, then put it on the table and took off the cape she'd put around Jaden. "What do you think?" she asked the women.

"Perfect, as always," Roxie said. "From a distance, Jaden will pass for me."

Jaden opened her eyes. "I guess it's spell time."

Roxie met her gaze. "Are you ready for this?"

The men joined them as Jaden nodded and put her glasses on. She wanted to be able to see everything Roxie did. "Let's do it."

After opening one of the wipes, Roxie rubbed the inside of her elbow with it before she took off the top of the syringe and stuck the needle into her skin. She pulled out the plunger and filled it with some of her blood. Guessing at what was to come next, Jaden held out her right arm, turned so the inside of her elbow was facing up. Roxie used the other wipe, then jabbed the needle into Jaden's arm.

Once she pushed the plunger to inject the blood, Roxie said the words of the spell. "The magic of the wolf's blood is now in thee. A wolf you become to run wild and free. Where once there were two, now only one we see."

Jaden gasped while Roxie chanted. The words seemed to resonate inside her. The place where Roxie had injected her burned. Then, moving like quicksilver, the feeling swept through her whole body. It felt as if Jaden was on fire from the inside out. She bit her bottom lip until she tasted blood, to keep herself from yelling in pain.

Once she thought she wouldn't be able to take anymore, the burning sensation slowly eased until it disappeared completely. Jaden shook with the aftereffects and took a few deep breaths. She looked at everyone crowded around her and found her sight was blurry, so she pulled off the glasses she no longer needed.

She gave everyone a shaky smile. "It worked. I can't see

through these anymore." She put her glasses on the table.

Saskia came and hugged her. "Welcome to the family, Jaden." She sharply pulled away from Jaden and gasped.

"What?" Jaden asked, scared that something had gone wrong with the spell after all.

"Your scent is different, and not just because you're now a werewolf. It's subtle, but it's enough for me to smell it." Saskia's gaze ran over her face with shock. "Your scent is similar to Miles's."

"Are you sure?" Jager asked. At Saskia's nod, he leaned in to Jaden and took a deep breath. "Holy crap. You're right."

Feeling uncomfortable, Jaden said, "How can I smell like Miles? I don't know him, and I've never been near him."

"Jaden, who is your father?" Saskia asked softly.

"I have no idea. My mother never told me. She never spoke of him. After she died, I never found anything in her belongings about him, either."

"I know who he is. Miles is your father, which makes you my niece."

Shocked, Jaden asked, "How can you tell that just by my scent?"

"Werewolf offspring carry the scent of their mother and father. It's something that doesn't go away, even after they reach adulthood. Because of that, we always know the paternity of our children. I guess you being born as a mortal had somehow masked Miles's scent, but you are most definitely his daughter."

Learning her father was the man who'd taken her mate and threatened to kill him was just not something Jaden needed. She'd always wondered what he was like, but right now, she wished he'd remained a mystery.

CHAPTER ELEVEN

They all moved to the living room, waiting for Miles to call. No one had been able to sleep. Jaden hadn't been able to even sit down for any length of time. She'd take a seat for a few minutes, then have to get up and pace once again. No one said anything about it. There was nothing they could really do to help her. Only being with Leif would end her torment.

Precisely at dawn, Saskia's cell phone rang.

Jaden crossed to stand in front of Saskia, where she sat on one of the couches next to Eli. Saskia answered the call and put it on hands-free. "Hello, Miles."

"My, aren't we polite?" he said back. "Have you thought over my offer?"

Jaden listened to the sound of her father's voice, wishing like hell she could reach through the phone and strangle him. He sounded too smug for her liking.

"Yes," Saskia replied. "We'll make the trade. Tell us where and when."

"Really? You're willing to hand over the foretold one just like that?"

"It's the way she wants to do it. She rules the packs, so I really don't have any say in the matter, now do I?"

Roxie silently gave Saskia a thumbs-up. They'd known full well Miles wouldn't believe they were that willing to hand her over. There had to be a pretty good reason behind their decision.

Obviously, Miles bought it, because he said, "And, of course, you wouldn't be able to ignore a direct order from her. Doesn't that just work out to my advantage?"

"Would you stop crowing about it, and tell me where you want to make the trade?" Saskia snapped.

"Watch how you speak to me, sister dear. I said I would give you Leif if you gave me the foretold one, but I never said what condition he'd be in when we make the trade."

Jaden bit the inside of her mouth to stop from whimpering. Her mind formed one image after another of Leif bloodied and badly beaten.

"Where, Miles?" Saskia asked impatiently.

"The warehouse you forced me to destroy. In one hour." He ended the call.

Saskia stood. "Roxie and Beowulf, I suggest you go home. And don't fight me on this, Rox. You're pregnant, and need your sleep. I'll send Dirk with you two. Even though Miles will be a little busy dealing with us, I still don't want you unprotected. The rest of us will take Jaden to make the trade."

Roxie grumbled under her breath, but did as Saskia said. Before she left, she made them promise to call her once they had Leif back. Dirk followed the couple out. Saskia motioned for everyone else to follow her.

Jaden told herself to take deep, even breaths as she followed the Protectors outside to the detached garage. Once Skylar backed the SUV out, she climbed inside with Kye, Saskia, Eli, Roan, and Ansley. Jager and Daylen were going to ride in Jager's car. After they'd all piled in, they sped toward the Golden Gate Bridge.

Jaden sat by one of the windows and pressed her forehead to the glass, concentrating on watching the scenery go by. Her hands were tightly fisted on her lap. The closer they came to the city, the worse her anxiety became. At the feel of a large male hand closing over her fists, she turned her head to look at Kye.

"It'll be all right, Jaden," he said kindly. "You'll get through this."

She gave him a wavering smile. Right now, she didn't feel as if it would ever end. It seemed as if she'd been suffering forever.

Once they reached the warehouse district of the city, Skylar drove to a burned-out site where an older warehouse had once stood. Jager followed them. After he parked in front of the ruin, everyone climbed out of the SUV, except for Ansley. Roan gave his mate a quick kiss and then told her to stay put.

Jaden walked toward what was left of the warehouse, with the Protectors surrounding her, and told herself over and over again she could do this. It was the only way to get Leif back. She couldn't let herself think she would be coming face-to-face with her father for the first time, or how much of a bastard he really was.

Once they'd come to what would have been the back of the building, their group stopped a distance away from a smaller group. It consisted of one man out in front, with two men behind him and off to the side, holding Leif hanging limply between them. With her much-improved vision, she saw he'd been beaten. She forced her gaze to the man who was in front—her father.

The sun glinted off the same white-blond hair he shared with his sister. His looks were similar to Saskia's as well. The only difference was, his violet eyes had a hard, cruel edge his sister's didn't have. Like the rest of his kind, he had a werewolf's super good-looks.

Miles took a step away from his men and held up his hand. "That'll be far enough. Send over the foretold one."

Even though the distance separating them would have had a mortal shouting to be heard, Jaden had no problems hearing what Miles had said.

"Give us Leif first," Saskia said back.

Miles motioned back toward his men and Leif. "I'm afraid Leif isn't in any condition to be walking now."

"What did you do to him?"

"Nothing that'll cause permanent damage. I just gave him something to keep him asleep. No more stalling. Send her over. Now."

Before Saskia could say anything more, Jaden stepped up behind her and tapped her shoulder. "I'll go."

Saskia turned her back to Miles, blocking his view of Jaden. "I don't like the idea of sending you out there alone. There's no telling what Miles will do."

"You said you recognized me as his daughter from his scent on me. He'll be able to tell as well. Let's hope his meeting a daughter he never knew he had, distracts him enough for you to get Leif free."

Saskia silently searched her face. "It might work. Miles definitely won't be expecting that. Leif may be drugged, but I don't think he'll stay under when he scents you. You being Leif's mate will be another surprise for Miles when he finds himself confronted by an enraged, mated male. His two men won't be able to hold Leif back."

With a nod, counting on everything Saskia had said to be true, Jaden straightened her back, and with her head held high, slowly walked toward her father. Just before she reached him, the wind shifted direction so it was no longer blowing in her face, but at her back.

She knew the instant Miles smelled her scent. His brows drew together in confusion, then his gaze locked on her. He seemed frozen in place as she closed the distance between them and stopped to stand in front of him.

"Hello, Father," she said, meeting his gaze.

"Sarah," Miles whispered.

Hearing him say her mother's name so reverently, Jaden resisted the urge to slap him. He had no right to say it like that. He obviously had abandoned her mom when she needed him the most.

Jaden reined back her temper and shifted her gaze to Leif, then back to Miles. "I've come for my mate."

"Your mate?" her father asked dumbly and reached out a shaky hand toward her. "You're my daughter."

Jaden slapped his hand away before he made contact with her cheek. "Don't touch me," she said harshly.

A loud growl ripped through the air, then everything exploded in utter chaos.

Leif threw off the men holding him and launched himself at Miles. Jaden jumped out of the way just as he landed on Miles's back. Leif's eyes glowed and his upper lip curved in a snarl as he pummeled her father with his fists. Both men shifted to their wolf forms, using sharp claws and teeth to fight.

Before Miles's men could join in the fray, the Protectors surrounded them. Soon, the only one who hadn't shifted into a wolf was Jaden. She listened with only half an ear to the second fight that had broken out. She kept her gaze locked on Leif and Miles as they tore into each other. Neither one of them seemed to be gaining the upper hand. Each of them bore bloody claw marks on their sides that glistened through their fur. She could easily tell which wolf was which since her father was a white wolf.

Then her worst fears were realized. Miles somehow managed to get Leif onto his back and took his throat in his jaws. Knowing what would come next, Jaden ran to them and pulled on the fur on Miles's neck.

"Stop it!" she screamed. "If you had any feelings for my mother at all, you will not take my mate from me." Miles's wolf eyes shifted toward her. "Please," she pleaded as tears dripped down her face. "Please don't do this to me."

Miles seemed to hesitate. It was enough for Leif to break out of his hold. He would have attacked her father again, but Jaden moved to stand between the two wolves. "No, Leif. Enough. I need you."

Once Leif shifted to his human form, Jaden just about went down on her knees as a wave of longing and arousal washed over her, one so intense it left her gasping. The separation anxiety she'd felt became replaced with the need to join her body with Leif's, to reaffirm the mating bond between them.

Leif panted, and ran his gaze up and down her body. "Jaden?"

When Miles whispered her name behind her, Leif snarled and whirled to go after her father once again. Jaden blocked him and grabbed his arms. "No. He's my father."

"But, Jaden, we—"

"You'll do as I say, Leif," she said in her best authoritative voice. "As the foretold one, I'm telling you to let him go."

Leif's gaze shot to her face. "What?"

"You heard her, Leif," Saskia said. "The foretold one has given you an order."

Jaden met his gaze and stared at him, her eyes pleading for Leif to follow along. "Let him go."

Leif shuddered once, then dragged her into his arms. Jaden clung to him, needing to be closer. Now that they touched, she found what little control she had over herself slipped away.

"We have to get out of here—now," Leif said against her hair as he plastered himself to her.

His erection pressing against her had Jaden unable to hold back the moan that pushed out of her. She ached, her pussy throbbing in time with her rapidly beating heart.

Jager jangled his car keys. "Here, take my car."

Leif snatched them out of Jager's hand and scooped her up into his arms before he took off at a run. Jaden looked over his shoulder one last time at her father. He silently watched them leave.

Once Leif got them into the car, he peeled away with the tires squealing. Jaden couldn't control her panting. Her body was on fire. "Leif? I need—"

"I know, baby. Just hold on. I feel it too. It's because of the separation. It won't take long to get to your place."

True to his word, they arrived at her basement apartment in record time. Jaden shot out of the car and then went to the entrance. Once she turned the knob and found it locked, she remembered her keys were at the mansion. Leif pushed her hand away, gave the knob a hard turn, breaking the tumblers, and pushed it open. He did the same to the door at the bottom of the stairs.

Inside, he kicked the door shut and had her back in his arms. Aroused to the point of pain, Jaden tugged at Leif's T-shirt. Not used to her new strength, she ripped it down the middle and tore it off him.

Leif didn't seem to mind. His lips slammed down onto hers, kissing her with desperate hunger. The sounds of her shirt and bra being ripped from her body filled the room. While he continued to nip and suck on her lips, they rid themselves of their pants. Completely naked, he took her down onto the bed. His hips landed between her thighs. Jaden made an animal-like growl as the tip of his cock brushed against her wet pussy. She dug her fingers into the tops of his shoulders and pushed down just as he surged inside her. He took her hard and fast. His hips thrust against her as he pumped his cock between her legs. With three strokes, her climax barreled up to meet her.

Just before it hit, she panted. "God, I love you, Leif."

He groaned. "I love you too. Come for me, Jaden. I can't hold back. I need you too much."

She wrapped her legs around his waist. "Just a little bit more." She let out a keening moan, her orgasm tearing through her like a freight train.

Leif quickly followed, throwing back his head, and howling as his cock filled her with his cum. Out of breath, he collapsed on top of her, his still-hard shaft keeping them joined.

After they could breathe evenly again, Leif raised himself on his bent arms and stared at her. "Roxie turned you."

"It was the only way I could stand in for Roxie when we made the trade."

He fingered her hair. "I guess that also explains why your hair is cut and colored to match hers."

"We didn't know if my father had seen Roxie from a distance."

Leif searched her face. "How do you feel about all this? Being my mate, being turned into a werewolf, and Miles as your father?"

She reached up and cupped his cheek. "I want to be your mate, and I wasn't going to give up the two thousand years we can have together. How do you feel about having Miles's daughter as your mate?"

He gently brushed her lips with his. "I'll love you no matter who your father is. You're mine."

"Yes, I'm yours, and you're mine." She shifted her hips and grinned. "How about you show me how much you love me? Or, as the stand-in foretold one, do I have to order you to take me again?"

Leif smiled and slowly moved in and out of her. "That will be one thing you'll never have to order me to do."

He showed her over and over again what she had to look forward to for the next couple thousand years.

EPILOGUE

Alone in his high-rise apartment, Miles went to his bedroom closet and took out a box he hadn't looked in for a very long time. With shaking hands, he carried it to his bed and sat.

It wasn't very big, but contained some items he held dear. He'd tried to throw them away once, but hadn't been able to do it. They were mementos from a time in his life when he'd thought he could be a better man. That was before it had all fallen apart.

He took off the lid, reached inside, and took out a photograph that had been taken twenty-eight years before. The last time he'd looked at it had been eleven years ago. He stared at the woman with long, brown hair who smiled from the picture, and gently brushed her cheek with the tip of his finger. It was a picture of Sarah, the mother of his daughter. She hadn't been his mate, but he'd loved her just the same. And she'd loved him until he'd let his greed and need to find the foretold one come between them.

For years, he'd tried to push her out of his mind, and for a while, he had succeeded. Then in a moment of weakness eleven years before, he'd taken out her picture only to have a vision showing him her death. He'd had no idea she left a daughter behind. Their daughter.

Jaden looked more like her mother than like him. It had been a shock to smell his scent mixed in with hers. He'd never thought of himself as a parent, but knowing a part of Sarah lived on in Jaden, he longed to get to know her better. The chances of that were slim. She was the mate of one of the Protectors, as well as the foretold one.

Learning his daughter was the one he'd sought to use and control for so long left him not knowing what to do. He might have taken the dark road of life, but the part of him that Sarah had made feel human had never really died. When it came to his daughter, he had a conscience, after all. Ripping her away from her mate to bend her to his will, making her suffer, was something he couldn't bring himself to do.

Stuck between what he knew was right and the ambitions he'd lived with for centuries, Miles stared at the one woman who had expected him to be more than what he was. With the knowledge of his daughter's position, his life would never be same. What was he supposed to do now?

The End

SKYLAR'S DEVOTION

A famous Victoria's Secret fashion model, Braelyn comes home to visit her parents after being away for a year. On a shopping trip, a man on a motorcycle at a red light snags her attention while she crosses the street. Once she draws even with him, he flips open the visor of his helmet, and she instantly forgets what she's doing. A blast from a car horn makes her aware she's standing in the middle of the crosswalk, and she quickly gets moving.

Skylar follows the beautiful blonde with his gaze, watching where she goes. Sitting at a red light is not the place he expects to run into his would-be mate, but there she was. Determined not to let her get away, he follows her. He finds it hard enough to deal with her being mortal and not knowing anything about werewolves, but the bigger problem is the stalker who wants to do his famous mate more harm than good.

CHAPTER ONE

Braelyn walked down the street of San Francisco's Financial District where the fashionable clothing stores were located. She stopped in front of one of the storefronts and looked in the display window. The stores weren't as ritzy as the ones found in Los Angeles — where she now lived — but clothes shopping was one of her favorite things to do. Being one of the top fashion models in the country didn't help with her addiction much either.

She caught her reflection in the glass and pushed her dark sunglasses higher up on her nose before she tightened the ponytail she'd created when she'd scraped her hair back. So far, none of the people she'd passed on the street had recognized her, which suited her just fine. She was in San Francisco to visit her family. It'd been almost a year since the last time she'd been back to see her parents. Her modeling schedule kept her busy since she was in such high demand, and some of her shoots had her traveling halfway around the world. At twenty-four, Braelyn had to ride her success for as long as it lasted. There would come a day when a younger, prettier girl would take her place.

Continuing on her way, Braelyn passed a couple walking arm in arm, so into each other they hardly noticed the people around them. She'd never fallen for a man that hard before, where he seemed entirely devoted to her, and she to him. Most of her relationships ended up being nothing more than a passing fancy.

She'd dated a few male models, but she'd found some of them to be vainer than their female counterparts. And regular guys, well, they tended to only want to date her because of her model status. They were the ones who tried to get her into bed halfway through a date. Just because she had to pose naked at times—with all the important body parts strategically hidden—it did not mean she would be an easy lay.

Braelyn reached a crosswalk, stopped at the curb and waited for the light to change. Once it did, she stepped onto the street and headed for the clothing stores on the other side.

At almost the halfway point, she noticed the black motorcycle stopped at the red light for the oncoming traffic and the man who rode it. The closer she came Braelyn noticed the way his dark blue jeans stretched across his thighs, outlining the heavy muscles there. He wore a black leather jacket, and his shoulders were wide and looked just as heavily muscled. The only thing she couldn't see was his face since he wore a helmet with the dark visor pulled down.

Just as she drew even with the motorcycle, the rider flipped open the visor, drawing her attention. Braelyn's steps faltered, and she sucked in a sharp breath when her gaze encountered a pair of light blue eyes staring at her with hunger. Her heart beat faster as she took in the gorgeous face that came with them. The longer they stared at each other the more aware her body became of the man who had yet to pull his gaze from hers.

The sound of a horn blaring broke the spell around her. Abruptly yanking her gaze away, Braelyn saw the crossing light flashed. Quickly remembering what she was supposed to be doing, she crossed the rest of the distance to the other side of the street.

* * * *

Skylar had taken his recently purchased Kawasaki Ninja ZX-14 motorcycle out for a spin with no real destination in mind. It was a nice sunny day, and since he didn't have protection duty until that night, he'd decided to take advantage of it.

The drive from his home in Marin County to San Francisco had given him the chance to open the bike up a bit. He hadn't had much opportunity to make this trip just for the pleasure of it. As one of the Protectors who watched over Roxie—the foretold one who ruled over all the werewolf packs—he took his duty seriously, which meant long rides on his motorcycle, just for himself, were few and far between.

In the heart of the Financial District, Skylar geared down his bike as the light up ahead changed to amber. He shifted into neutral once he came to a stop just as it turned red and sat straight. He used his leg muscles to keep the bike balanced. Inside his mind, he heard Leif's voice knocking how low the handlebars were. He smiled to himself. His brother-in-arms might think they were a back-breaker, but Skylar liked the speed of the racing bike and didn't mind having to bend low to ride it.

With his next breath, a scent slammed into him like a sledgehammer over the head. He drew in a deeper breath and filtered out the smells of the numerous car exhausts around him, leaving only the one scent behind. Out of the corner of his eye, he caught sight of a leggy blonde using the crosswalk, coming toward him. Skylar turned his head as she looked in his direction. It was her scent that had his mating urge kicking in, making his body go haywire.

He flipped open his visor to more easily draw her scent into his lungs. Skylar couldn't stop himself from staring at the woman who was to be his mate. The mating urge had to show in his eyes, but he was powerless to stop it. Their gazes met, and her steps slowed.

His cock had gone rock-hard the instant he'd caught a whiff of her scent, but locking his gaze to hers through the dark sunglasses she wore had it twitching. Shifting his gaze to take her all in, Skylar noted her slim, curvy body encased in light blue skinny jeans and a sky-blue scoop-necked T-shirt that showed off her modest breasts. Long, strawberry-blonde hair had been pulled back into a high ponytail. He looked at her face. She was a beauty beyond compare. Werewolves were known for their supermodel good-looks, and the woman before him rivaled any female of his kind.

The driver of the car next to him honked. Skylar barely resisted the urge to growl and snap his teeth at the driver as the woman startled, then continued to cross the street. Not about to let his mate get away, he watched her gain the curb on the other side of the street and walk toward the row of clothing stores there.

Once the light turned green, Skylar revved his motorcycle, and making sure there weren't any cops around, did an illegal U-turn. He turned down the same street the woman had gone and then parked his bike in the first empty spot at the curb just as she walked into a store a couple of doors down.

Skylar put down the kickstand and then pulled off his helmet. He put it on the gas tank between his legs before he reached up to smooth his hair. With a couple of tugs, he straightened the ponytail at his nape.

He picked up his helmet, swung a leg over his bike and stepped onto the sidewalk. He easily followed the scent trail the woman had left in her wake. Skylar didn't even bother to look at what type of store it was as he pulled open the door and then walked inside. His gaze automatically searched for the woman, and he found her near the back of the store. Focused only on her, he headed in her direction.

A saleswoman stopped him before he got very far. "Can I help you find something, sir?"

He didn't shift his gaze from the blonde woman. "No, I've already found what I came for."

"Are you buying for a wife or a girlfriend?"

That question had Skylar turning his head to look at the saleswoman. She was young-looking and wore a friendly expression. It was also then he saw the racks of sexy-looking bras and panties all around him. He blinked. He stood in the middle of a lingerie store and was the only male on the premises.

"Ah...ah..." he stammered.

His brain seemed to stop functioning after he spied a red, practically see-through, scrap of lace that would show more of a woman's body than it would cover. The sight of it did nothing to cool his libido. If anything, it jacked it up several notches, causing his cock to strain uncomfortably against his jeans zipper.

The saleswoman gave him a smile. "Are you sure you don't need any help?"

Slightly embarrassed about the situation he'd gotten himself into, Skylar took a few steps away, determined to carry on with his plan to meet the woman who'd stirred his mating urge to life.

"I'm sure. I'll call you if I need you," he said quickly before continuing to the back of the store.

As he closed in on the blonde, he drew in deeper gulps of her scent, burning it to his memory. That done, he'd now be able to recognize it and use it to find her. Skylar greedily drank in the back view of her body as she looked through a rack of bras. After she pulled one off and held it up to look at, he had to stop the growl of need that threatened to rumble out of his chest. The undergarment was another see-through piece, only it was a pale shade of blush. As he pictured what she'd look like wearing it with only a pair of matching panties, his mating urge sank deeper claws into him. He must have made a small sound, because she turned to face him. She slowly lowered the bra and stared at him.

Skylar wanted nothing more than to pull the dark sunglasses off so he could see the color of her eyes, but forced himself to stay where he was. "Hi," he said.

It was hard to form a coherent thought when all the blood in his body seemed to be rushing to his cock.

"Hi," she said back slowly.

"I saw you outside."

She glanced at the helmet he held. "You were on the motorcycle."

"Yeah."

A small smile pulled at the corners of her mouth. "Did you follow me in here or do you just like to shop for women's lingerie?"

It was on the tip of his tongue to say he only liked to shop in a store like this if he could buy for her, but he'd more than likely get slapped for that if he said it out loud. She didn't know him and had no idea what she would be to him.

"Believe me," he said with a chuckle, "I don't make it a habit of coming to shop in stores that carry women's intimate apparel. Actually, this is my first time stepping foot in one."

"Then you followed me," she stated simply.

"You could say that. I found myself unable to let you just walk away without getting to know you." He ran his gaze over her face, letting some of his arousal show in his eyes.

She swallowed. "Really?" she asked quietly. "So you decided to chase me down? What if I don't want to get to know you?"

Skylar crowded her until her back hit the rack behind her. No longer able to stand the sunglasses blocking his view of her gaze, he plucked them off her face. He stared into a pair of beautiful emerald-green eyes. She didn't wear any makeup, but that didn't make her looks any less amazing. Now that he saw all her features, he found her vaguely familiar, though he knew he hadn't met her before. He'd have remembered that.

He leaned in a bit and dragged more of her scent into his lungs. There was the unmistakable tinge of arousal mixed in with it now. "Since you hadn't run from me in the first place, I hardly could have chased you down. And I most definitely think you want to get to know me better."

"You're awfully sure of yourself," she said in a voice that had dropped an octave to a sexy murmur. It seemed to wrap around his cock, stroking it.

He crowded even closer so they were toe-to-toe. "Sometimes you have to have enough confidence in yourself to succeed. How about we start with introductions? I'm Skylar."

His soon-to-be mate opened her mouth to reply, but before she could, the saleswoman returned. "Oh, my god," the woman said excitedly. "I know who you are. You're Braelyn Whitmore, the fashion model."

"Yes, I am," said the woman he wanted to claim as his own.

The saleswoman squealed, then shoved him out of the way so she stood in front of Braelyn. "I can't believe you're here. I watched you on TV last week on the Victoria's Secret Fashion Show. I personally think you were the best model on it."

That's when it hit Skylar why Braelyn looked familiar. While taking his turn to guard Roxie one evening the other week, she'd insisted he watch the very show the saleswoman had mentioned. He'd spent most of the broadcast trying to hide the erection he'd gotten when one model had walked down the runway in nothing but a bra and panties. It'd been Braelyn. Since he hadn't been able to smell her scent, he hadn't known then why she'd affected him more than the other scantily clad models.

The sudden thought of how many viewers, how many *male* viewers, had watched that fashion show had Skylar gritting his teeth to hold back another growl. It didn't sit well with him to think of what those males could have been thinking—let alone doing—while they'd watched Braelyn strut her stuff on the runway.

Obviously, unaware of the tension inside him, Braelyn smiled at the saleswoman. "Thanks. I enjoyed it."

"What are you doing in San Francisco? Are you working?"

"No. I'm on a bit of a break before my next assignment. I have family here."

Once it looked as if the saleswoman would continue to monopolize all of Braelyn's attention, Skylar butted into the conversation. "Sorry to interrupt, but you were talking to me first."

Braelyn turned to look at him and grinned. "Feeling neglected?"

"Would it help if I said just a little?"

She flashed him a smile. Had he been in wolf form it would have had him looking up at her with adoring eyes and his tongue hanging out while he panted for her attention. It had Skylar fighting to maintain what little control the mating urge allowed him to have. If it slipped, he'd be staring at her with his eyes glowing mutedly, something they did whenever he became very aroused or angry.

"Maybe a tiny bit," she said. Braelyn turned to the saleswoman. "It was nice meeting you, but I really don't want to draw too much attention to myself. Think of me as any other customer who walks through the door. I'm going to look around, and if I need any help, I'll be sure to ask."

The saleswoman nodded. "Sure. I understand." She glanced at Skylar. "I'm sure you already have more than enough help right now." The woman walked toward the front of the store.

Braelyn turned back to the rack of bras and rehung the one she'd been holding. She shifted through others, looking as if she really intended to continue shopping.

"You're still going to shop?" he asked. "What about us getting to know each other better?"

Braelyn peered over her shoulder. "We can still do that at the same time. There's one thing you should know about me—when I'm on one of my shopping trips, it would take a herd of horses to pull me away." She looked him up and down. "And from the looks of you, you'll be more than capable of carrying all that I buy."

"Ah...all right. I guess I'm okay with that, but can't we at least go to another store that isn't quite so...provocative?"

She gave him a sultry expression, the same one she'd used on TV when she'd reached the end of the runway and done her pose. It'd gotten his libido going every time he'd seen it. "I'm not finished here yet, and maybe I'd like your male opinion on which bra or panty you find sexier." Braelyn turned back to the rack and pulled out another lacy bra before she swiveled in his direction again and held it in front of her. "What do you think? Does this do anything for you?"

Skylar groaned. God, she was going to kill him or make it so he had blue balls by the time they left the store. He'd just met his would-be mate, and already she strung him along. And seeing the look of mischief in her eyes, he could tell she knew exactly what she did to him. At this rate, she'd have him a mess before he could claim her as his own.

CHAPTER TWO

Braelyn loaded Skylar down with a few more bags that held her most recent purchases. He accepted them without complaint, juggling the others he already held so he wouldn't drop anything. Once it looked as if he'd manage, she turned on her heel and headed for the store's exit. He fell into step behind her.

After they were out on the sidewalk and walking side by side, Braelyn smiled to herself as she looked at Skylar from the corner of her eye. It wasn't too hard to see he'd almost reached the point where he'd become fed up with all the shopping. She'd decided to take pity on him after they made one last stop at a shoe store.

"Where to now?" Skylar asked.

"The shoe store at the end of this block."

He glanced at her feet. "Is there something wrong with the ones you have on?"

She looked at the Jimmy Choo blush-colored suede clog sandals she wore. They had a one-inch platform and a four-inch heel that pushed her five-foot-nine height to almost six feet. Even with that lift, Skylar still had at least nine inches on her.

Braelyn met his gaze. "No, there isn't anything wrong with my shoes."

"Then why do you need to shop for more?"

She gave him a look that said he had to be kidding. "You can never have enough shoes."

He rolled his eyes. "Are you at least going to buy something more practical than those ankle-breakers you have on?"

"Hey, I happen to like theses shoes—a lot. They make my legs look long and sexy. Don't you think so?"

Skylar's heated gaze ran down the length of her legs, leaving a trail of warmth behind. It had her body standing up and begging for some attention. He really was gorgeous with his heavily muscled body, light blue eyes and long, light brown hair he wore pulled back in a ponytail that hung between his shoulder blades. His chiseled good-looks matched those of any male model, but unlike them, he didn't act as if his face would land him any woman he wanted.

If anything, he'd stayed completely focused on her, not really looking at another woman, for the hour they'd been shopping together. She was used to men making her the center of their attention, but Skylar was different. He didn't just look at her with lust in his eyes—though he did do a fair amount of that. He looked at her as if he'd found some great treasure. The combination of those two types of looks left her feeling edgy with arousal. His heated stares made her pussy ache and her nipples grow taut beneath her shirt. When he happened to stand behind her, she felt the warmth of his body seep into hers. That sensation only increased the desire that built inside her.

Braelyn broke out of her thoughts when Skylar spoke in a husky voice. "Do you really want me to answer that? Because if you do, you'll find yourself thrown against the nearest wall and kissed senseless."

Her heart beat a little faster, and she swallowed as they stopped in the middle of the sidewalk, facing each other. She had to lick her suddenly dry lips. Skylar's gaze locked on to her mouth.

"Is that a threat or a promise?" she asked, her voice a bit breathless.

"It depends on what you want it to be."

For a split second, Braelyn thought she saw Skylar's eyes take on a strange, muted glow, but it disappeared so quickly she could only assume it were hers playing tricks on her.

"And if I took it as a promise?" She played with fire, but with the turn of their conversation, she'd become more turned-on.

He shifted as close as the bags he held allowed. "Skip the shoe store and let's go someplace more private and I'll show you."

Tempting, so tempting, but she wasn't ready to take him up on his offer just yet. She'd had too many men think she was easy in the past. If Skylar wanted to get to first base, he had to prove he was interested in her for more than a quick lay or because she had a pretty face. That being the case, he would have to jump through some hoops first. Some of her friends thought she was just being a bitch when she did that with the men she'd become attracted to, but it was no surprise to Braelyn how well it worked to weed out the ones who really weren't interested in forming a relationship with her.

She took a step back. "Oh no, I'm not going to give up the shoe store." Braelyn started walking again, and Skylar fell into step beside her.

"All right. You can do the shoe store, but I get a kiss for being so cooperative."

Braelyn shook her head. "No kiss. Not until after you take me out for dinner tonight."

"How about this? We go to the shoe store, you give me that kiss and then I'll take you out to dinner."

She weakened when Skylar's arm brushed against hers as he moved out of the way of a pedestrian coming toward him. Every time he accidently did that or touched her, a tingly sensation, as if a low voltage of electricity had passed between them, hit her. This time, like all the others, she managed not to show any kind of reaction.

Braelyn cleared her throat, making sure any huskiness from arousal didn't show, and said, "Shoe shopping, one kiss where you can touch me only with your lips and nothing else, then you take me out for dinner tonight."

"Deal," Skylar answered quickly.

At the shoe store, he rushed her inside.

"You know, it's still early in the day. Since you won't be taking me out for that meal for hours, we can take our time," she said as he gave her an impatient stare.

"That may be so, but I get to claim that kiss as soon as you're done in here."

"I never said when you'd get your kiss."

Skylar shook his head. "I think I deserve to get it when I want it, especially after you tortured me with all those bras and panties."

She chuckled. "You didn't appear to be suffering too much at the time."

Actually, she'd known she'd put him through hell. She'd selected some of the slinkiest bras and panties the store had to offer and had Skylar tell her if they would suit her as she held them against her. Even though she really didn't know him that well, she was comfortable enough to play with him a bit. And not once had he lost his cool with her. In some ways, it almost felt as if they'd been made for each other. Their personalities seemed to be basically the same and meshed. Then there was the sexual attraction between them. She couldn't deny that the thought of getting naked and having some mind-blowing sex with him hadn't crossed her mind. Braelyn would have to be dead not to be affected by him. The man practically oozed testosterone.

Skylar took a noticeably deep breath. "Can we just hurry it up? Talking about the lingerie store has made me want that kiss even more."

Braelyn sighed dramatically. "If you insist."

She turned from Skylar and walked to the section of the store that held the expensive designer shoes. She looked at the ones on display and stopped when she came to a light brown high-heeled ankle boot in suede. It had a lattice detail that would wrap around her ankle with a zipper up the back. The heel was almost four inches, just the way she liked them. The designer was Manolo Blahnik, and after looking at the price tag, she saw it was on sale.

Braelyn grabbed the boot off the shelf, then turned in search of a salesperson, catching the eye of the woman who was behind the counter not too far away. Once she came over, Braelyn asked for a pair of the boots in her size. The saleswoman nodded, then walked to the backroom to get them.

Skylar made a choking noise, drawing Braelyn's attention. He stood in front of the display where she'd gotten the boot. "What?"

"Are you seriously thinking of buying those?"

"Yes. Why?"

"Did you look at the price?" he asked incredulously.

"Of course. That's why I'm more than likely going to get them. They're on sale."

"Maybe so, but they're still over seven hundred dollars. What the hell would the price be if they weren't discounted?"

She shook her head over his naiveté. "Over a thousand dollars. The boots are Manolo Blahniks." When Skylar gave her a blank look, she sighed. "Manolo Blahnik is one of the top shoe designers."

"That would have no bearing on me. I still wouldn't pay that price." He looked down and stuck out his foot, giving her a good view of the black shit-kicker boot he wore. "These are what I call boots, and they sure as hell didn't cost as much as that heeled contraption you want to try on."

The saleswoman returned. She put the box she carried on the floor in front of one of the chairs against a nearby wall and then opened the lid. Braelyn went and sat as the woman pulled the boots out. She slipped off her shoes and put on the boots. Standing, she walked back and forth before she stopped at the small mirror sitting on the floor. The angle of it gave her a perfect view of her feet and legs. She nodded. The boots looked good with her skinny jeans, and they were comfortable to wear.

She walked back to the chair and slipped them off. "I'll take these."

The saleswoman took the boots, put them back into the box and then headed for the register near the front of the store while Braelyn slipped her shoes on. At the counter, she opened her purse and took out her credit card.

Skylar had followed her. "I just did the mental math, adding up what you bought today. Do you spend this kind of money every time you go shopping?"

Braelyn shrugged. "Sometimes. It's not as if I spend beyond my means. And the business I'm in, it's all about keeping up with the latest fashion. I think of it as a work expense."

"A very expensive work expense," Skylar grumbled.

With the boots paid for and the credit receipt handed to her, Braelyn took the bag from the saleswoman and then headed out of the store with Skylar in her wake. "I guess that's it."

"Good. Let's get all these bags put into your car. Where are you parked?"

"In one of the lots a couple blocks from where you parked your motorcycle." She'd seen it at the curb when they'd left the lingerie store.

With a nod, Skylar got them moving in that direction. He seemed to be in a hurry. Braelyn found herself having to almost trot in just to keep up with his long strides, but that didn't cause him to slow any.

*

Skylar kept up the quick pace until he saw the lot where Braelyn had parked her car. A short glance around showed they were the only ones there, which suited his purposes. He intended to get his kiss from her as soon as they reached her car. His mating urge had been pushing him to kiss her, take her in his arms and show her exactly what she did to his body, and to his peace of mind.

It would only get worse until he finally claimed her as his own. His mating urge would continue to ride him until the mating bond formed between them. That would only happen when they made love for the first time. Once bonded, werewolf mates couldn't stand to be away from each other for any length of time. One hour apart felt like months. Their minds would play tricks on them and make them think something had happened to the other. And, once they were together again, hot, intense sex followed shortly thereafter.

Never having been mated before, Skylar so far hadn't experienced what mates went through when separated. His sister-in-arms, Saskia, his true brothers, Roan and Jager, and his brother-in-arms, Leif, all mated, they'd done a pretty good job of describing it. Apparently it was a bitch to go through, and an experience that should be avoided at all costs, especially when it came to the newly mated. Over time, the separation would become easier to handle, but that took over a year, at least.

As soon as they entered the parking lot, he asked, "Which one is your car?"

He would be more than happy to get rid of all the shopping bags he'd been toting around for the last hour and get Braelyn into his arms. She'd promised him a kiss, and he intended to get it.

She pointed to the end of the line of cars in the aisle where they walked. "Mine is the blue BMW."

Skylar looked where Braelyn had indicated and spotted the dark blue BMW M3 coupe. The car was obviously a newer model, and something he totally expected his soon-to-be mate to drive. She liked the best things out of life, be it clothes, shoes or cars. It was a good thing he had more money than he knew what to do with—being alive for a little over a thousand years had allowed him to amass a fortune—and would be able to provide her with whatever her heart desired.

At her car, she reached into her purse and then pulled out a ring of keys. She pushed a button on the remote, and the BMW's trunk popped open. Braelyn lifted the lid all the way before she stepped aside for Skylar to put the bags inside. She placed the single one she held next to the others and then closed the trunk.

Before she could turn around, Skylar stepped up behind her and wrapped his arms around her waist, pulling her back against him. He nuzzled the side of her neck with his nose. "Now about that kiss," he said.

"Are you sure you don't want to wait until after dinner to claim it?"

She leaned into him and put her hands on top his arms. Skylar bit back a moan of need as a rush of intense arousal surged through him. Her scent wrapped around him, making him drunk on it. His cock, now fully erect, pressed against the small of her back. She had to be able to feel it. He wasn't exactly small, by any means.

"No," he said, barely managing to keep a growl from his voice.

Braelyn spun in his arms and put her hands on his chest. She lifted her gaze to his. "One kiss only. For now."

Skylar tightened his arms around her and did what he'd been dying to do since he'd first seen her crossing the street. He took her mouth in a heated kiss, angling his mouth until he had a tighter fit. Her lips softened under his when he swept the seam with his tongue, begging for entrance. Once she let him in, he groaned deep in his throat at his first real taste of her. Their tongues twined, tasting and stroking. Braelyn moaned softly as he rocked his hips into her, his cock throbbing in time with the surging of his blood.

The kiss seemed to go on and on. One taste of her would never be enough. It took a considerable amount of control not to take the kiss further, regardless of them being outside in a public place. And when she balled her hands into the front of his T-shirt as she deepened their kiss, he found himself hanging on by a mere thread. He'd finally found his mate, and having her in his arms, he wanted to claim her, make her irrevocably his.

If Braelyn had been a female of his kind and not a mortal, they'd have already been well on the way to becoming mates. Since she wasn't, it meant he'd have to take things a little slower, no matter how hard his mating urge pushed him to make her his.

Finding the willpower to break the kiss, Skylar lifted his head. They were breathing at a quick pace. With each deep breath Braelyn took, it brushed her taut nipples against his chest. He met her gaze and saw a dazed look in her eyes. She might not be a werewolf, and she might have been unable to sense his mating urge, but that didn't mean she was any less affected by their kiss. The smell of her arousal wafted around them, giving proof to the fact she was as hungry for him as he was for her.

Skylar loosened his hold on Braelyn, not yet ready to let her go completely. "Where would you like to go for dinner?"

She blinked. "What...what?"

"I promised I'd take you out for dinner tonight. We need to decide where and what time. I have to work tonight so it can't be too late."

Braelyn released her hold on his shirt and leaned back into the circle of his embrace. "Right. Okay. How about you pick me up at seven? And why don't we eat at the Supperclub? You know the restaurant where you get to recline on beds while you eat instead of sitting at tables?"

Skylar wasn't sure if it would be such a good idea to be anywhere near a bed with Braelyn when they would be doing nothing but eating. He'd be more tempted by her than the food.

At his hesitation, Braelyn asked, "Have you ever been there before?"

"No. I can say I have never eaten food on a bed in a restaurant."

She smiled. "Then we should go." Braelyn used a finger to

draw circles on his chest. "It'll be fun. We could take turns lying down and feeding each other." Her eyes took on a sexy, slumberous look. "Wouldn't you like me to hand-feed you, Skylar?"

Could his cock get any harder? Her words, and seeing the look in her eyes, were enough to have his dick hard enough to leave a permanent mark of his zipper on it. And the idea of her feeding him while he lay on a bed next to her made him want to throw back his head in a long, loud howl.

"The Supperclub it is then," he said.

"Great." Braelyn rattled off her address. "I'll see you at seven."

As she stepped back, Skylar dropped his arms and followed her to the driver's side of the BMW. After Braelyn got in, he moved out of the way as she drove out of the parking lot. Once she disappeared, he walked to the sidewalk and then headed in the direction where he'd parked his motorcycle. He had more than enough time to return to the Protectors' mansion and get ready for his date. And, if he were lucky, leave again with his family being none the wiser about him finding his mate.

CHAPTER THREE

After Skylar arrived at the mansion in Marin County, he groaned when he saw the black Mercedes-Benz parked in the drive near the large detached garage. The car belonged to Beowulf, Roxie's mate, which more than likely meant the pair of them were there. With her due date a week away, Beowulf accompanied his mate wherever she went.

Skylar parked his motorcycle in the garage and then headed for the front door. Roxie's presence would make things a little more difficult for him to slip back out unnoticed. She'd see him dressed for his date and would start with the third degree. Actually, he'd be lucky if he could even make it to his room before she cornered him. With Braelyn's scent all over him, the others would be able to smell it. Werewolf sense of smell was three times stronger than a mortal's. His family might let him get away without questioning him about whom he'd been with, but the same couldn't be said about Roxie.

If she realized his mating urge rode him, she'd try to lay down the law regarding how he should act around his mate. Roxie had come up with a bunch of rules she expected the males in the house to follow when it came to claiming their mortal mates. If her rules weren't followed, she tended to get pissed.

Skylar walked into the mansion before he quietly shut the door behind him. No one was in the large open-concept foyer. He crossed the black-and-white checked marble floor and made a beeline line for the blond oak staircase that curved to the upper level. He'd just managed to put one foot on the bottom step when someone behind him loudly cleared their throat.

Recognizing that someone's scent, Skylar stepped back down and turned to face the one person he'd hoped to avoid. "Hey, Roxie. Where's Beowulf?"

She put a hand on her distended belly. "He's with the others in the kitchen."

In an attempt to shoo Roxie off before she asked questions he really didn't want to answer, he said, "Then don't let me stop you from going to him."

Roxie narrowed her eyes. "Are you trying to get rid of me?"

"No. I'm just in a bit of a hurry is all. I have to go back out soon."

"Really now. And does your soon-to-be quick departure have anything to do with the woman whose scent you're wearing?"

Shit. Skylar didn't think he'd be able to talk his way out of that one, but it didn't mean he still wouldn't try. "Maybe it does and maybe it doesn't. I just have to go out for a while, but I'll be back in time to take my shift at your place."

"Uh-huh. And why do I get the feeling you want to avoid the whole topic of the new scent I smell on you? Whoever she is, she's not a werewolf. Is there something you'd like to tell me, Skylar?"

"Not particularly. If you must know, I have a date. Nothing more."

"A date? With the mortal woman?"

"Yes. What of it?"

"So you're telling me you just have a simple date with a mortal woman, and there isn't a chance of her being your mate?"

He nodded. "Yeah, that's about it."

Roxie closed some of the distance between them. "All right. Then prove it."

"Excuse me?"

"Then prove to me you haven't found your mate."

He crossed his arms over his chest. "And how would you want me to do that?"

"Easy. I want you to take the front of your shirt, hold it up to your nose and take a big old whiff of it. I have a feeling that's where the woman's scent is the strongest from you holding her against you."

Double shit. "And what do you expect to happen if I do it?"

"If she's your mate, your mating urge will be riding you. A good strong dose of her scent will be enough to get a reaction out of you. I'm betting it'll make your eyes glow, and you won't be able to control it."

"I'm not going to smell my shirt."

"Yes, you will, because if you don't, I'm going to assume you're too chicken. Come on. I dare you to do it."

Skylar gritted his teeth. He was no chicken, and daring him to do anything usually meant he'd do it just to prove to the person doing the daring he could. "Fine, I'll do your silly test."

Mentally bracing himself so he hopefully wouldn't react to Braelyn's scent, Skylar jerked up the front of his T-shirt and buried his nose in it. He took a deep breath. The smell of his mate's scent mixed with his caused his control to slip. He closed his eyes and he drew in more and more of the mixture, filtering out his own scent until he fixated on Braelyn's. Against his will, his body reacted. His cock filled with blood until the front of his jeans became uncomfortably tight.

"Open your eyes, Skylar," Roxie said. "I need to see them, but as how other parts of you have suddenly gotten bigger, I'm pretty sure I know what I'll find."

He opened his eyes to find Roxie smiling while she gazed at him with a "I told you so" expression. After one last whiff, he dropped his shirt and tugged it back down into place.

"Not a word," he said to her.

"You're such a liar," she said with a smirk. "Those glowing peepers of yours tell the truth. Not to mention certain other body parts."

Skylar frowned and tried to turn the tables on Roxie. "That's twice now you've brought the subject of my manhood into the conversation. I wonder how Beowulf would feel about that."

She laughed. "Manhood? Now you're really showing your age. And keep Beowulf out of this. I know what you're trying to do. You just want to steer me off the topic of your mate. There is no use in denying it. The way you smelled your shirt, you looked like a starved man who'd just found a big, juicy steak."

"All right, you win. So I found my mate."

"And you spent the day with her, obviously. Since you haven't brought her home, you must not have claimed her yet, which is good. You know my rule about letting mortal mates have the chance to decide whether or not they want to be claimed. I'm going to assume you're well on your way to convincing her since your brothers did the same with their mates."

Thinking it would at least put him in Roxie's good graces, Skylar decided to tell her how he'd spent his time with Braelyn. "I'm working on it, yes, but not the way you think. I managed to get only one kiss out of her."

"Then what exactly did you do with the rest of your time?"

"Clothes shopping," he mumbled.

A smile tugged at Roxie's mouth. "What was that? I don't think I heard you right. Did you just say you went clothes shopping with your soon-to-be mate?"

"I know you heard me perfectly fine. And for your information, she considers it something she has to do to keep on top of her career."

"Okay, now you have me interested. What exactly does she do that requires her to shop for her job?"

Skylar felt certain Roxie would recognize Braelyn's name. "I guess you could call her a famous fashion model. She's Braelyn Whitmore."

"Oh, my god, your mate is Braelyn Whitmore," Roxie shouted. "*The* Braelyn Whitmore, the Victoria's Secret model?"

He winced. "Yes."

Considering how loud Roxie had shouted, Skylar didn't think it would be very long before everyone else in the mansion came to investigate. Sure enough, the sound of more than one set of footsteps sounded in the hall that led to the kitchen. He groaned when every single person he lived with, accompanied by Beowulf, filed into the foyer.

Beowulf went to his mate's side. "What's the shouting about, Rox?"

"Skylar found his mate, and she's Braelyn Whitmore."

Roxie's mate shook his head. "The name doesn't mean much to me. Should it?"

Ansley, who was mated to Roan, spoke up. "She's best known

as a Victoria's Secret model. She was also one of the models in their fashion show on TV the other night."

Roan put his arm around his mate's waist. "Ah, yes. I remember watching that, and picking out a number of bras and panties I thought would look incredibly sexy on you."

Even though Roan was his true brother, and mated, the thought of him seeing his mate so scantily clad had Skylar's hackles rising. It wasn't as if he had to worry about Roan making moves on Braelyn, but the mating urge wasn't letting him think too clearly. A low growl rumbled out of his chest before he could silence it.

Jager, his other true brother, loudly cleared his throat to get everyone's attention. "I think Skylar isn't exactly in the mood to hear how many of us watched that particular show now. If you know what I mean?"

The conversation, which had centered on his mate being famous and the Victoria's Secret Fashion Show, ended abruptly. Skylar met Jager's gaze and nodded in thanks.

Saskia, who was his sister-in-arms and the leader of the Protectors, said, "Jager's right. I don't think we need to torture Skylar like that." She turned in his direction. "Though I am going to say I'm thrilled to hear another one of us has found their mate. At this rate, all of us will be matched up very soon."

Kye, who stood at the back of the group, said, "Hey, I'm in no hurry. I'm quite happy just letting it happen when it happens."

Deciding to make a break for it before things started to get out of hand, Skylar backed up the stairs. As Roxie opened her mouth to say something, he quickly said, "We can continue this conversation another time. I have a date with Braelyn this evening, and I don't want to be late."

Turning, not waiting for any of them to respond, he moved at preternatural speed the rest of the way up the stairs. It wasn't until he was safely locked behind his bedroom door that he breathed a sigh of relief. He'd survived that close call. All he had to do was sneak out of the house before he became cornered again.

* * * *

Braelyn managed to get all the shopping bags from her trunk into her parents' modest two-story house in one trip. Her mom must have seen her pull into the driveway, because she opened the front door as soon as Braelyn stepped onto the porch.

"My, that's quite a load," her mother said after she shut the door behind her.

"You know me, shopping is one of my guilty pleasures."

"At least you can afford to indulge."

She headed up the stairs to what had been her bedroom while she'd been growing up. Her mom followed on her heels. Braelyn dumped the bags onto the bed and then looked through them for something. Once she found the new dress she'd bought, she took it from the bag and shook it out. It was a black, sleeveless cocktail mini that had beading along the bust. The form-fitting garment only reached her mid-thigh, and had had Skylar's eyes almost popping out of his head when she'd come out of the change room to ask his opinion on it.

"That's a lovely dress," her mom said. "Are you planning on wearing it to have dinner with your father and me? I think you might be a tad overdressed if you are."

Braelyn inwardly winced. She'd totally forgotten about her parents expecting her to eat with them. She'd only arrived in San Francisco the evening before. "Um, I kind of have a date for dinner," she said as she turned to face her mother. "I hope you don't mind."

"You're back only one day and you already have a date," her mom said with a chuckle. "No, I don't mind. So who is he?"

"His name is Skylar, and he's from around here."

"How did you meet him?"

She smiled. "It's kind of a funny story. He saw me crossing the street and followed me into a store—a lingerie store. Once he realized where we were, he got a little bit uncomfortable, especially when I asked him which bras and panties he liked."

Her mother shook her head. "You and your tests. Obviously, he passed or you wouldn't be seeing him this evening."

"He more than passed. Even though I dragged him to quite a few stores, not once did Skylar try to find a way to get out of it. I actually enjoyed having him with me."

"Seeing the number of shopping bags here—" her mom waved

her hand toward the bed — "you must have taken him on quite a shopping spree. You're going to introduce him to your father and me before you leave, right?"

"I suppose so, though you know I'm no longer a teenager and can go out without my parents having to check out my date first."

"I know. I'm just being nosy. And I know you have good taste in men."

"Well, in that case, I'll be sure to do the quick introductions and then usher Skylar out the door. That should satisfy your curiosity."

"Oh, and talking about curiosity, something came for you while you were out." Her mom left the bedroom and returned a minute later carrying a courier envelope.

Braelyn looked at who sent it and smiled. "It's from my modeling agency." She ripped open the envelope and pulled out a stack of smaller regular envelopes. "These must be fan letters. My agent had said she'd forward any that arrived while I was out here. She doesn't like to be burdened with taking care of them and gets her models to deal with their own fan mail however we see fit."

"I see. So I can expect more of these to arrive?"

"More than likely. I tend to see a bit of an influx after doing the Victoria's Secret Fashion Show. And most of them seem to come from teenage males."

Her mom laughed. "I guess I'll leave you to your fan mail and let you get ready for your date. I'll be downstairs getting dinner organized if you need me."

"All right."

After her mother left her alone, Braelyn pushed some of the bags aside and sat on the bed. Even though she mostly just sent out autographed pictures of herself to every person who wrote to her, she read every letter.

The first two letters turned out to be what she'd expected — teenage males writing to say how much they loved her. Braelyn put those aside to send a photo. The next envelope didn't have any return address on it. She ripped it open and pulled out the single folded sheet of paper. Unfolded, she scanned the words printed in a large font.

Braelyn swallowed as she reread the letter. It wasn't exactly a fan letter, and it wasn't the first of this type she'd received either. Only a few short sentences, it said she was nothing but a slut who would one day get what she deserved. It also said whoever had sent the letter would be the one to give it to her, and that she'd beg for more while it happened.

Even though there weren't any identifying marks to give any clues as to who had sent it, Braelyn felt sure this letter had been from the same person who'd sent her the two other similar ones the month before. The large font used was the same, and the subject of the letter almost identical.

She wanted nothing more than to rip the letter into shreds and burn it, but Braelyn refolded it instead and then put it back into the envelope. The other two letters were back in her apartment in LA, and she'd save this one as well. So far, all she'd gotten were the letters, but in case it turned out she had a stalker and things got progressively worse, she needed to keep them as evidence.

Feeling a bit spooked, Braelyn finished reading the rest of her fan mail. The offending one, she stuck in the very bottom of her suitcase. She didn't need one of her parents to find it. For now, she'd keep it to herself.

CHAPTER FOUR

B y the time Skylar was ready to head to San Francisco to pick up Braelyn, Roxie and Beowulf had already left the mansion. Dirk and Kye had gone with them. Later that night, Skylar would take Kye's place and stay the night along with Dirk. Until Roxie gave birth, Saskia had decided two Protectors needed to spend the night with the couple to be on hand in case their former brother-in-arms made a power play during that time.

Miles, who was Saskia's true brother and at one time a Protector, had gone to the dark side when he'd made the decision to make the switch five hundred years before. Instead of protecting the one they'd all sworn to do so with their lives, Miles wanted to gain control of the foretold one and use that person as a figurehead to rule the werewolf packs himself.

So far, they'd managed to keep Roxie's identity a secret from him. And, with the events that had occurred after Miles had taken Leif hostage, as far as Miles knew, his own daughter was the foretold one. It'd been Jaden's idea to pose as Roxie when her father had demanded the foretold one in exchange for Leif, her mate. At the time, none of them, not even Jaden, had known Miles was her father. When Roxie had turned Jaden before making the exchange, her scent had changed, bringing out some of Miles' recognizable scent that declared him her father.

As Skylar slipped out of the mansion and went to the garage, he pushed thoughts of Roxie, Miles and Jaden from his mind. He climbed into his charcoal gray Infiniti G37 sport coupe and then backed out onto the drive. Once he hit the street, he drove in the direction that would take him to the Golden Gate Bridge and San Francisco.

Thoughts of Braelyn surfaced while he made the drive. He'd done a lot of thinking about her during the hours he'd had to wait to see her again. It hadn't helped when he'd come out of the shower to find someone—more than likely Leif—had shoved a copy of the latest Victoria's Secret catalogue under his door. Skylar had looked through it a half dozen times at least, staring at every page Braelyn appeared on. It was bad enough he'd have erotic dreams of her when he slept that night—thanks to the mating urge—but the catalogue only added fuel to the fire of burning need that hadn't really left him since he'd met her.

Finally across the bridge and in the city, Skylar drove to the address Braelyn had given him. After he arrived, he pulled over to the curb and parked in front of the house. It was situated in a modest neighborhood. Braelyn's BWM was parked in the drive along with a Buick Regal. She'd said she'd come to San Francisco to visit family, and from the look of the house, he bet that was where her parents lived. It only made sense she would stay with them while there.

Skylar got out of the car and took a moment to straighten his clothes. He wore black jeans, a dark gray button-down shirt and his shit-kickers. When he'd gotten ready, he'd thought he would be dressed up enough for the Supperclub, but he hadn't thought about the chance of having to meet Braelyn's parents on their first date. He would have to at some point since she was his mate and he had no intention of walking away, but he'd figured it would be sometime down the road after he'd claimed her.

After he shut the car door and used the remote on his key ring to lock it, Skylar walked toward the house. On the porch, he smoothed his hand along his hair to make sure all of it was still inside the ponytail at his nape, then rang the bell.

The door opened, and Skylar met the gaze of a smiling woman who appeared to be close to fifty. She had the same emerald-green eyes as Braelyn and shared some of her looks. This obviously had to be his mate's mother.

"I'm here to pick up Braelyn," he said.

"You must be Skylar," she replied. "Come on in." Once he had, she closed the door behind him and then held out her hand. "I'm Braelyn's mom, Bev."

Skylar took her hand and gave it a shake before he released it. "Yes, I'm Skylar. And it's nice to meet you."

"Braelyn will just be a few minutes longer. Why don't you come and take a seat in the living room while you wait?"

He nodded and followed Bev into the room just off the front entranceway. The living room was done in light colors and had a loveseat, couch and armchair. He chose to sit on the couch. Braelyn's mom sat in the armchair kitty-corner to it.

"My husband is working late tonight, something spur of the moment, or you'd be meeting him as well," Bev said. "I'm sure you didn't count on having to meet Braelyn's parents when you asked her out."

Skylar smiled. "I can honestly say the thought hadn't crossed my mind."

"Well, don't worry too much about it. Neither my husband nor I are the type of parents who have to know everything our grown-up daughter is doing. So you won't be getting grilled this evening."

He relaxed. Bev reminded him a lot of Braelyn personality wise. They were down to earth and a bit on the laidback side. Skylar could see himself having no problem getting to know his mate's parents—at least her mother—better and grow to like them.

Just then, he heard someone walking down stairs. A few seconds later, Braelyn stepped into the room. It took everything he had not to jump up, take her in his arms and kiss her senseless in front of her mother. She wore the same short, black dress she'd bought that afternoon. He remembered it well since she'd modeled it in front of him. It showed off her long legs. He wanted them wrapped around his waist as he sank his cock into her pussy over and over again.

Desperately trying to pull his mind away from anything dealing with Braelyn and sex, Skylar swept his gaze up her body, starting with the black, strappy high heels she wore all the way to her face. She wore makeup, which she hadn't had on during the day, giving her a sexier look. A small smile played across her lips as if she knew exactly what he'd been thinking seconds before.

He stood and closed the distance between them. "Are you ready to go?"

Braelyn nodded. "Yes." She turned to look at her mother. "Sorry to leave you alone, Mom."

Bev waved her daughter's apology away with a flick of her hand. "I'll be fine. I'm used to being alone when your father has to work late. Go enjoy your date." She stood and walked to them. "It was nice meeting you, Skylar. If I were single and my daughter's age, I'd be making a play for you."

"Mom!" Braelyn said with a laugh. She turned back to Skylar. "Never mind her. She isn't serious. She's been head over heels in love with my father since they first met, and she wouldn't have it any other way."

"So true," Bev said. "There's no harm in me admiring a good-looking younger man like Skylar."

"All right, I think it's time we leave before my mom gets out of hand," Braelyn said as she shook her head.

He chuckled at the banter between his mate and her mother. They were obviously very close. If only they knew he was way older than they thought. They had no idea he'd celebrated his thousand and sixth birthday four months before.

With a goodbye to Braelyn's mom, Skylar guided Braelyn out of the house and then to his car. He held the passenger door open for her before he closed it once she slid in. He walked around the front and then climbed into the driver's side.

Skylar started the car before he pulled away from the curb. He took a quick glance at Braelyn. "Are you hungry?" He knew he was, and not just for food.

She turned her head in his direction. "Yeah, I'm starved."

"Now don't take this the wrong way, but you are going to order something more than a salad, right? I know most models tend not to eat enough to keep a bird alive."

Braelyn shook her head. "I'm not like that. I do have to watch I don't overindulge too often, but I've been blessed with a fast metabolism. I eat pretty much what I want so long as I do it responsibly."

"Good, because it takes a hell of a lot more than a small salad to fill me up."

Out of the corner of his eye, Skylar watched Braelyn look him up and down. "Seeing you, I never would have guessed," she said with a grin. "I would imagine you have the opposite problem from me — not getting enough food."

"More than you know. With five brothers who are as tall and as muscular as I am, and a brother-in-law who weight lifts, it's hard to keep food in the house. My sister and sisters-in-law are always complaining about the number of trips to the grocery store they have to make."

"You all still live together? That's a big family. My parents only had me so I can't picture what it would be like with that many siblings around."

"We've lived in the same place for quite a while now. I'm used to it. We all have our own separate rooms. If it gets to be too much, I can go to mine and lock myself in."

"Your house must be huge. Where do you live?"

"In one of the mansions in Marin County."

"I'm impressed."

"I'll take you there sometime and you can see it for yourself. Just be forewarned it will also mean I'll have to introduce you to my entire family. And it won't be the same experience I just had with your mom."

Braelyn laughed. "I'm sure it won't be that bad."

"You have no idea," he said drolly. "I have one brother, Jager, who basically says whatever crap is on his mind and doesn't care who he offends. Then, until recently, my other brother, Leif, used to consider himself a ladies' man and would flirt with anything female. Now that he's married, he no longer does it. The others will just be nosy."

"I think I can handle your family."

They fell silent as Skylar turned into the parking lot of the Supperclub. It looked on the full side, and he wondered if they'd be able to get in when he pulled into one of the few empty spaces. He hadn't thought about calling to make reservations.

Once he helped Braelyn out of the car, he said, "I don't know if we'll get a place to eat. It looks busy. I didn't think to get a reservation."

She wrapped her arm around his and walked them toward the

restaurant. "Don't worry about that. I took care of it. They were booked, but once I said who I was, they had a sudden opening."

Skylar chuckled. "I guess dating a famous model has its advantages."

"Yes, it does," Braelyn replied with a smile.

Inside the restaurant, he let her do the talking when they were in front of the hostess. The woman put on a big show of greeting Braelyn and then taking them to the bed reserved for them. Once they took a seat on the mattress, the hostess smiled, and with one last gushing welcome and the assurance their server would be with them shortly, she left them alone.

Skylar shifted closer to the center of the bed. "This should be an experience." He looked around, noticing how some of the other diners sat up like he did while still others reclined on their sides.

Braelyn folded her legs to the side and moved closer. "You're going to enjoy this. You don't get to order food. The menu is picked by their chef, and served throughout the night in small portions. As you can hear, they have a DJ playing music. They also have live performances."

He wasn't exactly sure if he liked the idea of the food coming at such a slow rate. He'd planned to get through a leisurely dinner, but not too leisurely, and then take Braelyn someplace for the rest of their date to get to know her even better. If it would take most of the night just to eat, he didn't think there would be time for it.

Looking at Braelyn, he found her expectantly watching him as if she waited for his reaction. This wasn't the first time he'd seen her do it, either. While shopping, he'd gotten the feeling she used some of the things she did or said to test him in some way. He had no problem with it. The only thing that bothered him was the fact she felt she had to do it in the first place. Something must have happened in her past that had her putting a new man through a series of tests. Who and what she was seemed his best guess for the root of it. A lot of men could be dumb fucks when it came to beautiful women.

"It sounds different," he said. "And should make for an enjoyable evening." Skylar watched the expectant expression on Braelyn's face turn into a bright smile.

"It will be. And the meal is basically all finger food." She leaned closer. "We'll have to share from the same plates."

"I guess that means I can't make a pig of myself and eat everything before you get your share," he said jokingly.

"If there's a chance of that, I guess I'll have to hand-feed you. That way I'll be sure to get my portion."

Skylar's cock twitched at the thought of Braelyn feeding him. He wouldn't be able to resist licking off every bit of food from her fingers while she did it. He'd then have to feed her, of course. He could almost feel the warm wetness of her mouth closing over his fingers.

Horny as hell from his thoughts, Skylar cupped the back of Braelyn's head and brought her lips to his. He kissed her thoroughly, sweeping the inside with his tongue before he released her. "You can feed me so long as I get to feed you in return," he said huskily.

"I'd like that," Braelyn said, her voice just above a whisper.

At that moment, their server arrived at their bed. She asked what they wanted to drink. After she took their orders, she left to get them and returned a short while later with his beer and Braelyn's glass of red wine.

Soon after that, their food arrived. Skylar only recognized half of what was on the plate for the first course. It figured it would be just as trendy as the restaurant itself. Having never been a picky eater, he didn't care one way or the other. As long as it tasted good, he'd eat it, especially if the food came from the hand of his mate.

Braelyn reached into the square dish that sat on the mattress between them and picked up a shrimp that had been cooked in a citrus-type sauce. The smell of lemon and lime filled his nose when she lifted it to his mouth. He opened it only wide enough for her to place the morsel inside. As soon as she did, he closed his lips around her finger and gave it a gentle suck as she pulled it free.

Skylar chewed and swallowed without really tasting. He became completely focused on Braelyn when he detected the faint smell of her arousal. Encouraged, he reached into the dish and plucked out a shrimp. His gaze focused on her mouth, and he fed it to her. Just as he'd done, Braelyn closed her lips around his finger, only she pushed the bite of food to the side of her mouth and swirled her tongue around the tip.

A low, almost silent growl rumbled out of his chest. His cock ached to have her tongue on it while Braelyn pleasured him with her mouth. Now fully engorged, he lifted a leg to hide his erection. He had to keep his arousal under control or he'd have to explain to a roomful of mortals why his eyes glowed mutedly. Not something he wanted or needed to happen.

Her mouthful finished, Braelyn chose something from the other dish the server had brought. "Let's see if you like this," she said.

Her voice had taken on a sexy timbre that seemed to hit him in the gut. "Feed it to me then."

She popped the piece of herb encrusted vegetable into his mouth. This time he nipped the very tip of her finger. Braelyn sucked in a breath as she worried her bottom lip with her teeth.

They continued to feed each other in that manner for an hour. With each new dish of food, the sexual tension between them grew greater. Skylar didn't know how much more he could take. He was coiled tighter than a spring, and he'd long since given up trying to hide the erection that caused a noticeable bulge in the front of his jeans. It didn't help that the scent of Braelyn's arousal had become strong enough to overshadow the smell of what they ate. If he didn't get to really touch her, kiss her, he'd go insane.

Hoping to push the game they played to the point where Braelyn would be more than ready to leave, Skylar put a bite of food between his lips, then leaned toward her. He pushed it into her mouth with his tongue, keeping it there long enough to stroke hers before he pulled back. She chewed and swallowed while her heavy-lidded gaze stayed focused on his mouth.

"I've had my fill of food," he said. "How about you?"

"So have I."

"Then let's get out of here."

At Braelyn's nod, Skylar caught the eye of their server and motioned her over. Once he'd paid their bill, he ushered Braelyn outside and into his car. Now he just had to figure out where he could take her so they could be alone together. Someplace where he wouldn't be tempted to make love to her and claim her as his without her knowing what he truly was, and what it meant to be a werewolf's mate.

CHAPTER FIVE

Braelyn had become so turned-on inside the restaurant she had a hard time not squirming as Skylar got into the driver's side and then started the car. She'd never expected to become this aroused just by hand-feeding him. Every time he'd sucked or nipped her finger, the sensation had gone straight to her pussy, causing it to clench with need. And unable to miss the large bulge in his pants, wetness had pooled and leaked into her panties. When he'd suggested they leave, she'd been more than ready to do so.

She barely heard Skylar say quietly, "Where to go?"

"Start driving and I'll give you directions to a place where we won't be disturbed. It's partway to my parents' house."

A lot of years had gone by since the last time Braelyn had been there with a member of the opposite sex, but it was the first thing that had popped into her mind. She was desperate to get her hands on Skylar, to touch and taste him. The other men she'd dated hadn't made her feel this needy. She'd experienced arousal and had slept with more than a couple guys, but none of them had made her feel as if she'd not survive another minute if she didn't have his hands and lips on her.

Once they hit the street, Braelyn gave directions to the spot she had in mind. It wasn't a long drive, but given the condition she was in, it felt as though it took twice as long to arrive at their destination.

After they reached the high school, Skylar pulled to a stop in front of it and turned his head to look at her. "A high school?" he asked with skepticism.

"It's either here or a hotel room, and honestly, I'm not ready to go that far yet, if you know what I mean? Not on the first date."

"Neither am I."

Skylar had just scored another point in his favor. "Then here it is. Drive around to the parking lot at the back of the school. When I was a teenager, that's where I used to make out with my boyfriends. A lot of us kids used it for that purpose."

"I've been reduced to using a teenager make-out spot."

Braelyn undid her seatbelt, then shifted as close as she could get to Skylar and gave him a quick, hard kiss. "The longer we sit here trying to figure out another place to go, the less time we'll have to be together before you have to leave for your job."

That seemed to do the trick. Skylar hit the gas and drove around to the back of the school. Braelyn barely had a chance to notice they were the only ones there before Skylar parked and then he had her in his arms.

A breathy sigh escaped her lips as his mouth closed over hers. Unlike the other kisses they'd shared, this one was hot and demanding. He reached between them and undid his seatbelt. Once free of it, he hauled her onto his lap. Her short dress rode up as she straddled Skylar's thighs. She let out a small squeak of surprise when his seat suddenly went back and she wound up lying on top of him.

Braelyn moaned and sucked on Skylar's tongue as her panty-clad pussy came in direct contact with his erection. He was thick and long against her. More of the wetness that had pooled in her core leaked into her panties as she rubbed herself against his hard cock. He ground against her, matching her movement.

Skylar shoved a hand down the front of her dress and fondled her breast. "You aren't wearing a bra," he said against her lips.

"The straps would have shown," she said in reply. "And I can get away without one."

He made a noise that sounded between a groan and a very animalistic growl. "If I'd known that during dinner, it would have driven me crazy."

She sat a little straighter and worked to undo the buttons on his shirt. "Enough talking and more touching."

Once she reached the top of his pants, she pulled the shirt out from the waistband and continued to undo the buttons until she'd opened the last one. Braelyn parted the material and sucked in a breath. She'd known Skylar was built, but the sight of his well-defined chest and stomach made her want to lick and kiss every inch of them. She ran her fingertips across his hairless chest and down his six-pack abs. He was a work of art. She'd never touched a man as heavily built as him before. The male models she'd gone out with had muscle tone, but were more on the skinny side, without Skylar's mass. Braelyn found his body more to her taste.

Bending, she kissed a trail across his upper chest. She ran her hands up his smooth skin and held on to the tops of his shoulders. The thought of exploring every inch of him while naked had her heart beating faster. Braelyn promised herself she'd do just that the next time they were together. This was neither the place nor the time to act out that fantasy.

It was her turn to let out a loud groan as Skylar lifted her higher and pushed his face between her breasts. He found the hidden zipper concealed in the side of her dress and pulled it down. Once the material loosened, he yanked on the front enough to bare her breasts. He made that strange half-groan/half-growl sound again as he circled a nipple with the tip of his tongue before he sucked it between his lips.

Braelyn pushed herself closer and let the pleasurable sensations coursing through her take over. She ground against Skylar's jean-covered cock, wanting the release that slowly built inside her pussy. It'd been a while since she'd last been with a man, and it wouldn't take much to send her into an orgasm.

Skylar switched to give her other breast equal attention. He ran his hands up the tops of her thighs, pushing her dress to her waist. He urged her lower body off his and traced the waist of her panties before he shoved a hand down the front.

At the first brush of a finger against the slick opening of her body, Braelyn gasped as it circled her clit. She shifted her hips, trying to show Skylar where she wanted him to touch her next.

He released her nipple, and said, "You're so wet, Braelyn. You make me ache to have you, but I'll settle for making you come."

She looked at Skylar and saw in the dim light that he had his eyes partially closed. "Do it," she said, breathless. "Then it'll be your turn."

A whimpered moan escaped her as he pushed a finger inside her pussy. He pumped it in and out a few times before a second joined the first. Braelyn panted, squeezing her inner walls to increase her pleasure. It wasn't until Skylar used a stroking motion, caressing a spot that made her cry out, that her climax took her over. She closed her eyes, riding the fingers that continued to pleasure her, and moaned.

After the last wave hit her, Skylar pulled his fingers out of her pussy. The sight of him bringing them to his mouth and licking her juices from each one caused an aftershock deep inside her core.

"Next time," he said in a voice rough with arousal, "I'm going to make you come with my mouth. You taste just as good as you smell."

Braelyn knew there would be a next time. And it wouldn't be inside Skylar's car. She shifted off his lap to the passenger seat, then righted her dress and did up the zipper. "Now I get to see what you have hidden inside those jeans of yours."

When Skylar would have reached to bring his seat up, she stopped him. "You stay just where you are."

Once he settled back down, she undid the button on his pants and then slowly tugged down the zipper. Skylar's cock sprang free as she parted the material. She took her bottom lip between her teeth. He was as large and thick as she'd thought he'd be. Her pussy clenched at the thought of how good it would be to have his shaft buried deep inside her. And given the way he'd just made her come, there was no question about him not knowing how to use it.

Gently, she trailed her fingers along his erection from base to tip. It jerked, and a bead of pre-cum appeared. Braelyn collected the bit of moisture on a fingertip and rubbed it into the satiny skin. Skylar moaned.

Normally, she didn't give blowjobs until she felt more comfortable around a man, but with Skylar, she wanted to feel his cock inside her mouth while she sucked on him. She needed to hear the sounds of pleasure he'd make while she brought him to completion.

She took hold of his erection and lifted it off Skylar's stomach. She leaned over him and licked the same trail her fingers had taken. At the flared head, she circled it with her tongue, flicking the very tip across the slit. The sound of his harsh breathing filled her ears as she opened her mouth and sucked him inside.

Skylar's hips lifted off the seat as he matched her in and out movements. Continuing to suck, she glanced at him. It had to be a trick of the dim light surrounding them, but she could have sworn his eyes glowed mutedly before he closed them completely.

His cock grew harder, and his groans of pleasure came more frequently. "Braelyn." He panted. "I'm close, so close." She sucked harder and took him almost to the back of her throat, and he said harshly, "Ah, fuck, I can't hold back. Feels too good."

Skylar cried out—the sound almost sounding like a wolf's howl—as his cock pulsed while he came. Braelyn took everything and didn't stop pleasuring him until he had no more to give. Once it was over, to her surprise, he stayed hard as if he'd never come.

She released her hold on the base of his cock and met his gaze. "You came, yet you're still—"

He cut her off by sitting up and taking her mouth in a kiss that had her toes curling. Once he pulled away, he said, "I'm fine. It was more than nice."

He stuffed his still-hard cock inside his jeans and then zipped them up. Braelyn gave him a dubious look. "Are you sure? It looks as if that will be painful if it doesn't go down soon."

Skylar chuckled and cupped the back of her head while he kissed her again. "Stop worrying. Let's call me not losing an erection a little talent of mine, all right? And when I take you to bed, I'll show you just how long I can keep it."

Braelyn's mouth went dry. If Skylar could stay hard, even after coming, sex would never be the same for her again. What woman wouldn't want a man who could keep it up, and then make her come over and over again? She sure as hell wanted that experience.

With one last brush of his lips across hers, Skylar released her. "It's getting late, and I have to go to work soon. I want to see you tomorrow."

She settled into her seat and put her seatbelt on. "I don't have anything else planned. What time are you thinking about?"

He put on his seatbelt and turned with a smile. "If I had my way, I'd be knocking on your door very early in the morning, but I doubt your parents will like that. How about around lunchtime? We can grab something to eat, then decide after that what to do next. So long as it doesn't involve torturing me at a lingerie store, I'm open to anything."

Braelyn laughed. "I promise I'll spare you that, but if you're working all night, don't you have to sleep most of the day?"

"I get to sleep where I work."

As Skylar started the car and then drove around the school, she asked, "What exactly do you do if you can work and sleep at the same time?"

"I guess the best way to describe it is bodyguard. Actually, it's kind of the family business."

The unsettling fan letter she'd received that day rose to the forefront of Braelyn's mind. If Skylar was a bodyguard, and if the letters increased in number, it would be good to have a boyfriend in his line of work. It also had her seriously considering showing him the letter. She'd have to play it by ear.

"Sounds like an interesting job. Have you been doing it for very long?"

"Sometimes it feels like forever, but I'd never give it up. It's something I vowed to do."

Vowed to do? That statement made it sound as if Skylar's job were very serious indeed. "Once in a while, I feel the same way about modeling, as if I've done it forever. I enjoy it, but I know I won't be able to do it until I'm old and gray."

"I imagine the competition can get pretty stiff."

"It can, but now that I've made it, it isn't as hard as when I tried to break into the business."

They arrived at her parents' house, and Skylar pulled over to the curb. Braelyn glanced toward the driveway. Her dad's older model Ford Taurus was parked behind her BMW.

Turning to Skylar, she said, "I guess I'll see you tomorrow around lunchtime." She took off her seatbelt and then reached across to pull Skylar toward her. She proceeded to kiss him until she was out of breath. Braelyn pulled away and smiled. "Something to make you dream about me tonight."

Skylar caressingly ran the back of his fingers across her cheek. "Don't worry, I will, guaranteed."

Braelyn gave him one last look, then opened the car door and got out. She waited until Skylar drove away to wave before she walked to the house. A smile spread across her face as she thought about how the night had gone.

Just before she reached the front door, she suddenly had the overwhelming feeling someone watched her. She stopped in the middle of the front lawn and turned in a circle, but didn't see anyone. Thinking it could be one of the neighbors being nosy, Braelyn shrugged to herself and went inside.

* * * *

He watched Braelyn walk toward the front door of her parents' house. Hidden in the dark shadows, she hadn't seen him. From where he stood, he'd seen everything. The whore had been putting on quite a display in the fancy car of the asshole she'd gone out with. Seeing them kiss like they couldn't get enough of each other had made him want to teach her how sluts like her should be treated.

Once Braelyn disappeared inside, he slowly slipped away. Her time would come. She had to have gotten his letters. And now that she'd taken up with a man—more than likely already had spread her legs for him—it was time to act. The only good whore was a dead whore.

CHAPTER SIX

After getting buzzed through the gated entrance to Roxie and Beowulf's mansion, Skylar drove up the long drive. Once he arrived at the house, he found Kye waiting outside. He parked his car in front of the large garage and then headed for his brother-in-arms.

"Itching to leave?" he asked Kye.

"The boredom is what's killing me, and the inactivity. I'll be glad when Roxie has her baby and we can relax a bit."

Skylar shook his head. Out of all of them, Kye was the one who hated having nothing to do. He always had to be doing something, be it sword practice or running errands. The man didn't like to sit still. That being the case, Skylar couldn't understand why Kye had insisted he watch over Roxie during the day. As a web designer, she spent a lot of time sitting behind a computer, working. Kye usually ended up falling asleep.

"Dirk still inside?" Skylar asked.

Dirk, who was into computers as much as Roxie, usually took on a lot of the shifts, mostly because he and Roxie got along so well. The two computer nerds did a lot of brainstorming, not that any of them dared called Roxie nerd to her face. Being the only werewolf who could shift into a half-human/half-wolf form, making her bigger than even he, she could pretty much whip their butts if she had a mind to.

"Yeah. He's with Roxie. They started talking all things computer and then went up to her office so she could show him some type of code, not that I understood anything of what they'd said. Beowulf is at Wulf's Den and should be home in an hour or so."

Wulf's Den was the nightclub Beowulf owned. He'd cut way back on the number of hours he spent at the club to be closer to Roxie. Carl, the onetime bouncer, had shifted into the position of managing the place when Beowulf wasn't there. The very large werewolf had the distinction of being mated to Candice, Roxie's best friend. Once mortal like her friend, Candice had finally allowed Roxie to turn her six months before.

"Sounds as if everything is under control," Skylar said.

"I don't expect you'll run into any problems, so I'm out of here." Kye gave him a wave and headed to where he'd parked his car.

Skylar went inside the mansion and shut the door behind him in time to watch Roxie and Dirk walk down the stairs from the upper floor, deep in conversation. From the sound of it, they were still on the topic of computers and the Internet. Dirk had been working on some kind of web design project for a few months, keeping the particulars to himself, though Skylar had a feeling Roxie knew all about it.

"Don't the two of you ever get sick of talking about computers?" he asked once they reached the bottom of the stairs.

"Of course not," Roxie replied. "Do you ever get sick of playing with your sword?"

He rolled his eyes. "It's not the same thing. Being a warrior is a part of who I am."

"Yes, it is. I can't ever see myself not wanting to work with computers or the Internet in some way."

"That's because you're an Internet junkie." Skylar nodded toward Dirk. "And it doesn't help when you have someone just as addicted as you hanging around all the time."

Dirk shrugged. "What can I say? It keeps me out of trouble."

Roxie stepped closer to Skylar. "So? How did your date with your mate go? Are you still being a good boy and holding off claiming her?"

"Yes, though I'm not sure how long that's going to last. It's not

320

exactly a walk in the park to resist what my mating urge is screaming at me to do. If I'm not careful, I'll end up in the same condition as Leif just before he claimed Jaden."

Leif had fought to the bitter end before he'd finally taken Jaden as his mate. On the last day, he'd agitatedly paced in his room, driving the rest of them nuts. Roan, Jager and he had been forced to put Leif into his car and send him on his way. With his mating urge riding him hard, Leif hadn't been able to stop himself from going to Jaden.

Roxie snorted. "That was just Leif being a dumbass. The man had delusions of grandeur thinking he could cheat fate by ignoring his mating urge, hoping it would go away."

"That might be true, but not claiming a mate as soon as she's found makes a mess of us males," Skylar said.

"Then I suggest you don't wait too long to explain what you are to Braelyn and give her a chance to decide whether or not she'll accept you as her mate."

Needing to change the subject of Braelyn and what she meant to him, he said, "I'm getting a beer. I have a feeling I'm going to be in store for a long, hard, sleepless night."

Skylar left Roxie and Dirk and went to the kitchen. He opened the fridge and took out a bottle of beer. He twisted off the cap and then took a long swallow. What Braelyn had said with her last kiss goodbye, to make sure he dreamed of her that night, it hadn't been necessary. Well into the throes of the mating urge, she'd dominate his dreams if he managed to get any sleep. Having her shatter in his arms made him ache to complete the mating bond. And the release she'd given him wouldn't help much to take the edge off either. Until he made love to her, he pretty much wouldn't be good for anything else. If it took more than a few days for him to explain everything to her and get her to accept him, he could easily see himself having to take himself out of the rotation of watching over Roxie. God forbid if anything happened to her because his mating urge wouldn't let him think straight.

* * * *

It was close to three in the morning before Skylar finally fell into bed. Being alone in the room he used when he stayed over at

Roxie's hadn't helped him keep his thoughts from Braelyn. If she could have seen them, she'd think he was some kind of obsessed stalker.

He rolled onto his side and punched the pillow a few times to get it into the shape he wanted. Skylar closed his eyes and forced himself to relax. He tried to clear his mind. Slowly, by degrees, sleep reached up to claim him.

The dream took him shortly thereafter. Skylar found himself sitting in a chair facing a long runway, like the kind models walked down during a fashion show. There were other chairs on either side of him, but he was the only one in the audience.

The lights dimmed, and music played in the background. He turned his attention to the entrance of the runway when a bright spotlight focused on it. From one side, Braelyn walked out. Flashes of light, like those from a camera, went off. Skylar looked around, but couldn't see where the photographers were. As she headed down the runway, using the same walk she'd used when he'd watched her on TV, he gave up on his search and focused entirely on her.

She wore one of the Victoria's Secret bra and panty sets she'd worn in the show, as well as the wings on her back. Braelyn strutted down toward the end, not once looking his way. Once she reached it, she put her hand on her hip and held a pose for a few seconds before she turned back the way she'd come.

Skylar thought she'd keep going on her return trip since Braelyn hadn't noticed him before, but that wasn't the case. When she drew even with where he sat, she stopped and turned to face him. A set of stairs magically appeared, and she stepped down them. With a sultry look, she walked to him.

His cock grew painfully hard when she stopped directly in front of his chair and reached up to the middle of her chest. She undid the front clasp of her bra and cupped her breasts, lifting them in offering. He took hold of her hips and guided Braelyn to sit on his lap, straddling his thighs. Burying his face between her breasts, he dragged in her scent, taking it deep into his lungs, before he took what she offered.

Braelyn's head fell back as he sucked a taut nipple into his mouth. She moaned and sank her fingers into his hair, holding him to her. He released her breast as she gently pushed him away.

She cupped his face and bent her head to kiss him, nipping his bottom lip before she sucked on his tongue. Not breaking contact with his lips, she dropped her hands to the waistband of his jeans, going even lower. She caressed him through them, wringing a growl of pleasure from him.

In the next second, they were naked. Skylar remained seated on the hard, straight-backed chair with Braelyn straddling his lap. Still wearing her high heels, her feet were able to reach the floor. Her gaze locked with his, and he saw his eyes mutedly glowing in the reflection of hers. Braelyn didn't react in any way. She used her feet and pushed herself slightly off his lap, positioning her pussy over his cock, which stuck out straight from his body. With her bottom lip between her teeth, she slowly lowered herself onto his shaft until she'd taken every bit of his length inside. Once she rode him, Skylar held on to her hips and thrust up to meet each of her strokes. The feel of her body taking his was the best feeling in the world.

Her pace becoming faster, Braelyn moaned, then said, "Skylar, wake up, damn you."

The incongruity of her words to the atmosphere of the erotic dream jerked Skylar awake. He opened his eyes to find Roxie standing over him, shaking his shoulder. It'd been her voice he'd heard in the dream instead of Braelyn's.

"Rox? What's the matter?"

She straightened. "The problem is you."

"Me?" Since he slept naked, Skylar checked to make sure the sheet still covered him. It was also then he noticed the raging hard-on he had. He quickly sat up and put his hands on his lap to cover it.

"Yes, you. Being a very pregnant woman who now finds it hard to get comfortable enough to sleep, the sound of you moaning in pleasure isn't conductive to sleep. God, I heard you through the whole house. In this instance, I wish werewolf hearing wasn't quite so sensitive."

Hearing that Roxie, and more than likely Beowulf and Dirk as well, had heard him moaning while he'd had dream sex with Braelyn, caused Skylar to do something he probably hadn't done since he was an untried youth—he blushed. His face grew warm with the heat of it. He shook his head, letting his loose hair hang down a bit in an attempt to hide his reaction. He wasn't an exhibitionist, and didn't like the idea of anyone overhearing what his mating urge caused him to go through.

Roxie sighed and took his chin in her hand to force him to look up at her. "It's nothing to be ashamed of. I'm just a bit on the touchy side when I can't sleep. I know you don't have any control over your dreams, especially now. If it makes you feel any better, I'm the only one who heard you. Beowulf and Dirk are out like lights. I checked."

Or they'd just ignored him and gone back to sleep. Dirk would have awakened. All the Protectors could come fully awake at the slightest noise like all well-trained warriors.

"I'm sorry if I woke you up," he said.

"You didn't. I was already awake. I'd gone down to the kitchen for some water." Roxie stared at him closely for a few seconds. "I think you need to be pulled off the rotation until you've claimed Braelyn."

"I haven't gotten that bad yet. I can still do my duty."

"I never said you were or that you couldn't. When the others went through this, they were pulled off rotation as well. Saskia might not be here to make the final decision, but I want you to do it anyway. It'll give you more time to be with Braelyn."

Skylar had to agree with that last part. If he didn't have to worry about taking his shift watching over Roxie, he could use the extra free time to get to know Braelyn better, and her him.

"All right, I'll do it, but only if you promise to help me break what I am to Braelyn. You apparently had a calming effect on Ansley when Roan told her and she freaked."

Roxie smiled. "It's a deal. Why don't you get up and go home? I'm sure you want to get a fresh set of clothes before you see your mate again. It's almost five now. I'll be fine with just Beowulf and Dirk to watch over me before Jager and Daylen arrive later this morning."

He obviously wouldn't be getting any more sleep, not when he knew Roxie would more than likely be awake to hear him have another erotic dream. "Fine, I'll go home."

"I'll leave you to get dressed then. And whenever you're ready to have me talk to Braelyn, just give me a call."

Roxie left the room, and Skylar blew out a breath. He hoped

today would bring him one step closer to making Braelyn his.

* * * *

After Skylar arrived at the Protectors' mansion, he went directly to his room and took a long shower. It did nothing for his semi-aroused state, but it helped to loosen some of the tension he had in his shoulders and back.

He turned off the taps with the thought of leaving the other people in the house some hot water and then stepped out of the glass-surround shower stall. Skylar dried himself and then used his hand to clear some of the steam fogging up the mirror over the sink. He combed out his hair and decided to let it dry naturally.

Naked, he walked into his room before he pulled on a clean pair of blue jeans along with a black T-shirt. After donning those, he sat on his bed and turned on the TV. It was still a bit early for anyone else to be up and around. If he stayed in his room long enough, and was lucky, one of the others would have started cooking some breakfast once he went downstairs.

At around eight, he heard a phone ringing and then multiple sets of footsteps heading down to the lower level. Skylar waited another fifteen minutes before he too left his room.

Thinking he'd timed it perfectly, he walked into the kitchen expecting to see one of his family members slaving over a hot stove. That wasn't exactly what he saw. Not only did the stove sit cold from lack of use, but all the members of the household, minus Dirk, sat at the table with grim looks on their faces.

"Did someone die?" he asked once he reached the group.

Saskia spoke first. "No, but the news could be just as bad. Miles phoned me on my cell this morning. He wants to see Jaden, tomorrow."

"Are you going to let him?" Skylar easily read the concern Saskia had for her niece when she glanced at Jaden.

"Jaden will have the final decision."

"Do you think that's wise?"

"That's what we discussed before you came down. I think it should be Jaden's decision. As long as Miles still thinks she's the foretold one, I don't see him being much of a threat. He might have turned to the wrong side, but he wouldn't harm his own child."

"I don't know," Leif said. "I don't like the idea of Jaden around the bastard."

Jaden gave her mate an exasperated stare. "He's still my father. I think Aunt Saskia is right. I don't think my dad would harm me. You didn't see the look on his face when he first saw me and called me by my mom's name. He might be a bastard, but he truly cared for my mother. And since I'm the last living connection to her, he won't do something stupid like trying to attack me."

"And," Saskia said, "it isn't as if we'd let you see him alone. Since you're supposed to be the foretold one, we have to act the role of your Protectors. Most, if not all, of us should be there."

"What about Roxie?" Roan asked. "We can't leave her totally unprotected. She's the real foretold one, after all."

"I'll watch her," Skylar quickly said. "Roxie pulled me off rotation this morning, but I don't think she'll mind spending some time with me and my mate."

Saskia nodded. "Then it's settled." She looked at Jaden. "That is if you still want to see Miles."

"I do," Jaden said. "If anything, I want to learn how he and my mom met and what caused them to break up before I was born."

Saskia stood. "All right. I'll call Miles and arrange a time and place of my choosing. Once I get off the phone with him, we can make further plans."

Skylar wasn't sure if this was a good idea or not, but it wasn't his place to deny Jaden the chance of getting to know her father. He just hoped it wouldn't blow up in their faces.

CHAPTER SEVEN

B raelyn made it to her parents' house from setting her plans into motion with only twenty minutes to spare before Skylar was to arrive. She raced inside the house and yelled a quick hello to her mother. Before she reached the stairs to the upper level, her mom stopped her.

"Wait a second, Braelyn."

"I'm in a bit of a hurry, Mom. Skylar will be here soon."

"This won't take long." She held out a plain white envelope. "I found it in the mailbox this morning while you were out doing your running around. It has our address on it but no stamp."

A sense of unease washed through Braelyn as she took the envelope from her mother. On the outside, she tried not to let it show. "I guess the person thought it would be faster to drop it by the house instead of putting it in the mail. I'll look at it upstairs."

With the letter clutched tightly, she ran up the stairs and then into her room. Braelyn shut the door behind her before she crossed to her bed. She sat and tore open the envelope, hoping it wasn't what she thought it was.

Her hands shook as she unfolded the single piece of paper and read the message printed out in a large font. It was from the same person who'd sent the other letters. She read the similar threats, but this time they'd escalated by calling her a whore and saying her sickening public displays with a man needed to stop—

permanently. And that her type of woman needed to be cleansed from the face of the Earth.

Braelyn forced herself to take deep, steady breaths and not to hyperventilate. Not only had the person who sent this letter more than likely watched her with Skylar, he or she also knew where her parents lived, and that she was there. She picked up the discarded envelope, and as her mother had said, there wasn't a stamp on it. The letter had indeed been hand delivered.

After shoving it back into the envelope, Braelyn put it inside her purse. She couldn't ignore those threats any longer. She needed protection, and who better to provide it than Skylar? At some point during their date, she'd show him the latest letter. Given the business he was in, surely he'd know what she should do to handle this situation discreetly. Making this public knowledge would only give the sender notoriety he or she didn't deserve.

That decided, Braelyn changed into a pair of dark blue skinny jeans and a tan short-sleeved silk blouse. She pulled on the new ankle boots she'd bought the day before. She'd just finished putting on a bit of makeup when her mom called up the stairs.

After giving herself one last inspection in the dresser mirror, and satisfied she didn't look white as a ghost, Braelyn snatched up her purse before she walked out of her room. Once she reached the bottom of the stairs, she ran her gaze over the man who waited for her just inside the front door. Skylar's gaze found hers, and he smiled.

The mere sight of him caused her body to react. For the rest of last night and then all this morning, he hadn't been very far from her thoughts. If she didn't know any better, she'd say she'd become obsessed with him, something she'd never done over a man before. It was during the small hours of the morning—not able to sleep because he dominated her thoughts so much—she'd come up with the plan of how she wanted her day with Skylar to go.

"All set?" he asked once she'd walked to him.

"Yes."

With a shouted goodbye to her mom, Braelyn let Skylar guide her out of the house with his hand on the small of her back. Being near him, the last of the unease she felt because of the letter drained away. When she was with him, she felt as if she were safe, protected. Maybe it had something to do with his large size. All she knew was she was more comfortable with him at her side.

Once they were inside Skylar's Infiniti, he started the ignition, and said, "So have you had a chance to think about where you want to go out to eat?"

She put on her seatbelt and turned her head to look at him. "Actually, I did better than that. I already have a reservation at the Roots restaurant at the Orchard Garden Hotel. It's for twelve thirty, so we have plenty of time to get there."

Skylar smiled. "It would seem you were more on the ball this morning than I was."

"I figured it would save some time if I went ahead and made the reservations."

"Sounds good. And since you said we don't have to hurry," he said as he leaned toward her, "I can take the time to do this."

He kissed her, taking her lips in a gentle exploration. As she returned it, moaning into his mouth, Skylar became more demanding. In a matter of seconds, the passion between them raged into a conflagration. The rest of the world seemed to disappear, leaving only the two of them in it. They were more than good together. The desire his touch caused inside her just reaffirmed she'd made the right choice with the plans she'd made for them after lunch.

In the middle of the heated kiss, Braelyn remembered what the letter had said about public displays. She stiffened and put her hand on Skylar's chest to push him away. Once he broke contact with her mouth, she scooted away as far as her seatbelt would allow.

Skylar gave her a confused look. "Is everything all right, Braelyn? I didn't do anything wrong, did I?"

She shook her head. "I'm fine, and no, you didn't do anything wrong." She put on what she hoped was a sexy smile. "If we don't stop now, I doubt I'll be able to get through lunch without mentally undressing you."

His eyes took on a heavy-lidded appearance. "We'll have to see about continuing this after we eat then."

"I'm game for that."

After they arrived and then parked in the hotel's parking lot,

Braelyn got out of the car before she met Skylar at the front of it. They walked into the hotel and headed for the restaurant situated off the lobby. Since she'd been there earlier to make the reservation in person, the host smiled brightly when he saw them.

Before she could say her name, he said, "Right this way, Miss Whitmore. Your table is ready."

After they were seated with menus in front of them, Skylar said, "I guess I'm going to have to get used to strange men recognizing my ma...girlfriend."

She caught the slight stumble in words when he'd spoken. "Are you the jealous type, Skylar?"

"When it comes to you, I'm afraid I will be a little. I've never taken out a woman who was famous before. I'll try not to make an ass of myself in front of you."

Braelyn chuckled. "Nothing wrong with a little jealousy. You might not be famous, but you do tend to draw a lot of female attention."

Skylar pinned her with a stare that would have caused her knees to give out if she hadn't already been seated. "They can look, but I belong only to you."

Hearing him say he was hers sent a thrill through her. They had only known each other for such a short period of time, but Braelyn already had thoughts of how their relationship would work once she returned to LA. She didn't want to give Skylar up. Even though she really had no idea what her ideal man would be like, he seemed to be everything she'd unknowingly been looking for. And any man who would happily follow her around on one of her shopping trips without uttering a single complaint was one she needed to hang on to.

Letting some of how she felt about him show in her eyes, she said softly, "Then I'll hold on tight and won't let go."

Their server came and took their orders and returned with the food in good time. They'd just finished their meals when he brought up the subject of what they would do with the rest of the day.

"Do you have any plans up your sleeve I should know about? I forgot to mention I have a few days off from work, starting tonight."

With the knowledge they could spend the night together as

well, a shot of excitement went through her. Skylar's time off couldn't have worked out any better. She picked up her purse and put it on the table next to her empty plate. She opened it. The first thing she spotted was the letter, but decided now wasn't the time to bring it up. She reached past the envelope and plucked out the keycard she'd put in there earlier.

Braelyn held it out for Skylar to see. "Since you didn't seem ready to take me to your place, and we can't very well be together at my parents' house, when I made the reservation this morning, I booked a room at the hotel for one night."

For a split second, she thought she saw Skylar's eyes glimmer with a shimmering light. It was faint but there nonetheless. She stared for a moment, but he briefly closed his eyes. Once he opened them again, whatever it was had gone.

He looked at her with hunger. "You booked us a room here in the hotel?"

"Yes."

"You do realize what will happen once we go there?"

Her body went up in flames, knowing full well what he implied. She'd counted on it. "Last night in your car was a taste. I now want all of it."

Barely louder than a whisper, so soft she had to strain to hear it, Skylar said under his breath, "I'm not that strong." He signaled their server to their table.

* * * *

Skylar kept telling himself he would be breaking one of Roxie's rules the whole time he ushered Braelyn out of the restaurant and to the other side of the lobby where the bank of elevators were. He knew what would happen as soon as he got her inside the room. And with the mating urge riding him hard, and his wolf demanding he claim his mate, he didn't think he could stop from taking the final step that would bind their souls together. It would be too much to ask of him not to make love to Braelyn.

After the elevator car arrived, they stepped inside and then silently rode it to the floor where their room was located. Skylar clenched his hands into tight fists to stop himself from dragging Braelyn into his arms and ravishing her right then and there as the scent of her arousal filled the small space. His cock strained against his zipper. No, he wasn't strong enough to resist the pull his mate had over him. And he didn't think oral sex would satisfy him enough to avoid completing the act this time. After the dream he'd had of making love to her early that morning, his body was too primed.

The elevator dinged once it reached their floor, and they stepped out. Since Braelyn had the keycard, he allowed her lead him as they walked down the long hall. He skimmed his gaze down the length of her body, staying a few extra seconds on her shapely ass encased in her tight jeans. He had to admit the exorbitant price she'd paid for the boots she wore had been well worth the money. They made her long legs look even sexier.

At the room, Braelyn stopped in front of it and swiped the keycard in the lock. The little light turned from red to green, and she pushed open the door. As soon as they were inside and it closed behind them, she turned and put her arms around his neck. With a couple of tugs, she pulled the hair elastic out and threw it aside as his hair fell around his shoulders.

Braelyn went on tiptoe and brushed her lips against his. "I've been dying to see what you would look like with your hair out of the ponytail."

"And?" he asked, voice lowered to a husky level.

"I think you look even better with it down."

She accentuated her words by placing a kiss on each of his cheeks and nipping his chin, nibbling a path along his jaw to the side of his neck. His libido increased the lower she went. There was no bigger turn-on for a male werewolf than to be bitten where the shoulder and neck met. One bite there and he'd be all over Braelyn before she knew what hit her.

"Ah...ah, I'll have to wear it down more often." She eased lower, using a hand to tug away the collar of his T-shirt and drag her tongue across the exact spot that would guarantee a complete slip of his control. "Oh, god, Braelyn." He sank his fingers into her hair at the back of her head to hold her to him. "Do that again, but use your teeth as well."

"You like it a little kinky, do you?" She gently nipped his skin.

"Christ." His chest rapidly rose and fell as he panted. "Harder. Do it harder."

At the sensation of Braelyn, his mate, biting him hard enough for him to really feel it, Skylar's eyes just about rolled back inside his head. A wolflike growl rumbled out of him, and their fates became set.

Skylar lifted her off her feet with an arm wrapped around her waist, and guiding her lips to his with the other, before he carried her to the king-size bed in the middle of the room. All the reasons he should slow things down rushed out of his mind as he kissed her deeply, not holding anything back. He wanted, he needed, to claim her as his. Now that he'd found her, there would never be another to take her place. He wanted to bind her to him, to make sure she would always be his. The instinct to join his soul to his mate's had become too strong to resist.

Skylar only took the time to roughly yank the covers back before he lowered Braelyn onto the bed. She lifted her arms, draping them around his neck, and pulled him down on top of her as she shoved her tongue into his mouth. She lifted her legs and encircled his waist as he settled between them. When his erection came in contact with her jean-clad pussy, she ground against him.

More growls he couldn't hold back pushed out of him. Braelyn might be mortal, but now, she was as aggressive as any female werewolf intent on making love to her mate. Her whimpered moans filled his ears while she shoved her hands up the back of his shirt and dug her nails into his skin.

Feeling almost crazed with lust and the mating urge, Skylar tore his mouth away from hers and quickly worked on unbuttoning her blouse. He shifted to kneel on the bed. Braelyn's legs dropped from around his waist, and he helped her sit up.

No longer pinned beneath him, he made short work of taking off her top. His gaze landed on the sheer white bra Braelyn wore. The material shimmered in the light of the room. It was so see-through he easily saw each of her taut, pale pink nipples through it. He bent his head and placed a kiss on one and then the other before he reached behind her and undid the hooks. He pushed the straps down her arms and then tossed the bra away.

Skylar covered her breasts with his hands and kneaded them. "So beautiful, and so mine," he said, lifting one and laving a nipple with the flat of his tongue.

Braelyn moaned. "We need to get out of our clothes. I want to run my hands all over your naked body."

By now, his eyes had to be mutedly glowing. He kept them averted and released her, yanking his T-shirt over his head. "I took off something. It's your turn."

Braelyn bent each leg toward her, then took off her boots before she threw them to the floor. Next she shifted so he no longer knelt between her legs and stripped off her jeans, leaving her panties on. They were a match for the bra. She leaned over to drop her pants over the side of the bed, and he noticed the panties were a thong.

When she would have shifted back, Skylar put his hands on her hips and rolled her to her stomach. He straddled the back of her thighs. "Not so fast. I get to enjoy the sight of you in a thong before I remove them—with my teeth."

"It's your turn to take off your pants." She turned her head to look at him.

He ducked his and pressed his lips to the back of her neck. "If I take them off now, that'll be the last article of clothing I'm wearing. I get the thong first."

Braelyn squirmed beneath him. "Do you always go commando?"

"Yes."

"I'm going to have to remember that."

She sucked in a sharp breath as he kissed a path down her spine. He shifted lower on her legs and nipped each globe of her ass. His cock aching to be inside her moist heat, he hooked his fingers into the top of her thong and pulled it down.

Free of it, he used one of his legs to spread hers apart enough for him to kneel between them once more. He skimmed his hands down her back to her ass. Continuing lower, he dipped his fingers between her thighs, encountering the wetness leaking from her pussy.

"I have to taste," he said, his voice hoarse. "Roll over for me."

"Not until you lose the pants."

Skylar slid off the end of the bed and toed off his boots. Braelyn rolled to her back and propped herself up on her elbows to watch him. He closed his eyes to mere slits and dropped his hands to the top of his jeans and undid them. He pushed them down past his hips and let them drop to pool at his ankles. He kicked out of them and then shoved them aside with his foot.

Braelyn's gaze appeared locked on his cock. She licked her lips, and it jerked in response. "God, Skylar. Your body is perfect. Big in all the right places."

He got onto the bed and crawled his way to her. "And you have the body of a goddess. I intend to worship every inch of it before we leave this room."

Skylar took Braelyn's lips in a demanding kiss until he had her whimpering. He shifted down her body, taking the time to lavish attention on her breasts on the way. At her flat belly, he circled the tip of his tongue into her bellybutton before moving closer to the prize he sought.

With his shoulders wedged between her thighs, Skylar spread Braelyn's folds and licked her pussy from bottom to top. The scent of her arousal and taste went straight to his head, almost making him drunk on it. He used his finger to stimulate her clit as he continued to lick the opening to her body. Her heavy breathing and whimpered cries for more filled his ears.

Switching to take her clit with his mouth as he pushed one, and then a second, finger inside her pussy, Skylar pumped them in and out. Braelyn's cries increased in volume. She lifted her hips, and sank her hands into his hair to hold him to her. He pleasured her for a minute more before he pulled away. She was close to coming, and he wanted to be deep inside her when she did that.

He rose between her legs and covered her with his body. His cock came to rest against her pussy, the head of it just at the entrance. He had a split second of conscience where he knew he would be taking Braelyn's choice from her. That soon ended as she took matters into her own hands and pushed down on him, taking the entire tip of his shaft into her pussy.

With a loud groan, he thrust forward until she'd taken his full length. The feel of her pussy closing around his cock had him fighting not to come. He propped himself on his bent arms and pumped his hips. He speared in and out of her with hard strokes. Braelyn clutched his shoulders as she lifted her hips to match the pace he set. She felt so good. It wouldn't take much more to send him into his orgasm.

As it inched closer, a piece of his soul reached out for Braelyn's.

He moaned, plunging faster and harder into her pussy. A quiet howl of triumph punched out of him when a part of her soul brushed against his, then wrapped around it.

Now truly mates, the mating bond in place, knowing Braelyn was his, Skylar took her faster. With a keening cry, she came just as he reached the point of no return. Her inner walls clutched the length of his shaft, and his orgasm tore through him. His groans mixed with her cries of pleasure as he filled her with his cum.

Skylar collapsed on top of Braelyn, but he was still hard inside her. Far from finished, he'd wait until they caught their breath, then he'd take her again, this time in the way his wolf demanded.

CHAPTER EIGHT

That had been incredible. Actually, it'd gone way beyond incredible. Braelyn lay beneath Skylar, stroking his back as her breathing slowly returned to normal. Making love to him had been the best sex of her life. And as he'd promised, his cock was still hard, buried deep inside her after climax.

Besides being the best she'd ever had, she also hadn't missed the something that had passed between them just before they'd reached orgasm. It almost felt as if a part of her had touched a part of Skylar, and then wouldn't let go. Whatever had happened, it made Braelyn feel even closer to him. The word love rose inside her mind, but she quickly pushed that away. It was too soon, and it had to be the great sex they'd shared that would have brought those thoughts to her.

Skylar kissed her forehead and pumped his hips in shallow strokes. She moaned as a wave of pleasure shot through her. "More?" She shivered when he buried his face into the crook of her neck and gently nipped her.

"More."

Braelyn gasped as he pulled out of her and then flipped her onto her stomach. With his hands placed on her hips, he urged her onto her hands and knees. Still at her side, he reached under and fondled her breasts. Just like that, she became fully aroused.

She moaned when he kneeled behind her and stroked his cock

against the outside of her pussy. Braelyn lifted her hips, wanting to feel the length of him slide inside her. As he pushed against her, she rubbed herself along the head of his cock. Skylar made another one of the growling sounds he'd done the first time they'd made love. The animalistic noise did nothing to kill her libido. If anything, it increased it.

When he continued to tease her, she moaned, "Skylar, no more. I want you inside me. Now."

"Yes."

He held her in place, positioned his cock at her entrance and pushed forward with one hard thrust. Her head hung down as he rocked behind her, the position allowing her to take even more of him. In and out he stroked. Another climax quickly built. Unlike the first time, she didn't feel the sensation of another part of them joining, but that didn't mean she felt any less connected to Skylar.

His cock grew even harder inside her pussy as he thrust faster. The grip he had on her hips held her in place while he just about pulled all the way out of her body only to slam back in.

Braelyn cried out at the first flutter of her orgasm. She moaned, pushing back to meet Skylar's strokes as she came, her pussy clutching his cock, milking him to his release. With a loud groan, he stiffened and pushed into her one final time, his shaft pulsing deep inside her.

Skylar put an arm around her waist and rolled them to their sides with him spooned around her. His cock hadn't softened a bit. She pressed deeper into his embrace. "You might be able to keep going, but I need a breather."

He chuckled and kissed the top of her head. "Rest. I don't want to wear you out yet."

Braelyn closed her eyes and relaxed against him. She'd take a little nap, then she'd be able to keep up with Skylar.

* * * *

They made love, slept and made love again. During the early evening, they broke that routine by ordering room service. Once the food was gone, Braelyn found herself back in Skylar's arms while he made her come. The man was insatiable. She lost count of how many times he'd reached climax without losing his erection. He could go for hours before it finally subsided. At the amount of calories she had to be burning, Braelyn didn't think she'd have to watch her food intake with him around. A good romp in bed would be all she'd need.

After the last time he'd made love to her, Braelyn had collapsed onto the bed, feeling as though she'd never move again. He'd taken her in every position imaginable. Her muscles were like jelly, and she'd more than likely be walking funny the next day. Not that she regretted what she'd done to get in that condition.

Skylar must have sensed she no longer had the energy to make love one more time since he suggested they watch a pay-for-view movie offered through the hotel. Braelyn quickly agreed. She chose one that had vampires and werewolves in it. She'd seen it before, but Skylar hadn't. Since she'd enjoyed it, he'd been quick to agree with her choice.

Sitting naked in bed, propped against Skylar while they watched TV, Braelyn couldn't help noticing how critical he was of the werewolves in the movie. He made more than a few comments of, "Yeah, right" and, "That's just plain stupid."

After he did it for the fifth time, she turned her head to look at him. "I have to say I've noticed you're quite critical when it comes to the werewolves, and yet you have nothing to say about the vampires. Is there a reason you're so harsh when it comes to the shifters?"

Skylar's gaze snapped to hers. "No reason. Why would I have one?"

"I don't know. Why don't you tell me? Do you have something against werewolves?"

"No. I actually like them."

"So you're just overly critical about this particular portrayal of them."

"Well, some of the things are a bit farfetched, don't you think? And why do they have to make them dumb beasts, hungering for the flesh of humans once they've shifted? And you can't tell me all of them instantly become killers after being turned. Being a werewolf does not mean you end up having a personality adjustment and go crazy."

Braelyn bit back a smile at Skylar's rant. He had such a serious expression. "Listening to you, I would have to say you sound like a werewolf expert."

"I guess you could say that."

"Oh, really now. And just where did you learn all things werewolf? Books, movies or did you happen across a real werewolf and pick his brain?" Skylar opened and closed his mouth a few times as if he weren't sure how to respond to her questions. Taking pity on him, she laughed. "The last part, about you meeting a real werewolf, was a joke. I know there isn't such a thing as a werewolf."

His face grew serious. "Since you're the one who brought the subject up, let's say werewolves were real. What would you think of them?"

She chuckled. "They aren't. It being a hypothetical question, I truly don't know how I would react if I happened to come across one."

"Okay, how about this? What if I were a werewolf and I kept it hidden from you? And say after you've gotten to know me better, I reveal that secret. Would your feelings for me change because of what I turned out to be?"

"All right, I'll play along." She took a few seconds to think it over as she gazed at Skylar. He wore an expectant look, as if how she answered would have some great meaning to him. "Okay, if you turned out to be a werewolf and could shift into a half-human/half-wolf bloodthirsty beast, it more than likely would freak me out."

"What if my type of werewolf isn't like the ones in the movie? What if I could control when I shifted, and when I did, I only shifted into a wolf?"

"Like the wolves in the wild?"

"Exactly."

"I would have to say I'd more than likely be able to handle that better. It would be closer to you being a dog."

Skylar looked at her indignantly. "A dog? My wolf does not compare to a mangy dog."

She laughed again. "For a hypothetical werewolf, you sure are touchy."

"Being referred to as a dog is a great insult to werewolves everywhere."

"I'll have to remember that. I wouldn't want to insult the

wrong werewolf and have him bite, thus turning me into one of his kind."

With a frown, Skylar said, "A bite from a werewolf doesn't turn a mortal. You have to be born a werewolf to be one. Or in some cases, know someone special who has more magic than the average werewolf and uses a spell. Then the mortal would be turned into one."

It was Braelyn's turn to frown. "Okay, now you have me a little worried here. You sound like one of the geeks from my high school who were really into role-playing games. That's all they ever talked about, and listening to them, you would swear they thought it was real. They sounded like you, talking about their make-believe world as if it were true life."

A panicked look crossed his face. "I…ah…" Right then, Braelyn heard the muffled sound of a cell phone ringing. Skylar quickly jumped out of bed and reached for his discarded jeans. "That's mine." Once he fished it out from the front pocket and looked at the call display, he said, "I'll take this in the bathroom so I won't interrupt the movie. It's my sister, Saskia."

Skylar walked into the bathroom, and her gaze lingered on his muscled ass. Once he shut the door behind him, she heard him speak to his sister.

She turned back to the TV, not really paying much attention to the movie. Skylar's reaction hadn't been what she'd expected. She'd thought he'd bluster a bit and try to prove in some way that he wasn't a geek. Panic. Not something she thought she'd ever see on his face. He was so sure of himself in an alpha male sort of way. And considering the topic of their conversation had centered on something that didn't exist, she felt he might have overreacted just a tad.

About ten minutes later, Skylar came out of the bathroom. He put his cell phone on the small table on his side of the bed and then climbed in next to her. When he saw her looking at him, he said, "As I said, that was my sister. She called to give me more details about a job I have to do tomorrow. Even though it's a family business, she's what you would call our boss."

"I thought you said you have the next few days off."

"I do, but since everyone else will be busy taking care of a sensitive matter, that only leaves me to pick up the slack. Actually, it's a job both of us will be doing."

"You want *me* to go with you when you do whatever you do while you're protecting someone?"

"Yes. If I don't... Let's just say I'd be too distracted to do my job. I'd only want to get back to you."

Braelyn couldn't stop the smile that spread across her face, or the warm feeling she got when Skylar had said that. She turned toward him and put her hand on his chest as she kissed him on the cheek. "In that case, I'd be more than happy to go with you. When do we have to do this job?"

He put his arm around her waist and held her close. "Late tomorrow morning. Roxie—the woman we have to watch—lives not too far from the hotel. So I figure after we check out, we'll pick her up and then go to your parents' house. You can change your clothes, then all three of us will go to my place."

"Has Roxie been using your family's protection services for very long? You must be pretty friendly with her if you would take her to your house." Braelyn didn't miss the jealous tone in her voice. Not normally someone prone to that emotion, she found when it came to Skylar she had a small twinge of it.

Skylar chuckled and kissed her forehead. "We've been with Roxie for over a year now. And you have nothing to worry about. I'm all yours, babe. After what we've done inside this room, you're my one and only. If it makes you feel any better, Roxie is married and is nine months pregnant with her first child. She's due any time now." She pinched his nipple—hard. "Ouch. What was that for?" he asked as he rubbed the offended area.

"That's for laughing at me," she said. "So I'm jealous. I can't help it." Braelyn met his gaze. "This is probably too soon, but I do have to go back to LA in a week." She took a deep breath and forged on. "I don't want this to be over after I leave San Francisco. I have feelings for you, Skylar. Strong feelings. Making love to you just seemed to reinforce them. The thought that once I go back home you could end up being with another woman upsets me."

Before she could blink, Skylar had her on her back with him stretched out on top of her. He kissed her long and deep, stoking the flames of her desire once more. After he broke contact with her lips, he ran his gaze over her face.

"There will never be another woman, Braelyn. Ever. You have no idea what you mean to me. And as for you going back to LA alone, it won't happen. You're stuck with me from here on out."

She looked him straight in the eyes and saw he meant every word he'd said. "What are you saying? It sounds as if you already have us as good as married."

"Would that be such a bad thing?"

Braelyn ran her gaze over Skylar's handsome face and knew she'd find it no hardship to make that kind of commitment with him. It scared her a bit to realize it since she really hadn't known him for very long, but she was never one to try to ignore how she truly felt about something or someone.

"No," she said, feeling a bit breathless with the wild emotions flitting through her. "It wouldn't be a bad thing at all. I take this to mean you'll be booking a seat on the same flight as me back to LA?"

Skylar used his thigh to spread her legs a little farther apart and settled between them. "Or we could take a later flight."

The tip of his cock brushed against her pussy. Skylar was hard again. "I have photo shoots to do, ones that can't be rescheduled. I won't give up my modeling career."

"I never asked you to." He lowered his head until his lips were a breath away from hers. "We'll talk further about this tomorrow when we have another type of discussion with Roxie. After we talk with her, it'll put things into a different perspective for you."

Braelyn was about to ask him what they had to discuss with Roxie when Skylar closed the space between their mouths and took her lips in a heated kiss. After that, she pretty much lost the ability to think properly as he made love to her once again.

CHAPTER NINE

The next morning Braelyn woke up feeling sore in places she didn't know could ache. She stretched, and some of her muscles protested the movement. She turned her head and found the spot where Skylar had slept next to her empty. Lifting her head, she looked around and saw the closed bathroom door. She heard the shower running.

Braelyn threw back the covers, sat up, then got out of bed. She walked to the bathroom door and tested the doorknob. It turned in her hand. With a smile, she stepped into the steam-filled room. She kept her gaze on the opaque closed shower curtain as she tried to cross stealthily to the bathtub.

About halfway there, Skylar said, "You have to do better than that, Braelyn, if you're going to sneak up on me. I heard you open the door, and I can smell your scent."

Braelyn froze in place. How could he have known she was there? The shower curtain was still drawn across the tub, and as for smelling her scent, he had to be exaggerating. The only one she smelled was the fragrance of the hotel shampoo he'd used to wash his hair.

No longer trying to be quiet, she crossed to the end of the tub before she pulled back the curtain. Her mouth went dry, and she had to swallow at the sight of Skylar gloriously naked. His water-slicked body called to her, making her want to run the bar of soap he held over every inch of him. During the night, she'd touched, licked and kissed all those enticing muscles now on display for her. She didn't think she'd ever get sick of exploring his body.

She held on to the shower curtain as she stepped into the bathtub and then closed it behind her. Braelyn shifted closer and put her hands on his chest. "I think you made that up."

He put the soap in the soap dish attached to the wall and then put his arms around her waist. "What exactly do you think I made up?"

"You being able to smell me before you saw me."

Skylar gave her a crooked grin. "I'm supposed to be a hypothetical werewolf so hypothetically that means my sense of smell is a lot better than a mere mortal's."

"Mortal, huh? So your werewolf is immortal?"

"No, not immortal. Just able to live for a very, very long time. Also very, very hard to kill."

"How long would my supposed werewolf live?"

"Three thousand years."

At least this time, Skylar didn't seem panicky when they talked about him being a hypothetical werewolf. There was more of a playful sound to his voice. "That's really ancient. Wouldn't my werewolf be old and decrepit once he reached his thousandth year?" She went on tiptoe and licked some water out of the hollow of his throat.

Skylar sucked in a breath. "No, he's at his prime at that age."

"So I wouldn't have to worry about my werewolf being too old to keep me satisfied in bed? If, by some chance, I actually lived to be that old." She skimmed her hands from his chest to his sides and dropped kisses down his pec to one of his nipples. She laved it with the flat of her tongue.

"Ah...ah, there would be nothing to worry about in that department." Skylar groaned as she gave the same attention to his other nipple. "God, Braelyn, you're making me horny again. I took a shower before you woke up, thinking to avoid this very thing. You, wet in a shower with me, I'm going to want you."

"It's still early. We have hours before we have to check out. That gives us plenty of time to put this shower to good use."

As she slowly went lower on his body, Skylar's hold on her waist slipped away. She dropped her hands to his hips and went down on her knees in front of him. She ended up eye level with his fully erect cock. Braelyn didn't think she'd ever get enough of it. Thick and long, it filled her pussy to capacity. And he knew how to use it to wring the most pleasure out of her.

Braelyn licked off a few beads of water from the tip of his cock as she cupped his balls. He moaned and thrust his hips forward. She started at the base of his shaft and dragged her tongue up toward the head. It twitched, and a bit of pre-cum leaked from the slit. Her pussy clenched as an ache built deep inside it.

With a firm grasp on him, she opened her mouth and took as much as she could handle inside. As if he were still pretending to be a werewolf, Skylar let loose with a loud wolflike growl. The sound went straight to her pussy, causing it to grow even wetter.

She bobbed her head as he slid in and out of her mouth. The salty taste, musky scent of him and the sounds he made had her blood heating. He grew even harder. With a strangled moan, Skylar pulled her away and yanked her to her feet. He lifted her, urging her to put her legs around his waist. He cupped her ass, held her in position and surged up into her pussy with one stroke.

Braelyn put her arms around his neck as he spread his feet to better brace himself and then moved her up and down his shaft. In a show of just how strong he was, Skylar thrust up into her as he continued to lift her. Her eyes drifted shut as wave after wave of pleasure washed through her, pushing her release closer to the surface.

"Keep going," she said with a moan. "Just a little bit more."

"Come for me, babe. I'm right there with you."

A few more strokes and they came at the same time. Her pussy clutched his cock as it pulsed deep inside her. Lost in the moment, drowning in the pleasurable sensations taking her over, Braelyn cried out, "Oh, god, I love you, Skylar."

After her body settled, she realized what she'd said. Embarrassed, thinking she might have jumped the gun a bit, she tried to put her head on Skylar's shoulder to hide her face, but he didn't let her get away with that.

"Look at me, Braelyn," he said in a low voice. When she reluctantly did, he ran his gaze over her face, his eyes shining with what she could only guess was the same emotion she felt. "You didn't say anything wrong. I love you too."

"It's too soon. I don't want you to think I only said it because you gave me an incredible night of sex."

He smiled. "It was that good, huh?" His face grew serious. "I'm a firm believer in when you've met the right person, you then know you want to spend the rest of your life with them. I want that with you, Braelyn, and knew the instant I saw you crossing that street. I'm not ever letting you go."

Not usually a crier, she choked up. "I'm good with that, because I doubt I could ever let you leave me. I'd end up being one of those women who stalks the man who dumped her and can't let go."

"There's no chance of that happening." Even though he was still hard, Skylar pulled out of her and set her onto her feet. She sighed in disappointment. "None of that now. There'll be plenty of time for making love after we've taken care of business with Roxie." He turned them and angled her under the spray of the shower. "That doesn't mean I have to give up the pleasure of washing every inch of you."

It ended up being the best shower Braelyn had ever had.

* * * *

Skylar couldn't stop sneaking looks at Braelyn as he drove them to Roxie's place to pick her up. Braelyn was his, all his. He hadn't expected to claim her as his mate quite so soon, or without her at least knowing what he truly was, but he couldn't complain about the result. She loved him, had even said so. And even though it had been sort of a game between them, she'd played along with him being a werewolf. Not that she had any inkling there was nothing hypothetical about him being one. He had high hopes she'd be able to accept him for what he was without any freaking out, especially since she'd said she would be able to handle seeing him in his wolf form. Even if she had compared him to a dog.

At the gated entrance to Beowulf and Roxie's property, Skylar buzzed to the house. Roxie's voice came over the intercom, telling him to come on up as the gate slowly swung open.

"Roxie has a nice place," Braelyn said as they drove along the drive.

"This was the family home of her husband, Beowulf. His parents left it to him. He used to live here with only his younger brother, Wade. Now that Wade is married as well, he lives in Napa Valley on the vineyard his wife, Taryn, runs. So now it's just Beowulf and Roxie, and the soon-to-be addition to their family."

"Sounds as if you know them pretty well."

"I do. So do the rest of my family. If we're not here, Beowulf and Roxie are at our place." Skylar parked the car in the circular part of the drive, close to the front door, and then turned off the engine. "A word of warning. Roxie is probably going to be a little pissed off with me. Just ignore her. She'll settle down once all three of us have had that talk I told you about last night. I think it would be better if we held off doing that until we go to my house."

He saw Braelyn didn't really understand what he'd meant by everything he'd said from the unsure expression she wore. "This chat you want to have with Roxie, it isn't anything bad, is it?" she asked.

"No," he said quickly to reassure her. "Not at all. It'll just be easier on me to have Roxie with us when we have this particular discussion."

"All right."

They got out of the car, and Skylar linked his hand with Braelyn's as they walked to the front door. He knocked once and then opened the door. "Roxie?" he called.

"I'm in the kitchen."

Skylar guided Braelyn through the house to the kitchen. Roxie was there drinking from a bottle of water. She smiled when she saw him, but it slipped a bit when her gaze landed on Braelyn.

"Skylar," she said slowly, "is there a reason you didn't come alone?"

He steeled himself for what would come next. "Yes, a very good one." At Roxie's glare, he rushed ahead with the introductions. "Braelyn, this is Roxie. Roxie, this is Braelyn."

Roxie turned her gaze onto Braelyn. "It's nice to meet you. I'd recognize you anywhere. You're even prettier in person."

"Thanks," Braelyn said. "It's nice to meet you as well. Skylar told me you've used his family's protection services for a while now."

Roxie's gaze briefly flitted to him to give him another glare, then returned to Braelyn. "It's true, though I was reluctant to have them around in the beginning. Now I'm used to it." She looked at him again. "So, Skylar, did you have that chat you were supposed to have with Braelyn first, or did you take a page from your brothers' book and went ahead and did it anyway?"

"I didn't, and I wasn't the only party involved. A man can only take so much before he loses his head and gives his woman what she wants."

Roxie rolled her eyes. "How convenient. I suppose we'll be having that chat with Braelyn later?"

"That's what I planned." Braelyn looked between him and Roxie, more than likely a bit lost in the conversation going on around her. He decided it would be best to change the subject. "Well, Roxie, are you almost ready to go? We have to stop by Braelyn's parents' house first so she can change, then we'll head to Marin County."

"I just have to grab my purse from the living room."

"Beowulf went with the others?" Saskia had told him when she'd phoned the night before that Beowulf and a few of his pack members were going to the meeting with Miles, but would stay out of sight unless things turned ugly and they were needed.

"Yeah. I should be okay for a few hours. I made him promise. I'm not in any condition to be going through *that* right now. I have enough going on."

The "that" Roxie spoke of was the separation anxiety she'd have to go through if Beowulf didn't show up on time. He didn't blame her for wanting to avoid it. Now that he was mated to Braelyn, he wanted to make damn sure they didn't have to go through it.

"Then I suggest we don't waste any more time," he said.

Roxie turned and put the bottle of water she held onto the counter. Once she turned back to face him and Braelyn, she put a hand on her stomach and sucked in a breath.

"Are you okay, Rox?"

She waved his question away. "I'm fine. I just turned too quickly and got a cramp. I've been getting them lately, especially today." She walked past him and out of the kitchen.

He and Braelyn followed her to the living room and then they went outside. Braelyn insisted Roxie sit in the front seat and she'd take the back. For her thoughtfulness, Skylar gave her a kiss, which turned into something longer than a simple meeting of lips.

The sound of his car horn blaring broke them apart. Skylar looked at Roxie who had yet to shut her door. "That wasn't necessary."

"Yes, it was. Either I did that or I'd sit here for god knows how long before the pair of you came up for air. I remember what it was like for Beowulf and me in the beginning. We couldn't keep our hands off each other. Actually, we still can't."

Skylar gave a disgusted snort. "As if I didn't already know that. I've been around both of you long enough to have witnessed it firsthand. Not that I really needed to see it."

Braelyn laughed. "The two of you sound more like brother and sister than mere friends."

Roxie chuckled. "What do you think, Skylar? Would you like to have me as your sister?"

"Not particularly. You'd have too much fun trying to make my life a living hell."

He shut Roxie's door and then held open the back one for Braelyn. Once she was settled, he shut it before he walked around to the driver's side.

All three of them made idle chitchat as he drove to Braelyn's parents' house. Roxie asked about the different fashion shoots and shows Braelyn had done. Listening to them, Skylar realized his mate had been to a lot of major cities all over the world for her career. He was just glad it wasn't something she could do for a long period of time. Once Roxie turned her, she'd stop aging at the normal mortal rate. Braelyn would have another ten years or so and then she'd have to drop out of the spotlight.

After they arrived, Skylar pulled into the driveway behind Braelyn's BMW, which was parked beside the Buick Regal he'd seen when he'd dropped her off after their shopping trip. After shutting off the car, he came around to help Roxie out. Braelyn led the way to the front door.

"It looks as if my mom is still home since her car is here," she said.

"You didn't think she would be?" he asked.

"No. It's Wednesday, and my mom usually goes grocery

shopping around this time."

"Maybe she waited for you to get home first."

"Maybe."

Braelyn opened the door and walked in. Skylar and Roxie followed her inside. He closed the door behind them. "Mom?" she called. When there wasn't any response, she said a little louder. "I'm home, Mom. Where are you?" They were still met with silence. "She doesn't seem to be here," Braelyn said. "With her car in the driveway, I don't know where she would be. Our neighbors aren't the type to invite her over for coffee."

Skylar sniffed the air. "She's here, Braelyn." He met Roxie's gaze. "And she isn't alone."

Roxie nodded. "One female and one male. Both mortals."

He looked at Braelyn to find her looking at him strangely. "It wouldn't be my dad. He'd be at work. And how would you two know there are a woman and man here? And mortals? That's what you called people who aren't a werewolf in our little game, Skylar. How would Roxie know that?"

"A werewolf game?" Roxie asked.

"Yes," he said. "A game where I was a hypothetical werewolf, and we were trying to decide whether or not Braelyn could handle finding out I was one."

Roxie smiled. "Smart."

Braelyn shook her head. "I get the feeling you two know something I don't."

Skylar took the women by their elbow and led them farther into the house. "Why don't we look for your mother, then we'll get to your questions."

A quick glance into the living room showed it was empty. The fresh scent of the mortal male and the recognizable one that was Braelyn's mother were there. Following a scent trail that headed in the direction of the flight of stairs to the upper level, he urged Roxie and Braelyn on.

Just as they reached the bottom of the staircase, something hard crack into the back of Skylar's head. He stumbled as Braelyn screamed. Before he could recover, he was struck again. This time it was enough to send him tumbling into darkness.

CHAPTER TEN

Braelyn screamed again as the strange man, who'd come up behind them, whacked Skylar on the back of the head a second time with the metal pipe he held. Helplessly, she watched Skylar collapse onto the floor. She didn't even have time to see if he still breathed before the intruder dropped his weapon and lunged for her.

She tried to run up the stairs, but he managed to grab a fistful of her hair and painfully pulled her toward him. A loud growl, similar to the ones Skylar made, sounded, and Braelyn's gaze shot to Roxie. Her upper lip curled back in a snarl as she growled once again. Her eyes seemed to softly glow.

Not taken aback by the strangeness of it all, the intruder pulled out a gun and aimed it at Roxie's distended belly. "I don't know how you're doing that shit," he told her, "but if you want your unborn brat to keep living, you'll knock it off." Once she did, he said, "Move. Into the living room."

With his grip tightening in her hair, he dragged Braelyn into the room while he kept the gun trained on Roxie. Once they reached the couch, he motioned for Roxie to sit on the floor and shoved Braelyn down next to her. "Turn around, both of you," he barked. "And don't try anything funny. I still have the gun on you."

As they turned their backs toward him, he pulled out some

large tie wraps. He jerked first Roxie's arms behind her, cinching the tie wraps tight around her wrists, then repeated the process with Braelyn.

"Turn back around and lean against the couch."

They did as ordered. He put another tie wrap around their ankles, effectively binding their legs together. Roxie sucked in a breath as if in pain. Braelyn caught her gaze, and she shook her head.

Finished with them, the intruder stood and looked down at Braelyn. "I'm going to get your boyfriend, whore. Don't move if you want your friend here to remain alive long enough to give birth."

He left the room and returned a few seconds later, dragging Skylar while he held him under his arms. The intruder had an average build and height. He grunted as he manhandled the much larger Skylar toward them and then dropped him once he reached them, not caring that the back of Skylar's head hit the floor — hard.

Using his foot, he pushed Skylar onto his stomach and used the same tie wraps to bind his wrists and ankles. With Skylar's face turned toward her, Braelyn searched it, looking for any sign of him waking up. There wasn't any.

Once the intruder came to stand in front of her again, she asked shakily, "Where's my mother?"

"She's tucked away safe upstairs. I'll bring her down in a few minutes."

"Why…why are you doing this? If you want to rob the place, take whatever you want and leave."

He squatted, bringing him to eye level with her. "Didn't you get my letters, Braelyn? Didn't I warn you what happens to whores like you?"

She felt all the blood drain out of her face. This was the person who'd been sending her the hate letters. God, why hadn't she shown Skylar the letter yesterday? Too caught up in their lovemaking, she hadn't remembered until they were on the road to Roxie's place. If she'd shown it to him earlier, maybe they would have been more on guard when they'd walked into the house and her mother hadn't answered her calls.

"I can see by your face that you *did* get my letters," he said with an ugly smile. "I do like to leave a lasting impression." He straightened to his full height. "I'll get your mother, and then I have preparations to make for the little party you and I are going to have before I rid the world of another whore." He laughed as if what he'd said were a big joke and walked out of the room.

Roxie, who was closest to Skylar, nudged him with her feet. "Skylar, wake up." He didn't as much as groan, but she did.

The intruder returned with her mother in tow. He forced her down beside Braelyn and then tore off the piece of duct tape across her mouth. "The three of you will sit here, and don't even think of trying anything. I'll just be in the next room and will be able to see you."

Since there wasn't any dining room, the living room was attached directly to the kitchen. A pair of French doors separated the two rooms. The intruder walked through them before he shut them behind him. He paced back and forth in front of the glass doors, loudly talking to himself, waving around the gun he held. Not only was he a stalker and potential killer, he also appeared to be psychotic.

"Mom, are you all right?" she asked in a low voice.

"Yes. I'm more concerned about what he'll do to you. He kept asking if you'd gotten the letters he'd sent."

"This is all my fault," she said, her voice choked with emotion. "I should have gone to the police when I received the first threatening letter. I just thought it was some harmless nutcase, and that getting hate mail was something I'd have to put up with."

"The police might not have done anything," Roxie said. "They more than likely would have taken note of it, but what else could they have done? I bet there isn't a return address on any of those letters."

"There wasn't."

"See? There would have been no way for the police to track down who sent them." Roxie suddenly stiffened. "Oh, crap."

"What's the matter?"

Roxie sucked in a sharp breath. "Crap, crap, crap. My water just broke. I guess what I thought were just cramps were early labor pains."

Braelyn looked at Roxie's lap. A large patch of wetness had darkened the material of the pants she wore. "We have to tell him you're in labor. Maybe he'll let you go."

"I wouldn't," her mother said. "There's no telling what that man will do. He's crazy. And I don't think he'll care about your friend going into labor."

"Roxie?" she asked as the other woman breathed a little faster.

"I'm okay. Just another pain." Once it seemed to pass, she said, "We just need Skylar to wake up and then the asshole in the other room will get something he never expected."

Braelyn ran her gaze over Skylar. "He hit him pretty hard with that pipe. Skylar might not wake up—ever."

Roxie chuckled. "Skylar has a hard head. Plus, it takes a lot more than that to permanently incapacitate one of my kind."

"One of your kind?"

"This was the talk Skylar wanted the three of us to have. Skylar and I aren't like you. We're werewolves."

"What did you just say you were, dear?" her mom asked.

"Werewolves."

"Um, Rox, are you sure your labor pains aren't messing with your mind?"

"They aren't that bad, yet. I'd shift to prove it to you both, but at this stage in my pregnancy, there is a chance it could harm the baby. And now that I'm in labor, I wouldn't be able to focus enough to tap into the magic inside me to make the shift. Crap, here comes another pain." Roxie took deep breaths until it passed.

Braelyn quickly glanced toward the kitchen. Their captor continued his mad pacing. "Do you know how farfetched that sounds? Werewolves can't exist."

"Why not? Just because most of the population doesn't think they can be real doesn't mean they aren't. Skylar said you and he played a game where he was hypothetically a werewolf. Whatever he told you about what his werewolf would be like, I'm sure he told you the truth." She sucked in a breath. "Another one."

Braelyn waited until Roxie breathed normally again. "The truth? Are you saying werewolves can live to be three thousand years old, can only shift into wolf form and they can't be turned unless someone special who has more magic than the average werewolf uses a spell?"

Roxie smiled. "He told you the truth. And that someone special would be me. Only I can use the spell that can turn a mortal. Now that you're mated to Skylar, you'll have to decide whether you want me to use it on you or not."

If she hadn't been in the middle of a hostage situation with a crazy man preparing to do god knew what to her, Braelyn would have laughed off what Roxie had said and told her she had to be kidding. Or delusional. "Mated to Skylar?"

"Yes. I'm sure your mom isn't going to like hearing about her daughter's sex life, so I'm going to apologize ahead of time. The first time you slept with Skylar, you had to have felt something out of the ordinary pass between you, and not just amazing sex."

Her mother groaned. "No, I definitely don't need to hear this."

"Sorry, Mom. And, yes, I felt something that first time."

Roxie nodded. "That sensation is the mating bond being formed. A piece of your soul joined with a piece of Skylar's. Once mated, there's no going back." She gasped, breathing with deep breaths.

"Ah, I hate to say this," her mom said. "But your labor pains are coming only two minutes apart. I don't think it's going to take hours before you deliver."

"I'm not going to have this baby while being held hostage by a man who needs to be locked up in a nut house." Roxie nudged Skylar with her feet again, hard enough to make his head move. "Come on, big guy. Wake up. You're supposed to be one of my Protectors. Right now, you're not doing your job." Skylar groaned. "That's it. You can do it."

Skylar blinked open his eyes and quickly shut them again with a groan. "The room is spinning, and I feel as if I'm going to throw up if I move."

"Just lie still," Roxie said. "Oh, god, here comes another one."

"Another what?" Skylar asked.

Braelyn answered for Roxie as she breathed in through her nose and out through her mouth. "She's in labor."

"Shit." Skylar's eyes snapped open, and he tried to move his arms. He froze when his bindings kept them in place. "What the hell is going on? All I remember is something slamming into the back of my head."

Able to talk once again, Roxie said, "It would seem your mate has a stalker. He has sent her threatening letters, and followed her here. He thinks she's a whore and wants to kill her. You need to shift to free yourself and take care of the asshole before he hurts her, or before I end up delivering this baby, which will be kind of hard to do with my legs tied together and my pants on."

Skylar's gaze shifted to Braelyn. "I guess now I should be telling you about me being—"

"No need to," Roxie interrupted. "I told her and her mom what we are, but I don't think either one believes me." She breathed deeply again. "Another one. They're coming closer together now."

"Don't you dare have this baby now," Skylar said to Roxie as he moved his gaze to her.

"Like I have any choice," she said with a loud growl.

Braelyn's gaze shot to the French doors. As she feared, their captor had heard the growl. He stopped pacing and yanked the doors open. "Keep it down in here," he barked and stalked to her. "Unless you're anxious to start our party now. I'm almost done setting everything up."

She quickly shook her head. "No, I can wait." Since he'd done nothing but pace and talk to himself, she had no idea what he was "setting up" in the first place.

"Good. It'll be better if I'm fully prepared." He bent and lifted his pant leg to show the large hunting knife strapped to his calf. He pulled it free and showed it to her while he kept the gun aimed in her direction. "I'm going to have fun cutting up all that pretty skin of yours."

Braelyn shivered when he squatted and ran the flat of the knife across her cheek. She bit her tongue to stop herself from whimpering in fear. The blade skimmed along her skin a second time before he stood and went back into the kitchen.

She shook so much her teeth chattered. They weren't going to be able to get out of this. The deranged man in the kitchen would kill her, and there wouldn't be anyone who could stop him.

"Braelyn," Skylar said. "Calm down. I'm going to take care of him before he ever lays a finger on you. Do you understand?"

"How? You're tied up like the rest of us."

"Not for long. I'm going to shift."

She fought the urge to laugh hysterically. "You can drop the act now, Skylar. It isn't fun anymore. You're not a werewolf, and neither is Roxie."

"Do it, Skylar," Roxie said with a groan. "Now. This baby is in a bit of a hurry."

He met Braelyn's gaze, then did what she thought was only stuff of Hollywood movies—he shifted. His eyes glowed, then his body gradually shimmered, blurring just before a wolf with the same colored fur as Skylar's light brown hair took his place.

Unable to truly believe what she'd just seen, Braelyn hurriedly looked at her mother, who had to be wearing the same shocked expression she wore.

"He's a wolf," her mom said weakly.

Now free since the tie wraps had fallen away during the shift, the wolf walked to her and put his head on her shoulder for a few seconds before he pulled away to look her directly in her face. Intelligence shone in the wolf's eyes.

"Don't be afraid," Roxie said. "It's still Skylar in there. He understands everything you say." She turned her attention on the wolf. "Time to finish this, Skylar."

The wolf bobbed his lupine head up and down, then trotted closer to the French doors. He sat, threw back his head and let out a long howl. Their captor rushed out of the kitchen and stared at the wolf.

"How the hell did that thing get in here? And where is your boyfriend?" He waved his gun around as his gaze darted around the room.

Much quicker than when he had shifted into a wolf, Skylar shifted to his human form. "I'm right here, asshole."

Moving almost faster than her eyes could follow, Skylar grabbed the gun out of their captor's hand. The hunting knife held in his other was quickly taken away as well. Now that the man was no longer armed, Skylar put him out of commission. His fist slammed into the other man's face, and the sound of crunching bone as his nose broke followed. He took punch after punch until he stood weaving on his feet.

Skylar pulled back his fist one last time. "Come near my mate again and I'll show you how well I can use my teeth and claws while I'm in my wolf form."

When he threw the punch, it landed on their captor's chin. His head flew back with the force, and his eyes rolled up into his head as he crumpled to the floor. Skylar sank to his knees next to him and searched his pockets until he found more tie wraps. He used them to bind the other man as he'd bound them.

With the knife, Skylar cut first Roxie's bindings before he set her mom free. Once he freed her, Braelyn met his worried gaze. "Say something, Braelyn. Anything."

She opened and closed her mouth a few times, trying to sort out the jumble of emotions inside her. Before she could organize her thoughts, Roxie let out a pained cry. All three of them rushed to her.

"Ah, god, I need to push," Roxie ground out as she tore at her pants.

Braelyn knelt next to Roxie as her mother took control of the situation. All business, she turned to Skylar first. "Go upstairs and, in the hall linen closet, grab a bedsheet and a couple towels." Once he took off at a run, moving unbelievably fast, her mom looked to her. "Braelyn, help me with Roxie's pants."

They'd managed to strip Roxie from the waist down when Skylar returned. Her mom snatched the bedsheet from him and then draped it over Roxie's waist. She shoved the towels at Braelyn.

"It's coming," Roxie shouted. "Skylar, call Beowulf and tell him to get his butt over here — now."

"I'm on it," he quickly said and pulled out his cell phone. He was only on it a minute before he hung up. "He's on his way. He'll call the midwife."

"This will be all over before either one of them arrive," her mom said as she knelt between Roxie's spread legs and looked under the sheet. "She's crowning already."

"You sound as if you've done this before."

Her mother smiled. "I have many times. I used to be a labor/delivery nurse for many years until Braelyn talked me into quitting. She didn't like the long hours I had to put in at the hospital." Roxie groaned as she pushed. "That's a girl. A few more of those and you'll be holding your baby in your arms."

Five minutes later, after giving six good pushes, a baby's high-pitched cries echoed in the room. Her mom put the baby on Roxie's stomach. "It's a girl," she said.

"A nice, healthy little girl. Braelyn, go to the kitchen and get the spool of string out of the junk drawer along with one of the knives from the butcher block. And the open bottle of white wine

I have in the fridge."

Going to get what her mother asked for, Braelyn had to walk past her stalker. He groaned when she drew near. She looked back at Skylar to find him already on his way toward her. He gave her stalker a punch to the back of his head, knocking him unconscious once again. She hurried by him and went into the kitchen.

It took her only a few seconds to collect what she needed and return to the living room. Her mom used the string and knife — that she'd sterilized with the wine — to cut the cord. She'd just finished when the doorbell rang. Skylar went to answer it and then came back with a large, dark-haired man who rushed straight to Roxie when he saw her.

Roxie pulled back the towel from around the baby she held in her arms. "We have a girl, Beowulf."

He gently touched the baby's cheek and then kissed Roxie on the forehead. "She's beautiful. And, of course, you couldn't do this the easy way, Rox, could you?"

"I do like to keep you on your toes."

"The midwife should be here any minute."

Now with all the excitement over, Braelyn looked at Skylar to find him intently watching her. He more than likely was worried about how she'd taken the news about him being a werewolf, and that they were mates, but she wasn't ready to face any of that right now. She turned from him and went to stand beside her mom.

CHAPTER ELEVEN

It wasn't until after everything had been taken care of that Skylar tried to get Braelyn all to himself. The midwife had arrived and taken over, declaring Roxie and her newborn daughter had managed to get through the birth with no complications. Mother and baby had then been bundled up in another one of Bev's cleans sheets, and Beowulf took his wife and child home with the midwife accompanying them.

As for Braelyn's stalker, after a phone call to Saskia, explaining what had happened, Jager and Daylen had been sent over. Being an ex-cop, Daylen had put a call in to one of her friends at her old station. He'd come with another police officer who took the stalker away in handcuffs. Daylen's friend questioned Braelyn. Skylar didn't know whether he wanted to shake her or hold her tight when he heard how many threatening letters she'd been sent and hadn't gone to the police about.

Her statement given—minus the part where he'd shapeshifted into his wolf form—the police officer had left. Jager and Daylen followed shortly after. That was when Skylar decided he needed to get Braelyn alone to talk to her. She had to be having a hard go of it in accepting what he was. Every time he caught her watching him, she quickly looked away. At least she didn't have fear in her eyes when she did it, but her reaction didn't reassure him too much.

Skylar went to the kitchen where Braelyn and her mother sat at the table. That was where Braelyn had given the officer her statement. His head still hurt like a motherfucker from the blows he'd received, but he pushed the pain aside.

He went to stand beside Braelyn's chair and held out his hand. "Will you come and talk with me?"

She shook her head. "Whatever you have to say, you can do so in front of my mom."

Bev cleared her throat. "Braelyn, I think Skylar would be more comfortable if it was just you."

"I wouldn't be, Mom. You know what he is. It's no longer a secret."

Skylar dropped his hand to his side and sat in the chair beside hers. "All right. We'll do it your way. So now you know the truth. I'm a werewolf, and I'm over a thousand years old. And we are mated."

Braelyn swallowed. "Roxie said that our being mated means a part of our souls joined, and that there's no going back."

"That's true. And it's true I knew you were the one meant for me when I first saw you crossing that street. When a male werewolf encounters the scent of his would-be mate, it jumpstarts his mating urge. It'll ride him until the mating bond is in place. And once it is, mated couples literally can't be apart from each other unless they want to suffer separation anxiety. An hour away from your mate feels like months. Your mind will play tricks on you, making you believe something bad has happened to the other. All you'll be able to think about is getting back to your mate."

"That's why you wanted me to come with you when you had to watch over Roxie," Braelyn said softly.

"Yes."

"If that's the case, why didn't Roxie go through it? She wasn't with Beowulf for at least an hour and didn't seem to suffer for it."

"That's because they've been mated for a little while. After a year or so, it isn't as bad as it is for newly mated couples. Roxie and Beowulf can be away from each other for a couple hours before it starts to set in."

"Roxie said she's the special someone you know who can use the spell to turn me."

"It will be your choice to make. And Roxie *is* special. She is the foretold one, and rules over all the werewolf packs. My family has trained for hundreds of years to be her Protectors."

Braelyn's mother, who had remained quiet, spoke up. "That's a big decision you've put on my daughter's shoulders, Skylar. I know you said you knew she was your mate when you first saw her, but I have ask, do you love her?"

Skylar locked gazes with Braelyn. "I've already told her that I do, but I'll say it again. I love her with every fiber in my being. I started to fall for her the instant I saw her. If that hadn't been possible, my mating urge never would have kicked in. And I'll continue to love her for the rest of my very long life. I'm utterly devoted to her, and would do everything in my power to keep her happy."

"That's all I needed to hear." Bev pushed back her chair and stood. She kissed her daughter on top of her head. "Braelyn, hold on to this one and don't ever let go. He's a keeper."

Braelyn looked up at her mom with a shocked expression. "You have no problem with Skylar being a werewolf?"

"Honey, if it weren't for him being one, you would more than likely be dead at the hands of that sick stalker. And the way he looks at you is the same way your father looks at me. He truly loves you. Considering this mating bond he talked about is more permanent than a marriage license, you'll never have to worry about him only being with you for your fame."

"And what about me being turned into a werewolf? Can you accept that as well, Mom?"

"Yes, I can. To be honest, I'm all for it. What mother wouldn't want their child to live for a few thousand years? Heck, if it were possible, I'd be getting in line right behind you for the spell. After I convinced your father to go through with it, of course."

Skylar cleared his throat. "Ah, that could probably be arranged. My sister-in-arms, Saskia, her mate, Eli, was a mortal like you and comes from a big family. His twin and his sister, Billie, also took werewolves for their mates and decided to be turned. They have two older brothers and a father who have remained mortal, but Roxie offered to turn them to keep the family together. They're all thinking about it."

"You would do that, Mom?" Braelyn asked. "You'd become a

werewolf if I decided to go through with it?"

"I'm not going to say I don't find the long-life aspect of it unappealing. Who would skip the chance to have it? We'd have to convince your father to do it, though. That's something we can talk about later. Right now, I think it's more important you and Skylar talk. Alone. I'm going clean up the mess in the living room." Before she left, she added, "And if you want to take him to your bedroom to have more privacy, I won't stop you."

Skylar was tempted to follow Bev out to the living room and give her a big kiss. Agreeing to the turn would hopefully make it easier for his mate to make the same decision as well. After what had happened there today, the thought of Braelyn not being a werewolf scared him. If she'd been turned, she would have been faster and stronger than the sicko who had wanted to kill her.

He met Braelyn's gaze. "Will you go upstairs with me? If you're not comfortable with that, I can take you to my place."

She shook her head. "That would just delay things. We'll finish our talk in my room."

Skylar followed her out of the kitchen and then up the stairs. Inside her bedroom, Braelyn shut the door behind them. He made a point of not sitting on the bed. He stayed in the middle of the room and waited for her to make the next move. He ached to hold her, to make love to her, but since she'd made no move to touch him since the truth about what he was had come out, he wouldn't push her until she was ready.

Braelyn shoved away from the back of the door that she'd been leaning against and slowly walked toward him. She stopped when she stood in front of him. "So much has happened today — the stalker, you being a werewolf and Roxie having her baby. I feel as though I should be sitting in a dark corner with my legs drawn to my chest while I rock myself, mumbling incoherently as tears run down my cheeks, but one thing is stopping me from doing it."

"What would that be?"

"You. Any time I start to feel panic setting in, I look at you and remember how safe I feel in your arms. How protected. And that you'll do anything to keep me that way. Knowing you're a werewolf just adds to that feeling." He went to reach for her, but Braelyn stopped him by holding up her hands. "Wait, I'm not finished yet. I know you love me, and that I love you, but I'm not exactly thrilled you mated us without telling me beforehand."

He blew out a breath. "I had the best intentions in the beginning, I swear. Roxie has a set of rules she tries to impose on male werewolves who have found their mortal mates. One of them is we have to tell them what we are and what it means to be mated to us before we claim them. Unfortunately, it's a counterproductive rule when it comes to the mating urge. Being female, Roxie doesn't really have a clue how bad it can get. And then you booked the hotel room, and I was lost, especially after you bit me on the neck."

"Why does me biting you have anything to do with it? And you were the one who told me to do it, I might add."

"A bite where the shoulder meets the neck during foreplay is the biggest turn-on for a male werewolf. And if the female bites hard enough to leave a mark, we like to proudly show it off so other females know we're taken." Braelyn's gaze landed on the exact spot on his neck he'd been talking about.

She stepped a little closer until they were toe-to-toe. "You mean like this?"

Braelyn went on tiptoe, tugged the collar of his shirt away and bit him where his shoulder and neck met, hard enough so there was no question of whether she'd marked his skin. He shuddered and wrapped his arms around her as his cock went instantly rock-hard.

"Braelyn. God, I have to be inside you." She bit him again, and he clutched her tighter, his cock jerking.

After she lifted her head, he took her lips in a bone-melting kiss. He poured all his need and love he had for her into it. She returned it with the same heat. With teeth and tongue, he deepened the contact. After coming so close to losing her, he needed the earthly affirmation of lovemaking to show him he hadn't. He wanted to hear his mate's cries of passion echoing in his ears as he took her over and over again.

Breaking the connection with his mouth, Braelyn grabbed the bottom of his shirt and yanked it up. "Naked. Now."

With little finesse, they managed to strip off all their clothes. Naked, they fell on her double bed in a tangle of limbs, their lips meeting once again. Braelyn pushed him onto his back and then straddled his hips.

She looked at him. "Your eyes are glowing."

"It means I'm aroused."

"Then I'd better do something about it."

She reached down, took hold of his cock and held it in position as she slowly lowered herself on it. Once she'd taken him to the hilt inside her pussy, she rode him. Low growls of pleasure rumbled out of him as she arched her hips to take him deeper. He reached up to cover her breasts, kneading them when she put her hands on top of his.

Faster she rode him, her inner muscles tightly gripping his shaft until he couldn't hold back any longer. At the first flutter of her orgasm, he let out a howl and surged up one final time as his cock emptied deep inside her pussy.

Braelyn collapsed on top of him. He put his arms around her and stroked her back as she shook. "Braelyn? Talk to me." When she didn't say anything and there was wetness against his chest, he shifted them until he sat with his back against the headboard. He cupped her face and forced her to look at him. "Don't cry."

"I was so scared," she whispered. "My mom was right. If it weren't for you, I wouldn't be alive now."

He kissed her forehead. "It's over now, and I won't let anything like that happen again. I am a Protector, after all."

She gave him a watery smile. "You might be one of Roxie's Protectors, but you belong to me now and I'm not giving you back."

"I'll make sure she knows that."

Braelyn wiped her eyes. "Good. Now kiss me and show me just how devoted you are to me again."

Skylar did just that and then some.

EPILOGUE

Skylar sat a table away from the three people he watched at a small coffee shop. Miles and Jaden were deep in conversation while Leif sat next to his mate, his stern gaze never leaving Miles. Father and daughter ignored him.

It'd been a month since Miles had first contacted Saskia about seeing Jaden. Since then, they'd met at least once a week in places like this coffee shop. For now, there was no question about Miles being allowed near their home in Marin County. They didn't need the risk of him seeing Roxie there and somehow figuring out she and not Jaden was the true foretold one. So far, it hadn't been a problem. Miles seemed more interested in being with his daughter than what she was supposed to be.

Skylar pulled his gaze from the other table when Braelyn sat next to him and put one of the coffees she carried in front of him. He leaned in and kissed her cheek. He still found it hard to believe she was his.

In this past month, a lot had changed for her, besides becoming his mate. They'd both flown to LA for her to do the couple of photo shoots she hadn't been able to cancel. After that, they'd come home and settled into their life together. She'd allowed Roxie to turn her, as did her parents. It turned out Braelyn and her mother hadn't had to do much convincing to get her father to go through with it. Once Skylar had explained everything werewolf to him and what it all meant, he'd been quick to agree since the women of his family were for it.

"I still find it kind of surreal that I can hear Jaden and Miles' conversation as if I sat at their table," Braelyn said.

He gave a quick shake of his head and lowered his voice. "Remember, the same can be said about them being able to hear us." Miles didn't know much of anything about the spell, and they wanted to keep it that way.

"Oops, sorry." She quickly glanced at the others. "Do you think Leif will ever unbend when it comes to Jaden seeing her father?"

Skylar chuckled. "I can't see that happening any time soon. To be honest, I don't blame him. We all know what Miles is capable of. We'd be stupid to let our guards down now that he's decided to play nice."

"For Jaden's sake, I hope he stays that way. And before I forget, you know who called and said she wants us and my parents to come over for dinner tonight."

The "you know who" was Roxie. She'd grown quite close to Braelyn and her mom. "All right. I just hope this time she doesn't make me change any messy diapers."

Somehow, whoever was on protection duty ended up getting roped into diaper duty at some point. Not that Skylar minded all that much since he loved little Nevaeh as if she were his own daughter. Holding her made him want one of his own, but that would have to wait for a little while yet. Braelyn wasn't ready and wanted a few more years of her career before they started a family and she retired to become a full-time mom.

Braelyn laughed. "You never know. I do have to say I love watching you with Nevaeh."

Skylar turned his attention back to the other table when Leif, Jaden and Miles stood. "Time to go, it would seem. At least Leif behaved himself again."

There had been a few close calls during the first couple meetings, which was understandable since Miles had taken Leif hostage not all that long ago. Skylar and Braelyn followed them as they left the coffee shop.

Outside on the sidewalk, Miles hugged Jaden. From where he stood, Skylar easily saw the love Miles had for his daughter showing in his eyes. Saskia was right. Leif didn't have to worry about her father ever trying to harm Jaden. Miles might have chosen to walk the dark side, but there was still a good part to him that seemed to come out with his daughter. If only that could mean Miles wasn't a total lost cause.

Putting his arm around Braelyn's shoulders, Skylar kissed the top of her head as they waited for Leif and Jaden to join them. When the other couple did, he started them walking toward the lot where they had parked. He sent up a silent prayer, grateful he never had to worry about Braelyn's father ever turning into one of the bad guys. He was just happy to have found his mate and been given the chance to share his very long life with her.

The End

KYE'S HEART

Kye's idea of fun doesn't include toting Roxie's three-month-old daughter to the zoo, but like the good little Protector he is, Kye travels to the land of exotic furballs with pup in tow...then smacks himself for not heading to the zoo ages ago. There, dressed in drab brown and looking more gorgeous than any woman he's ever seen, Kye finds his mate.

Being a zookeeper, Michaela is used to soothing the savage beast...not screaming babies. Feeling sorry for the hottie who's looking more panicked by the second, she's quick to offer her assistance in calming the little bundle of adorable he's holding. Of course Kye doesn't hesitate to show his appreciation by asking her out and giving her a kiss that sends her heart racing.

While Kye struggles to tell Michaela about his penchant for howling at the moon, he manages to toss her right into the middle of his secretive life as a Protector and all the fangs that entails. The question is: Can Michaela tolerate any more fur in her life, or is she going to trample all over Kye's heart?

CHAPTER ONE

The gates at the end of Roxie and Beowulf's long, curving drive swung open, and Kye drove his French racing blue Jaguar XKR-S coupe up it. It was the middle of the morning, and his turn to watch over Roxie and her family. Now that her baby had been born, the overnight protection duty had stopped. No longer pregnant, she could once again shift, which meant in her half-human and half-wolf form, she'd be a force to be reckoned with.

Kye parked in front of the large, detached garage next to Dirk's car. His brother-in-arms had arrived much earlier, which was his norm. Dirk and Roxie would probably already be holed up in her office doing something Kye didn't understand on the computer. That was if Roxie wasn't busy with her new daughter, Nevaeh.

After getting out of his car, Kye pushed the remote to lock it. He smiled as he thought about Roxie and Beowulf's baby. Being over a thousand years old, and living most of that time with the rest of the Protectors, he hadn't had much opportunity to be around little ones. Nevaeh was only three months old, and every time he held her, he felt as if he'd break her. He had to admit the little squirt was growing on him.

Walking right into the house, Kye decided to check upstairs. He didn't hear anyone moving around on the lower level. He took the stairs two at a time and headed for Roxie's office. The only one inside was Dirk, who looked away from the computer he worked on once he noticed Kye standing just inside the doorway.

"Where is everyone?" he asked.

Dirk turned the steno chair to face him. "Roxie is in Nevaeh's room, changing her. Beowulf is out in the backyard having his coffee."

Kye jerked his head in Dirk's direction. "I see you're busy doing whatever the hell it is you do on that damn thing. You and Roxie always seem preoccupied with something that involves the computer. Yet you never say what it is you're working on."

Dirk smiled. "You'll find out soon enough. It just took a while to set up and get rolling."

He shrugged. "Whatever. I'm sure it's something I won't understand. I guess I have to look forward to another day of sitting in here with you two, bored out of my fucking head."

"I don't think so," Dirk said with a knowing smile. "Roxie has thought of something else for you to do."

Kye wasn't sure he liked the sound of that. "What would that be exactly?"

His brother-in-arms chuckled. "I think it would be better if you ask Roxie yourself."

Deciding to do just that, he left the office and then walked down the hall to the baby's room. He found Roxie had just finished changing Nevaeh's diaper. The task done, she lifted her daughter onto her shoulder and turned in his direction.

"Good, you're here," Roxie said.

"Dirk said you had something else you wanted me to do today."

"I do."

Roxie closed the distance between them and placed Nevaeh in his arms. Kye automatically stiffened, afraid to move in case he hurt her.

"Ah," he said hesitantly, "what would that be?"

He glanced at the baby to find her staring up at him. She had the same ice-blue eyes her father had, along with his black hair. What she had of it. Kye thought she was bald. In looks, she took after her mother.

"As of today, you're to be Nevaeh's sole Protector."

Kye's gaze shot to Roxie. "What?"

"Saskia and I discussed it, and we decided you'll have the sole responsibility of protecting my daughter."

"Won't that be spreading the others kind of thin? There are supposed to be two of us watching over you with each shift."

"That was another thing Saskia and I talked about. Miles is no longer the threat he once was. He still thinks Jaden is the foretold one. And from what Saskia says, her brother loves his daughter. He won't make a move against her. He still hasn't a clue about me really being the one to rule over all the werewolf packs."

Jaden, the mate to Leif, another of his brothers-in-arms, had pretended to be the foretold one when her father, Miles, had taken Leif as a hostage. Since Miles had never seen Roxie, Jaden had taken her place. Finding out he had a daughter he'd never known existed had caused Miles to have a change of heart about gaining control over the foretold one. He had wanted to use her as a figurehead to rule the packs himself. Once a Protector and brother-in-arms, it was kind of a relief to see Miles step back from the dark side.

"That might be the case now," Kye said, "but we still need to be careful. Who knows what Miles will do if he ever finds out the truth."

"We'll make sure that never happens. Jaden is willing to keep up the charade indefinitely for her father, if need be. I still want you to be Nevaeh's Protector."

Kye looked again at the baby in his arms. "All right, since I really don't have any choice." Roxie did rule over the packs, after all. "In a way, I'll still be here to help protect you as well, since Nevaeh isn't exactly able to go anywhere without you. The only problem I have with it is I'll be on duty all day and most of the night, every day. I'm going to need a break at some point."

Roxie waved his concerns away with a flick of her hand. "Don't worry about that. One of the others can spell you out for a bit if it starts to be too much, but you'll take on the majority of the task. And you'll still be here in the house most of the time, but I want you to take Nevaeh out alone."

Kye gave her a look that said he thought she was crazy. "Ah, Rox, I know nothing at all about babies. You can't expect me to look after her by myself."

"I can and do. It'll force you to get used to taking care of

Nevaeh. And you *will* be taking care of her. Saskia and I think it's important for you to bond with the baby now, so she'll feel safe and secure with you." Roxie cleared her throat. "And it'll give me a bit of a break from time to time."

"So you want me to be a glorified babysitter?"

"Not really. Come on, Kye, it won't be that bad. I'm not nursing her anymore. Since I couldn't produce enough milk to keep her fed, she takes a bottle. That's one hurdle we don't have to worry about."

To say he was uneasy about the whole situation was an understatement. What if he messed up? "You're willing to put your only child in the hands of a man who could forget to feed and change her? Fuck, I don't even know how to hold her properly." He stretched out his arms to show her how stiffly he held Nevaeh.

Roxie glared at him. "No swearing in front of my daughter. You got that? I don't want her first word to be a swear word. And you just need some practice is all. Plus, you don't have to worry about those other things. Nevaeh will make sure you know when she needs to be changed or is hungry. She has a good set of lungs." She pushed back his arms and tucked the baby more firmly into the crook of the one Nevaeh was nestled in while his hand stayed under her bottom. "There. That's better. Now put her on your shoulder. She likes it."

Feeling like a blundering idiot, Kye somehow managed to get the small person on his shoulder. He winced when Nevaeh grabbed a handful of his hair that just reached the tops of his shoulders and gave it a good yank. He heard sucking noises.

"Is she sucking on my hair?" he asked horrified.

Roxie laughed. "You should see your face. And, yes, she is. You might want to consider pulling it back in a ponytail. Beowulf has gotten in the habit of doing it whenever he's going to hold her."

He winced again as Roxie untangled his hair from the baby's fist. "So this is what you have planned for me today? To learn how to take care of Nevaeh?"

"That, and I want you to take her to the zoo."

Kye scowled. "Why the hell would I do that? She's only three months old, for Christ's sake. What the fuck would she get out of it?" Roxie smacked him on the side of his head. "Ouch!"

"I told you to watch the swearing. She might not be an active participant, but she is a werewolf."

"So? I'm a werewolf too, and I've never been to a zoo."

"I want her to be comfortable with her wolf side. I want her to learn about other animals and nature. And if you haven't, then this should be a new experience for you as well."

He rolled his eyes. "God, you can tell how young you are with all that touchy feely crap. Back when I was your age, I swung a sword, fighting on battlefields."

"Good for you," she said sarcastically. "I still want you to take Nevaeh to the zoo today. It's nice out, and not too hot. Who knows, you might even enjoy yourself."

"I doubt it," he said under his breath. By the scowl Roxie gave him, she'd heard him. He breathed a deep sigh. "Fine, I'll go, but I don't want to push her in a stroller. That thing is nothing but a pain in the ass."

"Then don't take it. I have a baby sling. You can wear it across your chest. Nevaeh likes being carried in it."

In no time, Kye found himself being given a quick lesson on how to change a diaper and how to heat a bottle of formula. Before he was practically shoved out the door, carrying Nevaeh in her infant car seat, he was given the aforementioned baby sling and a diaper bag. Jesus, he'd never known how much stuff went along with a baby until Roxie had had her daughter. It seemed as if he almost took the whole house with him when he left.

Kye promised to return in a couple hours, then strapped the car seat into the back of his Jaguar. He got into the driver's side and then started the engine. As he drove to the San Francisco Zoo, he kept checking his rearview mirror, looking in the baby's direction. He could only see the back of the car seat, since it was strapped in facing the rear. So far, Nevaeh was quiet, which he hoped like hell would continue for the entire time he was out with her.

After arriving at the zoo, he parked the car and then got out. Since his was a two-door, he had to flip his seat forward to get to the baby. Kye took the seatbelt off the car seat and turned it so it faced him. Nevaeh was asleep. He smiled. She looked as cute as a button. He took out the sling and put it on the way Roxie had showed him. Then carefully, he unstrapped the infant before he picked her up. He felt awkward as he placed her inside the baby carrier. She squirmed and whimpered a bit, but settled once he rocked her for a few seconds. Before he locked the Jaguar, he took out the diaper bag and slung it over his shoulder.

Still thinking this was a stupid idea, Kye walked toward the zoo's entrance. Whoever heard of taking a baby to a place like this? It would have been better to wait until she was at least a year old. Right now, he'd be the only one who'd get anything out of the trip, if he did. He wasn't sure if it would have been better to sit bored, watching Roxie and Dirk on the computer all day.

Kye paid the fifteen-dollar admission for himself, and wouldn't you know it, the baby was free. Of course she was, since the zoo knew infants and children under four really wouldn't pay much attention to the things around them, just as he'd told Roxie. He looked at the brochure he'd been given and ran his finger down the list of animals on exhibit. There wasn't a damn wolf on it anywhere. Figured. There were lions and tigers, but no wolves.

He walked farther into the zoo, heading to the first group of exhibits. His nose twitched as he detected all the different animal scents in the air. They just about overrode everything else. Some of them he didn't even recognize.

Kye meandered from exhibit to exhibit. He had to admit some of the animals he saw were interesting. He particularly liked the polar bears, watching them dive into the water of their enclosure. Probably forty-five minutes had gone by when Nevaeh woke up. She squirmed inside her carrier, grunting. He stopped and looked at her. The baby made a loud sucking sound as she crammed her tiny fist into her mouth. Since she didn't seem upset, he continued on his way.

Another five minutes passed before the baby whimpered as she sucked even harder on her fingers. Kye looked around for a bench to sit on. There wasn't one in the general vicinity so he kept walking, hoping to find one farther on. Once he found what he looked for, Nevaeh's whimpers had turned into full-fledged cries. And she'd completely given up on sucking her hand.

Feeling a bit desperate, Kye sat, pulled Nevaeh out of the carrier and held her against his chest. He set the diaper bag beside him and opened it. He pulled out what Roxie had called an "on-the-go" bottle warmer and unzipped the smaller container. By now the baby's cries were almost ear-shattering to his sensitive hearing.

He noticed Nevaeh's wails of unhappiness had drawn the stares of the other people visiting the zoo. Not liking it, Kye put the warmer down and then patted the baby's back as Roxie had shown him. That seemed to quiet her a bit. He stopped the motion and went to reach for the bottle, which set Nevaeh off again.

"You look as if you need some help." The woman's voice came from a spot close to him.

Without looking up from where he reached, Kye said, "I need to get the bottle out of this warmer, but Nevaeh isn't cooperating with me."

"Here, let me."

A figure moved in front of him, blocking the sun. As her fingers brushed his, he filtered her scent from the stronger animal ones around him. It hit him like a ton of bricks. His head jerked up, and his cock went instantly hard, straining against the front of his jeans as his mating urge kicked in. Kye had to bite back a growl of need as he looked into the face of his would-be mate.

She was pretty in a cute way. She smiled, showing even white teeth as she returned his stare, her light blue eyes friendly. Her long, straight black hair had been pulled back into a high ponytail. He ran his gaze over her body as she straightened with the bottle in hand. It was hard to tell what it looked like underneath the zoo uniform she wore, but from what he could see of her arms not covered by the short-sleeved shirt, they were slim and toned. He assumed the rest of her would be as well, but the only way to be sure was for him to strip her out of her clothes, which his fingers itched to do. The baby let out a loud wail, breaking some of the sexual haze that had descended over him.

His would-be mate held out the bottle. "I think you'd better feed her."

He nodded as he clumsily settled Nevaeh into the crook of his arm. He reached for it, his fingers once again brushing the woman's, causing his cock to jerk. "Thanks." He placed the nipple against Nevaeh's lips. She opened her mouth and greedily latched on to it.

"Is this the first time you've been out with your daughter since she was born?"

Kye's head snapped up. "She's not my daughter. I'm her Pro...uncle."

"So you're babysitting," she said.

"You could say that." At that moment, Nevaeh decided to squirm against him, and what sounded like rolling thunder, emanated from her diaper along with the sound of something Kye did *not* want to handle in a million years.

Some of what he felt must have shown on his face, because his would-be mate laughed. "Why do I get the feeling you've never changed a diaper before?"

He looked at the baby, then jerked his head away as a foul odor hit him, making him wish he didn't have a werewolf's acute sense of smell. "Oh, Nevaeh." She continued to contentedly suck on her bottle as if there wasn't a stinky mess in her drawers. Kye lifted his gaze to the woman in front of him and answered her question. "Because I haven't." The idea of having to deal with his first diaper changing horrified him.

It also cooled his libido somewhat, even though the mating urge was still there, unable to be ignored. Kye felt pulled in two different directions. He wanted to be with the one who was meant to be his, but Nevaeh was his responsibility. He'd opened his mouth to say something that would prevent his would-be mate from walking away when she beat him to it.

"How about I take pity on you and help you with that too? There's an office close by we can use."

He nodded and smiled. "Thanks, I'd appreciate that."

Her gaze seemed to latch on to his mouth, making Kye wish they weren't in such a public place, or that he didn't hold a baby in his arms. As she stared at him, he took the opportunity to intensely gaze at her face, wanting nothing more than to taste her kissable lips. He wanted to see if she'd moan into his mouth as he explored her or use his hair to pull him closer, becoming more of the aggressor.

At a sound that was a cross between a moan and sigh, Kye lifted his gaze to her eyes and saw her pupils had dilated. There was a slight flush across her cheeks. He took a deep breath and detected the subtle scent of her arousal. He ground his teeth to hold back a wolf's howl that built inside him.

She gave herself a small shake, as if to break the spell between them. She cleared her throat. "Ah, if you want to come with me, I'll take you to that office."

He nodded and pulled the bottle out of Nevaeh's mouth only long enough to sling the diaper bag over his shoulder, then stood. "I'm Kye, by the way."

"I'm Michaela."

Kye fell into step with Michaela and prayed she wouldn't look down and see the raging hard-on he had. Having her think he was some kind of perv wasn't how he wanted to start things off with her.

CHAPTER TWO

Michaela's heart thudded against her ribs. Her blood still rushed hotly through her veins after that hungry look he'd given her. Her pussy clenched at the thought of it. She shot a glance at Kye from the corner of her eye as he walked beside her. He was gorgeous, the type of man she could stare at all day. He had male supermodel good-looks that would draw women in droves. At five-foot-eight, she considered herself to be tall for a woman, but he made her feel small. If she had to, she guessed his height to be six-foot-four. Sitting down, he'd looked big with his well-muscled body, but with the extra eight inches he had on her, he came across as even bigger.

"So what do you do here at the zoo?" Kye asked, bringing her back to reality.

"I'm one of the animal keepers."

"You help take care of all of them or just certain species?"

"I go where I'm needed."

"Then you mustn't be afraid to be around large wildlife."

Michaela turned her head to look at Kye. He stared at her intently as if he waited to hear what her reply would be. "No, I'm not afraid of them. I find them all beautiful, especially the big cats. If I didn't, I wouldn't be doing what I do." Something she said must have been what he'd wanted to hear, because he gave her a smile that turned him from gorgeous to a mouthwatering hunk.

Finally able to pry her gaze off Kye, Michaela walked beside him in silence, but she was more than aware of his presence. At first, seeing him holding the small baby, she'd thought for sure he was married. She hated to admit how glad she was when she'd found out he was only Nevaeh's uncle. That still didn't mean there was a chance he wasn't taken, but given how he'd looked at her, she had high hopes he'd be single.

At the office door, Michaela opened it and then allowed Kye to walk in ahead of her. She shut it behind her once she stepped inside. She pointed to the couch in the corner. "You can use that to change her."

"Okay. I thought you were going to do that."

She smiled. "By help, I meant give instructions if needed."

"Oh." Kye grimaced.

Kye walked past to where she'd indicated. Michaela had to hide a smile behind her hand as his gaze shifted from the baby to the couch, looking none too sure of himself. He pulled the now empty bottle from the Nevaeh's mouth and then stuck it into the open diaper bag. He knelt, then laid Nevaeh down. He kept one hand on her as he rifled through the bag and took out everything he needed to do a diaper change.

The poor man appeared to be a bit shell-shocked, looking as if he really had no idea where to start. Michaela crossed the room before she squatted beside Kye. "Put the changing pad under her, then you can take off her pants."

He nodded and did what she said. After getting Nevaeh down to her diaper, Michaela heard Kye say under his breath, "You can do this. You've faced worse things."

She bit the inside of her cheek to stop herself from laughing at his pep talk. With a deep breath, he reached for the tabs and quickly tugged them open. Gingerly, he pulled down the front of the diaper.

Kye just about gagged and looked away. "Roxie is going to owe me big time for this," he said. "This was her bright idea."

Michaela's hopes sank a bit at the sound of another woman's name. "Roxie? Is she your girlfriend?"

He snorted. "No, I don't have one. She's Nevaeh's mother and the person who talked me into taking her daughter to the zoo by myself. Roxie thought it would help me bond with the baby."

Her hopes flared once more. "So Roxie is your sister then?"

"Again, no. Nor is she my sister-in-law. I'm not Nevaeh's uncle by blood or marriage. I guess you could say I'm a very close friend to her mother and father."

"Ah, I see. Well, Roxie isn't here to do this, so can I suggest you grab the baby wipes and get to work?"

Kye gave her a pleading look. "Do you think you could do it for me?"

Michaela laughed. "No. Nevaeh is your responsibility, not mine. My job is to clean up after the animals here, not change a baby's dirty diaper."

He gave her a lopsided grin that almost had her leaning in to kiss him senseless. "Oh well," he said. "It was worth a shot."

With a big production of almost gagging and bemoaning his fate, Kye managed to change the diaper. The only help she gave was to point out he'd put the new one on a bit loose. Finished, he picked up Nevaeh and stood. Michaela rose with him as he lifted the baby to his shoulder to burp her. A few good taps and he brought up a good one, along with something extra. She struggled to maintain a straight face, but it was a losing battle when Kye shifted the baby to the crook of his arm and looked at his shoulder in disgust.

"Great," he said. "Now I smell like puke. If something isn't coming out of one end, it's coming out the other. Roxie made sure I brought a change of clothes for Nevaeh, but I don't have an extra shirt for me. I don't want to walk around with spit up on my shoulder for the rest of the time I'm here."

Michaela couldn't help it. She laughed. At the stern look Kye gave her, she laughed even harder. After she collected herself, she said, "I'm sorry. Really, I am."

"I'm glad someone can find the humor in this," he huffed.

"The gift shop sells T-shirts. I'm sure there will be one in your size."

"Good idea. Here, hold Nevaeh."

Kye passed her the infant, slipped off the baby sling, then tore his soiled dark gray T-shirt off over his head. Her jaw dropped as she took in the wide expanse of his bared chest. It was thickly padded with well-defined muscles to match those on his washboard abs. She'd only seen a male body like that in ads or on romance book covers. Michaela ran her gaze over every hard-muscled inch of his upper body and yearned to touch him. To trace him with her fingers, lips and tongue. Her nipples hardened to tight buds, and her pussy grew wet as she thought of what it would be like to be given free rein over him. To do whatever she wanted.

A small noise that sounded awfully like an animal's growl had her lifting her gaze to Kye's face. The heat she'd seen in his eyes before had returned. She slightly narrowed hers as she thought for a brief second Kye's mutedly glowed, but that couldn't be right. She soon became lost in his hungry gaze, nothing else mattering, except for the way he stared at her. Her pussy clenched with the need that thrummed through her, and she took a step closer.

"Ah hell," he said, his voice a low, husky growl.

He closed more of the space between their lips and cupped her face. He tipped her head up and brought his mouth down onto hers. He slanted his more firmly to get a tighter fit while he licked along the seam, as if asking her to open for him. Michaela didn't hesitate. She softly moaned as he slipped inside, tasting her, pushing her arousal to even greater heights. He kissed her as if he wouldn't survive his next breath without her.

She took a step nearer, wanting to be closer, her body aching for his, but the baby she held protested, letting out a small whimper. The sound brought her up short, and Kye abruptly broke away and dropped his hands to his sides.

His chest rapidly rose and fell as he panted. She was no better off than he. Her heart pounded loudly in her ears, and desire still had her in its grip. She wanted Kye—almost desperately. No man had ever turned her on to that degree with a single kiss. He hadn't touched her intimately, yet Michaela felt as if it wouldn't take much else to push her over the edge into orgasm.

"I want to see you. Alone," Kye said huskily. "After you're done with work."

She nodded. "You can come to my place."

Michaela didn't normally invite men she'd just met over to her apartment, but Kye was different. She didn't want him to slip through her fingers. She wanted to explore this instant attraction that had flared between them. She usually had a good sense about people, and she had a positive one about the man who stood in front of her. The way he was with Nevaeh, he couldn't be bad.

He gave her a curt nod. "I'll be there around seven. Nevaeh should be asleep for the night by then. Just give me your address."

She passed the baby back to Kye and then turned to the desk behind her. She glanced over the surface until she found a scratch pad and pen. Michaela scribbled her address onto the paper before she tore off the top sheet. She passed it to Kye, who crammed it into the front pocket of his jeans.

"Seven will be fine," she said. "I guess I should take you to the gift shop for a new T-shirt, then get back to work."

He nodded. "I've monopolized your time enough already. I don't want to get you in trouble. I could always go there by myself."

"It's okay. I don't think they'll look too kindly on you going inside without a shirt on, anyway. Plus, it's part of my job to help the visitors at the zoo."

Kye shoved his dirty one into the diaper bag, then picked it up and grabbed the baby sling. He followed her out of the office. Once they arrived at the gift shop, he gave her some money for a new shirt and waited outside with the baby while she bought it. After she returned, she held Nevaeh only long enough for Kye to put on the black T-shirt stenciled with the name of the zoo in large gold lettering.

"I should get back to work," Michaela said. "I'll see you tonight."

He looked as if he wanted to kiss her again, but she took a step back before she became too tempted to let him. Outside where anybody could see them wasn't exactly the place to let herself get carried away. Being caught kissing one of the visitors to the zoo was more than likely a surefire way to lose her job or, at the very least, to get reprimanded. She liked doing what she did. Even though some people wouldn't think cleaning cages and looking after animals would be a dream job, it was hers. And as she'd told Kye, she loved working with the big cats.

Kye nodded. "And I should finish looking at some of the exhibits, then get Nevaeh home. Though I think I'll be returning to the zoo very soon, since I've now found something here I like." He gave her a heated look, which set her heart pounding once more. "I'll be at your place at seven sharp."

Kye walk away. He now had the baby safely tucked into the sling across his chest. There was something about a man that large carrying such a small infant she found even more attractive. With a sigh, she turned and headed to her next task. She just hoped the hours wouldn't drag before she was able to see Kye again.

* * * *

Kye spent another half hour looking at the animals. Nevaeh, now fed and changed, peacefully slept in the carrier. As he wandered, his thoughts kept going back to Michaela. He'd found his mate. And to think she worked at a zoo. The fact she was an animal keeper gave him high hopes she'd have an easier time accepting him as a werewolf. She was used to being around wild animals, and had even said she loved the big cats. Well, his wolf wasn't nearly as large as those beasts and nowhere near as unpredictable, since he retained human thought in that form.

He took a deep breath and was still able to smell Michaela's scent on his skin. The mating urge continued to ride him hard and would do so until he finally claimed her as his. Fully making love to her would cause their souls to join, cementing the mating bond between them. After that happened, they wouldn't be able to stand being apart. One hour away would feel like a month, and their minds would play tricks on them, making them think something bad had happened to the other. And once they came together again, depending on how long the separation had been, it usually ended with explosive sex, the best way to reaffirm the bond. Having never been mated before, Kye had no such experience with any of it, but having watched his brothers-in-arms as well as his sister-in-arms go through their matings, he knew what to expect.

Before he left the zoo, Kye debated on whether or not to see if he could find Michaela one last time. In the end, he decided not to torture himself. And it wasn't as if he wouldn't be seeing her later. When he did, he could indulge in his need to touch and taste her. He might not be able to make love to her fully, but that didn't mean he wouldn't strip her naked and make her come. Oral sex would more than likely ramp up his mating urge. Still, it was a price he was more than willing to pay.

After getting Nevaeh strapped into her car seat, Kye drove to Roxie and Beowulf's place. The baby just started to fuss as he parked in front of the garage. He quickly got out and then pushed his seat forward to gain access to the back. As he took Nevaeh out, he made a mental note to sell his two-door car and buy a four-door once he had a baby of his own. That thought sort of brought him up short. The idea of him having kids had really never come up before that moment. Now that he'd met his mate, the chances were good they'd be an eventuality.

Kye headed toward the house with Nevaeh. He shook his head. He was getting a little ahead of himself. Having Michaela accept him as her mate wasn't exactly a foregone conclusion. She was the one meant for him—his mating urge wouldn't have kicked in otherwise—but she didn't know he was hers. And with her being a mortal, he'd have to tread carefully to win her over.

Once inside, Kye found Dirk in the kitchen with his head stuck in the fridge. That was one thing Kye loved about Roxie—she kept a well-stocked refrigerator and allowed them to eat whatever they wanted.

"Hey, Dirk," he said as he put Nevaeh, still inside her car seat, onto the kitchen table. "Is Roxie upstairs?" The baby fussed, slowly working herself into a cry. Kye unstrapped her and then picked her up. She settled and stared at him with her big blue eyes.

Dirk closed the fridge before he turned toward him. "Yeah, but Beowulf is with her, if you know what I mean."

Kye rolled his eyes. "Have they been going at it the entire time I was gone?"

"No," Dirk said with a laugh. "For a while, Roxie slept and Beowulf and I hung out. It wasn't until he decided to see if she was awake. When he didn't come back downstairs, I figured they were making good use of their time alone together."

That was the thing about mated couples. Most of the time they could be found all over each other. It'd never really bothered Kye in the past, but now that he'd met Michaela, it just made him long for her more. He wanted to be the one locked inside his bedroom, making love to his mate.

"I guess this is what Roxie meant about getting 'a break,'" he said a bit grumpily.

Dirk seemed to be giving him a closer look. "You appear a little strained. Didn't the trip to the zoo with Nevaeh go well? I have to say, you seem more comfortable holding the baby."

Kye looked at Nevaeh and stuck out his index finger for her to clutch. She smiled, and he felt her burrow a little deeper inside his heart. He kept his gaze on her and answered Dirk. "It was great."

"Great? Really? I figured you'd be bored as hell."

He looked at his brother-in-arms and grinned. "It would seem I should have made this trip to the zoo a long time ago. I found something there that'll have me going back more than likely every day."

Dirk shook his head and chuckled. "Crap, you found your mate."

"Yes." Kye patted the baby's diapered behind. "And I have Nevaeh to thank for that. If she hadn't fussed and cried, my soon-to-be mate wouldn't have taken pity on me and come to help get Nevaeh settled."

"Maybe I should take her out for a walk sometime and see if I stumble across mine as well," said Dirk. He went to reach for the baby, but Kye jerked out of reach.

"Keep your paws to yourself, Dirk. Nevaeh is my little good luck charm. Go get your own."

"Look, Beowulf," Roxie said as she and her mate walked into the room. "Our daughter already has men fighting over her. I told you she'd be a heartbreaker."

Beowulf shook his head. "Not if I have anything to do with it."

"I thought you two were otherwise occupied," Kye said.

"We were." Roxie gave Beowulf a smile before she turned back to Kye. "I heard you down here, and I wanted to get Nevaeh. So, what's this about my daughter being your good luck charm?"

Kye cringed inwardly. Once he told Roxie about finding his mate, he knew what would come next. She had "rules" that she wanted each of them to follow while they tried to win over their mortal mates. So far, all his brothers-in-arms, except Dirk, had broken what she considered the "biggest one"—telling a mate what they were before claiming her as his own.

"Well," he said slowly, "I guess I got something out of the zoo, after all."

"Like what? You learned you need to be locked away with the

rest of the wild animals?" Roxie asked.

Kye scowled. "Do you know you drive me up the fucking wall sometimes?"

Roxie took Nevaeh out of his arms. "Watch your language. Baby ears in the room. Gee, Kye, can't you take a joke?"

"I'm not exactly in the mood to be ridiculed. I have other things on my mind." He paused for a second. "Like getting myself mated."

Roxie let out a little shriek, threw her free arm around his neck and hugged him. Nevaeh whimpered at being wedged between them. "Oh, Kye, that is fantastic news."

Beowulf stepped to them and took the baby from his mate's arms. "I'll hold her until you've settled down a bit, Rox. And since she feels and smells as if she's wet, I'll go upstairs and change her."

Roxie waved Beowulf off before she linked an arm through Kye's and led him out of the room. "Let's sit in the living room for our little chat."

He rolled his eyes. "Roxie, I already know about your stupid rules. You don't need to tell me."

Inside the room, she pushed him onto the couch before she settled next to him. "Too bad for you. You're still going to hear them. Rule number one, don't take mate claiming advice from Beowulf."

"I never said I would, did I?"

"Still, don't bother. His ideas contradict my rules."

"Whatever," Kye said with an exasperated sigh.

"Rule number two, and the final one, you won't claim your mate until you've told her what you are and what being mated to a werewolf entails. So far, no one has taken this one to heart. Here's your chance to come out better than the rest of your brothers-in-arms."

"I don't think any of us can forget that one, Rox. And I'll do my best to not break it."

She shook her head. "Not good enough. You'll do better than try. Do you understand me? You just have to have better control over yourself and the mating urge."

Kye gave her a dubious look. Ever since meeting Michaela, he'd walked around with a hard-on, or at least been semihard.

Desire and need for her were like living, breathing things deep inside him. The instinct to claim his mate demanded he act on it, but he had it under control for now. That wouldn't remain the case, though. As each day went by and he didn't make Michaela his, the mating urge would only get worse, making it harder and harder on him.

"Rox, you have no idea what it's like to be ridden by a mating urge. This isn't just something I can tell myself to ignore. And I'm sure it'll only get worse after I go out with Michaela tonight."

She sighed. "Just do your best, okay? So your mate's name is Michaela. Does she work at the zoo or was she just visiting like you?"

Kye was relieved Roxie had let the subject of her rules drop. "She works there. She's an animal keeper." Rox appeared to try to hold back a laugh, but she ended up failing. "What's so damn funny about what Michaela does?"

It took a few seconds for Roxie to get herself quieted. "I just figure, given her line of work, she'll be able to manage you in your wolf form quite well. It shouldn't be a problem for her to chain your ass up in the backyard if you piss her off."

He scowled, something he tended to do a lot around Roxie. "I doubt she'll be doing any such thing. As far as I know, chaining up werewolves in their wolf form in a backyard as if they were dogs as punishment is something only you do."

"And I must say it's quite effective."

"As long as I'm not on the receiving end of it, I'm not going to say too much about it one way or the other. Now that you've given me your rules, I'm going back to the kitchen and grab something to eat. To give you the heads-up, I have to pick Michaela up at seven, so I'll be leaving shortly after Nevaeh goes to bed."

"That won't be a problem. I don't expect you to stay here overnight. Beowulf and I are quite capable of watching over her then."

"Good. Now I'll go satisfy the one hunger I can."

Kye stood and headed for the kitchen. He could put an end to the hankering he had for food, but the one he had for Michaela wouldn't be remedied quite so easily.

CHAPTER THREE

She was nervous. Michaela looked at the clock for the hundredth time, at least. It still didn't show it any closer to seven than when she'd looked at it five seconds before. According to it, Kye would arrive in the next ten minutes.

Michaela had spent the rest of her day at the zoo reminiscing about her time with Kye, especially about the kiss they'd shared. It caused her to have more than one daydream about what it would be like to sleep with him. If he made love half as well as he kissed, she'd be one happy and satisfied woman. She hadn't made up her mind about how far she wanted things to go tonight, but she was willing to go along with all the options.

Now, with only five minutes left, Michaela gave her living room one final inspection. After coming home from work, she'd done a quick cleaning job of dusting and vacuuming before taking a shower. It still looked respectable. Her apartment wasn't large, by any means, but she didn't want anything bigger. She thought it was just the right size for her.

With a deep breath, she sat on the couch. She had some beers cooling in the fridge, and if Kye wanted anything to snack on, there were some frozen finger-type foods in the freezer she could throw into the oven. As for entertainment, there were a few good movies on The Movie Channel she hadn't seen yet.

At two minutes to seven, her telephone rang. Since she could use it to buzz people into the building, there were butterflies in her stomach as she answered it. "Hello?"

"Hi, Michaela. It's Kye. I'm here."

"I'll let you in. I'm on the sixth floor in apartment six ten." She punched in the code to let Kye through, then hung up.

A few minutes later, a knock sounded on her door. Michaela wiped her sweaty palms down her jean-clad thighs before crossing to it. It was stupid to be so nervous, but it mostly stemmed from her not wanting to blow it with Kye. She'd never had a chance to date a man as good-looking as him, and doubted she'd ever get to again if things didn't work out between them.

She smiled and pulled open the door. Kye just about took her breath away as her gaze landed on him. He was still dressed in the same clothes he'd worn the last time she'd seen him, right down to the T-shirt she'd bought for him in the zoo's gift shop. Staring him in the face, he was even better looking than she'd remembered. How the hell she'd ended up attracting a man like him, she had no idea. She just thanked her lucky stars she had.

Michaela took a step back, and said, "Hi, Kye. Come on in."

"Thanks for inviting me over," he replied as he stepped inside.

She closed the door and locked it behind him. "I'm glad you could come. How did the rest of your visit to the zoo with Nevaeh go?"

He smiled. "Pretty good, considering she slept through it."

She motioned him to follow her as she led him into the living room, then took a seat on the couch. Once he lowered himself next to her, she asked, "Do you look after Nevaeh often?"

"I haven't in the past, but it looks as if I'll be doing a lot more of it from here on out."

"Won't it interfere with your work?" Realizing that had been a pretty forward question, considering she didn't know Kye all that well, Michaela felt her cheeks heat in a blush. "Sorry, I should have held that back."

Kye chuckled. "No need to apologize. I didn't mind. Actually, it won't, since it really *is* my job."

"You mean babysitting is what you do for a living?"

"No," he said with a laugh. "I'm in the protection business. I guess you would call me a bodyguard. Roxie, Nevaeh's mom, is sort of a client as well as a good friend. Today, she decided I'm to be her daughter's personal protector."

"Ah, I get it. So that means you got a crash course in looking after a baby."

He nodded. "And as you saw, I still need some work in that department."

"You didn't do all that bad for your first time."

"What about you?" he asked. "Have you worked at the zoo long?"

"A couple of years now. I love it. Being an animal keeper is something I've always wanted to do. When the opening came up, I jumped on it."

"So you're good with animals then?"

"Yeah. I used to drive my mom nuts when I was younger. I'd bring home all the strays I'd find. And sometimes, they weren't really strays but the neighbors' pets."

"And I figure they knew which house to go to if their dogs and cats came up missing," Kye said with a smile.

Michaela nodded. "At least they never got upset with me."

"If you were anything like you are now as a kid, I can't see anyone getting upset with you."

She felt herself blush again at what Kye had said, but especially from the way he stared into her eyes. He looked at her as if she were something special. "Thanks. Ah, would you like something to drink? I have some beers in the fridge. I can even whip up some snack food if you're hungry."

"The drink would be great. Don't worry about the food unless you want something."

With a nod, Michaela got up and went to the kitchen. She took two beers out of the fridge and then twisted off the caps. Not bothering with glasses, she returned to the living room and handed one to Kye before sitting beside him once more.

After taking a couple sips, Michaela picked up the TV remote. "I figured we could watch a movie on The Movie Channel, if you're interested."

Kye shifted a little closer, and said, "Sure. Whatever you want to see is fine with me."

She turned on the television and switched it to the right channel. Figuring Kye would be more into an action flick than a romantic drama, she selected that and settled against the couch.

He'd put his arm along the back so his fingers brushed her shoulder. A small thrill shot through her at so simple a touch. As the movie started, she found she had a hard time concentrating on it, all too aware of the man sitting close to her.

Michaela drank her beer and watched what was on the TV at the same time. The scent of Kye's aftershave filled her head, making her want to turn toward him, press her nose to the hollow of his throat and breathe deep. She didn't, not wanting to be the one to make the first move.

Once she was close to finishing her drink, she turned her head to ask Kye if he wanted another. The words died on her tongue when she saw he wasn't watching the movie, but had his gaze totally focused on her. There was an intensity in his eyes that had her pussy clenching. She felt herself falling into them, unable to look away.

Michaela swallowed and licked her suddenly dry lips as Kye reached over and took her beer from her. He set both bottles on the end table next to his side of the couch. He turned back and leaned in toward her. As his lips descended to meet hers, she met him halfway.

She shifted on the couch so she was in his direction, her hands sinking into his longish hair to pull him closer. Her taut nipples brushed against his hard chest, causing them to tighten even more. Michaela opened her mouth for his tongue, sucking on it before stroking it with hers. Arousal pulsed through her body, an ache building deep inside her pussy.

In a quick move, Kye wrapped his arms around her and pulled her onto his lap to straddle him as he shifted to sit with his back against the couch. She moaned at the feel of the hard length of his cock pressed against the spot where she wanted to be filled. He deepened their kiss, put his hands on her hips and ground against her pussy. Michaela couldn't hold back the moan that pushed out of her. Wetness leaked into her panties.

All awkwardness disappeared as she rubbed herself against the large bulge in Kye's jeans. He made a sound, a cross between an animal-like growl and a groan.

Completely turned-on, she broke their kiss and straightened. She kept her gaze locked on his eyes, which were open to mere slits, and reached for the bottom of her T-shirt.

She pulled it up and off over her head. "More, Kye. Touch me."

"I intend to do a lot of touching, baby," he said in a deep, husky voice.

He reached around her back and undid the hooks to her bra. His large hands skimmed from her shoulders and down her arms, taking the straps with him. Michaela tossed the garment to the floor.

Kye cupped her head and brought her mouth down to his. He thoroughly kissed her until her breath came in short pants. He dragged his lips along her jaw and down the column of her neck, making a trail to the top of her chest. He licked his way to one of her nipples. He flicked it with the tip of his tongue before circling the whole thing. His breath blew against it, then he sucked it inside his mouth.

Michaela threaded her fingers through his hair and held him to her. The sensation of him sucking her nipple caused a corresponding pull deep inside her pussy. She ached to have him take her with his cock.

He switched to her other one and gave it the same attention. She rocked against him, making her even wetter. As Kye pulled away, Michaela fisted the front of his shirt and lifted it. She needed to feel his skin next to hers.

He yanked it over his head and tossed it to the floor before he leaned back against the couch and spread his muscular arms along the top of it. "How about you do a little touching of your own?"

She didn't hesitate. All that bared male flesh was too much of a temptation to resist. She traced his well-defined pecs with her fingers as she leaned in and nibbled on his chin. She took the same exploratory path Kye had on her and trailed her lips along his square jaw and down. She sucked and licked his skin until she reached where his neck and shoulder met. A large hand sank into her hair at the back of her head and held her there as he loudly panted. She bit him gently and dragged her tongue over the same spot.

Kye bucked his hips as he ground his erection against her. "God, Michaela. I love the feel of your mouth on me."

And she liked it there as well. Growing bolder at his words, she continued downward. His wide, hairless chest was a whole new terrain for her to explore. She made sure not to leave his flat nipples out, laving them with her tongue as she slowly worked her way farther down his body.

Michaela slid off his lap to kneel between his legs. She learned the ridges of his abs with her mouth while she busily undid his jeans. Once she had the zipper down, she reached inside the parted material. A smile spread across her lips when she found Kye had gone commando.

With nothing else to get in the way, she wrapped her fingers around the hot, hard length of his cock and stroked up and down. Kye groaned. Michaela looked up and found he had his eyes closed and his head leaning back against the couch. His features were tight with what she assumed had to be arousal. It gave her a sense of power to know that she was capable of bringing a man as large as he to this state.

She turned her attention back to what she held and released his cock only long enough to pull his jeans down past his hips. Satisfied that she now had better access to him, she gripped him at the base of his shaft and dragged her tongue up his full length. Another animalistic growl filled the air as Michaela circled the broad head before taking him inside her mouth.

She sucked him in and out, stroking what she couldn't take with her hand. The taste of pre-cum hit her tongue as Kye groaned, rocking his hips to match the pace she'd set.

He buried his hand in her hair to hold her to him as he fucked her mouth. "Just like that… Christ, I'm going to come soon. Don't stop," he said thickly.

She increased the suction, almost taking him to the back of her throat. His cock grew harder, each breath he took harsher than the last. He moaned, his fingers tightening in her hair as he stiffened and came. Michaela took everything he had to give. Her arousal increased, and her pussy throbbed in time with her rapidly beating heart.

She released his cock and looked down to find it still hard, even though he'd climaxed. She'd never known a guy who could do that. With no recovery time needed, it meant she didn't have to wait to have Kye. Michaela rose to her feet and undid her jeans, then shimmied out of them until she kicked them away. Her panties quickly followed.

Aching with need, Michaela moved to climb up to straddle Kye's hips. His erect cock stuck out straight from his body, and she intended to ride him until they reached orgasm. She had one knee on the couch beside his thigh when he caught her around the waist and took her to her back, onto the carpeted floor.

He kissed her, using his teeth and tongue until she clutched his shoulders. As he shifted down her body, she panted, "Please, Kye. I need..." She gasped when Kye sucked a nipple into his mouth.

After he released the taut peak, he said, "I know, babe. I'm going to give you what you want. I have to taste you. If I don't, I think I'll go crazy."

Michaela shifted restlessly under Kye as he drove *her* insane with his lips and tongue. She whimpered as he nibbled her hipbone before inching down to the top of her thigh. As he settled between her legs, his broad shoulders forcing her to open wider, she raised her hips in offering.

With a low growl, Kye dipped his head and dragged his tongue along her pussy. Michaela's eyes just about rolled back into her head as he circled her clit with the tip of his tongue before sucking on it. He licked and sucked, then slipped a finger inside her slick opening. She moaned, riding it as he moved it in and out. Once a second joined the first, and Kye laved her clit at the same time, it was all she needed to fall over the edge into climax. Accompanied by a loud, keening moan, she shattered, her pussy clutching the fingers that still worked her.

After the last spasm subsided, Michaela went limp. She had to give Kye credit. He sure as hell knew how to give a woman an orgasm with just his mouth. She'd never come this hard during oral sex before.

Kye rose between her legs and rolled them until she lay sprawled, completely boneless, along his chest. His erection pressed between them against her stomach. Michaela lifted her head to look at him. He had his eyes closed and he breathed hard. He didn't look like a man who was sated. More than willing to take what they started further, she brushed a hand down his side and over his hip until she reached the top of his jeans. Clutching it, she pushed down, but Kye stopped her before she got too far.

"No, Michaela."

At the sound of the strain in his voice, she asked, "Why? You're still hard. Obviously, you're still worked up. I know I want all of you."

He opened his eyes and met her gaze. "I want nothing more than to sink my cock into your pussy and ride you until you scream my name, but I think we should wait."

"Why?"

"Because it'll be better that way."

The arousal that had rebuilt inside her slowly died. What man would refuse sex? Especially one who not only was extremely turned-on—given the hardness of his erection—but had a naked and willing woman on top of him? Maybe one who found himself with said naked woman and had second thoughts about sleeping with her. At least that was what shot through Michaela's mind.

She pushed off Kye and stood. "Okay. I see. Look, you don't have to feel obligated to stay. We don't have to make this an uncomfortable situation, any more than it is already. If you don't want to sleep with me, you just have to say so. You don't have to make up some silly excuse about it being better if we waited."

Michaela felt like a fool. It'd been too good to be true to have a guy who looked like Kye want to be with her. She didn't think she was bad in the looks department, but she in no way compared to him. Hell, he could leave her apartment right now and get a woman to finish him off in a blink of an eye.

She avoided looking at him and collected her clothes off the floor. Kye's continued silence gave her the impression her words had rung true. The excitement of what they'd just done disappeared, making her feel hollow inside. She was about to head to the bathroom to change when a large hand wrapped around her ankle and stopped her before she could take more than a couple steps. She looked down to see he was still on the floor and twisted in her direction.

"Where are you going?" he asked.

"To the bathroom to get dressed."

"Shit, I've upset you."

Michaela held her clothes in front of her like a shield. She gave her foot a kick, but Kye didn't release her. "You think?" she asked sarcastically.

His hand slipped off her ankle, and he jumped to his feet so fast she hardly saw him move. Kye cupped her face and forced her to meet his gaze. "My hesitance right now isn't some lame excuse because I'm changing my mind about how I feel. The problem is I want you too much. I'm not going to rush things because I want more than a night of sex. Do you understand?"

She stared into his brown eyes and saw longing in their depths. That and something else. Not just hunger, though that was there as well, but something that made her want to believe what he said.

Michaela swallowed. "What do you mean by more?" she asked in a small voice.

"I mean you're the woman I've waited for all of my life, and I don't think I can ever let you go."

She pushed Kye's hands off her face and took a step back. "Now I know you're just shooting me a line of crap. We hardly know each other. You can't possibly think I mean that much to you in such a short amount of time. We just met today."

Kye ran a hand over his face, his frustration easy to read in the stiff way he held himself. "This isn't supposed to be happening like this. Damn it."

"What isn't? You're not getting your jollies from leading me on?"

Michaela found herself trapped against Kye's hard body, one of his arms wrapped around her waist like a steel band. A large hand sank into her hair, holding her prisoner as he plundered her mouth with his. This kiss wasn't anything like the others they'd shared. It was more carnal and demanding, his desperation evident in every stroke of his tongue against hers. If he hadn't held her up, she would have dropped to the floor at his feet, her legs no longer able to hold her upright. He didn't allow her a breath of air until he had her moaning with need once more and pressing as close to him as she could get.

They were both breathing heavy. Michaela thought she saw that strange glow in Kye's eyes again, but it disappeared before it could fully register.

"Now," he said huskily, "did that feel like a kiss a man would give you if he only wanted to lead you on?"

"N-No," she croaked.

"Because it wasn't. I'm going to do this right, which means we'll wait until we know each other better. You have no idea how hard this is going to be for me. I've never wanted another woman as I want you, Michaela. Your looks, gorgeous body and scent just make me want you more." He took a deep breath. "Get dressed, then we'll watch the rest of the movie. Once it's over, I'll leave. I don't want to. I'd rather stay the night just to have you sleep in my arms, but I can't trust myself not to do more than that."

Feeling as if she'd just been swept off her feet, Michaela could only nod. Once Kye let her go, she stumbled to the bathroom and then shut the door behind her. She held out her hand and found it shaking, not from fear, but from the strong emotions that surged through her. If she hadn't hoped for this date to be more than one night with him before, she sure as hell did now. The man made her feel wanted, needed and protected all in one. None of the other guys she'd dated had managed that feat. In this day and age, some women wouldn't be thrilled with his alpha-male tactics, but she found them downright sexy. She hadn't felt as feminine as she did right now.

Michaela used the toilet, splashed some cool water on her heated cheeks and dressed. Kye had better have told her the truth about everything he'd said, because she wasn't going to let him just walk out of her life without a fight.

CHAPTER FOUR

K ye sat on the couch next to Michaela, trying to appear as if nothing was wrong, but inside he fought to keep a tight rein over his mating urge. As he'd predicted, letting her give him a blowjob had made it worse rather than giving him a bit of respite.

He focused his gaze on the TV. It wasn't doing much to distract him. Michaela's scent filled his nose with each breath he took, and with her sitting beside him, her back resting against his chest while he had his arm around her, the feel of her body kept his cock hard and aching. He didn't think the damn thing would ever go down. The taste of her was still in his mouth.

Making her come, the sound of her pleasured cries echoing in his ears, had had both him and his wolf wanting to pounce and claim her as theirs. It'd been the hardest thing he'd ever done to stop Michaela when she'd tried to tug his jeans the rest of the way off so they could finish what they'd started. What he found in his would-be mate's arms was beyond better than any other sexual encounter he'd had.

Then he'd gone and almost messed up everything with his comment about her being the only one for him. Of course she'd at first thought he'd fed her a line of bullshit. Not being a werewolf, she hadn't a clue his mating urge wouldn't have kicked in if she hadn't been the right woman for him. From his perspective, there was no question about it—she was his. And there was no question he'd soon fall head over heels for her, and that no other would ever take her place in his heart. Once again, if there were no chance of that, the mating urge would have stayed dormant.

At least he'd been able to convince Michaela he'd been dead serious. He'd poured all of the pounding need that rode him into the kiss, not holding anything back. Kye had risked the control over himself, but it'd worked in the end. Now he had the job of getting her more comfortable with him before he revealed what he truly was. And since time would be ticking down to the point where he would no longer be able to keep from claiming her, he had to work quickly. The longer he ignored the mating urge the worse it would ride his ass until he'd act on blind instinct alone. She snuggled closer, and he bit back a groan. The next few days weren't going to be a cakewalk.

She turned her head and looked at him. "Are you comfortable with me sitting like this?"

"Of course. Why would you think I wasn't?"

Michaela looked pointedly at his crotch where there was no mistaking the large bulge there. "Well, for one thing, that hasn't settled down the whole time we've sat here. I know you want to wait, but I don't want you to feel tortured with me so close to you."

"Ignore it. I'll be fine." Even if he hadn't had the mating urge riding his ass, his cock would have remained hard after their bout of heavy petting and oral sex. Being a male werewolf had its perks, one being the ability to keep an erection for hours at a time, even after coming more than once.

"Really? Because that looks as if it could be painful after a while. Maybe I could help you with it the same way I did before."

He groaned loudly. "Believe me that would just make it worse. And with you offering, it isn't exactly making this any easier."

"Well, it remains open."

"Sure, torture me some more, why don't you," he said with a chuckle.

"So when will I see you again?"

"Will tomorrow be good?"

"I have to work, but after that I'm free."

"How about Nevaeh and I visit you there during the day, then

I'll take you out to eat around seven."

Michaela smiled. "Sure. Does this mean you're going to bring the baby to the zoo every day I'm working?"

"Why not? It's a public place. Besides, I didn't get to see all the animals yet." Kye kissed her forehead and decided to test the waters a bit. "Too bad the zoo doesn't have any wolves. I have an affinity for them."

"I know what you mean. I wish they had some as well. Out of all my favorite species, wolves come in at a close second to big cats."

Kye marked that as an invisible point for him. If Michaela already liked wolves, she should really like him in his wolf form. He was slightly bigger than his wild cousins, but other than that, he was basically the same. He figured the greatest hurdle he'd have to get over would be getting her to accept the fact he could shapeshift into one.

He glanced at the TV. The end credits of the movie scrolled on the screen. A quick look showed it was only ten o'clock. It was still on the early side, but if Michaela had to work in the morning, it would be better if he left to let her get some sleep. At least one of them should. He'd be lucky to get a few hours of solid shuteye. Until he claimed her, every time he slept, he'd have erotic dreams about her, ones that would leave him aching even more.

He brushed his lips across hers. "I should go. You have work in the morning, and I have to be at Roxie's around ten."

"Well, if you insist." Michaela stood when he did. "I'll keep my eye out for you and Nevaeh tomorrow."

She walked him to the apartment entrance. Kye really didn't want to leave, but it was for the best. He'd already pushed his luck enough for one night. He pulled Michaela into his arms and kissed her, reveling in the feel of her against him. Once their embrace verged on the edge of blazing out of control, he released her and then opened the door.

"See you tomorrow, Michaela."

Without looking back, Kye walked out before he shut the door between him and the woman who would soon become his heart.

* * * *

Kye arrived at the mansion in Marin County where he and his fellow Protectors and their mates lived and parked his car in the large detached garage for the night. Much to his surprise, it looked as if the rest of his "family" were at home already, which wasn't typical. It was too early for Roxie to be unguarded. Beowulf, who owned a nightclub called Wulf's Den, wouldn't be home yet. He usually stayed a couple hours at the club, but returned to his house before he and Roxie felt the separation anxiety.

Kye walked into the large foyer, closed the door behind him and headed to the living room where he heard voices. He stepped inside and saw Saskia and her mate, Eli, talking with Leif and his mate, Jaden. They fell silent when they saw him.

"Hey, what's up?" he asked. "I couldn't help noticing everyone is home. Shouldn't someone be with Roxie?"

Saskia shook her head. "Beowulf didn't go to the club tonight, so Roxie sent Roan, Ansley, Jager and Daylen home a couple hours ago."

"Oh. Is anything else happening? All of you looked pretty serious about something when I came in."

Leif was the one who answered. "We're discussing Miles."

"Has he found out something he shouldn't?"

"No, nothing like that." Leif looked at Jaden before he turned back to Kye, and said, "He, ah, wants to share some of the duties of guarding the foretold one, since Jaden is his daughter."

"Shit," Kye said. "After all he's done in the past, and the not-so-distant one at that, Miles can't expect us to just accept him back with open arms. He walked away from being a Protector." Even though he balked at the idea, his sister-in-arms had the ultimate say on the matter since she was the leader of the Protectors.

Saskia sighed. "Leif and the others feel the same way you do, but Jaden and I are leaning toward allowing him to take on some of it in a small capacity. If we don't, it could backfire on us. All we need is for him to become suspicious, and he might do some digging where we don't want him to."

"Okay, say you let Miles watch over Jaden, where exactly would he be doing it? So far, she's only been with him in public places. Are you going to want him here in the mansion?"

"Since Jaden has come into his life, Miles hasn't done anything to harm her," Saskia said. "It's been months. I know you don't want to hear it, but I think knowing he has a daughter has changed him."

Leif snorted loudly. "You know how I feel about that bullshit. Once an asshole, always an asshole." He grunted as his mate dug her elbow into his stomach.

"That asshole also happens to be my father. Your father-in-law. I don't see him as the evil lone wolf you do."

"Of course you don't. You only want to see the good in him because of what he is to you."

The way Jaden scowled at Leif, it didn't take much deducing to figure out Leif had just waved a red flag in front of his mate's face.

"Oh, you've done it now, Leif," Eli said with a laugh. "You'd better do some ass kissing right quick."

As if he'd just noticed the furious look on Jaden's face, Leif gave her a sheepish smile. "Now, babe, you know I really didn't mean anything by that. It's just it'll be kind of hard for you to be unbiased when it comes to your father."

Jaden's eyes seemed to shoot daggers at Leif. "What do you want me to do? Change the blood that runs in my veins? Well, I can't, any more than you can. And I'm sorry for wanting to see the good in my dad, a man who wasn't part of my life when I was growing up. I know perfectly well what he's done, and what he did to you, but I still love him. I just hope your *biased* opinions don't make you think any less of our baby."

"Baby?" Leif echoed, looking for all the world as if his brain had suddenly stopped functioning.

Jaden pushed off the couch to stand and glared at her mate. "Yes, Leif, a baby. I'd thought to tell you later when we were alone, but... Surprise, you're going to be a father."

With that said, she turned and stomped out of the room. Leif still looked completely stunned before he shot to his feet and went after Jaden. Saskia, Eli and Kye stared at each other. Kye had a feeling he wore the same surprised expression the other two did.

"Did Jaden just say she was pregnant?" Eli asked.

"Yes," Saskia said. A large smile spread across her face. "I'm going to be a great-aunt."

"Ah hell. That means I'll be a great-uncle," her mate said. "I'm still having a hard time getting my head around the fact I have a niece who's only six years younger than I am."

Saskia leaned in and gave Eli a quick kiss on the lips. "Hon, in another few hundred years, that won't mean anything. Believe me." She laughed. "Being pregnant would also explain why Jaden was so quick to fly off the handle. Hormones can be a bitch. And I just love the fact Leif has gone from chasing anything in a skirt to finding his mate, and now he's a soon-to-be father."

Kye thought over what his sister-in-arms had said and couldn't hold back his laughter as well. Eli soon joined in. It looked as if fate was getting back at Leif for fighting the mating urge tooth and nail after he'd first met Jaden. The poor bugger was still adjusting to being a claimed male.

Once his laughter died, Kye said, "I guess I'm going to call it a night. I'll be up in my room, watching TV if you need me."

"Not so fast," Saskia said.

Kye had turned to leave, but changed direction at his sister-in-arms' words. He had a feeling he knew what she was going to say. "What?"

"Dirk and Roxie told all of us the good news about you finding your mate. How are you managing?"

"I have a grip on it. Are you thinking of pulling me off rotation?" The mating urge being such a distraction, Saskia had told the others to take some downtime, telling them they wouldn't be any use as Protectors until they'd claimed their mates.

"No, I'm not. It would be different if Roxie hadn't assigned you as Nevaeh's personal Protector, though. You might not be totally on your game, but changing diapers and doing bottle feedings shouldn't be too hard for you."

He snorted. "True. Actually, I really do have to thank you for putting me on babysitting duty. If Roxie hadn't had the silly idea of me taking Nevaeh to the zoo today, I never would have met Michaela."

"So I guess that means you're no longer pissed with me for agreeing with Roxie."

Kye chuckled. "No, I'm not." He backed away. "I'm going up to my room. I have another big day planned for tomorrow."

He spun on his heel and left Saskia and Eli alone. He shook his head as he thought about Jaden being pregnant. The dynamics of his "family" were going to change once again after the baby arrived.

CHAPTER FIVE

Michaela prepared buckets of fish for the penguins in a workroom near their exhibit. It was late morning, and she expected Kye would more than likely arrive soon. She couldn't wait to see him again.

Ever since he'd left her the night before, she'd done almost nothing but think about him. She couldn't seem to get him out of her head. And every time the remembrance of what it was like to be held in his arms, having him touch her in the most intimate of places, played in her mind, it made her body heat with desire. It also made her long to have more of Kye.

Michaela had done a lot of thinking about Kye's declaration of wanting a long and lasting relationship with her. She still found it hard to believe he could know his feelings were that solid for her after only a day. She had to admit, though, she had deeper feelings for him than she'd ever experienced with another man she'd just met.

Finished filling the buckets of fish, Michaela took them outside for another animal keeper to feed the penguins. She ducked back into the workroom and then washed her hands.

Outside again, she left the habitat and headed for her next job at the other end of the zoo. At this time of day, it wasn't too crowded, which made it easier for her to look at the faces of all the people who wandered nearby. So far, she hadn't found the one she wanted to see.

She arrived at the big cat exhibit and a wide smile spread across her face when she saw Kye standing a little away from the lions' habitat. She increased her stride until she stood directly behind him.

"So you did come," she said.

Kye turned to face her. He looked at her, heat seeming to flare in his eyes. "There you are. I wondered if I would have to search the entire zoo to find you. I took a lucky guess you'd be with the big cats."

"Actually, I just got here. I was at the penguin exhibit. I helped get their morning meal ready."

He sniffed the air. "That would explain the faint fish odor surrounding you."

Michaela lifted her hands to her face and breathed in, but only picked up on the scent of the soap she'd used. "Really? You can smell fish on me? I can't."

"It's not strong or anything. I just have a sensitive nose when it comes to things like that."

"Just as long as I don't reek."

Kye chuckled and stepped closer. Leaning in—leaving some space for Nevaeh, who he carried in her baby sling across his chest—he gave her a kiss that made her wish they were alone. "No, you definitely don't reek."

"Good." She took a quick look around to see if anyone watched them, and asked, "So, how is Nevaeh today? Is she more alert this morning?"

He looked down at the baby. "She's awake. And so far, she hasn't decided to make a mess in her drawers for me, thank god."

Michaela stroked a finger along Nevaeh's soft cheek. The baby smiled. "She does seem happy. I have to say she has gorgeous blue eyes. I think she's going to be a heartbreaker when she grows up."

Kye chuckled. "That's what her mother thinks. Her father hopes that won't happen. He's already not liking the idea of his daughter dating."

"I don't think any dad does," she said with a laugh. "I had to sneak out for dates when I was a teenager. If mine had his way, I still wouldn't be allowed to go out with a man."

"From my standpoint, I'm quite happy he doesn't."

Michaela chuckled. "Yes, I can see why you would." She stepped closer to the chain-link fence as one of the male lions came near it. "So, have you had a chance to look at the exhibit?"

Kye shook his head. "Not yet. I'd just arrived when you did."

"Well, take a look. Isn't he gorgeous?"

"He is a majestic-looking beast. I don't know if I like you calling another male gorgeous, though."

"Would you feel better if I said I'm more attracted to you than him?" she asked with a giggle.

Kye shifted closer until he stood at her side. "Most definitely."

The male lion opened his mouth, showing his sharp teeth, and in an aggressive manner, rushed at the fence directly in front of where Kye stood. His loud growl filled the air. Both jumped back, and Nevaeh whimpered. Kye took a few more steps away from the fence, and the lion seemed to settle right down.

"I wonder what got into him," she said. "Tunya usually doesn't act like that."

Kye shrugged. "Maybe he took an instant disliking to me. I think I'll give him some space and stay back here."

"Yeah, that might be a good idea. Do you want to see the tigers?"

"Actually, I think I'd prefer to skip the rest of the big cats today."

"All right. Sorry to say it, but I have some work to do here. If you're still going to be around in an hour, I'll be on my lunch break."

"I'll be around then. Should I meet you here?"

"I can join up with you at the café, if you want."

"Sure. I don't want my presence to piss off any more lions. One of them might try to escape just so he can take a chunk out of me."

Michaela grinned. "We can't have that happening. It wouldn't look very good for the zoo."

"I guess not. I'll let you get back to work. I think I'll show Nevaeh the penguins."

"I'll see you later then."

She lifted her face for the kiss Kye brushed across her lips just before he walked away. Michaela turned to look at Tunya. He'd moved off farther inside the enclosure. She still had no idea what had gotten into him, but whatever it was, it hadn't lasted very long.

* * * *

Kye resisted the urge to adjust himself inside his jeans. Christ, just being beside Michaela gave him a hard-on. And it hadn't helped any that, as predicted, he'd had one erotic dream after another of her during the night. He'd taken a cold shower this morning, hoping it'd cool his libido, but all it did was cause him to break out in goosebumps.

Being with Michaela again, all he'd wanted to do was pull her to him and kiss her until neither one of them remembered their name. Of course he couldn't, given the fact that, one, they were in a public place where she worked, and two, he had a baby strapped across his chest. He didn't think Roxie or Beowulf would appreciate Kye giving her a lesson in human sexuality, not that Nevaeh would care one way or the other. Nor would she even remember it.

He arrived at the penguin exhibit in time to see them being fed by another animal keeper. It was kind of cute the way the birds clumsily waddled around, but in the water, the clumsiness ended. They could swim, turning on a dime, not once colliding with the others around them.

Next, Kye went to see the kangaroos and koalas. His presence didn't seem to disturb them as it had the lion. He had a feeling the male had acted so aggressively because he'd smelled another predator. Kye would have been deemed as competition. It didn't matter that he was in his human form. He still carried a werewolf's scent.

The hour nearly up, Kye changed Nevaeh's diaper in the men's restroom. They had one of those baby-changing tables that folded up against the wall when not in use. And lucky for him, Nevaeh was only wet this time.

That chore done, he pulled his cell phone out of his front jeans pocket and saw he'd have just enough time to get to the café to meet Michaela. He put it away as he headed in the direction of the small restaurant.

He walked through the entrance, stopping just inside the door, and searched for Michaela. Spotting her, Kye headed to the table where she sat. Just before he reached her, a woman approached his mate.

"Michaela? Michaela Jones, is that you?" she asked rather loudly.

Kye came to a standstill. Michaela looked none too thrilled to see the other female. In fact, from the slight change in his mate's scent, she was a little leery of her, even though she smiled.

"Yes, I'm Michaela Jones."

"I thought it was you. It's been years since I've seen you. I think it was in high school. Do you remember me? I'm Katy Adams."

Michaela's smile shifted partway into a grimace. "Of course I remember you." Under her breath, she said sarcastically, "How could I not?" The other woman didn't seem to hear it.

Seeing the expression on his mate's face, and hearing her hushed words, it didn't take Kye long to figure out Michaela hadn't gotten along with this Katy during high school.

Deciding Michaela needed some rescuing, Kye crossed the rest of the distance to her table, and interrupting what Katy had been about to say, he kissed the top of his would-be mate's head. "Hi, honey. I brought someone who missed her mama." He took Nevaeh out of the baby sling and put her into Michaela's arms. He pulled out a chair next to hers, then placed his arm around her shoulders.

Katy's jaw dropped as she openly stared at him. "Ah, hi," she said.

"Hi," he replied. "I couldn't help overhearing you're one of the people my wife knew in high school."

"*You're* Michaela's husband?" From her tone, he got the impression Katy didn't think it was possible.

"Yes. My name is Kye. And this," he nodded toward the baby, "is our daughter, Nevaeh."

Katy's gaze went from him to Michaela and back again, as if she couldn't quite believe he'd be Michaela's husband. "Oh, ah, nice to meet you both." She focused on Michaela. "So, you work here at the zoo?"

Michaela nodded. "Yes. I'm an animal keeper. Last I heard you'd gone away to college."

"I see. And I did. I'm only back to visit my sister and her brats." Katy motioned to a table behind her that had a stressed-out looking woman, who shared a family resemblance, sitting with three young boys who argued noisily.

"Well, I shouldn't hold you up then," Michaela said. "I'm on my lunch break, and I'd like to spend some time with Kye and Nevaeh before it's over."

"Sure. Hey, I'm going to be here for a few days. How about the three of us go out for dinner tonight? We could catch up on old times, Michaela. That is, if you can get a sitter."

Thinking a dinner out with Katy would be the perfect time to knock her down a peg or two, before Michaela could answer, Kye quickly said, "We'd love to."

Michaela reached under the table and dug her nails into his thigh. He pried her hand off his leg and clasped it in his. She turned her head and gave him a stern look.

"Didn't we already have plans to go out to dinner? Just the two of us?" she asked.

"Then you do have a sitter already," Katy interjected. "That's perfect. I can just tag along. It'll be my treat, and I won't take no for an answer."

"See, hon?" Kye said. "Katy is willing to pay and everything. How can we refuse her generous offer?"

Katy's laugh sounded phony. "Then it's decided. How about we meet at The Cliff House restaurant? Say around seven thirty?"

"We'll be there," he answered.

"Great. See you then." Katy paused, then looked him up and down. "I'm looking forward to getting to know you, Kye."

With a smile, Katy turned and walked to the table where her sister sat. The entire group left the restaurant a few seconds later, the kids wailing and complaining as they went.

Once Katy and her crew were gone, Michaela slapped him on the chest. "What the hell was that?" she asked.

"What do you mean?" Kye removed his arm from around her shoulders and placed the diaper bag he carried on the table to take out a bottle of formula.

"You know exactly what I mean. Why would you accept Katy's offer to go out for dinner tonight? If you couldn't tell, I'm not comfortable being around her. She was the bane of my existence in high school. One year, I ended up with no friends because of her. She was a mean, spiteful bitch back then, and I doubt she's changed over the years. If anything, she could be worse. Plus, I saw the way she looked at you. That just pissed me off."

Kye gave Michaela a heated look. "So you don't like another woman checking me out?"

"Of course not," she said softly.

He gave her a hard, fast kiss, then took Nevaeh out of her arms. "Good, because you're the only woman I want groping me with her gaze." Kye waggled his eyebrows.

She shook her head and chuckled. "You're bad."

"And you like it." He took the bottle out of the portable warmer and then fed Nevaeh.

"True. Even though I don't like that we now have to go out with Katy, thanks for the other thing you did. Pretending to be my husband and saying Nevaeh is our daughter."

"Thanks aren't necessary. I couldn't help noticing you weren't thrilled to see her. I was able to put two and two together after I heard her say you went to high school together."

"Well, thanks, anyway."

Michaela leaned in and kissed him softly, lingering a little longer over him than a short peck would entail. It had Kye fighting his mating urge. God, did he want her. Now that he'd found her, he couldn't picture a future without her in his life. If only she weren't mortal, she'd be his already.

He cleared his throat, forcing the instinct to mate aside. "So, you really aren't angry about us seeing Katy later, are you? I have a reason that I accepted her offer, and it's not because she's going to pick up the bill. I figured at the restaurant I'd bring her down a peg or two."

"No, not really, but I'm not looking forward to dinner as much as I was when it would have been just the two of us. And what exactly do you have planned to accomplish that feat?"

Kye smiled. "Easy. I'm going to show her what a loving and doting husband I am to you while I look down my nose at her. If she thinks I'd give her a second look, she's mistaken. She comes across as having a big ego. My failure to fall for her charms should be a blow to it."

Michaela laughed. "Yeah, she does have one. Katy was on the

cheerleading squad and was prom queen. You could say her ego is huge. She'd find it inconceivable that a man like you would be more interested in me than her."

He pulled the nipple to the now empty bottle from between the baby's lips and then put her on his shoulder to burp. His gaze locked on Michaela's, and his voice dropped to a husky timbre with the desire he felt for her. "Remember, I already told you that you're the only woman for me. And I don't really care if she thinks I should be attracted to her. All that matters is that you know she can try her best to come between us, but it won't change how I feel about you."

Michaela audibly swallowed. Her eyelids seemed to grow heavy, and he once again smelled the delicate scent of her arousal in the air around them. His cock jerked, throbbing in time with his accelerated heart rate. The way things were going he'd end up with blue balls. It also pushed home the fact he'd have to screw up enough courage in the next day or so to tell her what he was. The mating urge tortured him too much as it was.

The spell that took hold of him, making everyone in the café but his would-be mate just disappear for him, broke when Nevaeh let out burp that would do a beer-guzzling truck driver proud. He and Michaela laughed.

"I don't think I've ever heard a baby burp that loud," Michaela said while chuckling.

"It was a whopper."

Kye spent the rest of Michaela's lunch hour with her. Once it was over and they'd left the café, he pulled her to a relatively quiet and out-of-the-way place. He hungrily took her lips. Reluctantly, he let her go, promising he'd pick her up at her apartment for dinner.

CHAPTER SIX

Twenty minutes before they were to meet Katy at the restaurant, Kye buzzed up to Michaela's apartment. After letting him know she'd meet him downstairs, she gave herself a quick check in the bathroom mirror. Even though he'd reassured her he wanted only her, she felt she still had to do a little something to keep herself in the running with Katy. Not one for wearing any makeup, Michaela had put some on just to accentuate her eyes and lips. She tugged at her blue short-sleeved silk blouse before running her hands down her black skinny jeans. On her feet, she wore black high-heeled sling backs. Heels were something else she rarely wore, but she had to admit they made her legs look longer. And the extra height wouldn't hurt, since he was so tall.

After picking up her purse on the way out, Michaela stepped into the hallway and then locked her apartment door behind her. A short elevator ride down, and she was in the lobby. Kye was in the vestibule, waiting.

Michaela pulled open the glass door and joined him. She kissed him and then stood back to get a good look at him. She ran her gaze over his dark gray button-down shirt and dark blue jeans. The material hugged his broad shoulders and wide chest to perfection, leaving no doubt about his muscular physique. The pants were tight-fitting and outlined him just right.

Kye held out his arms straight from his sides. "Do you want me to spin around so you can get the full picture?"

She shook her head. "No, I don't think that'll be necessary, though you do look very nice this evening."

He took his turn running his gaze over her. It was so intense it almost felt like a physical touch. "Not that there's anything wrong with how you normally dress, but I have to say you're looking particularly fetching."

She laughed. "Fetching? I don't think a man has ever used that term about me before. It sounds kind of old-fashioned."

Kye stepped closer until there was almost no space between them. "Maybe I'm just an old-fashioned man at heart." His gaze focused on her mouth. "We'll get this dinner over and done with, then we can come back here and I can get to the fun stuff. I'm going to enjoy stripping you out of those very tight jeans of yours."

Michaela's cheeks heated, not from embarrassment, but with the surge of arousal that had shot through her at Kye's words. "As long as I get to strip you out of yours too," she said huskily.

He grabbed her hand and pulled her to the outside door. "Time to leave before I do something stupid like take you right here and now against the wall. I'm sure that'd be enough to have one of your neighbors calling the cops."

She took a deep breath, trying to slow her rapid breathing, and allowed Kye to lead her to the visitors parking lot at the front of the building. Her steps slowed a bit when he took out his keys and then aimed the remote at a blue Jaguar. The two-door car looked new and expensive. All she could think was the protection business must pay well. Very well. On her salary from the zoo, she'd never make enough money to buy a car like that in a million years.

Kye let go of her hand and pulled open the passenger door, holding it for her. Michaela got in and snuggled into the leather seat. Once he closed her in, he came around the back and then climbed into the driver's side. After turning the key in the ignition, the vehicle came to life, sounding like the expensive sports car it was.

On the street, Kye drove in the direction of The Cliff House restaurant. Michaela still dreaded the thought of having to spend any time with Katy. At least she wasn't the skinny, ostracized teenager whom Katy had once taken great joy in bullying. And having Kye at her side helped. Michaela turned to look at him. It probably got the bitch's goat to see him with her. All she could say about that was *good*. Katy deserved it.

Kye parked in an empty space next to the restaurant and then turned off the car. Michaela got out and waited for him to join her before they headed inside. Katy was already there, waiting for them. Michaela silently groaned when her nemesis spotted them and animatedly waved them over.

"You made it," Katy said. "I called earlier and got a reservation."

"Great," Michaela said unenthusiastically. She looked the other woman over, noticing she wore something similar to what she'd chosen, only her blouse was much lower cut. And she had on more makeup.

Katy talked to the hostess, and soon after, they were led to their table. It was round with four chairs. They took their seats, but Kye jumped up when Katy made sure to sit next to him. He went and sat on Michaela's other side and shifted closer to her.

Michaela looked at Katy and had to bite the inside of her cheek to stop from laughing. Her nemesis' smile had slipped a little, and the look in her eyes said she wasn't too happy about Kye's change in seating.

A waitress came and took their drink orders before leaving them alone again. Michaela bent her head to the menu, trying to decide what she wanted to eat. Kye's shoulder brushed hers as he opened his to do the same. The waitress returned with their beverages, then left after taking their food orders. Soon after, Katy started what Michaela decided to call "putting her moves on Kye."

"So, Kye," Katy said, smiling while she leaned in closer to the table, giving a better view of her cleavage she had showing. "What do you do for a living?"

He placed his arm around Michaela's shoulders, stroking along the top of her arm. "I'm in the protection business."

"What kind? Like security systems and whatnot?"

"No. I'm more of what you'd call a personal bodyguard."

Katy blatantly ran her gaze over his chest and arms before she licked her lips and looked back at his face. "I see. I must say, you," she gave another pointed stare, "have the body for it. Have you been in the business long?"

"It seems like forever. Not that I don't like the job because I do."

"Where did you meet Michaela?" Katy took a sip of her white wine.

"At the zoo," Kye answered, turning his head to meet Michaela's gaze. "I saw her and instantly knew she was the woman I wanted to spend the rest of my life with. I fell head over heels at first glance. I'd waited a very long time to find her. She completes me."

Michaela felt as if she were falling into Kye's eyes as he'd spoken. She couldn't shake the impression he meant every word he'd said, that it wasn't just for Katy's benefit, and he was telling her what was truly in his heart. He'd told her more than once she was the woman he wanted, but he'd never said it with such feeling before. She believed him now. Unable to look from his gaze, what she felt for him deepened a little more. It made her wish she could drag him out of the restaurant right now, take him to her apartment and make love to him for the rest of the night. The thought had her pussy growing wet.

"Really?" Katy asked. "Not once did you second-guess yourself?"

Kye took a deep breath, and his grip tightened on Michaela ever so slightly, pulling her closer. "Really," he said, his voice sounding a bit strained. "And why would I regret being with Michaela?"

Katy snorted. "Come on, with your looks? No offense to Michaela, but you could get someone prettier with a snap of your fingers."

Kye's head whipped around in Katy's direction. From his deep scowl, there was no mistaking the fact he'd taken offense to what the other woman had said. "Just because you say you don't mean any offense to my wife doesn't mean what you say will be excused."

Katy was saved from answering as the waitress showed up with their food, but Michaela saw the shocked expression her nemesis wore. She bet no one had talked to Katy like that in a long time, if ever. Kye had brought her down a peg or two with his comment.

Even though some of the company wasn't her choosing, Michaela enjoyed her meal. And when Kye fed her from his fork, Katy gave them a look of disgust.

It was after they'd finished eating, but the dishes had yet to be taken away, that Kye stood and said he wanted to use the restroom. The uncomfortable feeling that washed through her at the thought of being left alone with Katy vanished as the other woman stood after Kye had gone and excused herself for the same reason. Michaela breathed a silent sigh of relief. She and Kye could ditch Katy soon and spend the rest of the night enjoying each other's company.

* * * *

After washing his hands, Kye turned off the water in the sink. He glanced at his reflection in the mirror on the wall in front of him. He didn't see the telltale sign of the arousal coursing through him. He hated leaving Michaela alone with Katy, but he'd needed to use the toilet and put some space between them to get a better grip on his control. Sitting close to her, totally focusing on her alone, confessing his true feelings—even though she probably thought he'd put on a show for their dinner companion—had gotten him all worked up. At least the meal was over, and he could get away from the self-centered woman and take his soon-to-be mate home.

Michaela had been right about Katy being a bitch. He'd never wanted to slap a female as much as he did her, especially after her rude comment about Michaela. She had some nerve to say he'd basically settled for his mate. As if he'd ever want Katy instead. She wasn't ugly, by any means, but her personality made her less attractive. At least for him it did. His Michaela was just as beautiful on the inside as she was on the outside. He didn't think she'd ever say something spiteful to anyone.

After he dried his hands, Kye headed out of the restroom and exited into a short hallway, which was hidden from the main part of the restaurant by a short stretch of wall. Much to his disgust, Katy stood close to the doorway, waiting for him.

"I'm glad I caught you alone," she said.

"Why?" The word came out clipped.

She took a step nearer, giving him what she probably thought was a sultry smile. It did nothing for Kye. If anything, it annoyed the hell out of him.

"Without Michaela around, you can talk more freely. Say how you truly feel without having to worry about the consequences."

He narrowed his eyes. "I'm not sure what you mean."

Katy came even closer. "There's no need to play stupid, Kye. It's just the two of us. I know the things you said about being so in love with Michaela were just for her benefit. She's a nobody, and will always be one. She's not even that pretty." She dropped her hand and cupped his cock. Katy licked her lips and smiled. "I knew you were attracted to me. You're hard." She moaned. "I'm going to enjoy riding you."

Completely pissed off, Kye put his hand around her wrist and squeezed, painfully. He also let the anger he felt show in his eyes. The widening of hers told him his mutedly glowed.

With a borderline growl lacing his words, he said, "You'll take your hand off me unless you want it broken." She released his dick, but he didn't let go of her wrist. "Just to set things straight, I wouldn't want you if you were the last woman on Earth. Now you're going back to the table and apologize to my wife for insulting her. I also suggest you leave, never to see Michaela again."

Kye released her with a shove. Katy stood there, her mouth working as she tried to find a response. To get her moving, he snarled, his upper lip curling, and growled softly. With a squeak, she turned and hurried away.

"Now that's what I call putting a woman in her place," a man's voice said from the entrance of the hallway.

Kye looked in that direction and stiffened at the sight of Miles standing there. "What do you want?"

Miles stepped farther into the hall. "I'm not following you, if that's what you think. I'm here with friends. I happened to need to use the restroom, and here you are."

"Friends? I didn't think you had any of those, unless you count all the lone wolves you've recruited to your side."

Miles' eyes glowed for a split second with anger. "Those days are done. I no longer associate with the likes of them."

"So you expect me to believe that since finding out your daughter is the foretold one, you've turned over a completely new leaf? That one day you won't up and change your mind about wanting to rule the packs yourself through Jaden?"

"I have, and I'd never do anything like that to her. She's my flesh and blood."

"So is Saskia, your own sister, and that didn't stop you from sending one of your thugs to kill her mate. Eli barely survived."

Kye just stopped himself from saying the only thing that had saved Eli's life had been his transformation into a werewolf. As far as Miles knew, it wasn't possible. He had no idea there was a spell that would change a mortal into one of their kind, one only Roxie could use since she was the true foretold one.

Miles sighed deeply. "I've come to regret that decision. I've apologized, even though it doesn't make up for it. Believe me, those days are behind me. I want to be a better man for my daughter. I want to keep her safe just as much as all of you do. I know you won't accept me back into the ranks of the Protectors, but I'm willing to take whatever you allow me."

"Does this newfound sense of duty extend to Saskia? And to Jaden's unborn child?"

"What?" Miles asked with a shocked expression. "Jaden is pregnant?"

Oh shit. Leif and Jaden obviously hadn't yet told Miles about their good news. Hopefully, Leif wouldn't want to kill him for telling his father-in-law about the baby. It didn't matter anyway since Kye couldn't take it back.

"Ah, yeah, she is," he said. "We just found out."

A wide smile broke across Miles' face, then he hugged Kye, making him feel extremely uncomfortable. Kye had never taken Miles for the type to put on outward displays of emotion like that.

Miles released him. "I'm going to be a grandfather," he said exuberantly. "I have to call Jaden."

With another glowing smile, Miles turned on his heel and walked away. Kye hoped to hell he hadn't messed things up for Jaden and Leif. He took a big breath as he returned to his table.

Michaela was alone with Katy nowhere in sight. She smiled. "There you are. I wondered if everything was all right, especially after Katy came back from the restroom, mumbled an apology and almost ran out of here."

"Sorry," he said as he sat next to Michaela. "I was held up by a couple people." At that moment, Miles walked by the table with his cell phone held to his ear and gave him the thumbs-up sign.

"Who's that? Was he one of the people you mentioned?"

Kye waited until Miles left the restaurant. "He's an old acquaintance. And yeah, he was one of them."

"And the other person?"

"Let's just say Katy decided to corner me, but I convinced her she'd made a terrible mistake. I doubt you'll ever see or hear from her again. I wasn't exactly nice about it."

"What did she do?" Michaela asked.

Kye put his arm around her shoulders and brushed a kiss across her lips, quite happy to see his mate's indignant expression on his behalf. "She basically offered herself to me and got a little grabby."

Michaela narrowed her eyes. "Grabby how?"

He took a quick look around the restaurant to make sure no one watched, then took Michaela's hand and placed it on the bulge in the front of his jeans. "She mistakenly thought she had me in this condition. I set her straight, though. It's all for you."

Seeing the hungry look in Michaela's eyes, his cock jerked under her hand. A very quiet, breathy moan pushed past her lips as she tightened her grip on him. It took everything Kye had not to shove the dirty plates off the table and strip her naked so he could finally ease the raging desire she stirred inside him.

His voice rough with need, he moved her hand away, and said, "Let's get out of here. You're my dessert, and I want it now."

Michaela silently nodded, but with his acute hearing, he was able to hear how fast her heart beat. He looked around the room, caught sight of their waitress and waved her to the table.

Once she stood next to him, he asked, "Can we have the bill?"

"That won't be necessary, sir. The woman who was with your party paid it on her way out."

"In that case, here's a tip for you." Kye took out his wallet and then handed her some money.

"Thanks, and I hope you enjoy the rest of your evening."

"Oh, we will," he said as he helped Michaela to her feet before ushering her out of the restaurant.

CHAPTER SEVEN

The ride back to her apartment just seemed to blur all together for Michaela. One moment Kye was helping her into his car and then the next thing she knew he'd pulled into a visitors parking spot at her building. Granted, she'd spent the entire trip staring hungrily at him. After feeling how hard he'd been at the restaurant, all she wanted was his big cock buried deep inside her.

And this time she wouldn't be denied. There really wasn't any reason to wait. She felt as if she knew a fair amount about Kye, and making love would only bring them closer.

It didn't take them long to arrive at her apartment door. Michaela unlocked and pushed it open, then she strode in ahead of Kye. Once he was inside, she shut it and locked it. They walked into the living room where she threw her purse onto the couch. The next thing she knew, he pulled her into his embrace and his mouth came down on hers.

Michaela wrapped her arms around his neck and kissed him with all the repressed lust coursing through her body. Her pussy throbbed, aching to be filled, as wetness pooled between her legs. She threaded her fingers through the hair on the back of Kye's head and angled her mouth over his for a tighter fit. His tongue pushed past her lips and stroked hers, the taste of him making her moan.

Kye's hand came up and covered one of her breasts, plucking

the nipple through the material of her blouse. It grew taut in response. Michaela pushed against him, rubbing along the hard length of his cock. He sucked on her tongue, groaning as he dropped his other hand to her ass, hauling her even closer.

The sound of their heavy breathing filled the room. Kye's kiss turned more demanding, taking her lips like a starving man. Michaela clung to him, becoming more turned-on, wanting what only he could give her.

She broke contact with his mouth and stepped out of his arms. "I want you naked and on my bed," she said as she reached for his hand.

"I can't think of anything else I want more than stripping you out of your clothes," he huskily replied.

Once his fingers closed around hers, Michaela led Kye to her bedroom, heading straight for the bed. She stood at the end of it and locked gazes with him. She reached for the buttons on his shirt and undid each one. She parted the material, slid it over his shoulders and down his arms. She didn't think she'd ever get enough of looking at his body.

After taking a step forward, she placed kisses across his wide chest. At his flat nipples, she dragged her tongue across each one. They pebbled beneath it. She set to work opening his jeans. That job done, she pushed them past his hips until they fell down his legs to pool at his ankles. Kye toed off his shoes, stepped out of his pants and kicked them away.

Michaela's gaze drifted along his body. It became focused on his cock. He was fully erect, his shaft sticking out straight from his body. She licked her lips at the sight of the small bead of pre-cum that appeared at the slit.

"Your turn." Kye's voice came across as a sexy rumble.

As she'd done to him, he undid the buttons on her blouse and then took it off. The bra she wore soon followed. He worked on her jeans, and she used her toes to push down the straps of her high-heeled shoes before she kicked them away. Kye took hold of the now open waistband of her pants and shoved them past her hips. He continued to follow them downward until he kneeled at her feet to help her remove them.

His large hands dragged down her panties. Michaela held on to Kye's shoulders for balance as she stepped out of them. She only had a second to tighten her grip as he nudged her legs farther apart and licked her pussy. He sucked and lapped, sending her body into overdrive. Her legs shook the higher he pushed her arousal. If not for his hands on her hips, holding her steady, she wouldn't have remained upright.

Kye drove her to the very brink of climax before he pulled away. Michaela whimpered, feeling the loss of his tongue. He stood and lifted her off her feet at the same time. He brought her down onto the bed and stretched out on his side next to her. He claimed her lips in a heated kiss.

Needing to touch Kye, Michaela trailed her fingers down his chest. His stomach muscles jumped as she caressed his abs, moving lower until she brushed against the head of his cock. He moaned into her mouth when she wrapped her hand around his shaft and stroked up and down. The feel of him made her pussy ache to be filled.

Michaela shifted to lie facing Kye. She continued to pump his erection as her wetness leaked onto her inner thighs. She wanted him. Wanted him buried so deeply inside her she wouldn't be able to tell where she ended and he began. He'd give her a good ride. His cock was big enough he'd fill her all the way up.

Remembering from the last time how Kye had liked it when she'd licked where his shoulder and neck met, she broke contact with his mouth. Michaela kissed a trail down to his chin, taking the time to gently nip it before going lower until she reached that particular spot. As he'd done the first time, he buried his fingers into her hair to hold her against him. His whole body stiffened as if in anticipation.

"Michaela, you have no idea what you're doing to me," Kye said gruffly. She dragged her teeth along his skin. "Shit," he hissed. "More. Let me feel more of your teeth."

Prepared to give him what he wanted, she sucked the area before giving Kye a harder-than-gentle nip. That one bite seemed to be all he'd needed to let go of his restraint.

Michaela found herself flipped onto her back with Kye's hips wedged between her legs. The tip of his cock brushed against her slick opening. She spread her thighs wider, hoping to urge him to push home. She looked at him and found he had his eyes closed and the veins in his neck stood out as he held himself rigid.

"I…I can't," he said through gritted teeth.

Not about to let things end there, Michaela grabbed his ass and pulled him forward as she pushed down, taking the head of his shaft inside her. With what sounded like a quiet wolf's howl, Kye sank his entire length into her pussy. She wrapped her legs around his waist, locking her heels at the small of his back as he plunged in and out of her.

Michaela's eyes drifted shut so she could better focus on the pleasure from having him take her with his cock. She hadn't been wrong—he fit perfectly inside her. She squeezed her inner muscles around his pumping shaft, and it grew harder.

She lifted her hips, matching each of Kye's strokes. It wasn't going to take much to make her come. Already her orgasm built deep inside her, working its way to the surface. Michaela clutched his biceps, holding on as he lifted to support himself on his hands to angle his cock just where she needed him.

As she came closer to teetering on the edge of finding her release, Michaela felt something else. Something she'd never experienced before during lovemaking. It was almost as if a part of her reached out for Kye. Not in the physical sense, but more like her essence, her soul, searched for his. She gasped in response when it was enveloped and then seemed to join with a part of Kye's spirit, binding them.

Whatever it was, the instant the essences became one, her pussy climaxed around his plunging cock. Michaela let out a whimpered moan, riding the waves of intense pleasure that washed over her. Kye stiffened above her and groaned as he too came.

After it was over, he collapsed on top her. She didn't mind his heavy weight pushing her farther into the mattress. She wound her arms around his back and shifted under him, feeling the still-hard length of his cock buried deep inside her. Just as he'd done the night before, Kye kept his erection after orgasm.

Michaela relaxed and kissed his shoulder. Kye propped himself up on his bent arms and brushed his lips across hers before he deepened the contact. He had her breathing hard again once he pulled away.

"Don't get too comfortable there," he said. "I haven't had all of my dessert yet."

He pulled out of her and shifted them both until they were on their sides with her back pressed against his chest. His erect shaft came to rest between her legs. Kye rocked forward, rubbing the head of it against her clit. She pushed back on him, becoming more aroused.

"Kye," she panted. "I want you inside me again."

"Don't worry. You'll get what you need."

He lifted her leg and put it on top his. Kye continued to rub himself along her pussy until he was slickly wet with her juices, then he sheathed himself to the hilt. Michaela moaned at the sensation of his thickness filling her, stretching her. What she thought sounded like a low growl rumbled out of him. It turned her on even more.

His pace became faster and harder as he took her from behind. Michaela gripped his plunging cock with her inner walls, loving the feel of him inside her. Kye reached around her and found her clit. He plucked at the small bundle of nerves, and it was enough to send her flying again. Once more, he came the same time she did. His erection pulsed, filling her with his cum.

Michaela was surprised to feel Kye remained hard, even though he'd come twice. He pulled out of her and nestled her against him, tucking her head under his chin. An arm settled over her waist and held her tight. His cock pressed along her bottom.

Kye kissed the top of her head. "I think a nap is in order, because I intend to put the rest of the night to good use."

She smiled. "In other words, I'm not going to get much sleep?"

"It's underrated when we can use those hours in a more enjoyable way."

"Mmm, I think I have to agree with you on that. It's a good thing I don't have to work tomorrow."

"Perfect. Now nap, because I'll be waking you very soon."

Michaela closed her eyes and relaxed against Kye. Surrounded by him, liking exactly where she was, she drifted off into slumber.

*

Michaela relaxed even more as she slept. Kye held her close, relishing the feel of her in his arms. It hadn't been his intention, but he'd claimed her as his mate. One little bite from her where his shoulder and neck met, and all his plans had gone totally out the window. He'd played with fire when he'd urged her to use her teeth on that spot. For a male werewolf, it was the biggest turn-on to have his mate bite him there. If a mark was left behind, all the better, because it was a sign to warn off other females, and to show he was taken.

The sensation of Michaela nipping him had wreaked havoc on his control over the mating urge. It'd amped it up to the point where he'd barely hung on by the skin of his teeth. Then having her take the head of his cock inside her pussy, it'd been too much. There had been no stopping what had happened next. Not that he regretted it. He'd just hoped he'd have been over the sticky part of explaining about being a werewolf first.

Be that as it may, Kye couldn't get around it. Plus, there was the bonus of the mating urge no longer riding his ass since he'd made Michaela his. The only drawback was he had to make sure he stayed near her at all times. At this stage, having to go through separation anxiety wouldn't be something he'd want his mate to experience. She wouldn't have a clue what happened to her.

With her not having to work in the morning, Kye decided he'd wait to tell her his secret for at least a day. He was going to have the job of convincing Michaela his feelings for her were true and that he wanted her to move into the Protectors' mansion with him. He loved her, and even without the threat of what would happen to them if they were apart, he didn't want to be away from her. With the mating bond in place, how he felt about her had solidified even more.

Kye kissed the top of Michaela's head again, taking a deep breath of her scent, and settled more comfortably behind her. He'd sleep, then make love to her again. Each time he did, it'd make the bond between them only stronger. And hopefully, when the time came for him to reveal what he truly was, his mate would be more inclined to accept him.

CHAPTER EIGHT

You're completely serious, aren't you?" Michaela asked, unable to keep some of her skepticism out of her voice. "You really want me to move in with you?"

Kye nodded. "Of course I am. I know you might think I'm hurrying our relationship, but I've never had such strong feelings for a woman as I do for you. I just know giving it a few months, a few weeks, hell, even a few days, isn't going to change how I feel for you."

They'd been sitting at her kitchen table, eating the late breakfast she'd cooked when Kye had dropped that bombshell on her about wanting her to live with him. It wasn't as though she found the proposal unappealing, because it wasn't, and he'd told her before how he felt for her, but this would be a big step. One, if it didn't work out, could have an adverse effect on her. Apartments she could afford, and as nice as the one she now had, were kind of hard to come by.

After their marathon of sex during the night, she felt closer to Kye. More so than she'd ever had for any other man. Quite a few times during the long hours he'd made love to her, it'd been on the tip of her tongue to tell him she loved him.

Kye reached over and took her hand. "You're awfully quiet, Michaela. I hope I didn't spook you."

"Not really. As you said, it does seem as if you're rushing

430

things. This would be a huge step for us, and only after knowing each other for three days at that. I'd have to give up my apartment. Where would I go if we ever break up?"

He locked gazes with her. "Trust me on this, I know that won't happen. I want you by my side — always."

"So does that mean you'll be getting down on one knee now and asking me to marry you?"

Kye gave her a crooked grin. "If you want me to, I will."

She shook her head. "I wasn't joking, Kye."

His expression grew serious. "I'm not either."

Michaela didn't know what to say to that. A marriage proposal at this stage in the game wasn't something she was ready for. She'd heard about too many divorces caused by the couple jumping into the "death do us part" thing too quickly. If she said "I do" to any man, she wanted to be sure she'd want to stick it out for the long haul.

At Kye's expectant look, Michaela finally said, "Don't, okay?" When he opened his mouth to say something in return, she quickly cut him off. "I'm not saying it isn't an option in the future, but not right now. I don't feel ready to be discussing marriage with you at this point."

Kye nodded, then squeezed the hand he still held. "It's all right, Michaela. Truly. I still want you to move in with me. I'd feel better if we lived in the same place. I don't like the thought of you being alone."

"I've been for some years now, Kye. I'm twenty-nine years old."

"That's not exactly what I mean. You know I'm like a bodyguard, a protector, right?"

"Yeah," she said, not sure where he was going with this.

"Well, the people I guard against, let's just say they'd use any means at their disposal to remove me."

Michaela eyes widened. "Are you saying I could be in danger because you're my boyfriend?"

"Not right now, but there's always the possibility."

He had her going there for a bit, thinking she'd have to look over her shoulder for bad guys. "If I were to say yes — I'm still not ready to agree just yet — I'd want to see your place first before I make any decision."

Kye smiled. "That's fair. And I think you should meet my family as well."

"Your family? Don't you think it might be a little soon?"

"Yeah, I guess I forgot to mention that we all live together. We also work in the same business."

"You live with your entire family?" Kye still couldn't be living with his parents at his age. He looked to be at least thirty.

"Actually, we're really not related, well, except for Roan, Jager and Skylar. They're true brothers. We just like to think of ourselves as one big family."

"How many of you are there?"

"In total, including myself, twelve of us. Sorry, make that almost thirteen, since Leif's wife, Jaden, recently found out she's pregnant."

"So married couples live with you as well?"

"They're the majority. It's just Dirk and I, but now that I've met you, I don't consider myself single."

That last part made Michaela feel good. She wasn't going to deny it. Hearing a man like Kye say he was no longer up for grabs, and that basically he was hers, sent a thrill through her.

Michaela leaned over and kissed Kye. She brushed her tongue along the seam of his lips, and when he opened, she pushed inside. She took his mouth, loving the taste of him. After a few more seconds, she pulled back.

"What was that for?" Kye asked huskily.

"I just wanted to. If I'm near you, I don't think I can go for too long without touching you in some way."

The sexy smile he shot her had her pussy clenching. "I feel the same. And it's just another reason I want you living with me. I want you in my bed every night and to wake up holding you in my arms each morning."

That was something Michaela wanted as well, to be able to sleep next to Kye all the time. She could quickly get used to waking up in the mornings surrounded by his heat and snuggled in his embrace.

"All right," she said. "Take me to your house and let me meet your family."

Kye gave her a short, hard kiss. "You know I'm going to do my best to make you say yes."

She chuckled. "I figured you would." She thought of something. "Shouldn't you be looking after Nevaeh right now?"

"Roxie gave me a few days off. She said she wanted to give me time to spend with you. One of my family members will pick up the slack for me so it isn't a problem. And she wants to meet you."

"Okay, but let's get the family introductions over with first."

"Sounds good. I'll call home and let them know we'll be coming. That way, at least one of them will wait for us."

Michaela followed Kye with her gaze as he stood and walked into the living room. He pulled his cell phone out of his jeans pocket. She cleaned up their dirty plates, only listening to what he said with half an ear. The thought of meeting his family made her feel a little nervous, but she wouldn't back out.

After he finished his call, Kye helped her wash the dishes. Once they were done, he soon ushered her out of the apartment and then down to visitors parking. Seated inside his expensive car, Michaela wondered what type of house he and his family lived in. It obviously had to be large. With that many people under one roof, they all wouldn't fit otherwise.

As they drove, she looked at the passing scenery. Seeing the Golden Gate Bridge coming into view, she had a suspicion where they were going. "You live in Marin County, don't you?"

Kye shot her a quick look before he turned his gaze back onto the road. "How did you know?"

"It was a lucky guess. The car you drive, and the direction we're headed, it wasn't too hard to figure out. You and your family are rich, right?" Gazing at Kye's profile, she saw him smile.

"You could say that."

Michaela turned her head to look out the side window again. Silence stretched between her and Kye, but it wasn't, by any means, uncomfortable. After arriving in Marin County, the houses got progressively bigger and grander. She sat straighter when the car turned onto a long drive for one of the mansions. At her first sight of his home, she found herself speechless. She took in the well-maintained grounds and gardens that had brightly-colored flowers artistically planted. The house was large, way bigger than she'd expected.

She kept staring at the huge edifice the closer they came. Kye drove past it and parked in front of a big detached garage.

Michaela scrambled out once he shut off the engine and had opened his door. She walked around the back of the car to join him.

"Well," he said, "what do you think? Can you picture yourself living in a place like this?"

Michaela looked from the house to Kye. "You're kidding me, right? You live in a freaking mansion."

He snaked his arms around her waist and pulled her close. He grinned. "So, does that mean you're swaying more toward saying yes?"

"It does put my dumpy little apartment to shame."

"Come on, I'll take you inside."

Kye kissed her forehead, then released her. Michaela took the hand he held out, and they walked toward the front door. They stepped inside a large foyer that had a black-and-white checkered marble floor. Her gaze lifted to the fair-sized crystal chandelier that hung from the center of the cathedral ceiling. She swallowed as she next took in the blond banister that lined the outside of the staircase, curving up to the floor above. Of what she'd seen so far, the place smacked of extreme affluence.

Michaela hadn't realized she had her mouth hanging open until Kye used a finger under her chin to close it. He quietly chuckled as she met his gaze. "You look as if you don't know quite what to say."

"I don't. You really want me to live here, with you?"

"Of course I want that."

"You want me to live in your mansion? A place I never thought I'd ever be able to step foot in, much less call home in my lifetime?"

"Yes. You might not have as much privacy as you would at your apartment, but we do have a lot of space."

Hell, the issue of lack of privacy hadn't even crossed her mind. Moving in with Kye would give her a dream home and Prince Charming all rolled into one. And from the looks of the place, he wasn't just loaded — he was filthy rich.

"Show me more," she said.

Kye linked their hands before he took her to the spacious living room that had a big LED television and black leather couches and armchairs. No one was in the room, but she could picture his family sitting around, watching TV. Next, he showed her the kitchen with its stainless-steel appliances and large table. There were twelve chairs around it. If she hadn't already known how large his family was, that would have given it away.

Kye let go of her hand, crossed to the window above the sink and looked out. "That's where they are."

He motioned for her to follow as he went to the single door that led outside to the backyard. The first thing she heard was the sound of metal hitting metal. The next was a woman's voice yelling, "Come on, Roan. You're not going to let your brother whoop your ass, are you?"

After a quick grin aimed her way, Kye took her hand again and hurriedly pulled her around the corner of the house in the direction the sounds had come from. "You have to see this," he said.

Michaela's steps faltered slightly when they came into view of two very large men going at each other with swords. She had to blink just to make sure she truly saw what she thought she'd seen. She had. Those were real, and they swung them as if they did it every day.

As Michaela walked closer with Kye, she noticed the two men had strikingly similar features, and they were extremely good-looking. They had to be two of the three true brothers Kye had told her about. The only difference was one wore his hair longer, pulled into a ponytail that ended at the middle of his back. She spotted two women who stood on the sidelines, cheering them on.

Just before they reached the small group, who stood in the middle of the lawn, Kye said, "Roan is going to lose. Jager, his brother and the one with the long ponytail, usually does beat him, and the rest of us, on a regular basis. His sword is such a part of him that when he was single he used to sleep with it in his bed."

Before Michaela could get a chance to ask if by "the rest of us" Kye meant he knew how to sword fight as well, he'd brought them to the two women and introduced her. "Ladies, this is Michaela. Michaela this is Ansley, Roan's wife." He nodded to the woman with long, straight dark brown hair. "And next to her is Daylen, who is Jager's." Daylen had shoulder-length hair as well, but hers was reddish brown.

Michaela smiled at the two women. "Hi."

Before she could say anything more, Kye said, "Now that the three of you have been introduced, I'll be right back."

"Wait. Where are you..." Kye left at a run.

"He won't be gone long," Daylen said with a chuckle. "Kye has more than likely gone into the house to get his sword."

"Do they do this a lot?" she asked. "Fight in the middle of the backyard with replica swords? At first, I thought they were real, but they can't be. Can they?"

"Yes, but those aren't replicas. They're the real deal."

"You mean the blades are sharp enough to cut?" Michaela's gaze swung toward Roan and Jager. Watching them cross blades took on a whole new meaning now that she knew they weren't blunted.

"It's all right," Ansley said. "They rarely hurt each other. They're what you'd call experts, and have done this for years."

Michaela turned at the sound of Kye returning. Sure enough, he carried a sword that appeared to be a match to the ones Jager and Roan had. He'd also changed his button-down shirt for a black T-shirt.

He met her gaze. "You look a little worried about something."

Ansley answered before she could. "Daylen just told Michaela you guys don't use blunted replicas."

He smiled at Michaela. "You have nothing to worry about, babe. This is just practice so we're always careful."

At that moment, there was the sound of something heavy hitting the ground, accompanied by a loud groan. Michaela sucked in a breath when she saw Jager standing over the fallen Roan with the point of his sword leveled at his brother's throat.

"Damn, Jager," Roan said. "When the hell did you learn that move?"

His brother stepped back and held out his hand to help Roan to his feet. Jager grinned. "Daylen has taught me some karate moves. Having a wife who has a black belt does have its advantages."

"Well, shit, now you're going to be even harder to beat."

"Now it's my turn," Kye said as he walked toward the two men. "Which one of you wants to take me on?"

Jager pointed at Roan. "Since he was the loser, you can fight him."

"Hey," Roan said, "shouldn't it be the winner who accepts the challenge of any and all contenders?"

"Not today it isn't." Jager went to his wife and put his free arm around her shoulders. "I promised Daylen I'd take her out for lunch since we have the evening shift at Roxie's." He turned Michaela's way. "And you must be Michaela. Kye has talked about you."

"I am," she said. "I'd offer to shake your hand, but I don't want to end up on the business end of your sword."

Jager looked down at where he held it, then up at her with a chuckle. "I usually take it wherever I go so I sometimes forget I have it." He squeezed his wife closer. "When Daylen and I first met, she tried to arrest me for carrying it. She used to be a cop."

Michaela took in Daylen's slim, toned body and could easily picture her as a police officer. And that would explain why she had a black belt in karate. "So you aren't a cop anymore, Daylen?"

The woman shook her head. "No, I gave it up. I enjoy being a Protector more. Plus, that way I don't have to worry about being apart from Jager. As a police officer, I worked long shifts, mostly nights."

"I see."

"All right, enough standing around, talking," Kye said. "I guess it's you and I, Roan."

As Kye and Roan crossed swords, from the corner of her eye, Michaela vaguely saw Jager and Daylen walk away. She was too focused on the two men nearby as they blocked each other's hits with the edges of their blades. She'd seen lots of movies where the actors fought with swords, but their steps were all choreographed. Such wasn't the case with Kye and Roan. All it would take would be a single misstep and one of them could be seriously hurt. She couldn't stop the shiver that ran through her at the thought.

"Don't worry so much, Michaela," Ansley said. "If you watch closely, you'll be able to see they really aren't trying to do any damage. I think of it as a kind of dance the guys do."

Doing as Ansley suggested, she paid closer attention to each strike Kye and Roan made. It looked as if each man held back some of his strength, though it didn't mean they stopped trying to find an opening to disarm their opponent.

In the end, they called the contest a draw, neither man able to get the advantage since they were so evenly matched. Kye and

Roan breathed heavily as they crossed the short distance to Michaela and Ansley.

Kye pulled his shirt off over his head. "Now I need a shower."

Sweat beaded his forehead and made his wide chest sheen. The muscles on his arms appeared to be pumped up. If Kye practiced with a sword on a regular basis, it was no wonder he was ripped. Even though the men swung them as if they weighed nothing, she had a feeling she'd hardly be able to lift one.

"Where is everyone else?" he asked Roan, which caused her to stop ogling Kye's chest and focus on the others around her.

"Saskia and Eli are at Roxie and Beowulf's place. Skylar and Braelyn left early this morning to catch a flight to Paris. Braelyn had a photo shoot. Dirk is off doing who knows what since Saskia ordered him to take some time off. And Leif and Jaden are holed up in their room. From what I understand, Leif is doing his best to make her forget she got angry at him for what he'd said about her dad."

"Hmm," Ansley said to Roan. "Maybe I should get mad at you and have you make it up to me in the same way."

In a sudden move, Roan slung his wife over his shoulder. "You don't need to pick a fight to get that." With sword in hand, he walked toward the house and then disappeared around the corner.

Kye shook his head. "Does he do that to Ansley often? Just throw her over his shoulder and go?" she asked.

"Actually, no. Only once in a while. Anyway, those are a few members of my family. You can meet the others later, though not Skylar and Braelyn, since they probably won't be home for a couple days."

"Braelyn is a model?"

"Yeah. Does the name Braelyn Whitmore mean anything to you?"

Michaela nodded. "She's a Victoria's Secret model. You mean to say she's married to Skylar?"

Kye grinned. "She is. They haven't been together for very long, though."

"I do have to say your family isn't exactly like everyone else's, with sword practice in the backyard and famous models in residence."

"No, we aren't the conventional family, by any means. Let's go inside and I'll show you my room, which will also be yours."

"Only if I agree to move in."

Kye leaned in and kissed the tip of her nose. "I'm going to work on that right after I have my shower."

With his T-shirt draped over his shoulder, he put his arm around her waist and guided her toward the mansion. Michaela's heart sped up just thinking of the ways Kye would try to persuade her to say yes.

CHAPTER NINE

Kye didn't let Michaela go until he'd taken her upstairs and had them locked behind his bedroom door. He crossed to his walk-in closet and threw his sweaty T-shirt into the laundry hamper inside. He sheathed his sword in the scabbard hanging up among his clothes. That done, he turned back to Michaela. She stood in the middle of the room.

"So?" he asked. "What do you think?"

She looked around, her gaze lingering a bit longer on the king-size bed than the rest of the furniture. If he had his way, and figured he would, Kye would have her spread out naked on the thick mattress in the next little while.

Michaela closed most of the distance between them, staring at him. "Well, it looks as if you have lots of extra space for two people to comfortably share the room. Even the bed."

Kye focused on her mouth. "It really does. After my shower, how about we test it to see just how well the two of us fit on it?"

She placed a hand on his chest and stroked her thumb back and forth. "Better yet, why don't I join you, then we can move to the bed? I could use a good wash."

His cock twitched, hardening at Michaela's offer. "Really now? I happen to be the perfect man for the job. I'll make sure no part of you gets missed."

Michaela gave him a sexy smile. "I had a feeling you wouldn't turn it down."

Kye took her hand and led her into the en suite bathroom. Even though they'd made love numerous times during the night, he still wanted her as desperately as he had then. The desire to possess his mate was almost a living, breathing thing that would always remain a part of him. With the mating bond firmly in place, there would never be anyone else for him. He was as much Michaela's as she was his. He loved her with his whole heart and soul. He would do anything to keep her happy and safe, to the point of sacrificing his own life if need be. Mated male werewolves were noted for being overprotective of their claimed females at times. It was how they were wired.

After taking two towels from the shelf on the wall and then putting them on the vanity counter, Kye turned back around to find Michaela already stripping out of her clothes. God, she was gorgeous. He'd never get sick of looking at her. Once she was down to her bra and panties, he brushed her hands away to remove the last articles of clothing himself.

He kissed her leisurely before he nibbled a path down the side of her neck. All the while, he worked on unhooking her bra. "Have I told you how much your body turns me on?" he asked against her skin.

Michaela chuckled, the sound low and husky. "Maybe a few times last night, but I don't mind hearing it again."

"Good, because I'll probably say it a lot, especially when I have you almost naked in my arms like this."

Kye straightened and skimmed Michaela's bra straps down her arms and then off. His gaze latched on to her more-than-a-handful breasts with their taut, rosy nipples. He bent and sucked one into his mouth, loving the feel of his mate's fingers sinking into his hair to hold him exactly where she wanted him.

He switched to the other breast, hooked his fingers into the sides of her panties and pushed them down until they fell to pool at her feet. Michaela stepped out of them and then kicked the silky material away.

Once he had her moaning, Kye released her nipple, straightening to his full height. Michaela's cheeks were already blushed with arousal, and her eyes were heavy-lidded. "I'll turn on the water to get it warm," he said.

He turned his back to her, pulled his cell phone out of his pants pocket and placed it on the counter near the towels. He opened the door of the glass-enclosed shower. He stepped inside and turned the single knob on the faucet. Kye fiddled with it until the water was the correct temperature. Before he faced in the other direction to step out, Michaela's arms came around him from behind. Her hands skimmed down his abs to the top of his jeans.

"I figured since you're already in here, and you'll probably want to change your jeans anyway, I'd just take them off for you now," she said while pressing kisses to his back.

Kye sucked in a breath as she opened his pants and reached inside for his cock. She wrapped her fingers around it and stroked up and down his shaft. While she worked him, she shoved her other hand down the back of his jeans and grabbed his ass. A low growl rumbled out of him.

She continued to fondle him until he rocked his hips forward in time with her strokes, pushing himself tighter into her hand. He groaned, growing even harder. Michaela released him and tugged at his jeans, which were now soaking wet. It took her a couple tries since, at first, the material wouldn't cooperate. With a flick of his foot, he kicked the garment into the corner. She once again took hold of his cock. He let her pump it a few times before he pulled her hand away.

"Not that what you're doing doesn't feel good, because it does, but I think we'd better get to the washing first before I want to skip it entirely," he said.

Michaela's arms slipped from around him, and she shifted to stand at his front. "Oh, I don't want that to happen. You're not going to deprive me of getting to soap up that hard body of yours."

After taking hold of his arms, she turned him so he was directly under the spray of warm water. She released him and grabbed the bottle of shampoo that sat on a recessed corner shelf. Kye wet his hair before slicking it back. Michaela motioned for him to lean down, then proceeded to wash and condition it. He did the same for her, relishing the feel of running his fingers through her silky locks.

He would have reached for the soap first, but Michaela beat him to it. She shook her finger at him with a playful grin. She held the bar under the water before she worked up a lather.

Michaela's soapy hands glided along the top of his chest, then she worked lower, seeming to not to miss any part of him. He moaned once she stopped just short of his cock and reached for one of his arms. She took her time running the soap along it, doing the same to the other.

Kye hadn't thought his cock could get any harder until Michaela went down onto her knees in front of him. She looked up while she rolled the bar between her hands. He closed his eyes to a squint, knowing they had to be mutedly glowing by now. She had him too worked up for them not to be. As she licked her lips, his erection bobbed. Instead of taking him into her mouth as he wished, she lowered her gaze and soaped his leg.

"I don't think I've ever had such a torturous shower in my entire life," he said in a gruff voice.

"You're tough. I'm sure you can handle a little torture," she replied with a small laugh.

"If you tease me too much, don't be surprised if you find yourself pressed against the wall while I take you from behind."

"Who says I wouldn't want that?"

Kye groaned as Michaela continued to wash his other leg. Once she was done, she rose to her feet. She lathered her hands again before she reached for his cock. He closed his eyes, holding back the loud growl that built inside him. The feel of her slippery hands surrounding him, stroking him, made him fight to hold back his orgasm.

All too soon, her fingers disappeared from his shaft, and Michaela turned him around so his front faced the water. Her hands slid over his back, inching their way lower and lower. Kye fisted his hands at his sides to stop himself from pulling her to him. He'd let her finish, then it'd be his turn.

At his ass, she pressed closer, and the tips of her breasts brushed against his skin. Michaela kneaded and squeezed each of his butt cheeks until he couldn't take any more. Kye spun around and took the bar of soap from her.

"I think I'm clean enough," he said huskily. "Now I get to do everything you did to me."

He positioned her under the water before he lathered his hands. Kye took the same path she'd taken on him, starting at her breasts and working his way down to her legs. He skimmed up the inside of her thighs, but avoided touching her pussy. Even through the water, he was able to smell the scent of her arousal. She whimpered as one of his knuckles accidentally brushed against her.

That one sound seemed to wrap around his cock and squeeze. Faster than he'd intended, Kye turned Michaela and finished washing her, saving her pussy for last. He slipped a soapy finger between her nether lips and stroked. She panted and moaned, her bottom pushing back against his hard-on.

"Kye. Now who's teasing whom?" Michaela reached around him and grabbed his ass.

That was it. He couldn't take any more. He needed to be inside her right now. He held her under the spray and rinsed her off before turning Michaela so she faced one of the walls. Kye ran his hands down her arms until he reached hers. Those, he placed flat on the glass in front of her. He took hold of her hips and pulled them toward him so she was slightly bent forward. With a knee between her legs, he spread them farther apart.

Kye kept his grip on her, angled his cock and slowly sank his length inside Michaela's pussy. The sensation of her silken walls closing around him, gripping him tight, had him moaning. He reared back and pulled almost all the way out before sliding back in so he was balls deep. She fit him perfectly, sheathing him like a glove. Sex had been good before he found Michaela, but it was even better now with her. He was addicted to her, as if she were his drug of choice. He'd never get enough of her, and would do anything to get his next fix.

He pistoned his hips, taking her harder and faster. Their breathy gasps and moans rose in volume until they were louder than the sound of the running water. Michaela pushed back, matching each of his strokes, her pussy squeezing tighter around his plunging cock.

All too soon, the point of no return rushed up to meet him. He skimmed a hand from her hip to her front and between her legs. Finding her clit, he stroked it in time with his thrusts. "Come for me, Michaela. I can't hold back much longer."

She moaned. "I'm there. Oh, god, don't stop."

Her inner walls rhythmically clutched his shaft, milking him to his own orgasm. He pushed inside her one final time and held her tightly to him as his cock pulsed deep inside her pussy, his release tearing through him.

After the last tremor tapered off, Kye pulled out of Michaela, turned her and wrapped her in his embrace. "I think it's time to test out the bed."

She nipped his chin and smiled. "You won't find me arguing, though I do have to say your shower passed with flying colors."

Kye turned off the water and then carried Michaela out through the glass door. He dried them both before he took his mate to bed. He proceeded to show her exactly what he could do with the extra room on the mattress.

* * * *

Michaela awoke to the sensation of her stomach growling. She wasn't sure what time it was, but it'd been hours since she'd last had anything to eat. And with the amount of calories she and Kye had burned in his bed, it wasn't any wonder she felt starved. At the rate they were going, she'd never have to worry about getting fat.

A quiet snore in her ear told her Kye still slept. She smiled. She'd probably worn him out, not that it was entirely her fault. The man kept an erection for so long he just seemed to keep going and going. He'd ruined her for other men. To be honest, she didn't want another. She hadn't told him yet, but she'd already made up her mind about moving in with him. He'd won her over to that idea. She'd move in with him tomorrow if he wanted. The only drawback would be her commute to work, but she was sure she'd get used to it. After all, she'd come home every day to the man she loved and a mansion.

Michaela lifted Kye's arm where it was draped over her waist and rolled toward him. He let out a loud snort but didn't awaken. She kissed him. "Kye, wake up." He mumbled something she couldn't understand, still mostly asleep. "Come on, sleepy head. I'm hungry. Are you going to let me starve?"

His brown eyes blinked open. "What time is it?" he asked groggily.

"I have no idea, but we've been in your room for hours."

He gave her a crooked smile. "True. So what's the final verdict? Was I able to have you side in my favor?"

She couldn't help but grin at Kye's playful expression. "Hmm, let me think." She brushed her lips against his. "I don't know if you did enough convincing or not."

Kye rolled her to her back, landing on top her. "Woman, we'll never leave this room if you want me to give you more reasons for saying yes."

Michaela giggled. "Did you just call me 'woman?'"

"Yes, because you're mine. So, woman, are you going to put me out of my misery? Or do I have to kill myself pleasuring you for hours on end since you're so demanding?"

"As if you'd find that a hardship. And I'm not demanding. If I recall correctly, it was you who kept things going, if you know what I mean?"

"Well, are you going to answer my question or not?"

With a dramatic sigh, she said, "If you insist. I've reached a decision." She paused for effect. "I think my dresser is going to clash horribly with yours, unless you want to buy me a new one."

Kye dropped his head and took her lips in a long, hot kiss that had her wanting him all over again. He finally pulled away and locked gazes with her. "I'll buy you one and anything else you want. I'll make sure you never regret moving in with me."

She wrapped her arms around his neck and played with the back of his hair. "How could I when I'll be with the man who somehow won my heart in a matter of days?"

"And I promise to keep it safe." He kissed the tip of her nose. "Just so you know, you won mine the first time I saw you. I love you, Michaela. Don't ever doubt it."

"I love you too, Kye. And I won't."

Hoping he'd do more than kiss her after they'd just confessed their feelings for one another, Michaela groaned as Kye pulled out of her embrace and then slipped off the bed. She ran her gaze over his body, lingering on his once again hard cock.

"Forget it," he said. "We're going to get dressed and find something to eat downstairs. Then once you're fed, we're off to your apartment to pack your clothes."

She sat up. "You want to start moving me in today?"

Kye walked to the closet and disappeared for a few seconds.

He came back out with a fresh pair of jeans. "Damn right I do. I can't sleep without you now. I'd probably lose my mind if I did." He pulled on his pants, but left them undone.

He sounded so serious she had to laugh. "Well, I guess that's a good thing, being wanted and needed that much."

"Good, because I wasn't going to take no for an answer." Kye leaned over and caressed her cheek. "Where you go, I go." He straightened and then went to his dresser.

He took out a gray T-shirt and then tugged it on. "Okay, but how are you going to manage that while I'm at work?" she asked with humor in her voice. "Are you going to follow me around the zoo all day?"

Kye turned in her direction, and Michaela felt her smile disappear by degrees at the serious expression he wore. "Quit," he said simply.

"Quit?"

"Yes."

"You want me to leave the zoo and do what?" She'd just come to terms with moving in with Kye and then he'd decided to drop another bombshell.

He crossed to the bed and sat beside her. He cupped her face and stroked his thumb along her cheek. "Do nothing, if that's what you want. I'm not exactly hard up for money, as you know. I want to look after you. Let me. Please."

"I don't know if I like the idea of depending totally on you financially. Plus, there's the fact I love my job. I love working with the animals. I'd miss it, and I'd hate to quit, then later down the road regret that decision."

"What if I were to come up with an alternative? Something that'd allow you to do what you're doing now, only here at the mansion."

She looked at Kye as if to say she didn't think that'd be possible. "What would that be? Unless you're willing to open a wild animal rescue or something."

He smiled. "We'll figure something out, but I want you to seriously consider quitting."

"All right."

"Good." He released her and stood. "Get dressed, then we'll see what I can whip up for us in the kitchen."

Michaela slipped off the bed and then headed for the bathroom. If Kye didn't stop throwing life-altering offers at her, she'd be a basket case in no time.

CHAPTER TEN

After they'd eaten, Kye had driven them to her apartment. Surprisingly, it didn't take too long for Michaela to pack the two large suitcases she owned with her clothes. What didn't fit, she'd put in black garbage bags. He took out things hanging in her closet in bundles and then placed them on the backseat of his car. She'd also packed a few other necessities. The rest of her belongings could stay in her apartment for now until she figured out what she wanted to do with them. She'd have to give the landlord her month's notice as well.

With her suitcases loaded into his trunk, they made the drive to Marin County and the mansion. Kye parked closer to the front door, and Michaela got out. She gathered some of her clothes from the backseat while he went around to the trunk and took out her two suitcases.

They'd just made it through the door when a woman with almost white-blonde hair stepped into the foyer. She smiled as she came closer. "You must be Michaela." Her gaze skipped over the things Michaela and Kye held. "And it looks as if you're making a good start of moving in. I'm Saskia."

"Nice to finally meet you," Michaela said. "And yes, but it's just my clothes for now."

"It's something." Saskia's gaze skipped over to Kye. "Just to give you the heads-up, Miles is here, so behave yourself."

Kye groaned. "Saskia, are you sure this is really wise?"

"Yes, I am. He's my brother, Kye. If being with Jaden like this will help keep him on our side, I'm not going to deny him."

Michaela looked from Saskia to Kye. She had no idea what this "on our side" meant, but from their expressions, it had to be something serious.

"I know," Kye said. "We can't let our guard down. For me, the bastard has to prove himself — that he's no longer what he used to be — before I even think of welcoming him back."

"I never said we shouldn't stay vigilant. I know exactly what Miles is capable of as much as the rest of you. I just want this to work, so in other words, no going out of your way to fuck things up. Got it?"

"Yes, boss. I guess when Michaela and I finish unloading my car, we'll come down and join everyone else."

Saskia nodded. "When you're ready, we're sitting outside on the patio." She turned and walked toward the back of the house.

"Are you going to tell me what that was all about?" Michaela asked as she and Kye walked up the stairs to his bedroom.

"Ah...not right now."

At the hesitancy in Kye's voice, Michaela put the clothes she held onto the bed and then turned to face him. "Does it have something to do with you protecting Roxie and her family?"

Kye closed the distance between them and put a hand over her mouth. "Shh. We don't need Miles to overhear you talking about Roxie, all right?"

She nodded, even though the chances of anyone hearing what she'd said were impossible. She and Kye were alone in his room and the others were outside. And even if someone was downstairs, they still wouldn't have been able to hear her.

He took his hand away. "There are some things I have to explain to you, but not while Miles is here." Kye took a deep breath and let it out on a long sigh. "Once he's gone, we're going to have a little chat, you and I."

"Okay. And I promise I won't say anything about...you know who."

Kye smiled. "Good. You'll understand more once I tell you everything."

They finished taking the rest of her clothes up to Kye's room.

Until she picked out a new dresser—he insisted she get one—she'd be living out of her suitcases. The things that could be hung up were now in his walk-in closet along with his stuff. It was a start to making Michaela feel as if it was her room too.

After Kye moved his car to the garage, they headed for the backyard patio. It was later in the day, but darkness hadn't yet descended. There were five people sitting around the wrought-iron table, talking. Saskia was there, but Michaela hadn't met the others yet. Her gaze landed on one of the men, who she recognized from the restaurant the night before. He had the same light blond hair and similar features as Saskia. Michaela assumed that had to be Miles, Saskia's brother.

Once they reached the table, Kye introduced her to Eli, Saskia's husband, then to Leif and Jaden, leaving Miles for last. She and Kye took the two remaining empty chairs, which had Michaela sitting next to Eli.

After the introductions were over, Leif turned to Kye, and said, "I guess I should thank you for telling Miles about Jaden being pregnant."

Kye cringed. "I wasn't thinking, all right? I was a bit...distracted, trying to handle something else at the time. I didn't mean to ruin the surprise."

"From the looks of you and Michaela, I'd say you two worked through your distraction," Miles said with a laugh. "I assume congr—" He stopped talking, reached down to rub his leg under the table and looked over at Jaden. "What did you kick me for?"

Jaden glared at him, giving an almost infinitesimal nod in Michaela's direction. "Dad, you don't want to say something that will embarrass Kye's *girlfriend*, do you?"

Michaela's gaze shot to Miles. There was no way he could be Jaden's father. He didn't look much older than her. And Michaela thought the way Jaden had stressed the word "girlfriend" a bit strange.

"Oh, sorry," Miles quickly said in return. "I didn't mean to do that."

Jaden nodded, then looked at Kye. "It's okay you told my dad about me being pregnant. I wasn't upset by it." She glared at her husband. "Not like someone else."

Leif held up his hands in surrender. "Hey, don't look at me like that. I only thought you might want to wait until you were a little bit further along. You're only four weeks pregnant."

"So? I might not go around telling the whole world, but I'd planned to tell my dad."

Leif ran a hand over his face. "I think I'm just going to shut my mouth now since every time I open it I seem to bury myself in deeper shit."

One minute they were all chuckling over what Leif had said and the next everyone, except for Michaela, instantly quieted. They appeared to sniff the air, and a low animalistic growl rumbled out of everyone but her and Jaden. Michaela couldn't overlook the sound this time as she'd managed to do every time Kye had done it.

She stiffened as a group of seven men suddenly arrived on the lawn a short distance away. They moved so fast Michaela had a hard time tracking them. It wasn't normal.

All the men and Saskia shot to their feet as one man from the other group stepped forward and spoke. "Did you think you could just drop us like crap on your shoe, Miles? Did you think we'd just walk away?"

"Leave, Curtis, or this isn't going to end well for you and the others," Miles snapped back.

Curtis laughed. "You think we're afraid of you and a few Protectors? You promised us that once you had the foretold one in your possession, things would be different in the packs. That we, the lone wolves, would have all the control. Just because it's your daughter doesn't mean we still don't want what you promised when we joined you."

Miles snarled his lip and snapped his teeth. "The foretold one being my daughter *does* change everything. She has opened my eyes to the path my life had taken, one that would have ended in my destruction."

Curtis slowly clapped. "Ah, isn't that sweet, but that doesn't get me the status or money you promised us."

A scream locked in Michaela's throat as Curtis and the men behind him turned into wolves. She looked at the others around her as they too, one by one, became wolves. She couldn't pull her gaze away as Kye's eyes glowed mutedly just before his body shimmered and blurred, taking on the form of a wolf with very light brown fur.

The two groups of wolves launched themselves at each other. Michaela found herself unable to move, her mind having a hard time processing what she saw. A large hand wrapped around her arm and pulled her away from the table.

"Get back!" Leif shouted. She turned to find him and Jaden close by. He let go of her and cupped his wife's face. "Promise me you won't shift."

Jaden shook her head. "It's still early enough in the pregnancy that I can without hurting the baby."

"I don't care, Jaden. I don't want you in the fight. You've never had to face anything like this before. Just do as I ask. Please."

Jaden closed her eyes for a few seconds and nodded. "All right. Just be careful."

Michaela couldn't hold back a startled yelp as Leif too became a wolf in a matter of seconds, then ran off to join the fray. "What…what are you people?"

"I'm sure this isn't how Kye wanted you to find out, Michaela, but we're all werewolves," Jaden said.

"You're one too?"

"Yes." Jaden looked toward the battle taking place on the lawn. "God, they're outnumbered. If anything happens to Leif or my dad, I don't know what I'll do."

Seeing how upset Jaden was helped bring Michaela out of some of the numbness that had descended over her. They were two women with no way to protect themselves as a group of wolves tore into each other with teeth and claws.

She looked around for something to use as a weapon, or at least as a deterrent. They might be werewolves, but they were still just wolves with the same weakness as the wild variety from the looks of it, though they were slightly bigger. Relying on her training from the zoo, she knew she should never confront an aggressive animal empty-handed. It was too bad there wasn't a tranquilizer gun nearby.

Michaela spotted the metal straight-edged rake learning against the brick wall of the house. She ran to it and then snatched it up. It wasn't much, but its points would hurt. She'd just turned to go back to Jaden when the other woman screamed.

"Dad! No!"

Michaela looked in the direction Jaden stared. A white wolf was pinned down at the back of his neck by the jaws of a darker one. Now that she'd convinced herself to think of them as just normal wolves, her fear evaporated. Having dealt with larger and potentially more dangerous animals at the zoo, she had no qualms about going in to help the white wolf she'd seen Miles shift into.

She ran to the pair, swung the rake at the darker wolf's head and knocked him away from the white one. He turned and snapped at her, but she shoved her makeshift weapon in his face. "Don't even try it. I've faced down a pissed-off tiger before, and you're nothing compared to that."

Michaela hovered over the white wolf as he slowly got up onto his feet. His assailant looked as if he wanted to try to come at her again, but a loud howl preceded a form covered in light brown fur launching itself at him. The fight between them was vicious and over quickly with the second wolf being the victor. After that, the battle wound down. It seemed Kye and his family were more skilled fighters than their combatants. They appeared to find a weakness in their opponents and took advantage of it.

"Thanks."

Michaela turned her head to see Miles once again human, standing where the white wolf had been. He bled from many places. "You're welcome."

"Weren't you afraid? Most mortals would think twice before wading into the middle of a wolf fight."

She shrugged. "I'm an animal keeper at the zoo. I deal with wild animals every day."

Miles threw back his head and laughed. "I have to say you're the perfect mate for a werewolf."

At the sound of her name being called, Michaela looked to see Kye in human form, standing over the defeated wolf. He had a few bite and claw marks on him, but he looked relatively unharmed. She dropped the rake and ran into his open arms.

"It's okay," he said as he held her close. "It's over."

"I should be losing my mind right now, but during the fight, all I could think about was what I'd do if something like this ever happened at the zoo. And that I needed a tranquilizer gun."

Kye laughed. "I hope you didn't want to tranq my ass."

She leaned back in his arms and looked at him. "Werewolf,

huh?"

"I had planned to tell you later tonight."

"Too late for that."

"Come on, let's go talk." He looked around them. "The others seem to have everything under control here."

Seeing Curtis and what was left of his group being tied up, she nodded and let Kye lead her away. She didn't say anything as he guided her into the house and then up to his room. Nor did she speak as he continued into the bathroom and shut them in.

"I'm going to make this short since Miles is still here and I don't want him to learn some of what I'm about to tell you. Besides being a werewolf, I'm over a thousand years old. I've waited a long time for you, my mate."

He proceeded to tell her what it meant to be his, how the mating bond formed between them the first time they'd made love and how with it in place they wouldn't be able to bear being apart.

"Now this is the part Miles can't ever know," Kye said. "As far as he knows, Jaden is the foretold one. She isn't. Roxie is. That's why we're her Protectors."

"What's the foretold one?"

"It's the individual who was prophesized to one day rule over all the werewolf packs. At one time, Miles wanted to control the foretold one to rule himself, using her as a figurehead. Since Jaden had taken on the role for his benefit, he no longer wants that, but it doesn't mean we can be any less vigilant when it comes to Roxie." He paused. "Being what she is, she can do things others of our kind can't. One of them is she can use a spell to turn a mortal into a werewolf." His gaze locked on Michaela's. "Do you know what I'm saying?"

She blinked a few times as understanding settled over her. "You want Roxie to use the spell on me so we can be mates in every sense of the word."

"Yes, but I won't push you. Just let me tell you that Eli, Ansley, Jaden and Braelyn already made that choice to be like their mates."

Michaela searched Kye's eyes, seeing the hope there that she'd agree to the spell. Did she want to become a werewolf? Looking at the man who'd come to mean so much to her, she realized the thought of having a couple thousand years with him instead of what she'd have as a mortal was more than she could have ever imagined.

Somehow, all she'd learned wasn't freaking her out. She wanted to accept it. Slowly, she nodded. "I'll do it. As long as I have you at my side, I can accept this new way of life."

He dragged her into his arms and crushed her against him. Kye kissed the top of her head. "You're my heart, Michaela. I'll make sure you never regret this for the rest of our days."

With all her heart and soul, she believed him. "You're mine, Kye."

The End

DIRK'S LOVE

Dirk has worked tirelessly to create an online dating service to help male werewolves find their mortal mates. Having hired a mortal female to assist him, when he meets her face-to-face for the very first time, he's smitten with her beauty and finds himself breathless as he realizes the very thing he's spent a lifetime looking for—his mate—is finally within his reach. Her proximity alone sets his mating urge off in an instant.

Ryann, completely absorbed with raising her precious son for the last two years, has been without a man in her life for far too long. When she sees Dirk in person for the very first time, and he reawakens the sexual cravings of her neglected body, she hungers not only for his touch, but also yearns for the day her new boss will think of her as more than just his employee. She doesn't have long to wait. It turns out Dirk has been searching for her his whole life.

CHAPTER ONE

irk walked into the upstairs room Roxie used as her office. The two of them had spent so many hours working on his secret project—including the time he was on duty protecting her—he felt as if he practically lived in the beautiful mansion she shared with her mate, Beowulf. Now that they'd completed what they'd worked so hard on, he didn't know if he should feel sad about it or not. He'd rather enjoyed his time brainstorming with her.

As she typed on her desktop computer, he smiled. Roxie was just as much an Internet junkie as he was. She was also an exceptional web designer. She'd taught him everything he knew about HTML and coding pages.

"Hey, Rox," he said as he stepped farther into the room.

She turned her head away from the computer monitor, her hands still moving on the keyboard. "Hi, Dirk. Are you ready for your big reveal?"

He groaned to himself. He still didn't think this was such a great idea, but Roxie had insisted. And since she was the foretold one who ruled over all the werewolf packs, he pretty much had to do whatever she said. Dirk was just one of her Protectors.

"I'm still not keen on it," he said. "The others are going to think I'm an idiot for doing this. You know that's the main reason I've kept my mouth shut about this project for the last year. And why I swore you to secrecy."

Roxie rose and walked around the desk until she stood in front of him. "There's no backing out. You should be proud of what you've accomplished. I think you came up with something that'll help a lot of male werewolves. If your brothers-in-arms can't handle it, then they're the fools. And I left Saskia out of that group on purpose. I know she'll side with me."

Saskia was the leader of the Protectors while Roan, Jager, Leif, Skylar, Kye and he made up the rest of the group. They were so close they'd basically formed their own pack and lived together in a mansion in Marin County.

"It's a given that Leif will say something. He won't be able to help himself. Jaden may have reined him back a bit, but he still talks shit when the mood strikes him, or if he wants to rile one of us up."

Roxie waved his concerns away with a flick of her hand. "Forget about Leif. If he knows what's good for him, he'll keep his comments to himself. You've worked very hard on this, and I won't let him spoil your moment. If he does try to be a jackass, I'll order him to shift into his wolf form, then use my magic to keep him like that for a day so I can chain his butt outside in the backyard."

Being the foretold one, Roxie had more magic inside her than the typical werewolf. Her trick of chaining a werewolf out in her backyard like a dog had been used a few times already. To be on the receiving end was humiliating, to say the least.

"That still doesn't make me feel any more confident," Dirk said.

Roxie punched him in the arm. "Stop doing that to yourself."

He rubbed the spot where she'd hit him. "Ow. And doing what to myself?"

"Feeling as if you should be ashamed. You should feel proud instead."

"Fine. I guess I'll do it your way, not that you've left me with any choice in the matter."

"No, I didn't. If I had, you wouldn't tell them."

Damn right he wouldn't have. He was nine hundred and fifty years old, and had spent most of his adult years — which were many — fighting with a sword. His little project was so beyond that it wasn't even funny. He was a warrior through and through, but this could quite possibly make him look like a big wuss in his brothers-in-arms' eyes.

Roxie turned back to her desk and picked up the closed laptop resting on its surface. "Come on, let's go downstairs and make your big reveal."

She brushed past him and headed out the door. Dirk slowly followed Roxie. He'd bite the bullet and get it over with as quickly as possible.

Once they reached the bottom of the stairs, he fell in behind her as she walked toward the living room where his entire "family" sat, waiting. More than one of them had asked him what this "meeting" was all about, but he'd given nothing away.

"About time you two came down," Kye said as Dirk and Roxie came to a stop in the middle of the room.

Kye sat on one of the couches while his mate, Michaela, was next to him. They'd been mated for only the last six months. The others in the room were Saskia and Eli, Roan and Ansley, Jager and Daylen, Skylar and Braelyn and Leif and Jaden. Jaden sat on her mate's lap while Leif's large hand rubbed her six-month pregnant belly. Roxie's mate, Beowulf, sat on the floor playing with their nine-month-old daughter, Nevaeh, and her toys. The gang was all there, and there would be no getting out of it now.

"Yeah, we wondered if you two got sidetracked upstairs and forgot about us," Roan said. "It wouldn't be the first time."

Roxie gave him a pointed stare and cleared her throat. She didn't respond to Roan's comment, and said, "You're all probably wondering why I asked you to come to this meeting."

Jager groaned. "Please don't tell me you're pregnant again."

Roxie sighed. "No, Jager, I'm not expecting another baby. This has to do with Dirk, not me."

Dirk felt all eyes turn his way. Stupidly, a wave of uncertainty washed through him. He had a feeling this was going to blow up in his face. He just knew it. He opened his mouth to tell Roxie to forget about what she'd planned, but she spoke again.

"It's finally time to reveal the project I've helped Dirk bring to fruition," she said with a smile.

She opened the laptop and shifted to a spot where everyone would be able to see it. The others leaned in for a closer look as

Beowulf picked up Nevaeh, then stood so he was nearer.

"Mate Connection. What the hell is that?" Jager asked, blunt as usual.

"Oh. Oh, I know," Ansley said. "It's an online dating service. Right?"

At Dirk's nod, Leif burst out laughing. It didn't help that the rest of his brothers-in-arms laughed along with him. The only males in the room who didn't were Beowulf and Eli, mostly because their mates looked at them, just daring them to join in. Dirk felt as if he should climb under a rock somewhere.

"Oh, god," Leif said between laughs. "An online dating service? Really? Couldn't you come up with something better than that?" He laughed again, but harder.

"Shut up," Roxie said with a loud growl. "All of you." The room instantly went silent. "Listen up, boneheads. No more laughing at Dirk or you'll get better acquainted with my backyard, if you know what I mean. It was seeing each one of you find your mates—your mortal mates—that prompted Dirk to come up with this idea to have a website where male werewolves can look around to find potential mortal women."

"I think that's a wonderful idea," Jaden said as she gave her mate a smack to the back of the head. Leif cringed in response.

The rest of the women quickly agreed, which made Dirk feel a trifle better. At least the females of his family sided with him. It was a start.

"Okay, I can see that having some merit," Skylar said. "What makes your service any different than the mortal ones already out there? Male werewolves could search them just as easily as yours."

"Good question," Roxie replied. She turned to Dirk. "Well, Dirk, why don't you answer Skylar since you haven't said a word yet."

He took a deep breath. "All right. What makes mine different is that the questionnaire the females have to fill out is geared more toward a male werewolf. It isn't obvious, but the answers the women give will determine whether or not they'd be acceptable to one of our kind."

"How did you go about compiling those kinds of questions?" Beowulf asked.

Dirk smiled. "It was easy enough. I hired a psychologist, who also happens to be a werewolf, to write them up for me. And I think she hit the nail right on the head."

"So I take it you're going to somehow get word of the website out to the packs," said Roan. "If it starts to take off, aren't you going to find it hard to keep up with your protection duties as well?"

"Not really. I've already hired an employee. She'll be working from home, and taking on some of the responsibilities."

"You've hired a woman?" Jager asked. "A mortal woman, I take it?"

Dirk nodded. "Yes, she's mortal. Her name is Ryann. Every time I've talked to her on the phone she seems like a real go-getter."

"You gave her the job without meeting her face-to-face?"

"Nowadays, especially with an Internet business, everything is done online. Even the hiring of employees," Dirk said. "Not that I should have to explain myself to you, Jager."

"Dirk, are you hoping you can meet your mate through it as well?" Daylen asked softly.

He nodded again. "Yeah, I am."

Being the last member of his family to become mated sucked. He hadn't said anything to any of them, but he yearned for what all of them had found. He hated being alone. Dirk had been doing a lot of searching for the one woman meant for him ever since his brothers-in-arms found their mates. So far, he'd come up empty-handed. Even Beowulf's nightclub, Wulf's Den, hadn't worked for him. Longing for his would-be mate, and wanting to find her, was just part of the reason he'd come up with the idea for his online dating service. He'd been the first person to fill out a Mate Connection questionnaire.

Ansley sighed. "I think you'll find her, Dirk. It sounds as if you have the whole site well on its way to doing what you set it up for. I wish you the best of luck with it."

"Thanks, Ansley."

Roxie closed the laptop. "Now that you all know, I guess this meeting is over." She turned to Dirk. "Don't you have another one to get to soon, Mr. Boss?"

He smiled. "I do. I'm meeting Ryann for lunch in about twenty minutes."

"Then what are you waiting for? Get going."

More than relieved to have this part of his day over, Dirk nodded, then turned and walked out of the room. He headed for the front door, thinking he'd have plenty of time to get to the restaurant ahead of Ryann. He wanted to be there before she arrived to organize his thoughts on how he wanted their first meeting in person to go.

It wasn't too far of a drive from Roxie and Beowulf's place. It was a nice and bright San Francisco day. Dirk slipped on a pair of sunglasses and then took the top down on his gray metallic BMW 335is convertible. He looked forward to seeing Ryann. They'd talked so much over the phone since he'd hired her two weeks before, he felt as if he'd known her for a lot longer than that. They worked well together. With her background, she was just the kind of person he needed to help with the service.

He pulled into the lot of the Japanese restaurant he'd chosen and then parked. Dirk had become hooked on sushi about six months before, and couldn't get enough of the stuff. He found himself coming to this place at least once a week to feed his new addiction.

After getting out of his car, Dirk walked to the entrance of the restaurant, stepped inside the vestibule, then pulled open the glass door that led to the main section. The place had a definite Asian flare to it. As usual, already quite a few people were there, eating. He'd learned early on to make sure he had a reservation.

Greeted by the hostess, he gave his name, saying he'd have another person joining him shortly. The woman led him to a booth and left two menus on the table. Dirk's stomach growled as he looked one over, promptly deciding what he'd order first. The thing he loved about this sushi place was that it was all-you-can-eat. Each menu item had a number, which had to be filled out on a form with the amount desired on a small slip of paper. The waitstaff — whoever happened to see it first — picked it up, and shortly after that, the freshly prepared food arrived at the table. Someone could order as much and as many things as they wanted, so long as they finished everything before ordering more. Not that he had any problem in that regard.

Dirk pulled in a deep breath, his mouth watering at the smell of raw fish, rice and the other items the restaurant served. Being a werewolf, he liked any kind of meat practically uncooked, so raw fish was right up his alley.

As Dirk tried to think through what he wanted to say to Ryann, he drew in another breath, then one more quickly after that. His whole body stiffened — along with his cock — when he detected a new scent added to the mix of others around him. He held the menu tighter as the one thing he'd longed to feel surged through him, roaring to life — his mating urge.

He looked up to find a woman standing at the side of the table, smiling. Dirk latched his gaze on to hers, unable to do anything but stare. She was gorgeous with long, black hair that fell over her shoulders. Friendly-looking light blue eyes gazed back at him. He filled his lungs again with her scent, reveling in the fact she was the one meant for him. His mating urge rode his ass hard, making it almost impossible to think beyond the need to claim her as his.

She stuck out her hand. "You must be Dirk. I'm Ryann."

Dirk stood and wrapped his much larger one around hers and shook it. He had to fight with himself not to yank her forward and devour her with his mouth. His cock throbbed in time with his rapidly beating heart, pushing against the zipper of his jeans.

"Nice to finally meet you, Ryann," he said in a voice that had gone husky as he forced himself to let go.

"It's nice to put a face to the voice. Just to start off, I have to apologize. My sitter bailed on me at the last minute. I hope you don't mind that I had to bring my son along. This is Tyler."

Dirk's gaze dropped to the small boy who stood next to Ryann, clutching her hand. The first thing that popped into his mind was — *Oh shit. My mate is already married.*

CHAPTER TWO

Ryann waited to see what Dirk's reaction would be after she told him about Tyler. When it came, she hadn't expected to see his face turn slightly white as he stared down at her son.

A bit uncomfortable, she waited for Dirk to say something first. She used the opportunity to study him closer. He was so good-looking she wouldn't have been surprised to find herself drooling over him. He had looks that would put a model to shame. And his body. *Damn.* His muscles filled out the formfitting black T-shirt and blue jeans he wore quite nicely. He also was tall, really tall. Ryann guessed him to be around six-foot-six. At five-foot-eight, there weren't too many men who could make her feel short, but he did. And throw in his long—past his shoulders—dark brown hair with blond highlights and dark green eyes, it was all she could do not to stare at him with her tongue hanging out.

Finally, Dirk brought his gaze back up to her face. His eyes were filled with such longing her knees weakened. He blinked, and it was gone. He motioned for her to take the banquette seat across from him.

"That's okay," he said in a deep voice. Once they were all seated, he added, "I didn't realize you had a son. Or that you were married."

Ryann made sure Tyler couldn't get at anything on the table that he could make a mess with before she turned her attention back to Dirk. "Well, that wasn't one of the questions you asked when I applied for the job. And I'm not, by the way."

"You're not what?"

"Married. Tyler's father and I've been divorced for two years. My ex decided he wanted out when Tyler was a year old. I guess that's what I get for wanting the whole marriage thing at twenty-one."

"How long were you married?"

"Three years." Ryann couldn't help noticing as she'd told Dirk about her ex he'd regained some color. If anything, he seemed to be more comfortable being around her and Tyler.

"Sorry to hear that."

She chuckled. "Don't be. It's worked out for the best, believe me. We have shared custody of Tyler, with Mack getting him every other weekend, but my ex is good for getting out of it when he has other plans."

"It must be hard on you, raising your son basically alone."

She shrugged. "I'm not going to lie and say it's all a cakewalk." Ryann quickly snagged the bottle of soy sauce Tyler had managed to grab off the table before he dumped it everywhere. "Having a three-year-old to chase after can be tiring. That's why I'm happy to work for you. I can spend more time with Tyler, and not feel as though half my wages are going for a sitter."

"Good save on the bottle," Dirk said with a smile. "You were the best candidate for the position." He glanced at Tyler. "Will he like anything here? We could have rescheduled for a better day."

"Thanks, and he'll eat fried rice and noodles. No, it's fine. You have no idea how much I've looked forward to this. I don't get out to do a lot of adult things, so I don't let the opportunity slip through my fingers when it comes along. I know, pretty pathetic, huh?"

Dirk chuckled. "Actually, no. I've been looking forward to this meeting as well. I feel as if I've known you for a long time through our phone conversations. And now that we've met, I look forward to getting to know you even better."

Ryann forgot to breathe as Dirk stared at her as if she were a piece of sushi on the menu. Her body instantly went up in flames, her pussy clenching, aching to be filled. It'd been so long since she'd been intimate with a man. The last one she'd slept with had been her ex-husband. Having a guy like Dirk showing interest in her was waking her sex-starved body from its extended hibernation.

Her lungs protesting the lack of oxygen, Ryann let out her breath and yanked her gaze from Dirk's. She focused on the menu in front of her. "So, do you see something that's turning your crank more than others?" She realized what she'd just asked could be taken in another context, and quickly added, "I mean the food."

"I know what you're asking. Yes, there is." Dirk paused. "And I don't mean the food."

Ryann jerked her head up to find Dirk giving her a sexy grin. Oh shit. Was he hitting on her? If he were, she was so out of practice it wasn't even funny. She racked her brain to think of something to say in return when Tyler reminded her she didn't just have herself to think about.

"Mommy," he whined. "I'm hungry."

"I know, buddy," she said. "I'll order something for you in a minute."

Dirk shifted his gaze to her son and held out his hand, palm up to him. "I never did say a proper hello to you, Tyler. I'm Dirk."

Tyler smiled and slapped Dirk's hand. "You're a lot bigger than my daddy."

Ryann groaned to herself. Tyler didn't have a lot of interaction with the male gender, except for his father and grandfather, her father. So he tended to compare other men to his dad. If Dirk were interested in her, he didn't need the constant reminder she'd been married before. Some guys didn't like the baggage an ex-husband entailed, especially one she'd had a child with. Not that she'd even dated a man since divorcing Mack. Raising Tyler had become her number-one priority.

Dirk grinned at her son. "I am, am I?"

Tyler nodded. "Uh-huh. You're super tall. I want to be really tall like you when I grow up."

"Well, then you'd better make sure you eat lots of lunch to help make you grow."

Tyler turned to Ryann. "Mommy, order me lots so I'll get bigger like Dirk."

She laughed. "All right."

Dirk filled out the slip of paper as she told him what she and Tyler wanted. Once a waitress grabbed it, silence reigned, except for the sound of Tyler playing with his toy car on top the table after she'd fished it out of her purse to keep him entertained.

"So—" she started.

"What—" Dirk said at the same time.

They laughed. "You can go first," she said.

"I just wanted to know what you'd be up to tomorrow afternoon."

"Nothing much. Why?" Ryann's heart beat a little faster. Was this Dirk's way of asking her out on a date? The idea that he might sent a little thrill rushing through her. He answered her, and she felt a bit of a letdown, not that she let it show.

"I've decided you need to have a better computer. The one you said you have really isn't up-to-date enough for the type of work you'll be doing for me. At least it won't be fast enough. So I've decided a new desktop comes with your job, at my expense. If you'll be around tomorrow, I'll buy one and bring it over. I'll even set it up for you."

"Really? You want to buy me a new computer?"

"Yes. I was thinking of an all-in-one with a twenty-three-inch touch screen. I recently bought myself one, and I love it. It's nice not having a tower and a ton of cables to deal with."

"I guess I can't turn down one of those. And if for some unforeseeable reason I have to leave my position, I'll be sure to give it back."

Dirk shook his head. "No, it's yours to keep." His gaze met hers again, and Ryann felt as if she were falling into it. "Though I really can't see ever letting you go."

She stared back at Dirk, feeling as if his gaze ate her up again. An ache throbbed deep inside her pussy. God, he turned her on with just one look. If they weren't in the middle of a restaurant, and she didn't have Tyler with her, Ryann would be tempted to throw herself at him. Professionalism be damned. She wanted him. Wanted to have some hot, dirty sex with him, something she'd been sorely missing in her life. Sometimes she wanted to feel like a sexy woman instead of a mommy. And she had a feeling he'd be more than willing to give her exactly what she longed for.

The first plates of their food arrived, and the spell that had taken her over broke. While they ate, the conversation centered more on Dirk's online dating service, which was the purpose of the whole lunch meeting. Ryann kept an eye on Tyler, thankful the mess he made with his food wasn't hers to clean up. She had to hand it to Dirk—he didn't bat an eye when some of Tyler's rice ended up flung to his side of the table.

Even though Ryann considered herself a big eater, Dirk put her to shame. She'd reached her limit long before he did. The last two rolls he'd ordered had just been placed on the table. He picked up one piece with his chopsticks and then popped it into his mouth, sighing with pleasure. It sent of shiver of desire down her back. She wondered if he'd make the same sound in bed. She quickly pulled her thoughts from that topic before they got out of hand.

Dirk swallowed before he asked, "Are you sure you've had enough?"

She nodded. "Definitely. I eat another bite and I'll blow up, but you go ahead."

He plucked up another piece. "Oh, I will. I'm addicted to this stuff. When I come here, I make sure I get more than my money's worth."

She laughed. "I bet you do. And I bet they're happy to see you go."

"Well, being so big," Dirk winked at Tyler, "I have a healthy appetite."

"I'm glad I'm not responsible for feeding you. You'd eat me out of house and home really quickly."

"To make sure that never happens, you'd just have to move in with me. That way, I'd be the one who'd have to feed you instead."

"What about me, Dirk?" Tyler chimed in. "Would you let me move in with you too?"

"Of course I would. I'd make sure you had your own room, and I have a huge backyard you could run around in all day if you wanted."

"Really?" Tyler asked excitedly. "Can my mom and me move in today?"

Ryann felt her face heat. "Tyler, Dirk was only joking. We really can't move into his house with him. Dirk's my boss. It's because of him I don't have to leave you during the day."

Tyler's face fell. "Oh."

Dirk reached across the table and ruffled Tyler's hair. "How about you come for a visit. Would that be okay?" He looked at Ryann. "If it'd be all right with your mom, that is."

"Don't feel as if you have to," she quickly said.

"I know. I want to. Besides, there could be times where we might have to work in person. Tyler is welcome to come along."

"Are you sure you want a three-year-old running around your place? He can get rambunctious. I'd feel bad if he ended up breaking something."

Dirk laughed. "You don't have to worry about that, and you'll see why when you come for your first visit."

"All right, don't say I didn't warn you."

After finishing the last of his rolls, Dirk asked, "How does sometime tomorrow afternoon sound for me to bring the computer? I'll give you a call when I'm on my way."

"That'll be fine. I guess I'll see you tomorrow then."

"Yes. Don't worry about the bill. I'll take care of it on my way out."

"Okay." Ryann slid out of the booth and took hold of Tyler's hand after he stood beside her. "Thanks for lunch. I'm glad we could finally meet face-to-face."

"You're welcome. And same here."

Not able to think of something else to add, Ryann turned Tyler toward the restaurant's entrance and walked away. As she pulled open the glass door, she commended herself for not turning around and looking at Dirk one last time. Even though he'd given her a couple toe-curling looks, that didn't mean anything. The way he looked, he didn't need a divorced woman who came with a child.

* * * *

Dirk waited until Ryann and Tyler walked out of the door before he signaled one of the waitresses to bring him the check. He slightly relaxed the hold he had over himself. He thought he'd done a great job of acting as if nothing out of the ordinary was happening while he'd sat across from Ryann. On the inside, that had been the furthest thing from the truth.

His mating urge rode his ass — hard. The whole time he'd been with Ryann, her scent had filled his head. What ramped it up even more was when he'd caught the perfumed smell of her arousal a few times. He was glad they'd been seated with a table between them. He swore he spent the entire meal with a hard-on, one that was just slowly going down. Not that his cock would behave now that Ryann had left. Until he claimed her as his mate, he had to look forward to walking around with an erection, or at least being semi-hard.

He took a deep breath. He already missed Ryann. When he'd at first thought she was married, he'd felt as if the fates were playing a cruel trick on him. She couldn't belong to another man and be his. With a child involved, there was no way in hell Dirk would've tried to come between Ryann and her husband. Regardless of how badly it'd affect him.

Once she'd said she was divorced, a sense of relief had surged through Dirk. There wouldn't be any other man standing between him and Ryann. His would-be mate already having a child didn't bother him in the least. He loved kids. That he'd have an instant family once he became mated to her was fine with him.

After leaving enough money to cover the bill and tip, Dirk left the restaurant. Once in his car, he headed in the direction of Marin County. There wasn't much point in returning to Roxie and Beowulf's place. He wasn't on duty to watch over Roxie today. She'd forced him to take a few days off since he'd spent more time at her house working on his online dating service than doing anything else.

Dirk arrived at the Protectors' mansion and then parked his car in the large detached garage before going inside. He stood in the foyer as voices came from the living room. From the fresh scents in the air, he knew Leif and Jaden were home, and Jaden's father, Miles, was around as well.

Dirk stepped into the living room and found all three of them there. Leif and Miles laughed at something, but quickly stopped when he walked into the room. Jaden sat on the couch next to her mate, taking turns scowling at the men. He had the sneaky suspicion the two males had been laughing about something to do with him.

His thoughts were confirmed when Miles said with a grin,

"Jaden and Leif were just telling me about your latest...endeavor. Did you get bored with your online trading before deciding to do something so...so different?"

He stared at the other man and scowled a bit. He still wasn't used to the idea of Miles being in his home whenever the man felt like it. As Saskia's true brother, Miles had been a Protector at one time. Then he'd gone to the dark side, wanting to find the foretold one himself to use whomever it was as a figurehead so he could rule over the werewolf packs. They'd considered him the enemy for a very long time. Now that Miles thought Jaden was that foretold one—knowing nothing about Roxie—he seemed to have turned over a new leaf. He wanted to take on some of the duties of protecting his daughter. If Miles were to ever find out Jaden was only posing as the one they were to watch over, Dirk had a feeling it'd all end very badly.

"I figured my service would be something a lot of male werewolves would find useful," Dirk said. He wasn't about to give more of an explanation than that, especially when Leif and Miles laughed again.

"Enough, the both of you," Jaden said over their laughter. "You're acting like two teenage boys instead of men who've lived to see a thousand years. I think Dirk had a great idea when he came up with this. He hopes he'll be able to find his mate through it." She looked directly at Miles. "And, Dad, I think you should be signing up to use it as well."

Miles stopped laughing and gave Jaden a shocked look. "What? You can't be serious."

This made Leif laugh even harder. "Miles, you should see your face," he said between gales of laughter. "It's priceless."

Miles and Jaden ignored Leif. Jaden sighed and rolled her eyes before she said, "Yes, I'm serious, Dad. Mom wasn't your mate. You loved her, yes, but you never had the mate bond with her. That means there's a woman somewhere out there who's meant for you. I'd like to see my father as happily mated as I am. You've been alone for too long."

Miles looked even more shell-shocked. "You want me to go on the Internet to find my mate?"

All this mate talk played havoc with Dirk's nerves. He was already having a hard time being apart from Ryann, knowing what she was to him. Having to wait twenty-four hours to see her again was going to be damn tough to go through. Though he had to admit Miles' reaction to Jaden telling him she wanted him to sign up for Mate Connection was humorous. Dirk decided to keep his mouth shut about it, figuring it'd only set Leif off again.

"What's wrong with that?" Jaden asked. "You'd be surprised how many people meet their future husbands and wives that way." She looked at Dirk. "You'd have no problem signing my dad up, would you, Dirk? That way both of you can hopefully find mates."

"Sure," he said. "If he'd be willing to fill out the questionnaire. I won't force him to do that."

"Then I choose not to," Miles interjected. "I'd rather do it the old-fashioned way by letting it happen all on its own."

Jaden shook her head. "So you'd be willing to wait years, maybe hundreds of them, to find her? Well, I think that's stupid when Dirk's service could help even the odds in your favor."

"Still not interested."

"What if it works?"

"Then you'd have to prove it to me." Miles looked at Dirk. "If he finds his mate through his online dating service, I'll sign up the very next day."

"You're on, Dad," Jaden quickly said.

Dirk had to say something. "Ah, Jaden, I'd hold off on that if I were you."

"Why? Please don't tell me you've changed your mind about finding your mate that way."

"It's not like that." He paused. Just thinking about Ryann ramped him up again, making his mating urge dig its claws harder into him. "Well, you see, I've already found her."

"What? You did? When? Who is she? Is she from your site?" Jaden barraged him with questions as she got off the couch to stand in front of him, wearing a wide smile.

He chuckled. "Slow down. One question at a time. First of all, she isn't one of the women who signed up for the service, though she's connected with it. It's Ryann, the woman I hired to assist me with running it."

Jaden scowled. "Wait a minute. Are you saying you've walked around this entire time in the throes of the mating urge and no one noticed? You hired Ryann a couple weeks ago, at least that's what you said."

"No, it hasn't been like that. And yes, it was that long ago that I first 'met' Ryann." Dirk made air quotes. "Remember, I didn't meet her face-to-face until this afternoon when we had lunch together."

"I guess I'm off the hook then," Miles said with a smile.

Jaden sighed. "Darn. It's too bad Ryann never filled out a questionnaire. We could've at least compared it to the one you did, Dirk, to see if the outcome would've been the two of you being a good match."

"Actually, she did," Dirk said.

"She did?"

"I wanted someone to test the site as if they were signing up. Since I hadn't told any of you about the service, I asked Ryann to do it. Once she did, I only looked it over to make sure everything had worked."

"Let's look at it then," Jaden said excitedly.

"We'd have to go upstairs to my room to use my computer."

Jaden hooked her arm through his. "That's fine." She looked over her shoulder. "Come on, Dad and Leif. And no backing out now, Dad."

Leif stood, then came and tugged Jaden away from Dirk, tucking her under his arm. Miles also gained his feet before he followed them out of the room. Dirk heard him mutter under his breath, asking what he'd gotten himself into.

Upstairs in his room, Dirk walked to the desk he'd set up in the corner and then sat behind it. He moved the mouse to turn off the screensaver, then launched his browser. It only took him a few clicks to get into Mate Connection and his profile. He clicked on the link that would take him to his possible matches. Since he really hadn't gotten the service out to the public yet, seeing Ryann listed hadn't made him think anything of it. He thought it was a glitch he'd have to work out, that the program had put her there because she was the only female who'd signed up.

Dirk clicked on Ryann's name and was instantly brought to her profile. There wasn't a picture of her since he'd told her not to worry about it. He'd been more concerned about whether the info she filled out in the questionnaire had worked. He'd ignored the bottom of the page on both of their profiles where it gave a percentage of how compatible she'd be with him. He went back to his to look. It was ninety-nine point nine.

He pointed to the number on the screen. "Holy shit, it worked." Dirk had it programmed so it would, but there had been a small part of him that had thought it wouldn't be that accurate.

"There you go," Jaden said behind him as she leaned over his shoulder for a closer look at the screen. Once she straightened, she turned to face her father. "No point in waiting, Dad. Dirk already has the website open, so you might as well take his seat and fill out the form."

Dirk spun his steno chair around and then stood. He gestured for Miles to take his spot. Miles didn't look at all happy about being forced into signing up. Even though this man had been an asshole for hundreds of years, Dirk couldn't help feeling a smidge sorry for him.

"Look, Miles, if you really don't want to do this, then don't. There's no point if you aren't willing to go through the whole process," he said.

Miles shook his head. "No, it's fine. If this is what Jaden wants, I'll do it." He smiled. "She might be my daughter, but she's still the foretold one, after all. I have to do what she wants, since she rules and all that."

Dirk, Leif and Jaden laughed quietly. Dirk knew what was going through the others' minds, because the same thought ran through his—Jaden didn't rule.

Miles slowly sat on the chair and sighed as he turned to face the computer.

Leif laughed, and said, "It's not as if you're a dead man walking, Miles. Who knows, maybe you won't find anyone this way either."

Jaden scowled at her mate. "Don't say that or you'll jinx him for sure."

"Whatever." Leif looked at Dirk. "I'm going to leave you three to it. Once you're done, we can go out back and get some sword practice in. I know you must be feeling keyed up with the mating urge riding your ass. I remember what it was like."

Dirk nodded. "All right. I'll meet you in the backyard in a bit."

After Leif left, Dirk got Miles set up on the computer before he backed up a bit to watch father and daughter while Miles filled out the questionnaire. He saw the love the ex-Protector had for Jaden was real. It was in his eyes for anyone to see every time Miles looked at her. And becoming a grandfather seemed to bring more and more of the old Miles back, the man he'd been when they'd first formed the Protectors. Dirk had liked him then. They all had. He just hoped for Saskia's sake, and especially Jaden's, that Miles didn't revert back to what he'd been. It'd more than likely break the hearts of the two women.

CHAPTER THREE

The next day Ryann finished packing the last of Tyler's things he'd need over the weekend at his dad's into his backpack. Mack was supposed to pick him up after he finished work. So far, she hadn't gotten any phone calls from him to say otherwise, so she figured he'd still be taking Tyler.

She left the backpack in Tyler's bedroom and went to the living room. Her son sat on the floor in the middle of the room with a pile of building blocks surrounding him. He snapped the plastic pieces together to form a tall tower. Once he had it as tall as he wanted, he'd knock it down just to build it again. One of his favorite pastimes.

Tyler looked up when he noticed her watching him. "Mommy, when's Dirk coming?"

She smiled and shook her head as she sank onto the floor to join him. He'd done nothing but talk about Dirk since they'd had lunch with him the day before. And Tyler wasn't the only one who seemed obsessed with him, either. Ryann hadn't been able to get Dirk out of her mind. The thought of him coming to her apartment excited her—a lot. More than it should. She had to keep reminding herself he was her boss. He'd given her a great job, and she didn't want to do anything to screw it up. It was ideal for her and Tyler.

"Well, when is he?" Tyler asked again.

"It shouldn't be too much longer. It's after lunch, so I suspect he'll come sometime this afternoon."

"I hope he comes before Daddy does. I want to play blocks with Dirk."

"Now don't be disappointed if he doesn't. Remember, he's coming here for a reason. He's giving me a brand new computer for my job with him."

"I know. He still might. I'll even ask nicely."

Ryann leaned across and gave Tyler a big kiss. "I'm sure you will."

At that moment, someone buzzed up to her apartment. She had a feeling it was Dirk since Mack wasn't expected for hours yet. She stood, then walked to the panel by the apartment door before she pushed the intercom button.

"Hello?"

"Hi, Ryann. It's Dirk. Can I come up? I have the computer with me."

"Sure, I'll buzz you in. Do you need help bringing it all up?"

"No, I can manage."

"All right."

She hit the button to let Dirk in. She unlocked the apartment door and waited there for him. At the prospect of seeing him again, her heart had sped up. Ryann resisted the urge to reach up and fix her hair. It wouldn't have mattered if it were stuck up on end. He wasn't there for a date. She took a deep, calming breath. She'd keep her cool and not stare at him like a sex-deprived woman who hadn't slept with a man in years. Wait a minute, that *was* exactly who she was.

A short time later, Dirk knocked. Ryann opened the door and then held it as he stepped inside, carrying a box that was large, but not very wide. She shut and locked it behind him before she turned to face him. Tyler had already come to them.

"So this is the computer," she said. "Is that all of it?"

Dirk smiled. "Yes. I told you I'd be getting you an all-in-one."

"Lemme see, lemme see, lemme see," Tyler chanted.

"Relax, Tyler," Ryann said. To Dirk, she added, "Come on, I'll take you to where my other one is set up. We just have to switch them out. I'm sure that must be getting heavy."

"It's not that bad. Lead away."

She headed to the room that was hers. Dirk followed her. Tyler suddenly pushed past her once they reached the doorway and ran to the small computer desk tucked in the corner.

"Here, Dirk," he said. "It goes here."

"Well, thank you, Tyler," he replied as he set the box on the floor. "How would you like to help me move the old computer?"

Her son nodded enthusiastically. "I'd like that. I'm strong too." Tyler lifted his skinny little arm and flexed his biceps.

Dirk squatted in front of him and squeezed her son's muscle. "Oh, you are." He stood. "Let's get started."

Ryann shifted out of the way as Dirk and her son worked together. Dirk was good with Tyler. He didn't get impatient with the three-year-old's incessant questions, unlike Tyler's father. What she'd learned of Dirk from talking to him on the phone almost every day for the last couple weeks, and now seeing how he was with Tyler, she knew he was the type of man she'd want as a stepfather to her son. He was patient, gentle and kind. All the things her little boy needed. Not that she thought that would ever happen.

Dirk bent over, and Ryann's gaze landed directly on his tight ass. His jeans molded it to perfection. She bit her bottom lip to keep the moan inside that threatened to bubble up. She imagined his body was a piece of art hidden underneath his clothes. The idea of stripping him naked to see it sent her pulse racing. Her pussy clenched at the thought of seeing his cock, hard and ready.

It was around that time that Ryann remembered they were inside her bedroom, and the bed became a looming presence. If Tyler were gone with his dad right now, she'd do her damnedest to let Dirk know she was more than interested in him. Short of jumping his bones and having her way with him, that is.

Dirk suddenly straightened, turned his head and looked over his shoulder at her. His nostrils flared as he took a deep breath. His gaze latched on to hers, making her pussy clench again at the intensity that lurked in his eyes. It was as if he'd known what dirty thoughts she'd had about him.

Ryann quickly broke eye contact with Dirk and set her attention on Tyler, who was busy taking the old keyboard off the sliding tray on the computer table. When she looked back at Dirk, he'd again turned his focus to what he'd been doing.

Since the new computer was so easy to set up, it didn't take Dirk long to get it up and running. Ryann came closer to examine it. It was one she'd looked at before, but had thought she'd have to wait a few years to get.

"Well, do you want to give it a go?" Dirk asked.

Ryann blinked and tried to pull her mind out of the gutter as she took what he said in a totally sexual meaning. "Sure."

She walked past Dirk to sit in the steno chair in front of the computer desk. Since he didn't move—if anything, she swore he took a half step in her direction—her side brushed against his on her way by. Her body reacted as if he'd touched her intimately. Her pussy grew wet while her nipples tightened into stiff peaks.

As she sat, Dirk drew in another deep breath, then let it out on what sounded damn close to an animalistic growl. With Tyler in the room, she decided to act as if she hadn't heard.

She reached up and touched the screen, launched the browser and checked her e-mail. After going to a few more websites, including Mate Connection, Ryann spun the chair around to face Dirk. He expectantly looked at her.

"Thanks, Dirk," she said. "I love it. It's so much faster than my other one."

He gave her a smile that just about melted all her bones. "I knew you would."

Ryann's gaze met Dirk's as she looked at him, and she felt as if she were falling into his eyes. The heated stare he'd given her the day before at the restaurant was back. It made her breath catch. Her body, so long denied, ached to feel him skin-to-skin. She gave herself a mental shake. She was only working herself up for nothing.

Tyler stepped to Dirk's side and took hold of his hand, giving it a few tugs. "Are you done, Dirk? I want you to play blocks with me."

The spell broken, Dirk looked at her son. "Sure, buddy. I'd love to." He turned his gaze to Ryann. "As long as it's okay with your mom if I hang around longer."

Ryann stood. "Of course you can. Stay as long as you want." Hell, he could stay overnight if he wanted to, in her bed, while she joined him.

"Hurray," Tyler yelled as he pulled on Dirk's hand, trying to steer him out of the room.

She chuckled softly as Dirk allowed Tyler to tow him away. At least if anything ever did happen between her and Dirk, she wouldn't have to worry about her son not liking him. If anything, Tyler was just as taken with him as she.

Ryann followed them into the living room. Dirk didn't seem to have a problem with sitting on the floor as he took the blocks Tyler handed him. She sat on the couch and watched. It was a scene she'd like to see happen more often. Her son hadn't had much male influence in his short life. Mack was useless as a father, really. He did the basics and nothing more.

Time slipped away from her as Tyler and Dirk built tower after tower. Tyler was particularly thrilled when Dirk used his tall height to build one as high as the number of blocks they had would allow. Before she knew it, the sound of her apartment buzzer going off could be heard.

She looked at the clock on the digital TV box and realized how late it'd gotten. It had to be Mack. Without a word, Ryann went to the panel on the wall and pressed the intercom. At the sound of her ex's voice, she buzzed him up.

Ryann turned back to the living room, and said, "That's your dad, Tyler. Time to put the blocks away and get your things for your weekend with him."

Tyler groaned. "Do I have to go? I'd rather stay here with Dirk."

She shook her head. "Sorry, you do. It's only for two nights and then you're back home again. I'm sure Dirk will come see you some other time."

There was a loud knock that signaled Mack's arrival. Knowing how he didn't like her keeping him waiting in the hall, she opened the door and let him in. He sailed into the apartment as if he owned the place.

"Is Tyler ready?" he asked without even saying hello.

"Just about," she replied coolly.

Ryann left Mack at the door and went to the living room. Dirk was just finishing helping Tyler put away his blocks. Once that chore was done, he stood as Tyler rushed off to his bedroom to get his backpack.

"Who the hell are you?" Mack asked in a rude tone.

She turned back to face her ex. Dirk came to stand at her side. "Not that it's any of your business, this is Dirk."

Mack stared at Dirk, doing his usual act of trying to intimidate someone he felt threatened by. "Do you really think it's a good idea to have a strange man around my son, Ryann?"

"He may be a stranger to you, Mack, but he isn't to me. So cut it out."

"Then who exactly is he?"

Before she could answer, Dirk spoke up. "I'm Ryann's new boss." He then did something Ryann hadn't expected at all. He put an arm around her shoulders and tucked her tightly against his side. "I'm also the man who intends to take your place in her life."

Her head snapped up to gaze at Dirk. Had she heard him correctly? He didn't look at her, but continued to stare at Mack as if he were a bug he'd like to squash.

"Is that so?" Mack asked in a hard tone. "You'll have some pretty big shoes to fill."

"I'm sure I can manage since I'm bigger than you are, according to Tyler."

Just then, Tyler came back into the room, dragging his backpack behind him. He walked to his dad and sighed dramatically. "I guess I'm ready to go."

Mack took Tyler's backpack and ignored him. His gaze stayed on Ryann and Dirk. "So what are you going to do for the rest of the day?" He directed his question at Ryann. "And the rest of the weekend?"

She bit back a retort along the lines that he hadn't cared in the past, so why should he now? "As I said before, it's really none of your business."

"The hell it isn't. I'll have Tyler. I need to know where you'll be if anything should happen. Aren't you always telling me I should be a better parent? I'd think wanting to know what my son's mother is up to in case there's an emergency would classify as such."

Ryann knew it had nothing to do with that at all. "Fine, since you're obviously not going to back down, I'll be—"

Before she could finish her sentence, Dirk cut in. "She'll be with me all weekend. I'm going to take Ryann out for a nice dinner tonight and tomorrow. The rest of the time, well, I'm not going to say since Tyler's in the room."

Images of what Dirk had just insinuated flitted through Ryann's mind—them naked, having hands-down great sex. She told herself he was more than likely saying those things and acting possessive of her for Mack's benefit. None of what he'd said was real, but that didn't stop her body from thinking so. It was practically jumping up and down in excitement. Not wanting to spoil any of the effect, she kept her features even as she stared at her ex, showing none of the roiling emotions deep inside her.

Mack glared at her, showing her exactly how much he didn't like anything Dirk had said. That caused anger to quell some of her arousal. How dare he be jealous now? That was exactly what had him so upset. It was okay for her ex to hop from one woman's bed to another, not caring how she felt about it, but when it came to her, he had double standards. It was quite an eye-opener for her, though it really wasn't that much of a shock. It proved Mack might not want her anymore, but he sure as hell didn't like that someone else did.

Her ex took Tyler's hand. "You'd better be here when I drop Tyler off on Sunday." With those parting words, Mack led their son out of the apartment, shutting the door behind them harder than he needed to.

Ryann sighed, ready to apologize to Dirk, and to thank him for what he'd tried to do, basically saying he was her new boyfriend. His arm stayed around her, still holding her tight. She turned to look him in the face and all the air rushed out of her lungs. He stared at her with what she could only describe as intense desire. For one brief moment, she thought his eyes took on a muted glow, but he blinked and it was gone.

She swallowed, doing her best not to show her body's reaction. "I have to apologize for—"

Dirk cupped the side of her face and cut off her words with his lips. Her body erupted into flames as he kissed her as if he'd never get enough of her. All she could do was hang on to his waist and hope he didn't stop.

CHAPTER FOUR

Dirk turned Ryann in his arms so she faced him and deepened his kiss. He pushed his tongue between her lips and bit back the growl that hovered near the surface at the taste of her. He was sure he was going too fast for her, but he couldn't hold himself back.

He hadn't meant for it to go so far. He'd only thought to show her ass of an ex-husband that Ryann wasn't going to be alone for much longer. Dirk had hated the way Mack had waltzed into the apartment, barely being civil to Ryann. He'd seen plenty of men like Mack, who thought they were god's gift to women, and that the opposite sex was only good for one thing.

Dirk pulled his soon-to-be mate closer and pressed his erection against her stomach. God, he wanted her. Right there, right now. Having smelled the scent of Ryann's arousal off and on since he'd arrived at her place, it'd played havoc with his control. He was well into the throes of his mating urge, and each day he didn't claim her as his it'd only increase. He'd had erotic dream after erotic dream of her during the night. He'd awakened this morning with his cock achingly hard. Even though it hadn't done anything to relieve him, which he'd known it wouldn't, he'd brought himself to release in the shower.

Now with his would-be mate in his arms, her kissing him back, he only felt the pounding need to make her his. Dirk rocked his lower body into her, unable to hold back. She perfectly fit against him, as if they'd been made as a matching pair. The scent of her arousal increased with each second that went by. The urge to strip her out of her clothes and lick every inch of her was almost too strong to ignore.

Realistically, he should slow things down. He'd gone from just being Ryann's boss to getting hot and heavy with her. He bet she thought he'd only put on an act for Mack. To her, this must've come totally from left field.

He was about to lift his head, but Ryann had other ideas. She shoved her hands up the back of his T-shirt and dragged her nails along his skin. She sucked on his tongue at the same time, just ramping him up even more. Okay, so she didn't want to take things down a notch. He was all for giving her what she wanted.

Dirk lifted one of his hands to cover her breast. He rubbed his thumb across her nipple, feeling it grow taut beneath her shirt. Ryann nipped his bottom lip, causing a low growl he couldn't hold back to rumble out of him. He couldn't get himself too worked up. He had to keep his head. Fully making love to her now would only make a mess of things. They could fool around and bring each other to release another way, though.

He rested his hands on her waist, then slowly pushed up the sides of her T-shirt. He skimmed his palms along her soft skin the higher he went. Once he reached her breasts, Ryann let him go and lifted her arms above her head for him to pull her shirt off all the way.

After doing just that, Dirk paused to look at what he'd bared. Ryann wore a silky-looking white bra that slightly pushed up her more-than-a-handful breasts. He could just see a hint of her rosy nipples through the thin material. His cock twitched as he thought of seeing more of her curvy body.

Dirk looked back at Ryann's face. Her eyes appeared heavy, and her cheeks were flushed with her growing desire. He reached up and ran his thumb along her bottom lip, which was puffy from his kisses.

"I want you to know I'm not taking advantage of the situation," he said in a husky voice. "What I told Mack is true. I really do want to spend the weekend with you. Take you out for dinner and whatever else you'll let me do."

Ryann smiled. "I hoped you would, though I must admit I thought you were putting on a show for my ex."

He dropped his hand to one of her breasts and circled the nipple with his index finger. She sucked in a breath. "No, I wasn't," he said. "Since I first saw you yesterday in the restaurant, I haven't been able to stop thinking about you. I even dreamed about touching and tasting you."

She moaned. "I'm not going to stop you from doing that. It's been so very long since I last had a man in my bed."

Dirk bent his head down and kissed the corner of her mouth. "How long?"

Ryann brushed his lips with hers. "Mack. He was the last man I've slept with."

"Then that's something I have to remedy."

He gathered her close and took her mouth in a heated kiss once again. Dirk picked her up off her feet and carried her to her bedroom. He didn't put her down until he had her stretched out in the middle of the bed. He followed her down to the mattress, coming to rest on his side next to her. He looked at her and still found it hard to believe she'd finally come into his life.

With featherlight kisses, Dirk worked his way across Ryann's cheek, down to her jaw and side of her neck. She turned her head away to give him better access. One of her arms came up, and she clutched his biceps. He licked and sucked a path to the hollow of her throat where he lingered for a few seconds longer, dragging her scent deeper into his lungs.

Once again finding himself in contact with her chest, he reached under her and undid the clasp of her bra at her back as he laved a taut nipple through the material. It only took a couple tugs to remove the piece of clothing and bare her beautiful breasts to his sight. The tight peaks that tipped them were a rosy pink, just begging for him to suck them. Dirk flicked one with the tip of his tongue before he opened his mouth and took it inside. Ryann arched her back on a moan, pressing closer.

Dirk switched to the other side, showering that nipple with the same attention. His cock pressed painfully against the zipper of his jeans. He was so hard he longed to open his pants to free his erection. Instead he ignored it, wanting to give Ryann pleasure, focusing totally on her needs.

She shoved a hand up the front of his shirt. "Take this off," she said in a soft voice. "I want to touch you too."

Dirk shifted so he kneeled while straddling her thighs, grasped the back of his T-shirt and yanked it off. He tossed it over the side of the bed, not looking at where it landed. Ryann sat up and placed a kiss to the center of his chest. He breathed at a rapid pace as she continued to explore him with her lips and tongue. It felt so damn good to have his would-be mate touching him like that.

She licked one of his nipples as she dropped a hand to the bulge in his jeans. She stroked him through the material from root to tip. Ryann continued to fondle him until Dirk thought he was going to lose his mind. She undid his pants and touched his cock with nothing to hinder her.

Dirk had thought to make Ryann come first, but he found it hard to get back on track when she fisted his shaft and pumped up and down, squeezing tight. He was having a hard enough time not pushing her flat onto her back, tearing her jeans off and sinking his aching dick into her warm, wet pussy.

Lost in a haze of desire, Dirk did nothing to stop Ryann when she shoved his jeans down past his hips. Knowing his eyes had to be mutedly glowing now—something he had no control over when he became very aroused or angry—he shut them, not wanting her to see. They soon snapped open at the sensation of her circling the head of his cock with her tongue.

"Christ," he groaned. "That feels so good."

"Then you'll like this."

Ryann took his dick inside her mouth and sucked him as far as she could take him. Dirk's eyes practically rolled back in his head in ecstasy. He looked to see her head bobbing up and down as she took him in and out. As she raised her eyes to peer at him, he quickly shuttered his to mere slits.

His cock grew harder, his orgasm pushing ever nearer to the surface. God, he didn't want Ryann to stop pleasuring him in that way. He wanted to come, give her everything he had. Being a werewolf, he wouldn't lose his erection after climax. He could stay hard for hours at a time, unlike his mortal counterparts.

Dirk rocked his hips, matching the pace she set. Just before he was about to reach the point of no return, he ground out, "Ryann, you're going to make me come."

In response, she sucked his cock harder and used her hand to squeeze him at the base of his shaft. That was all he needed to push him into his release. He moaned at the pure pleasure of it and came as she kept him inside her mouth.

After the last spasm took him, Ryann released his still-hard cock. Her gaze remained locked on it. "No recovery time?" she asked.

In answer, Dirk used his body to push her back onto the bed. He nuzzled the crook of her neck as he worked on getting her out of her jeans. "No. Now it's my turn to pleasure you."

The pants were sent sailing to the floor, and he only took a few seconds to see that Ryann's panties matched the bra she'd worn before they too followed. He wasted no time working his way down her body, learning it with his lips as he went. The scent of her arousal drove him crazy. He had to have a taste of her — *now*.

He used his shoulders to push her legs farther apart as he settled between them. He growled softly at the sight of her pussy all wet for him. He bent his head and dragged the flat of his tongue along the opening to her body. Another growl rumbled out of him. Her taste rivaled her scent, both going straight to his head. He was pretty sure he'd never get enough of touching and tasting Ryann.

Dirk spread her pussy lips and licked her from bottom to top, circling her clit, then sucked on it. Ryann moaned as she raised her hips, rocking against his mouth. He pushed a finger and then another inside her, moving them in and out. He alternated between licking and sucking on the bundle of nerves that were the center of her pleasure. Her inner walls clenched around the digits he used to work her.

"Mmm, yes," Ryann moaned. She panted, "So close."

He slightly lifted his head, continuing to move his fingers in and out of her. "Let go. I want to feel you come on my hand."

Dirk looked up her body to find Ryann had her eyes closed with her hands tightly fisted in the sheets under her. She breathed in short pants. He angled his strokes higher so he hit her G-spot and pushed her into climax. Her pussy rhythmically clenched and unclenched around his plunging fingers. He let out a sound that was a combination of a groan and a growl, wishing it were his cock deep inside her, riding out her orgasm.

Dirk ignored his dick, which throbbed once again, and rose between Ryann's legs. He wrapped his arms around her before he rolled to his back, taking her with him. She ended up sprawled atop him. The perfect place where he wanted her.

Slowly, Ryann's breathing returned to normal. She ran her fingers up and down his sides as she lay there with her head pillowed on his chest. He moved his hand in circles on her back.

Ryann eventually lifted her head and looked at him. "Are we stopping?"

"For now." Dirk laughed at the disappointed expression that formed on her gorgeous face. "Don't look at me like that."

She wiggled, his erection trapped between them. "Do we have to? You're still ready to go, if you know what I mean. The oral sex was great and all, but you're looking at a woman who's done without it for far too long. You woke up the beast, so you have to feed it now."

He chuckled. "The beast?"

"Yeah, you know, my urge to have sex. I've kind of suppressed it for the last couple years, being busy raising Tyler on my own and all. After this, I don't think that's going to work anymore."

Dirk cupped her face and brought her mouth to his. He kissed her thoroughly before he let her up for air. "Well, the beast is going to have to be satisfied with the taste it got. I want us to spend more of today together, talking, before I take you to bed and not let you out of it for maybe a day."

Ryann groaned. "Do you have any idea what you're doing to me? We've done nothing but talk to each other for the last two weeks."

"Yeah, but only over the phone. Plus, we really didn't discuss anything personal. It was mostly about the website. I still want to take you out for dinner. If I let this go any further, that won't be happening, I can assure you."

She sighed dramatically. "All right, you win. What do you have in mind to fill the rest of the time?"

Dirk kissed the tip of her nose before he slid out from under her and got off the bed. He quickly tucked his still-hard cock inside his jeans and then did them up before he turned to face Ryann. She lay on the mattress in all her naked glory, making him almost rethink what he'd just told her. Almost.

"I thought we could work on some ads for the launch of the website," he said, doing his best to hide the fact that seeing her like that, stretched out in open invitation, made him horny as hell.

She smiled coyly. "Are you absolutely sure that's what you'd rather be doing? We could always work on them sometime later."

Ryann didn't know it, but she played havoc with his good intentions of easing her into his world first before taking her as his mate. She had no idea how much he wanted to climb back onto that bed and finish what they'd started. Already, his mating urge had dug its claws even deeper into him because he'd only come in her mouth.

Instead, Dirk forced those thoughts away. "Positive. I'm not going to mess up what we've started."

"Fine," she said with a pout as she slid from the bed. "Have it your way, but all I have to say is we're off to a pretty good start, in my opinion."

He was about to answer her when his cell phone rang. Dirk reached inside his front jeans pocket and took it out. Seeing the number, he silently groaned to himself. It didn't take a brainiac to figure out why she called.

He hit the button to answer, and said, "Hello, Roxie."

"Good, you answered," she replied. "That must mean I'm not too late."

"Too late for what?"

"To make sure you don't forget about my rules when it comes to mortal mates. I know Ryann is yours. Since you're the last of the Protectors to get matched up, I'm going to make sure you do everything by the book."

He sighed. "So far so good. Okay?" Dirk followed Ryann's movements as she gathered up her clothes before she put them on. With each bit of skin she covered, he wanted to groan in disappointment.

"I guess, but the question is, how long will that last?" Roxie asked. "All your brothers-in-arms caved. Are you with Ryann now?"

"Yes."

"What are the two of you doing for dinner?"

"I'd planned to take Ryann out somewhere."

"Come to my place. Have dinner with Beowulf and me. Jager

and Daylen will be here as well."

"I don't know, Rox. I promised I'd take her someplace nice."

He was met with a short silence before Roxie said, "Are you insinuating my house isn't? Or that I'm not a good cook? You've eaten enough of my meals to know that's not the case."

"You know that's not what I meant. Gee, don't bite my head off or anything."

"Then you two will come over. And just so you know, that's an order from the foretold one."

"I guess my answer has to be yes, doesn't it? Since you really haven't given me much choice. I'm still going to ask Ryann first if it's all right with her."

Dirk covered the mouthpiece of his cell with his hand and spoke to his soon-to-be mate. "It's Roxie, and she's invited the two of us to come over and have dinner with her and her husband, Beowulf. I know it won't be just the two of us going out for a meal, but it should be fun." Not. He had a feeling Roxie would be watching him like a hawk to make sure he followed her rules.

Ryann nodded. "Sure, I'd love to. I know she's a good friend of yours, and that she helped you set up Mate Connection."

He pulled away his hand, then said into his phone, "Rox, Ryann said she's fine with it. So I guess we'll see you for dinner. What time do you want us over?"

"How about we have a late meal, say around seven? That way I can get the baby to bed beforehand so I can eat with no interruptions."

"Sounds good. We'll be there. Bye."

Dirk ended the call and then put his cell phone back into his pocket. He closed the distance between him and Ryann and wrapped his arms around her waist to hold her close.

"Thanks for agreeing to go over to Roxie's. She was quite insistent about it. Knowing her, if I refused, she would've just kept calling until she'd worn me down. She really does want to meet you."

Ryann laughed. "No worries. So, what time are we going over there?"

"She wants us to arrive at seven."

Ryann went on tiptoes and kissed his chin. "Then we'd better get cracking on those ads you want to work on. Maybe we should have a little something to snack on now to tide us over until then. I make some mean nachos."

Dirk smiled. "I'm not one for turning down food."

As he walked with Ryann out of the bedroom, he hoped Roxie wouldn't hover over him too much this evening. He loved her like the sister he never had, but the state he was in, he'd only be able to stand so much.

CHAPTER FIVE

Ryann sat in the passenger side of Dirk's BMW convertible with the top down, enjoying the wind in her hair as he drove them to Roxie's place. Since it wouldn't be dark for another couple hours, and he'd asked if it was okay if he put the top down, she'd quickly agreed. She'd never ridden in a convertible before or a BMW, for that matter. She had had a feeling her new boss had money, considering some of the things he'd said while they'd talked on the phone. The first and foremost giveaway had been the fact he lived in Marin County.

Dirk sent a quick look her way before he focused back on the road. "Is it too windy for you?"

Ryann tucked her hair behind her ears. "No, it's fine."

"Just let me know if it is and I'll put the top up."

"I will."

They drove in silence for a little while until Ryann noticed the neighborhood they were in. "Ah, I take it Roxie is rich like you."

He gave her a quick smile. "You could say that, but mostly because of Beowulf. You could say he comes from very old money."

"If that's the case, I hope he isn't one of those stuck-up rich people."

Dirk laughed. "I can assure you Beowulf is nothing like that. He's a pretty laid-back guy. He even owns a nightclub. You

493

might've heard of it. Wulf's Den?"

Ryann shifted in her seat to better face Dirk. "Are you kidding me? I've heard of Wulf's Den. Where I used to work, that's all the single girls talked about. How the hottest guys could be found there. Like off the pages of *GQ* hot. I think some of them went to the club every Saturday night, hoping to get lucky with one."

"Yeah, it does have a reputation for that," he said with a chuckle. "Beowulf says it's very good for business. So did any of those girls hook up with one of the guys?"

"Only one, supposedly."

"What do you mean by that?"

"Well, she came back to the office that Monday, bragging about how the guy could keep it up for hours, even after he came repeatedly. We, of course, thought she was full of crap." Ryann looked at Dirk's profile. "After what we shared in my apartment, I'm starting to rethink that. She could've very well told the truth. Though I think I might have to do a little more research into it before I fully believe it. Do some testing of that theory on my own."

The glance Dirk shot her was heated, making a thrill shoot through her from her head to her toes.

"You can use me as your guinea pig any time you want," he said huskily. "I'm sure you'll be more than satisfied with the results."

If they hadn't been in a car, driving on the road, Ryann would've jumped him and thrown herself on top of Dirk. Her pussy grew wet as her imagination ran wild with all the things she'd do to him to test her theory. She was so very tempted to tell him to turn the car around and go back to her apartment, to forget about Roxie's dinner invitation. From Dirk's tight expression, she had a feeling he'd have no problem going along with it.

His knuckles turned white as he gripped the steering wheel tighter. "God, you have no idea how much you're killing me here. If it were anyone but Roxie, I'd be saying the hell with it."

"She wouldn't understand?"

"Not even close." He reached across and squeezed her leg. "We'll get this over with, then leave shortly after the meal is done."

"I'm going to hold you to that."

Dirk put on his indicator to turn left before he pulled into a gated drive. He rolled down his window and then punched in a series of numbers on the security pad located near the entrance, and the black iron gate swung open.

"You must come here a lot if you know the code to get in," she said.

"There are times I feel I practically live here, especially when Roxie helped me set up the website."

Dirk drove up the long drive, then parked in front of the garage next to a black Chevy Camaro. Once he turned off the car, Ryann got out and walked around to his side. He took her hand and linked their fingers together as he guided her to the mansion's front door. It'd been years since she'd walked with a man like that. She'd missed it.

Dirk didn't bother to knock and just walked inside. He called, "Rox?"

"We're in the living room, Dirk," a woman answered.

Still walking hand in hand, Ryann allowed Dirk to move her in the direction the voice had come from. Once they stepped inside the room, the two couples already there seemed to turn their gazes directly on her. She found it a bit disconcerting to be the center of attention to a bunch of people she'd never met. They didn't stare at her in a mean way, more of a curious one.

As they came closer, a woman with long, golden-brown hair got up from the couch where she'd sat with a man with long, black hair. She headed straight for Ryann with a big friendly smile.

"It's nice to finally meet you, Ryann," the woman said when she came to stand in front of her. "Dirk's talked a lot about you these last couple weeks. I'm Roxie."

Ryann returned her smile. "I can say the same about you."

"Well, don't just stand there. I'll introduce you to the others."

Dirk and Ryann followed Roxie to the two couches. Once they were all seated, Roxie made the introductions. Ryann learned that the man with the black hair was Roxie's husband, Beowulf. The other two people were Jager and Daylen, another husband and wife.

She couldn't help but stare a bit at Jager and Beowulf. The two men were tall, muscular and had supermodel looks just like Dirk.

Their spouses were pretty but didn't look like models found on a fashion runway. Ryann was thankful for that. At least she wouldn't stick out like a sore thumb when it came to the looks department.

Ryann had just sat back as Dirk put his arm around her shoulders when Jager said, "So, have the two of you slept together yet?"

"Jager!" Daylen and Roxie said sharply at the same time.

"What?" he asked. "I know you're both dying to know, well, at least Roxie is."

Daylen shook her head and rolled her eyes. "Just ignore him, Ryann. My husband has the bad habit of saying whatever the hell is on his mind, regardless of how bad it sounds coming out of his mouth."

With his long, light brown hair pulled back in a ponytail and tough-looking exterior, he had the appearance of a man you wouldn't want to meet in a dark alley. Jager's expression softened, showing the feelings he had for his wife when he looked at Daylen.

"That's part of the reason you love me," he said with a smile.

Next to Ryann, Dirk groaned. "As another person who lives in the same house as you, I can definitely say it doesn't make me want to love you. Sometimes it actually has the opposite effect."

As the others laughed at Dirk's quip, Ryann turned her head to look at him. "Jager and Daylen are your roommates? I thought you lived alone."

The laughter petered out as he answered. "They're not roommates, more like family. I like to think of them as the siblings I never had. Along with the others we live with."

"There's more than just the three of you?"

Dirk nodded. "Altogether, including the new baby Jaden and Leif are expecting, there are fourteen of us."

Ryann looked at him, feeling very much surprised. "That's one big family. I don't know if I could live with that many people. I'm so used to it just being Tyler and I."

"Don't worry, Ryann," Jager said. "You'll think nothing of it once you've moved in." He grunted when his wife elbowed him in the side.

"Would you shut up, Jager?" Daylen asked. She looked at

Ryann. "As I said before, ignore him. Who's Tyler?"

Ryann couldn't help the smile that formed. "He's my three-year-old son." She quickly added, "I'm divorced."

"Where is he now?" Roxie asked. "You could've brought him along instead of leaving him with a sitter. We have plenty of room here for him to sleep, if and when he got tired."

"He's with his dad for the weekend."

"Oh, so you don't have to rush home?"

"I suppose not," Ryann said, though getting Dirk alone again was something she planned to do as soon as she could without being rude.

Roxie stood. "I think the food should be done. Why don't the rest of you head to the dining room while I get everything ready to serve?"

"Do you need any help, Rox?" Daylen asked.

"Nope, I'm good."

Once Roxie left, Beowulf got up and led the rest of them to the dining area. The table was long with more than enough room for six people to sit comfortably. A dark blue tablecloth covered it, and places had already been set.

From another doorway that must have been connected to the kitchen, Roxie came in, carrying a large pan of piping hot lasagna. She placed it in the center of the table on a cooling rack.

She took off the oven mitts she wore before she said, "I'll just get the garlic bread and then we can dish up."

The smell of garlic preceded Roxie once she returned. Ryann's stomach growled in anticipation. She had a weakness for Italian food. All heads turned her way, and she felt herself blush. She hadn't thought the sound of her stomach grumbling had been that loud.

She looked at Roxie. "It smells delicious. I guess I'm hungrier than I thought."

"Well, help yourself, and eat as much as you want. I made lots."

No one spoke as the food was dished up on the plates. Once she had hers, Ryann picked up her piece of garlic bread and took a bite. It was good, and so was the lasagna when she'd tasted some of that.

While they ate, a large bottle of red wine was passed around, everyone filling the wineglass next to their plate. As the meal progressed, it went around a second time. Once that was emptied and another bottle had been opened, Ryann knew there was no way she'd be able to keep up with the others at the table. Two glasses were her max, especially if she wanted to remain sober for later. She wasn't one of those drunks who could liven up a party. No, finding a corner somewhere and going to sleep was more her style. She doubted Dirk would enjoy that.

Once the food was all gone and everyone was on their fifth glass of wine—not that any of them appeared to feel the effects of the alcohol—Ryann was still amazed by how much they'd had. It made her think that Dirk really couldn't be in any condition to drive. After having her two glasses, she didn't want to get behind the wheel either.

Trying not to be too blatant about it, she leaned toward Dirk, and whispered, "When you want to leave, I think we should call a cab. Neither one of us should be driving."

He smiled and replied just as quietly, "I'm fine. I can drive."

"I don't know if that's such a good idea. We don't need you to get a DUI."

From the end of the table, Roxie said, "Ryann's right, Dirk. You don't need one of those. You two can stay over. So can Jager and Daylen." Her gaze seemed to lock on Dirk's. "I insist."

"Really?" Dirk asked. "You're going to do it like that?"

Roxie smiled. "I'm afraid so. I told you I was going to watch you."

Ryann got the distinct impression she missed out on part of what Dirk and Roxie's conversation really meant. She had a feeling some of it didn't have to do with him driving while under the influence, but she didn't say anything.

"Fine," Dirk said with a sigh. "I guess we'll be staying the night." He turned to Ryann. "You don't mind, do you?"

She shook her head. "If you want to stay, I'm fine with it."

There was no way she'd pass up the chance to spend the entire night with Dirk in a bed. It didn't matter where it was, so long as he was in it.

CHAPTER SIX

After dinner, Dirk kept shooting Roxie looks that let her know he wasn't exactly thrilled with what she'd done. He hadn't counted on having to stay the night at her place with Ryann. Actually, he hadn't planned on spending the entire night with Ryann at all. It'd just be asking too much of him. He was only a man, and with the mating urge riding his ass, the desire to make love to his mate would be extremely hard to resist.

Well, Roxie had just made sure he was put in a situation that he, and especially she, wanted to avoid. He could've driven without having to worry about blowing over. All his kind metabolized alcohol differently than mortals. For him to be in the range where he'd get nailed with a DUI, he'd have had to drink all day. Roxie knew that, being a werewolf herself.

Not that he could've told Ryann any of that since she had no clue what he was, or the fact she spent her evening with a bunch of werewolves. Though with Jager around, and never knowing what he'd say next, he could let the truth slip. That wasn't how Dirk wanted Ryann to find out.

Dirk probably would've enjoyed the evening more if he hadn't felt so on edge. It didn't help matters that Roxie watched him like a hawk, as if he'd take Ryann to the floor and claim her right in front of everyone. The only good thing was that Ryann didn't seem to notice.

She'd warmed up to everyone as if she'd known them for a long time. She and Roxie talked about their kids while Ryann had Daylen talking about her days as a police officer. She'd even had Beowulf telling her about Wulf's Den and Jager telling her about swords, though Ryann thought he was just a collector. She had no idea his brother-in-arms was rarely without his sword strapped around his waist. Even though Jager wasn't wearing it right now, that didn't mean it wasn't stashed somewhere close by. At one time, before meeting Daylen, he used to sleep with the damn thing tucked in beside him in his bed.

Once it grew late enough for everyone to call it a night, Dirk was more than anxious to get Ryann alone. From the heated looks she'd sent his way when no one was looking, he knew she felt the same way.

Dirk stood and turned before he offered Ryann his hand. She quickly took it and let him help her to her feet. "I guess we'll see you all in the morning," he said, wanting to make a fast getaway. "We'll take the room I normally use when I stay over."

Roxie stopped Dirk and Ryann before they'd taken more than a couple steps toward the living room's entrance. "Are you sure that's what Ryann wants to do? She might feel more comfortable in a room by herself."

He turned and scowled at Roxie. "That won't be necessary." He looked at Ryann. "You're fine with sharing a bed with me, right?"

Ryann nodded. "I don't mind staying with Dirk."

"Are you sure? We have enough rooms if —"

Beowulf cut her off. "Enough already, Rox. Let it go."

Using the opportunity to leave before Roxie thought of something else to say, Dirk steered Ryann out of the room. Once they were out of sight, he scooped her up into his arms, and with a tiny burst of werewolf speed, took the stairs to the upper level two at a time. She giggled as she wrapped her arms around his neck and held on.

After stepping into the bedroom and then flipping on the light, Dirk quietly closed the door behind them before he turned the lock. He wouldn't put it past Roxie to try to barge in. That done, he put Ryann on her feet. She kept her arms around his neck and shifted so she was pressed to the front of him from chest to knees.

The scent of her arousal bloomed around them. His cock hardened in an instant.

"I've been dying to do this all night," Ryann said in a husky voice.

She went on tiptoe and took his mouth in a heated kiss. She pushed her tongue between his lips, stroking his. She tasted of the wine they'd been drinking. Her fingers curled into the hair at his nape. Dirk ground his aching cock against Ryann, making them moan.

His hunger rose for the woman who'd be his mate. Dirk went to wrap his arms around her, but Ryann had other plans. She broke their kiss and pushed him back against the door with a hard shove. It banged when he made contact with it. Then she was on him again.

Ryann lifted the front of his T-shirt with one hand and dragged the flat of her tongue along his pec. Nimble fingers worked on the button and zipper on his pants and soon were inside them, wrapping around his thick shaft. She pumped him, forcing another groan that bordered on a wolflike growl. He tried to take hold of her, but she shoved him once more, which made the door bang again.

Dirk took the hint that she wanted him to stay right where he was as Ryann slowly went down on her knees in front of him. His breath sawed in and out of his lungs while his heart beat at a rapid pace when she jerked his jeans down far enough to spring his cock.

He couldn't tear his gaze from her. The sight of her opening her mouth and taking his dick inside had him wanting to howl in pleasure. The feel of her sucking him just about did him in. Desire surged through him, his cock hardening even more.

The door rattled at his back as someone knocked on it. Knowing full well who that someone was, Dirk ignored her. He just prayed she'd take the hint and go away.

"Dirk," Roxie said through the door, "you better not be doing something you shouldn't in there."

Ryann swirled her tongue around the head of his cock before she sucked him almost to the back of her throat. Dirk couldn't hold back the growl that rumbled out of his chest. He wasn't doing anything he shouldn't. It felt too fucking perfect.

Through gritted teeth, he said, "Go away, Roxie. Now isn't a good time." The last word ended on a moan. Ryann fondled his balls. "Definitely not now."

"Dirk, open this door."

"Go. Away. Roxie."

If she didn't leave him alone, Dirk wasn't going to be responsible for what he did. The grip he had on his control was tenuous at best. And Roxie wasn't helping matters, to say the least. Much to Dirk's relief, he heard Beowulf's voice next.

"Rox, what did I say about doing something like this?" Beowulf asked. "You're taking it a little too far."

"I just want to make sure he plays by the rules."

"I think I need to show you how pleasurable it can be when you don't."

Roxie let out a little shriek, then the sound of Beowulf's heavier footsteps walking away down the hall sounded. It wasn't hard to guess he had slung his mate over his shoulder and carried her away, something he did when she was prone to ignore him.

On the brink of coming, Dirk tugged on Ryann's shoulder to get her to release his cock before he pulled her up onto her feet. It was his turn to pleasure her. In a move Beowulf had just used on Roxie, he picked her up and swung her over his shoulder. He crossed the short distance to the bed and then flipped her onto the mattress. She giggled as she bounced.

He grabbed hold of Ryann's legs and pulled her down to the end of the bed where he stood. He undid her jeans before he peeled them off her. Dirk hooked his fingers into the waistband of her panties and slowly removed that article of clothing.

Staring at her pussy, seeing her juices on her inner thighs, he licked his lips. "Now I get to eat what I've been craving."

Dirk kneeled and used his hands to push her legs farther apart. Her pussy was pink and swollen with arousal. He dragged a finger through her wetness before he swirled it around her clit.

Ryann lifted her hips. "More. Give me more."

"Don't worry, babe. I will."

He lapped at her slick opening, enjoying the taste of her. His cock throbbed in time with his rapidly beating heart, aching to be buried deep inside Ryann's wet heat. It beat at him, making him clamp down even harder on his control.

Dirk used two fingers to push inside her pussy, pumping them in and out. Ryann's cries of passion rang in his ears as she matched him stroke for stroke. Her inner muscles clamped around his digits, her juices coating them as he worked her.

He sucked and licked her clit, and when it seemed as if she hovered close to the edge, he pushed her higher, stroking her G-spot. Ryann cried out, her body clenching around his fingers.

Dirk rose to his feet and climbed onto the bed. Still breathing heavy, Ryann pushed back until she was in the center of the mattress. She tore off her shirt and then quickly shed her bra. He ran his gaze over her, getting even more turned-on by her nakedness.

She turned to him, inching closer on her knees. If Ryann had been a werewolf, he would've sworn she stalked him from the way she held his gaze while moving slowly.

Once she reached him, Ryann grabbed the top of his jeans and pushed them farther down his legs. "Pants off," she said in a husky voice. "You promised I could use you as a guinea pig. I'm thinking now's a good time to run my little experiment. It's going to be called 'How many times I can make Dirk come before he loses his erection.'"

He swallowed against the howl that wanted to break free. "How about we make it even more interesting and say you can only do that with your mouth and hands?" It'd kill him, make his mating urge go straight through the roof, but it'd be well worth it.

She smiled. "Deal, just as long as I get to come too. Now get rid of the jeans."

Dirk quickly shucked his pants and dropped them over the side of the bed. "Oh, don't worry. You won't be left out."

He soon grunted in surprise as he found himself flat on his back with Ryann hovering over him. With a smile that said she was ready to play, she worked her way down his body. Her hot breath fanned over his cock, making it jerk.

Dirk lifted his head to watch. A bead of pre-cum leaked out of the head of his dick as Ryann took hold of him. The tip of her tongue came out, and she licked it off. She moaned as if it were the best thing she'd ever tasted.

He closed his eyes and laid his head back. It wasn't going to take much for him to find his first release. He was primed and ready to go. Dirk gritted his teeth to keep his howls of pleasure from escaping when Ryann sucked his cock into her mouth. Her teeth lightly scraped against his skin as she took him in and out. So close now, he held the back of her head and pumped his hips, fucking her mouth.

She hummed, the vibration running along his entire length, and that was all he needed to reach completion. Dirk growled low, arching his hips, coming in Ryann's mouth, giving her all he had. Once the last shudder had gone through him, he was on her, playing her body like a finely tuned instrument.

They made each other come three more times before Dirk collapsed on top Ryann, trying to catch his breath. He had to admit he was in trouble. Coming so many times without being inside her had his mating urge spiraling almost out of control. It didn't help that his wolf had risen to the surface, demanding he claim his mate.

Dirk buried his face in the crook of Ryann's neck, fighting to calm down. The smell of sex on her skin only heightened his need. She shifted beneath him so his hips became wedged between her thighs. She lifted her legs and wrapped them around his waist, anchoring him there. The tip of his cock brushed her wet pussy. A deep shudder racked him.

Ryann shifted again, this time taking the head of his dick inside her. "The experiment is finished. I need you to fill me. Now."

As if a damn had broken, Dirk lost the battle. He surged into Ryann's pussy, sheathing himself to the hilt with one stroke. From the number of times he'd made her come, she was more than wet enough to take him. Her inner muscles clamped around his pistoning cock as he rode her hard and fast. He was beyond being able to take it slow. Growl after growl rumbled out of him, the sounds as much wolf as man.

"Oh, god. Yes," Ryann keened. "Don't stop."

He couldn't even if he tried. Dirk had played with fire, and been engulfed by an inferno. He plunged into her pussy again and again, the pleasure unlike any he'd ever felt. Being inside his mate, claiming her, nothing was better.

Wanting Ryann to leave her mark on him, Dirk gathered her tightly into his arms and brought her with him as he shifted so he sat back on his heels. His dick still buried deep inside her, he urged her to ride him with a hand on her hip. He placed the other on the back of her head to lead her mouth to the spot where his neck and shoulder met.

"Bite me," he growled. "Hard." Once she bit too gently, he added, "Harder. Sink your teeth into me."

He continued to spear into her pussy. When she did bite him hard enough to leave a mark, Dirk felt the beginning of the mating bond form between them. A piece of his soul reached out for Ryann's. Continuing to growl, he took her faster, harder, until the two parts wrapped around each other and became one. He and Ryann were thrown into instant climax as the mating bond snapped into place. She called out his name on a keening moan, throwing back her head as her pussy clutched his cock, milking it, prolonging the pleasure surging through him.

Once it was over, Ryann collapsed against his chest with her head on his shoulder. Dirk wrapped his arms around her, holding her tight, his cock still hard and buried deep inside her pussy. She was now his, and there would be no going back.

CHAPTER SEVEN

For the life of her, Ryann didn't want to move. Actually, she doubted she had the energy to accomplish that feat. Holy shit, sex had never been this intense for her—ever. She felt as if she'd been thoroughly loved. That was how it'd seemed to her. That it hadn't just been sex. As Dirk had finally joined their bodies, she'd been more than desperate for him. Then something had happened between them, something she'd never felt before. Even now she had a hard time trying to describe it to herself. Whatever it was, it'd sent a feeling of being somehow connected to him shooting through her. How she felt about him had solidified even more, becoming stronger.

She hoped to god it wasn't a side effect of her sleeping with the first man since her divorce. In no way did she want Dirk to think it was more than sex if that wasn't what he intended. She didn't want him to think she was clingy. That had been Mack's biggest complaint about her. That she clung to him and was too needy. Ryann didn't think she was either of those things, but it'd be kind of a blow to her ego if Dirk thought so.

Dirk shifted to bring his legs out from under him so they were stretched in front. Ryann moaned softly. The man was still hard, buried deep inside her. He'd come five times, and he'd somehow managed to keep his erection. She had no idea how it was possible. Her little experiment had more than proved that the girl she had once worked with hadn't lied one bit. He had just done what had seemed so farfetched.

He nudged her with his shoulder. "You're so quiet. Either you're half asleep or you're thinking too much about something. I hope you're not regretting what we just did."

Ryann sat up and cupped Dirk's face. She kissed him deeply before she pulled away. "It's probably a little bit of both — tiredness and just lost in thought, though not with regret. I'm not much of a night owl anymore. Not with Tyler sometimes waking me up at the crack of dawn."

He reached up and tucked her hair behind her ear. "Yeah, I can see how he could put a damper on any late nights. At least here you can sleep in. Now, what are you thinking about?"

She hesitated, wondering if it'd be such a good idea to say anything at all. She didn't want whatever this was to start off with her holding back. Mack had been the problem in their relationship, not her. He'd chosen to leave her, to see if life would be better without her in it.

"Well," she started, "I was just thinking about us. How good we're together. I don't want to do anything to jeopardize what we have going here with being too clingy. That's what Mack said I was like while we were married." Ryann took a deep breath. "Now don't think this is stemming from the fact you're the first man I've had sex with since my ex, but I'm finding I have strong feelings for you already. I know it's sudden and all."

Ryann would've said more, but Dirk cut her off with a kiss that had her pussy clutching his hard cock. Unbelievably, arousal rose inside her once again. Going from thinking she wouldn't be able to move again, she now wanted Dirk to make love to her once more.

He released her lips and stared into her eyes. "You have nothing to worry about. I mean it. I'll never find you too clingy. If anything, you'll think I may be at times. As for how I feel about you, well, you're the woman I've waited to show up in my life. For a very long time. I'm afraid you're stuck with me."

She blinked in astonishment. "You mean like forever? And here I thought I was rushing things. Remember, I don't come alone. I have Tyler."

He leaned in and kissed the corner of her mouth. "Yes, I mean as in forever. I know you come with Tyler. I have to say I really like the little guy. So I end up with an instant family. I won't find that a hardship. It might seem as if I'm rushing into this, but I'm not. This was meant to be. You're mine now, and I keep what's mine."

A thrill shot through Ryann at Dirk's words. The way he looked at her while he said them, all possessive, made her want him even more. They could make this work. She wanted it to. She'd been alone for way the hell too long. He was just the man she wanted in her life.

"Then I guess I'm yours," she said slowly.

Heat flared in Dirk's eyes just before he claimed her mouth in a kiss so carnal she craved him once more, wanted him to take her over and over again. To let him know what she wanted, Ryann rose onto her knees before she slowly sank onto his cock. A deep, growly moan pushed out of his chest, like so many he'd made before while in the throes of passion. The sound turned her on.

Dirk broke contact with her lips and lifted one of her breasts before he sucked on the taut nipple. A corresponding pull of pleasure contracted her pussy at the same time. She put her hands on his shoulders and slowly rode him up and down, his cock growing even harder inside her.

He released her nipple, held on to Ryann's hips and lifted her off him. She made a small sound of protest, but soon realized he wasn't done with her yet. He guided her onto her hands and knees on the center of the mattress before he came to kneel behind her. With a heavily muscled thigh, he spread her legs farther apart.

The tip of his cock brushed against her pussy. Ryann moaned and rocked back, wanting him deep inside her again. He didn't make her wait. With a thrust of his hips, he sheathed himself balls deep. She tightened her inner walls around his thick length, heightening her pleasure.

Dirk set a slow and steady pace as he reared back until he was almost free of her body before pushing all the way into her again. Ryann rocked back, matching him stroke for stroke. She loved the feel of his hard cock stretching her, filling her all the way up. In and out he pumped, pushing her ever closer to her climax. She panted. He'd just spoiled her for other men. No other would measure up to his standards.

Another animalistic growl rumbled out of Dirk. He reached around her body and found her clit as he continued to pump in and out. Rubbing the small bundle of nerves as he pounded her from behind, she let herself go. Moaning, she came, her pussy rhythmically clasping the hard cock embedded in her. He thrust once, twice, then stiffened as he found his release, filling her with his cum.

He kept his arm around her and brought them to their sides. This time, his shaft softened and slipped free of her body. Exhausted and completely satiated, Ryann closed her eyes and fell into a deep sleep.

* * * *

The next morning Dirk managed to get them out of there without being cornered by Roxie. Of course she would've known—same as everyone else who'd been in the house—that he'd claimed his mate. With werewolf hearing being so acute, it was inevitable. Not that he regretted any of what he'd done last night. She could be pissed off at him for breaking her rules, but she might as well have asked him to jump over the moon. The mating urge was what it was, and it was something no male werewolf had much control over.

Now at Ryann's apartment, Dirk had the day to slowly work out how he was going to tell her about being his mate and get up the nerve to do it. She'd accepted him last night when he'd said he wanted to keep her forever, and he didn't want that to change once he revealed what he truly was. The one thing he knew was he had to do it before Tyler came home the next day.

Now with the mating bond firmly in place, and growing stronger each time they made love, neither he nor Ryann would be able to stand to be apart. That meant he'd have to move his new family into the Protector's mansion as soon as he could manage it. His protection duties would have to be worked out as well. Having a son meant Dirk could no longer do any of the evening shifts. Ryann would have to come with him so they didn't suffer the separation anxiety that all mated couples had to avoid. Wherever she'd go, so would Tyler.

It was late in the afternoon, and Dirk and Ryann sat in the living room, watching TV. They'd already made love a couple times since returning, once in the shower and the other time on her bed. Not really paying too much attention to the show on the screen, they talked about anything and everything.

During one such conversation, Ryann's telephone rang. She picked it up and looked at the caller ID. She scowled. "It's Mack. I'd better take it." Ryann pressed the talk button. "Hello, Mack. What's up? Is everything okay with Tyler?"

With his hearing, Dirk could easily hear Mack's response.

"Tyler's fine," Mack said. "Since your new boyfriend mentioned he was taking you out for dinner tonight, I thought I'd call and find out what time and where you'll be."

"Why?" Ryann asked. "If you need to get a hold of me, I'll have my cell phone."

"Can you just tell me? That way if your cell dies or something I'll still know where you are."

Ryann sighed. "Fine, if it'll get you off my back. Hold on, I'll ask." She covered the mouthpiece with her hand and looked at Dirk. "Mack wants to know where you're taking me out to dinner tonight and what time we'll be there."

"I was thinking around six. I'm going to take you to this small out-of-the-way place called King Crab if you like seafood."

"I love it." Ryann pulled her hand away and relayed that info to Mack.

After finding out how Tyler was doing, and getting the assurance that her ex would drop off their son around lunchtime the next day, she hung up.

The rest of the day sped by, and Dirk still hadn't told Ryann about him being a werewolf. Since it was already close to six, and they were getting ready to go to the restaurant, he figured he'd wait until after they returned to the apartment to come clean.

After arriving at the restaurant, Dirk pulled into the parking lot at the back of the building and chose a spot farthest away from any other cars.

"I hope you don't mind the walk," he said. "I don't like parking near anyone. I'd rather a hike than have someone ding my car with their door."

She chuckled. "I don't mind. If I had one like yours, I'd do the same thing."

Another car drove into the lot and parked four spots over as Dirk and Ryann got out of the BMW. He didn't think anything of it, and waited for Ryann to meet up with him on his side. Once she did, he took her hand and got them walking toward the restaurant.

They'd only taken a few steps when Ryann stiffened and came to a complete standstill. Dirk stopped and looked at her. "What's wrong?"

She nodded in the direction where the other car was parked. "It's Mack, and he's not alone."

Dirk swung his gaze to where Ryann indicated and saw she was right. It was her ex, along with two large men. All three of them walked toward Dirk and Ryann, looking none too friendly.

"Mack, what the hell are you doing here?" Ryann asked as they drew near. "And where's Tyler?"

Not sparing her a glance, Mack said, "Tyler's fine. I came to warn your prick of a boyfriend off."

"What? You have no right. We're divorced. I can see whomever I want."

"Not this guy, you won't," Mack said in a hard voice. "I've had to listen to Tyler go on and on about this asshole for the last two days. I don't want any man trying to take my place in my son's life."

"Well, you should've thought of that before you left me."

"Shut up, Ryann," Mack snapped.

Not liking how her ex had spoken to her, Dirk growled low in his throat, not holding anything back. He felt all eyes on him. "I suggest you watch how you speak to Ryann. She's mine now. Not yours. Keep it up and I'll make sure you regret it."

Mack laughed with no humor in it. "Really? I doubt it. You see, I brought my two friends along to make you rethink going anywhere near Ryann and Tyler."

With that, the two large men dove for Dirk. He just had enough time to push Ryann out of the way before they were on him. Not giving a shit if they saw what he truly was, Dirk growled and ducked as one man took a swing at his head. He snarled his upper lip, snapped his teeth and turned his gaze on them, knowing full well his eyes had to be mutedly glowing with the anger that surged through him. They were taken aback a bit, but not for long. Though they were strong for mortals, they were no match against a werewolf. He clipped one on the jaw, and the man went down like a ton of bricks.

Just as the other moved in to take another swing at him, Ryann yelled, "Tyler's in the car! You brought him along while you did something like this?"

Dirk took a quick look at the vehicle the men had left and saw Tyler's little face pressed against the side window in the backseat. He focused his attention back on his attacker, and with a one-two combination to the gut, along with a hook to the jaw, the second man was out for the count.

That left only Mack. Dirk turned to find him going after Ryann as she headed for the car. Her ex grabbed her by the arm and roughly pulled her to a stop. She let out a cry of pain as Mack gave her a good shake.

Something snapped inside Dirk at the sight of another man touching his mate in such a way. He growled loud enough to capture Mack's and Ryann's attentions. He drew on the spark of magic inside him and shifted to his wolf form. He thrilled at the way Mack's eyes widened, and his scent became laden in fear. Dirk knew what Mack saw. As a wolf, he was much bigger than the ones found in the wild.

He padded to Mack and growled, his hackles rising as he came to stand between the other man and Ryann. Babbling nonsense, Mack backed off. Dirk turned to look at Ryann. She was as white as a ghost, her wide-eyed gaze riveted on him. He'd have to deal with her fear after this was all over. Right now, he needed to get Tyler out of the other car.

Knowing he was more of a threat in his wolf form, Dirk remained in it as he loped over to the vehicle. He looked at Tyler and let his tongue hang out, giving the boy a wolflike grin. He hoped Tyler would come out without him having to shift to convince him to. He counted on the fact that kids seemed to accept out of the ordinary things better than adults usually did.

He didn't have long to wait before Tyler opened the back door and slid out. Showing no fear whatsoever, he threw his arms around Dirk's furry neck and hugged him.

"You're a wolf, Dirk!" he shouted. "That's cool."

As Dirk turned to head to Ryann, a small hand gripped the fur at his neck as Tyler pulled himself up onto his back. The boy kicked his small heels into his sides as if he were a horse. Laughing inside, he walked back to his mate.

Ryann was still staring at him wide-eyed. Mack, on the other hand, was busy rousing his friends. Once he managed to get them onto their feet, all three men hightailed it to the car, and in a matter of minutes, burned rubber out of the parking lot.

Dirk sat on his haunches, causing Tyler to slide down his back. Once the boy got off, he shifted to his human form. He closed the distance between him and Ryann. She still hadn't made a sound. She seemed almost frozen in place.

"Say something," he said as he cupped her face.

"A wolf? You're-you're a wolf," she stammered.

"A werewolf, to be exact."

"I-I don't know if I..." Ryann held herself stiffly and looked about ready to lose it.

"I know it's a lot for you to take in. Will you at least let me take you to the apartment and explain everything?"

"You won't hurt me?"

Dirk leaned in and kissed her. "You're my mate, Ryann. I could no more hurt you than pull my heart out."

Before she answered, Tyler said, "Let's go, Mommy. I want to ride Dirk the wolf again."

Dirk laughed. "I have a feeling I'm going to have a sore back for many days to come in the near future."

With a big sigh, seeming to push back what fear she had to be feeling, Ryann nodded. "Okay, you can come to the apartment. I guess if Tyler isn't afraid of you, I shouldn't be either."

"That's all I can ask," he said, scooping up Tyler before he placed his son and mate into his car.

* * * *

"Damn, my back's getting sore just from watching him," Leif said.

Jaden nudged him. "Just wait until our baby's old enough to ask for wolfy rides. You'll be doing exactly what Dirk is."

Ryann chuckled at Jaden's words before she turned her

attention on her mate and son. Tyler had two good fistfuls of Dirk's fur and laughed as his stepfather trotted around the large backyard of the Protector's mansion. Something he had to do at least once a day, at Tyler's request.

It'd been a week since the incident in the restaurant parking lot, and now she and Tyler lived with the others in Dirk's family mansion. It'd been a lot for her to accept once he'd told her everything about him being a nine-hundred-and-fifty-year-old werewolf. In the end, her strong feelings for him had helped her accept him for what he was.

Tyler laughed as Dirk got down onto the ground on his belly and shook him off. Her mate shifted to his human form and then tickled their son until Tyler shrieked with laughter. God, she loved Dirk. And he loved her. She hadn't realized how much she'd been missing in her life until he'd come around. She sent up thanks every day that she'd answered his ad for the position at his online dating service.

Ryann left Leif and Jaden and headed for the two males who were the loves of her life. Tonight would be the real start of her new life with Dirk. They were going to Roxie's where she'd use the spell to turn Ryann into a werewolf. When Tyler was old enough to make the decision for himself, Roxie would turn him as well.

Once she reached her family, Dirk pulled her down into his arms and gave her a kiss while he tickled her as well. With Tyler joining in, the two of them ganging up on her, Ryann knew her life was perfect. Falling in love with a werewolf was one of the best things that had ever happened to her. It ranked right up there with Tyler's birth. She finally had the family she'd always dreamed of for her son.

The End

MILES'S REDEMPTION

Miles knew using Dirk's online dating service wouldn't be the best way to find his mate and is proven right when his date stands him up. But his bad luck turns to good when his would-be mate walks through the restaurant's doors.

Kareena has been on a dating dry streak since her fiancé of seven years dumped her the year before. She wants the hottie who sits close to her and her friends' table to be the one to end it, but she doesn't have enough nerve to go up and talk to him. After meeting Miles, her life ends up going in a direction she never thought would exist. She soon learns she's the only thing that can secure Miles' redemption.

CHAPTER ONE

Miles shut off the engine on his black Audi and let out a loud breath. He looked at the building in front of him. He had no idea why he'd allowed Jaden to talk him into this. It wasn't going to work, no matter how accurate Dirk thought his online dating service was. There was no way in hell Miles would find his mate this way.

He got out of the car and then pushed the button on the remote on his keychain to lock it. To make Jaden happy, and to make her stop bugging the crap out of him, Miles had finally caved and set up a date with the mortal woman who was supposedly his closest match. From her picture on the dating service's website, this Gail looked attractive enough, but he really had his doubts she'd end up being his mate. For one thing, she was mortal. Her lifespan was so much shorter than his. He was almost a thousand years old, and was guaranteed to see another two thousand birthdays. And he knew, along with the rest of the werewolf population, there was no way to turn a mortal into one of their kind. He'd prefer his mate to be a werewolf so he wouldn't have to suffer through losing her too early.

Miles headed for the entrance to the restaurant-slash-bar where he'd chosen to meet with his date. He snorted. He'd never thought he'd "date" anyone again. Ever since his relationship with Jaden's mother — who hadn't been his mate — had ended, he'd only sought out women who'd be happy with a quick tumble in the sack and then moved on. He hadn't wanted anything else until Jaden had brought up the subject of him finding his mate. Deep down inside, he wanted what his daughter had with her mate, Leif.

He stepped inside the restaurant and went to the hostess, who smiled as he approached. "I have a reservation for two," Miles said and then gave his name.

She took him to a table in the center of the room and then placed two menus on its surface before she left. As Miles snagged one and pulled it in front of him, he hoped his date wouldn't keep him waiting long. A quick look at his watch told him he was a few minutes early.

A waiter appeared and asked if Miles would like to order a drink. He decided he might as well and asked for a beer. A minute or so later, the waiter came back with his drink before leaving Miles alone once again.

More people came into the restaurant, but none of them was his date. Having an excellent view of the entrance from where he sat, Miles looked in that direction each time the door opened. And each time he didn't see the mortal who was to meet with him.

Fifteen minutes went by and then a half hour. Miles was already on his second beer when he reached the conclusion that he'd more than likely been stood up. Just to make sure, he took out his smart phone and checked the e-mail account he'd set up just for communicating with his would-be "dates." Sure enough, there was an e-mail from Gail sent forty-five minutes earlier, saying she had to cancel and asking if they could arrange to meet another time.

Miles mentally crossed her off the list, not that there were any others on it besides Gail. That gave him another reason the online dating service wasn't for him. He didn't like being stood up by a woman he hadn't even met and had only communicated with through the Internet.

With a sigh full of disgust, Miles lifted his bottle of beer to his lips and took a swallow. He'd finish this, then go home. There was no point hanging around. Maybe he'd even order something from the restaurant for takeout.

He'd just looked at the menu in front of him to see what he'd like when a new scent barreled into him like a speeding train. His head snapped up, and he focused on the entrance. His grip on the bottle tightened as his cock went instantly rock hard, his mating urge slamming into him and riding his ass hard. Miles had to hold back a growl that threatened to punch out of him as he spotted a group of four women who'd just come into the restaurant. One of them was his would-be mate. He separated her scent from all the others in the large open space and dragged it in deep, memorizing it.

As the hostess led the small group farther into the room, Miles kept his gaze glued to them. They came closer to his table. It was then he was able to zero in on which woman was meant to be his. He focused solely on her. The urge to go to her and drag her into his arms was hard to resist.

Instead, he settled for taking in everything about her. Shoulder-length light brown hair shined in the overhead lighting. Miles guessed her to be around five-foot-seven, tall for a mortal woman. Her dark brown eyes flashed as she laughed at something one of the other females had said. He ran his gaze down her from her beautiful face to a slim, curvy body and long, toned legs showcased in a pair of snug-fitting black jeans.

Miles's cock jerked as he drew in another lungful of her scent as she walked past his table. He continued to follow her with his gaze, pleased to see the group snaked around tables and ended up sitting at a booth straight across from where he sat. He had an excellent view of his would-be mate as she slipped onto the bench seating.

He drained the last bit of his beer, then set the bottle on the table. A short while later, his waiter approached. This time Miles ordered something off the menu, not for takeout, and another beer. He'd be staying right where he was until the woman who was meant for him showed signs of leaving the restaurant. Drawn to her, the mating urge making it hard to focus on anything else, he wouldn't be going home until he'd taken steps to have them on the road to becoming mates.

*

"Here's to the birthday girl," Kareena said as she lifted her glass of wine toward her friend, Alice. "And to Lacy, who finally woke up, realized how much of an asshole her boyfriend was and dumped his ass." Kareena, Alice, Lacy and their other friend, Natalie, took sips of their drinks.

"I guess that's something to celebrate besides me being one year older," Alice said. She looked at Lacy. "Kareena is right, though. Evan was an asshole, and you can do so much better."

Lacy sighed. "I know, I know. All I can say is the sex had been pretty damn good, and I stupidly turned a blind eye to Evan's bad points because of it."

"At least you came to your senses before you wasted years with him," Natalie said. "He was the type of guy who'd keep you around until he'd found something better."

Kareena nodded. "Yeah, count yourself lucky. From firsthand experience, it's not fun having to go through that."

Up until last year, Kareena had been engaged for seven damn long years. Her ex had asked her to marry him when she'd been twenty-four. They'd been together for a year at that point. She'd been so happy, and had agreed when Victor suggested a long engagement. Kareena had figured it'd give her plenty of time to plan the wedding of her dreams. She'd never expected it to be quite so long. After a while, she'd wondered if he really wanted to get married. She'd put some pressure on him to settle on a date. That had blown up in her face when he'd suddenly decided he didn't want to be with her anymore. Now at thirty-two, Kareena figured he'd taken some of the best years of her life. Ones she'd never get back.

Lacy, who sat next to Kareena, patted Kareena's hand. "Your ex was an asshole too. He has no idea what he gave up, but it's his loss."

"Thanks, Lacy," Kareena said. "Now no more negative thoughts. Let's get this celebration going."

With their food and second round of drinks served, Kareena relaxed and set out to enjoy herself. She and her girlfriends didn't get together like this as often as they used to. With all of them busy in their jobs, it was hard to find time when they all could meet without someone's schedule coming into conflict. Being an ER nurse, Kareena's was the hardest one to work around.

On her fourth glass of wine, and feeling a bit on the drunk side, Kareena figured one more drink would be her limit. She'd take a cab home, so it wasn't as if she had to drive. After a week of twelve-hour shifts at the hospital, she needed to let her hair down and unwind.

Natalie, who sat on the opposite bench and on the outside like Kareena, cleared her throat. "Ah, Kareena, I think you've caught the notice of the hottie sitting alone a couple tables away."

"What?" she asked as she went to turn her head to look. Natalie stopped her before she could even get a glimpse.

"Don't look," her friend said. "At least don't be blatant about it. Don't make it appear as if you've noticed him. Make him work for it."

Kareena rolled her eyes. Natalie was the type of woman who liked to make a man practically jump through hoops before she agreed to go out with him. Kareena wasn't like that, but to make her friend happy, she did a slow sweep of the room, her gaze lingering for a few seconds longer on the table Natalie had indicated before finishing with the rest.

She met her friend's gaze. "Holy shit. You weren't kidding when you called him a hottie. He's freaking gorgeous."

Natalie smiled. "I told you. He's stared at you since we sat down."

Her other friends made sounds of appreciation as they too looked at the man. He wasn't hard to miss with his blond hair so light it almost appeared white and his cover-model face. From what Kareena had seen of his upper body, the guy was muscular, his wide shoulders and chest filling out the dark blue button-down shirt he wore to perfection.

"Who's to say he's looking at me?" Kareena asked. "He could be watching any of you as well."

Alice shook her head. "Nope, his gaze is right on you." She moaned. "Oh, god, he just smiled, which makes him even better looking."

Kareena had to look again to see if Alice was right or not about him being only focused on her. She turned her head in his direction, then had to bite back a groan. He did indeed seem to only stare at her. Their gazes met, and her body responded with arousal. Her pussy clenched, and her nipples grew taut when she thought she saw hunger flash in his eyes even from the distance between him. Her blood heated, and she felt her face grow flush.

She had a hard time tearing her gaze off him.

"I think you should pick him up," Lacy said.

Kareena stared at her friend as if she'd lost her mind. Kareena was drunk but not *that* drunk. "No," she said firmly. "I'd have to have a hell of a lot more than this to drink to even consider it."

Natalie pushed her drink to Kareena. "Here, have mine. Pound it back, then go over to his table."

"Go on," Alice added.

"You can't let him get away," Lacy said, making it so all her friends had ganged up on her.

She couldn't believe she even considered doing it. Kareena reached for the drink Natalie had given her and drank it down in a few swallows. She grimaced at the taste. Her friend's drink had been vodka mixed with cranberry juice. Kareena hated cranberries, but the vodka would hit her harder than the wine.

"All right, here I go," she said as she slid off the bench and stood.

Kareena found she wasn't very steady on her feet as she slowly headed in the hunk's direction. She was thankful she hadn't worn high heels. She'd have already ended up on her ass if she had. And wouldn't that have made a great first impression?

Her heart beat faster as she neared his table. *You can do this*, she told herself as a pep talk. As his gaze latched on to her and didn't waver, Kareena lost her nerve. She quickly changed direction and walked as fast as she could in her drunken state to the women's washroom.

Once she was closed inside, she groaned as she silently called herself all kinds of vile names. While she was there, she used the toilet. Kareena was sure her friends were all shaking their heads at her. She hadn't always been like this. Before her ex, she'd been more outgoing with the opposite sex, but since her breakup, she'd found she couldn't get back into her old groove. Even though it'd been a year, she hadn't been out on a single date. With her busy work schedule, and trying to get over being dumped by her fiancé, she hadn't made a point of getting back into the dating world. And being over thirty, she didn't think that'd be an easy task, anyway.

She washed her hands and took some deep, calming breaths. She'd march back out and walk straight to the guy's table. She'd introduce herself and then ask him to take her to his place and screw her brains out. No. Kareena wouldn't say that. Maybe he'd be more interested in sneaking her into the men's room and taking her against the washroom stall door. She shook her head, which only made the room spin a bit. Where the hell had that idea come from? The men's room? Ah, gross. She had to be drunker than she'd thought. Or horny enough to do the hunk anywhere. It *had* been a year since she'd last done the horizontal mambo, after all.

Kareena left the washroom and headed once more in the direction of the table where, thank god, the hottie still sat. His gaze latched on to her, and it felt as if he physically touched her breasts when it lingered there. She forgot to breathe as her pussy grew wet, an ache building deep inside.

In her inattention, she stumbled into a chair, which made a screech as the legs dragged across the hardwood floor. Embarrassed by her klutziness, Kareena lost her nerve again and made a beeline for the table where her friends sat. She couldn't even look at the hunk to see what his reaction was.

She slid onto the bench seat, grateful to see a full glass of wine on the table in her spot. Kareena picked it up and took a big sip. She looked at all her friends and found them giving her disappointed looks.

Kareena shrugged. "All right, I'm chicken shit and couldn't do it."

"You need to get out of the slump you're in," Alice said.

"I will. It just won't be with him unless he comes to talk to me."

"If he doesn't?"

"Then it wasn't meant to be."

There was still disapproval on her friends' faces, but they didn't say anything else. Kareena finished her wine, knowing full well she'd gone over her limit and would probably come to regret it in the morning. Right now, she just felt way too good to give a crap.

Once they'd taken care of the bill, all four of them slipped off the seats, then headed for the restaurant's entrance. Kareena was not very steady on her feet, but she managed to keep in a straight line.

It didn't remain that way when she reached the doors. She stepped back so Lacy could open them, and Kareena's sense of balance went all out of whack. She would have fallen, but a set of strong arms wrapped around her waist from behind and pulled her against a hard, male body. She turned her head to look at who held her and saw it was the hunk. Her mouth suddenly went dry, especially when the unmistakable ridge of his erection pressed into the small of her back. Arousal tore through her, making her knees even weaker.

He smiled. "I've got you."

"Hi," she said, the one word coming out a bit slurred.

"Let me help you outside."

Kareena didn't say a word as he shifted her to his side and tucked her under his arm. He was tall—at least six-foot-three. She liked tall men since she was no munchkin. The heat from his body seemed to envelope her as she put her arm around his waist to anchor herself. The scent of his cologne hit her nose, and she dragged in a lungful, liking the smell.

Outside, her friends gave her encouraging smiles and said their goodbyes, leaving Kareena alone with the hottie. She was sure she'd get phone calls from all of them tomorrow.

She looked at the hunk and found him intently watching her. Her pussy clenching with need, Kareena said the first thing that came to her mind. "I'm Kareena. Why don't you take me to your place?" Of course all her words kind of slurred together, but the smile he flashed her said he didn't seem to mind.

"I'm Miles," he said in his deep voice. "Are you sure you're in any condition for that?"

"I'll admit I'm a bit drunk, but I'm good."

"How about I drive you home instead?"

"Okay. You can spend the night with me."

He chuckled and walked her to the parking lot and a fancy black Audi. With a push of a button, he had the car unlocked. Once he had the passenger door open, he helped her onto the leather seat and waited until she'd buckled her seatbelt before he closed her inside. In a matter of seconds, he was behind the wheel and starting the engine.

Kareena settled deeper into the seat as Miles backed up and then drove out of the parking lot. Her eyes grew heavy as he merged with the traffic. Unable to keep them open any longer, she fell into a deep sleep.

CHAPTER TWO

Miles glanced at Kareena and opened his mouth to ask for her address, but closed it when he saw she was fast asleep. He nudged her a couple times without getting any response. It looked as if his would-be mate had passed out, which didn't really surprise him. She was more than a little drunk. If she'd been a werewolf, the amount of alcohol she'd consumed wouldn't have had any effect on her. His kind had to drink a crap load of it to get drunk. Enough to more than likely give a mortal alcohol poisoning.

He nudged Kareena again, but she didn't awaken. All she did was let out a soft snore. Well, so much for taking her home. She hadn't given him her address before she'd fallen asleep. Since he couldn't get her roused, that left him with only one option—he'd have to take her to his penthouse. Hopefully, she wouldn't wake up in the morning and be too upset about it. It wasn't as if he he'd just dump her into the street somewhere. She was his mate, his to protect and care for.

Being inside the small, closed space of the car with Kareena made her scent stronger, which had Miles's libido going haywire and his mating urge riding him harder. The need to claim her as his beat at him, but he wouldn't. For one thing, she wasn't in any condition for him to make love to her. And for another, she was mortal and had no idea he was a werewolf. He'd have to tell her the truth about him before he let things get too far. Hiding it wouldn't do him any favors. He'd learned that with Jaden's mother. She hadn't taken the news too well.

That hadn't been the reason she'd left him when she'd first become pregnant with Jaden without telling him about it. It had been his inability to give up his quest to find the foretold one who'd rule over all the werewolf packs. For a great many years, he'd looked for this special werewolf, wanting to use him or her as a figurehead so Miles could rule. That was behind him now, though. Jaden, his own daughter, had turned out to be the foretold one. There was no way he'd do anything to hurt her. She was the love of his life, as was her unborn child.

Miles glanced at Kareena as he arrived at his penthouse. Now he had his mate to add to his list of people he'd do anything to see happy. His sister, Saskia, who was the leader of the Protectors, who watched over the foretold one, was right up there as well. She hadn't been for years, but with the new leaf he'd turned over, he worked on rebuilding the connection he'd once had with her.

He parked in the underground garage. Miles scooped up Kareena from the passenger seat before he headed for the elevator. Once it arrived, he stepped inside and hit the button for the penthouse. On the ride up, she snuggled deeper into his arms. She felt right. He ached to take her pouty lips in a searing kiss, but he wanted her awake and aware when he did that.

At the very top floor, the elevator doors silently slid open. Miles walked the short distance down the hall to his door. Easily holding Kareena with one arm, he unlocked it and then pushed it open. After stepping inside the penthouse, he kicked the door shut with his foot. He didn't bother to turn on any lights since he could see in the dark as if it were daytime.

Inside his bedroom, Miles pulled back the covers on his bed before he put Kareena on it. He took off her shoes and then tucked her in, leaving her completely dressed. Undressing her wasn't an option. It'd only upset her if she were to wake up and find herself only in her panties and bra. There was the fact that it'd just make his mating urge worse, seeing her almost naked. He was just a man and could take only so much before he lost the tenuous hold he had on his control.

As he straightened, his cell phone vibrated in his jeans pocket.

He'd turned off the ringer in anticipation of his date. Deciding to answer it out of the bedroom so he wouldn't disturb Kareena, he quickly left the room and then shut the door behind him as he took out his phone.

He smiled when he saw it was his daughter calling. "Hello, Jaden."

"Hi, Dad. So how did your date go? Is she your mate? Did she set off your mating urge?"

Miles chuckled. "One question at a time. In answer to your first one, the date didn't go."

"What do you mean?"

"I mean she stood me up. She sent me an e-mail just before she was to meet me, saying she couldn't make it. She wanted to set up another date, but I won't be doing that."

"All right. We'll just have to try the other matches that came up on Dirk's dating service."

"No, that won't be necessary."

"Dad, you can't give up so soon just because your first date didn't go as planned. Your mate is out there waiting for you to find her."

Miles smiled, even though Jaden couldn't see it. "I already found her."

There was a short stretch of silence and then Jaden asked, "What did you say?"

"I said I already found my mate. She arrived at the restaurant where I was to meet my date."

He had to pull the phone away from his ear as Jaden let out an excited-sounding shriek. In the background Miles heard Leif complaining about Jaden bursting his eardrums with her yelling. His daughter ignored her mate.

"I'm so happy for you, Dad. I knew you'd find her. So what's she like? When will you see her again? And most importantly, when will I get to meet her?" she asked excitedly.

"Calm down, Jaden. You're almost a week away from your due date. Do you want to have your baby right now?"

"I'm fine. You're just as bad as Leif. He thinks anything and everything is going to start my labor. The baby will come when it's ready. Now tell me when you're going to see your mate again."

"Actually, Kareena is here at my place."

"Then what are you doing talking to me on the phone?"

Miles chuckled. "Well, she had a little too much to drink at the restaurant. She was there with three of her friends, celebrating one of their birthdays and another's breakup from her boyfriend. From what I heard, he was a bit of a jerk. I offered Kareena a ride home, and she passed out in my car before I could get her address. She's asleep in my bed right now."

"Then I guess you haven't claimed her yet, which is good."

"No, I haven't. Why is it good? I thought you wanted me to be mated."

"I don't mean it that way. It's just that, as the foretold one, I have a rule I like male werewolves to follow when they find out their mates are mortals. No claiming her until she knows exactly what you are so you can give her the choice."

"Okay," he said slowly. "This is something new to me, but I had planned to tell Kareena first, anyway."

"Good. I'll let you go now. I can't wait to meet your mate."

After saying goodbye, Miles ended the call and then put his cell back into his pocket. Drawn to Kareena, he returned to the bedroom. She was still fast asleep. He stepped closer to the bed and stared down at her. He traced her features with his gaze, memorizing each one. She really was pretty, not supermodel pretty as the females of his kind were, but she was no less gorgeous to him.

Figuring it'd be a long night, Miles brought one of the armchairs from the sitting area of the bedroom closer to the bed at the side Kareena slept on. He wanted nothing more than to get under the covers next to her and hold her close as she slept, but that would only push his luck. Now that his mating urge had kicked into high gear, he was guaranteed to have erotic dreams of her, and would continue to have them every night until he'd claimed her as his own. Still in a semi-aroused state – something else he'd have to suffer through until he'd made her his – he was already walking too close to the line. It was better to be uncomfortable on the chair than closer to temptation.

Miles settled onto the chair's thick cushion and slouched into a somewhat more comfortable position. He continued to watch over Kareena for a few hours before he attempted to fall asleep. At least with her there in his bed, she'd be the last thing he saw when he went to sleep and the first thing he'd see come morning.

* * * *

Something had caused Kareena to slowly rise out of the deep slumber she'd been in. She hovered between sleep and wakefulness. She rolled to her side and tried to sink further into sleep's warm embrace. She didn't want to get up yet. She wanted to stay where she was.

Again, something brought her back to wakefulness. This time she cracked open her eyes, then immediately regretted it as she closed them once more. There was only dim light inside the room, but it was enough to make the headache she had throb more painfully in her temples. It felt as if someone had taken a jackhammer to her head. She rolled onto her back and swallowed. Her mouth tasted as if something had crawled inside it and died. It was also dry.

She remembered her time out with her friends. She'd had way too much to drink, especially after working long nightshifts. Kareena usually knew better and stopped before she got drunk. Now she paid the price for the overindulgence.

A noise that sounded unmistakably like a male moan—not of pain but of pleasure—had Kareena cracking open her eyelids once again. The first thing that hit her was that she didn't recognize the room. She turned her head and her gaze landed on the large man sitting in an armchair fast asleep. The position he was in was bound to give him a sore neck. She remembered him from the night before at the restaurant. His name was Miles.

Even though the sudden movement made her head feel as if it were about to fall off, Kareena bolted upright. She looked down at herself and breathed a sigh of relief when she saw she still wore the clothes from last night. The last thing she remembered was Miles putting her into his car so he could drive her home. She cringed when the memory of her telling him he could spend the night with her at her place surfaced. All that alcohol had made her bold. She'd basically propositioned him. Thank goodness he was gentleman enough not to take advantage of a shitfaced drunk woman who threw herself at him.

Miles moaned again, and the sound seemed to go straight to Kareena's pussy, making it clench to be filled. The masculine noise was of pleasure. He still slept, so he must be having one hell of an erotic dream. Even though she told herself not to look, she did. He had a hard-on that caused a large bulge in the front of his jeans. Men had five erections, on average, at night while they slept. This obviously was one of them for him.

She licked her lips as she tried to guess how big he was by the size of the bulge. Yup, he appeared to be just as large there as the rest of him. An ache deep inside her pussy throbbed as wetness pooled. God, the idea of jumping onto his lap and taking what she wanted was one sexual daydream she wished she could act on. Just the sight of him sleeping in the chair turned her on.

He groaned and his nostrils flared slightly as he drew in a deep breath. Kareena bit back a gasp as his eyes snapped open, and for a split second, they appeared to almost mutedly glow. It happened so fast she wasn't sure she saw what she'd seen. She soon didn't have time to think about that any further as he sat straighter and leaned closer. He drew in another big breath as if he smelled her.

"Ah, hi," she said. She figured her breath had to smell as bad as her mouth tasted and tried not to say too much.

"Hi," Miles said with a drop-dead gorgeous smile. "Did you sleep well?"

She nodded. "Yeah. This your place?"

"Yes. You kind of fell asleep in the car before I could ask you where you lived. I had no choice but to bring you here. Don't worry, nothing happened. You just slept."

"Thanks," she said sheepishly. "I don't normally drink like that. The late-night shifts at work did me in so I was just a disaster waiting to happen."

"What do you do?"

"I'm an ER nurse at San Francisco General Hospital."

"That must be a rewarding job."

"It can be." Right at that moment, Kareena needed to empty her bladder before it burst. "I need to use the…ah…bathroom."

"The en suite is just through that door." Miles pointed to the open doorway across from the bed. "There will be some spare toothbrushes in the medicine cabinet."

Kareena nodded as she slipped off the bed and headed for the en suite. She really had to have some killer bad breath if Miles told her where to find a toothbrush. Feeling her face heat with embarrassment, she closed the door behind her. She used the toilet, then washed her hands. A look in the medicine cabinet showed a couple brand-new toothbrushes still in packaging and a tube of toothpaste. She grabbed one of the brushes and the paste and the bottle of Ibuprofen she saw in there as well.

She downed one of the pills before she brushed her teeth. While she was at it, Kareena splashed some water on her face. She dried it with one of the hand towels and then peered at her reflection in the mirror. She didn't look too bad for being hung over. It was too bad she didn't have any makeup with her. She never wore the stuff, but with hot Miles in the other room and her not at her best, she would have liked to get rid of those dark circles under her eyes. Not much she could do about them, though.

She dismissed how rough she looked and stepped into the main room. Miles still sat in the armchair close to the bed. The sight of him almost took her breath away, especially when he ran his gaze over her body as if he wanted to eat her up. She had a wicked thought of his light blond head between her legs, making her come with his mouth.

Kareena yanked her mind out of the gutter and crossed to Miles. He stood, coming to stand almost toe-to-toe with her. Her gaze zeroed in on his lips. She wanted them on hers. As if he'd read her mind, he bent his head until his mouth hovered above hers. She sucked in a breath, taking his exhale into her lungs. With a groan, he claimed her lips.

She reached up and put her arms around his neck as his came around her waist and tugged her so she was flush against him. He swept the seam of her lips with his tongue before she opened for him. Kareena was more than glad she'd brushed her teeth when Miles thoroughly explored the inside of her mouth, their tongues dueling.

The ache inside her pussy was back and so was the pooling wetness. She pressed herself against Miles's erection, causing the ache to intensify. She wanted his big cock buried deep inside her. A year was a damn long time to be on a dry spell. He was the man who could end it for her.

He held her tighter, kissing her deeper. Her nipples grew taut under her blouse, the hard points brushing against his chest. Her body was on board with the idea of having sex with Miles. It was primed and raring to go. Even though she hardly knew him, Kareena was more than willing to hop into the sack with him. He couldn't be that bad of a guy since he'd taken care of her last night. They'd hardly spoken at that point, and he'd made sure she was okay.

Miles lifted her off her feet so her mouth was now level with his. She moaned as he fed from her lips. Her arousal shot through the roof. Kareena lifted her legs and put them around his waist, locking her ankles just above his ass. Her pussy came down on top of his hard cock. A surge of desire tore through her at the pleasure that contact made. She ground against him, wanting more.

He groaned, turned and the mattress rose to meet her back. She continued to cling to him as he came down with her and repositioned her to the middle of the bed. Miles's hips settled more firmly between her thighs as he moved against her. More wetness leaked into her panties the more turned-on she became.

Kareena pulled away from Miles's mouth and reached up to undo the top buttons on his shirt. "I want to touch you," she said in a breathy voice.

He lifted his upper body off her to give her better access. "I've been dying all night to have your hands on me."

She made quick work of the rest of the buttons and yanked the ends of his shirt out of his jeans. Kareena spread the material and sucked in a breath. Miles's chest and abs were lickable with all the ridges and valleys of his well-defined muscles. His broad shoulders flexed as he took off his shirt and tossed it away.

She feasted her eyes on all that bared, male flesh. Kareena ran her fingertips over his chest, circling each flat nipple as she came to it. Miles groaned when she reached his six-pack abs and continued lower. She looked up to see he had his eyes closed, his lips parted as he breathed at a quick pace. In the throes of desire, he made her want him even more.

Kareena reached for the waistband of his jeans, but he brushed her hand away and lowered himself on one bent arm. He used his other hand to work the first button free on her blouse.

"Not yet," he said in a gruff voice. His eyes were open to mere slits. "I get to take your top off and explore you. Then I'm going to make you come with my mouth."

"Yes," she panted. She wasn't going to turn down oral sex, or the chance of an orgasm, especially if a man as good-looking as Miles was the one giving it to her.

CHAPTER THREE

T he scent of Kareena's arousal and the feel of her under him had Miles wound tight. His cock ached with the need to take her, but he ignored it as much as he could. He was going to pleasure his would-be mate first before he thought of himself. He wanted to hear her cries of passion as he brought her to climax.

He finished undoing the buttons on her blouse and then peeled it off her with Kareena's help. Once she lay back down, he stared at her chest. Her breasts looked to be more than a handful, and were covered in a simple white cotton bra. It wasn't meant to be sexy, but it turned his crank.

Miles made sure to keep his gaze lowered as he ran a finger between Kareena's breasts to the front clasp of her bra. His eyes would assuredly be mutedly glowing. They only did that when he was very aroused or angry. He was most definitely aroused. She didn't need to see them like that just yet.

He undid the clasp before he brushed the material away. A low growl rumbled out of him. Her breasts were perfect, tipped with rose-pink nipples that were taut, just begging for him to suck on them. He lowered himself to his other arm, coming closer to the objects of his desire.

Miles bent his head and licked a nipple before he blew a breath on it. Kareena moaned and arched her back. He did it again, then took the tight bud into his mouth. She sank her fingers into his hair as he sucked, her breath coming in pants. He loved how responsive his would-be mate was to his touch. It made his cock strain against the front of his jeans.

He released her nipple and kissed a trail across her chest to the other one. He sucked it into his mouth. Kareena scraped her nails against his scalp as she ground her pussy against him. The scent of her arousal grew stronger. She was wet. He'd bet anything her juices soaked into her panties. He was going to lick her, lapping it all up like a cat did with cream.

The need to taste her coursing through him, Miles let go of her breast and shifted to his side. He undid Kareena's pants and then peeled them down her long legs. He hooked her panties with a finger and took them off as well. He gazed at what he'd revealed. She took his breath away.

He settled between her legs and inched lower on her body until he reached her pussy. He spread her thighs even wider, opening her to his gaze. Her sex glistened with her juices. He couldn't hold back another soft growl. His cock jerked. The urge to tear them open and sink into her wetness was almost too hard to ignore. He managed to beat it back.

Miles used his thumbs to spread her pussy lips and took his first lick. Kareena gasped, fisting the blanket under her. He closed his eyes and groaned. Her taste went straight to his head. He wanted to throw it back and howl. Instead, he lapped at her, swallowing down her wetness. She moaned, her hips lifting off the bed.

He licked and sucked, making sure to pay attention to her clit as he did so. The sounds Kareena made turned into keening moans as she ground her pussy against his mouth. Miles focused on her clit and pushed a finger inside her. Her inner walls clamped down around it as he slid in and out. He soon used two as he worked her. She was close. So very close.

Miles set a faster pace and sucked on the little bundle of nerves that was the center of her pleasure. Kareena rode his fingers, the movement of her hips jerky. He felt a rippling along her inner walls and then she was there. She moaned loudly as her pussy rhythmically clutched the digits he still moved inside her. He didn't stop until he'd wrung everything out of her.

He pulled his fingers free of her body and then licked them

clean as he rose from between her legs. Miles buried his face in the crook of Kareena's neck. His body was on fire for her, his cock aching for release. The thought of sinking deep inside her pussy made it ache even more. If she'd been a werewolf, he wouldn't have held himself back. He'd have taken her without a second thought, but she wasn't. She didn't know what would happen if he did. Once the mating bond formed between them, neither one of them would be able to stand to be apart from the other. Separation anxiety would ride them hard, and any absence would make them think something terrible had happened to their mate. All they'd be able to think about was being together again.

Kareena shifted under him. "Miles? You stopped. You don't have to."

Oh yes, he did. "It's all right." He reined back on his arousal and mating urge. Sure his eyes would no longer be mutedly glowing, he lifted his head to look at her. He brushed her lips with his. "This one was all for you."

"You're still hard."

"It doesn't matter. I'll be fine."

"At least let me give you some relief."

She reached for the button on his jeans, but he caught her wrist and lifted her hand away. It was very tempting. The only problem with letting her make him come was he really wouldn't get any relief. That would only happen when he made love to her fully. Any other way would only cause his mating urge to ride his ass harder. Plus, it wouldn't get rid of his erection. As a male werewolf, he could keep it for hours, coming multiple times before he'd soften.

"No," he said softly. "That will just make my good intentions fly out the window. There's no need to rush. I'd like to get to know you better before we go any further."

"Wow." She blinked. "Are you for real?"

He gave her a cautious look, not sure if she were being sarcastic. "What do you mean?"

"Most guys I know wouldn't have stopped. They wouldn't have given a damn and would have taken it all the way."

He smiled. "Then you must know a lot of jerks."

"Well, that about sums them up, especially my ex. He was the biggest one of them all. I guess I attract that kind of men."

Miles cocked an eyebrow. "You didn't this time."

Her cheeks turned a becoming shade of pink. "Crap. I didn't mean you were a jerk. I know you aren't. Damn. I sometimes don't think before I open my mouth and say whatever is on my mind. I haven't put you in the same class as my ex."

"I'm glad to hear that," he said with a chuckle. "It's okay. I was just having a bit of fun with you, but since you really don't know me that well, you wouldn't realize that."

"You're right."

He pulled away and slid off the bed to stand next to it. "Why don't you get dressed while I get us something for breakfast?"

"I really don't know if my stomach will be able to handle food just yet. If you have tea, I'd love a cup or two of that."

Miles smiled. "I do have tea. I'll put the kettle on."

He turned and walked out of the room without a backward glance. Seeing Kareena naked and lying on his bed made him want to forget what he'd told her. Miles went to the kitchen and put the kettle on to boil.

It'd been a long time since he'd awakened to a woman under his roof, at least one he cared about. The last female had been Jaden's mother. Even though he knew relatively nothing about Kareena, he did care about her. The mating urge had made sure of that. It wouldn't have been set off if there wasn't a chance of him falling in love with her. The only thing that still niggled at the back of his mind was the fact she was mortal. He could possibly have a hard time getting her to accept what he was. What he really was worried about was the fact he was so long-lived, and she had what seemed like only a handful of years compared to his lifespan.

He didn't know if he could stand the thought of losing her so soon. It'd been hard enough when Sarah, his daughter's mother, had walked out on him. Giving Kareena his heart, then having death claim her, would hurt even worse. The mating bond would make it so.

Arms wrapped around his middle as Kareena came up behind him. "You must be lost in thought about something serious. I said your name, but you didn't hear me."

He turned and dragged her closer before he gave her a quick kiss. "I was lost in thought, but nothing too serious. Why don't you sit at the table? The kettle should be just about boiled."

She dropped her arms and did as he'd suggested. "You have a great place here. Is it a penthouse?"

The kettle shut off once it reached a boil. He took out a teapot and then put two teabags into it before he filled it with the heated water. "Yes, it is." Miles brought the pot and two mugs to the table, then sat next to Kareena.

"I told you what I do for a living, but you haven't said where you work," she said.

"I don't have what you'd call a job, though I'm easing my way back into my sister's protection business. I used to work with her many years ago."

"The bodyguard business must be good. Do you enjoy it?"

"It's nice to be doing it again, and to work with my sister once more. Saskia and I haven't been close for a long time because of the way I left. I'm trying to remedy that. Do you like being an ER nurse?"

"Yeah, though it can be stressful at times. The long shifts can be a killer, especially the night ones. I've been a nurse for a while. I went to San Francisco State University's School of Nursing right after high school."

Once they mated, Kareena would have to give up her career. There was no way either of them would be able to handle the separation while she did a long shift at the hospital. He had more than enough money to financially support them.

The tea steeped, Miles poured some into their mugs. "Do you want milk?"

Kareena nodded. "Please."

He took the jug out of the fridge and then poured some into a creamer before he returned to the table. He waited until after Kareena had used it, then added some milk to his tea. She took a sip of hers and sighed.

"Going down okay?" he asked with a smile.

"Yes. I'll say it again. I don't normally drink as much as I did last night. I should have probably not had those last two drinks. They did me in."

"You and your friends looked as if you were celebrating something."

Kareena smiled, and Miles resisted the urge to drag her into his arms and kiss her senseless. He couldn't remember the last time he'd sat with a woman and had a conversation. Since Sarah, he'd made sure not to form any attachments to the opposite sex. Much to his shame, he'd be the first to admit he'd been too busy doing despicable things that he wasn't proud of. He'd let his lust for power get the better of him.

"We were celebrating," Kareena said. "It was Alice's birthday. And Lacy had dumped her asshole boyfriend."

Miles had known those things. Werewolf hearing was so acute he'd had no problem hearing the conversation at Kareena's table. "So your friend breaking up was a cause for celebration?"

"Most definitely. We all hated her boyfriend. He didn't treat Lacy very well. It took her a while to see it, but in the end, she did."

"What about you and your ex? Were you together long?"

Kareena blew out a breath. "You could say that. He's my ex-fiancé. We were engaged for seven years before he decided he didn't want to get married, after all. That was about a year ago." She gave him a shy look. "I haven't dated anyone else since then, except you, of course."

"Well, we haven't had a real date, have we? That's something I want to have with you, though. Are you free this evening?"

"Yes. I'm off work for the next two days."

"Then how does going to see a movie or something sound to you?"

She turned toward Miles and kissed him, just a mere brush of her lips that left him wanting a whole lot more. "It's a date. A movie sounds good. I haven't been to the theater in ages."

"A movie it is."

Kareena finished her tea, then placed the mug on the table. "I really should go home so I can change out of these clothes. Plus, I need to get ready for our hot date."

Miles chuckled. "I'll drive you. Your purse is still in the bedroom. I guess I could have gone through it to check your ID for your address, but I didn't think you'd appreciate it if I did. It gave me an excuse to bring you to my place."

"Yeah, we women have a thing about our purses," she said with a laugh. "I'm glad you didn't look for my address. I wouldn't have had the chance to get to know you better."

"Oh, you wouldn't have gotten rid of me that easily. I would have showed up at your door today, no matter what."

She wrapped her hand around his nape and brought his mouth to hers. Kareena gave him a thorough kiss that jacked his libido up another level. It'd been at a low simmer as it was.

After she pulled away, she said, "I'm glad I met you, Miles. I'm looking forward to this evening. Maybe we can take up where we left off earlier."

Miles groaned. "You're trying to kill me, aren't you? Now I won't be able to think about anything else but that for the rest of the day."

Kareena stood. "Anticipation is a good thing. I'll get my purse, then we can leave whenever you're ready."

She walked out of the kitchen. God, he wanted her. He just hoped like hell he'd be able to hold her off for a little while longer. If it looked as if he couldn't rein back on his instinct to claim Kareena as his mate, he'd have to tell her the truth about him tonight. Considering how well things were going with her right now, he'd hate to have that throw it off, but it wasn't something he couldn't do. He'd have to tell her. It'd be a test to see just how strong his control was.

CHAPTER FOUR

Kareena directed Miles to her apartment building. This time she was awake for the ride in his car. She still felt a little embarrassed about passing out on him the night before. What a way to meet someone.

She looked at Miles's profile as he drove. Kareena traced his handsome features with her gaze. She could stare at him all day. And to think she'd been naked in his arms as he'd pleasured her. Hopefully, there'd be a lot more of that during their date that evening. As she'd told him earlier, anticipation wasn't a bad thing.

Miles pulled up to the front of her building and then put the car into park. He turned toward her and leaned across the seats to claim her lips. His tongue slipped inside her mouth as he cupped the back of her head, holding her just where he wanted her. Kareena moaned softly as she returned the kiss, her body craving more of his touch. All too soon he ended it.

"I'll pick you up around six. Decide on what movie you'd like to see. Afterward, we can go someplace for a drink."

"All right. I promise not to get drunk tonight," Kareena said with a laugh. "Instead of going out to a restaurant or bar, how about we come back here? I'll make us some snack-type food."

Miles smiled. "I'd like that. I'll supply the drinks."

She leaned toward him and gave him another kiss. "Don't worry about the drinks. I'll get those as well. See you later then."

Kareena opened the car door and then got out. Once she closed it, Miles gave her a wave before he drove away. She went inside the building and then took the elevator up to her floor. The sound of a phone ringing inside her apartment reached as she unlocked it. Quickly, she opened the door and raced to get the cordless.

She smiled when she saw Lacy's number on the call display. "Hi, Lacy."

"Finally, you're home. I was worried sick."

"Why?" Kareena shut her apartment door before she locked it.

"Why, she asks. I've only tried to get a hold of you since last night. I even tried your cell phone, but it keeps going straight to your voice mail."

Kareena fished her cell out of her purse. The battery had died. "I have to charge it. Why were you calling last night? I thought you'd at least wait until today."

"We all saw you leave with the hottie and get into his car. You were kind of drunk last night. I didn't think it was such a smart thing to let you go with a guy you just met, but Alice said you'd be fine. She said she *felt* he was no threat, and that you'd be okay."

Alice had this uncanny intuition when it came to people. She could tell just by observing them if they could be trusted or not. She claimed this ability ran in her family on her mother's side, dating back to an Irish gypsy relative.

"Then you shouldn't have worried," Kareena said. "Alice is never wrong."

"I know. So where were you all night?"

"With Miles."

"The hottie?"

"Yes. I spent the night at his penthouse."

"Damn. Good-looking and rich. You sure landed on your feet all right. Was he great in bed? He looks like the type of guy who'd keep a woman up all night."

"Well, we didn't get quite that far, though we did fool around a bit this morning, which was really nice."

"So you actually didn't sleep with him?"

"No. You were right about me being drunk. I ended up passing out on him in his car. Since I hadn't told Miles where I lived before that, he took me to his place to sleep it off."

"You didn't," Lacy said with a laugh.

"Yeah, I did." Her friend burst into gales of laughter. "It isn't that funny. I'm actually a little embarrassed by it."

"Oh yes, it is. You land yourself a guy who looks as if he could be a cover model, and you pass out on him. I wonder if you snored."

"I don't snore."

"Yes, you do when you've had too much to drink. During our college days when we'd overindulge and stay overnight at one of our places, you always snored. Not loud enough to rattle the windows or anything, but you still did it."

Kareena cringed. "Great. Now you have me all worried about that. I must have made a real good impression on Miles with the whole being drunk and snoring. I'm surprised he wants to go out on a date this evening."

Lacy laughed again. "If he wants to see you again, I guess it didn't bother him."

"Still, ugh. I'd better be on my best behavior tonight or he might rethink that."

"Hey, if he's still interested after all that, he must be really into you."

"I know I'm really into him. The man knows how to kiss, amongst other things."

"Not something I needed to hear, especially now that I'm single again."

"You won't be for long. Unlike me, you won't wait a year before you move on to the next guy."

"So true. I'm already on the prowl."

Kareena laughed. "Then all the single men out there better watch out."

"I'll let you go since you have a date this evening. I'm just glad you're okay, and that *you* have finally moved on. I'll talk to you later, and I'll give the others the good news that you've managed to snag the hunk."

"Talk to you later then."

She hung up and shook her head. Out of all her friends, Lacy was the one who liked to gossip. If any of them wanted to know what was up with the others, they just had to call Lacy. It didn't bother any of them. They all knew it was just a part of their friend's personality.

Kareena headed toward her bedroom and shook her head again as she thought of how fast her other friends would hear about Miles. She wouldn't be surprised if they called her next, wanting all the juicy details.

She tossed her purse onto her bed before she stripped out of her clothes for a shower. Kareena had some primping to do before Miles picked her up for their date.

* * * *

Instead of going to his place, Miles decided to make the drive to Marin County to check in on Jaden. With her due date so close, he wanted to make sure she still felt well. He looked forward to being a grandfather. Having not been involved in bringing Jaden up, he didn't want to miss out on anything when it came to her child.

He pulled onto the drive of the Protectors' mansion and then parked in front of the garage before he headed for the front door. He usually called ahead to let Jaden know he'd be showing up, but since this was a spur of the moment thing, he hadn't bothered. He didn't think his daughter would mind. He'd been slowly working his way back into his old life, and had even taken over some of the protection duties. Though he didn't think watching over her was a chore. It just gave him more time to spend with her.

Miles knocked once on the door, then opened it. He stepped into the large, open-concept foyer. "Hello? Anyone home?" he called as a courtesy. He knew there was, because he could smell the scents of each individual inside the mansion. His daughter's was one of them, but there were three he hadn't encountered before.

Without waiting for someone to greet him, Miles headed for the living room. Inside were a couple and a small child he'd never met, all werewolves. The woman had the same coloring and build as Jaden. The man had long, black hair. The female child looked to be a year old. The man and woman seemed to stiffen as Miles walked farther into the room. The scent of anxiousness suddenly came off the adult female.

He slowed his steps, stopping before he came too close. The

man shifted slightly, as if he tried to place himself between his family and Miles. Miles put on a smile that would show he wasn't any kind of threat. Some males could be overprotective of their mates, especially when they had young with them.

"Hi," Miles said. "I didn't mean to startle you. I'm Miles. Saskia is my sister and Jaden is my daughter."

The man answered. "I'm Beowulf, and this is my mate, Roxie, and our daughter, Nevaeh."

Miles nodded at Roxie. "Nice to meet you all. I just stopped by to see Jaden."

Before he could say anything more, Saskia came rushing into the room. Her gaze flicked to the couple on the couch. Miles could have sworn his sister wore a panicked expression for a split second, but it was gone too quickly. She turned her focus on him.

"Miles, what a nice surprise. We weren't expecting you today, what with you finding your mate last night and all. We thought you'd be busy with her."

He smiled. "I dropped Kareena off at her place, then decided to pop in to check up on Jaden. I'm not staying long. I'm taking Kareena to a movie this evening."

Saskia closed the distance between them and gave him a hug. "I'm so happy for you. How do you feel about Kareena being mortal?"

"She's my mate. It really doesn't matter that she's not a werewolf. It doesn't seem to be a problem now. I'm worried about her being able to accept what I am and the differences in our life spans. I don't want to think about that, though."

"I wish there was some way I could help you with the last part."

Miles took a deep breath and let it out. "So do I. Though I met Kareena less than twenty-four hours ago, my feelings for her are growing stronger. A lot faster than they did with Jaden's mother. The idea of losing Kareena to old age makes my gut knot. I'd give anything to have her become a werewolf, but we all know that isn't possible. She'd have to be born one."

Roxie cleared her throat. "She's your mate. That's why your feelings for her are already so strong. I take it you haven't claimed her yet."

Miles looked at Roxie. "No. Jaden told me her rule about how she wants male werewolves with mortal mates to tell them what they are first to give them a choice. She said that was a rule given as the foretold one. So I really don't have any choice but to obey."

Roxie smiled. "Jaden is very smart. That's a perfect rule. I couldn't have come up with a better one." Beowulf snorted, and his mate gave him an elbow in the stomach for it.

"I heard someone say my name," Jaden said as she waddled into the room with Leif at her side.

"I just told your dad how smart I thought you were for telling him about the rule you have about mortal mates," Roxie replied.

"Oh. Nothing bad then." Jaden came to Miles and kissed him. "What are you doing here, Dad?"

"I wanted to check up on you and the little one." He placed his hand on his daughter's distended belly and was rewarded with a kick. He smiled.

"As you can see, we're doing fine. How about we go out back and visit? It's a nice day. I figure I won't get too many chances to just sit and enjoy the outside once the baby comes. I'll be too busy."

Miles nodded. He turned to Beowulf and Roxie. "I hope to see you again."

He followed Jaden and Leif through the house and then outside to the back patio. It was a gorgeous day with the sun shining brightly and hardly a cloud in the sky. Miles sat at the wrought-iron patio table as Jaden sank onto the chair next to Leif with a sigh.

"Are you sure you're fine?" Miles asked Jaden.

"Yes. I'm just ready to have this baby. Plus, I'm feeling cooped up in the house."

"Tell you what. I recently bought a cottage that borders the Point Reyes National Seashore land. It's on the secluded side, but it's quiet. You and Leif can spend a couple days there with me and Kareena."

"I don't know," Leif said. "Jaden is close to giving birth. There is the whole question of it being safe for her up there."

"Between the two of us, I think we can watch over Jaden well enough," Miles quickly assured his daughter's mate. "Kareena is an ER nurse. So if anything should happen in regards to the baby, she should be able to help. We're only going to be an hour-drive away."

Jaden looked at Leif. "This sounds like a great idea. I'd love to go. I'm sure Aunt Saskia won't have a problem with it. I promise I'll take it easy and rest."

Of course Saskia would have to be consulted about the trip. As the leader of the Protectors, she had the final say when it came to the safety of the foretold one.

Leif stared at Jaden while she gave him a pleading look. "God, I hate when you look at me like that," he said. "I can never tell you no."

Jaden took her mate's hand. "Does that mean we can go?"

"Yes. So long as Saskia agrees."

"When would you like to go?" Jaden asked Miles.

"I was thinking tomorrow or the next day. I'll talk it over with Kareena tonight and see if she can get time off work."

"Then let's tell Saskia what we have planned," Jaden said as she pushed off her chair and stood.

They filed back into the house and then went to the living room. Saskia was still there along with Beowulf, Roxie and their daughter. Jaden explained what they wanted to do. As Miles had predicted, his sister agreed with their plans. Shortly after that, he said his goodbyes and left. He couldn't think of a better way for his mate and daughter to get to know each other better. He just hoped Kareena would say yes as well.

* * * *

After the sound of Miles's car on the driveway could no longer be heard, Saskia blew out a breath. "That was too damn close. I'm sorry, Roxie. I never expected Miles to show up like that. He usually calls before he drops in."

Roxie waved her concerns away with a flick of her hand. "Don't worry about it. No harm done. I'm sure your brother is more than a little distracted with his mating urge riding him. I doubt he'd have thought Beowulf and I were anything more than just friends."

"Still it was a risk."

"He's changed," Roxie said, then paused. "I think we have to tell him the truth."

Saskia, Beowulf and Leif all said "No!" at the same time. Saskia shook her head. "No, Roxie. We can't. He's only changed because he thinks Jaden is the foretold one. I don't know if that will last once he finds out we've lied to him."

"Your brother has found his mate. His *mortal* mate. Is it really fair to let him continue to think Kareena can't have the same lifespan as him when I can turn her into a werewolf?"

"I don't," Jaden said in a quiet voice. "My dad has done terrible things in his past, but he's trying to make up for that. I don't think he'll ever go back to what he was, no matter the circumstances. If you don't want to tell him the truth, then at least let him know Roxie is special and can use a spell to change Kareena into a werewolf. He doesn't need to know the other things she can do."

"I think that's a great idea," Roxie said. "Miles shouldn't think it too strange that I can work the spell. After all, his own grandmother was the one who saw my coming and wrote the prophecy about the foretold one. You have the sight as well, Saskia."

Saskia thought it over, then nodded. "All right. We can tell him about the spell, and that's it. I just hope it doesn't backfire on us, but I can see how it'd appear unfair to keep this from Miles. He has as much right to be as happy with his mate as the rest of us."

"I'll tell him when we're at his cottage," Jaden said. "I think it'd be better if he heard it from me. I'm supposed to be the foretold one, after all. I should be the one who decides who gets to be in on the know about the spell."

"Wait until he's claimed his mate. I wouldn't be surprised if Miles decides to use this trip away to tell Kareena about his being a werewolf. He might think she'll have an easier time of accepting it with you there, Jaden."

"Then it's decided," Roxie said. "We tell Miles about the spell and nothing else."

"Once you've done the spell, Rox, you're going to avoid seeing Miles again. I don't want to take any unnecessary risks. He's my brother, but that doesn't mean he's earned back all my trust. I still have the responsibility to keep you safe."

Roxie nodded. Saskia just hoped they weren't making a huge mistake by telling Miles about the spell. Hopefully, he'd be so thrilled by the fact his mate was no longer mortal, he'd just accept

Roxie as they wanted her to appear to him—a special werewolf with an extra bit of magic. Saskia would get him to swear on his life that he'd keep the spell a secret.

CHAPTER FIVE

Kareena was ready for her date with Miles at exactly six o'clock. After she'd taken a shower and changed her clothes, she'd gone to the grocery store to pick up some snack food and drinks. Not sure what he liked, she bought a six-pack of beer along with a bottle of white wine. She'd spent the rest of the afternoon making the snacks so she wouldn't have to fuss around too much in the kitchen while he was there.

Once Miles buzzed up to apartment, Kareena told him she'd meet him at the door through the intercom. She locked up and then took the elevator down to the front entrance. Her gaze landed on him where he waited. Even though it'd only been half a day since she'd last seen him, he still took her breath away. She missed him. He hadn't strayed very far from her thoughts. She'd caught herself daydreaming about him while she'd been busy in the kitchen. She was lucky she hadn't sliced off a finger.

She walked to the door to the vestibule before she stepped through it. Miles swept her up into his arms and gave her a kiss that had Kareena practically moaning. It felt too good to be pressed against his hard body.

"We should go," Miles said, his voice a bit on the husky side. "Have you decided what you want to see?"

Kareena linked her fingers with his as Miles took her hand. They walked out of the building and then headed for the visitors parking. "Well, there is one I wanted to watch, but I doubt you'd be interested in it. It's a vampire movie that's more along the line of a young adult romance. I won't force you to sit through it."

"If that's what you really want to see, I don't mind." He helped her into the car. Once he was behind the steering wheel, he said, "So, you're into vampires or are you just into romances?"

"I'd have to say I'm into both. Actually, I've been hooked on reading paranormal romances for the last couple years, especially ones about werewolves and vampires." Kareena felt her face heat as she spoke. Her ex had liked to make fun of the genre she loved to read.

Miles started the car and turned his head to look at her before he backed out of the parking spot. "Werewolves, huh?"

"I know it's stupid. My ex thought I was an idiot for reading them. One day I got angry and told him he needed to read one since he had no idea what real romance was."

"I bet he didn't take that too well," Miles said with a laugh.

Kareena chuckled and shook her head. "No, not very. He said my expectations were too high, because of all the crap in the books. He also said I had a problem if I thought werewolves were sexy. His idea of a werewolf was of the one in horror movies."

"Those movies give werewolves a bad rep."

"You think that, huh?"

"Yes. Why can't they be sexy? If a vampire can been seen that way—a being that has to drink human blood to stay alive—why can't a werewolf?"

She smiled as Miles glanced her way. "Hmm, I might have to keep you around if you keep saying things like that."

Miles reached across, placed his hand on her thigh and gave it a squeeze. "Good, because I plan to be with you for as long as I can."

A warm sensation washed through Kareena at his words. If she had anything to say about it, it'd be a very, very long time. Now that she'd met him, she had to think her ex had done her a favor by dumping her. If he hadn't, they might have already been married, maybe, and she never would have met Miles. So for the first time since their breakup, she sent her ex a silent thank you instead of calling him every vile name she knew.

At the movie theater, Miles took her hand once again and

guided her into the building. There were more than a few people already waiting in line, but it didn't take very long before it was their turn. He paid for two tickets for the vampire movie she wanted to see, then walked her to the counter where the popcorn and soda were sold. Since she had snacks back at her apartment, Kareena only ordered a soda. He did the same.

Inside the theater where their movie would be showing, Miles guided Kareena up the stairs close to the back. They settled into seats in the middle of the row. There was still time before the show would start.

Miles took a sip of his drink before he placed it in the cup holder on the armrest. "I haven't been to a theater in years."

"Since I started working as a nurse, I don't have as much time for it either. When my friends and I were going to school, we used to come frequently. That was before I started seeing my ex."

"Then we'll have to do this more often."

With most of the seats taken, the lights dimmed, and the trailers played on the large widescreen at the front of the room. There were a couple movies Kareena wouldn't mind seeing.

The movie started, and Miles put his arm around her shoulders. Kareena snuggled in as close as the armrest would allow. It'd been a long time since she'd sat in the dark at the back of a movie theater with a guy she liked. She might not be a teenager any longer, but the idea of making out with him seemed like a great idea.

Kareena got caught up in the movie, but never forgot Miles sat next to her. With his arm still around her shoulders, he played with her hair, the tips of his fingers brushing against her cheek from time to time. Watching the romantic scenes play out on the screen, she wished she could snuggle closer.

At the end of the movie, and as the credits played, Kareena turned her head to ask Miles if he'd enjoyed it. She didn't manage to get the words out. His lips covered hers, his tongue pushing inside her mouth. He thoroughly tasted her, deepening the kiss. Her body melted with arousal.

He pulled back and rested his forehead against hers. "Let's get out of here before I do something that'll get us both arrested."

She nodded. "That wouldn't be too good, and it sure would put a damper on the date."

Miles kissed the tip of her nose, then stood and held out his hand. She slipped hers into his, and he pulled her to her feet. Kareena looked around the theater. The lights had come on as they'd kissed. There were only a few people who were sticking around to watch right through until the end of the credits. None were very close to where they'd sat. She doubted they'd been seen. Not that she really cared if they had.

They headed out of the theater and were soon in his car. He drove straight to her apartment. The closer they came the more Kareena couldn't wait to get him behind closed doors. Her body was starved for sex, and after she'd gotten a taste of what it'd be like with him, she craved more of his touch. She wanted to explore parts of him she hadn't gotten to see that morning.

Once they were inside her apartment, Kareena closed and locked the door behind them. "I have some snack food I can whip up pretty quick. Would you like something to eat and drink? I have beer and white wine in the fridge."

"Later. There's something else I'm hungry for."

Kareena found herself wrapped in Miles's arms with his lips claiming hers in a heated kiss. She dropped her purse onto the floor and placed her hands onto his chest. She fisted his shirt as she tried to get closer, his mouth angling over hers for a deeper kiss. Just like that, she went up in flames, her pussy aching to be filled. This morning had been an appetizer. Now her body demanded the full-course meal.

She hungrily kissed Miles, sucking on his tongue as she tunneled her fingers through his light blond hair. He groaned and pulled her tighter against him, his hard cock pressing against her belly. Wetness pooled between her legs at the thought of having it inside her. She wanted him to take her over and over again until she couldn't move.

Kareena made a sound of approval deep inside her throat as Miles picked her up and carried her in the direction of her bedroom. Just another thing she really liked about him—he could carry her around as if she weighed nothing. There was something to be said about having a muscular man for a lover.

Miles walked into her room and headed straight for the bed. He took her down to the mattress, not breaking contact with her mouth, and stretched out on top her. His hips wedged between her legs. Kareena moaned at the feel of his erection coming to rest along her pussy. He rocked his hips, which sent a surge of pleasure straight through her.

He made short work of stripping her out of her top and bra. Kareena's nipples grew taut as Miles stared down at her breasts. He cupped one and dragged his tongue over the tight peak before he sucked it into his mouth. She felt a hint of teeth as he drew on it hard, causing a corresponding pull deep inside her pussy.

So turned-on, Kareena could no longer stay still. She rubbed against his cock. He switched his attention to her other breast and cupped her bottom in both hands. He lifted her slightly and ground his erection in just the right spot. If he kept it up, she'd come. She didn't want that, though. She wanted nothing between them when she reached orgasm.

Kareena pushed at his chest until he released her nipple and lifted slightly off her. He looked at her with eyes only open to slits. "My turn to be on top," she said in a husky voice. "You're not the only one who gets to do some exploring."

He wrapped an arm around her waist and rolled to his back, taking her with him. "Be my guest." His voice was rough. "I'm all yours."

Yes, he was. Kareena planned to keep it that way if she could. Now where she wanted to be, the first thing she did was lift Miles's shirt up and off over his head. She tossed it over the side of the bed before she once again admired his muscular chest and abs. What she traced with her gaze, she did the same with her lips and tongue. His skin was smooth and warm beneath her touch. The scent of his cologne filled her nose.

She shifted so she straddled his thighs instead of his hips. As she nibbled on his well-defined abs, Kareena worked on undoing Miles's jeans. She'd been dying to get inside them to see just how large he was. Once she'd accomplished what she'd set out to do, she parted the material, springing his cock.

There was no underwear to come between it and her hand. His shaft jerked as she trailed her fingers up his full length and circled the head. Encountering a bead of pre-cum at the slit, she rubbed it into his skin. Miles made a sound that suspiciously sounded like an animal growling.

Kareena looked up his body. He held himself stiff as if in

anticipation of her next move. She teased Miles a little bit more by bending her head and swirling her tongue around the very tip of his cock. It jerked, and more pre-cum leaked from it. She lapped it up, moaning at the taste.

"Kareena," Miles said through gritted teeth. "I thought you wanted to explore, not arouse me to the point of insanity."

"This is exploring. I'm finding out what you like."

"I'd like it even more if you'd —"

His words cut off in a sharp moan as Kareena opened her mouth and took his cock inside. She sucked him as far back as she could manage before sliding him almost all the way out. She used the flat of her tongue to stroke the sensitive spot just under the flared head. She held him at his base while she kept him in a tight grip and sucked him in and out. His erection hardened even more. The growls he'd made before continued to rumble out of him, louder and sounding more animalistic the longer she pleasured him.

She continued to take him in and out of her mouth as she reached between his legs and fondled his balls. Kareena gave them a small tug before she gently cupped them. Miles thrust his hips in time with her movements. Her juices leaked into her panties. He breathed in rapid growling pants, which aroused her even more. She was getting to him — bad.

It wasn't too long before Miles ground out, "Enough."

Once she pulled away from his cock, he rose to a sitting position and grabbed her. He took her to her back, his lips leaving a searing trail wherever they touched as he worked on stripping her out of her jeans. Her panties were yanked down and off in a matter of seconds.

Miles was between her legs, spreading her open to his sight in a blink of an eye. He kissed up the inside of her thigh. Once he reached her pussy, he gave it one lick before he continued down her other leg.

Kareena groaned. "Miles, what did you say about teasing?"

"Just a little payback."

He continued to torture her with licks until she whimpered with need. She lifted her hips off the bed each time his mouth came in contact with her wet pussy. Miles finally relented and stroked her the way she wanted. He stiffened his tongue and plunged it into her opening the same way she needed his cock to move inside her. She was so close all it took to send her over the edge into release was for him to rub her clit with the tip of a finger. Kareena let out a keening moan, her climax tearing through her. He lapped at her pussy until the last tremor shook her.

Still breathing hard, she watched Miles shift to her side and push out of his jeans. She thought for sure he'd settle back on top of her and sink his cock inside her. He didn't. Instead, he lay on his back. She ran her gaze over his body. His erection was thick and long.

"I want your lips wrapped around my cock when I come," he said in a strained voice.

If that was what he wanted, she'd give it to him. They still had a lot of hours of the night left. Kareena straddled his thighs once more and fisted the base of his erection. She wasted no time taking him into her mouth. She sucked on him hard and felt her cheeks hollowing out.

"Don't stop," he panted. "I'm close."

Unbelievably, his cock grew even harder and bigger. She bobbed her head as she took him in and out. He surged inside her mouth one final time, hips arching off the bed, his shaft pulsing with his climax. She took everything he had to give. Once it was over, she released him. He was still hard, as if he'd never come. He pulled her into his embrace with her stretched out on top him. Her pussy was mere inches away from his cock, but he made no move to join their bodies. Kareena decided she'd let him catch his breath and then she'd make sure they took it to the next level.

*

Miles was so close to having his control snap it wasn't even funny. He felt Kareena's moist heat against his skin, his dick so close to her pussy. His mating urge was worse than before they'd started. It'd been bad enough with all the erotic dreams he'd had of her during the night while she'd slept in his bed. Coming had made it worse, as he'd known it would, but he hadn't expected it to be this bad. His whole body shook with the strain of holding himself back. With the scent of his would-be mate's arousal in the air, and the taste of her juices on his tongue, it made it harder to remember why he couldn't claim her as his.

Kareena shifted. Just the head of his cock entered her, causing his control to slip even more. He was barely hanging on by the skin of his teeth. It felt like torture lying there, not moving, when all he wanted to do was thrust up into her and bury his full length inside her pussy.

Miles put his hands on her hips to hold her still, to make sure she didn't take any more of him. At this point, he could pull out before it was too late. At least he thought he had that kind of willpower. Kareena had ideas of her own, though. She didn't try to push down on him, but rolled her pelvis in such a way his eyes practically rolled back into his head. That move was like a nuclear bomb exploding on top of his control.

Instead of stopping her with his grip on her hips, Miles put her right where he wanted and surged up, sheathing himself to the hilt inside her pussy with one stroke. The feel of her inner walls wrapping around his cock was pure bliss. Already too late to prevent what was about to happen, he lifted her up and then pushed her down on his shaft.

Kareena placed her hands on his chest and rode him, her pussy squeezing him. She did that roll with her pelvis again, and the top of his head just about blew off. He set a faster pace, lifting his hips to meet hers. She took him in longer strokes, grinding her clit against his pelvic bone with each downward one.

Just as his balls drew closer to his body, and the point of no return edged ever nearer, a piece of his soul brushed against Kareena's. She gasped, then moaned in pleasure as the two pieces became one. The mating bond formed and snapped into place between them. Miles let out a growl. She was his now. Nothing would change that, and there was no going back.

Kareena let out a keening moan as she threw back her head. Her pussy convulsed around his cock, milking him to his own orgasm. He filled her with his cum, the pleasure going on and on. She collapsed on top of him, breathing as if she'd just run a great distance, and he did the same. His cock, still hard, remained buried deep inside her.

Miles held her close until their hearts no longer raced. He'd broken Jaden's rule, but he didn't know how she expected any male in the throes of the mating urge to be able to restrain himself enough to follow it. The instinct to claim a mate was just too strong. Since Jaden was a werewolf, her mate hadn't had to go through it. Leif would have gotten one sniff of her scent, known what she was to him and would have made her his shortly thereafter. Christ, Miles had barely lasted twenty-four hours. He couldn't have seen him being able to hold out for days.

Kareena stirred on top him and lifted her head to look at him. "Ah, Miles, you're still hard."

He grinned. "I know."

"I don't mean to put a downer on things, but I'm a little concerned."

His brows drew together. "About what?"

"About you staying erect for so long. It isn't normal. The ER nurse in me thinks you should have a doctor check you out in case there's something wrong."

He kissed her and smiled. "Let me assure you there is nothing wrong with me."

"All right. Then did you take one of those pills that give a man an erection?"

Now he felt slightly affronted. "Hell no. I don't need anything like that. This is all me." He pushed up into Kareena for an added effect.

It did nothing to wipe the concern off her face. "Okay, you didn't take anything. You have to know if an erection lasts too long it can cause capillaries to burst in your penis, which can cause permanent damage."

This was the first time Miles had a woman so concerned about how long he could keep an erection. The few mortal women he'd slept with in the past couldn't have cared less why it happened. They'd just liked that he could keep going even after coming several times.

It did make him feel good that his mate cared enough to feel worried. Right at that moment, he didn't want to tell Kareena the truth about him being a werewolf, and that staying hard was normal for the males of his kind. Now that they were mated, he saw no reason to hold back. He still wanted her.

Miles lifted Kareena off him and settled her on her side next to him. He shifted behind her and sank his cock back inside her pussy. He palmed a breast, tugging the nipple, and stroked in and out of her.

"I'll show you that I'll soften. It's just going to take some time."

He proceeded to show Kareena just how long a male werewolf could pleasure his mate without needing time to recover in between.

CHAPTER SIX

K areena awoke to a dark room. She'd fallen asleep, which wasn't surprising, considering how long she and Miles had had sex. He'd just about worn her out. He'd eventually lost his erection, as he'd said he would, but that had taken another four orgasms. He'd made her climax every time he'd had one. She'd never thought she was capable of coming that many times during one bout of lovemaking. He'd shown her she could.

After a quick look to see Miles was still sleeping, Kareena slipped out of bed and blindly felt around the floor for something to wear. She ended up picking up his T-shirt and pulled it on. The bottom of it hit her around mid-thigh, and the sleeves reached her elbows.

She tiptoed out of the room and headed for the kitchen. After all that exercise in bed, she was hungry again. She figured Miles would be as well. There was no point wasting the snack food she'd prepared earlier. It was around midnight, but Kareena didn't care.

She turned on the oven to preheat, then went to the fridge and took out the baking sheet that she'd assembled nachos on earlier that day. It wouldn't take very long to melt the shredded cheese on the chips. Her stomach growled at the thought of how good they'd taste. She'd loaded them up with cheese, jalapeño peppers, chopped tomato and black olives. Then there was sour cream and salsa to dip them in.

The oven beeped to let her know it was finished preheating. Kareena opened the door and bent to put the nachos inside. A hand ran up the outside of her bare leg as a male pelvis snuggled against her bottom.

"Got hungry?" Miles asked.

She closed the oven door and then turned to face him. He looked sexy as hell wearing only his jeans with the button undone. She gazed at him, wishing she could burrow under his skin so she could get even closer. Since they'd made love—in so many positions she didn't think there were any left to try—her feelings for Miles had become even stronger. The scary thing about it was what she felt was along the lines of love. It was too soon for that, though. She wasn't the type of woman who instantly fell in love with the guy she happened to have sex with. Something had passed between her and Miles just before they'd come the first time he'd been inside her. She had no idea what it was, but it felt as if she were more connected to him than she'd been before. If that made any sense.

Kareena put her arms around his waist. "Yes, I'm hungry. I think I burned a ton of calories in bed with you. I need to refuel. I'm making nachos. You want a beer?"

"I could go for nachos. I'd love that beer. I worked up quite an appetite."

She let him go, then went to the fridge for the beers. She handed one to Miles. He twisted off the cap before he removed hers. Kareena had to admit the cold beer was good going down.

A quick look in the oven showed the food was just about ready. "Another minute and these should be done." She went about putting the salsa and sour cream into small bowls.

"Once we're eating," Miles said as he watched her, "I want to ask you something."

"Okay. Here take these and put them on the coffee table in the living room," she said as she handed Miles the bowls once he'd put his beer on the counter. "I'll bring in the nachos."

He took them and walked out of the kitchen. Kareena got out a wire rack and then put the nachos on it once she took them out of the oven. She carried the rack and all into the living room where Miles waited for her on the couch. She made one more trip back to the kitchen to get their beers.

She settled on the couch beside Miles. "So what did you want to ask me?"

Miles turned to face her. "Do you think you can get a couple days off work?"

"Probably. Human resources has been bugging me to use up some of my vacation time. Why?"

"I have a cottage that borders the Point Reyes National Seashore land. I want to take you there tomorrow for a few days with another couple I know. I really want you to meet them, and I thought you might enjoy the change in scenery."

Actually, the thought of going away with Miles, even if it wasn't that far away, was something Kareena was all for. The chance of meeting some of his friends meant he must have some strong feelings for her as well.

"I was supposed to work Monday, but I can call the head nurse tomorrow and talk to her. She can handle contacting human resources about me having a few days off. I'm sure it won't be a problem. I've covered some shifts for a couple coworkers recently, so they won't mind doing the same for me."

"Great. We'll leave right after lunch. That should give you enough time to arrange time off." Miles leaned back and took his cell phone out of the front pocket of his jeans. "I'll text Jaden and Leif now so they know when we want to go. They already said they'd come when I spoke to them about it earlier."

"So you had this all planned before you asked me."

Miles sent his text, then placed his phone on the coffee table. He smiled. "Of course. I had a feeling you'd say yes. Just so you know, I plan to stay the night here with you. Tomorrow, after you've made your phone call and you're packed, we'll go to my place so I can throw some things into a bag. I'll suggest to Jaden and Leif that I drive so we don't have to take two cars."

"You really do have this all planned out."

"This should be fun. I have a feeling you and Jaden will hit it off. She's pregnant with her first child."

"I can't wait to meet her and Leif." Kareena leaned in and gave Miles a kiss. "Now let's eat before the nachos get cold."

They dug into their food. Kareena turned on the TV to watch while they ate. She didn't think this night could get any better. She sat next to a man who she was falling for in nothing but his T-shirt. It felt comfortable and right. She could see them doing this very thing on a regular basis for years, just enjoying each other's company. She already felt closer to Miles than she ever had with her ex, and she'd been with him for eight years. She and Miles being together was meant to be.

* * * *

The next morning Miles called Jaden while Kareena was on the phone to the hospital. Even though Leif had texted him back the night before to say he and Jaden were fine with the plans, Miles wanted to make sure everything was still a go. Jaden reassured him she hadn't unexpectedly gone into labor. She told him that she and Leif would be ready when Miles and Kareena came to pick them up.

He'd just disconnected the call when Kareena came into the living room. She'd gone into the kitchen to make hers. "Well?" he asked.

"I have the time off. Actually, I have the whole week off. The head nurse said she didn't want to hear any arguments about it since I haven't used up any of my vacation time. So I took the week."

"That's great. I just finished talking to Jaden. She and Leif are all ready to go. You need to pack a bag."

"I'm on it."

Miles followed Kareena into the bedroom and then sat on the bed to watch her pack what she wanted to take with her to the cottage. He was pleased that she had a week off rather than only a couple days. He planned to tell her about what he was later today. After he explained what it meant to be his mate, he'd have to tell her that her days as an ER nurse were over. Neither one of them would be able to handle the separation anxiety now that the mating bond was in place. Plus, there was no way he could hang out in the ER department every time she had a shift. It'd get a little noticeable after a while.

He hoped like hell Kareena would be able to accept his being a werewolf. Miles thought maybe his mate would have an easier time of accepting it all with Jaden there when he told her.

Kareena finished packing, and they headed down to the visitors parking. A stop off at his penthouse for Miles to change clothes and pack what he needed didn't take very long. Then they were on the road to Marin County.

After arriving at the Protectors' mansion, Kareena said, "Your friends have a nice place. It's huge."

"Jaden and Leif aren't the only ones who live here. They have what they call their 'extended family' living with them as well. There are seven couples, including Jaden and Leif."

"Wow. Are you friends with the others as well?"

"Yes, and I have family here too. My sister lives here with her husband."

"I guess I'll get to meet her before we leave."

Miles parked as close to the front door as he could so Jaden wouldn't have to walk too far. He looked out the window and smiled. "That's a given since Saskia is standing by the door, waiting for us."

Kareena looked in the direction he'd indicated. "She's beautiful. There's no mistaking you as siblings. You're very similar in looks, right down to the same hair color."

"Saskia is four years older than me."

"You'd never know it. You both look to be around the same age."

"That's a family thing. We tend to age better than others." Most mortals would be shocked to know Saskia was over a thousand years old and that Miles had just about reached that milestone as well.

Miles and Kareena got out of the car and then went to meet Saskia. His sister gave Kareena a big smile as they approached. "It's nice to meet you, Kareena," Saskia said. "Miles came by yesterday and told us all about you."

"It's nice to meet you too. I was telling Miles you have a beautiful home."

"Thanks. Come on in. Jaden and Leif are inside, waiting." Saskia looked at Miles. "I think inviting them to go away was a great idea. Jaden really needed this, especially with the baby coming soon."

"When is she due?" Kareena asked.

"In a week."

"Good thing we won't be too far away if she should go into early labor."

Miles put his arm around Kareena's shoulders. "We also have our very own ER nurse if that should happen."

"It's a good thing I started working in labor and delivery before I switched to the ER."

"Then Jaden should be in good hands," Saskia said before she opened the front door and then stepped inside.

Kareena and Miles followed her. He noticed the suitcase near the entrance, obviously the one his daughter and her mate planned to take away. Only Leif was in the living room.

"Where's Jaden?" Miles asked.

"Using the bathroom," Leif said with a chuckle. "What else is new? Since you haven't introduced me, I'm Leif," he said as he smiled at Kareena.

"Kareena," Kareena said in return.

"Sorry," Jaden said when she came into the room. "I feel as if I spend half the day in the bathroom. Hi, Kareena. I'm Jaden."

Kareena introduced herself before Miles had a chance to. Seeing his daughter and mate together, he had high hopes they'd become close. He wondered how Kareena would take the news when she learned she was going to be a step-grandmother.

Miles suggested they get on the road. Leif stood to get the suitcase to take outside while Miles said his goodbyes to Saskia. Once Jaden and Leif's suitcase was in the trunk and they were all in the car, Miles pulled out of the drive.

During the trip, Jaden and Kareena kept up a steady flow of conversation, bringing Leif and Miles into it from time to time. Before Miles knew it, they were at the cottage he'd decided to buy with the thought of having a place for his grandchild to come and explore. It was secluded enough that going wolf and having mortals see wasn't a problem.

They piled out of the car, and Miles opened the door for Jaden and Kareena to go inside while he and Leif retrieved the luggage from the trunk. Miles took his and Kareena's bags up to the master bedroom and told Leif he could pick whichever guestroom he wanted to use. Even though Miles hadn't yet spent much time at the cottage, he paid to have someone in to clean once a week. Plus, the last time he'd come there he'd brought some nonperishable food and meat that he'd put in the freezer.

That done, Leif and Miles returned to the main floor and their mates. The two women sat on the couch with bottles of water in their hands.

"We raided the fridge for something to drink. I hope you don't mind," Jaden said.

Miles nodded. "That's fine. You can help yourself to anything you want. I haven't stocked up much so we'll have to take a run to the local grocery store tomorrow."

Jaden pushed to her feet. "Well, I want to go for a walk along the shore since your cottage backs on to Tomales Bay. Come with me, Leif."

As his daughter and her mate walked out the back sliding door, Miles knew Jaden had given him some time alone with Kareena. Right now would have been a perfect opportunity to tell Kareena what he was, but he wasn't ready to do that yet. He wasn't at all sure he wanted to do it without at least Jaden being there as well. Plus, they'd only just arrived. There was no point in spoiling what they had.

Kareena closed the distance between them and took his hand. "A walk sounds like a great idea. We'll go the opposite way they did." She went on tiptoe and kissed him. "They do say the sea air is supposed to give you an appetite." She winked.

Miles knew exactly what kind of appetite she referred to. He guided her outside, thankful he had a small reprieve before he tested the waters of how strongly Kareena felt for him.

CHAPTER SEVEN

Kareena couldn't have picked a better place to get away than being at Miles's cottage. Plus, she thought Leif and Jaden were great. It was obvious they were very much in love from the way they looked at each other. They were constantly touching in some way.

"It's really nice here," Kareena said as she walked down the sandy shore, holding his hand.

"I'm glad you like it. I'll have to take you here again sometime."

"So you want me to stick around for a while then."

Miles tugged Kareena to a stop and pulled her around so she stood facing him. He cupped her face and gently caressed her cheekbones with his thumbs. His face grew serious.

"I want it to be longer than just 'a while,'" he said. "I don't think I'll let you go any time soon."

Kareena gulped. She'd known her feelings for Miles had been headed that way, but she'd never been too sure how he felt about her. Hearing him say he wanted her to stay with him made her heart beat a little faster.

"You want me to stay with you?" she asked in a quiet voice.

"Yes. If you haven't already noticed, I've fallen for you. I haven't always done right in my life, but being with you is one of the best things that have happened to me. You make me feel things that at one time I thought I'd lost forever. That the wrong turn I'd taken made it so I'd never have what I have with you. I love you, Kareena."

Kareena wasn't a crier, but unshed tears burned the backs of her eyes. She swallowed, fighting not to lose it. She reached up and placed her hands over his. "I didn't think I'd ever be able to trust another man enough to fall in love again after what my ex did to me, but you have shown me I can." She took a deep breath. "I love you too." She paused. "Just don't make me regret it."

"I'd never hurt you. You own my heart, and always will." Miles claimed her lips in a kiss that was so sweet and tender it had Kareena fighting back tears again.

Miles finally pulled away. "Let's go back to the cottage. Maybe we can sneak upstairs before Jaden and Leif come back."

Kareena smiled. "I'll race you back."

She took off running, not waiting for his response. Ho took after her, but let her keep the lead. It wasn't until they reached the sliding back doors of the cottage that he closed the distance between them and caught her around the waist. They barreled into the house.

Kareena drew up short when she spotted Jaden and Leif in the living room, kissing. The couple broke apart. Her mouth dropped open at the sight of their eyes mutedly glowing. There was no mistaking what she saw. It slowly faded as she stared at them.

"Their eyes. They glowed," Kareena said as she tried to back up. All she managed to do was press even closer to Miles, who stood behind her.

"It's all right, Kareena," he said. "That's normal."

She tore herself out of Miles's embrace and looked from him, to the couple and back to him again. "Normal for what? Not once in all the time I've worked at the hospital have I ever seen anyone's eyes do that."

Miles sighed. "It's normal for werewolves, which the three of us are."

"Werewolves? You honestly can't expect me to believe that."

"It's true. I planned to tell you later today."

"You can't be serious."

"Very."

Kareena found herself frozen in place as his body blurred and shimmered while it took on another form. One minute the man she'd come to love stood in front of her, and the next, a white wolf had taken his place. Her gaze shot to Jaden and Leif just in time to see Leif change into a wolf as well.

Jaden gave her a small smile. "I'd shift as well, but I can't because of the baby."

Kareena kept frantically shifting her gaze between the two wolves. She panicked as she breathed too fast, and her heart raced. This wasn't happening. Werewolves weren't supposed to exist. She shouldn't be in a room with three of them.

The white wolf took a couple steps closer to Kareena, and that was enough to unfreeze her. She turned to get ready to bolt outside, but ended up going nowhere when Jaden just suddenly appeared in front of her. For being pregnant, she could move very fast. The other woman took hold of her upper arms. Kareena tried to wrench away, but Jaden was much stronger than she looked, and Kareena couldn't break free.

"Calm down," Jaden said. "I know this is a lot to accept. It might be scary, but my dad would never do anything to hurt you. You're his mate."

"Your dad? That's impossible. Miles isn't that much older than you. He can't be your father."

"Werewolves live a very long time. I'm in my twenties, but my dad has seen many, many more years than that."

Kareena was used to working under stressful situations in the ER. She'd been trained to never panic, to stay calm and do what needed to be done, but nothing could have prepared her for this. How did she get over the fact that the man she'd just proclaimed to love had turned out to be a creature that should be found only in fiction, not real life.

Her gaze was drawn to the wolf Leif had turned into as its body blurred and he became a man once more. He took a few steps toward her, holding his hands up in a gesture to pacify her.

"It'll be all right, Kareena. Miles is still in there. We keep our human intelligence once we shift, and understand every word spoken to us. As a wolf, Miles still loves you as much as he does while in his human form. As Jaden said, he'd never do anything to harm you. You're his mate. Your souls joined when the mating bond formed between you."

Kareena wanted to move away, but there was nowhere to go. Jaden still stood in front of her, Miles the wolf was close to her one side and Leif converged on her other. At her back were the sliding glass doors, but having seen how fast Jaden could move, Kareena doubted she'd ever make it without one of the others catching up with her first.

"Do you realize how freaky that sounds? Souls don't join," she said. Her voice shook ever so slightly.

"I know this is hard for you to accept," Leif said as he came closer. "You have to. You're already in our world. There's no changing that. Once a mating bond has formed, there's no breaking it. It's for life."

A cold nose touched her hand, and Kareena let out a surprised yelp. She tried to jump away when she saw it was the white wolf that had touched her, but once again, she was stopped. Leif used her distraction to take her gently into his arms. She struggled, even though she didn't stand a chance of getting free.

Leif easily subdued her and wrapped one of his hands around her wrist. He turned her and forced her fingers to sink into the fur on the white wolf's back. "Touch him, Kareena. Get to know Miles in this form." He ran her hand up to the wolf's head, making her scratch behind Miles's ears, which he seemed to like since he leaned into her, pressing his furry side against her leg.

The longer Leif forced Kareena to pet Miles the less scared she felt. Miles didn't try to bite her. He just stared at her with the same violet eyes he had as a human. His gaze seemed to plead with her to get over her fear. Eventually, Leif released her, and she petted the wolf all on her own.

Out of the corner of her eye, Kareena saw Leif and Jaden leave the room. After they were gone, the white wolf's body blurred and shimmered, and Miles was once more himself. Even though her heart tried to beat out of her chest, she held her ground. She decided freaking out wouldn't get her anywhere. Instead, she focused on all the unanswered questions about everything she'd seen.

Miles reached out and ran the backs of his fingers along her cheek. Kareena jumped but didn't jerk away. He must have taken that as a good sign, because he stepped closer and cupped her face.

"Are you okay?" he asked.

"I don't really know. A part of me still wants to run out of here screaming."

"I know, but I'm glad you aren't." He gently kissed her forehead. "Let's sit on the couch and I'll try to answer all the questions I'm sure you have."

He released her and went and sat in the middle of the couch, which gave Kareena only one choice, to sit beside him. She did and waited for Miles to begin. Her thoughts were a jumbled mess.

"I guess I should start with some of the things Jaden and Leif already told you. Yes, Jaden is my daughter, and I am old enough to be her father. I'm nine hundred and ninety-eight years old. Werewolves live to the age of around three thousand. You are my mate. I knew the instant I smelled your scent in the restaurant and it set off my mating urge. The first time we made love, the mating bond formed between us, our souls becoming one. Now we won't be able to stand to be apart for long periods of time or we'll suffer through separation anxiety. I've never experienced it, but no one wants to go through it." He met and held her gaze. "I do love you, Kareena. You're still one of the best things that has ever happened to me. It ranks up there with me finding out about Jaden almost two years ago."

"You didn't know her before that?"

He shook his head. "No. Jaden's mother left me without telling me she was pregnant. She was mortal like you."

"Did she leave because you were a werewolf?"

"No." Miles sighed. "She'd come to accept that. It was the path I'd chosen for my life that she couldn't condone. As I told you before, I've done some dark things. When I'd met Jaden's mother, for a time, I pulled myself back to what I'd once been. It didn't last for long. I let my ambitions get in the way. She died when my daughter was young."

"Was she your mate?"

"No, but I did love her. I just didn't love her the way she deserved." He paused, then said, "In my past, I've done some pretty despicable things. Having Jaden in my life has shown me I was on a path of destruction. Now I have you to love, to protect."

Sitting beside Miles, listening to him talk, Kareena became numb. She was having a hard time getting over the fact he was a werewolf and almost a thousand years old. Then it hit her. He'd said his kind lived up to three thousand years. He'd even called her a mortal. She'd die first. He'd stay young-looking and live on for another two thousand years without her.

Kareena wrapped her arms around her middle as the full impact of it sorted itself out in her mind. "This can't work."

Miles turned to face her. "What won't?"

"Us. Unless you can turn me into a werewolf, which I'm not sure I'd want, anyway. It's not as if we can have a happily ever after together. My lifespan is nothing compared to yours."

"There's no way for me to turn you. You have to be born a werewolf. We'll still have lots of years to be with one another. I'd rather have that than nothing at all. You're my mate. There will be no one else for me. Ever."

"Will you feel that way when I'm old?"

He cupped her face and looked intently into her eyes. "Of course I will. My feelings for you will never change."

Jaden stepped into the room. "Dad, I need—" She looked down at her feet, then her gaze flew to their faces. "I think my water just broke." She moaned and placed a hand on her stomach.

Seeing the puddle at Jaden's feet, Kareena went into automatic nurse mode. She pushed away from Miles and went to the other woman. "Are you having a contraction?"

"I think so. It feels like a really bad period cramp."

"Yup, that's a contraction. Just breathe through it. Since this is your first baby, I don't think we have to worry about you delivering before we can get you to the hospital."

Jaden shook her head. "No hospital. I have a midwife." She turned her head toward the stairs and called for her mate. "Leif, I need you."

Leif raced down the steps at a speed no mortal would be capable of. "What's the matter?" He seemed to take in the water at Jaden's feet. "It's time? The baby's coming?"

"Yes. Call the midwife and tell her to meet us at the house."

Miles came to stand at Kareena's side and looked at Jaden as Leif took out his cell phone to make the call. "Is there anything you need me to do?" Miles asked.

"You can take my hand, because here comes another one," Jaden said on a moan and held out her right hand for Miles to take. He shifted around to his daughter's other side and took it.

"Slow down your breathing a bit, Jaden. You don't want to hyperventilate," Kareena said. "I'm going to check your pulse."

Kareena took Jaden's left wrist and tried to shove up the wide leather cuff-like bracelet she wore so she could get to her pulse point, but it didn't move enough. She unsnapped the dome that held it together and then removed it.

A loud wolflike growl rumbled out of Miles. Kareena's gaze jerked to his face. His eyes were mutedly glowing as he stared at Jaden's wrist. There was no mistaking his anger by his scowl.

"You lied," he said through gritted teeth. "My own daughter lied to me."

Kareena hadn't a clue what had set Miles off. One minute he was very solicitous of Jaden, and the next, he was angry with her. She opened her mouth to say something that would diffuse the situation, knowing his anger wouldn't be good for Jaden right now, but Leif took it to the next level.

With a low growl, he tore Miles away from Jaden and threw him against the closest wall. Miles sprang back on his feet, his eyes glowing and his upper lip curled in a snarl as he snapped his teeth in Leif's direction.

"Don't fucking do this now," Leif said on a growl. "Jaden doesn't need you slipping to the dark side while she's in labor. Let's get her home. After the baby is born, we'll get this all out in the open. Until then, keep it together. For once, don't be a selfish bastard. If you've forgotten, your new mate is watching this."

Jaden moaned and held her hand out. "Leif."

Her mate returned to her side and picked her up into his arms. "I have you. I'll help you get into some dry pants, then we'll leave." Leif walked at a fast clip as he carried Jaden away.

Alone with Miles, Kareena turned to him. His eyes still mutedly glowed, and he gazed in the direction the other couple had gone. She cleared her throat to draw his attention.

Once she had it, she said, "I don't know what this is all about, but I don't really care right now. Jaden is the one I have to look after until we can get her home and into the hands of her midwife. Whatever set you off, get it under wraps. Now. If you truly love your daughter, you won't put her through this when she's in such a vulnerable state. So pull it together and get ready to leave. I'll get our bags."

She walked out of the room and didn't give Miles a second look. He'd either behave or he'd see how tough of a nurse she could be when warranted.

CHAPTER EIGHT

Miles stood against the wall in the now empty room as a number of emotions whirled inside him. He was angry and shocked, as if someone had just ripped a carpet out from under him, but he mostly felt betrayed. How could Jaden have lied to him all this time? She wasn't the foretold one. She didn't bear the mark around her left wrist that he thought she hid under her leather bracelet. The absence of it meant she wasn't what she said she was.

The old Miles wouldn't have cared who Jaden was to him, or that she was in labor. He would have forced her to tell him who the true foretold one was, whom it was she protected with her lie. He hated to admit it, but very deep down inside, the old him wasn't entirely gone.

Kareena came back into the room, carrying their bags. Seeing him, she said, "Leif and Jaden are going to be down in a minute. Pull your head out of your ass and get the car unlocked. We have time, but if we delay any longer, there's still a slim chance I'll be delivering your grandchild at the side of the road. So move it."

His mate's words dragged him out of the downward spiral Miles had been stuck in. Kareena was right. He had to pull it together. Jaden had lied to him, but that didn't mean he wanted to put her or the baby in any risk. He tamped down his anger and headed outside to his car. Kareena followed.

He'd just put their bags into the trunk when Leif appeared, carrying Jaden. She appeared to be having another contraction. Miles took the suitcase Leif carried as well and then put it with his and Kareena's.

No one said a word as they got into the car. Miles started it and then pulled out of the drive. The trip to Marin County seemed to take longer than it should have. With each moan of pain Jaden made, it set his nerves on edge. He hated to see his daughter suffering, but there was nothing he could do for her. Kareena kept telling Jaden how well she was doing and to remember to breathe in through her nose and out through her mouth. Miles caught sight of Leif in the rearview mirror. The other man suffered right along with Jaden when each contraction hit.

They arrived at the Protectors' mansion to Saskia, Jager and Roan waiting outside at the front door. Obviously, Leif must have called them before they'd left the cottage.

Leif confirmed it when he simply said, "They know."

Miles brought the car to a stop and then shut off the engine. Leif carried Jaden out and into the house. Saskia, Jager and Roan didn't follow. Miles knew they waited for him. Kareena got out, and he did the same. He walked around to confront his sister.

"Saskia," he said.

"Bring your mate inside, Miles. The midwife is already here." She gave him a sharp look.

He nodded at the other two Protectors who stood on either side of her. "Are Jager and Roan here to make sure I cooperate?"

"Take it any way you want, but you're coming inside."

Kareena looked at him and then at Saskia and back again. There was no mistaking the tension between him and his sister. Kareena being his mate, he'd dropped her right in the middle of things.

He gave a nod, walked past Saskia and into the house. Kareena silently followed. He should be reassuring her, but he couldn't find the words to do it. His emotions were still in turmoil. For too many years he'd walked the dark side, as Leif had said, compared to the new path he'd chosen after finding Jaden. The pull was still there. The only thing stopping him from going over was Kareena. He never wanted her to see what he'd been like. He wanted her to see him as a good man. She deserved him to be one.

They filed into the living room. With his acute werewolf hearing, Miles heard everything that happened upstairs. Kareena took a seat on the couch, but he couldn't sit. He paced the room, hoping Jaden's labor would be quick.

Saskia's, Jager's and Roan's mates joined them. Everyone introduced themselves to Kareena, but they basically ignored him. Miles knew that didn't mean the Protectors weren't keeping a close eye on him, though. As he paced, he felt Kareena's gaze on him from time to time. She made no move to come to him, which in a way was good. He didn't know if he'd end up snapping at her. Since they really hadn't had time for her to accept everything, he probably would end up doing more damage than good.

Two hours later, Miles heard the wails of a newborn coming from the upper level. He stopped pacing as the others in the room fell silent. They all turned their gazes to the entrance to the living room. After twenty minutes had gone by, Leif appeared in it, holding a blanket-wrapped baby.

Leif walked straight to Miles. He placed the infant into his arms. "Say hello to your grandson. We're calling him Cole."

Miles looked down at the newborn's face. Cole had his eyes open and looked up at him. His heart melted. He pulled the blanket aside and touched the tiny hand with the tip of his finger. The baby gripped it. He instantly fell in love. He now had a third person he'd do anything to protect.

"She wants to see you," Leif said.

"How do you feel about that?"

"I'm not happy about it, but I'd never try to keep you two apart. Even though I don't trust you, you're still my mate's father."

Miles kissed the baby's forehead before he passed Cole to Leif. "Tell Jaden I can't right now. I need some time to come to terms with what she did."

"You really are a cold-hearted bastard," Leif said in a quiet tone. "So she lied to you about her being the foretold one. She wouldn't have if you hadn't taken me captive, beaten the shit out of me and threatened to kill me if we didn't hand the foretold one over to you. It was Jaden's idea to take on that role. Once Saskia realized what Jaden was to you, Jaden volunteered. Not once did she think she'd be playing that part for months to come. None of us expected you to try to redeem yourself. If it weren't for Jaden, you'd be kept on the outside even today. She wanted you in her life."

Miles brushed past Leif and headed for the entrance to the living room. He was fighting an internal battle as the good and bad inside him vied for dominance. It'd be so much easier to let the bad win and walk away, slip back into his old ways. Being good took a lot more work.

"Where are you going?" Saskia called.

He slowed his steps. "Outside to the backyard. I need to be alone for a while."

"Don't go too far. Remember you're mated now."

Miles walked out of the room. He hadn't forgotten about Kareena. It was best that he put as much space as the mating bond would allow between them for now.

* * * *

After Miles left the room, Jager asked, "Should I watch him?"

Saskia shook her head. "Leave him be for now. Miles isn't going anywhere as long as Kareena is here."

"I'm going back up to Jaden," Leif said. "I'm not going to relish telling her that her father doesn't want to see her." He left, cuddling his newborn son close.

Kareena still was a little lost as to what was going on. All she knew was that Jaden had pretended to be this foretold one to stop Miles from killing Leif. Miles had told her he'd done some pretty bad things in his past, but she hadn't realized he'd been capable of murdering someone to get something he wanted. The idea sent a chill through her and sent home that she really didn't know him. If he ever went back to being that type of person, she couldn't stay mated to him. Somehow, she'd have to find a way out.

She lifted her head and found everyone in the room watching her. She looked at each couple—Saskia and Eli, Jager and Daylen, Roan and Ansley. There was pity in their eyes.

After swallowing, Kareena said, "All right. Give it to me straight. Don't hold anything back. Tell me what's going on between all of you and Miles. I might as well have this all out on the table today. A few hours ago, I found out werewolves exist and that I'm a mate to one. Now this."

Saskia sighed. "You have no idea how I wish I didn't have to tell you this, but you do need to understand since you're Miles's mate. My grandmother had the sight, and foresaw that a werewolf would be born who'd have more magic than the rest of us. This werewolf would rule over all the packs, and a special mark on his or her left wrist would proclaim him or her as the foretold one. My grandmother saw that this special werewolf would need protection so she formed the Protectors. Originally it was me, Roan, Jager, Skylar, Leif, Kye, Dirk and Miles. Hundreds of years ago, Miles decided he'd rather find the foretold one himself, keep this werewolf under his control and rule the packs through him or her. I'm not going to sugarcoat it. He turned bad. I won't list all the things he did, but killing was acceptable to him."

"Then he found out about Jaden," Kareena added.

"Yes, then he found out he had a daughter. We had no idea who she was, and neither did she since she'd never met her father. After she was turned into a werewolf, her scent changed, and that was enough for me to realize who she was."

Kareena interrupted. "Wait a minute. Miles told me a mortal can't be turned, that to be a werewolf you have to be born one."

"Well, before we found the foretold one that was true. Roxie, who is the foretold one, learned of a spell that turned her. Now it only works if she's the one using it. She turned Eli, Daylen and Ansley."

"What about me?"

"We planned to tell Miles that Roxie had the spell and nothing else. We'd hoped he'd accept that she just had a little something extra when it came to magic. Our grandmother did since she had the sight, as do I."

"So I don't have to worry about growing old and dying and leaving him behind?"

Saskia smiled. "No. Roxie already said she'd turn you, if that's what you want." She looked Kareena right in the eyes. "I can't tell you to do it, but I strongly urge you to. Miles loves you. Having a mate can be life changing. I think you're the only one who'll be able to keep him from going to the dark side again. Do you love my brother?"

Kareena didn't even think about it. "Yes, but if he goes back to being bad, I can't be with him." A sudden feeling that something had happened to Miles swept through her. She ignored it as Saskia spoke once more.

"I'm hoping the mating bond will stop that from ever happening. It's instinct for a male werewolf to protect his mate. If he goes to the dark side, he'll be putting you in jeopardy."

"Then I'll become a werewolf." Kareena's brows drew together. Talking about Miles made her feel as if she hadn't seen him in a very long time. She felt as if she should get up and look for him. She needed to be with him. The sensation was so strong she shifted on the couch.

Saskia eyed her. "Is something wrong, Kareena?"

"I don't know. All of a sudden I have this need to be with Miles. I feel as if something bad has happened to him. I miss him."

"Shit, he wouldn't have," Jager said.

"He must have," Saskia replied. "Roan, see if Miles is still out back."

Roan left the room at a run. All the people in the room turned their gazes to Kareena. The stares of pity they'd given her earlier were now replaced with concern.

"What's the matter?" Kareena asked.

"Did Miles tell you what happens when mates are separated for long periods of time? About the separation anxiety that happens with it?"

"Yes. He told me we won't be able to stand to be apart."

"Well, what you're feeling is the separation anxiety. It looks as if my idiot brother is no longer in the backyard. Roan has just gone to confirm that, but from what you're feeling, I know he isn't there."

The thought of Miles leaving her behind had Kareena feeling a tad on the desperate side. He wouldn't have dumped her, would he? They were mated. He'd told her he loved her. Would this be her ex-fiancé all over again? Only this time it'd be much, much worse.

Roan came into the room. "He's not out back, but his car is still parked at the front of the house. So he didn't leave the property."

"He's probably gone to the very back of it," Eli said. "It's far enough to have both of them feeling it."

Kareena shifted on the couch cushion again. "Maybe I should

go to him."

"No," Saskia said. "Let him come to you. I know this won't be fun for you, but letting Miles go through the separation anxiety will remind him of what he has now. That he has a reason to stay clear of the dark side."

"How bad will this get?"

Ansley gave her a pained look. "It can get pretty bad the longer he stays away."

"Have you and Miles been together since he told you what he is?" Saskia asked.

Kareena shook her head. "If you mean have we had sex, no. When Jaden went into labor, I was still feeling freaked and having a hard time accepting what he told me. The only reason I'm not feeling like that now is because so much has happened since."

"If Miles stays away long enough, when you two are together again...let's just say you'll want to reconnect in the most elemental of ways. You won't be able to help yourselves."

Great. So she'd end up having sex with Miles with a houseful of people knowing exactly what they were doing.

As the need to be with him grew, Kareena found she didn't care all that much. She wanted Miles to come back. Eventually, she had to get up and pace. It was beyond her to sit still. He'd been gone a half hour, but to her, it felt as if she hadn't seen him in months. She literally felt as if she were going nuts. Another half hour went by, and she was about ready to climb the walls.

Then she heard it, a long, drawn-out wolf's howl coming from the back of the house. Kareena ran out of the room, knowing it had to be Miles. She didn't stop until she'd reached a pair of French doors. On the other side stood a white wolf—Miles. The sight of him in his wolf form didn't affect her as it had the first time she'd seem him in it. All she cared about was that he was there. Arousal slammed into her, making it hard to think of anything else.

Kareena opened the door and let the wolf in. Behind her, Saskia said, "You can use Eli's and my bedroom. Miles knows which one it is. Follow him."

She should have felt embarrassed by Saskia basically telling her where she could go with Miles to have sex, but Kareena didn't. Her pussy ached to be filled. The need to have him inside her was a beast that clawed at her. Already, wetness leaked into her panties.

Still in wolf form, Miles gently took her wrist between his jaws and tugged her into motion. Kareena went with him, leaving the others behind. She hurried up the stairs and then into the bedroom he led her to. Once he released her, she closed and locked the door behind them.

The wolf's body blurred and shimmered, then there stood Miles. He was completely naked and very aroused. His cock jutted from his body, and already a bead of pre-cum had leaked from the tip. Her arousal increased, the ache deep in her pussy intensifying.

Miles was on her a heartbeat later. His lips claimed hers with hunger and desperation as he almost tore her clothes off her. He didn't stop until he had her as naked as he.

His hands roamed her body while he walked her to the middle of the room. "I can't wait, Kareena. I need inside you."

"God, yes," she moaned into his mouth.

Miles took her to the floor, used a thigh to spread her legs, then surged into her to the hilt with one stroke. Kareena reached around and grabbed his thrusting ass, urging him to take her faster and harder as he pumped between her thighs. Loud wolf growls rumbled out of him with each thrust of his hips. She squeezed her inner walls around his hard cock. It felt so good to have him inside her. Her moans of pleasure were just about as loud as his growls.

Kareena lifted her hips to meet each of Miles's strokes. Her climax built like a runaway freight train, her body coiling tighter with each thrust. His cock grew even harder inside her, stretching her, filling her to capacity.

Her orgasm slammed into her, taking her breath away. Intense pleasure tore through her, seeming to go on forever. Miles pumped once, twice, then howled. His cock pulsed as he came, hot jets of his cum filling her.

He wasn't done with her yet. His cock remained hard. Miles pulled out of her and got her up on her hands and knees. He positioned himself behind her and pushed into her, taking her in hard thrusts. All Kareena could do was moan and match his strokes. Even though she'd just come, another orgasm gathered steam. She panted his name as it grew and grew. He reached around her and found her clit. He plucked the bundle of nerves and sent her flying, but he didn't come with her.

He changed their positions again. This time he sat on the floor with her straddling his hips. He pushed up into her and had her ride him. His cock hit her G-spot, and she took him deeper. Unbelievably, her body coiled tight, readying itself for another release.

Miles wrapped a hand around the back of her neck and brought her mouth down to his. He pushed his tongue inside, mimicking what his cock did to her pussy. He soon pulled away, but kept his hand where it was.

"I want you to bite me, Kareena."

"I can't bite you."

He thrust up into her hard. "Yes, you can. Bite me where my shoulder and neck meet. Mark me as yours. It's a male werewolf's biggest turn-on to have his female bite him there, leaving teeth marks to show her male is claimed."

Exerting slight pressure on the back of her neck, Miles positioned her mouth at the side of his neck where it met his shoulder. He stiffened as she kissed him and licked him there. His cock grew even harder. He put his hands on her hips and had her ride him faster. She dragged her teeth across the spot, and he groaned with a growl mixed into it.

"Kareena," he begged. "Do it."

She did it. She bit him hard just as he wanted her to. The effect it had over Miles was instantaneous. He slammed her down onto his cock and bellowed as he came. The movement threw Kareena into climax as well. Once it was over, she collapsed against him. He held her close and lay back on the floor. He was still hard, but just continued to hold her in his arms.

Once she could breathe without puffing, she rested her chin on her stacked hands and looked at him. "Saskia told me everything. What you used to be like, some of the things you've done."

"I figured she would. That was part of the reason I went wolf and put more distance than I should have between us."

"If you ever do that again, I'm going to kick your ass."

He chuckled. "I promise I won't."

"Good. While I'm laying down the law, you *will* stay good. The days of you trying to control the foretold one are over. You're going to meet her, and do whatever you have to do to show you'll stay loyal to her."

"Bossy, aren't you?" He grew serious. "There's still a small part of me that wants me to use her for my own purposes."

"Well, you tell that asshole part of you it no longer has the control. You'll always play nice with Roxie from here on out since she's the one who can turn me into a werewolf so I can have those thousands of years with you."

Miles jerked up to a sitting position, taking Kareena with him. "She can do that?"

She nodded. "Jaden was born mortal, Miles. Roxie turned her. Apparently, she has a spell that only she can use that turns us mortals into your kind. So you're not going to do anything to piss her off. I want to stay with my mate for a very, very long time."

He kissed her, which soon became hot and heavy, but he pulled away before it went too far, even though his cock was still hard and their bodies were joined. "I promise not to do anything to hold back the gift she'll give us."

"So you'll prove to her that you'll never turn to the dark side again?"

"Yes. I'll swear fealty to her, whatever she wants."

"Just what I wanted to hear." Kareena used her weight to push Miles flat onto the floor. "We'll arrange to meet Roxie later. Right now, I want to make love to my mate again."

* * * *

Later that night Kareena stood with the Protectors and their mates, except for Jaden and Leif, as Miles swore fealty to Roxie as the foretold one. The Protectors watched him with a close eye, but Kareena knew they didn't have to worry about her mate being a threat any longer. His dark days were over for good. She was his redemption, and she'd make sure he never strayed to his dark side.

After Roxie accepted the pledge Miles gave her, she motioned to Kareena to join them. Kareena knew what would come next. The foretold one would use the spell that would make Miles and Kareena true mates.

With no hesitation, Kareena stepped forward. She met Miles's gaze with her own and saw the love he had for her shining in his eyes. He was her future, one she thought she'd never have. She placed her hand in his when he held it out to her and turned to Roxie, ready to take the next step in her life with Miles.

The End

ABOUT THE AUTHOR

Marisa Chenery was always a lover of books, but after reading her first historical romance novel she found herself hooked. Having inherited a love for the written word, she soon started writing her own novels.

She now writes young adult books and erotic romances.

Marisa lives in Ontario, Canada, with her boyfriend, Steve, four children, four grandchildren (she's a young grandma in her fifties) and rabbit and dog.

www.marisachenery.com

www.ingramcontent.com/pod-product-compliance
Lightning Source LLC
Chambersburg PA
CBHW020820030726
47496CB00001B/22